THE TICK-TOCK TRILOGY

DAVID B. LYONS

THE TICK-TOCK TRILOGY COMPRISES THREE NOVELS THAT ALL TAKE PLACE IN THE SPACE OF FIVE-HOUR TIMEFRAMES

MIDDAY

by David B. Lyons

WHATEVER HAPPENED TO BETSY BLAKE?

by David B. Lyons

THE SUICIDE PACT

by David B. Lyons

1

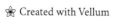 Created with Vellum

BOOK I

MIDDAY

By David B. Lyons.

I included the 'B' in my author name so you can come on this journey
with me.

07:00

Vincent

As soon as I wake up I let out a sigh that probably sounds as if I'm disappointed to be alive. There used to be a time when I wouldn't care if I woke up or not. But not now. Not with the excitement that envelops me these days.

I tap the screen of my iPhone to put an end to the beep. I purposely chose the most annoying alarm tone so it would force me to sit up when it goes off. There's no need to look at the clock. It's seven a.m. – the same time the alarm sounds every weekday morning. I wipe my hand over my face before throwing my feet over the side of the bed. I always rest them on the carpet before mustering the energy to lift my body to a standing position. A shower will refresh me. I open the Spotify app on my phone and pause for a moment. Some days, this is the hardest decision I make.

What will the soundtrack to the morning be?

I scroll until I see Beyoncé's name. This is nothing new. Her songs have so much energy in them that they are the perfect tonic for a wake-up call. 'Love on Top' begins as I shuffle my way to the en suite. I don't even look behind at what I've left in the bedroom. It's the same scene every morning. A crack of light forms from a gap in our blinds and casts itself over our king-size bed. Ryan will be curled up in foetus position, contemplating what to do with himself today. He'll be well aware that I've got up, but turning over to wish me a good morning won't have crossed his mind. It's way too early for him to talk.

The sensors turn the light on in the en suite for me as I head straight

8

for the mirror. I don't know why it's the first thing I do every morning. I look my worst at this time of the day. Everybody does. My eyes are swollen and my face appears puffy. I check my hairline again. If I stare at it every day I don't notice it receding too much. But who am I kidding? I'm going to be a bona fide bald man soon. I've trimmed my hair as much as I can. It's long enough to look like I have some hair on my head but short enough to look like I'm not trying to hide the baldness. I turn the shower on and decide to dance my way into the spray. 'Love on Top' is a great song. The tempo builds and builds. I contemplate the day ahead before getting annoyed with myself. I shower for two reasons – to wash and to refresh. This cubicle doesn't entertain thoughts about work. To distract myself, I imagine I'm on stage at the 3Arena prancing around in high heels in front of twenty thousand obsessed fans. I snatch at the blue bottle of body wash and use it as my microphone. I love these lyrics. It's one of those songs that you can really put everything in to.

Now I'm awake!

I stop singing when I get out of the shower. I know it annoys Ryan. I think I've got a decent singing voice, but I've noticed him wince every now and then when he hears me harmonising around the penthouse. Instead, I pick up my iPhone again and, having turned off the music, I turn the kettle on. That's my favourite use of the iPhone – the fact that I can turn the kettle on in my kitchen, while in another room, through a Bluetooth device. It's hugely pointless, but it brings me a little joy. I wrap the towel around my waist and make my way through the bedroom towards our open-plan kitchen and living room. It's the perfect time of the morning to wake up on an April day in this old town.

The sun has just risen and thin rays of gold are beaming their way into our penthouse. We have floor-to-ceiling windows all around the living quarters of this place. The living room and kitchen are flooded with light in the daytime. I love these two minutes to myself. I use them to stare out onto the rooftops of the city. The disorganised mess of architecture appears silhouetted at this time of the day. I love Dublin. Well, I used to love Dublin. It's lost its charm for me a little, but there's no getting away from the fact that it's ruggedly handsome. It shouldn't be, but it is. We can make out a lot of the iconic buildings around the town from our vantage point. The top of the Spire creeps its way above everything in the distance. I think it's a deadly sculpture. It's striking to look at – isn't that what art is supposed to be? I can't get over the fuckwits who moaned about the cost of the Spire. We were always a population of easy-going jokers in Ireland, but we've turned into a right crowd of moaners in recent times. We adopted a lot of traits from the Brits over the centuries, but we always stayed clear of their miserableness – up until we got money. Now we're just a tiny replica of our big brother across the Irish Sea – a bunch of moaners and groaners. I don't like to moan. I always try to look at the positive. Such as this view. I can never get enough of it.

What does Dublin have to offer me today?

I stay at the window until a click confirms that the kettle has boiled before I pour both myself and Ryan a fresh mug of coffee.

'Mornin', gorgeous,' I call out as I re-enter the bedroom to place the mug on his bedside table. I get a grunt in return.

Some mornings I feel like throwing the hot coffee into his pretty little face.

07:00

Ryan

I HATE THAT FUCKIN ALARM. I'M CERTAIN VINCENT CHOSE THE MOST annoying tone on his phone just to make sure I start every day in a miserable mood. He takes his time turning it off each morning too.

I lie in bed contemplating another long day stuck in this penthouse. At least I used to wake up with aspirations for the day, a year or so ago, even though I knew that I wouldn't go on to fulfil them. But now I can't even bother to lie to myself. I'm going to get out of bed, not long after Vincent brings me my coffee in about ten minutes' time, to watch morning television with him over a bowl of Corn Flakes. He'll leave for work at about seven forty-five and I'll climb back into bed. I'll probably stay here until midday with only the urge to masturbate at least once disturbing my lie in. I agreed to get up with Vincent at seven every morning when I left my job almost two years ago. Vincent thinks I spend eight hours a day on my laptop writing a future bestseller. I can't bring myself to tell him that I've written one page of notes in the past twenty months. That's it. I've lost my ability to write, but more annoying than that is the fact that I've lost my passion to write. I was always full of great ideas. I had a strong imagination when I was younger, but my creativity receded so much as soon as I started to work in media. My writing was forced to become formulaic. I use the laptop Vincent bought for me to scroll through Facebook and to watch porn. I'm useless. I do nothing with my days and I'm no longer afraid to admit that to myself.

I'd fall back asleep contemplating my failing life if it wasn't for the fact that I have to put up with Vincent singing in the shower. He thinks I can't hear him over the noise of the water, but I can. His voice is genuinely shit. There's only about three-quarters of an hour left until he heads off. Seven forty-five is my favourite time of the day. In fairness to him, he stops singing once the shower is turned off. He does that for me. I love him and loathe him in equal measure. Sometimes I just wish he wasn't successful. That way, we'd both be useless together and I wouldn't feel so inadequate. But then again, we wouldn't be living in a place like this if Vincent wasn't so brilliant at what he does. I constantly have to remind myself that I shouldn't blame him for my depression. It's all on me.

I can hear him pour coffee into our favourite mugs and I know he's coming to wake me up. He loves me so much. His dedication to our relationship has never diminished. He does all the right things. I feel really grateful when he places the mug of coffee on the bedside table beside me and I know it's cute that he still calls me 'gorgeous'.

But some mornings I just want to throw the hot coffee back into his ageing face.

07:05

Darragh

I've been lookin' forward to this day for months. But now it's all about to go down, I'm nervous – or anxious. Maybe both. I don't think I know what the fuckin difference is between those two feelings anyway.

I stand at the corner of Blood Stoney Road and Horse Fair, leaning against a lamppost so I can stare up at their apartment. It looks like a pretty cool place to live in. This building's seven storeys high and made entirely of glass. The sun's just popped up in the sky and the reflection from the windows is starting to blind me. I know I have everything in me bag because I checked it at least five times before I left me bedsit an hour ago. But I tap the inside of me jacket pocket to assure meself that the gun is still with me. Then I rub at me jeans pocket to feel for the mobile phone JR handed over to me last week. I'm good to go. I'm just waitin' on that phone to ring.

Me mind flashes through what could happen throughout the morning. Part of me hopes I don't have to kill again and that everything goes according to plan. If that's the case, I'll be a millionaire by midday. But another part of me won't be bothered at all if I do have to shoot Ryan. That'd be murder number three for me. I really am turning into a proper fuckin gangster.

A light turns on in their apartment and I know for certain that the fags are awake. JR has this down to a T. These jammy fuckers must have a lot of money to live in a place like this. The first two floors of the building used to be a warehouse but were turned into a marble lobby on the ground floor, and a posh bar and restaurant on the first. Some investor, about twenty years ago, pumped a fair few quid into this area of Dublin. He musta made a fuckin fortune. They're all pretty cool-lookin' buildings around here now. It looks like a mini New York City. But there's no doubt that this is the most jaw-dropping mini tower round the place. And these pricks live at the very top of it. JR knows everything about these fags. He even knows everything about their neighbours. Fat Barry and Ugly Janice, who live on the sixth floor, spend most of their time in London and won't be around this week – this is just one of many apartments they have around Europe. Keith and Sean, who live on the fifth floor – and who we also believe to be fags – will both be in their art studio further down the street on Clare Lane. I watched them leave about ten minutes ago. They don't normally come back until around five o'clock. I'll be grand anyway. The noises I make will be minimal. There'll be no raised voices and I have a silencer for the gun. There isn't a need for me to worry. JR and I have done our homework. This will be a walk in the park for me. I've hardly any work to do. It's Vincent who will be doing all the hard graft after all.

I'm glancing around the area again for no other reason but to pass some time when the phone finally buzzes.

'All good?' asks JR.

'All good, boss. Beautiful morning, isn't it?' I reply.

'You in place?'

'Been waiting on your call. I've had a good look around. Everything is as we said it would be. It's ten past seven, do you want me to make the move now?'

'Go ahead. Don't take the lift.'

'Of course I won't take the lift.'

JR's amazin'. He's taken me under his wing over the past few months and taught me so many things I've always wanted to learn. But sometimes he treats me like I'm an idiot. Of course I won't take the lift. That's been drilled into me as part of the plan for months. There are cameras in the lifts. There are also cameras in the reception area of the building, but we figured out a way to get by them. Besides, with this disguise on, nobody would be able to recognise me anyway. I walk slowly towards the entrance of the building and pause for a minute until I see the receptionist face in the opposite direction. As soon as she crouches down, I quietly push at the big glass door and make me way into the lobby – staying to the left as planned. I stoop low to crawl behind the wide leather couch before entering the jacks. There's two doors immediately inside the jacks: one that leads into the urinals and another that has a sign on it, which reads 'Staff Only'. I take out the library card from me back jeans pocket and wrestle with the second door handle before it releases. Another door faces me now I've walked into this pokey room which isn't locked and allows me access straight to the stairwell. I trip over a bucket as I make my way towards the stairs, causing a racket to echo through the room. Me heart races for a few beats. I wait until there's absolute silence before heading towards them. The receptionist didn't notice me entering the lobby and I dodged all the cameras. Job done. I'll be able to climb to the fags' apartment from here without any fear.

07:10

Vincent

I TURN ON THE LIGHT IN THE LIVING ROOM SO I CAN JOT DOWN SOME notes. I have a touch of OCD when it comes to work and I need to know where I am going to be at any point during the day. My work life used to be stressful, but I've managed to take control of my routine and have everything and everybody in line. My career is at a stage now where I just observe all of my staff stressing on my behalf. If I'm brilliant at anything, it's delegating.

Ryan is draped on our couch watching the adverts between *Good Morning Britain* segments. I like the fact that he has a small crush on Piers Morgan. People tell me I look a lot like him. I can see it. We're almost the same age and happen to have the same shaped head. He probably has a little more hair than I do, but we share a rosy complexion. Both of us scrub up well, too. I wonder if Piers looks as dishevelled as I do first thing in the morning before he puts his suit on?

I finish my notes as *Good Morning Britain* restarts and notice Piers is wearing a midnight blue suit with a blue tie. That's what I decide to wear today too as I make my way towards the bedroom. I find my iPhone on our bed and press play on Spotify. Beyoncé is back! 'Halo' begins to play, but fuck that. I want something more upbeat and scroll through the playlist until I find 'Freedom'. I bizarrely have my own dance routine for this song that I can somehow still pull off as I dress. My moves aren't bad for a forty-nine-year-old. I act like a straight bloke everywhere except in my own bedroom and en suite. I can really ham it up in the comfort of my own home. I take a crisp white shirt from a hanger in the wardrobe and dance my arms into it. Just as I fasten the top button I'm certain I hear a knock at the door. That's unusual. I mute Beyoncé and squint my eyes in surprise.

'That you, Ryan?' I shout out.

'It's the door,' he replies.

He can be so fuckin' lazy. He heard the knock for certain and is still slouched on our couch purring over Piers Morgan with a bowl of Corn Flakes resting on his chest.

'I'll get it, I guess,' I say sarcastically as I pace past him towards the front door.

I look through the peephole to see a young guy with an ugly haircut staring back at me.

What the hell does he want?

As soon as I open the door a wave of panic hits me. I'm shoved straight back into the hallway and bounce off the wall before landing face first on the floor. I blink my eyes open in shock to find the ugly prick pointing a gun at me. His other hand is lifted to his mouth, with his index finger stretched up to his lips, signalling that I should shut the fuck up. I hear Ryan's heavy breaths as he sprints towards us. It must be the quickest he's moved in a couple of years. The ugly prick points the gun at my boyfriend before back-kicking our front door closed behind him.

'Not a word, you two. In the sitting room, now,' he orders, motioning the gun up and down. I crawl to a standing position, my body trembling with disbelief.

'Sit down!' he orders again once we're at the couch. The stranger grins at us before dropping his gym bag to the ground. He reaches inside and takes out a reel of duct tape. I stare over at Ryan. He looks petrified.

'Is there anything ...' I begin to say before being told to shut up by virtue of the gun being shoved back into my face. My heart races as I try to take in what's happening.

'You,' screams the stranger, pointing the gun at Ryan. 'On the fuckin' floor, now. On your stomach. Spread your arms and legs out as wide as ya can.'

He has the strangest mongrel accent. I'm pretty sure it's half Cork, half Dublin. I'd bet any money that he grew up in Cork but moved to Dublin half his lifetime ago. I stare at his face. He has a bizarre blond hairdo that would have even looked dated in the eighties. You can tell by looking at him that he's had a hard life. I can see it in his bloodshot eyes. Yet he's still only a kid. About eighteen or nineteen, I'd guess. He can barely grow a moustache, but he is trying. And his face is still producing fresh acne. Ryan does as he's told while the kid waves the gun back at me, motioning that it's my turn to get up. Sliding one hand over a chair in our kitchen, he nods at me to sit in it. I notice my hands shake while I slip into the seat. I'm afraid to say anything as he wraps the thick tape around my wrists, fastening them to the arms of the chair. He keeps an eye on Ryan as he's doing this, but my boyfriend is clearly too afraid to try anything. He'll do as he's told. When the kid's finished taping both of my wrists, he slaps me across the face. That boils my blood more so than having the gun pointed at me. He then reaches for the back of Ryan's neck and pulls him to his feet.

'Sit in that other chair, fag,' he says, grinning.

Fag? Have we just rewound the clock by a decade?

The prick ties Ryan to the chair in much the same manner he tied me, but then proceeds a little further. Ryan's ankles are also taped down and I figure he must have missed that part of the process with me.

'We'll cooperate with you,' I finally manage to say. 'We'll do whatever it is you want, just don't hurt us, please!'

He walks over to me with a grin gurning across his face.

'Too fuckin' right you'll cooperate with me. Whether I hurt you or not. Now shut the fuck up.'

Turning his back on us, he reaches further into his bag. My eyes widen. I have no idea what he has in store for us. I look over at Ryan again. He looks like a rabbit caught in the headlights of an oncoming truck. At this moment I am more worried about him than I am for myself. And that's unusual. My default is normally selfish. At least I can admit that. Ryan's much weaker than I am. I'm relieved to see that the kid has only removed an old mobile phone from his bag.

He walks towards Ryan and wraps more tape tightly around the back of his head and across his mouth at least eight times. Ryan keeps his head still, but he can't help grunting in fear. When he's done, the smug fucker strolls towards me.

'This is for you, big boy,' he says, shoving the phone into the breast pocket of my shirt before falling back onto our couch.

'Here's what's gonna happen,' he says.

Ah … I know what's going on.

07:20

Jack

I TAKE A QUICK PEEK AT MY WATCH AS I LEAN AGAINST A LAMPPOST ON Horse Fair across from their apartment. It's less than five hours until the deadline. I know it's still early but I'm agitated. I take the mobile phone out of my jeans pocket and stare at the home screen again. Still no missed call. For some reason I don't believe the phone and click into the call history to double check. I notice a strange number that makes me squint for a second before I realise it was me who dialled it. It's the number for the reception on the ground floor of the apartment building. I rang there ten minutes or so ago asking for a form that I knew would make the receptionist turn around. But since then there's been no activity on my phone. I hope everything has gone as it's supposed to. I can't stop worrying. More things could have gone wrong in the first ten minutes of this morning than I believe they will over the next five hours. My mind races through all possibilities.

Did the receptionist see Darragh? Did he fail to open the staff door? Is he still making his way up the stairs? Did Vincent or Ryan get the better of him after he pushed his way into their apartment?

I dismiss these notions and conclude that I'm just being way too impatient. Darragh will ring me when he's ready. I wish I was a fly on the wall up there. I'd love to see Vincent and Ryan's faces as Darragh explains to them what a tiger kidnapping is.

I check my watch again and sigh loudly. Only one minute has passed since I last looked at it. I decide to take a slow stroll around Sir John Rogerson's Quay to try to relax. I catch a glimpse of myself in a car windscreen as I cross the street. A beard suits me. I don't like the black wig so much but it's amazing how many years the beard has taken off me. I thought it would have made me look older. I might grow one for real, but I suppose that would defeat the purpose of why I'm wearing one today.

Checking out the Sir John Rogerson's Quay area over the past few months has made me dig deep into my memory bank. I was eight years of age when we moved out of this place. It looked a lot different then. My da used to work in a bakery on the corner of Lotts Road, near the dog track. His boss rented us the small flat above it. Every time I smell cinnamon, it brings me back to my tiny bedroom; just enough room for the bed itself and a tiny cabinet. This area has changed so much in the four decades since we lived here. It's a nice modern area of Dublin now, but back in my day it was quite rough. At least I was led to believe it was rough. I don't remember seeing anything bad happen around here. My ma did her very best to make sure we didn't become friends with the Luciano kids. Their father was supposedly involved in the Italian mafia. I'm pretty certain that was just a rumour. They were the only Italians in the neighbourhood, so they were just labelled 'mafia'. They may well have been the nicest family around, but nobody knows because nobody got to know them. My parents would come down hard on me if I wasn't improving at school. They both took a big interest in anything I did. When my da forced me to join the local underage GAA team, he made sure I didn't miss one training session. It wasn't that he thought I was going to be the next Kevin Heffernan or anything like that, he just wanted to make sure I wasn't mixing with the wrong kids. My folks spent hundreds of hours of my young life making sure I'd grow up to be a respected member of the community. I was always grateful for that. I wonder what they'd think of me now, if they were looking down from whatever heaven my ma pretended to believe in, as I orchestrate the greatest bank robbery in the history of this old country of ours.

During my stroll around the block of City Quay and Grand Canal Street, and making my way back towards the penthouse, I manage to calm down. Morning fresh air is a remedy for almost all head-fucks. Darragh's not a bright lad, but he's determined and loyal. He'll do exactly as I tell him. He's loyal to a bad cause. If he thinks it's criminal, he's in until the end. He's a weird little boy. I couldn't have a weirder little boy on this job. He'll see it all through for me, I'm certain of that. I've been anxious over the past month or so and didn't really sleep last night; I was rolling around in bed desperate to get back to my dreams. Ironically, today is the type of day I have dreamt about for years.

07:20

Darragh

I can see the terror in both of their eyes. Ryan looks the most frightened though. He doesn't know whether to stare at me in fear or at Vincent for help. Neither of them has any idea what I'm up to. It's hilarious. They nearly shat themselves a few minutes ago when I went searching in me bag for the first time. I was only lookin' for the tape. Fuckin idiots. Vincent keeps trying to speak up but I'm keeping control. Ryan is too stunned to open his mouth. Whatever he'd try to mumble wouldn't make sense anyway. He's all taped up now. But I need to talk with Vincent. That's why I've only taped his hands to the chair. I reach back into the bag and take out the second mobile phone.

'This is for you, big boy,' I say, shoving it into the breast pocket of his shirt. At least this gay fucker is dressed. The other fag only has his boxer shorts on. It's actually a bit sickening to look at. I take a moment, on purpose, to sound as cool as fuck as I fall back onto their couch.

'Here's what's gonna happen. Vincent, you're going to withdraw two million euros from each of the four branches of ACB you run and return to me here with all eight million by midday. If you don't, I'll kill your little fuck buddy here.'

I deliver my lines perfectly, just as I've rehearsed hundreds of times over the past few weeks. Vincent looks stunned. His jaw is practically on the floor.

'But ... but ... I, eh,' he stutters. I don't have time for this shit. Well, he doesn't have time for it. Time ain't on his side.

'Shut the fuck up, ya little cunt,' I demand, as I sit more upright on the couch. I need to get angry. 'I know for a fact that you are authorised to take two mill from each bank so don't even pretend you can't or I'll shoot you both dead right now.'

Perfectly delivered again. That stopped Vincent in his tracks.

'You need to get this all done within the time frame, d'ye hear me? You have until midday. Not one minute past. Any wrong moves and he'll get a bullet straight to the head. And then we'll come back for you. Do you understand me, fag? If this doesn't go according to plan you'll both be killed. Tick, tock!'

I'm delighted with how cool I'm handling all of this. This is the first time I've ever carried out a kidnapping. JR calls it a tiger kidnapping. I'd never heard of it before. It makes perfect sense. JR is a fuckin genius. That's the hardest part of my morning over. I have both of these fags in place now.

I've tried to play out how the morning would go in my head countless times but there's not much I can predict. I'll be sitting here keepin' an eye on Ryan until I'm told otherwise by JR. While the two fags are taking in everything I've told them, I take a look round their apartment. It's pretty cool, I have to say. They've got one helluva massive television screen. I guess that's what my eyes will be on all morning. JR has been drilling into me for months about not lettin' Ryan get into my head. But what can he do? He looks a lot more terrified than Vincent. I was told this would be the case. Vincent already seems like a bit of a smug cunt. I bet he's one of those fuckers who just thinks he knows it all. I hate that sort of prick. Ryan just looks like a little rent boy. That's all he is now anyway. A kept little fag. It's almost sad. What a shitty life that must be. They're both surprisingly silent as I pace round their couch. They don't know what to do. I go over everything in my head again, one final time. I'm pretty sure I've explained it all perfectly. Vincent knows full well what he has to do and he hasn't flipped out. I get the impression he feels he can do this. The excitement seems to be getting the better of the anxiousness in my stomach at last. It looks like me and JR are gonna be millionaires in just a few hours' time.

07:25

Vincent

I GET INTO CHARACTER STRAIGHT AWAY. THE CULCHIE IS STILL MUMBLING some big-man bullshit but I'm just thinking of the task in hand. I need to get around each of the four branches of ACB in the next five hours and take two million euros from each of the vaults. I have access to those vaults, of course, but I can't get in there alone. They can only be opened with a double key card system. I have one key, being manager of all four banks, while my assistant managers – who work at each of the branches – have the sister keys. I know for certain that three of them won't even question me, but I'm wary of Noah Voss, who is the new assistant manager of Church Street. He was appointed about three months ago against my wishes; the board felt his experience as head of a successful branch of Barclays in London made him the ideal man for the job. I still haven't figured him out. He asks a lot of odd questions. Plus, he's a Christian. I can't stand Christians. How can you trust somebody who believes in fairy tales?

I've totally calmed down since the prick smacked me across the face earlier.

'Any wrong moves and he'll get a bullet straight to the head,' I was told as our captor nodded towards Ryan about five minutes ago. 'And then we'll come back for you. Do you hear me? If this doesn't go according to plan you'll both be killed.'

I've figured in the past few minutes, after the shock receded, that I can handle the task at hand. I just need to get into character. I'm playing myself like it's any other day. That can't be hard. I just need to keep calm despite the surreal situation. If I stay cool, I can do this. There should be no need to worry.

'Is there a route you want me to take?' I ask our captor to his surprise. He was just pacing around our couch muttering to himself at the time.

'Well ... what's the quickest way?' he asks me as an answer.

'Nassau Street, Camden Street, Church Street and then back to the IFSC branch,' I reply rapidly. I've been thinking about it.

'Alright,' he says, looking a bit flustered. 'That makes sense. Work your way around that way. I don't really care what way you work it once you come back with all the cash. But I don't want any mistakes, d'ye hear me?' he asks, his Cork accent coming through the angrier he gets.

'I'll be back with the money before midday,' I assure him. 'Just please don't hurt him. I promise I'll be back.'

'If you're not back at midday ... boom!' he says, mock shooting Ryan.

I stare over at my boyfriend. His eyes aren't as wide as they were a few minutes ago. I think he's been calmed by the fact that I seem confident I can do this. A tear that I noticed running down his face earlier has dried into his skin. He hasn't been able to say anything, but what could he say that would interest our captor? This is all in my hands. I'm the one who has to carry out the robbery. I'm acting composed because I want to be in character. If I give anything away to any of my employees then this will all fall apart. I'm also selfishly thinking that there is no immediate threat to my life. I will be getting on with my day, free as a bird, as if it were a normal Tuesday morning. It's Ryan's life that is directly at stake this morning, not mine. That sounds harsh but it's an honest feeling. My stomach may be in knots, but I won't let that be known on the surface. Not to Ryan, not to our captor, and certainly not to anyone in ACB.

'What time is it?' I ask.

'It's almost half past. You leave for work in about fifteen minutes, right?'

Wow, this fella knows my routine off by heart. I nod a reply before eyeing my taped hands. He gets the gist. The kid walks over to me and bends down to undo the tape. He begins the process with the pistol still glued to his left hand. But after struggling for a few seconds he decides to leave it on the ground beside him. It's about a yard away from my left foot. Once my hands are free, I'm pretty certain I can make it to the gun before him. The possibility races through my mind as he releases my right wrist before turning his attention to my other arm. I stare up at Ryan. He knows what I'm thinking and shakes his head in a disapproving manner.

He's right of course. Our captor still has an advantage over me. The gun is nearer to him even if I genuinely feel I could get there first. I have no intention of doing it, though. He unties my left wrist and reaches for the pistol straight away. The only muscles I move are in my hands to ease some of the numbness. Then I stand up.

'Calm down, big boy,' I am told. 'Where you off to?'

'To finish getting dressed for work. I assume that's why you untied me,' I reply smartly.

'Yeah, of course,' he says. 'But on my fuckin' terms, okay?'

I figure our captor isn't that bright. It disappoints me somewhat. How could the two of us have been turned over by this loser?

'I'll follow you. Where are your clothes?' he asks.

I point towards our bedroom. I already have my shirt and trousers on. I just need to knot my tie and throw my jacket, my shoes and my glasses on before I'm all set. I stare at myself in the bedroom mirror as I slide a dark blue tie under the collar of my shirt. I can see my captor behind me pointing the gun at me. He appears nervous. But he's also unpredictable. Trying to take him on wouldn't make any sense. He could unload the barrel of that pistol into me without hesitation. I finish the process of getting dressed and turn to him.

'How do I look?' I ask, surprising him again.

'Like eight million euros,' he replies, making a tiny laugh shoot out of my nose. Not a bad retort. Perhaps he isn't as stupid as he looks.

07:35

Ryan

I CAN'T BREATHE. MY NOSE CAN'T TAKE IN THE AMOUNT OF OXYGEN IT needs right now. I have to get this tape off my mouth but nobody seems to be listening to my muffled screaming. I wonder what those two are up to in the bedroom. I'm not surprised how calm Vincent is acting while I'm all tied up. That's his character in a nutshell. Some little prick has broken into our home and is pointing a gun at us, yet Vincent is still going on like he's in control. I decide to stop focusing on my breathing and think this whole thing through. I stare at the digits on the microwave oven that I can see from where I'm sitting – 7.35. I do the maths in my head. Vincent has four and a half hours to go to his office, make some phone calls and then visit the four banks he plans to rob of two million euros each. My breathing becomes panicky again. My head shakes back and forth frantically. I need to calm down. I think of the yoga classes I used to attend years ago before I even met Vincent.

Breathe in slowly, visualise each breath coming in through the nostrils, filling the back of the throat and drifting slowly down the chest cavity before it enters the lungs. Feel the lungs expand. And then visualise the air going in the opposite direction as you breathe out.

It seems to be working. I miss yoga. I miss a lot of things from my years gone by, even if my past was mainly a huge struggle.

Every time my breaths get panicky, it brings me back to the afternoon I sat in my bedroom determined to tell my folks that I fancied men. It was about time I told them. I was nineteen years of age and I'd known I was gay for at least five years. I'd sat on the end of my bed with my head in my hands, breathing just as I had been seconds ago, too heavy and too panicky. My chest ached but that wasn't going to stop me. I stood up and walked down the thirteen stairs of our terraced red brick house before entering the sitting room. Me da was watching horse racing, annoying me ma with tuts and sighs as she tried to read some tabloid rag. Our sitting room was the same scene every Saturday afternoon.

'I'd like to talk to you two,' I said in a way that already spelt out drama.

'In the middle of the fuckin' racin'?' me da asked.

'Dessie!' me ma said sternly. It didn't matter. Me oul fella ruled the roost.

'Wait till this race is over!'

I sat beside me ma on our shabby couch and felt her stare inquisitively at me as she folded the newspaper to put away. She knew something wasn't right. I looked up at her, fully aware I was putting on 'pity me' eyes.

'Ah, fuck ya!' me oul fella shouted out, cursing that his horse didn't win. He jumped off his armchair in a rage and clicked the television off.

'What do you want, son?' he said, standing over me. He was peering down at me as if I'd already ruined his day. He had no idea what was coming next. I knew it wouldn't go well. Me da called gay people 'queers' when he saw them on TV and he genuinely thought homosexuality was a disease. It was a generational thing, I suppose. Telling him his only son was gay was no easy feat. But he didn't say a thing when I finally got the words out. Me ma didn't either, but she leaned in to me and wrapped both of her arms around my shoulders. She was trying to hide it, but I could tell she was crying. She was worried about what the neighbours would think. I knew that would be her only concern. It's the only concern of any Dublin housewife. Me oul fella spun around and lashed at the TV standby button again, turning the horse racing back on. Then he sat down in his chair as if nothing happened over the past two minutes.

'Give me that newspaper, Anne, will ye? I wanna see who I've bet on in the next one.'

My sexuality was never mentioned again in that house. I only ever spoke to me ma about it when she came to see me in the bedsit I'd rented in Mount Brown. She didn't quite understand what being gay meant but to her credit she tried to learn about it. It turned out that coming out to my parents wasn't as painful as coming out to me mates. I thought people of my generation would be more understanding, but I noticed my so-called pals slowly but surely drift away from me as weeks and months went by. I'd visit gay bars in town to try to generate new friends but I found it very difficult. I was used and abused by some I'd hoped to become pally with, and genuinely contemplated suicide on two separate occasions. They were just thoughts back then, but I was so depressed. So down. I really didn't like my life at all. That was until the bank manager I had met a few times to discuss a loan suggested we meet for a bite to eat outside office hours.

I watch Vincent walk out of our bedroom in his favourite navy-blue suit. It would look like any other morning but for the gunman behind him. My boyfriend winks over at me to suggest everything will be okay. He can be a bit arrogant, but heroes normally are the arrogant type. I trust him implicitly. I am the weak character in our relationship. But I know more than anyone that Vincent isn't as clever as he thinks he is. I know he will feel confident he can get back here in four hours with all the money in tow. But I am sure it's a more difficult task than he will feel it is. He walks over to me, shadowed by our captor, and kisses me on the forehead.

'I'll be back, baby,' he assures me. 'Please just relax. I can get this done.'

I swing my head from side to side in the hope of getting the gunman to remove the tape from my mouth, but he doesn't even react. He just watches as Vincent holds my head still to kiss me again.

'I love you,' he says. I nod and blink some tears out as a response. I want to tell him I love him too.

'You guys are fuckin' sick,' says our captor, pulling Vincent away from me. 'Now, go get me my fuckin' money.'

07:45

Jack

WHEN I HANG UP THE PHONE, ADRENALINE RUSHES THROUGH MY BODY. Darragh has done exactly as asked. Vincent should be coming down the elevator and out of the building any minute now. I was worried about the first part of the day because it was the only part I didn't have full control over. It was all on Darragh. But the boy's done well. Now it's all back in my hands. I haven't had a rush like this in years. And even back then I wasn't enjoying it as much as I seem to be right now.

Before I married Karyn I was inducted into the Dublin gang scene. I didn't like it, but I loved her. Karyn's whole family were involved in organised crime and if I was going to be part of the Ritchie family, I'd have to get involved too. I'll never forget her da wrapping his arm around my shoulders on the first tee at Deer Park golf course one freezing morning back in 1985. He was puffing on one those ridiculously oversized cigars he used to smoke for show. It felt like something you'd see in a mob movie. That's the thing with these guys, they try to live up to the stereotype Hollywood invents for them. The movies aren't a retelling of organised crime, organised crime is a retelling of the movies. And the Irish newspapers do their best to glamorise it as much as they can too, just to jump on the bandwagon. I find it all quite cringeworthy, to be honest.

'Now listen here, kid,' he said, exhaling rancid cigar smoke. 'Ye gotta do what you gotta do. But if you wanna be part of this family then you gotta do a little of what I want you to do.'

It felt like I was an extra in a parody of a poor mob movie but I didn't dare suggest that. Instead, I nodded in agreement and acted like a puppy dog around Harry Ritchie. Everybody did. He was actually a very friendly guy and quite warm, but he was assertive and strict when I first met him. He was probably laying down a marker, but he had an amazing ability to get everybody on his side. I made it quite clear to him that his daughter was my main concern in life, but if there was anything he needed from me, I'd never let him down. He respected my honesty and for that reason, I was always on the periphery of affairs and not fully involved in the heavy-duty stuff. For the first couple of years, I was used as 'body' – that was it. I'd visit restaurants and bars, that my brothers-in-law or other members of the 'family' would break into, to demand protection money. I've always been a big guy. I was six foot three inches tall at just sixteen years of age, and I have always had broad shoulders. I was known as the Friendly Giant through the last couple of years of secondary school and often wondered what those kids would have thought if they'd seen me hanging around with The Ghost. I just stayed in the background as those braver than me would smash a bar manager's face in until he handed over every penny he had in the tills. I didn't get involved in the physical activities for the first eight months or so but after a while, some of the landlords decided to fight back and I'd be called on to sort them or their friends out. I think I'd only ever thrown one punch in my life up until that point, which was aimed at my old best mate in a school corridor when we were both in fifth year. I enjoyed the thrill of the fights because I always knew we could handle them. But I'd go home at night and feel sorrow for what I'd been involved in. Karyn hated the fact that I'd got involved in her family's business. But she knew all too well that I had no choice. Besides, the money was good. I'd personally take home around a thousand pounds in one week, which was huge money back then. I once calculated that Harry's empire was collecting close to a hundred thousand a week. And that was only in protection money. He had loads of other activities on the go at any one time.

I hide behind a parked Rav 4 as I watch Vincent push open the glass door to exit his apartment building. He really likes that blue suit. I've seen it on him several times recently. His face appears paler than normal but I have no doubt that he will be able to carry out his orders. He has to. He is mainly based at an office at the IFSC, on Harbourmaster Place, which is a twenty-two-minute walk from here. He doesn't order his driver to take him to work. He likes to take in the fresh River Liffey air, for some reason. He'll walk straight over Sean O'Casey Bridge and continue past the two moats in the IFSC until he turns slightly left onto George's Dock. Once there, he'll be only a few hundred yards away from his office. He normally arrives between 8.05 a.m. and 8.15 a.m. By the looks of things, he'll be there at the earlier time this morning. His chauffeur-driven car will be waiting for him in the car park under his office. He'll certainly be using it today. The banks he'll rob won't open until nine o'clock, but he'll spend the guts of the first hour of his morning organising access to the vaults through four phone calls.

I'd already decided that I'd head towards Nassau Street after I'd watched him cross the bridge towards his office. I know where I'll be standing when he walks out of that first branch with two million euros. I've been spending the money in my head for the past few months. We've already planned our perfect life together as millionaires.

08:00

Darragh

I DON'T HAVE MUCH TO DO UNTIL VINCENT RINGS ME TO CONFIRM HE'S organised his visits to the banks. He'll be arriving at his office in the next ten minutes or so. It will probably be another half an hour or forty minutes before he gives me the go-ahead that everything is set up. From what JR has told me, none of this should be a problem. Vincent is the boss of ACB.

I pass some of the time by taking a stroll around the apartment. I want a place like this when I'm rich. The living area is somethin' else. It's one big, bright large space with a huge L-shaped leather couch taking up the middle of the floor. It faces what must be a fifty-inch TV screen. Just off that is a pretty cool kitchen. I think it's the biggest kitchen I have ever seen. A big floating table thingy separates the living room and the kitchen. The colours wouldn't be to my taste, it's all creams and whites throughout the whole space. I like blues and blacks. Dark colours. Probably because I have a dark mind. A faggoty perfume smell fills the place. This has the look and feel of a gay couple's apartment except for the sports magazines and newspapers that are thrown across both the floating table thingy and the couch. It's a clean home but it's untidy. Ryan mustn't be doing his job properly as a little fairy housemaid. According to JR, this little fag hasn't worked in a couple of years.

I stare over at him as I walk around his table thingy. He no longer looks petrified. He looks depressed. Maybe he doesn't trust that Vincent will get the job done. I imagine shovin' the gun into Ryan's face at midday and blowing his brains all over the massive window behind him. Part of me wants to kill him, but what we really want is Vincent to get round to all four banks in time to give me and JR a payday we could only ever dream of. If he does, Ryan will survive. JR is tailing Vincent all day; I'm certain the job will be completed without fuss.

I'm not all bad. I do have pangs of guilt every now and then, especially with regards to the first young fella I killed. He didn't deserve to die, but Bob did. He was a sick fuck – a rapist! JR came up with a plan for us to confront Bob with all the information we knew and demand money from him. Take it, then shoot him. Bob was adamant he hadn't raped anyone, but JR had it on good authority that it was true. He has great links with the Dublin mob and they have allowed him to take the lead on a new arm of their gang, of which I am the first newbie. It's a dream come true for me. Most young guys want to be professional footballers or rock stars, Hollywood icons, or some shit like that when they grow up. Me? I always wanted to be Henry Hill. *Goodfellas* has been my favourite movie since I was twelve years old. I must've watched it at least a hundred times by now.

My job was to have the sick rapist empty his safe of cash before blowin' his head off. Everything JR said to me came true. He knew the cunt would deny the allegations and he knew he'd have about fifty thousand euros in the safe. We split it down the middle.

'You have the wrong guy, you have the wrong guy,' he kept repeating. I didn't have the wrong guy. JR's research is always spot on. I shoved the gun into his mouth and asked him a question.

'Any last requests?' I said, not giving him time to answer before pulling the trigger. I figured that could be the line I mutter before I kill people in the future. I could become known for it. It could be my catchphrase. I looked at the hole in the top of his head and licked my lips. I unscrewed the silencer while standing over his body and placed both the silencer and the pistol in my bag before slinging it over my shoulder and making my way out of his tiny gaff. I could hear the soundtrack to *Goodfellas* playing in my head as I strolled away from the garden. I allowed myself a smile. Since then I've had feelings of guilt, but there are also times when adrenaline rushes through me, knowing full well that I am a real-life hitman.

As far back as I can remember I always wanted to be a gangster.

I often repeat that line over and over to myself in Ray Liotta's accent.

Good Morning Britain is still showing on the TV I muted earlier. I notice Susanna what's 'er name is wearing one of those low-cut tops she likes to tease us with every now and then. She's a dirty lookin' bitch. I bet she's savage in the sack. How sexy can one woman be? She is big where all women should be big: lips, tits, hips and ass. She's not great without make-up on, I saw that when she did that celebrity dancin' shite on the BBC a few years back, but there's something in those eyes that screams 'fuck me now'. The white dress she has on today is makin' me dick twitch. I reach for the TV remote and unmute the volume. I instantly hear her voice. That husky British accent was designed for men's ears. Well, most men. Not this fag tied up in the chair just ten feet away from me.

'How can she not turn you on?' I say, looking at Ryan. He doesn't even respond with a head nod. He just sits there feeling sorry for himself. I snigger through my nose when an idea crosses my mind. It's equally funny as it is sick. I unbutton my jeans and slide them down past my ass. I begin to rub on the outside of my boxers, making my dick stiffen.

'See how sexy I find her?' I say, pointing me dick at Ryan. Susanna continues to talk about some British education bullshit but I'm not hearing the words, I'm just hearing that husky voice. She's often awoken my morning glory. I giggle to meself as I walk over to Ryan with my hand wrapped round me whole package.

'See that, fag, bet you never had one that big, did ye?'

I'm not even sure whether me dick is big or not, to be honest. It's seven and a half inches long when hard. I measured it once with a ruler. I think that's a decent size. Google says the average size of a penis is just over five inches when on a boner so I must be fuckin well hung. But when I watch porn I end up a little bit confused. My dick is tiny compared to the guys that fuck on camera for a living. Maybe the camera adds length.

'Oh yeah, mutha fucker,' I say to Ryan while grabbing at my balls. I stare over at the TV screen. Susanna what's 'er name has turned into Piers Morgan. That's one sure-fire way to lose an erection. But for some reason I'm still turned on. I don't normally get this horny this quickly, but I think the strange environment for wanking has added to the excitement. I've never had somebody in the same room as me while I whack one off. Within a minute I spray a load of cum all over the screen, laughin' as I do it. When I'm done cumming I stare over my shoulder at Ryan. His chin is resting on his chest looking down, but I'm sure he had a peek up just to see if I finished the job all over his fifty-inch TV screen.

'That's what real men do, Harkness,' I say to him. He allows himself a look at me, perhaps in surprise that I know his surname. 'You're missin' out on pussy and tits, you little freak.'

I fall back on the couch and sigh deeply, just as I always do after a wank. The thrill of whackin' off is deadly but I always get a depressed feeling instantly afterwards. I don't know if all men get that. I pull my boxer shorts back up over my dick and button my jeans back up just in time for the phone to ring. I answer, expecting to hear Vincent's voice, but it's not him.

08:05

Ryan

I WISH I LISTENED TO VINCENT MORE OFTEN. I'VE NO IDEA WHAT TIME HE gets to work. But if he leaves at seven forty-five each morning I'm guessing it only takes him about twenty minutes to walk there. He should be arriving at his office about now. This morning is the first morning in ages I wish he hadn't left me. I've been a lot more nervous since he headed off.

I've refused to stare over at this spotty prick but he's just turned the volume back up on the TV and I can't help but give him a glance.

'How can she not turn you on?' he asks, pointing at Susanna Reid on *Good Morning Britain*. I answer by looking away again. But I can't help but draw my eyes back to him when I notice he's pulling his trousers down.

What the fuck is he doing?

He begins to rub at his dick right in front of me. This guy is fuckin' insane. My eyes widen as I see him take his dick out of his boxer shorts. I don't look but I know he's tugging away at it. He must be just trying to freak me out. If he is, it's working. But after a few seconds of being disgusted I will him on in my mind to complete the job.

Cum, you stupid prick. Go on, spray a load.

He strolls away from me towards the TV, giving it everything. This is weird for a million different reasons, but none more so than the fact that he's now jacking off to Piers Morgan's smug face. He's not relenting. I hear his spunk slap against our TV screen and I almost laugh to myself.

Way to leave your DNA at a crime scene, you fucking idiot!

I can't believe somebody would be that stupid. It begins to frustrate me that Vincent and I were held captive by somebody with such a low IQ. I think the whole thing through. This can't be for real, can it? I look at his face for the first time since this morning as he falls back into our couch sporting an ugly grin, and realise that he must be some form of retard. And that's when I get really frightened. This guy is so unhinged that he will have no problem blowing my brains out as he promised he would if Vincent doesn't arrive back here by midday. I immediately think of my yoga breathing techniques again as the panic attack resurfaces. My yoga instructor used to always start by saying 'breathe in through the nose'. Right now, I have no fuckin' choice.

Just as I'm calming my breaths, his phone rings. I assume straight away that it's Vincent, as he is supposed to give this guy the okay after he's contacted his assistant managers. But I can hear the screech of an unfamiliar voice on the other end of the phone and I know it's not my boyfriend.

'Good, good,' says the freak next to me. It gives nothing away. 'He's a little tied up at the minute,' he then says while looking over at me. He thinks that line's hilarious, which probably proves again how dumb he really is. 'Great stuff. He should ring me in about twenty minutes then, I guess, like?'

He already told us somebody would be keeping a close eye on Vincent to make sure he's looking after everything from his end. This must be that guy on the other end of the line. His partner in crime. I wonder if they are as stupid as each other. I also begin to wonder how two stupid people could come up with such a plan, and immediately feel that this has to be an inside job. Somebody Vincent knows must be in on this.

'That was my man,' says the greasy prick to me after he hangs up the phone. 'Your pussy-ass boyfriend is in his office. All's going on time. Your life could be spared yet.'

I try to think of people Vincent works with and immediately get frustrated that I zone out every time he opens his mouth about work. I know there's a guy called Jonathan, who he mentions quite a lot and then there's Michelle, of course, who I know quite well. But neither of them would be the type to get involved in this sort of thing. Vincent also has a secretary called Belinda but as far as I'm aware she's as innocent as they come. It must be somebody I've never heard of. Some low-ranking official from one of the banks or the head office. There's no way they're going to get away with this. Certainly not with this dumb fuck leaving his baby-making juice all over our living room.

I notice him walking around the apartment, taking it all in. I'm willing him to leave more DNA around the place, but in truth he's probably already delivered enough.

'What the fuck do you do around here all day, Harkness, huh?' he shouts out to me. 'I mean it's a nice place, I wouldn't mind hanging out here myself all day, but you must get bored.'

That's the second time he's mentioned my surname. He knows everything about us. This is a well-planned job. I don't answer him. I can't answer him. Instead, I feel justified in knowing that this is an inside job. How does he know I sit around the apartment most days? This guy is leaving me clues every two minutes. He is so stupid that by the time Vincent comes back I may have this case solved.

'Lover boy keep you, does he? You don't have to work because he brings home enough bacon, huh?'

I continue to ignore him. He's right in his assessment though. I haven't had a job for twenty months now. Vincent and I were only dating for about two months when he asked me what my dream job would be.

'I'm a good writer,' I said. 'I enjoy writing. I always wanted to write books but I don't have the discipline. There's also no money to be made from writing unless you pen a masterpiece.'

'There are plenty of ways to make money from writing,' replied Vincent. 'What about creative writing in an advertising agency or something like that? Journalism?'

'I'd love to be a journalist. I just don't have the qualifications.'

With that, Vincent whipped out his laptop and started searching on Google.

'Here ye go,' he said, turning the laptop towards me. 'DCU do a specialised journalism course. Let's see if we can get you on it this September.'

'Nah, I … I …'

'You … what?' he said, looking at me with a raised eyebrow. I just shrugged as an answer before smiling back at him. Within eight weeks of knowing him, Vincent was already an inspiration to me in more ways than I ever thought possible. He leaned over to kiss my smile and I knew right there and then that I was in love with him.

My eyes refocus towards the clock on the microwave. I panic slightly. 8:15. The last quarter of an hour has flown by. I hope the minutes tick by slower throughout the morning. My heavy breaths begin to consume me again and the tape feels tighter around my mouth. I allowed myself to get carried away assuming we were dealing with Ireland's dumbest criminals, but maybe dumb criminals are the most dangerous kind to be dealing with. I can't keep my eyes off the blinking colon in the middle of the 8 and the 15. There is no noise, but I can hear it inside my head. *Tick, tock. Tick, tock.*

08:15

Vincent

I'M ALWAYS THE FIRST PERSON TO ARRIVE AT THE OFFICE. I SIT HERE ALONE until about quarter to nine almost every weekday morning. I've often remarked how quiet and peaceful these few minutes are to my colleagues when they finally arrive in. But today I can hear the ticking of Belinda's clock just outside my office door as if it's ringing right next to my ear.

Tick, tock, tick, tock.

It is literally a timely reminder. I need to get a move on. I take a deep breath to refocus and get back into character before picking up the phone. I must remain cool. *This is an ordinary Tuesday. This is an ordinary Tuesday.*

'Hello, Vincent,' screeches Michelle as she answers after just one ring. I don't normally call her this early.

'Hey, Chelle,' I say in a friendly tone. We've been close for years. Well, she thinks we're really close but I just play along. I think she likes the fact that I'm gay. She likes telling her friends that she has a gay friend. Whatever floats her boat. I've never played the gay card at all, except when I'm listening to Beyoncé in my own home. I don't want to be any woman's gay best friend. The idea repulses me. I never have been, nor ever will be, the sort of person who will sit around sipping coffee whilst bitching about people who aren't in my company. Fuck that! That's for people who have nothing going on in their own lives. I've got plenty of things going on in my own little world that I don't have much time to dissect other people's. And even if I did have the time, I'd fill it in a more

41

productive way. The one stereotype that annoys me most about gay men is the one that says we're all bitches. It's simply not true. I've known quite a number of gay people in my lifetime and have socialised in gay circles for years. I'd say a low percentage of gay men meet that stereotype. But Chelle thinks I'm a cute accessory to her life and I'm happy to go along with it once she toes my line professionally. She'd do anything for me.

'Nassau Street are low. Just a miscalculation on Jonathan's part coupled with a monumental number of big withdrawals last week. We'll need to shift some notes from your vault.'

'No problem,' she says breezily. 'How much do you need?'

'Two mill,' I reply, while holding my breath.

'Jesus, two million? Wow! That's more than you've ever asked me for before.'

'I was thinking that this morning after Jonathan rang me,' I say, backing it up with a confident giggle. 'But I'll have it back in your vault within forty-eight hours. It's just one of those strange coincidences. There was over one point five mill withdrawn from Nassau Street alone in the past five days,' I lie. 'That's three times the regular amount. They're just really low at the moment.'

'Okay, well I'm about fifteen minutes from the bank. When will your guys be coming to collect it?'

'I'll be transferring it myself,' I say. This is the tricky part. I shift massive amounts of notes between the branches on a regular basis but Securicor, our security firm, normally looks after the transfers for us. Especially the big ones. I've personally shifted some small amounts here or there but nothing coming close to two million euros. I grind my teeth during the silence between my saying that and Chelle's response.

'Really, two mill all by yourself?'

'Ah, he needs it as soon as possible. It's no problem. I have the cases here and will use my car. I'll get to you around nine, just as you open.'

'Okay,' she replies slowly.

I hang up and let out a small sigh of relief. Chelle will be the easiest to get around today. I know Jonathan and Ken will play ball too, even if better explanations are required, but I'm still worried about Noah. I rest my face on my forearm, leaning on the desk. I was thinking of how to approach things with Noah as I walked to work this morning and feel I should just be assertive as his boss. Rather than ask him for the transfer, just tell him it's happening. Who's he going to go complaining to anyway? I'm his only superior. He doesn't have the contacts for any of our bank's board members and, even if he did, they wouldn't have the time to get back to him in any urgent manner. It takes them at least forty-eight hours to return any of my calls and I'm in charge of all four of their Irish branches. I should be fine. I need to channel my acting skills and get in the zone. I can't give anything away. I'm a method actor anyway. Playing myself is a walk in the park.

Jonathan is next on my list of calls. As I pick up the receiver to call him I notice the time on the digital screen on my phone. The flashing colon in the middle of the 8 and the 21 makes me hear Belinda's wall clock again. *Tick, tock.*

Jonathan hasn't answered. I play around with the idea of leaving him a voicemail as his cheesy message plays, but I hang up just before the beep sounds. He'll get back to me when he's ready. Jonathan is always on the ball. I lean my head back on my swish leather chair waiting for Jonathan's call. I'm taking a moment to myself when I immediately sit back upright and reach for the phone. A quote I have lived by professionally for decades enters my head:

If you have to eat more than one frog, eat the big one first.

Get the toughest job done early.

I puff out my cheeks as I hear the ringing tone. He's one of those chumps who answers the phone by saying his full name. I can't stand those sorts of people. What is the fucking point of that?

'Noah Voss ...'

08:25

Jack

THE SOLES OF THESE SHOES ARE GOING TO BE WORN OUT BY THE END OF THE day. It's no big deal. I'll be able to afford a walk-in wardrobe for shoes alone soon enough. I'm annoying myself by pacing back and forward on the pathways of Westland Row. I've been lacking patience all my life. I surprised myself by holding off on this heist as long as I could, though. I needed everything to be perfect. And today is ideal. Even God would be telling me so, should the fucker exist. The sun is belting down on Dublin's city centre and I find myself in a jovial mood despite the fact that I am in the midst of the biggest bank robbery in the history of our country. I begin to whistle the tune of 'Under the Moon of Love' by Showaddywaddy and it takes me back to my youth. I must have been eighteen years old when that song was a big hit. It would have been just before I met Karyn. I was a really nice guy up until that point, even if I do think so myself.

I grew up in a tiny detached bungalow on Carpenter's Road after we left town when I was about eight. We used to say our address was Castleknock, but I'm not sure it really was. It was outside Castleknock, really. Anyway, our post always found us and our house price was slightly higher than it should have been. Our gaff was only a five-minute drive to Elm Green golf course. My old man was a member and we used to bond over eighteen holes every Sunday morning. We were huge golf fans. We'd watch as much golf as we could on the TV at the weekends, too, annoying my ma. I was always my dad's favourite for that reason. My old man used

44

to cheer on all the Irish golfers, but I was struck by Gary Player. I just loved the man. He seemed like a movie star playing golf to me, such was his aura through the screen. I used to have posters of him on my wall. Sounds fucking pathetic now. A golfer? When I was in my early teens, Gary Player replaced Jesus Christ as my hero. Like everybody else in the whole of Ireland, I fell for the bullshit that is the Bible for the first fourteen years of my life. My parents were happy for me to toe the conventional line, but there was no way on earth my father ever bought into the nonsense. My ma died believing that crap, my da certainly didn't. My old man was such a great guy, looking back. He worked his ass off to provide for the three of us. Like almost everyone, I hadn't a clue how great my old man was until it was too late to tell him. He was probably more obsessed with golf than I was. It's such a shame – the Irish golfers were pretty shit through his entire lifetime and these days they can't stop fucking winning. If an afterlife exists, then I'm sure my old man would be looking up from hell delighted at the country's successes since the turn of the century. But, of course, there is no afterlife. There is no proof of an afterlife whatsoever, which is why you have to make your years on earth count. That's what I'm doing today. I'm going to make sure the rest of my life is as enjoyable as it possibly can be.

My da passed away after suffering a heart attack in his bedroom aged just fifty-eight. I'm seven short years off that age now. I somehow managed to get over his passing quite rapidly due to my fascination with Karyn Ritchie. My mind was on a new life, not my old one. I think it hurt my ma even more that I dealt with the tragedy quite well and for that reason alone I don't think she ever took to Karyn. I, on the other hand, was obsessed with her from the moment I saw her across the room at Trolli's Dance Hall. I could tell straight away that her eyes were green. I don't know how, she was about fifty yards away from me in a low-lit room, but she stood out in such an obvious way. It was almost as if it was meant to be. I don't believe in any of that bullshit but I'd be stumped to explain with words just how much I was drawn to her that night. I couldn't understand why every other man in the room wasn't staring at the brunette in the blue dress. I'd always been labelled a handsome guy but I found it difficult to find a girlfriend. People used to tell me I was just too shy. I think I was just too picky. It was unusual I'd really fancy a girl. My standards were high. But I distinctly remember the urge I had to speak to Karyn that night. I thought I was being pretty cool by throwing my cigarette in front of me, stamping on it and making my way over to the girl in the blue dress. It was like it all happened in slow motion.

'Fancy a dance?' I asked, feeling a little Clarke Gable-esque for the first time ever.

'No thanks,' she said, embarrassing me in front of all her friends. 'I have a boyfriend.'

I smiled for years afterwards thinking about that moment. I'd never known what fancying somebody felt like until that night in Trolli's. The only thing I could relate it to was my fascination with Gary Player.

I whistle 'Under the Moon of Love' again through my smile when I feel the phone buzz from the inside pocket of my jacket.

'How a ye, JR?' says Darragh in an upbeat tone. It always amuses me how he pronounces the R with his West Cork accent – as if he's saying 'are'. 'Vincent rang me there. Everything is good to go. He said he has authorised to take the money from each of the banks. He'll be setting off in about twenty minutes or so to get to the first one for nine o'clock. He's going to Nassau Street first, okay?'

I can't really make out what he's saying due to the noise of the traffic so I ask him to repeat himself. Plus, my mind is wandering through the possibilities of the rest of the morning. The excitement builds in my stomach as I realise Darragh is telling me all is in order.

'Great work, Darragh,' I say, ending the call.

I look at my watch. 8:35. If I stroll from here to Nassau Street I should arrive just before Vincent and his chauffeur pull up in their BMW. I can't wait to see the look on Vincent's face as he walks out the front door of that bank with two million euros cuffed to his hands. A rush of adrenaline hits me. Instead of whistling, I sing quietly to myself.

'*Let's go for a little walk ...*'

08:30

Vincent

JONATHAN REILLY HAS ALWAYS BEEN EASY-GOING. I CAN'T BELIEVE HE questioned me so vigorously about the money transfer. I transfer money to and from his bank on a regular basis. Besides, it's not his bank. It's my fuckin' bank. Fair enough, I've never asked him for two million, but I'm a little annoyed that he went against the grain. He usually bows to my every demand. Noah Voss also surprised me. He did bow to my demand, without question. My phone call to him lasted about three minutes with him concluding he would have everything ready when I popped by at around ten thirty. Strange. Everything this fucker does is odd to me. He's a Christian, after all. I can't stand believers of faith. They're so bloody arrogant. Imagine having the arrogance to think you know the answer to life's greatest questions.

Where do we come from? What happens after death?

These fuckin' idiots walk around with a smug persona thinking they know it all. They know as much as anybody else. In fact, they know less than non-believers. Non-believers like to research and seek answers to these questions, believers don't. They are stuck with an answer – a wrong answer – and as a result are totally narrow-minded on the whole issue. Believers are the last kind of people you should listen to when it comes to life's biggest questions. Christianity bothers me more than any other religion probably because I'm surrounded by it in Ireland. I bet most of these guys have never even researched the book they believe to be the word of some creator. The Bible is actually a book filled with plagiarism.

The story of Jesus Christ coming down to earth is a total rip off of the story of Horas that was written decades before. Horas, like Jesus, was born miraculously to a virgin, they were both the son of 'God', an angel came down from the skies to inform the mother of her pregnancy, their birth was heralded by a shining star, there is no telling what happened to both between the ages of twelve and thirty, they both had twelve disciples, both performed miracles. Oh yeah, and both were crucified to death before rising again three days later. And then there are stories of other gods such as Attis, Dionysus and Mithra who cover the same bloody plot lines that were written before the Bible. You couldn't make it up. Actually, you could. They did. How can anyone of sound mind believe the Bible is a unique book when the Bible is plagiarised from fictional tales? The truth is, Christians aren't of sound mind. They are liars. They lie to themselves. I don't trust them. I don't fuckin' trust Noah Voss. He's a snake. I didn't like him in his initial interview despite the fact that he had a perfect CV. He had an arrogance that made me instantly dislike him. He told the story of how he grew up in Nigeria before he and his twin sister took refuge in London when they were just thirteen years old, leaving the rest of the family behind. They had not one single penny to their name. He was determined to make a success of himself and managed to obtain education to degree level before becoming a bank clerk. The board members of ACB fell for his sob story. I didn't give a shit. We've all been through our own difficulties. Appointing him as assistant manager of the Church Street branch wasn't my decision but I was outvoted. He hasn't caused me any hassle since he was appointed but I know trouble is on the horizon. I bet this prick is eyeing my job. The feedback I'm getting from our employees in Church Street is that Noah is quite a fair boss, but I'm sure they'll see through his 'pity me' bullshit in time.

I pick up the phone and dial two. That's the quick way to get hold of John. He is the most loyal man I know. We share the same sense of humour. He's been chauffeuring me for the past decade.

'You're gonna be busy this morning, John boy,' I inform him. 'I'll be visiting every branch. I'll head down to the car park around ten to nine-ish and we can head straight to Nassau Street. Is that okay?'

'No problem, boss,' he says to me. 'I'm just arriving at the offices now. I'll give you a call in about fifteen minutes and you can come down to the car.'

My heart rate quickens up. Fifteen minutes. Wow! In fifteen minutes' time I'll begin a robbery that will be all over the news tomorrow morning. According to the spotty little shit who broke into my penthouse this morning, I have a little over three hours to get back and save my boyfriend's life. I stare at my iPhone after taking it out of my pocket and think about leaving it here throughout the day. I can't be distracted. I suck on my teeth while I stew the thought over in my head before deciding to just turn the power off and bring it with me.

Then I take out the cheap-ass mobile the ugly prick gave to me this morning and ring him with the good news.

'All is in order,' I tell him.

'Good little fag,' he snarls back. That was it. He hung up.

'You look like you've seen a ghost, Vincent, are you okay?' Belinda asks as she enters my office. I hope she didn't hear me on that last phone call. But then again, I didn't say much.

'Yeah, fine,' I say, smiling back at her.

'You're white.'

'It's the blue suit,' I reply. 'I shouldn't wear it. It flushes my colour out.'

'Will I make you a coffee?' she asks, fake laughing at my retort. 'It might redden those cheeks a bit.'

'A quick one, please. I've to head out in a few minutes.'

'Oh yeah, Jonathan said you were calling over to him in an hour so, you want to take two million from him to transfer?'

The sneaky prick. He got on to my secretary to make sure everything was legit? He shouldn't be discussing any bank business with Belinda without my saying so.

'Belinda,' I say, agitated as I stand up. 'I need you to stay off the phones today. My office is a mess and I'll be out all morning. Could you organise these files into alphabetical order for me and clean up my emails? It won't take long. Just up until lunchtime.'

'Sure thing,' she replies as she walks back out of my office to put the kettle on. I lift up a number of paper files from the shelves behind my desk and shuffle them around. I always have everything in perfect working order so messing these up causes my temples to sting slightly. But I need to keep Belinda away from Jonathan while I visit the banks this morning. When our apartment was broken into just over an hour ago and this robbery was forced on me, I had a number of reservations about how it would go down. But Jonathan Reilly fucking it up never crossed my mind.

08:35

Darragh

It was only a short conversation but I could feel JR wasn't his usual self. He seemed quite nervy or somethin', almost as if he wasn't listening to me. Everything is goin' as planned. Vincent has got the green light from all four banks to take the cash so I'm not sure why JR would have been off. He kept askin' me to repeat meself. His nervousness is making me a bit tense now. I'd been doing okay up until that call. I'm sure he'll be alright. JR knows what he's doing. I pick up the TV remote control and start flickin' through the channels. There's fuck all on to watch. These pricks have the full deal – around two hundred channels in all. I didn't know fags were into sports, but they must have every sports package ye can get. I manage to click through each channel twice before blowing out me cheeks. I'm bored already. I've only been here about an hour and a half but it seems a lot longer than that.

Suddenly the apartment doesn't seem so big anymore. Ryan hasn't lifted his chin from his chest since he caught me whacking one off to Susannah what's 'er name about twenty minutes ago. I think about removing the tape from his mouth so I have somebody to talk to. At least it'll keep me entertained for the morning. But I know it's not the right thing to do. I'm desperate to not reach inside me jacket pocket. I promised meself I wouldn't, but I just don't think I can get through the morning without doing it. I obviously brought it with me for a reason. I knew in the back of my head that I'd want it. Ryan's eyes almost pop out of his head as I brush by him to make my way to the kitchen table thingy where I'd tossed me jacket earlier. Me fashion choices, if you can call them that, haven't changed since I was twelve years old. I was wearin' a very similar black leather bomber jacket the day I arrived in Dublin.

I miss Cork a little bit. Everyone keeps telling me West Cork is the prettiest place in the world, but I don't remember it that way. I grew up in a red-brick estate. Maybe me memories of the whole area are sketchy, but I remember the neighbours really well – Cork people genuinely are a more straightforward bunch. I had some great friends when I was younger. I would have even considered me da to be one of me best friends until I walked in on him beatin' me ma to a pulp one Friday afternoon. Despite protests from me ma I didn't hesitate in ringing the cops as soon as me old man left the house to go back to the pub. I learned over the next few weeks that beatin wasn't a one off. Me ma pressed charges under pressure from some family members and me old man was sentenced to fifteen months in prison. Within a matter of days of him going behind bars me ma had all our bags packed. We were off to Dublin. Me Uncle Mick had organised everything. He'd been living in Dublin since I was one, and looked after his little sister by arranging' work and a small flat for her and her three kids. It was just off the main Cabra Road. Me ma, me two sisters and meself were cooked up in a tiny two-bedroom flat over a newsagents on the Fassaugh Road. I liked the fact that we were livin' in Dublin for about two months before boredom set in. I had no friends. I hung out with me older cousin, Michael Junior, and his gang of fuckwits for the first few weeks but they soon lost interest in me. The novelty of me Cork accent only bought me so much time with them. They were fifteen and sixteen years old and were too cool to hang around with a kid like me. I didn't make friends in school. I was too new to join any gang. I know most kids say they don't like school, but I really fuckin hated it. I used to ditch it on regular occasions to sit at home watching movies while me ma was out working in a launderette in Glasnevin. *Goodfellas* is two and a half hours long but I learned every single bit of dialogue in that film within a couple of months of being in Dublin.

I've only really had one friend in my nine years in this city – Piotr Simienksi, who I met about four years in. I think we found comfort in each other having gone through similar stories. Me family and me arrived in a car from Cork to escape our past life, Piotr's family arrived on a plane from Poland to escape theirs. As luck would have it, me only mate in the world could barely speak a word of English. He had learned enough to get by, but his accent was so thick that we ended up communicating through actions most of the time. We had our own language, I suppose. When we were both seventeen we managed to get our hands on some really good fake IDs and after a day spent knocking door to door in the estates close to where we lived, offering to do odd jobs around people's homes, we would spend our evenings and the money we earned knocking back warm beer in The Hut on the Phibsborough Road. We used to laugh a lot but I didn't know what we were laughing at most of the time. Neither did Piotr. I think we were just both relieved to have a friend. I sometimes miss those days.

I reach inside me jacket pocket and pinch at the small plastic bag. I fuckin love cocaine. Piotr gave me me first line of the stuff about five years ago and I can barely get through one day without getting high now. I thought I might have the patience to get through this morning without it as I need a clear head, but the boredom coupled with the nervousness is proving too much for the sober me. I grab one of the sports magazines scattered on the kitchen table thingy and bring it over to the couch with me. Ryan's head cocks up when he hears me choppin' at me coke. Choppin' coke is the only reason I have a library card. But just as I'm about to roll up me five-euro note to snort the line, Ryan starts making bizarre noises. He's fuckin shaking. It looks as if he's havin' a fit.

08:40

Ryan

I ONLY MOVE MY EYES TO CATCH THE TIME. 8:40. I'M NOT SURE IF THE morning is going really slow or really fast. I seem to look at the clock every two minutes to subtract the difference between what it says and midday. Three hours, twenty minutes is the current calculation. I puff out my cheeks quietly and rest my chin further into my chest. I'm not the only one in the room puffing out their cheeks. This little prick's been agitated ever since he made that phone call a few minutes ago. I wish he'd stop flicking through the channels. It's so bloody torturous hearing one-second snippets of TV shows. He's just skimmed by the start of an old Champions League match that I'd love to watch again. It would help pass the time. He leaves the TV on a music channel that's blaring out one of the most ridiculous songs I've ever heard by a female artist I've never seen before. Then he abruptly stands up. I feel a waft of dread shoot through my body as he brushes by me. He paces over to the kitchen where I hear him fumble around in his jacket. What are the chances he's packing it in and going home? Zero. He just got a phone call from Vincent ten minutes ago saying everything is on track before ringing his partner in crime to inform him of the good news. I wonder what Vincent is up to now and how much he's worrying about me. I get distracted when my captor sits on the couch and begins pouring what I can only describe as the lumpiest looking line of cocaine I've ever seen onto one of my sports magazines. There can't be much money in kidnapping thefts. That is nasty, cheap-looking coke. I should know. In PR you need three things with you at all times; a notepad, a phone and bag of coke. Every PR representative and journalist I know snorts a line or two to get them through the day. PR reps have the biggest egos. They're all like Patrick Bateman from that movie *American Psycho*. They think they're much more important than they actually are. It's cringeworthy.

I tried to get into most newspapers when I graduated from DCU but it was difficult to find employment in that specific area. I wanted to work on a sports desk, but so did the other thousand journalism graduates from that year and every other year before that. I did the odd shift at the *Evening Herald*, but I could never nail down a position. That's when I decided to turn my 'attentions to PR. I harassed the MD of Wow PR in Harcourt Street until he eventually invited me in to talk to him. I began as an intern but soon found myself climbing the ladder somewhat into an account management position. Wow PR specialised in sport so I felt I'd reached my goal in some way. It was great hanging out with people such as Brian O'Driscoll and Robbie Keane for press calls in the early days, but that soon lost its charm. I was earning little or no money at the beginning but Vincent didn't seem to mind. He moved me into the apartment he was renting in Ringsend while the new penthouse he had just bought from the plans was being built. PR – as I began to find out after a few months in the industry – is full of arse lickers. I can't be that kind of person, my sexual activity aside. The industry is full of pretty little people who will fuck anything that moves – sports stars, sports journalists, other PR staff. It's a horny industry. That wasn't necessarily the part about it that bothered me. I just couldn't stand the fact that PR is full of self-centred pricks. You are either hanging out with PR reps who are too full of their own importance, or worse, journalists. Journalists are a law unto themselves. I swear most of them think they're celebrities in their own right. I found it all a little bit mortifying to be honest. Though I have to say, the one good thing about working in media is the fact that the social life can be pretty epic. I didn't get along with most of my colleagues but that didn't stop me snorting line after line of coke with them in almost every nightclub Dublin's city centre has to offer.

As I watch my captor roll up a used five-euro note to do a line of his own, an idea crosses my mind. I call out to him as loud as I can, mumbling through the duct tape. I manage to lift the chair up and stamp it to the ground. I catch his attention in seconds and flick my head as if calling him over.

'What the fuck's wrong with you, fag boy?' he asks, lifting my magazine from his lap to head towards me.

I eyeball him and mumble further in the hope that he'll remove the tape. It works. He yanks at it, taking most of the facial hair from my cheeks with it. The loop of duct tape loosens and falls around my neck. It allows me to breathe properly for the first time in over ninety minutes. I pant heavily before speaking.

'That's cheap-ass bullshit coke you got there, man. Go into the bedroom and bring out the silver box from the bedside drawer. The one on the far side of the bed. I've got some proper powder for ya.'

08:40

Vincent

I'M RARELY STERN WITH BELINDA BUT, AS SHE PLACES A MUG OF COFFEE ON my desk, I give her a look that I hope suggests I'm deadly serious.

'Be, I really need these files in alpha order by lunchtime today. It's imperative. I just haven't been keeping them in file order these past couple of weeks and I need to use them for reference later today.'

'Sure, that's no problem,' she replies as expected. Belinda has always been a very professional secretary. I've managed her really well. I've nailed that fine line between fear and fawning. It's called respect. She has a ton of respect for me.

'Don't worry about the phone. Let everything go to voicemail and we'll go through any outstanding work between us when I get back, okay?'

I'm concerned that she's aware I'm taking a huge sum from Jonathan's branch. If she gets one more phone call about the withdrawals from any of the other assistant managers she would have every right to be suspicious. It's important she stays away from the phones. I do worry that Jonathan can reach her through her personal mobile phone. He's a happily married man, but he's had a huge crush on Belinda for years. She's way out of his league, of course, but she seems to enjoy the fact that he drools over her. I hope their flirtatious relationship doesn't fuck all of this up. Their immature dalliance could be responsible for Ryan having his brains blown out before midday. I emphasise to Belinda what I expect from her over the next few hours before I head out of my office door, leaving the mug of coffee she poured for me cooling on my desk. She knows what I've asked her to do is unusual, but she's in no way suspicious that anything extraordinary is going on. I take a moment to refocus when I'm in the lift. I have to act normal when I see John. He probably knows me better than anybody at ACB. But acting comes easy to me. I thought I was coming out to my parents when I told them I wanted to be an actor, having achieved mediocre Leaving Cert results from Saint Brigid's National School, but they didn't quite understand my ambition.

'Acting? That's not a career,' me da would tell me over and over again. 'Ninety-nine per cent of actors are unemployed right now.'

I knew he was right, but I felt I was so talented that I would ease into the one per cent without much bother at all. Neither of my parents had one iota of a clue that I was gay. Nobody really did. I am as straight a gay guy as you could meet. I always have been. I loved acting as soon as I took my first drama class in school. During the final year of school, I used to stay back two days a week with Mr Hanrahan to perfect my acting techniques. He had praised me for my lead performances in some of the school plays. I even landed a professional role in a production of *Who's Afraid of Virginia Woolf?* in the Pavilion Theatre within months of leaving school. Mr Hanrahan had arranged an audition for me and I nailed it. I had decided I was a method actor and took my role as Nick so seriously that I lived as the character for the full eight weeks of the play's run. This annoyed my folks somewhat as they now had a stranger living with them, but I didn't shrug Nick for one whole minute of those two months. The local newspaper's review was admittedly average but everyone I knew was largely complimentary of my performance – except me da of course.

'You were decent, but can't you get a good steady job like your old man?' he said to me. 'I can get you a job in our bank.'

I had zero interest in working in banking for the rest of my life. I was a method actor. The planks of Broadway and the hills of Hollywood were waiting for me.

Today is the first day I've acted in decades. If I can nail Nick from *Who's Afraid of Virginia Woolf?* then playing Vincent Butler on a normal Tuesday morning shouldn't be a problem at all. I have to rid myself of the tension I'm feeling and forget about any outside influences. I have to take two million euros from each of our four banks, acting as if it's a normal procedure, and then I have to return to my apartment before midday. It can't be that difficult.

I am not nervous. I am not under pressure.

I repeat that into the mirrored wall of the lift over and over again as it takes me down to the underground car park. I let out one big sigh before the sliding doors open and I make my way towards a smiling John.

'Mornin', Vincent,' he says, tipping the peak of his cap at me. His Dublin accent as thick as ever.

'All good, John boy?' I ask, as composed as I am every other morning.

'Yes, sir.'

'Can you pop the boot for me? I've a few withdrawals to make today and I need to make sure I've enough cases.'

I do. I look inside the boot of the car and see eight cases. There are always eight cases. That's exactly how many I need. They each pack up to a million euros. Hopefully they'll all be full in the next few hours. I don't have to worry about John. He has absolutely no idea how the banking system works. It's unusual that I'd drive around all four banks to withdraw money in one morning, but John will barely notice. He's just always happy to be out and about rather than sitting around a small office sipping coffee while waiting on me to decide to go somewhere. He's been driving me around for over a decade and has actually been employed by ACB longer than I have. There used to be fourteen bank branches in Dublin before the crisis hit in 2008. I was manager of the Drumcondra branch before it closed and was given John as a chauffeur when I first took the job in 2004. When we restructured in early 2010 the board decided to cut some of the large wage bill by closing down the ten branches that were scattered around the Dublin suburbs, leaving just the four that operated in the city centre. They were the only ones making money. They let go all thirteen of the bank managers, leaving me to run all the four remaining branches. They would hire assistant managers on lower wages to assist in the everyday running of the banks, but I would be the man mainly responsible for the entire Irish operation. The restructure saved ACB almost three million a year in wages and expenses and the Irish branch of the company just about managed to survive. You would think that being the manager of four branches rather than just one would have meant a huge pay rise for me. Not so. I was told I'd be taking a salary cut. I didn't mind, initially. I was just so proud to be the only manager kept on. I felt valued. I hadn't felt as proud of myself since I won the audition to play Nick all those years ago.

'So, where we off te?' asks John as he opens the back door for me.

'Church Street first, John, please,' I reply before I realise I'm making a mistake. 'No, Camden, no, Nassau Street. Yeah, Nassau first, John, thanks.'

'Y'alrigh', Vincent?' he asks, staring at me through the open door. 'You don't seem yerself today.'

I nod my head in response before breathing heavily. In the time it takes him to walk around to his side of the car I feel panic setting in. Maybe I'm not as good an actor as I always assumed I was. I look at my watch and grind my teeth. It is genuinely the first time I've lost my composure since leaving the apartment. The digital clock on the car dashboard just blinked to 8:50. Time to start robbing some banks.

08:50

Jack

WATCHING TEENAGERS HANGING AROUND THE BOTTOM OF GRAFTON Street makes me wonder what other people are up to today. It's the mid-term holidays. Most kids are enjoying their break from school. Most adults are probably cooped up in some office or factory in a job they hate. For almost every one of the million people in this city, today is just another Tuesday morning. Dublin has no idea that the subtlest bank robbery in the history of this city is under way. Bank robberies used to be a big deal in Dublin. If one occurred, it would make national headlines. But that's hardly the case anymore. They estimate that thirty-five bank robberies happen in Ireland every year. It's not a huge number, but it's significant enough to not have news editors drop their jaw each time one happens. This will be a different story altogether though. Nothing like this has ever happened in this country. It'll go down in folklore. Mostly because the guys that did it got away with it.

A brunette pushing a pram past the side wall of Trinity College reminds me of Karyn. They share the same shaggy, curly mop of brown hair. I twist my neck to take a peek at the baby and notice she must be only a few months old. I think it's a girl. She has a bright yellow bib on. That's all I can go on. Karyn never pushed a baby that young.

A week after my failed attempt at asking her for a dance at Trolli's Dance Hall, my father informed me on my return home from work that some girl had phoned looking for me. He squinted as he tried to make out his own handwriting.

'Karyn Ritchie,' he said, as butterflies swarmed around my stomach. He handed me the small note and I immediately ran to the home phone under the stairs. I didn't hesitate in dialling the number.

'You asked me for a dance last week,' she said smartly after I had told her who was calling. I rang so quickly that I didn't give myself the opportunity to get nervous.

'Yes, I did,' I responded, unsure what she would say next.

'Well, I don't really like to dance, but I do like Italian food. In fact, I really like the Italian food in Pirlo's restaurant on Dame Street. And I would particularly like their food this Friday night at seven o'clock.'

I was stumped. I wasn't sure if the confidence in this girl made me fall in love with her or feel intimidated by her. Either way, I was fascinated.

'Don't you have a boyfriend, Karyn?' I asked sheepishly.

'I might do by Saturday,' she responded, before hanging up.

How bloody cool is she? I couldn't compete with this shit, could I? It turns out I could compete with it. I had a few days to play it cool and managed to gain a pinch of confidence before I met her for our first date. We bounced off each other as if we were an experienced comedy double act. We literally fell into each other's arms laughing. It was as if the script for our first date had been written by Billy Crystal for some Oscar-winning romantic comedy.

Karyn lived about a half an hour from my parents' house and I needed to take two buses to see her. I didn't mind. When I wasn't working in the print factory I would be hanging out with Karyn. We were each other's best friend immediately. The relationship wasn't very physical. She was a strict Catholic girl but it genuinely didn't bother me that we weren't having sex. The relationship wasn't about that, it was about finding somebody who mirrored me and who I knew I could spend the rest of my life with. We shared the exact same sense of humour and brought the best out in each other. A successful relationship isn't about finding someone you can't live without, it's about finding somebody you can live with. I was working extra shifts at the factory just to save enough money for us to afford a flat together, but in order for that to happen, we would need to speak to her father first.

'That's no problem, he can't be that strict, can he?' I distinctly remember asking her after we'd been going out for three months. 'I mean, we're both nearly twenty, we're adults.'

'You know I told you his name is Harold, right?' she said, arching an eyebrow. 'And you know my second name is Ritchie?'

I nodded, hanging my bottom lip out in confusion.

'Harry Ritchie!' she emphasised.

'Holy shit!' I responded before dropping my mouth open in shock. 'You're Harry Ritchie's daughter? Well, that's it, we need to break up. Break up now!'

We both laughed. This was the kind of stuff that made us giggle, but behind the wide grin on my face lay a deep fear. I only knew about Harry Ritchie through stories lads would tell down the pub. It wasn't really a secret in Dublin that the gangland boss – who the tabloid newspapers nicknamed The Ghost – was Harry Ritchie from Crumlin. It was just sorta known by everyone. The papers couldn't name Harry for legal reasons. So they nicknamed him, just like they nicknamed anyone else involved in gangland crime. The cops couldn't get near him. He kept his hands too clean. I never bothered to read about gangland crime in Dublin. The subject never really interested me. But now it would have to. If I were to get my one true wish in life, which was to get this young woman to accept my ring on her finger, I would literally be marrying into the mob. That would be some transition for somebody who used to be an altar boy in St Peter's Church.

I'm not sure if it's nerves or excitement that hits me when I stroll onto Nassau Street. Rather than walk by the ACB building, I stop at the wall of College Park where I can glance over at the entrance to the bank without looking suspicious. I perch myself against the brick wall and play with my phone. I could easily be waiting on one of the many buses that pull in here on a minute-by-minute basis. There are no CCTV cameras pointing in this direction. I'd planned to sit here when the Nassau robbery was going on. In fact, I know where I'll be for each of the four thefts today. I've sat here on quite a few occasions over the past months, imagining Vincent walking out of the bank with two full cases. I'll be watching that image for real in the next half hour or so. The bank's still not open, but I notice that there are two parking spots available directly outside and I expect John will be pulling up to park in one of them very soon. I look at my watch. 8:58. There's three hours left. It should take Vincent at least half an hour in each bank to go through the procedure required to withdraw money from the vaults. Taking driving time between branches into consideration, we really have given him a tight deadline. But we did that for a reason. The longer this process goes on, the more likely it is that somebody will notice something odd is going on. Plus, I want the deadline to be tight. I need it to be tight. Vincent isn't supposed to complete the task we've set him. I'm mentally trying to play the full morning out in my mind once again when I notice a black BMW indicate right and pull into one of the empty spaces in front of the bank. I know John to see. He climbs out of the far side of the car before walking around to open the door for his boss. I watched Vincent walk out of his apartment earlier this morning looking quite composed; I wonder if he still feels the same way. But the fact he doesn't instantly get out of the car worries me. He seems to be in conversation with John. I hope nothing funny is going on. When I finally see Vincent emerge from the car he doesn't look right. He's really pale. He seems faint. As he and John walk towards the back of the car to retrieve the cases Vincent collapses to the ground on all fours.

What the hell is going on?

08:50

Darragh

I HOLD A FINGER TOWARDS ME NOSTRILS AS I WALK INTO THEIR BEDROOM just in case I can smell the gay sex. It's a big bedroom but I know the waft of bum fuckin must be floatin' round here somewhere. I step over some old clothes at the edge of the bed to get to the far side of the room where Ryan told me his coke was. I don't get angry with him when I can't find it in his big-ass bedside cabinet. I know it's probably just me. Any time I have to look for something in a drawer or a cabinet I somehow manage to see everything in there bar the one thing I'm lookin' for.

'A silver tin,' I whisper to meself over and over again as I root through old newspapers and gadgets. This fucker must collect watches for a living. There must be at least a dozen old watches in this cabinet alone. Me mind gets distracted by a black Hublot that has the coolest lookin' face. Everything on it is a different shade of black: the face, the hands, the numbers, the date scroll. I throw it round me wrist. It suits me.

'What the fuck are you talkin' about, boy?' I scream out of the bedroom towards Ryan. Me accent goes all Cork when I'm cursin'.

'The silver tin,' he shouts back.

I slam the cabinet door shut, get up off my knees and storm out to the fag. I reach for the gun resting on the table in front of him and point it straight into his face.

'If you're fuckin playing me for a fool I'll end your life right now,' I snarl at him. He's practically shitting himself. 'There's no fuckin silver tin in there,' I snap.

'It's there, it's there,' he stutters back.

I've no doubt he's telling the truth. I probably wouldn't have noticed a beach ball in that cabinet if it was the one thing I was looking for. I don't know what my problem is. I guess me mind just likes playing tricks on me. I crouch down and yank at the tape strapping Ryan's legs to the chair and, after a struggle, I free both of his ankles. I then pull at the tape round his wrists and set him free. He doesn't budge an inch when I release all the tape. I have the gun resting in the waistband of my jeans behind my back. I reach for it as soon as I'm done with the tape and point it at him again.

'I'm stayin' right behind you, fag,' I say. 'Go get it for me.'

I was in his position once. Piotr and I went a step further with our addiction to coke about three years back. We managed to do a deal with our drug dealer who introduced us to his boss. He talked us into taking five kilos of coke that we were expected to sell over the course of a month on the streets of North Dublin. We were given our own little patch to work on. I was super excited about the deal because I worked out that we could take in around two and a half grand profit each week. Piotr and I drove out to an old warehouse on the way to Enfield to pick up our package. It was explained to us how we should chop it up into sellable sizes that would bring in around €120,000 in total. We'd just have to return in four weeks' time with a hundred thousand euros to The Boss, pocketing the extra twenty thousand for us to split between ourselves. Easy dough.

'We're trusting you to deliver,' we were told. 'Any false moves and you'll both be dead before you even realise we're in the same room as you.'

Dublin gangsters are kinda funny but they're also scary as fuck. They all seem to wear tracksuits that are too big for them. Big, grey, baggy pants with a massive bunch of keys in the pockets. I've never worked out why Dublin people carry around massive bunches of keys. Despite looking a bit like clowns, gangsters are genuinely intimidating. But me and Piotr were really happy to get involved with them. We drove away from the warehouse with a trunk full of coke and talked for ages about what we were gonna do with the money. It was when we were driving through Lucan on our way home that Piotr pulled over and reached for the glove compartment. I genuinely thought he was joking when he grabbed a gun and pointed it at me. I think I laughed out loud.

'Get out,' he said in his thick Polish accent.

The smile dropped from my face when I realised he was serious. He followed me out of the car and walked behind me with the gun held against my spine for about three hundred yards into a small forest. I heard the gun click in his hand.

Is my best friend about to kill me?

'I'm sorry, Darragh,' he said before spinning on his heels and sprintin' back to the car. Lanky prick. I never saw him again. I don't think anybody did.

I hold the gun to the back of Ryan's head as he leans his left arm on the bed to crouch towards his cabinet. He pulls out a tiny casing that looks more green than silver to me. It's decorated with some sort of Scottish tartan. I remember brushing past it as I repeated the words 'silver tin' to meself just a few minutes ago.

'Here,' he says, taking the lid from it.

I take a look inside and see a massive bag of fluffy powder that forces a wide grin across me face.

'Good lad,' I reply before nodding at him to walk out of the room. I keep the gun at his back but I can't keep me eyes off the coke. It looks like snow. This guy certainly buys straight from the mixer. The fag is mumbling something, along the lines of, 'Please don't hurt me', as I force him to sit back down on the kitchen chair again, but I'm not listening. A thought crosses my paranoid mind that this powder may be something other than coke and that this little prick is tryna poison me. Had he somehow planned that somebody would kidnap him so he thought of hiding a bag of poison in his bedroom to pass off as coke to his captor? Course not, but I'm gonna play it safe.

After re-taping both of his legs, but just one of his arms, to the kitchen chair I pour out a small hill of coke onto the magazine before givin' it a little chop of me library card. I don't need to chop this stuff up much. This is as fluffy as it could possibly get. I reach for my old five-euro note and offer it to Ryan.

'You first,' I say, eyeballing him. It's the first time I've seen a glint in his eyes all morning.

08:55

Vincent

I PULL AT THE COLLAR OF MY SHIRT TO ALLOW SOME OF THE COLD AIR circulating in the car to creep inside. I am sweating everywhere: my armpits, my neck, my chest, my back, my forehead. I never sweat like this. I have the air conditioning turned up so high in the back of the car that it sounds as if a small aircraft is flying by my ears.

'You sure you're okay, Vincent?' John shouts back again, eyeballing me in the rear-view mirror. I don't answer him this time. I pretend I can't hear him. Instead I concentrate on my breathing but I'm sure I'm doing it all wrong. I'm breathing way too quickly. I wish I'd accepted Ryan's constant requests for us to go to yoga classes together over the years. I try to calm myself by thinking in the same selfish manner I have been thinking in this morning.

My life is not immediately under threat.

But it's not working. The calm, composed figure I managed to portray back at the penthouse in front of Ryan's kidnapper is proving elusive. I catch a glimpse of myself in the reflection of the car's tinted windows. I can make out a glistening across my forehead. I remove my glasses and wipe my whole face with the sleeve of my expensive suit. Just as I'm dampening down the sweat on the back of my neck with the other sleeve our car pulls right and comes to a halt. Holy shit. We're outside the Nassau Street branch already. That was quick. I stare up at the windowed building and try to force myself to calm down.

This is my bank. I am in complete control. Relax!

I am trying to slow my breathing down when the car door opens.

'Here you are, Mr Butler,' says John.

Since I've known him, I've suggested that he should call me Vincent at all times, but when we are on official duty in the office or at any of the branches he insists on being formal. I find it funny because he doesn't pronounce the 't' in Butler.

'I'll be one moment, John, I just … I seem to …' I stutter.

'Mr Butler, will I take ya home? You clearly aren't well.'

'I'll be okay in a second, John.'

I take three deep breaths before swinging my legs out of the car and rising to a standing position. I assumed I'd be fine once I got outside of the car, but the brightness of the morning sun seems to affect me instantly. My head feels a little dizzy. I try to shrug it off by following John to the boot, though I keep a hand on the car just to ensure my balance. But just as he's about to hand me the two cases I've requested the dizziness proves too much to bear. I feel myself falling to my knees in slow motion. The path I'm staring at seems to be changing colour and a humming sound pierces my ears. I can hear John calling out to me but it sounds as if he's way off in the distance.

'Mr Butler, Mr Butler,' he repeats.

'I'm alright, John,' I finally say when the humming seems to suddenly stop. After a few seconds I manage to sit up on the kerb, staring at John's kneecaps.

'I can call an ambulance, or I can drive ya straight to the hospital?' he says in a worried tone.

'John, trust me,' I say, raising my head to look him in the eye. 'I am genuinely okay. I jogged to work this morning and it was too hot for that kind of exercise. It's my own fault. I'm just a little dehydrated,' I lie.

John disappears, and within a few seconds reappears with a bottle of water. I laugh at him.

'You're always on hand, John boy,' I say before taking a swig from the bottle. The water's warm but I don't mind. I'm much warier of Chelle coming out and catching me sitting on the kerb. She's more likely to cause a fuss over my dizziness than John is. I twist my neck to look behind me and notice that the branch is now open. I stare at the ACB logo etched on the glass doors and feel relieved that nobody has come out to greet me yet. Sometimes Chelle can be out front waiting on me with open arms if she's privy to my arrival. I guess I gave her very short notice this morning. She's probably ordering her staff to have every area of the bank spotless, telling them Mr Butler is on the way. I need to get to my feet before she comes out. John offers me his right forearm and helps lift me up just in time. As I stand and face the bank I make out Chelle's figure caught between the first glass door entrance and the second. She has to wait for the initial door to close before the next one opens. I don't think she saw me sitting on the ground. As she's staring out at me, John is tapping at my ass as if he's a dog desperate to get my attention.

'What the fuck are you doing?' I ask, half laughing.

'Your pants are filthy, Mr Butler,' he retorts. We both giggle. It puts me at ease.

'Vincent, good morning,' bellows Chelle as she paces towards me in her high heels. We kiss on both cheeks as if we're better than everyone else. The fact that she loves me so much kind of annoys me. So much of it is pretentious.

'I'll wait here, Mr Butler,' says John, handing me both the cases and a wink. I tap him on the shoulder and wink back. He's so loyal that he won't give anyone any hints that two minutes ago I almost had a full-on panic attack. As Chelle and I walk towards the entrance of the bank, I'm aware a slight grin is etching itself onto my face, knowing that John will be staring at my assistant manager's ass. He's mentioned his fascination with her figure to me before. Michelle Dewey is forty-four years old and, while you would guess she is around that age, there's no denying that she looks superb for it. She's given birth to two kids and her body has bloated somewhat as a result. But it has bloated in all the right areas. Her hips and ass look like they belong to another body compared to her waist. Her chest is over-voluptuous too. John's often remarked to me, in the privacy of the car, that he thinks she's the hottest woman he's ever known in all his sixty-five years. I have to give it to him. If you are into hourglass figures than they don't come much better than Chelle's. If I was being bitchy I would say that her face isn't a match for her body, but I'm no bitch.

I've known Chelle for seven years. I hired her as a bank clerk for our Drumcondra branch and she impressed me so much that she was promoted four times in her first five years of service. When the board of directors at ACB brought me in to discuss the restructure I had no hesitation in nominating Chelle as one of the assistant managers. Her appointment has been justified since. Our Nassau Street branch is operating like clockwork in comparison to the other three. I know it's in safe hands. Even though we've always had a professional partnership, Chelle has never been shy in trying to double it up as a personal relationship too. Even in the early days she would insist that I'd keep at least one lunchtime free per week just for her. She would obsess about work over a Panini and would pick my brains for any hints or tips on how to improve her role. She's an impressive, hard-working woman. I had to hit the brakes on our social outings though. I felt it was going beyond a line. I did it subtly. I remember sitting on a kitchen chair in her Terenure terraced home with Ryan, celebrating her twin boys' fourth birthday one Saturday afternoon, thinking *what the fuck am I doing here?* I hate kids. Ryan had been asking a similar question on the way over. Enough was enough. Chelle and I still do the odd lunch but that's as far as our social activities go these days. I just make excuses that I'm too busy or want to spend more time with Ryan any time she asks me to do something involving her family or circle of friends. I do like Chelle a lot, and I have a ton of respect for her – she's been through the mill, her daughter went missing what must be fifteen or sixteen years ago now, so she'll always have my sympathy - but I felt our relationship was turning into a gay-guy, straight-gal cliché. We're both better than that.

'Now, you want two million euros?' she asks, squinting, as we stand inside the first door waiting on the second one to buzz us through. 'Is Jonathan alright?'

It's typical Chelle. She'd love it if Jonathan's branch was failing. It would make her look even better.

'He's fine,' I say. 'He just had a substantial amount of withdrawals last week. Holiday season, I guess.'

The bank floor is empty but for the nine staff who all stand in their rightful positions smiling over at me as if I'm going to take note of their smiles and reflect my impression in their next pay review.

'I really must do this quickly,' I whisper over to Chelle, letting her know I have no time to stand around small talking to her staff.

'Of course,' she responds before shouting over at her personal assistant. 'Janice, do you have that paperwork for me?'

Janice looks petrified.

'Sorry, Mrs Dewey, but the printer is out of ink.'

I almost laugh at the ridiculousness of it all. There is zero chance of me withdrawing any money from this branch without all the necessary paperwork being filled out. If I even remotely hint at that, Chelle would call in either the cops or some mental doctor – and rightly so, too.

'It should be just another five or ten minutes,' Janice says, fidgeting.

'Fuckin' typical,' I mutter softly as I walk away from Chelle and Janice towards the assistant manager's office at the back corner of the bank floor. I shake my head and smile at the thought of Ryan being killed due to a lack of ink in the office printer.

'I'll just wait in here,' I shout back out to the floor in an impatient tone before I slam my arm on the desk and my forehead onto my arm. I sigh deeply and begin to think things through.

What the fuck am I doing?

Earlier on I was somewhat intrigued by what I was being forced to act out. I walked to the office this morning thinking about how I could secure the money and strategising about getting back to the penthouse before midday. But ever since I set out in the car to begin the robberies I have felt nauseous. The more involved in this I'm getting, the less confident I feel. Maybe I am all show and no action. I take out the cheap mobile phone from my jacket pocket and stare at it. I'm trying to think what I can do before I start these robberies when it suddenly buzzes in my hand.

'Now you fuckin' listen to me, cunt hole …' roars the mongrel accent.

08:55

Ryan

I OPEN UP THE TIN AND TIP IT SLIGHTLY SO IT SHOWS HIM WHAT'S INSIDE. HE beams like a little kid being offered his favourite sweets.

'Good lad,' he says to me in such a patronising tone that it makes me wince.

He's let his guard down somewhat. The gun he's gripping in his left hand isn't his main concern right now. I think about trying to knock it out of his grip by punching at his hand, but I genuinely have never thrown a punch in my life. I could be dead in one second if I attempt to take this prick on. He takes the tin from me and nods towards the living quarters of the penthouse. Pointing the gun in my back, he leads me towards the same kitchen chair I'd been sitting on for the past couple of hours. He shoves me back down into it and turns around to reach into his bag. After removing the duct tape again, he wraps my ankles to the chair legs. He follows that up by taping my left wrist to the arm of the chair but for some reason he leaves my right hand free. The stupidity of this guy is really wrangling with me. I can't quite get my head around somebody trusting a guy this dumb to take charge of an eight-million-euro theft. I watch the smug fucker pouring my cocaine onto one of my magazines before he rolls up his dirty note.

'You first,' he says, handing me the bill. I stare at him, confused. 'Go ahead, fag.'

He holds the magazine with two thick lines of coke under my face and I lift the five-euro note to my nostril before snorting the smaller of the two lines. As I'm doing this I allow myself a look at the microwave clock. 8:59. This is early, even for me. I don't normally take my first line until after midday. I've become a bit of a bum, but I'm a disciplined bum. The rush of cocaine is instant. I love it. You can feel it burn the back of your nose within a split second before the rush makes its way to the brain. After I snort a line of coke I like to dab my finger into the remains of the powder and rub it around my tongue and gums. The instant numbing of the mouth is a great sensation. I don't get to do that this time though. My captor grins into my face as he pulls the magazine away from me and sits down on the couch. He is about to re-roll the five-euro note when his phone rings. I can feel my heart rate rise significantly but that could be down to the coke as much as the phone call. I wonder if it's Vincent calling. I hope he's okay.

Vincent doesn't like me doing coke. It's a bit unfair considering he used to enjoy a line himself. I'm eleven years younger than my boyfriend, but when he was my age he liked to use the drug on regular nights out. He thinks that's all I use it for now – the odd session. He has no idea I snort a couple of lines every day just to get me through the realities of life. The last time Vincent used coke was at our penthouse warming. We moved in four months later than scheduled due to some unexpected mishaps with the building work, but it was so worth it. The penthouse looked just as good in reality as it did in our imaginations. Vincent had worked so hard and deserved an amazing place to live in. I was really chuffed for him and immensely proud. When we first moved to the city centre I was still studying journalism at DCU. I promised that I would pay my way some day, but Vincent seemed content with being the main provider in our relationship. Even when I was earning decent money he made sure I spent it how I pleased. After all, he was earning six times the wages I was. I couldn't believe the size of the penthouse when I first walked into it completed. I had taken walks through the building while it was being renovated but I didn't have a good enough vision to realise how it would be once the kitchen was installed and all the rooms were painted and decorated.

Vincent got so high the night we opened the penthouse up to our friends. He hid in the bathroom to do line after line of coke so his work colleagues wouldn't know. But they must have noticed something was different. He was not only strangely full of energy but he was wiping and snorting his nose at any given opportunity. I remember giggling to myself as he spoke to Michelle and her husband Jake at the kitchen table while constantly fidgeting with his right nostril. If Michelle or Jake knew anything about the use of cocaine it would have been plainly obvious that Vincent was on it. I chuckled constantly thinking about it the next day but Vincent wasn't in the mood for laughing. His cocktail of coke, whisky and wine had his head throbbing. I had to leave a bucket beside the bed for him to puke into as he moaned and groaned his way through the day.

'I'm never fuckin' doin' coke again,' he screamed on several occasions in quick succession while pinching at his temples.

'Try giving up the whisky and the wine,' I roared back at him. 'It's not the coke that has your head splitting.'

He kept to his word. He's never taken any drugs since that night. He wouldn't even take a drag of a joint these days. The fun seems to have snuck out of his being. I've often thought it's just his age. Vincent is a middle-aged man now. He's only six months off half a century. Yuck!

'Relax. Sorry,' my captor says, startled, into his phone. 'I was in the bedroom … I was … I was just walking around the apartment. I left the phone on the couch. Everything is alright here. Chill out.'

I can't make out what his accomplice is saying on the other end of the line but I know there's panic in his voice due to the raised volume. He's treating this greasy little fuck like a kid. I guess he is a kid.

'But what … he what? What are you saying?' my captor mumbles. He seems really confused. 'What do you mean, he collapsed?' he asks after another moment of silence.

My breathing starts to get panicky again. I'm not entirely sure if I'm initially worried about Vincent or myself. If Vincent has had some sort of panic attack and can't get on with the job, am I going to be shot right now?

'So he's in the bank now – everything must be okay?'

The person on the other end of the line seems to have calmed down. So too has my heart.

'Okay, okay. I'll ring him and make sure he's not up to any funny business. I'll give you a shout back in a minute or two.'

I've no idea what Vincent is playing at, and I'm concerned. He doesn't have a history of fainting. But then again, he doesn't have a history of robbing his own banks of eight million euros, either.

My captor and I eyeball each other when he hangs up. He seems worried. As he lifts the phone to his ear again he holds my stare. That's my fucking black Hublot he has on his wrist!

'Now you fuckin' listen to me, cunt hole,' he snaps down the phone.

09:00

Jack

JOHN SEEMS TO BE SLAPPING VINCENT ON THE ASS FOR SOME REASON. HE must be just shaking off the concrete dust. At least I hope that's all that's going on. That's some service.

I watch through a gap between two parked buses as Michelle greets Vincent. He finally looks to have steadied himself. But I'm still a little shook up about him collapsing onto all fours. I remove the phone from my jacket pocket and speed-dial Darragh. My teeth grind as the tone rings out. My panic begins to grow. What the hell could have gone wrong at the apartment? Three minutes ago, everything was going perfectly; now it all seems to be falling apart. I have one collapsed man who is supposed to be taking the money and one accomplice in charge of the kidnapping who can't answer his bloody phone. Huffing, I spin on my heels to take my frustration out on the grey brick wall I had been leaning against. It's kicked repeatedly before I try to compose myself. I need to stay calm. I can't draw any notice to myself. I'm staring at my phone willing it to ring back when, in my peripheral vision, I notice Vincent entering the bank with Michelle. I'm worried about him cracking up once he's in there. Maybe he isn't as strong as we both think he is. I'm desperate to find out what's going on. I speed-dial Darragh once again. This time the spotty prick answers within three dials.

'Where the hell have you been?' I scream down the line. He mutters some response about walking around the bedrooms. The little shit has one job to do – keep a gun on Ryan until midday. How hard can that be? Suddenly he's telling *me* to calm down.

'Listen,' I say sternly. 'Vincent bloody collapsed when he arrived at the bank.' I can tell Darragh's in shock. 'He fell to the ground. He got up, though, and is in the bank now. But I need you to call him straight away and make sure he's not breaking down in there and ruining this for us. Tell him you're going to kill his little boyfriend if there's any more messing.'

I wait for Darragh to hang up but he's still breathing down the line.

'Bloody ring him!' I shout so loud that a pedestrian walking by glances at me.

I'm not too bothered. My disguise really is so good that I can't imagine anybody would recognise me. There is no way any witness could conjure up any sort of photofit that would look even remotely like me. The sun is out in all its spring glory, which allows me to wear my sunglasses without any suspicion whatsoever. Most people on the streets are wearing sunglasses today. Coupled with my wig and false beard, my whole face is covered up.

I only ever had a real beard for about six months in my early twenties. It was about two years into my marriage to Karyn. She claimed she liked the look of it but didn't like kissing me with it. That was fine by me. Our relationship never really took off in a physical sense. I was dreading having the conversation with her but managed to sit her down before we got married to explain I was impotent. Some days we would try to fool around and I would climax but it was a very low percentage of the time. I still pleased Karyn on occasion and we would be intimate in some small way almost every night. We often fell asleep in each other's arms. But I was ashamed and stressed out that my dick didn't work. She was very understanding. It didn't become an issue at all until we wanted to have kids. We read a lot of self-help books and visited doctors about my condition. But after four years of frustratingly failing to conceive, we had to admit defeat. Karyn had looked into adoption for almost eighteen months before I accepted the idea. I didn't know anybody who had been adopted and thought it would be an admission to all our family and friends that my dick didn't work. But Karyn had talked me around and even introduced me to a few people who were either adopted or had adopted. I realised there was no stigma attached to this type of thing in the nineties.

Karyn's family connections helped us to skip some of the dragging protocol when we applied for adoption. That's almost unbelievable. A life of crime got us to the top of the queue to be responsible for a baby. I felt it was totally immoral but not to the extent that I said it to anyone. We'd only have to wait around six months to get our child, not the usual two to three years it took everybody else. We got a phone call one Monday afternoon on the tenth of September in 1993 to tell us we could pick up our son. He had been born four months earlier and was in Sacred Heart in Cork. His mother had been a heavy drug user but we were assured everything was fine with Frank. We named him after Karyn's grandfather. It wasn't forced on me. I'm a huge Sinatra fan and calling my kid after the Chairman of the Board was A-okay with me. Karyn and I were like two hyper kids on the three-hour drive to Blackrock. But we instantly grew up as soon as we met him. My life changed in that instant. I'd never known love like it before.

My mind continues to race, thinking of what Vincent could be doing inside that bank. Even if he has composed himself and is doing as asked he will be at least a half an hour in there. I know the protocol and exactly what's required for him to take the money out of the vaults. I decide to take a little walk and head towards Merrion Square. There's a casual little walkway down there that could help calm my mind while I wait on Darragh to get back to me. If Vincent doesn't pick up, we'll have a big decision to make. The heat forces me to take my jacket off for the walk. I make sure to remove the phone from the inside pocket and cling on to it in my left hand while my right hand holds the neck of the coat over my shoulder. My strategy for something going wrong at Vincent's end is to exit as soon as possible. I'd walk east away from all the banks towards the 3Arena before hailing a taxi back west towards Drimnagh where I'm supposed to meet with Dinah later. I would ask the taxi driver to leave me past my destination at the Luas Stop on the Naas Road, meaning I'd have a twenty-minute walk back on myself. I have it all worked out, but this is not a strategy I want to use today. I have to trust that Vincent is okay, but part of me thinks he may have confessed everything inside that bank. I'm starting to feel a little sorry for myself when the phone eventually buzzes in my hand.

09:05

Darragh

'Now you fuckin listen to me, cunt hole,' I shout down the phone before he even has the time to say hello. 'If you keep messin' I'll blow your baby's head off.'

I walk over to Ryan and hold the barrel of the gun against his forehead.

'Scream for your sugar daddy,' I order.

'Vincent, Vincent, are you okay?' Ryan screeches down the line.

I have the gun pointed at his brain yet he's more worried about his boyfriend. I'm obviously not gonna kill him, not yet anyway. I'm aware that the safety is still on.

'Vincent, Vincent … he's gonna shoot me. He's gonna shoot me,' he cries. That's what I wanted. I take the phone back up to my ear and grin.

'Did you hear that, lover boy?' I say. 'Any more messin' and bang! Now what the fuck went wrong?'

'I-I just felt a little overcome by the whole situation but I'm fine. I just needed to lie down and get some air before I got on with the show. I'm meeting with the assistant bank manager now. Everything is going as you want it to go. I'll be filling out the paperwork to take the first two million out in the next few minutes.'

'Good girl yerself. Call me as soon as you're done,' I say before hanging up. 'Relax, boy,' I tell Ryan, who seems to be putting on the crocodile tears just to please me. 'Here, have this line as well,' I follow up with, and hold the magazine under his chin while handing him the five-euro note. He doesn't hesitate. 'We'll have some fun while your fagotty boyfriend robs us some money, huh?'

As Ryan is getting his nose dirty I speed-dial JR. He'll be delighted I'm returning his call so quickly.

'It's all good,' I say to him. 'He's in the bank now and is meeting with the branch manager. He's fine. He just said he needed to take a little time out. He's gonna ring me as soon as he's done, like. He's just about to sign the papers to get the cash. There's no funny business goin' on.'

'Great stuff, Darragh. That's a relief,' replies JR. I can hear in his voice that he seems much calmer. 'Thanks, buddy. You're doing a super job.'

I'm always chuffed to receive praise from JR. I look up to him so much. My relationship with him is vastly different to the relationship I had with me first boss; it didn't take long for his gang to catch up with me. It was literally within ten minutes. They had been tailing Piotr's car and watched on as he walked me into the forest before spinning on his heels. I was shoved into their car and taken back to The Boss. I sat, just as Ryan is now, with me hands tied to a chair in the old warehouse I'd left just an hour before when The Boss walked towards me.

'You two have to be the dumbest mutha fuckers I've ever come across,' he barked. 'Within an hour you fuck yourselves right up. Did you think we wouldn't be following you and keeping tabs on our merchandise?'

'Please, sir,' I said, tryna sound polite. 'I had no idea Piotr was going to rob me. To rob you. My intentions were always to make you money. To make me money. I want this. I don't know what happened. I'm as surprised as you are.'

I received an open-handed slap across the face from The Boss before he put me at ease.

'I believe you,' he said. 'But you still deserve a slap. We watched it all go down. What the fuck were you doing teaming up with a guy so fuckin stupid that he would try to rob me?'

'I don't know,' I replied, shaking me head. 'We've been friends for years. I ... I ...' I stumbled. I'm sure The Boss could tell I was being genuine. I should have been filled with fear having one of the most notorious drug lords standing over me, but I was mostly feelin' heartbroken. I was devastated that me only friend tried to rob me and left me for dead in the hands of these gangsters. I couldn't get Piotr out of me mind.

'We caught up with your friend,' The Boss told me. 'The deal is still alive. He's not. We thought the two of you had concocted some sort of plan but he told us right before we dealt with him that you had no part in this whatsoever.'

This caused me jaw to drop towards me chest. Did they kill Piotr? After a moment of silence, I looked up through my wet eyes at The Boss.

'Good,' I said. 'Fuck him!'

'We're gonna spare your life. But your life is ours now, do ya understand?'

I stare over at Ryan. I can tell he is as high as a kite. His eyes are starting to redden and he's constantly wrinkling his nose. I want to join in. I reach for the plastic bag of coke that I'd put back into the tin and pour a thick line onto the magazine for meself. It looks so good.

'That's some good shit,' I say, smiling over at Ryan after I snort as much of it up one nostril as I can. 'You and I could become good friends.'

09:10

Vincent

I'VE BEEN SITTING UPRIGHT IN CHELLE'S OFFICE CHAIR WAITING ON HER TO come in with the paperwork for the past six minutes. I know it's exactly six minutes because I haven't stopped looking at my watch. I need to get this job done. I'm not committing a crime here. I am acting under duress to save my partner's life. Ryan sounded petrified when he called down the phone to me. But I need to put his cries out of my mind. I'm just going to do as his captor says. No messing about. I need I get back into character.

'I'm so sorry about this, Vincent,' Chelle says from the doorway of her office.

I wonder how long she's been standing there.

'I'm so embarrassed. Janice has had to run out to get some ink. She shouldn't be long.'

'What?' I reply a little too dramatically, slapping the palm of my right hand against her oak desk. It stings. Chelle looks stunned. I feel I need to justify my reaction.

'I told you Jonathan needs this money as soon as possible. He's very low, Chelle.'

'How about I give him a quick call myself to apologise and tell him we'll get it over as soon as we can?'

'No. Jesus, no. Listen, I'll look after everything Jonathan's end. You just get me the paperwork as soon as you can. Where has Janice gone to?'

'There's a place that sells ink on Frederick Street. She'll be back in ten minutes. I'm mortified we've run out of ink. I don't recall this ever happening before.'

I look at my watch. Janice probably won't be back until around nine twenty-five. This is a terrible start to the morning.

'Chelle,' I say, rubbing my forehead. 'Just get me a coffee will you, please?'

I stare around her office and notice her qualifications framed on the walls. She actually has more certificates than I have. I fuckin' hated studying. I auditioned for at least forty roles after landing the part of Nick in *Who's Afraid of Virginia Woolf?* but didn't land one of them. After that play, I spent eighteen months unemployed and living off my parents. My da was getting tetchy. I was the only one of my friends that wasn't moving on to pastures new as we were turning twenty-one. Bennett, one of my closest friends through secondary school, moved to London to take up an internship with a tech company called Black Castle. My very best friend, Keith, had been studying in Galway since we left school and still had another two years of his marketing masters to go. They were literally going places while my life seemed to be stagnating. I just had to get out of my parents' house but the only light at the end of that tunnel seemed to come from accepting my father's invitation to work at his bank. I hated the type of work I was doing from day one, but I somehow got talked into studying accountancy at night to ensure I could be on the big bucks in the future.

It amazes me that not enough people follow their dream. We only have eighty years on this planet, on average, yet most of us spend forty hours of our weeks working on something we fuckin' despise. How does that make sense? Why would we do that? Yet I'm one of those dumb schmucks who spends half the time I'm awake doing something I don't like doing. As soon as I received my degree in accountancy in 1992 I left TSB. I didn't want to be working with me da. He understood and saw to it that I got a great reference, which helped me get through my interview for a banking official's position with ACB. I've never liked banking but I have to admit that it suits my natural skill sets. I'm very straight up and immensely efficient. My brain is also dialled up to deal with numbers. I've learned over the years that I don't have a great creative brain. That disappoints me so much. All through my teens I figured I was one of the creative types. I guess I was wrong. I was only twenty-eight years old when I was appointed assistant manager of ACB's Drumcondra branch, having worked at the company for less than five years. I was the youngest person ever to reach that position. The board of directors thought highly of me and the feeling was mutual. Unfortunately, the old guys have either retired or passed away since then, leaving their spoilt little snotty offspring in charge of decisions they just don't care enough about. They are so clueless that it stuns me on a regular basis. ACB is back running a healthy business in Ireland. I know for sure it's because of me. I think the board assume it's because of them. Fuckin' idiots.

Chelle is full of apologies again as she returns with my coffee. I don't budge off her big-ass leather chair, leaving her to sit in the more uncomfortable visitor's seat. I huff a bit of puff to remind her how frustrated I am, but we soon get talking about our lives. Chelle has always been fascinated with Ryan. She can't wait to read his novel.

'It's coming along well,' I lie to her.

I sometimes wonder if Chelle only asks me about Ryan so that I return the politeness by asking about her perfect little family. I don't this morning. Instead, I allow an awkward silence to fill the room after I'm done lying about Ryan's book. She's clearly aware that I'm upset with her. This must be killing her inside.

Darragh

THIS COKE IS SO FUCKIN GOOD. I ROLL UP THE NOTE AGAIN TO TAKE another small line and promise meself as I'm doing it that I shouldn't get too carried away. I'm only supposed to be taking this to relieve the boredom and to help me relax. This isn't about partying it up. I shake me head with delight as the coke hits me brain again.

'Where do you get this stuff from, fag?' I ask Ryan.

'I know a guy,' he answers. 'I can sort you out. I can keep you in this type of pure coke every day for the rest of your life if you just let me go.'

I stare at his face and fake laugh as loud as I can.

'Dude, in about three hours' time I'm gonna have millions to me name. Why the fuck do you think I would give that up for a little splash of your coke every now and then, like? Where I'm goin' and what I'm gonna be able to do will give me the best of every world. Don't have any fears that I won't be enjoyin' life after I leave here today, boy.'

'What's your plan?' he asks.

He must think I'm stupid. 'Now why the fuck would I tell you that, fag boy?'

The truth is I don't actually have a plan. JR and I have been obsessing about this robbery for months but I never really got to the point where I figured out what I want to do when it's all over. I just want to stay a gangster. I want to be a hitman for JR. The money is insignificant to me. Once I have enough cash for a few beers and a few lines of coke every evening, that's enough for me. I get me real kicks out of carrying out thefts or killing people. I'm not sure why I haven't thought it through, but the coke is helping to open me mind further. I start to wonder about JR and what he'll do after we steal this eight mill. I hope he's not planning on retiring. As far as I'm concerned, we're just getting' started. I know JR has never pulled off a heist that brought in this amount of money before, but I never thought to ask him what he plans on doing with the cash once he has his hands on it. JR's been a gangster most of his life. I'm sure that's not gonna end today. Once a gangster, always a gangster. Me old boss must've had millions to his name but that didn't stop him continuing in his job.

I was just a common street drug dealer for him but I always figured it was my first rung on the ladder to gangland fame. I was lucky they believed Piotr's story about me and that my life was spared. I was grateful that Piotr stuck up for me but me mourning for him didn't last too long. According to The Boss, I owed him big time so I was forced to sell his merch on the streets of north inner-Dublin for little or no profit comin' in my direction. I'd have to prove meself trustworthy before the initial deal offered to me and Piotr would be put back on the table. But once it was, I would be pocketing the full twenty grand profit every month for meself. Sounded good to me. I had to work up a load of contacts in the area to sell to, but despite a slow start I began to talk to the proper lads in the area. They were intimidating at first but once they understood I was selling for The Boss it earned me an awful lot of respect. It also kept rival drug dealers away from me. They didn't want to start a patch war with my gang. It made me feel like I was finally worth somethin'.

In each of the first three months, I returned to The Boss having sold around eighty per cent of the drugs. He'd rant and rave, saying it wasn't enough, but I'm pretty sure he was impressed that I could shift this much in an area I didn't really know that well. I was delighted to be a drug dealer but passing small bags of coke to guys outside bars and through car windows wasn't really pushing me buttons after a while. I was involved with a feared gang, and I wanted to get my hands really dirty. While my eyes were on bigger prizes I was determined not to get complacent. I'd learned through me new mates that the cops could smell complacency from miles away. Durin' one shitty evening I was cornered by two guys waving their Garda badges at me. I had sold a lot of my merch already that day but I was still left with a few small bags in the boot of the car. I felt confident they wouldn't find it when they searched but the younger of the two cops lifted my spare wheel with one hand and checked inside the tyre.

'Looks like you're fucked!' he said to me and grinned. 'Get inside the car, now.'

The two of them spoke to me for about an hour, insisting they wouldn't arrest me if I gave up some bigger fish. They wanted me to rat out me mates in order for me to be set free. Fuck that. I'd learned from *Goodfellas* that you never rat on your friends. As it turned out, I was talking to two of them. I'd no idea. They were friends of The Boss and had set me up just to check out whether I could be trusted or not. I passed with flyin' colours. It was some relief. I was shittin' it sitting inside that car but I never wavered. Not for one second did I think about dobbin' the boys in.

'Can you twist my chair around so that it's facing the TV straight on?' Ryan asks.

It makes me laugh. Probably because I'm super high. Ryan laughs along with me. This genuinely is some super-hot coke. We both sit in the plush apartment laughing loudly before we realise the ridiculousness of it all.

'Why not?' I say, having calmed down. I lift my ass up off the couch and twist at the legs of his kitchen chair so that he can see the TV clearly. 'Here ya go, boy,' I say, handing him the TV remote control. 'Throw on what you want.'

'You like football?' he asks me.

'Ah, I used to,' I reply. I did. I used to watch a tiny bit of football back in Cork, but I haven't seen a game in years.

He flashes a TV guide menu onto the screen before scrolling down to some sports channel. When he turns it on I notice the words 'Man U' in the score line up on the top left-hand corner.

'That's Man United, right?' I ask him. Ironically that was the team I used to support as a kid. Me old man was mad into them.

'Yep, they're playing Bayern Munich. This is the Champions League semi-final.'

'I know of Man United but that's about as far as my football knowledge goes, fag,' I say.

'Well watch this, you might as well. We have the time. Let me tell you how the game works.'

I look at him, confused, but I'm also aware that a wide smile is starting to spread across my face. It's the coke. Picking up me phone from the arm of the couch I press at a button just so the face lights up and I can make out the time. 9:16. Fuck it, I'll watch the game. What else is there to do?

09:10

Jack

I watch a young girl leave the bank and head in the direction of Grafton Street. I don't find it suspicious in any way but I decide to keep an eye on her from across the street. I feel so relieved since I hung up the phone. I was seriously thinking of implementing my exit strategy and cursing my luck, but Darragh has assured me everything is okay. Vincent should be filling out the paperwork about now. The excitement has returned to my bones. I'm confident once again that we will be millionaires in just three hours' time. I stay about a hundred feet behind the young girl but she's walking at a brisk pace and it's not easy to stay on her tail, given the fact that parked buses are obscuring my view of her. Having followed her along the wall of the college, I notice her turn onto Frederick Street. I figure she's just doing an errand for the bank and decide I no longer need to follow her. I make my way back to the grey brick wall I had been kicking in frustration just ten minutes ago. I'll wait there until Vincent leaves. I had thought about going for a stroll around Merrion Square earlier but I turned around when Darragh rang me. I don't want to miss the look on Vincent's face when he walks out with those two cases.

Becoming a father changed me dramatically. I would stay awake at night just to watch Frank breathing in his cot. I was overcome with emotion. Karyn spoke to her father on my behalf, asking him to only use me for jobs when it was necessary. He agreed, but I was still required to carry out the odd protection run with my brothers-in-law at least once a week. Harry's sons were called Leo and Craig. They were both okay to me, but they could be nasty fuckers to other people. My splitting from the group wasn't solely down to the fact that I had a young son – I genuinely didn't want to be involved in crime. I was working forty hours a week at the print factory as it was. Harry was happy for me to have an honest job, but it took him a while to get used to it. The Ritchies didn't do honest labour. Harry was fine with me most of the time. I think he was delighted that his daughter had fallen for a regular guy. I was different to the sort of men she would have grown up with.

As the years went by Harry used me sparingly, as promised, but he would fume at me once or twice after being informed I wasn't as forceful as I could have been on the job. There were a couple of scary moments but we always seemed to get by. Harry didn't tell me too much but I'm pretty sure he had some cops on his payroll. He kept insisting we didn't have to be fearful in that regard. But I was always more fearful that rival gangs would begin some sort of turf war with us. The thought of Frank growing up without a father was just not an option as far as I was concerned. Frank's youngest years seemed to go by so fast. I'd fill with pride watching him walk off to school. It nearly killed me when, at seven years old, he turned around to me one day and insisted I didn't walk him to the school gates. Leaving him to his own devices scared me but it was all part of him growing up. It was only a six-minute walk to school anyway, but it was a body blow to me. It's the simple things that break your heart as a parent.

It sounds conceited but Frank, Karyn and I were as happy as any family I've ever known. There are plenty of days that stand out for me during my son's childhood, but certainly none more than the day he was set to make his football debut for the school team. He wasn't as tall as I had been at nine years of age but he was still taller than the rest of his year. The coach had stopped him in the school corridor two months earlier and asked him to trial as a goalkeeper. He impressed the coach so much that not only was he asked to be the team's number one, but he was also given the captain's armband. He had Karyn's personality traits to thank for that. He was as loud and as forthright as his mother. A doctor's appointment meant Karyn couldn't attend the game but I brought the family camcorder with me to record the action. I remember following the game up and down the touchline with perfectly steady hands. I felt guilty about wishing the other team to play well for the fact that it would involve Frank more in the game. He didn't do anything wrong, nor did he do anything outstanding that I could catch on tape to bring home to his mother. The highlight of the footage was the smile he beamed at me before kick-off when he noticed where I was standing. I was out of his mind as soon as the game started though. He was immersed in what was going on in front of him. The game seemed to be petering out to a nil-all draw when an opposition player broke free from the defence and raced towards my son. Frank's teammate desperately tried to get back at the attacker but when he slid to deny him the ball, he missed and brought the player crashing down instead. The referee pointed to the penalty spot to roars of disappointment from parents beside me. I closed my eyes in a deep squint of disappointment before I realised this could be Frank's big moment. I managed to creep around to behind Frank's goal to get myself a good shot of the penalty kick. When we watched that footage back I could be heard whispering, 'Save it, save it, save it!' And he did. Frank dived to his right, guessing where the penalty taker would kick the ball, and stuck out his hand to tip it around the post. His teammates reacted by bear-hugging him. The referee blew the final whistle there and then. He had literally saved his team from a loss in the dying moment. I knew he was looking over at me while he was being smothered in celebration, but I couldn't look back at him. I was in tears. The pride I felt that day has never been matched. By the time Frank had dressed and joined me in the car for the trip home I had composed myself. We must have spoken about the penalty save for the full duration of our drive, stopping twice to view the footage on the camcorder. Karyn smiled solemnly at us as we both chanted Frank's name on returning to the house.

'You have to see this, you have to see this,' I said to her, turning the camcorder back on. The three of us sat around our kitchen table and replayed the save at least a dozen times. Tears welled up in Karyn's eyes but I was able to hold mine in in front of Frank.

'I'm so proud of you,' she told him before asking him to go and take a shower. 'You stink of sweat and effort.'

I watched his tiny ass make his way upstairs before turning to my wife. Tears continued to roll down her face.

'I'm dying, Jack,' she said, staring into my eyes. 'Cancer. It's gone right through me.'

09:15

Ryan

I THOUGHT HE'D LAUGH AT SUCH A REQUEST SO I'M SURPRISED WHEN HE reaches towards the two legs of my chair to spin me around to face the TV. If I look sharply right I can still make out the clock on the microwave. He then hands me the remote control and tells me to watch what I want. He must be very grateful for that cocaine. I know I should have a lot going through my mind right now but I still want to watch that Champions League match. That's why I giggled at his shit joke earlier. This guy's a sucker.

'You like football?' I ask, hoping to spark up some conversation with him now that I don't have the tape wrapped around my mouth. Let's see how gullible he really is. Suddenly I'm teaching him about the sport he says he used to like when he was a kid. This exchange makes me wonder whether I should aim for his heart or for his mind in my attempts to get free. I could get personal with him and bring him to a level where he sees me as a human being and not as a pawn in his game. Maybe I could pull on his heartstrings to get out of this mess. Or maybe I should start playing mind games with him. I could just tell him out straight that he's already fucked. That the cum he tried to wipe from the TV screen earlier this morning hasn't really covered his tracks. I should inform him that cleaning the TV and the carpet beneath it a hundred times still wouldn't ensure that his DNA was not left behind. If I tell him all this and get him to realise he's so fucking dumb that he's already tripped himself up, he might decide to abandon the operation. But I decide playing to his heart is probably my best option. For now, anyway. If I confront him over the cum he may react aggressively. And he's so stupid I'm not sure what actions he would take. The TV screen is smudged slightly but it's not interfering with my watching of the game.

We only bought that TV about five months ago. I say we; I mean Vincent. He owns practically everything in here. I used to love this apartment so much. It was great to leave it in the mornings to earn a crust because coming home was always a fulfilling experience. To take the elevator up this building and to walk through the front door of the penthouse used to be a thrill. But waking up in this place and remaining here until I go back to bed at night has dimmed my fascination with it. Sometimes it feels a bit like a prison. It certainly does today. Vincent and I have fucked in every corner of this place.

We were both on such a high when we first moved in and the high didn't seem to waver for the first four years or so. I think I started to feel down once I got my promotion at work. The thrill of PR seemed to end for me once I gained a decent bit of responsibility. It also didn't help that I hated most of the guys I had to deal with on a daily basis now that I was a senior member of the team. The higher up in PR you go, the more wankers you have to endure. I found a soul mate in Ruairi though. He seemed to share my opinions on the egos of our fellow employees. He noticed it as soon as he walked in the door, despite being just a kid. He was an intern the company signed up for a year. I liked him. We used to bitch about the place on a regular basis and became good pals because of it. Bitching is such a great way to bond with somebody. Ruairi was content with his job but he didn't feel married to PR. He thought bigger and brighter things were out there waiting for him. Despite the fact he was thirteen years younger than me, he was the only person in the office I felt comfortable around. He was a likeable chap and no doubt always in great form because he was engaged to a girl who, I have to admit, was the most perfect-looking bird I have ever seen – and that includes celebrities. Her skin was flawless. Ruairi was happy that his position at Wow was bringing in a steady, albeit tiny, income for the two of them.

A junior account manager is the best position to be in. You get the perks that come along with the job without much of the responsibility and pressure. I used to stare at Ruairi at work with envy. He and I would sneak to the toilets at least twice a day to shoot a line of coke up our noses. I'm guilty of getting him hooked. But like me, he was disciplined with it, despite the fact he was only twenty-one. Neither of us got so high that we couldn't function through our working day. We saw it as a recreational drug and it helped us get through the monotony of rehashing shite press releases some famous sports star had their personal assistant type up. Sports stars are so fucking drab due to the media training they endure these days. They are afraid to say anything that doesn't toe the professional line.

If it hadn't been for Ruairi's friendship I would have given up my job at Wow sooner. In the end, he was the reason I left. One night, when he was staying back to wait for some golf tournament to finish before getting a quote for a press release, I decided to hang back with him. We could watch the end of the tournament in the company of a few lines of coke. It was unusual that we'd get this high in the office. Everybody else was long gone and we knew Ruairi only had one small paragraph of text to waffle through. I'm not a huge golf fan and can't even remember how the play unfolded but it was a memorable evening for me for a very different reason. As I sat perched on Ruairi's desk, laughing at something he tried to say that came out wrong, he leapt up and kissed me. Never in a billion years did I see that coming. I wasn't even sure if Ruairi knew that I was gay. We took advantage of the deserted office and fooled around all night on his desk, only stopping so that he could write up the last bit of copy and email it on to some newspaper editors. We didn't fuck, but we did everything else we could think of. Ruairi was a seriously handsome young man. Any guilt I felt was overridden by the excitement of it all. Whenever Vincent popped into my mind I would dive down to the desk and sniff another line of coke.

I've already done two lines, but I must keep a level head if I'm to somehow talk my way out of this situation.

'So how come you like Manchester United then if you're not a big footie fan?' I ask, looking at him.

'Me da was a fan, back in the day,' he replies.

'Are you from Kerry originally? There's a lot of United fans down in the Kingdom.'

'I'm not from fuckin' Kerry,' he replies like only a Cork man would. 'Stop fuckin' askin' me questions about meself or I'll tape your gob back up, do ye hear me?'

I nod as a reply and stare back at the TV. I thought he'd be dumb enough to give me more details about himself.

Out of the corner of my eye, I can tell he's glued to the football. Because I'm adjacent to him, he would have to twist his neck to see what I am doing with my right hand. While still maintaining a posture that suggests I'm watching the match I can reach down to pick at the tape around my right ankle. For fear of making a noise while trying to release some of the tape, I increase the volume on the television. It doesn't raise any suspicion.

'Great atmosphere at Old Trafford,' I say, looking at him. When he turns to me I can tell his eyes are glazed over from the coke. He just glares at my face before turning his attention back to the screen. His high is helping him to get engrossed in the game. I'm glad I'm such a lazy bastard that I don't cut my fingernails regularly enough. My scratching at the tape is certainly working. I feel my ankle release somewhat and an adrenaline rush hits me. I take a moment to reassess. His gun is on the glass table in front of him. If I could free this leg before turning my attention to my left side, I'm certain I could get to it before him. I take another peek at my captor before slowly reaching back down. I'm gonna be the hero for once in my life.

09:15

Vincent

CHELLE'S OFFICE WOULD BE QUITE ROOMY IF IT WASN'T FOR THE ENORMOUS oak desk she placed in the middle of it. I drum my fingers against it in anticipation of Janice returning with the ink. Chelle doesn't know what to do with herself. She's fuming. I'm not sure if it's the noise I am making with my fingers or the fact that I haven't said a word to her for five whole minutes that's niggling her mind the most. I've rarely been upset with her. I've never really had a professional reason to be upset with her. She's such a great employee. The printer's run out of ink and she doesn't have any spare in the supply room – big deal. It happens. It's not even Chelle's fault. If she was worried about the ink gauges on her printers then I'd be worried about her priorities.

I stare at the family portrait on her desk as I continue to tap my fingers. The photograph must have been taken about four years ago. Her twin sons are only babies in it. Jake looks as handsome as ever; Chelle's husband is an estate agent and possesses both the charm and the smile required for such a cheesy career. They met travelling through Europe. Chelle and I actually share a mutual fascination with Rome. That's where she met Jake. Aesthetically, it's such a stunning city, but only a small part of the magic of that city lies in its architecture. The pace of life is totally different there. There's a deep understanding away from the tourist traps that life is about contentment. The Romans don't get too high, and as a result, they don't get too low either. Their mentality towards life is in total contrast to the rest of Europe. Probably the rest of the world. Both

94

Chelle and Jake were actually married to other people when they first met. Intrigued by the coincidence of hearing a fellow Irish accent on a tiny rooftop bar in a different country, Chelle couldn't help flirting with the handsome man sipping on a whisky cocktail. Before the end of the trip, they had shared a kiss and were plotting to meet up when they arrived home. I christened him Jake the Snake and giggled when Chelle filled me in on the story for the first time. Having got to know him well since then, I'd have to admit that he's no snake. He is a genuinely charming man. His jokes are a bit shit, but he's easy to like. Ryan and I would often go on double dates with them but we haven't hung out in a couple of years. Ryan and Jake used to obsess about sports over dinner while Chelle and I would roll our eyes at each other. There are a few reasons why the four of us don't socialise as much these days. Part of it is to do with the fact that Ryan seemed to get himself into a state of depression having left Wow PR and rarely has the inclination to go out anymore. And part of it has to do with me getting pissed off with Chelle's fascination with my sexuality. We all remain on good terms, but we just don't see each other as often as we used to.

I pick up the framed photograph and finally remove Chelle from her discomfort. 'How's Jake?' I ask.

'He's doing well, thanks,' she replies with a smile. 'He's away on business today. Up in Belfast at a big consultancy conference.'

'And the kids?' I ask.

'Good. Oliver is gearing up to start school this September and George is just happy once we put a football at his feet. He did really well in his first school exams.'

I wink at her to relieve the tension. I actually don't care about her kids that much. I don't really care for any kids. Like everybody else, I find bold kids repulsive but I'm not a fan of good kids either. I just happen to be one of those people who can't stand children. Unlike Ryan.

I see Janice before Chelle does. It's only twenty past nine. She must have run to Frederick Street and back.

'Hi, Michelle, hi, Mr Butler,' she says breathlessly as she enters the office. 'I've got the ink.'

'Well go put it into the printer,' Chelle says firmly, passing my original annoyance back on to her personal assistant. 'And get me those papers in the next three minutes.'

Filling out paperwork for such a task seems old school considering the evolution in digital technology. However, every transfer from branch to branch needs to be accounted for in both hard copy and in our complicated computer system. It's a lengthier process than is actually required but I can understand the board's strategy in this regard. It works. It's very rare for any money to get mixed up between the banks. Every new and used note is accounted for in both of our systems. It's used notes I'll be taking from the banks today. Ryan's captor told me what he wanted. Used notes can't be traced outside our branches. Once they leave our banks they can be used anywhere. The dizziness seems to enter my head once again as the thought of the robbery takes over my mind. I've got to get my feelings under control. I'll have to go through some simple paperwork with Chelle here in her office before we take a little trip to the vault. There, we will have to count out the amount of cash between us. We have to do that four times before updating the computer system. I should be out of here in about twenty-five minutes' time, I reckon.

'Two mill is a hell of a sum,' Chelle mentions once again while we await the paperwork. 'Are you sure you're okay transferring it yourself?'

'Ah, it's fine,' I say. 'John is at the doorstep waiting on me. Plus, someone's gonna have to chop my hands off, aren't they?' I say, wiggling the two handcuffs chained to the cases.

'I'd cut your hands off for two mill in used notes.' Chelle laughs.

'Yeah, fuck it, so would I.' I giggle back before noticing Janice is standing in the doorway to the office. I normally act super professional around all employees. I'm not sure whether she heard me swear, but she certainly doesn't let on that she did.

'Here you go, Michelle, Mr Butler,' she says, placing the paperwork in front of us. She then picks up a pen from Chelle's desk and hands it to me. I take a deep breath. Here we go.

09:25

Darragh

THE FOOTBALL IS MAKING ME REFLECT ON THE TIME I FIRST MOVED UP TO Dublin. I really missed home for a month or two. I've only ever driven through Cork since I've been in the capital, I've never actually gone back. Us Galligans don't do holidays. The fact that I'm watching Man United is quite ironic. Me old man used to make me watch them in the early days, but I guess I didn't show enough interest. I'm enjoyin' this though. But that's probably all down to the coke. I noticed that I was smiling ear to ear just a few moments ago and had to check meself before squinting towards Ryan, making sure he didn't catch me in the moment. He was talking me through the game earlier but he seems to have gone quiet now. I'd love to know who he buys his coke from.

After about four months of selling on the streets of North Dublin, part of the profit seemed to be winging its way into me pockets. The Boss would only ask for about ninety per cent of what I'd taken and would wink at me as he handed back some of the notes.

'You're doing well, Darragh,' he said to me one day. It was unusual to get a compliment from him. 'We might get you involved in some of the fun stuff, huh?'

'I'd love that,' I said. 'I want to get involved as deep as I can, like.'

The fact that I passed the mock arrest test with flying colours seemed to get me closer to the lads. I got the sense that The Boss was hesitant in involving me any further but the rest of the gang seemed to put in a good word for me. Pretty soon afterwards I was being called into their meetings to discuss shipments. They knew they could trust me. I began transferrin' large quantities of the drug to Belfast. It was a long three-hour drive to Clifton, but I was happy to do it alone. At times I'd have up to twelve kilos of coke in the boot of a rented car, which would have resulted in me spending around fifteen years behind bars had I been caught. But I felt invincible. I didn't even go to any great lengths to hide my merch. I would just pack the trunk of the car with the bags of coke and throw a blanket over them. I wasn't being paid well, but the few quid I did pocket was enough for me. The Boss also didn't mind me skimming the odd bit of coke from the packages for myself as long as I didn't go overboard. The rental on the car was legitimate but The Boss had sorted me out with a very convincing fake driving licence. I didn't need to produce it at any stage of my dozen or so trips over the border. But for some reason, I ended up doing a run to Limerick one Wednesday morning and ended up almost shittin' me cacks.

The Boss asked me to drive to an estate to deliver ten kilos of coke to a new connection of his. I had a fear that something would go wrong from the outset. I never felt comfortable. I had to try to convince meself that I was just out on a drive. What could possibly go wrong? A broken fucking tail light! I was literally ten miles from the estate when I heard a siren blare behind me. In a split second me mind flipped between stepping on the accelerator and stepping on the brake. The fact that the siren only sounded for a second and so asking me, rather than telling me, to pull over made me mind up. I figured that the cop must have just noticed me committing a minor road offence I didn't even know I'd committed.

'Licence,' said the grumpy-lookin' fuck after he'd strolled slowly up to my rolled-down window.

'Here ya are, Garda,' I responded politely. 'Did I do something wrong?'

He squinted looking at me licence. 'That a Kerry accent, Mr Chomsky?'

I was about to reply with a polite 'no', when I realised that was exactly where Grant Chomsky was from.

'Eh, yes,' I say with a smile. 'Dingle.'

'Ah, my wife's from Tralee,' he replied. 'You know your driver's side tail light is out, Chomsky?'

I felt such a relief with his words. I had stayed composed but I could still feel beads of sweat forming on my forehead as he held that licence.

'I'm just heading to Limerick city for a bit of a work errand,' I said. 'I'll stop at the first mechanic I find on me route and make sure I get the bulb sorted. I promise.'

'Wouldn't get it fixed in Limerick city, if you know what I mean,' he replied. I think he was joking. So I laughed. Maybe I laughed too loudly. It made him look up at me for the first time.

'You got bad dandruff or is that cocaine on your shirt?' he asked, poking his head closer to me.

Shit! I'd been doing a couple of lines on the drive.

'Get out of the car.'

I managed to brush some of the powder from me chest as I got out, but I knew he was going to search me. I had a tiny bit of powder in me jeans pocket. It was nothing compared to what was in the boot. After asking me to rest my hands on the top of the car he searched my pockets. He held the small plastic bag up in front of me face. I focused to look at it and gritted me teeth. There was literally enough for two decent-sized lines left in it.

'Just to get me through Limerick city,' I said, smiling. My joke didn't work.

He opened my car door and knelt inside to have a look around. He didn't find anything but sweet wrappers and an empty water bottle. I was delighted to see him crawl his heavy ass back out without having reached for the boot popper. But then he asked me to turn around and face him.

'Open your boot for me,' he said as he walked to the back of the car.

Bollocks.

'Sure,' I said kneeling back into the car. I stared at him in the rear-view mirror before I swung me legs into position in the driver's seat and lashed on the ignition. I clicked the gear stick into reverse and heard the bumper crash against his kneecaps before I sped off. At no time did I feel afraid. I was lovin' it. The thrill of a car chase is insane. I watched in the rear-view mirror as he called for assistance on his walkie-talkie while hobbling to his car. I easily had a quarter of a mile head start on him. His sirens were in full flow but he didn't make any ground on me. I wasn't sure whether he'd recorded me licence plate. I had to assume he did, so I knew I needed to get out of the car as quickly as I could. I made a sharp left off the motorway towards Clyduff and sped into a kip of an industrial estate. There were dozens of cars parked in and around the warehouses. As quickly as I could, I parked my car up, broke into another and switched the coke over. I was out of there in two minutes. The Boss had taught me how to do that. I delivered the merch as expected and even made it back to Dublin in a different stolen car. The gang were fuckin delighted. I'd been in touch with The Boss the whole ride through, keeping him updated after I'd nearly got done. He was filling me in and helping me get back safely by recommending different routes and opportunities to change cars. He hugged me like I was his brother when I returned. These gangland guys really don't respect you until you nearly get caught. It's incredible. You have to be bad enough to almost get arrested before they will realise you're good enough.

'You're a fuckin superstar, Darragh Galligan,' The Boss said, kissing me on the forehead. 'Let's have a celebration. You got any plans tonight?'

'Nah, nothin',' I said, high as a kite.

'Well you do now. We're taking you out, kid.'

I'm certain it's not my fondness for Manchester United that has my heart racing. I'm enjoying the match but I know I've probably taken too much of this shit. If I was lying about at home I wouldn't be panicking about being high but I need to keep a level head today. I fuckin swore to meself I wouldn't overdo it this morning. I look at Ryan. He hasn't budged an inch. He's just sitting there enjoying the game. I puff out me cheeks before getting up off the couch. I need to splash some water on me face. The last thing I need to do right now is have a full-on fuckin panic attack.

09:25

Ryan

I CAN SEE THE GREASY LITTLE SHIT OUT OF THE CORNER OF MY EYE. HE'S grinning to himself as wide as I've ever seen anybody grin. He's super high. You can snort coke every day of your life and still not be immune to a new batch. It's the same with most drugs. Some new formula that you haven't tried before can really fuck you up. Unfortunately, he's only taken two lines of the stuff so far. That's not enough to tip him over the edge. But I don't think he's going to have any more. He can't be that stupid. Either way, I need to somehow release my right ankle before turning my attention to my left side. The coke is probably giving me the focus I need to get this tape off my wrist and ankles, but it may also be responsible for me eventually getting caught. I can't get too erratic with my approach. It's important I stay calm. I'm trying to figure out in my head whether I can reach the gun if I just release my right ankle. I'd have a clunky kitchen chair holding my left side down and I wouldn't be able to put one foot in front of the other to walk. But if I could leap forward and somehow grab the gun, I'd hold all the aces. My gut feeling tells me I would make the leap towards the gun and end up falling flat on my face against the corner of the glass table while this prick laughs at me. The table is about three large strides away from where I'm sitting now. It's just too far to leap in one go. I need to release both sides from the chair. After ten minutes of picking away I'm making good progress on my right ankle, but this could take a while. I peek at the clock on the microwave again. 9:26. Two and a half hours left. Reaching my right hand back down I try to tug at the tape instead of scraping at it. But it's just not doing me any good. The tape is just too strong. I need to pick away at each layer of it with my nails, and work my way through it that way. There must be at least ten layers. This'll take a while.

To my surprise, the fantasy night with Ruairi didn't make things awkward between us the following day. I texted him in the morning with a feeling of dread, thinking he wouldn't get back to me. But in a matter of seconds he replied telling me he enjoyed the night. When we met in the office later that evening he winked at me. Butterflies filled my stomach. I felt just as excited as I did when I first fell in love with Vincent. Ruairi and I ended up going for drinks on a regular basis. It normally ended in us fooling around, but we never had full-on sex, despite my pleas. We were both enjoying our new relationship, even though Ruairi would often piss me off with his 'I'm not gay' insistence. The guy fuckin' loved cock. About one month into our affair I began to dream of a life with him. It wasn't fair on Vincent at all. Vincent had turned me from a nobody into a somebody and I owed him all the joy I had in life. Besides, I was living in one of the hottest and trendiest places in the whole of Dublin. There was never any guarantee that Ruairi would leave his girlfriend for me, but it didn't stop me thinking about the possibilities. My relationship with Vincent wasn't in dire straits. We weren't arguing or even that sick of each other. Our bond just seemed to plateau after a few years. We weren't keeping things fresh enough. Fooling around with Ruairi gave my life the spark it needed. That was why, when he came to me to say he no longer wanted to see me outside the office, I spiralled into depression.

'Listen, I've enjoyed it and had some fun, but it was just experimental on my part,' he said, staring into my eyes while at our favourite pub one evening. 'I'm in love with my girlfriend. I can't do this anymore.'

I stayed silent initially. I had a million ways to approach this with him but I couldn't figure out which one to choose. In the end I opted for defensive and arrogant.

'Your girlfriend will find out you're a fuckin' cock lover eventually, you piece of shit,' I shouted at him as I stood up to leave. Everybody in the pub turned to face us. I was too hurt to care.

My anger soon turned to bitterness before genuine heartache set in. It was only a swift affair but I got caught up in the emotion of it all. What made it even worse was having to work with him. Although he worked shifts, I'd still have to see his face and hear his voice in the office at least three times a week. I made excuses to not turn up in the early days of the heartache but soon after I had to face up to the torture. The worst part about getting your heart broken from an affair is the fact that you can't actually confide in anybody. I couldn't talk to any colleagues about the fling nor could I tell any of my friends. All my friends were Vincent's friends anyway. I tried to immerse myself in my computer screen when I was at work, but at home I'd just curl up into a ball on either the bed or the couch and cry myself to sleep. I'd wake up each morning and convince myself that today was the day I would finally get over Ruairi but I knew deep down I was kidding myself. To numb the pain, I promoted cocaine from a social drug to a daily habit. I contacted an old student friend of mine who made the greatest coke ever, to get so wasted I would forget Ruairi's handsome face. Vincent could tell I wasn't myself but he believed me when I told him I was just dejected with my career. That was partly true. I had, after all, fallen out of love with PR way before I'd fallen in love with Ruairi.

I'm getting a bit paranoid that my captor will notice my right hand missing any time he looks up at me. I have to reach lower now, right to the bottom of my ankle, to finish the job. If he looks over at me he'll notice I'm slightly hunched, but I suppose my posture isn't anything out of the ordinary. My face is still towards the screen, watching the match as I pick away at the tape. The high definition big screen and the sound the fans are creating in the stadium seems to be distracting him. It's imperative I get this tape loosened as soon as I can. I freeze, though, when I notice him sit more upright. After rubbing his eyes, he stares over at me before standing up slowly. He takes a walk behind the couch and heads towards our main bathroom. He's left the gun on the glass table right beside his phone. This guy is a full-on fucking moron. When I hear the tap turn on in the bathroom I think about making the leap towards the gun. I won't reach it in one go, but with him at least fifteen feet away from me, I'll have a few seconds to crawl my way towards it. I need to do this now. I force the balls of my feet deep into our carpeted floor and begin to count myself down.

09:25

Jack

My ass is growing numb perched on this wall. I've stood up to stretch my back so many times that I'm starting to get paranoid somebody has noticed I'm up to no good.

I check my watch again. I've estimated that Vincent should be coming out of the bank at around nine-thirty; that's only five minutes from now. I'm afraid to go for a walk, in case I miss his exit. I just need to know he's doing okay. His collapse is continuing to worry me despite Darragh confirming everything is back on track. I know Vincent's next port of call is Camden Street. That's another twenty to twenty-five-minute walk for me. He'll arrive there with his driver, John, before I do. In an ideal world I'll observe Vincent entering and exiting each bank, but I can't physically stay on his tail too much. I'm wary of getting public transport because there are cameras on buses, and taxi drivers will be asked about their fares as part of the investigation into this robbery. I'd made a decision early on in this process that I would walk to each of the branches and I must continue to follow through with that. It's a long walk and a lot of effort, but the pay-off will be oh so worth it. Sticking to the plan is paramount. I'm absolutely sure there is no way I can get caught. I've covered each and every possibility. Another look at my watch causes me to blow out my cheeks. Only seconds have gone by.

Some people say, spending time with a loved one when you know they have limited time left to live is rewarding. I think that's bullshit. I loved Karyn dearly, but the pain it caused my heart to leave the hospital every night feeling that I'd said my final goodbye was monstrous. The doctors told me one afternoon in late June 2005 that my wife would only last another three months. She shocked them by staying alive for another half a year. But from that day up until the night she passed away, just two days into 2006, was torturous for me. I felt really selfish for feeling such pain when it was Karyn who was dying, but I couldn't help it. I hate saying goodbye. I must have said at least a hundred goodbyes to Karyn. A part of me wished that she had died in a car crash and I just had to receive a terrible phone call. It would be shocking and painful in other respects, but losing my wife in that way wouldn't have been as mentally challenging and exhausting for me. The whole process was very hard on poor Frank who really didn't understand what was going on. I didn't fill him in on every detail but he knew his mother was close to death. He wasn't stupid. She looked like she was close to death. Karyn decided to take a large course of chemotherapy in the hope that a miracle would occur, which made her face appear gaunt in her final months. I remember being angry that she chose to have the treatment. It prolonged her passing. Selfishly, I just wanted her to die so Frank and I could move on with our lives. Her family were very supportive. They really are a super-tight bunch. Harry and his third wife, Yvonne, visited the hospital almost as often as I did. I used to hear them praying in the ward. That always amused me. These guys had no problem ordering people to be murdered, yet they somehow still believed there was a God up there who would answer their prayers. On the day Karyn finally passed, Harry sat me down and told me he considered me as part of the family still, and he would look after me in any way I sought. I thanked him but insisted I'd stay away from organised crime for Frank's sake.

'You made my daughter very happy for nearly twenty years. So I will make you happy in any way you want. If you ever need me, you just call, okay?' he said before hugging me and walking away. But I knew that wasn't the end of the conversation.

I'm finding myself clicking through this old phone. I miss my iPhone. I left it at home for a very valid reason. Mobile phones can be easily traced. It amazes me the amount of times I read about idiots being found guilty of certain crimes because their phone was traced to the scene. How stupid can you be? There is nothing on this cheap phone except today's call history and a game called Snake. It's a boring little graphic but it beats staring at the doors of ACB across the street. I finish a couple levels of the game before staring at the time on the top of the phone again. It's nine thirty-one and there has been no movement out of the bank. I know I'm impatient, but I feel like I have to ring Darragh to get some information.

'Have you not got your phone right beside you?' I ask when he finally answers. He has annoyed me again by taking his time picking up. 'Any word from Vincent?'

He hasn't heard a thing. I'm not surprised. It's literally one minute past the time we thought Vincent would exit. But that doesn't stop me from acting the hard man.

'Listen, I'm worried about him. Give him a call for me, will ya? Tell him he shouldn't be messing about or you'll kill that little darling of his, alright?'

09:30

Ryan

As I lean slightly forward, allowing my toes to take most of the weight, the two hind legs of the chair lift up. I play the jump forward in my head. I figure I will make one giant leap that will leave me about four feet from the gun. From there, I should be able to pull myself up on the edge of the glass table and grab it with my right hand. I puff out my cheeks three times fast and count myself down in my head. *Three ... two ...* The noise of his phone rattling off the glass table scares the shit out of me. The legs of the chair immediately fall back down to the carpet and I look backwards to see if my captor is coming from the bathroom to answer the phone. I shake my head in amazement at the timing of the call.

'That my phone?' he shouts out as I hear him turn the tap off.

I sigh. 'Yeah.'

Why the fuck am I helping him?

He sprints out of the bathroom and scoops the phone up as quickly as he can.

'Hello? Yes, I have the phone here beside me all the time,' he says after a pause. Seems like his partner in crime is ranting at him again. They're like fuckin' Laurel and Hardy. 'No, he hasn't been onto me yet. It's just gone half nine now, he shouldn't be too long.

'Okay, I'll give him a ring now,' he says, sounding exhausted after another pause.

They're getting worried. But it should be me who's most worried. It's my life at stake, after all. I notice my captor fumbling at the phone to make an outside call. He's obviously trying to get onto Vincent, but he doesn't seem to be able to get an answer. Vincent is at the bank with colleagues. Why would he answer that cheap-ass phone you gave him in front of them? Idiots! Vincent would hate to be seen with such a cheap mobile phone. He's a bit of a snob in those respects.

The pain of seeing Ruairi almost every time I went into the office proved too much for me in the end. Vincent could see the depression etched on my face. I had to tell him that I hated being in PR and I hated the people I worked with. He bought it. The fact that I'd been bitching to him about my colleagues over the years paid off. He had insisted for a long time that I should write a novel. I always have ideas for stories, but I totally lack the discipline to be that kind of writer. Even before I handed in my notice at Wow I knew all too well that I wouldn't get up in the mornings and motivate myself to write a few chapters of a book. Vincent set out a plan that meant I would have to wake up with him when his alarm went off at seven o'clock every morning. And after he headed to his office, I would open the new MacBook Air he bought for me to work on my novel. A few ideas that I had in my head for years made it onto a Word document in the early days of my working from home, but that was literally it. Ideas. I had one story concept in my mind about a celebrity paparazzo, which had a chilling twist, and another one about a stunning blonde bombshell who was also an amazing slutty private investigator. She would sleep with all the men she was investigating to get the details she was looking for over pillow talk. I wasn't bad for ideas, but I was pathetic when it came to work ethic. PR doesn't help you become a good writer. In fact, it does the opposite. It teaches you how to write shit formulaic copy as quickly as you can. The creative promise I had before I joined Wow was wiped out within a couple of months of working there.

It's just over nineteen months since I left media to write a book. I have added little to those two story concepts on that Word document since. That's pathetic in its own right, but it's not as pathetic as the reasons for which I now use that MacBook Air. I have zero career ambition. I feel like my old twenty-year-old self again. A no-hoper. Only this time I'm lacking hope in the more comfortable surroundings of a glorious penthouse as opposed to a tiny, untidy bedsit.

He looks a little frustrated that he can't reach Vincent on the phone, but he also seems a bit lost. He's scrunching his nose up again, a habit all coke users have after snorting a line.

'Where was I?' he asks himself before spinning around. He looks over at me before picking up his gun and placing it in the band of his jeans. He then makes his way back towards the bathroom. I hear the tap turn on again and curse to myself.

How the fuck did that other cunt happen to ring at the exact moment I was about to leap for the gun?

Staring over at the television, I continue to watch the match before remembering what I had been up to. With my captor out of the room, I can work on my right ankle with more vigour. I reach down and begin to tug really hard at the tape. It's loosening its grip of my ankle to the leg of the chair but I still can't remove my foot fully. I pick away at the tape with my nails as quickly as I can. Doing this without fear of making any noise is much more effective. I seem to be making huge progress when I hear the tap turn off. The bathroom door closes and I feel the presence of my captor back in the room. He lets out a satisfied yelp before throwing himself back on the couch, placing both the phone and the gun down on the glass coffee table in almost the exact same positions they occupied a minute ago. I stare at him but he hasn't even noticed me. He's now watching Paul Pogba running one-on-one with Bayern Munich goalkeeper Manuel Neuer and smacking a ten-yard effort off the inside of the post.

'Ouch,' he says while still staring at the screen. 'I would have scored that.'

The atmosphere in the Old Trafford stadium rises in volume and, as it does, I allow myself a strong tug at the remaining thin sliver of tape until finally I feel it snap. Relief fills my whole body as my foot releases. My whole right side is now free. I'm halfway to getting myself and Vincent out of this mess.

09:35

Vincent

NEITHER CHELLE NOR I WANT TO READ THROUGH THE PAPERWORK, BUT IT'S a legal requirement. We've read through this jargon thousands of times over the years. But Chelle knows that I would demand she follows protocol at all times. So rushing her through it today would look suspicious. The fact that I'm taking out two million euros is suspicious enough. We flick over page after page as Chelle mumbles through the contents and then we each sign on the dotted lines at the bottom. There are eleven pages in all and each of them must be signed by both of us. To be fair to Chelle, she is getting through it as quickly as she can. She's still cringing about the ink.

'… to extract two million euros,' she reads with emphasis while raising an eyebrow at me. She keeps mentioning this, but then again, she should. This is a hell of a lot of money to be transferring from one branch to another.

As she twirls the paperwork towards me for another signature I feel the cheap phone vibrate in my suit pocket. There's no way I can answer it. Chelle would piss herself laughing if I took out an old Nokia phone to take a call. Besides, if I did answer it, what sort of conversation could we have in Chelle's company? I'll have to excuse myself later and pretend to go to the bathroom or something and call this prick back. I try to calm down after the vibrating stops but it doesn't last long. The gobshite tries to ring me back straight away. He really is one thick fuck.

Although my professional life had taken off, my personal life had taken a bit of a step backwards. I had frequented the gay bars around the city for a full six years but I had to force myself to stop going out after I'd become manager of the Drumcondra branch. It wasn't just the responsibility of the new job that made my mind up for me. I genuinely couldn't cope with the hangovers anymore. Something chemical happens in your body after you get into your late twenties when it comes to alcohol. Suddenly hangovers, which used to last a morning, start to stay with you for two or three full days. But that didn't stop me getting back on the party bus after I met Ryan. We were both just high on life in those days. I'd had two semi-serious boyfriends in my twenties. I dated Seamus Gaughran for all of a year before I found out he was fucking as many blokes behind my back as he possibly could. Then there was Simon O'Dea. I met him on a trip to Sligo. We stayed close for a couple of years but it got tiring for the two of us. The west of Ireland is a great place to travel to, but it's a pain in the ass to drive there. That trip on a regular basis is so monotonous. After Simon, I was celibate for almost three years, bar four guilt-riddled one-night stands. I'm not sure why I felt so guilty about having sex with strangers. I was free and single. But one-night stands – which I had been fond of fifteen years prior – just seemed so juvenile to me. I knew I'd be a great catch for somebody but I couldn't seem to find any man I'd like to live with. I was earning over €250,000 a year and was just about to complete the purchase of one of the trendiest penthouses in the whole of Dublin, yet I had nobody to share all that with. There was one guy who interested me, but I was afraid to ask him out. He'd been in and out of my bank on a few occasions to discuss a possible loan. I could see an awful lot of potential in his look, despite the fact that he had the appearance of an early nineties boy band member. His curtains-style haircut was so wrong in 2002. But under his hanging fringe beamed a really cute smile. He had dimples that sunk into his cheeks when he smiled, but smiling seemed like an irregular occurrence for him. He had heavy eyes. I felt straight away that he came across as if he wasn't enjoying his life. That part of it was actually a turn-on for me. The opportunity to kick-start this guy's life really was quite fascinating. I started to become a little infatuated with him. There's little more exciting in life than really fancying somebody. I knew by his manner that he was gay. You wouldn't place Ryan in the 'camp' category but you wouldn't have to possess the greatest gaydar on the planet to recognise his sexuality.

'Would you be interested in discussing this over dinner some evening?' I asked him while checking over my shoulder one Wednesday afternoon. I knew I was taking a risk. It was a totally unprofessional thing to do, especially for somebody like me. He looked at me as if I had two heads. He'd later tell me that he didn't realise I was asking him out on a date. He genuinely thought it was a service I was offering as a bank manager.

'… and last one,' Chelle says, spinning the paperwork back over to me. I sign it with extra emphasis on the cross of my 't' before grinning at her. She tidies the paperwork with a quick bounce of the sheets off her desk before standing up. She then leads me out of her office towards the back of the building.

'You got your key, Vincent?' she asks as we stand either side of the vault door. I answer her by waving my card at her. 'Three, two, one,' she counts down, just before we swipe at the double lock entrance.

As the vault door opens I take another look at my watch. It's twenty to ten. I can feel my phone buzzing again. I think about dismissing myself to ring that asshole back but I've gone too far now. He'll have to wait. Chelle and I came straight to the vault after completing the paperwork so I think it would look rather odd if I headed off to the toilets now. I'll only be in here for another ten minutes or so. The prick will be happy enough when I ring him back. I'll have the first two million with me in the car. The first vault door brings us into a small corridor that holds a lot of the bank's paperwork. There are six shelves on each side filled with heavy files of stuff nobody will ever read. There's a small steel door at the other end of this corridor that will lead us to the cash. Chelle keys in a five-digit code that allows the door to click open. You can smell the banknotes as soon as she pushes through. It's a scent I've never become immune to. There are all sorts of bonds and notes neatly packaged in eight large vaults but it's the vault at the front right corner of this heavy-lit room that I need to make my withdrawal from today. This vault houses the cash that the bank uses on a daily basis. Used notes.

'You wanna do the first count?' Chelle asks as she turns to a computer screen on the right side of the small room.

'Sure,' I say. 'Will that take long?' I'm asking about the computer system. I know it only takes a few minutes but I'm really suggesting she works quicker than normal. She gets the gist.

'I'll be as quick as I can,' she answers.

You would think counting out two million euros would take a fair bit of time, but when the notes are neatly packed into ten-thousand-euro piles already it's quite a straightforward task. I just need to pull two hundred of these packs out of the vault and place them on the countertop beside me. I'm done counting the money before Michelle has updated the database.

'Jaysus, two mill doesn't look that much when it's laid out like that,' she says turning to me, laughing. 'Now, let's see. There should be two hundred packs, right?'

'Yep,' I answer with a sigh.

I know we have to do this two times each as part of the protocol. On Chelle's second go, we count the notes into my cases. On each of the four counts we manage to make up the two million without any errors. You'd want to be fucking stupid not to be able to count to two hundred, after all.

'It's all there,' she says as I pack up the second case before tightening the handcuff around my wrist.

'Chelle, it's been an adventure,' I say sarcastically.

'I'm so sorry about the ink,' she says. 'I feel awful about—'

'Don't worry about it,' I interrupt, then kiss her on both cheeks. 'I really need to get going to Jonathan. I'll call you later, okay?'

I don't hear her answering. I'm too busy rushing out of the vault and through the large steel doors before pacing onto the bank floor. A couple of employees wish me goodbye. I only offer a fake smile in return. As I stand in the glass hallway between the two exit doors I can see John reading his newspaper in the driver's seat of the car. I let out another big sigh before murmuring to myself, 'What the fuck are you doing, Vincent?'

Adrenaline pumps through my veins as the second door beeps open. When I push through I feel the heat of the morning sun hit me straight in the face.

What a fucking day this is.

09:35

Darragh

I'M JUST ABOUT TO FILL THE CUP ME HANDS ARE FORMING WITH COLD WATER when I'm sure I hear me phone ringing.

'That my phone?' I call out after turning off the tap.

'Yeah,' he answers. Fuckin idiot.

I race out to answer it with me hands still wringing wet.

'Have you not got your phone right beside you?' JR shouts down the line at me.

'Yes, I have the phone here beside me all the time,' I lie. This is the second time I've left the phone behind while I'm out of the room. I need to get me fuckin act together. This is not how proper gangsters do it.

'Have you heard from Vincent?'

'No, he hasn't been onto me yet. It's just gone nine-thirty, like, he shouldn't be too long.'

'Listen, I'm worried about him. Give him a call for me now. Tell him he shouldn't be fuckin about or you'll kill that little darling of his, alright?'

'Okay, I'll give him a call now,' I say before hanging up.

It's literally five minutes past the estimated time Vincent should be coming out of the bank. And even at that, nine-thirty was just a rough guess. JR is certainly lacking patience. When we were planning all this, JR said Vincent will be thirty to forty minutes in each bank. He's given him thirty-five minutes in the first one and I already have to get in touch. Maybe he's freaking out because Vincent collapsed earlier. I'd almost forgotten about that. Bleedin' coke.

JR has the number for the phone we gave Vincent stored in as number two on the speed dial, but I can't seem to get my head together to dial it. I wipe my wet hands on my T-shirt. After a fumble, I manage to dial his phone, but it's ringing out. I kick the floor in frustration and try him again. He's still not picking up. He must be in the vaults filling his cases with notes. He fuckin better be. I'll leave it for a few minutes before I try him again. I'm about to put the phone back down on the coffee table to return to the bathroom when I realise I really should be bringing it with me. I pick the gun up too and force it into the waistband of me jeans. I need to be more careful. Ryan wouldn't be able to get to the gun, but I know I must get me head together and stop flutin' about. I stare into the mirror over the sink in their huge bathroom and shake my head. My eyes are fuckin purple. I need to chill. I twist at the cold tap again and let out a big sigh that clouds up the mirror. I gotta splash me face.

The Boss insisted I didn't put my hand in my pocket throughout the celebration night. He must have thrown his arm around me at least a hundred times. I felt like the young Henry Hill at the start of *Goodfellas* when De Niro greets him on the steps of the courthouse.

'You took your first pinch like a man and you learned the two greatest lessons in life – you never rat on your friends and you always keep your mouth shut.'

I'd performed even better than the young Henry Hill. I didn't even get pinched. I don't like champagne but the whole gang kept popping bottle after bottle in celebration. It wasn't just my heroics that we were celebrating. The Boss now had a major player from Limerick involved in his circle, which was likely to bring in another half a mill or so every year. The lines of coke were being shared among us as often as the bubbly was being poured out. If I remember correctly, there were twelve of us out celebrating that night. Every one of us was wasted. The Boss may have been talking drunk bullshit into me ear most of the time, but what he was saying was really getting' me excited. He wanted to start getting' me involved in a big money laundering scam he was starting up. He said it would bring me in a rake of dough every couple of months. It was the compliments more than the cash that got me pumped. I could finally sense that The Boss liked me. I think that was the first time I ever felt accepted. I remember the air hitting me when meself and two other lads left the club that night. The champagne went to me head instantly. One of me new mates, who we called Smack, started to take the piss out of a group of slutty-looking bitches because that's what Smack did for fun. He had a way with words. I don't think I've ever known anyone funnier than Smack, not even a professional comedian. I don't know why I ever thought I could outdo him. But I did try that night as we walked further down the Tallaght Road and came across a couple sucking the faces off each other outside one of those run-down gaffs.

'She must be easy, snoggin' an ugly fuck like you,' I shouted out to the laughter of me two mates. They were egging me on, especially after the fella stopped kissing his bird to stare back at me.

'What you lookin' at, you ugly piece of shit?' I barked over to him.

Then his girlfriend turned around.

'Ah, I see now,' I continued, laughing. 'She's ugly as fuck too.'

Me mates didn't really laugh at that one. I got the feeling even Smack felt I'd crossed the line. I felt so uncomfortable that I couldn't leave it there. The bloke wrapped his arm around the bird to walk away from me and for some reason I jogged towards them in a rage. I watched the girl fall to her knees as she began to run. The thought of picking her up crossed my mind for a split second before I noticed a fist coming at me. I just managed to dodge it with a quick turn of my head before responding with an upper cut of me own. I'd never caught anyone sweeter. I heard his jaw shatter. He fell backwards, smacking his head off the bottom step of a doorway. I can still hear the two noises today: the smack of my fist off his jaw and the smack of his head off the step. I remember every beat of that whole ordeal because I replayed it over and over in me head for months afterwards. Smack and Greggo grabbed me away from the scene as quickly as they could. I knew that bloke was dead there and then.

I seem to be able to focus a bit better now that I've splashed water on me eyes. This match is getting really interesting. United are desperately chasing a goal to advance to the next round and they seem to be getting closer each time they attack. They hit the post two minutes ago. I lean forward to check the time on my phone. 9:45. I seem to have got lost in this match. JR will be wondering what's going on. It's been nearly a quarter of an hour since I told him I'd get onto Vincent. As I lift the phone to my ear after dialling JR, I hear a strange beep piercing through the speaker. I take at a look at the screen to see if I can make out what's causing the noise.

Incoming call from 2

That's Vincent calling me. Perfect timing! I tap on the green button to answer it, hanging up from JR. He won't mind waiting. Not if it's good news.

'What up, fag?'

09:45

Vincent

I WINK AT JOHN AS I APPROACH THE CAR. I DON'T KNOW WHY I FEEL excited. Adrenaline is a bipolar hormone. It doesn't always relate to what the mind is thinking. John raises both his eyebrows at me before getting out of the car. He pops the boot just as I reach him and assists me in unlocking the two cases from my wrists.

'I got 'em,' he says as he grabs both before shoving them towards the back of the boot. 'Some day, huh?' he adds, gripping both of my shoulders.

'Sure is,' I reply. I realise the smile is still etched on my face as I say it.

'Now ... it's Camden Street you want to go to next, right?'

I hesitate. 'Yeah, Camden Street.'

John opens the back door and I immediately feel the cold waft from inside the vehicle hit me. John had left the air conditioning on while he waited on me. He was probably freezing. But I'm delighted. It's a welcome relief from the heat.

'Ye look a lot better,' he says, readjusting his rear-view mirror after climbing into the driver's seat.

'I feel it, John, thank you.'

The drive from here can take less than ten minutes, but the traffic around Stephen's Green is unpredictable. I check the time and realise I have less than two hours and fifteen minutes to complete the whole mission. That wipes the smile from my face. I take a peek at my reflection in the car window and stare into my own eyes. I let out a small sigh as I register with myself. Time to make a call. I hit speed dial one as instructed and squint my eyes as the tone rings through my ear. I haven't thought through what I'm going to say.

'What up, fag?' snarls the greasy little prick in my ear.

'It's all done,' I say quietly.

'Two mill?' he asks.

'Two mill,' I reply. 'I'm on my way to Camden Street now, should be there around ten. How is Ryan?'

'Ryan will be fine up until midday,' he snaps back at me. 'Call me once you're out of Camden Street with two more million, huh?'

I glare at the small screen of the phone after Ryan's captor hangs up. But that doesn't stop me from noticing John staring back at me through the rear-view mirror. He never questions anything I do and I know for certain that he won't ask anything today. But maybe my suspicious mood swings are playing on his mind. He's probably worried about me. To quell this feeling in both of us I offer a wide smile into the rear-view mirror just for him.

'I need a little pick me up, John boy,' I follow up with. 'You got some classical in the CD player?'

'You betcha,' he replies, reaching over to one of the many buttons on his dashboard. Ah … Tchaikovsky. He's no Beyoncé, but he'll do. Classical music can take the mind places.

Our first date went perfectly well. I've often told him that I fell in love with him at our very first dinner, but that's a bit of a lie. If I recall correctly, I was thinking he wasn't as cute as I initially thought he was when he dressed up in a shirt and tie to see me at the bank. He wore a T-shirt – that didn't fit – on our first date. The round neck was out of shape and one sleeve seemed longer than the other. It made me question whether I fancied him or not. I guess I used to be shallow. I went on our second date feeling it was make or break, and he somehow won me over by opening up. My instinctive observation of a sadness behind his eyes turned out to be true. His father sounded like a right stubborn prick while his mother, though dear to him, seemed weak. I felt this kid could do with a father figure and I knew the perfect man for the job. Me! I probably spilled the beans on my wealth a little too hastily, looking back. I couldn't help it. It made me realise I had an ego. People used to tell me I was vain but I never thought I was. I guess I figured telling him about the plans for my new penthouse and alluding to how much I got paid would help him fall in love with me. I didn't want to lose him. Especially not after I'd restyled him – finally getting rid of that stupid haircut. The new and improved Ryan looked absolutely delicious and I was only too delighted to show him off. He told me he didn't fall in love with me until I sorted out his career about four months later. After I'd gone to the trouble of finding him a journalism placement at DCU and filling out his application forms, he grew really close to me. I think I was the first person he really trusted. I would have been happy for Ryan to stay at home, but he felt he needed his own path. I wasn't surprised when he told me he wanted to be a writer, but I've never considered him very talented. I've never told him that, of course. I genuinely sensed from the outset that PR was the wrong profession for him. I felt he'd get eaten up and spat back out by the sharks in that game. I guess that's what happened in the end. Out of all the gobshites who worked in media that I met through Ryan I don't recall meeting anyone I liked. People who work in that industry tend to be cunts. For some reason, they have massive egos that don't equate to their status in society. They are literally middlemen. That's what media means: medium. Why the fuck would being a middleman afford you an ego? I could never understand that.

I think this one is from *Swan Lake*, though I'm only guessing. I like to listen to classical music but I'm no expert. John would be able to tell me which Tchaikovsky composition this is. He listens to this stuff whenever he can and is responsible for my recent fondness for it too. He keeps looking at me through the rear-view mirror. Perhaps he does this every day and I'm only noticing today due to paranoia. I can see his lips hum along to the strings of the violins. Inspired by the music, I stare out of the car window feeling like I'm in a movie. I've had a habit of doing this ever since I was a young boy. We're stuck in traffic at the back end of the Green. I watch people walking by almost in slow motion with Tchaikovsky's mid-tempo concerto as a backdrop. It helps me calm down.

I've got this.

Jonathan Reilly will be quick and professional. I should be in and out of the Camden Street branch in no time. I allow myself a peek at John's dashboard to read the time again. 9:51. I've definitely fallen behind but I can make it up in this next branch. It won't be long now until I have four million euros in the trunk of this car. That'll have me halfway there.

09:50

Jack

I'M WALKING TOO QUICKLY FOR THIS HEAT. BUT I CAN'T HELP IT. I'M agitated. It's 9:50 and I still haven't heard from Darragh, despite watching Vincent leave the first bank what must have been about ten minutes ago. It's just over a twenty-minute walk to the Camden Street branch from here, right through the Green. I should arrive there around about ten past ten. Hopefully Vincent will be well in the branch at that point. Just as I turn onto Kildare Street the phone finally buzzes in my hand, but when I answer it there's nobody on the other end of the line.

What the hell is Darragh up to?

We went through this whole plan countless times in meticulous detail. He can do the difficult tasks no problem, but he seems hopeless at being able to make or take phone calls. I hope Ryan isn't getting inside his head and changing his mind. Nobody knows more than I do just how gullible Darragh is.

Frank missed his mother for about two weeks before getting back to normal. Karyn hadn't been herself for months so he slowly got used to her not being in our home. She was mostly in hospital for her final half a year. I was relieved that I didn't have to go through much of the grieving process with him. I felt relief initially after Karyn passed but it soon turned to heartache about a month in. I just missed her presence so much. It hurt my heart. But I don't believe in looking backwards. It genuinely is a complete waste of time. I tried to be positive. I saw a bright future for Frank and me. I wanted us to be the best dad and son combination ever and to go out and take on the world. Unfortunately, taking on the world meant me having to take a job at a paint factory out in Blanchardstown. It was fine. It was a half-an-hour drive from where we were living but it was an okay way to make some honest money. They offered me a manager's position and it paid better than any normal job I'd had before.

The Ritchies were practically throwing money into my pockets for months after Karyn died. They went out of their way on a regular basis to make sure Frank was okay. I never minded them calling by to see him and I felt obliged to take their money offerings early on – for his sake, of course. Frank adored his grandparents and uncles. When I told Harry I wanted to go straight, he held his hands up and said it was understandable. I think he genuinely respects me. And I respect him. The Ritchies' generosity gave my bank balance a good cushion. It meant Frank and I never had to go without the necessities in life and things never got too tight. I was able to sit on the savings and felt positive we would have a bright future. Frank needed minding during the day while I worked. That was how Margarite came into our lives. She really was adorable. She was the very first person I interviewed for the position of minding Frank and I loved her straight away. She was mad about my son, and he her, from the very first moment they met. Margarite was one year older than me and possessed the kindest smile I think I've ever seen. She had Norwegian heritage, but that was from two generations back. I'm certain she used to be really pretty but by the time I met her, she had let herself go. I loved her, but I never fancied her. I'm sure people used to think we were an item but we never were. Margarite fancied me though. She never hid that fact even though she never actually said it out loud. I sometimes tried to will myself to be interested in her that way. It never worked. It would have made so much sense for us to be a couple. We were both otherwise free and single but for our dual responsibility of taking care of my son. I was happy being a single dad and assumed I'd stay that way forever. I was living a contented life, despite the tragedy that had struck me. After a while, the Ritchies started to phone us rather than knock, which made things more ideal for me. Harry was trying to stay low-key after the Criminal Assets Bureau kicked into gear in Ireland. He was afraid he'd lose all his money. He and Yvonne moved to London. It still didn't remove the niggle I had in my head that they would, one day when he was older, expect Frank to get involved with the family business. I always felt Harry's 'low-key' move to London was temporary. The last thing I wanted was for Frank to get involved in any sort of trouble. I lived every day to keep us out of it.

As I'm trying to call Darragh back for the fourth time, the phone starts to buzz in my hand again.

'Sorry, JR,' pants Darragh. 'Vincent rang me just as soon as I was about to ring you back, so I thought I'd take his call first.'

I pointlessly nod with approval while saying nothing, allowing Darragh to fill the silence.

'Well, he had no problem in Nassau Street apart from the delay. He has two mill in the car and should be arriving at Camden Street in the next few minutes.'

'Great stuff, Darragh. How are you getting on over there? Don't let Ryan get into your head.'

'Course I won't!' he grunts back. 'The little fag is helpless. He's just watching some poncey football match now, tied up in his chair. He knows there's nothing he can do but wait.'

Waves flow through my stomach as I watch the sunshine beat down on strange faces in the Green after I hang up. Dubliners of all ages are taking strolls around the pond. Wow. We already have two million euros. The morning has gone perfectly so far. I'm aware we're literally only one-quarter of the way through this process, but the fact that Darragh seems to have Ryan under control fills me with so much confidence. We're gonna pull this off! I whistle along to the tune of 'Let's Go for a Little Walk' yet again as I pass over the tiny O'Connell Bridge. I'm only about ten minutes away from the next bank. Vincent's driver should be pulling up outside there any second now.

09:50

Ryan

HE'S HAD THE PHONE UP AND DOWN TO HIS EAR FOR THE PAST COUPLE OF minutes. After hanging up on Vincent a few seconds ago he's now onto his partner in crime. Vincent has robbed one bank of two million euros. That's insane. The reality of the whole ordeal has been trying to take over my mind, but I won't let it. I have to stay focused on this one task – getting free. The tape is so fucking hard to rip off in a discreet manner, but I'll get through it before this dumb fuck notices.

'The little fag is helpless,' I hear him say as he stares straight at me with a straight face. 'He's just watching some poncey football match now. He knows there's nothing he can do but wait.'

He grins at me while he's hanging up.

'Pogba miss another chance there, yeah?' he asks, straight as a die.

What a dumb-ass prick! He didn't even have the decency to laugh after saying that. Was he trying to be funny or is he just that fucking stupid that he didn't realise he just called the game 'poncey' ten seconds ago? This guy is a fruit loop. But I'm confident I'll get the better of him once I'm free. I take a peek at the microwave clock. 9:51. There's just over two hours left. The maths isn't looking that great for Vincent to get to three more banks and back before midday. I wonder how he's feeling right now. I bet he's still playing it cool. So many things could go wrong his end. I need to get myself out of this situation. I need to be the hero. At least I've got something to do today.

It's amazing how doing nothing breeds into more doing nothing. You would think that the less you have to do, the more inclined you would be to do something. That's not true at all. The less you do, the less you want to do. It's staggering how addictive doing nothing can become. I have three pairs of what I call apartment pants. They're not apartment pants at all. They're just pyjama bottoms but I don't want to call them that. Pyjamas sounds a little bit more pathetic than apartment pants. I wear at least one pair of them every day sitting on that big-ass L-shaped couch. For some reason the TV's always on – I don't know why. I barely watch anything on it. I spend a bizarre number of hours each week clicking through each of the hundred odd channels we have. It's the same mid-morning bullshit on every bloody channel. Well, in fact there are two kinds of programmes on TV during the first hours of the day. There's either a live show being presented by a couple of dicks like Piers Morgan and Susanna Reid beaming their fake smiles into our living rooms. Or else there are straight news channels. And news channels only offer up bad news. They thrive on bad news. War and worry is big business for the media. So, there's an option of either sickening positivity or dour negativity on our screens every morning and afternoon. I can never decide which one I want to watch. That's why I keep changing the channels. I guess it reflects real life in some way. Life is either rosy or it's downright shit. I've only ever been really high or really low in life. I'm not sure a happy medium exists. Same as TV – there's just nowhere else to turn to. I guess that's why I spend so much time on my laptop. And that's what has me depressed the most.

I have a routine for surfing the web that's rather sad. It even saddens me. As soon as I open the lid of my laptop I search for sports news. It's an old habit I can't kill off. Why would I? Just because I'm no longer in sports PR doesn't mean I can't be a fan. But searching news updates doesn't take that long and I inevitably end up using the Internet for the same reason most people do – porn. The amount of porn, and different types of porn, I see on the Internet continues to astound me. People really are into all kinds of sick shit. From dwarfs fisting each other's assholes, to men shitting in women's mouths, you really can search for anything you want, whenever you want. Imagine that. Somebody invented a window to the world where we could access any information and entertainment we could possibly ever think of. And what do we do? We watch porn more than anything. I'd only ever been interested in regular intercourse. I'd watch videos of handsome men fucking for hours until I felt the need to orgasm myself. Everyone has their own fantasies. I always loved rugged, handsome faces. That's all. If a porn video included a really good-looking guy, that would do for me. I like dark hair and cute faces. John Stamos would be my ideal man. Vincent thinks my celebrity crush is Piers Morgan. I've no idea where he got that from. I think I said Piers looked well once. Vincent took it as a compliment, because he thinks he looks like him. There is a resemblance. They're both blotchy and bloaty. Vincent has never really been my 'type' but I love him so much. I used to type 'Italian men' into the search menu on porn sites. That's just genuinely what I was into. But it's easy to get dragged into the murkier world of porn online. There are so many hidden links that drag you down trapdoors. I wonder what sort of sick shit this spotty prick is into.

He's sat still staring at the game. I can see him glance towards the coke every now and then. He's dying for another line. I don't blame him. I know how he feels. One line should always be enough but it never is. I'm glad I know this match goes into extra time because it's keeping his attention away from me. Getting my free hand across to my left leg is a bit more difficult, but I'm pretty certain I'm being discreet. The arm of the couch is blocking his view to me somewhat, so I continue to scratch away at the tape. I try to play out the eventual scenario in my head but it all depends on where his gun is placed once I peel myself free. It's currently back on the glass coffee table but it's been in and out of the waistband of his pants on quite a few occasions. I guess that's down to his anxiousness. If the gun is on the table when I'm free from the tape, I'll get to it first.

A plucking technique, rather than the scratching I was using earlier, seems to work better. Tiny fragments of the tape are peeling off into my fingernails. I look at the time again. 9:58. I give myself a time frame. I want to have this left ankle free by half ten before I begin to work on my left wrist. All going according to plan, I should be shoving the gun into that dumb ass's face before eleven.

09:55

Darragh

'Pogba miss another chance there, yeah?' I ask the fag after I hang up the phone.

He sniffs an answer – almost as if he's laughing at me. Little cunt! I thought we were getting on just fine, too. He seems to be getting a little too quiet for my liking. But he can't get up to anything. He's just sitting there helpless. A rush fills my mind as I take in the fact that Vincent now has two mill in the boot of his car. Half of that is mine. That's unreal. I never thought I'd have that much money in me life. I'm literally a millionaire right now. My money just happens to be sitting in the trunk of a chauffeur-driven car rather than sittin' in my own bank account. But it's all fuckin mine. I think of that brilliant scene in *Goodfellas* where Ray Liotta opens his wardrobe to a fuck-load of designer suits. I guess that's what a millionaire gangster's life looks like. I think I'll buy one of those huge wardrobes and fill it with suits meself. I don't wear suits, but that doesn't matter. Maybe I'll start wearing 'em. I'll be a multi-millionaire, after all. I'll have to wait a while though. JR has told me I shouldn't flash the cash so soon after getting' me hands on it. He said we should both wait it out for around six months before spending. He knows his stuff. He has figured out every tiny piece of this jigsaw. He has both the brains and the brawn to be a perfect mob boss. I wish I was more like him. I hope he continues to teach me. By the time I'm his age, I'll be a fuckin mastermind in the criminal underworld. I wonder how old JR actually is. It's hard to put a number on him.

The Guards released a photofit of what the newspapers labelled the 'One-Punch Killer'. It looked nothing like me. I'm not sure if witnesses sent cops in the wrong direction in fear of The Boss; but surely the girl who was at the scene of the crime must have had a say in the image the police were putting out there. Perhaps it was too dark for her to remember what I looked like. The man in the photofit had the same colour hair as me but that was about it. I was so fuckin relieved to find out the cops had nothing to go on in their investigation. The Boss told me they were chasing shadows. He had a few contacts on the inside. He wasn't happy with me at all though. He didn't mind that I'd broken me duck but he was disappointed in how I did it. He kept saying I was really immature. And that accusation annoys me. It would annoy anyone. I kept apologising to him, but I wasn't even sure he was ever listening to me. I think the adrenaline I drowned in after the murder flicked a switch in me. I began to envisage killings almost every day. As I watch people, I can imagine I'm battering them to death. Not everybody I see, just when the moment takes me. It's normally men I imagine killing. Mostly smug men. But I never planned another murder for real until I met JR. The Boss told me to stay out of trouble for a while, so I kept meself to meself for a bit. My fascination with Netflix helped. I watched all five seasons of *Breaking Bad* in less than a week. I think there's over sixty episodes in that show. It was fuckin deadly. Aaron Paul's character is the bomb. I've never tried meth. It was never offered to me. I guess I probably would have tried it if someone did have some. All the boys I was hanging around with drank beer and snorted coke. That's all I've been introduced to over the years. It's fine by me. I love coke.

I'd fuckin love another line of Ryan's shit right now. But there's no need for me to do any more. I've done enough. I'll celebrate later. Ryan probably thinks I haven't noticed, but I can see him looking over to the clock on the microwave every few minutes. I don't mind. It's probably making him panic even more. I envisage blowin' his brains out yet again. Even if I was to do it now and walk away, I'd be a million euros richer. But there's more of that to come. Besides, I have no intention of swerving off course from JR's plan. I wonder what he's up to now. He never really told me exactly where he'd be for each bank robbery. I wonder how close to Vincent he's actually getting. I'm sure he's all okay. He knows how to swerve all the CCTV cameras. He even has an alibi. He sorted one out for me too. It's brilliant. I've left me mobile phone in me bedsit and my laptop programmed to log in to certain websites at certain times of the morning. JR is some genius. If we are ever caught for this in any way, shape or form then I can easily show proof I was at home all morning. The alibis are just a backup to the backup of a backup. They won't be needed at all. JR and me have this totally under control.

I take a look at the microwave clock meself. 10:03. I need to get this straight in me head. Vincent has three hours to rob four banks, yet one hour has passed and only one bank has been hit. That doesn't sound right. I wonder why JR hasn't mentioned this yet or why he hasn't been getting on at me about it. Surely Vincent is getting close to Camden Street now. The next I'll hear from him will be when he exits there. He'd want to hurry the fuck up. Time is ticking. I turn my eyes to look at Ryan sittin' in his chair like a pussy. Bang! I imagine his brains splat all over the window behind him again. This is really gonna happen. I can feel it. It'll be my third murder. I guess that'll make me a serial killer.

10:05

Vincent

I TURN THE AIR CONDITIONING BACK UP TO FULL AGAIN JUST AS JOHN TURNS into Camden Street. I don't fell as panicky anymore, but I just fancy one last blast of cold air before meeting Jonathan. I look calm in the reflection of the car window. I can see the ugliness of Camden Street behind my reflection. Camden Street is a typical example of tradition meeting contemporary to create ugliness. That mess of architecture is ripe around Dublin city. Some people love it. I don't. I love old-school Dublin. The city used to be full of character, but these modern buildings take some of that character away. I mean, it's fine around Sir John Rogerson's Quay where I live because it's full of modern buildings, but here, on Camden Street, they look out of place. The ACB branch on Lower Camden Street is almost directly across from Cassidy's pub, right next to Concern Charity's headquarters. The board of directors for some reason leased half of that new building and then replaced the clear windows with blacked-out glass. Their reasoning behind it was so people couldn't see inside from the outside. But you also can't see the outside from the inside because the windows they ordered were too dark. Fuckin' idiots! That was the decision of these young board members who earn a combined annual salary of almost a billion dollars. I genuinely think most of the multi-millionaires I've met through my life, and there's been a few, have all been a bit thick. Maybe they're good at playing thick and that's why they're so successful or maybe, as I suspect, they've just been fuckin' lucky.

The board of directors used to be perfect at ACB. They ran all the banks like clockwork and they had a real eagerness to agree on decisions. That was their best asset. But the current board take an age to make any decision at all. And they keep me at a huge distance. I used to be more involved with the important decisions made over in the States, but not anymore. There's one little spoilt prick on the board, Clyde Sneyd, who is only twenty-eight years old. I used to be close with his old man, Bernard. But Bernard's offspring has no respect for me whatsoever; I'm not sure he even has respect for himself. It seems he lives a very eccentric life in New York that I'm not sure even he's happy with. He brings that depressive attitude to his work. Sometimes it has taken the board over a week to even get him by phone. It's not just him, though. None of 'em seem to give a flying fuck. They think they're all heroes for taking the bank through the economic crash. It's a bit sad, really. Everyone else knows I'm the reason ACB pulled through in Ireland. They're a mismatch of spoilt personalities. It's such a shame. I genuinely couldn't give a shit anymore.

John doesn't always get a parking spot right outside the Camden Street branch but there's one available today. It allows me to take in the sorry building as we come to a stop. I often chuckle to myself looking at the blacked-out glass with the ACB logo flying proud above it. How the fuck can they be proud of this shit hole? Jonathan won't have known I've pulled up. He can't see out of the building! I need to head in as quickly as I can. My palms aren't even sweaty about this one. Tchaikovsky's been a big help. I've barely thought about reality on the way over here.

Ryan said he fell in love with me when I sorted out his career path, but I'm pretty sure the fact that I moved him into my brand-new penthouse helped too. We were both high on love and cocaine for the first two years we were together. I bought the penthouse from the building plans but not on a whim. I've never regretted it. ACB's mortgage expert, Dave Cauley, put me on to it. He said the area it was being built in was an up-and-coming trendy neighbourhood. His estimation then was that the penthouse would be worth almost two million in ten years' time. That was a bit inaccurate. The value of the penthouse was €1,100,000 a decade on. It's worth €1,200,000 now. It's still a great investment. I bought it for €650,000 and now only owe the bank a little over two hundred thousand. Nice. I guess that makes me a millionaire, in bricks and mortar at least. But nobody's told my bank account. I earn a quarter of a million a year, but you wouldn't think it because my money somehow seems to drift in and then quickly out of my bank account every month. All I've really got from all my years of hard work is the penthouse. I allowed Ryan to have a tiny bit of input into the finishing touches, but it is, and always has been, my design. I've got better taste than Ryan. He's not really into that sort of thing anyway. As long as he has a large TV screen, he's happy. I don't know why he insisted on a massive TV, though. He spends most of his time looking into his twenty-one-inch laptop screen. We used to host mammoth parties when we first moved in. I probably got carried away with the socialising aspect of life back then. Maybe I was a bit too old for it. But I wouldn't swap those days for anything. I'm sure there were lots of people who turned up for sessions at our place that neither I nor Ryan knew. The penthouse would be crammed some Saturday nights. Ryan often rounded up dozens of students from DCU and I'd invite some of the bank staff over on the odd occasion. The students used to bring the greatest cocaine anybody could ever have snorted. Not even Colombia could manufacture a purer dose. Three of them had set up a lab in their cheap student accommodation and were cashing in big time. They had their student loans paid for within two months of creating and selling their own coke. It was great while it lasted. But after a couple of years I started to feel a little down. It wasn't depression or anything but I knew I had to give up the partying lifestyle. I'm proud that I made a quick decision to cut down on the drugs and alcohol cold turkey. Ryan didn't seem to mind too much either. I think it was getting on top of us both. He had just got a job at Wow PR and wanted to take his career seriously. I was very proud of him, if a little fearful. We were finally two grown-ups in a serious relationship. Our lives became less fun, but boring can be rewarding in its own way.

I can see my own reflection in the bank's dark windows as soon as John lets me out of the car. I stare at myself walking towards the entrance, the two briefcases hanging from my arms. Somebody's just cut the grass on the small lawn in front of the building. That smell's eternal. The scent of freshly cut grass takes everybody back to their childhood. I let out a small sigh of warm air as I wait to be buzzed through the first door. The glass in the small entryway is clear, so I can finally see the staff at work. They're certainly not hard at it though because there are currently six members of staff and only two customers inside. I stare down towards the back offices to see if I can spot the seventh member of this team. Somebody must have told him I'm coming through the second door because Jonathan wheels out of his office on his chair to offer me a big smile.

'Hi, Mr Butler,' calls out one of the junior members of staff as I enter. I can't think of her name, despite sanctioning her employment about a month ago. I offer her a nod in return.

'Vincent!' Jonathan calls out a little bit louder than normal.

'Hey, Jonathan,' I say offering him my handcuffed hand as we make our way towards each other.

'Everything in order?' I ask before the small talk can begin.

'Yeah, yeah. You mean for the collection?'

'Of course I mean for the collection, Jonathan. I told you I needed it all as soon as poss—'

'Yeah, yeah,' he interrupts me. 'I have all the paperwork ready.'

He wraps one of his palms over the top of my left shoulder and practically escorts me into his office.

'Everythin' alrigh'?' he whispers to my annoyance.

I don't show that in my answer though. But I am pissed off that he's asking questions. This was supposed to be an easy branch.

'Of course, I'm just in a hurry. I can't believe Michelle's got so low. I could do without this today, to be honest,' I say, justifying why I'm coming across agitated.

'Ah … it happens,' he says. 'Not to the tune of two mill often. But it happens.'

'You've got a tan,' I say, changing the subject. It wasn't exactly seamless.

'Ah, the golf course does wonders for a tan,' he replies.

I didn't say out loud what I was thinking, but I would love to see Jonathan's reaction if he knew I was aware he uses sunbeds. Belinda told me. Jonathan is a nice guy, but he is definitely the sort that thinks he's a little more successful than he really is. There's plenty of these guys around Dublin. They're harmless. He likes to talk the talk. I don't really mind that to be honest. I think he's good at what he does. Just not as good as he thinks he is.

'Here ya go,' he says, handing me a pen. The paperwork is all ready on his desk. Perfect!

'Thanks, Jonathan,' I reply, offering him a wink. I could be out of here in the next twenty minutes.

10:15

Jack

I'M ABSOLUTELY SWEATIN'. I'VE PACED HERE WAY TOO BRISKLY FOR THIS kinda heat. I hope my walk didn't look suspicious. If anything, it looked nothing like my normal walk, so that's good, I suppose. Nobody would have been able to recognise me. I keep thinking people are suspicious, but it's just a pinch of paranoia. It's understandable I'd be slightly paranoid this morning, even though I'm one hundred per cent confident my plan will go perfectly. No one has any damn clue that this robbery is taking place. Two million is already gone and not one person in this city is any the wiser. My heart rate slows the more I think about how soundproof the whole plan is. I don't walk directly onto Camden Street. I walk up Harcourt Street and turn at the corner of the Bleeding Horse pub so I can stare down at the ACB branch. It's an odd-looking building. The first two floors are surrounded with black glass while the top floor has clear windows. It looks like a stubby pint of Guinness. I place myself at the entrance of a large apartment building with the phone to my ear. I don't look suspicious here at all. It's a massive apartment complex built over four buildings. There are so many people living in this place that nobody knows who their neighbours are. I could easily be one of them. I'm out of sight of the CCTV and I'm blending in with the passers-by. I planned this position months ago. I can see Vincent's car parked outside. I wonder what time he arrived at. It couldn't have been much before ten o'clock.

'Hey,' calls out a woman from inside the apartment building.

'Hi,' I reply, turning around. Holy shit! It's Antoinette. I'm staring at Karyn's cousin as she struggles to open her mailbox in the hallway.

'All good with you?' she asks. She can't possibly know it's me. Can she?

Harry and Yvonne cut their visits down to roughly one a month. The intimidation Harry used to invoke in me receded dramatically after Karyn's passing. He never mentioned business to me, but would often ask how I was getting on at the factory. If I hadn't flat-out refused more money from him years ago, he'd still be offering it to me now, I'm sure. I think Harry's a bit embarrassed to offer me money now. He totally understood that I wanted to fend for Frank on my own terms. Myself, Harry and Yvonne would sit and talk about golf for hours while Frank played around our feet. Yvonne's a bigger golfer than Harry, and probably me if I'm being honest. She'd be able to call Rory McIlroy's swing changes before I could. She had a real eye for the strategy of the sport and would often amaze me with her insights. Yvonne was a very interesting woman. She loved being a gangster's moll. She thrived on it. But I'd mostly describe her as having a decent heart. She loved Frank as if he were her own grandchild. She either really liked me or felt sorry for me. I could never quite figure out which it was. I think we got on well. Yvonne's only eight years older than I am. Harry has a good sixteen years on her. I'm pretty sure Yvonne's Dublin accent grew stronger the more she spent time with Harry. It was like she grew into her role as a gangster's wife. It was the only irritating thing about her, but Karyn and I used to laugh about it. A lot of men would probably find Yvonne attractive. I never did. She's not natural looking at all. But she's Harry's type and that's all that matters. Their marriage is still going strong after all these years and that doesn't surprise me one bit. I was impressed that Harry didn't mind Margarite being around Frank so much. He did ask me if we were an item at one stage, suggesting it in a jokey manner, but I answered him honestly. I also re-emphasised the point to Yvonne the next time they called over just so they knew for sure that I hadn't replaced Karyn. I used to get odd pangs of paranoia about Harry, but on many occasions, he let it be known that he appreciated what I was doing with my life. He said being in his line of business wasn't obligatory. When I asked one day if it would be obligatory for his grandson, he looked disappointed in me.

'He's your son,' he said. 'You raise him how you want. He's my grandson and I will love him whatever he does with his life.'

I felt instant relief when he said that to me. It was all I'd ever worried about. But days later the words 'whatever he does' started to reignite my paranoia. Did he mean Frank would be offered a choice?

I grunt a reply at Antoinette which was meant to sound like a polite way of saying 'I'm not interested in talking'. But she is still behind me going through her mail. She's changed somewhat. You would know she's middle-aged but she's still pretty. She has deep lines either side of her eyes but the eyes themselves haven't lost their sparkle. They're not unlike Karyn's. I had no idea she lived here. My heart is now racing quicker than at any moment it had done this morning. I keep playing what she said to me over and over in my head. *Hey.* And *All good with you?* Does she know it's me? She can't. Can she? My whole face is covered. And she barely even saw my face. She greeted me from behind. Shit! Perhaps that's where I'm recognisable. From behind. I didn't do anything to disguise myself from the back. Is my back even recognisable? Maybe I'm going mad. What if she does know it's me? The whole plan is fucked. Too many questions are spinning around my head. I feel like I need to talk to her, to find out for sure she doesn't know who I am. I check my watch. 10:21. I doubt Vincent's exit is imminent. Surely he'll be another ten minutes at least. I think I'll have to talk to Antoinette. I can't let her go not knowing for sure whether she recognised me or not. I take a bite of my bottom lip. I have seconds to make up my mind, then I find myself spinning towards her.

'Is your name Lisa?' I say, changing the pitch in my voice. Antoinette stares back at me.

'Sorry?' she asks. Shit! I've to repeat that.

'Is your name Lisa?' I reply. I think the pitch sounded the same.

'Oh.' She giggles. 'Sorry, I didn't hear you the first time. No, my name's not Lisa. Are you looking for somebody in particular?'

I feel relieved. She has no idea she's talking to me.

'Oh no. My neighbour upstairs is called Lisa and I have yet to meet her. I thought you were her. Sorry.' Brilliant. I have nothing to worry about. And I nailed the pitch in my voice again.

I hope she doesn't want to keep talking. I stare out of the apartment archway looking down the street as if I'm waiting on somebody to come and pick me up. Antoinette hasn't said anything in reply. She just offered a smile before turning her attention back to the envelopes in her hands. I can still hear her ruffling paperwork in the background. She must get a huge amount of mail. Or maybe she's just back from holidays and is getting her mail for the first time in a week or two. She looks glowing, she might have been away in the sun. To relieve myself of the discomfort, I pretend to make a call, surprising myself with my improvisational skills.

'Hey, sweetheart,' I say. Pause. 'Can't wait to see you.' Pause. 'I know it is going to be a long time. But just think how much it's going to be worth it.' I pause for ages this time, taking a glance to see if Antoinette has left the building. Shit. Maybe I'm pausing way too long now. But who am I pausing for? I look around and see nobody in earshot. It doesn't stop me from finishing my charade. 'Okay, I love you. Ciao.' I even pretend to hang up with a fake press of a button. My finger misses the phone by about two whole inches. It's unusual I make myself laugh. But I did this time. I'm still smiling when I finally look back at the apartment entrance and see Antoinette heading straight towards me with a smile of her own. Bollocks!

10:15

Vincent

JONATHAN SEEMS AS EAGER AS I AM TO READ THROUGH THE PAPERWORK. I'M supposed to be following along as he mumbles the jargon, but I can't help but look around his office. He thinks highly of himself. But it doesn't show on the walls of his workplace. It's a very muted office, painted what I could only call magnolia. It's probably some other bland shade of cream with a fancy name like pertwee off white or something or other. But I know it as magnolia. The only piece of artwork hanging on his wall is in contrast to the wall itself. He told me before who painted it, but I can't recall the name. I like the painting. It's like a 3D mix-match of colours that seems to form an eyeball, I think. I like how the blue evolves into purple down the bottom before it meets with red. But that's about as far as my art knowledge goes. I like colours, that's about it. The only photograph in the room sits on his desk. I can only see the back of the frame from here, but I know the photo. I've seen it before. It's a family portrait of Jonathan and his wife Sabrina with their two sons.

'Two million is a huge amount, Vincent,' he inevitably says to me as he gets down to the finer details of the paperwork.

'You're telling me?' I reply, rolling my eyes before taking a look at my watch. He knows too well that I just want to get a move on. We've both signed two pages so far.

'Don't worry,' he gurns. 'I'll get you into the vault soon.'

I like Jonathan. He doesn't run his branch as effectively as Chelle because he's too concerned with being liked rather than being successful.

But he still runs a steady ship here at Camden Street. The only thing that's ever really pissed me off about him is his fascination with Belinda. I wonder what she's up to now as I take a genuine glance at my watch. This time I actually want to know what it reads. 10:17. I wonder if Belinda's finished sorting my paperwork into alphabetical order. Perhaps she hasn't even started. Even if Jonathan gets me in and out of his vault in the next twenty minutes, I'd still be behind time. But I'm catching up. As Jonathan continues to murmur through the paperwork, I reach for the frame on his desk and turn it my way. I don't ask him how Sabrina, Kai and Taylor are, I just assume they're okay. I've often wondered if Sabrina really is okay. I think she's besotted with her two sons, but I wonder if she knows her husband isn't totally devoted to her. Jonathan and Sabrina have been together since they were both twenty-one. They met in their final year at UCD. I think couples tend to stay in the same mentality they are in when they first meet. Jonathan is a mature, professional man and Sabrina is very bright and articulate. But they seem to rub each other up the wrong way like twenty-one-year-olds do when they're together. They're still petty to each other. I've often heard Jonathan being short with Sabrina on the phone and have observed them at office get-togethers in a huff with each other. I'm sure Jonathan was very much in love with Sabrina once upon a time. Maybe he still is, but he doesn't show it – not to her. I'm not sure how she feels. I know Jonathan has cheated on her in the past. I watched him leave clubs with strange girls many years ago and he once hooked up with Ryan's cousin at one of the parties at our penthouse. Given a chance, I'm sure he'd fuck Belinda without a second's thought. But I do wonder if he'd ever leave his wife and kids for her. That's played on my mind often.

'They're keeping well,' he says to me.

'I didn't ask,' I joke back. 'You nearly done?'

'Jeez, you really are in a hurry. You okay?'

'I'll be happy when this morning's over with.'

'Ah, one of those days, huh?' Jonathan replies. 'You, eh … you just want me to sign this?'

'Jonathan,' I say really slowly, allowing myself time to think. 'Read through the bloody paperwork for me, let's sign all the pages and then get me out of here. Please.'

I'd love to skip all the obligatory reading and for us to get into the vault, but I have to toe the professional line. He knows I'm a little more tense than usual and I've let him know I'm in a hurry. I can't risk evoking any further suspicion in him.

'I'll be five more minutes,' he says, flicking through the rest of the papers. As I stand up to impatiently pace around Jonathan's office, I feel the cheap mobile phone buzz in my pocket. I immediately dismiss any notion of answering it, and then decide I can't take any more of Jonathan's murmurings.

'Sorry, Jon,' I say. 'Need to take this. Keep on reading. Finish it off.'

I walk outside his office and hit the green button on the phone.

'Gimme one second,' I say before palming the phone and pacing through the bank floor towards the exit. I don't want anyone to see this old thing. I wait until I'm buzzed through the first door before putting it back to my ear.

'I'm just in the Camden Street branch, what's up?'

'Don't "what's up" me, fag,' says Ryan's captor. 'What the fuck's going on? It's coming towards half past ten – you've gone beyond time.'

A rage fills up inside me.

'What the fu ...' I say, and stop myself. 'Listen ... I can't do anything more than I am. I can't make this process quicker. This is just how—'

'They're your fuckin' banks. Get the eight mill back here by midday or I'll splatter Ryan's brains all over this place.'

'I'll get back with the eight mill,' I reply, trying to catch my breath as I'm finally buzzed out of the second door. 'Forget about the time. I'll get it back once the whole process is done. Let me—'

'Midday,' he snaps down the phone at me. 'Get it back by midday or that's fucking it, boy.'

'I'm doing the best I can. Just ... just ... please, extend the time by another half an hour and I'll definitely be back,' I plead.

'Mid-fuckin'-day!'

I stare at the phone after he's hung up. This guy sounds like a lunatic. Fear engulfs me for the first time since I left Chelle. I'm not sure why I've been so relaxed over the last half an hour. I pace slowly back to the bank's entrance taking in my reflection once again. The reality of the whole situation flows through my mind as I stare into my own eyes for what seems like an age, until the mobile phone buzzing in my hand snaps me out of it.

'I'll ring you back in two minutes with an answer to your request,' he raps in his mongrel accent. Then he hangs up again.

I've no idea what to do. Do I go back inside to Jonathan or do I wait out here? I take a look towards my car but John isn't paying any attention to me. All I can do is stare past my reflection into this horrible black glass. If anyone could see out, they'd see a confused man. I remove my glasses and wipe my face to try to defuse my current state of mind. I wish I was throwing handfuls of cold water on my face. I need to chill out. I breathe slowly to stave off any signs of panic.

Think, Vincent, think.

I try to focus on the positive, but my stomach is starting to turn. So much for this being the easy branch to take money from. Jonathan was eager to get me in and out as quickly as possible and everything was going smoothly. Now I must look a little panicked and out of sorts. Jonathan will be wondering why I left at the tail end of a contract read-through. Especially after I'd just insisted we must follow protocol. I'm wondering why I left too. I wonder if he's finished reading through the paperwork. My phone doesn't seem to be ringing back. I'm not sure staring at it will help. The longer I stay out here, the more suspicious I look. Rather than think it, I say it to my reflection: 'What the fuck am I doing?' I can't stay out here much longer. I decide to stroll back into the bank, get the money out of the vault and then deal with any deadline discussions when I finally exit. I refocus my stare to look at myself one final time before heading for the door. I can see Jonathan eyeballing me after I get through the first entrance. He must have been on his way out to me. As I stand trapped inside the two doorways I don't know where to look.

What must Jonathan be thinking right now?

I would never leave a withdrawal read-through before it's finished. I can't bring myself to look at him. Then I hear the second door buzz me through.

'Let's go, boss,' he says, winking at me. 'Paperwork's done. Let's get you that money.'

10:25

Darragh

NEITHER OF US SEEMS TO BE TALKIN'. THAT'S FINE BY ME. I'M HAPPY TO JUST watch the match as my high wears off. It's looking like it will go into extra time. Both legs have finished one all. I only learned what 'legs' meant in football a half an hour ago. It's when a knockout is played over two different games, one in each team's home ground. Still don't get why they call it 'legs', like. But that's all the chatter me and Ryan have had over the past while. Small talk about football. I think the sport is winning me over again. I'm willing United to score. As the referee blows for another foul, I take the mobile phone from the table to make sure it hasn't been ringing while I was transfixed on the game. I would have heard it surely, but I am high, I guess. I don't want to miss another JR call. He'd go fuckin nuts. There's been no activity on the phone. I decide to palm it rather than place it back on the glass table just in case there is a call. I'll be able to feel it vibrate. I look at the clock on the microwave again. 10:26. I expect Vincent will be another fifteen minutes at least in the Camden Street branch. A distant ringtone makes me raise my eyebrow. I look to Ryan to see if he heard anything. Then at the TV. Maybe it was a noise from the football supporters? Then I realise the phone in my hand is dialling out. Shit! I lift it up to see that I am dialling two. That's a relief. I'm ringing Vincent, not JR. I don't want JR to think I'm losing it. I've no idea what I am going to say. Hanging up crosses me mind but that would look suspicious. He probably won't answer anyway.

'Gimme one second,' says Vincent abruptly down the line as I hear him walking.

What's going on?

'I'm just in the Camden Street branch, what's up?' he finally says.

'Don't "what's up" me, fag,' I bark back at him. Cheeky cunt. 'What the fuck's going on? It's coming towards half past ten – you've gone beyond time.'

He almost swears at me. He must be stressin' out big time.

'Listen … I can't do anything more than I am. I can't make this process quicker. This is just how … how—' he says, stuttering.

'They're your fuckin banks. Get the eight mill back here by midday or else I'll splatter Ryan's brains all over this place,' I reply cool as ice. I really am cut out for this kinda shit. I'm a natural gangster.

'I'll get back with the eight mill,' Vincent whines. 'Forget about the time. I'll get it back once the whole process is done. Let me—'

'Midday,' I snap. 'Get it back by midday or that's fuckin it.'

He stutters some other whiney bollocks before I repeat meself with a firmer tone.

'Mid-fuckin-day!' Then I hang up.

It might have sounded cool. Or maybe it was a little too dramatic. I'm not sure. I take notice of Ryan out of the corner of me eye, but he's not showing any reaction to the call at all. I swing my head at the microwave again. 10:29. There's no way Vincent can get in and out of all three remaining banks in the next hour and a half. I call him back immediately.

'I'll ring ya in two minutes with an answer to your request,' I say much more coolly before hanging up again.

Then I let out a sigh. JR will probably want to kill me if I bother him with requests from Vincent. But I think this is somethin' we need to talk about. If we want all eight million, we may have to give Vincent an extra half an hour. JR doesn't take long answering. Like me, he must have his phone in his hand waiting for it to ring.

'He's not out already, right?' he asks.

I decide to put my case forward straight away. 'No. Listen. Take your time to think about this. He's doing a good job but he needs more time.'

JR tries to stop my flow but I'm determined to make sure we give ourselves the best shot at getting all the money. Nobody knows more than I do just how much JR will want to stick to his plan.

'Think about it, JR. He's only in bank number two and it's almost ten-thirty. We can get all eight mill if we just give him a bit more time.'

'I'll think about it,' he says.

Great! JR has listened to me. He hangs up, leaving me grinning and almost skipping around the kitchen table thingy. We're a proper partnership, JR and me. He kinda needs to hurry up thinkin' 'bout it though. Vincent is waiting on me to call back.

I'd exhausted all the decent Netflix shows within a couple of months. It got boring. I wasn't sure how long The Boss wanted me to chill out but I was certain the cops were nowhere near finding the One-Punch Killer. All this lay-low bullshit was beginning to bug me. I'd call Smack every day pleading with him to speak to The Boss on my behalf, to tell him I was bored and eager to get back to work. But I'd rarely hear anythin' back. And after a while Smack's phone had a habit of dialling all the way through to his voicemail. I was starting to lose the will to live. I knew The Boss wouldn't be happy if I turned up at his club unannounced. I'd been told to stay away until he contacted me, but I couldn't sit around doing nothin' for the rest of me life. As soon as I walked into his club, though, I knew I was doing the wrong thing. I knew exactly where he'd be sitting, up in the back booth where he always is. I could feel, not see, the faces in the club staring at me. Before I got to his table, Smack raced towards me.

'What the fuck you doin' here?' he asked.

'I need to see him, Smack. I haven't heard a thing back from you and—'

'He'll fuckin kill you, Darragh. He told you to stay away. Trust me, for your own good, turn around and walk back out that door.'

I should've listened to him. I knew he was right but for some reason I tried to plead with Smack to let me talk to The Boss. But just as I was being pushed towards the exit, The Boss noticed me. He called on Smack to bring me towards him. Within a split second of me getting to the booth, I was thrown sideways by The Boss and pinned to the red leather couch. He had both his hands wrapped firmly around my neck.

'I told you never to come here, didn't I?'

I couldn't answer.

'You little fuck. Don't bring your shit near me. You hear?'

I felt like cryin'. This was heartbreak for me. A break-up. A break-up of the only relationship I ever wanted to have. I think The Boss could see my sadness. After releasing his grip on me, he clipped my face with the palm of his hand.

'Follow me, kid,' he said. I walked slowly behind him until we reached the back porch of the club. With one flick of his head The Boss cleared the porch of the two security men who were guarding the back entrance.

He sighed heavily before speaking. I took it as a sign his heart was a little broken too.

'We can't have you involved, Darragh. There was heat on us over that killing. I had to stave it off and in doing so I agreed to distance myself from you. You know you can't bring any heat near me and your fuckin freelance killing, nothing to do with my business, can't come near me. If I order a fuckin hit it's because I know everything is good to go. You can't go around killing people, Darragh. You fucked up.'

I hung my head in shame. He was right. I knew I fucked up.

'Stay here,' I was told. I didn't lift my chin from my chest in all the time I was alone in that porch. I was too saddened to even think about what might happen next. When The Boss burst back through the front door, he headed straight towards me.

'Twenty thousand,' he said shoving a wad of notes into my hands. 'Best of luck, Darragh. I enjoyed working with you.'

'I … I …' I stuttered.

'I enjoyed working with you,' he repeated, before going back inside.

I must have looked like a lost puppy. When I was outside the club moments later in the pouring rain, I thought about throwing the wad of notes back into the porch in anger. I'd never felt such a depression.

I can't pace around this kitchen table thingy any longer. I stare at the phone in my hand again. I need to know if the time is going to be extended. Vincent is waiting to hear back from me.

Ring me, JR, for fuck's sake.

10:30

Jack

'I THINK LISA'S THE WOMAN WITH THE RED HAIR,' SAYS ANTOINETTE, PACING towards me. I can't believe I'm looking into this face again. It's been years. She has no idea this is me. 'Are you on floor four?' she asks, not going away.

Now I have to remember the pitch in my fake voice again.

'No,' I say, missing the pitch by some distance. I hold six fingers up into her face. It's terribly rude. I feel really bad. Nobody should be rude to Antoinette. She's too lovely. But I can't bring myself to talk again.

'Oh, six,' she says offering another smile. This is so awkward. A huge silence fills the two yards between us. 'Okay, have a good day, sir,' she says, trying to defuse the awkwardness before walking off.

I cringe, but I let out a sigh of relief as she paces away. I know from her face that she didn't recognise me at all. I never should have engaged in conversation with her in the first place. But I had to know for sure she wasn't aware of who I was. I watch her walk in the opposite direction down Charlotte Way and stretch my bottom jaw in some sorrow. That's the last time I'll ever see her. I look at the buildings across the street and realise it will be the last time I'll ever see them too. I'll miss Dublin when I'm gone. I've equally loved and hated Dublin for as far back as I can remember. I'll miss the city centre more than anything but I've become a bit bored with it. Dublin used to be the prettiest little town, but it seems to have been swamped with homeless people and meth users over the past six or seven years. I don't know what happened, but overnight the druggies seemed to appear in the streets again. It seemed to coincide with the economic crash. The streets of Dublin are ugly now. I get a little embarrassed thinking of all the tourists from all over the world coming to Dublin only to be approached by a few skangers off their heads, asking their usual question: 'Any change, bud?' I won't miss that. I will miss the new modern architecture in Dublin, even though some of the buildings lack real character. I'll miss the thick Dublin accent. I love it. I'll miss spring here. Dublin's at its prettiest between April and June. I'll miss Pat Murray. He's the only employee from the factory that I've stayed in touch with after I left a few years ago. I'll miss his wise words. But I'm eager to take my life in a totally different direction. The excitement I've been feeling about this move is huge. But today, I'm anxious. My whole life – our whole lives – hang on what happens over the next ninety minutes. I'm still reminiscing about this old city when my phone rings. It's Darragh.

'He's not out already, is he?' I ask, staring back at the bank entrance.

'No. Listen. Take your time to think about this. He is doin' a good job but he needs more time.' Darragh's never spoken to me like this. I'm taken aback.

'Darragh…' I interject. But the kid is determined to keep talking.

I already know I'm not giving Vincent more time. But as Darragh continues to plead with me, I decide to play along, to keep him sweet. I don't want him feeling dejected. He needs to feel like he has some sort of control over this heist too.

'I'll think about it,' I say. Now Darragh sounds like he's the one taken aback. But it's a good tactic from me. It keeps his boredom at bay.

I can't believe I'm going to be a multi-millionaire in the next couple of hours. I don't necessarily want to be super rich. Wearing a Rolex watch or driving a Ferrari doesn't interest me one bit. I just want to see out the rest of my days in the most comfortable manner possible. We're going to have so much fun.

I remember the first time I went to Italy. I pleaded with the factory to allow me to take three weeks off work one summer when Frank just turned thirteen. I figured a trip around Europe would help broaden his mind. My boss at the factory was always good to me. I concocted an itinerary that would see us take in London, Rome and then Paris. We cut our Paris trip short by a few days because we loved Rome so much. It's steeped in history and really helps put life into perspective. Frank wasn't as amazed as I was, but I was very conscious of this precious time in our lives. This was our summer – the boys on tour. I set initial plans in motion for us both to move to Rome on a permanent basis but it just didn't make any sense. Neither of us could speak Italian, and Frank was still years from completing school. We'd have to wait. I don't need to wait much longer. In a couple months' time I'll be sipping expensive wine on a rooftop bar overlooking the ancient city.

Vincent shouldn't be much longer in this branch. John is waiting patiently for him outside. I take a look at the screen on the old phone. 10:36. I should ring Darragh back and give him the bad news, but I'll word it so that he feels as if I've taken his concerns on board and that I view him as a genuine partner in crime.

'Hey, JR,' he says, answering the phone rather quickly.

'Listen, Darragh. I've had a long think about this. I understand where you're coming from and I think you did the right thing talking to me about it. But you and I have planned this for so long and I think the only proper thing to do is to abide by the plans we drew up early on. We cannot go beyond the deadline. Not just today, but in any robbery we make from here on. We need to be strict.'

'I understand,' he replies.

I thought he'd be disappointed, but he's not. He's probably buzzing because I mentioned future robberies. He's often talked to me about the future, about being included over the long term. I think being a gangster is all he's ever wanted to be. He used to be involved with Alan Keating's gang a few years ago, until they let him down. He needs an excuse to be relevant. I'm his excuse right now.

'So, if it comes to midday and I order you to kill Ryan, what are you gonna do?' I ask in a tone similar to how a teacher speaks to a student in secondary school.

'Kill Ryan,' he says.

Correct answer.

'Exactly. Me and you, buddy, we're gonna be the most feared gangsters in the whole of Ireland. But we must stick to our plan, okay?'

'You got it, JR. You got it.'

10:35

Vincent

'YEP, TWO MILL AGAIN,' I SAY, HAVING COUNTED THE BUNDLES OF NOTES FOR the second time.

'Okay, one more time each,' Jonathan replies with a sigh.

He's going through this as quickly as he can. I really need to get a move on. I haven't checked the time in a while but it must be gone half ten by now. I swipe all two hundred bundles of notes towards his side of the counter and let out a sigh of my own.

'One, two, three, four,' he tries to whisper.

'Do it quietly, Jon, will you? My head's a little sensitive today.'

'Sorry, Vincent.'

It's very warm in this vault. It's a larger vault than the one on Nassau Street but this one is cooped up in a basement, and the air conditioning is as useful as a fart. The contrast in my anxiety is confusing me. It's up and down. When I arrived at Nassau Street I was really nervous and then I settled somewhat when I got to the vault. This time around it's been the complete opposite. I was relaxed coming into this branch but now my head is starting to feel faint again. It could be the heat but I've been feeling weak since I was outside fifteen minutes ago. The little fuck hasn't rung me back to extend the deadline. I'll probably be another five minutes in here, at least. It's going to be close to eleven when I reach Church Street. I really am cutting it close.

'Yeah, two hundred there,' Jon says, scooping as many bundles of notes as he can in one go towards me. Time for me to count to two hundred … again. Then we're done.

Our 'grown-up relationship' lasted several years. We were both happy with our lives, even if everything was vastly different to what we got up to when we started dating. Ryan was living the high of being involved in sports media. He'd get to hang out with big-name stars on odd occasions. I'd join him now and then. I'm kinda fascinated with celebrities. Even celebrities I didn't know existed. I'd often stand at the back of the room during press conferences tiddling the Press badge Ryan had signed over to me. The buzz from that lasted a couple of months. It had already dissipated in Ryan. He said he only enjoyed working in media when he was working as a junior account manager. As soon as he started working with the professionals, he realised how pointless his career actually was.

'It doesn't matter one fuckin' jot,' he'd say to me after another boring day at the agency. 'Football. Rugby. Who gives a shit?'

'You do,' I'd respond, trying to cheer him up.

I knew how he was feeling. I was starting to hate my own job but I didn't confide in Ryan. I knew he got bored any time I mentioned work. All the great men I admired at ACB started to resign in the wake of the global recession. I couldn't blame them. They'd had enough. I miss those men so much. They were real men. Not like their offspring. It was a huge compliment to be told I would be kept on and even promoted during the cuts. But I found it difficult to be excited about it. My lack of excitement didn't affect my work ethic though. Motivated to make the most of the four remaining Irish branches, I managed to get my way with all four assistant manager appointments, initially – making sure I was working with people I wanted to work with. There's nothing worse than working with people you detest. That's why Noah Voss's appointment – over my head last year – really pissed me off. I don't want to be working with fuckin' Christians. I was starting to feel content with my life again when the branches began to pull out of trouble. Inch by inch, we helped all four of them improve. But just as I was starting to feel good about myself again, Ryan's depression started to spiral out of control. I knew it was work related and insisted he hand his notice in at Wow, but he wasn't having any of it. Months later, I added two and two together. The little fucker was having an affair on me. I wasn't sure who was banging him, but it certainly wasn't me! Our sex life was dead – or perhaps barely breathing was the more appropriate way to phrase it back then. I'd give Ryan a good blowjob for his birthday. That was practically our sex life. I knew what was going on, but I decided to turn a blind eye. If he left me, he'd lose everything. On his shitty little PR wage, he wouldn't be able to afford an apartment one-eighth the size of ours. I wasn't actually in denial about his affair – I knew he was just having a small fling and it would end with him crying back into my arms. I was right. Of course I was right. I usually am. He told me, with tears rolling down his face one morning, that he couldn't face going into work.

'Fuck it!' I said to him. 'Fuck that place. You're better than that. Hand your notice in. I'm going to buy you a new laptop and you can work from home. All those book ideas you have … let's get one of them written, okay? You are now an author, you hear me?' I said, wiping a tear from his eye.

He smiled and nodded a reply. I knew I'd got my Ryan back there and then. We could return to being the popular couple everybody envied again. I'd got my way once more. I knew I could keep an eye on Ryan if he was at home all the time. What trouble could he get up to cooped up in our penthouse on his own all day?

'Yep, two hundred,' I say, winking at Jonathan. We pack a briefcase each with one hundred bundles before I wrap my arms around his shoulders.

'Thanks, Jonathan,' I say, surprising him.

'Gee, you alright?' he asks me. I'd never hugged him before in my life.

'Long morning,' I reply. 'Long morning.'

What the fuck was I thinking?

I must be emotional. I handcuff the two cases to my wrists and bid Jonathan farewell. The phone begins to buzz in my pocket just as I'm exiting the vault. I decide I'll ring the fucker back when I'm outside.

'I'll give you a shout this afternoon,' I holler back at Jonathan. 'I'll let you know when I can get this money back to you. Won't be long.'

'No rush,' he shouts after me as I pace across the bank floor. I just about hear him.

A rush hit me when I left Nassau Street with the first two million but I'm not sure how I feel right now. Ringing the kid back is my main priority. I wonder if he's going to extend the deadline.

10:35

Ryan

I PRETEND TO BE NOT BOTHERED BY THE TELEPHONE CONVERSATIONS THAT have just occurred. But I am. Vincent is clearly looking for more time. I think he might get it, but I can't wait around on the answer coming from this prick's partner in crime. JR, his name is. Yeah right! They've probably made up initials for each other. Perhaps this spotty little fuck is called BJ during this kidnapping. I couldn't even imagine getting a BJ from BJ. His skin is way too fuckin' greasy. He disgusts me. I can't even bring myself to look at him. I'm pretending I'm soaked up in this game, but my main priority is peeling the tape from my left ankle. Tape is flicking its way onto our carpet but it's bit by bit, literally. The game is moments away from going into extra time. That'll keep the prick occupied for an extra half hour. I think he'll be delighted that Manchester United end up winning. He seems to be urging them on.

The apartment is really hot today. The sun is scorching in through the windows. It must be over twenty degrees out there. It certainly feels like it from where I'm sitting. I was hoping to have released this ankle by ten-thirty but I've already missed that deadline. Just as the ninety-minute whistle blows in the game, his mobile phone rings again.

'Hey, JR,' he says.

I'm trying my best to hear what the cunt on the other end of the line is saying, but it's pointless.

'I understand,' replies my captor.

151

Shit. This isn't good. Maybe they're not going to offer Vincent more time after all.

'Kill Ryan,' he then says, staring over at me. I can see him in my peripherals, but I'm not showing him that I'm shitting it.

Kill Ryan. Holy fuck. Is this really happening or is he just running fear through me every so often on purpose?

I need to get myself out of this mess as soon as possible.

The Internet's corridors are plentiful. There are literally millions of little websites you can access with the click of a button that would almost have your eyes popping out of your head. From being only interested in straightforward pornography, I got lulled to the darkest of X-rated arts within a matter of weeks. It all started when I began posting on forums out of pure boredom. I'd discuss my innermost fantasies with random strangers who had even more random usernames. When I began discussions about my fascination with handsome dark-haired men, other posters thought I was being sarcastic. 'It's such a boring fantasy,' they would tell me. 'Open your mind.' I had no idea how much my mind was about to be opened. Within forty-eight hours of logging on to these forums, I was watching videos of all kinds of crazy shit. I watched one of the most beautiful women I've ever seen suck off a horse. She did her best to swallow the load too, only to gag on it and then throw up. I remember seeing a video, which has since been seen by millions of people around the world, of two Asian chicks puking and shitting into a cup before sharing the contents with each other. None of this weird shit turned me on. Whenever I fancied cracking out an orgasm, I'd return to my usual 'Italian men' search.

I had to be discreet though. Vincent wasn't particularly tech savvy, he knew what the best up-and-coming gadgets were, but he wouldn't know the ins and outs of how they operated. I've been deleting all the porn activity from my laptop anyway. It's easy to lose a browser's history. Besides, I never once saw Vincent opening the lid of the laptop he bought for me. He has his own to play with. I often wondered what he got up to online when left alone, but a sneaky search of his laptop's history provided no evidence of naughtiness. Vincent is only interested in hard news. I'm not sure he is aware of the full delights the Internet has to offer. And I don't just mean pornography. There's a wealth of information online that I know he'd love. But all he seems to log on to is the BBC News website. Oh, and Bill Maher clips on YouTube. He fuckin' loves Bill Maher. He cackles away to his old clips, nodding his head in agreement. Vincent thinks he's as liberal as Maher but the truth is, Vincent is a liberal *because* of Maher. I don't know why he's more interested in British and American politics than he is Irish politics. But I really don't give a shit. I wish my video viewing on the Internet was restricted to YouTube. Even YouPorn is old school for me now. YouPorn is boring. There's not much fun to be had on there anymore. It was YouPorn that attracted me to commenting on videos in the first place though. I got chatting to a few of the fellow contributors to that website and they led me to other forums. It got dark really quickly. I blame the coke. I couldn't give up my daily habit after I'd finished at Wow. I hid it from Vincent. Well, I didn't really hide it, I just never told him I was still snorting lines while he was hard at work. I thought the coke would initially help me with the novel. Instead, it assisted me in digging deeper into the world of pornography. None of it seemed to really turn me on, but I was still fascinated by it. From Kaiju porn through to clown porn and anime to bestiality, I watched it all. Just because I would rather do anything than write. A guy with the username TeenCum069 led me through most of the corridors. He would post the sickest videos on the forums and we'd chat shit about them for hours each day. Then he posted one video that turned my brain upside down. I will never forget the child's face. It was the innocence in his eyes that turned me on.

This prick has been pacing around the kitchen since the full-time whistle blew in the game. I can see him eyeballing the small mound of coke on the glass table again. His tension is creeping over to me. I've been particularly panicky since he got off the phone a few minutes ago. But I'm hiding it well. There's little over an hour and a quarter left until Vincent's deadline. I am hopeful I can get myself free of this tape and outmuscle this fucker. But even if I struggle, I still have the cum to fall back on. I can tell this fruitcake that he left his DNA at the crime scene, that he's fucked either way. That'll stop him in his tracks. It's my plan B.

Just when I think the tape around my left ankle is getting the better of me, I form a small gap in the top of it with the tip of my thumb. It's tight, but if I can force my thumb down the side of it, I should be able to snap the rest of the tape off. The sweat forming on my fingers due to anxiety is helping me. I manage to slide my thumb down the side of some of the tape and begin to tug at it. The prick is still pacing in the kitchen, humming some shit tune to himself. He's been trying to ring Vincent back to give him the bad news, but he's not answering. He must be in the second vault. I wonder how Vincent is feeling right now. He must be sick with worry but I bet he's not showing it.

'Your cock buddy better hurry the fuck up. You don't have much time left,' the prick shouts over to me. It's the first time he's spoken directly to me in ages.

'I … I …' I stutter before remembering I had been doing well ignoring him up until this point. 'Vincent will be back,' I eventually muster up. I shouldn't have bothered.

He points his finger at me.

'Bang,' he says, cocking his thumb.

My thumb is doing an exercise of its own. I feel it pop through the tape. My leg falls free and I feel my heart rate quicken instantly. Both my legs and my right arm are now free. It won't be long now until I can get to that gun. I remember my yoga breathing techniques again.

In through the nose, out through the mouth.

'Let's see, shall we?' I say in return. Prick!

10:40

Darragh

'EXACTLY,' HE SAYS. 'ME AND YOU, BUDDY, WE'RE GONNA BE THE MOST feared gangsters in the whole of Dublin.'

I feel a huge grin stretch across my face. That's all I've ever wanted to hear. JR is such a legend. I'm delighted that he sees a future for the two of us. I recall that sentence over and over in my head as I continue to pace around the kitchen table thingy. Kitchen island, that's it! That fuckin word's been on the tip of me tongue all mornin'. I try to ring Vincent back to give him the bad news but he's not picking up right now. He must be close to leaving the second bank. He better be. I stare over at the coke on the glass table again. I really shouldn't.

'Your cock buddy better hurry the fuck up. You don't have much time left,' I bark over at Ryan.

He looks shocked. I haven't said a word to him in ages. He's still sittin' there like a helpless pussy. Just as he's mumbling some stuttered response to me I point my finger at him and mock shoot him. His face is priceless. Poor fag. I take a peek at the time. 10:42. I can't see how Vincent is going to get to two more banks before midday. But I don't care anymore. Even if we come out of this with six million and one dead body, it'll be all worth it. Me and JR have a future together. I know that for certain now.

I didn't know what to do with the twenty grand The Boss gave me. I've never been good with money. I left it under me mattress. That's probably not very smart, but nobody ever comes into my bedsit but me anyway. And nobody would want to rob my bedsit, that's for sure. I thought about getting a better place to live in, to put a deposit down on a nice apartment, but I was comfortable where I was. I bought meself a new TV and a PlayStation 4 with some of the cash, but I soon got tired of sitting on the same old couch, pressing the same old buttons.

After a few more weeks cooped up in the bedsit all day, I decided to start a new daily routine for meself. I spent a lot of my afternoons in the Deer's Head on Parnell Street. I'd sip cold beers talking shit to either Aisling or Billy. They were the only two bar employees in the place. I didn't really like either of them, but they were the only company I had. I tried to sell weed for a local dealer but I'd only manage to get rid of a couple of twenty-euro bags a day. Seeing as my cut from each bag was only five euros, it really wasn't worth me while. But I wanted to be involved in some sort of underworld crime in any way I could. I missed the big time, but I didn't know who to turn to. I thought about investing the money in something worthwhile but I had no clue what that should be. All I knew was that I wanted a better life. But a better life to me wasn't a nice big gaff or a convertible car. I wanted to be a gangster. That's what a great life to me looks like. Somehow, I'd managed to get involved with the best criminal gang in Dublin and fucked it all up. And I did fuck it up. My unravelling was all my own fault. Moving to a different county crossed my mind regularly. Dublin had fuck all to offer me and I had fuck all to offer Dublin. But I'm glad I didn't move. Billy the barman told me one day that some geezer had been enquiring about buying weed in the area and asked if he could arrange a meeting between the two of us. Billy knew I flogged the odd bit of grass here and there.

'Well, you know I'm here every day from about two-ish,' I replied.

'Perfect, I'll let him know.'

It didn't take long for me to meet this guy. He dropped by the pub the very next day. I feared he was a cop straight away, but he convinced me he wasn't by showin' me his dirty fingernails. He told me he worked in an old paint factory. It's unusual to come across a middle-aged man looking to buy a small bag of weed in some city centre pub, but he seemed very cool to me straight away. Behind his odd haircut and strange beard, JR has kind eyes.

I stop pacing round the kitchen island and sling myself back onto the couch as extra time begins in the game. I have to remind myself constantly not to look at the coke. I take a sly look over at Ryan. I try to figure out if I feel sorry for him in some way. I don't. I don't know why I don't. I just don't. It's not because he's a fag. I don't mind fags as long as they keep their fuckin dicks away from me. Maybe I don't care about him because he's been such a jammy cunt. This guy doesn't even work yet he lives like a king. He's a little bitch, I guess. I like the way coke makes me think. I can dig deeper into my thoughts when I'm high. Me imagination runs wild. I come to the conclusion that this spoilt little asshole has had luck at every corner he's turned. I've been nothin' but unlucky all my life. Well, that changes today. I haven't done anything to scare Ryan since I whipped me cock out earlier this morning. Maybe I'll try somethin' in a while just to fuck with his head again. A few possibilities are skipping through my mind when his boyfriend calls back.

'Hello,' he whispers down the line to me.

'Midday is your deadline and that's it,' I say as straight as an arrow. This is my opportunity to act like a gangster again. But he stumps me.

'Whatever,' he snarls back.

His reply is a surprise. Fuckin fag! I'm about to hang up on him when I realise I need to ask if he's out of the second bank. I guess he is.

'Yep. I'm walking towards the car with another two million now,' he replies, tryna act as if he's not bothered.

'Well, hurry the fuck up,' I say, giving me the perfect opportunity to hang up in style yet again. I'm good at this shit. I toss the phone back onto the glass table, making a point, before realising I need it to ring JR back. I was almost cool then.

10:45

Vincent

B<small>EFORE</small> I'<small>M</small> <small>BUZZED</small> <small>OUT</small> <small>OF</small> <small>THE</small> <small>SECOND</small> <small>DOOR</small> I <small>HAVE</small> <small>THE</small> <small>PHONE</small> <small>TO</small> my ear.

I've barely finished saying 'Hello' before the fucker snaps at me.

'Midday is your deadline and that's it!' Fuck him.

'Whatever,' I say trying to act like I don't care. I think it stuns him. He falls silent for a few seconds before asking me if I'm finished in Camden Street.

'Yep. I'm walking towards the car with another two mill now.'

'Well, hurry the fuck up,' he snarls back before hanging up. I bet he thinks he's cool.

John rushes to the back of the car when he sees me approaching.

'You okay, boss?' he asks, with a touch of concern in his voice.

'I'm a hundred per cent,' I lie. I'm such a good actor.

John unlocks the two briefcases from my wrists and places them in the trunk for me.

'Church Street, John boy,' I say before climbing into the back of the car. Tchaikovsky's still playing and the air is as cool as it's been all morning.

Church Street then Mayor Street, half an hour in each plus at least twenty minutes of travelling time. That would take me just past midday.

I let out another sigh before winking at John through the rear-view mirror to try to act like I know what I'm doing. He must be wondering what the fuck is going on today but he won't dare ask. And I won't offer up any lie. I never divulge any information to John so it would only add to the oddness of the morning if I did. John doesn't add to any of my worries though. He'll just do as I ask him. It will take us about ten minutes to drive to Church Street. I wonder if Noah Voss has been trying to ring me. I take out my iPhone and turn it on. I dread to think how many voicemails I've received. I have to listen to the nonsense Vodafone robot calling out my own mobile phone number before I get my answer. Five voicemails. My heart races in anticipation of listening to them. I know from the mobile number being called out that the first is from Noah.

'Hello, Mr Butler,' he says. 'Just making sure you will be here at about ten-thirty like you said this morning. I have everything ready, sir. Look forward to seeing you.'

The next voicemail is from Derek Talbot. He's an old employee of mine who has tried to keep in touch with me ever since he left my old job a couple of decades ago. I like him. But I'm not really that interested in hanging on to our relationship. He rings every couple of months for a catch-up. That's okay with me, I guess. I never follow up with his loose plans for us to meet for a drink. He's part of my past.

The next call is from my office. Fuck! Belinda is looking for me.

'Vincent, I've just noticed six missed calls on your phone here. Do you want me to listen to them? Let me know. Talk soon.'

Bollocks! I hang up from my voicemail and ring her straight back. I wonder if she'll answer. I have asked her to stay away from the phones all morning but if she notices my mobile number ringing, she should pick up.

'Hi, Vincent,' she says.

'Belinda, leave the phone alone. Have you got that paperwork in order for me yet?'

'I'm still doing it, Vincent,' she says. 'It's taking a long time. I don't know how you got them in this mess …'

'I just haven't been keeping on top of paperwork, Be. If you can just concentrate on that for now and leave the phones until I get back, that'd be great.'

'Will do, boss. I did notice that Jonathan had been looking for you. It was his number that rang a few times.'

My blood boils instantly. I surprise even myself with the tone I take.

'Stay away from the phones, Be,' I say more sternly than I've ever said anything to her before.

'Okay, okay. I am, Vincent. I'm just keeping note when they do ring. I … I …'

'I know you are, darling,' I say, relieving the tension. 'I'm sorry. I'm having a crazy morning. I have a conference call with the board members later and I need to have all that paperwork in order. Please.'

'A conference call with the board? I didn't know anything about—'

'They contacted me directly first thing this morning, Be,' I say, making my story up on the spot. 'They're looking for a total update. I just need to have all in order.'

'Is there anything I can do to help?' asks Belinda.

'Yes. The paperwork,' I reply, laughing. 'Get those files in alphabetical order and stay away from the phones.'

She laughs in return.

'Just as you asked me this morning!'

'Exactly. Just as I asked this morning.'

'I'll have them sorted before you get back,' she says.

'Thanks, Be.'

I'm desperate to get back to my mobile phone voicemails. I grunt, having to go through the process of dialling into the system again. It seems to be taking ages.

Bollocks. It's Jonathan.

'Hi, Vincent, just making sure all is okay. You said you were heading over to Michelle straight from here but I noticed your car pull off in a different direction. Everything okay? I can't reach you and I can't reach Belinda by phone. Let me know what's up.'

This is so frustrating. I should have left my phone on through the morning. I was an idiot for turning it off. I need to quench these fires as soon as they come in. The voicemail informed me this call was made at ten-forty. Just eight minutes ago. I decide to listen to the last voicemail before getting back to Jonathan. It's Noah again.

'Mr Butler. It's gone ten-thirty now and I hope everything is okay with you. I am awaiting your visit. Your phone seems to be switched off. Call me back at your convenience to let me know.' Fuck off, Voss!

I liked the fact that Ryan was always home, initially. He used to work most evenings so it was great for the two of us to make the most of dinner dates. He'd search for the best restaurants in Dublin through TripAdvisor and we'd go and pay them a visit. It was great for us to rekindle our romance, but it did get kind of boring after a few months. We didn't have a whole lot to talk about. When we did talk he would spout some shit about wanting to move to Sydney. We'd travelled through Australia back in 2010 and while I certainly enjoyed it, I harboured no ambitions to move there full time. Ryan did, however. Ryan had some bizarre notions.

He never really thought things through. On the odd occasion that we would talk about something other than his dream move to Sydney, I'd mention his book. He explained the concept to me a couple of times and I think I understood it. It's about some paparazzo who stalks Hollywood stars. Doesn't sound very original to me. I was never sure Ryan was capable of writing a book but I wanted to support him. I bought him the latest Apple Mac and iPhone as a retirement present when he left Wow. He was so grateful. That shut him up about Sydney for a while.

I roll my eyes as I ring Jonathan back.

'Ah, Vincent, how are you? Is everything okay?' he asks.

'Jonathan. Calm down. What is going on? I just got your voicemail.'

'I just … I just thought I'd check everything was okay? I saw John pull away and—'

'Everything is great, Jonathan. Calm down. John was just getting some petrol in the tank before we headed over to Michelle. Are you okay?'

'I just couldn't reach you … or Belinda. I just thought I should keep trying.'

Ah, he's mostly upset because Belinda hasn't been returning his calls, I bet. I finish the call by telling him I have urgent engagements. I'm pretty certain he'll be okay for an hour or two while I get this completed. I stare out of the car window after I hang up. John has just turned right onto Church Street. I wonder how pissed off Noah is that I'm arriving twenty-five minutes later than I told him I would. I don't give a shit. I need to be bullish in here.

10:45

Jack

I can see him holding the phone to his ear as he exits. He must be ringing Darragh to let him now he has a further two mill in tow. A packed briefcase is hanging from each of his wrists. Vincent looks to be in control. It's a cocky approach, but I like it. John seems to be taking everything in his stride too. He greets Vincent at the trunk of the car and helps him place the cases inside. As they both climb back into the car, I take a look at my watch. They should be arriving at Church Street a little before eleven a.m. He's not really that far behind his deadline now. I won't be at Church Street. It's the only branch I'm not going to witness being robbed today. I have another appointment. And it's very important that I attend. As soon as I spin on my heels towards the South Circular Road, where my first car is parked, the phone buzzes in my hand.

'All looks good,' I say in an upbeat tone.

'Yeah, he has the other two mill,' bellows Darragh. 'And I told him the deadline is the deadline. He seems to be quickening up.'

'You're doing a great job, Darragh. In just over an hour we'll both be millionaires. Call me when Church Street is done.'

'Will do, chief.'

The giggle I allow myself after hanging up isn't supposed to be loud, but it is. It startles the old woman walking towards me. The car's a four-minute swift stroll from here. I've made this walk three times in the build-up to today. It'll take me ten minutes to drive to Dinah's from the South Circular Road.

I reminisce about my time travelling with Frank while I walk. We both suffered a little post-vacation depression when we finally arrived home from our first European trip. But it didn't take us long to get back into the swing of things. I don't think Frank loved golf as much as I did, but he never turned down the opportunity to have a round with his old man. I think he felt it was his obligation as a son. I'm not sure I would have minded if he told me he didn't love golf all that much. Or maybe I would. I'm not sure. Sometimes I felt he opened up more to Margarite than he did to me, but I never minded that either. In fact, I encouraged it. Margarite was a proper mother figure to him. I still stay in touch with her, though it's a rarity these days. She moved to Edinburgh about six years ago with her husband. She met Marcus two years prior. I liked Marcus. He was a good man. I'm sure he still is. Some people thought I was jealous that Margarite had met somebody else, but I genuinely wasn't. There were times when I felt I should be jealous but I couldn't bring myself to be. I was worried Frank would be heartbroken once Margarite moved on, but he proved to be of strong mind again. He was nearly sixteen when she left.

I get to the car twenty seconds shy of four minutes. I made a short appointment with Dinah, telling her I'd call by around eleven-ish. I wanted to leave the timing vague. I knew Vincent would be heading to Church Street any time between ten-thirty and eleven o'clock, and that would be my cue to head towards Dinah's. She's been amazing to me. She's really sorted my head out.

Frank may have been a cocky teenager but that's a much better trait in a child than that of lacking in confidence. He was a handsome young man and had a natural charm. He definitely got his gift of the gab from the Ritchies. I was never that charming. I told him once about my attempt at winning over his mother and he had to stop laughing just to breathe. We had our moments. Frank always felt like he knew it all, which was hard to deal with. But apart from the occasional spat, we were an ideal father and son combo. I've heard from other fathers that a father and son relationship is a lot tougher to control than a father and daughter. Daughters tend to adore their dads while mothers and sons have a preferable bond. It sounds about right. I would say on a scale of one to ten in father–son relationships mine and Frank's would rank at about an eight or nine. I was proud of my decisions in parenthood and watching Frank grow into a fine, albeit overly confident, young man filled me with joy. I'm always surprised by how quickly time flashes by when I'm thinking of my son.

I made sure not to go over the speed limit on the way to Drimnagh, but I must have got lucky with the traffic lights across the canal. I make it to Dinah's a full minute quicker than any time during my trial runs. I was quick getting my wig and beard off. It's four minutes past eleven now. I imagine Vincent is inside the Church Street branch by this stage, dealing with Noah Voss.

Community centres always look bleak from the outside. Yet inside this building everything is freshly decorated. I don't know why none of the budget goes on the exterior of these buildings. They always look uninviting, which is totally against the point of them. Dinah's room is the first on the left past the small reception. A dark-haired man I've never seen before greets me as I make my way towards her.

'How-a-ya?'

'Hello. Is … eh … is Dinah here?' I ask.

'She is,' replies the man. 'I've just finished a session with her. She works wonders.'

'She does, doesn't she?' I reply with a soft smile.

'Sorry. My name is Trevor. Trevor Kirwan. I … I lost my wife five months ago.'

'Oh, I'm sorry to hear that. Jack,' I reply, shaking the hand he held out to me. I don't offer any more until I notice him arch his eyebrows, willing me to open up. Fuck it. Why not? We're both in a bereavement help centre.

'I lost my wife too,' I say solemnly. 'And my son.'

10:50

Ryan

DAVID DE GEA'S LONG THROW TOWARDS MARCUS RASHFORD ON THE halfway line lets me know the winning goal is imminent. As I'm attempting to peel away at the tape wrapped tightly around my left wrist, I watch Rashford skip by two defenders before bearing down on Manuel Neuer in the Bayern Munich goal. The German's mistimed dive brings the United attacker tumbling to the ground. It's an obvious penalty kick. I've watched it a dozen times since it happened. The referee had no choice. But of course, the media made a meal of it, because it was a decision that went in favour of Manchester United. It takes a few moments for this prick to realise what's just happened before he leaps to his feet.

'Penalty kick, penalty kick,' he roars.

He really is into this. I haven't been able to tell him this match was played out two weeks ago. I figured it best to let him believe it's live. It has assisted in his infatuation with it, meaning he hasn't been paying me much attention. I know Paul Pogba will take the penalty kick and blast it straight down the middle of the goal while Neuer dives towards his left post. That's how Manchester United made it to the final of this year's Champions League to face Real Madrid. That game takes place in a couple weeks. I hope I'm fuckin' alive to see it. The prick roars with delight upon seeing Pogba almost break the net with the penalty. He barely glances at me as he celebrates. I think he asks me a question but I don't answer it.

'That's it, that's game over isn't it?' he says.

It is, yes. But he can figure that all out by himself. Bayern would have needed two goals in the final few minutes of extra time and they barely even registered two shots. I don't have to stretch as much to get my hand across to the remaining tape but it is a more difficult task. My arms are more visible to the prick than my legs are. But I can sit back in a relaxed state while I delicately peel at the tape. The gun is still sitting on the glass table next to his mobile phone. I hope it's still there when I free myself. Shouldn't be long now. I'm thinking through my plan of action once again when I notice him grab at the chair he had Vincent perched on this morning. He spins it around until it mirrors my chair, and then he plonks himself on it. His nose must be only two feet from mine. I can smell his breath. It smells like baked beans. I immediately curl my ankles around the front legs of my chair, hoping with all my might that he doesn't notice they are now free.

'Game over!' he says with a grin. 'Who will they play in the final?'

I think about not answering before deciding that's not the best route to take right now.

'Real Madrid play Juventus in the other semi-final tomorrow,' I offer up. 'Do you want to call by to watch that with me too?' He finds my retort funny.

'I'll be out spending my millions tomorrow, fag boy,' he responds. It's so juvenile to call anyone a fag. I'm glad he's immature. I can take this fucker down once I'm free. I'm certain of it. 'Who'll win that?'

'Real Madrid,' I answer with absolute positivity. I know. The game was actually played last week.

'Really? You think so?'

'I know so. They won the first leg one–nil and they'll see out a nil-all draw tomorrow to go through.'

He screws his nose up trying to take in what I say. I know the two legs thing still has him baffled despite me explaining it to him when he first settled down to watch the game. His silence is welcome. I'm wondering if he's going to leave it at that. I can see he's thinking about what to do. The palms of my hands are clammy with sweat. If he notices my ankles are no longer taped then all my morning's work will be undone. I glance at the microwave clock, ignoring his gaze. Anything to get away from the stench of his beans. 10:58.

Holy shit. Do I really have just an hour to live?

After a while the only videos that TeenCum069 was sharing with me involved kids. It was very strange watching them, but I found it quite addictive viewing. I was half turned on, half feeling sick with guilt. I remember feeling the same way when I watched "regular" porn for the very first time. I had the nerve when I was just fourteen years old to ask the local video rental guy if he had any porn movies. He didn't hesitate in ducking down behind his counter to show me what he had to offer. I'd heard of pornography then, but I'd never watched any of it. I pretended to school friends that I knew what sex was all about but I hadn't got a clue. I remember waiting on my mother to go to work that evening before placing the VHS in our dated video recorder. The film opened with a beautiful blonde girl stranded on the side of the road after her car broke down. Fast forward to three minutes later when the hero who stopped to help her began to unzip his jeans. I watched stunned as she took his hard dick to the back of her throat.

What the fuck's going on?

My stomach flipped upside down. I felt like throwing up. But so too did my dick. It stood on end. That mixed feeling between a sour stomach and horniness thrashes through my body every time I watch kiddie porn. TeenCum069 introduced me to other like-minded Internet scum. It wasn't long until they were teaching me how to contact kids online. I still can't believe how easy it is for us to interact with teens. Why the fuck do their parents allow them this sort of access online? I guess they can't help it. Every kid wants to have their own social media accounts and that is where they're most vulnerable. All it takes is for people like me to set up a fake account, using images of a hot young girl, and boys will do or say anything you ask them to. I'm pretty sure I wouldn't have been this gullible when I was ten or twelve years of age. Kids these days are more stupid than ever. Despite me contacting quite a few cute kids when I first set up my fake account, it was a ten-year-old named Brady Donovan who fell for my bullshit first. He was fascinated with Nicole Blake, my alter ego. It didn't take long for him to agree to meet me. But I kept putting it off. Every time we arranged a date, I would freeze. So many permutations crossed my mind. The guys in the forum tried to help me fight those fears. They'd all been through this countless times before. They knew how to deal with the fact that the boy was looking to meet a cute schoolgirl only to be met by a middle-aged man. They gave me all the lines, all the subtleties required. It was like being handed ammunition. I remember the date well because it etched itself on my mind. I arranged to meet Brady in the car park of the Travelodge in Derry on the sixth of December. That was about a year and a half ago now. I had a room booked in the hotel under the names of Charles and Brady Donovan – a father and son. When I first bumped into him in the car park, I figured straight away that the guys' hints and tips would work almost effortlessly.

'She can't make it,' I told Brady's disappointed face. 'I'm her uncle. She asked me to come and meet you just to make sure you can be a good enough boyfriend for her. If you come with me, she asked me to show you some things. She wants to know if you're ready. Ready to meet her. To really love her.'

'Okay,' he said, shrugging his shoulders.

'Cool,' I reply. 'I have a room booked up here in the Travelodge hotel. I have some videos for you that Nicole would like you to watch.'

'Let's do a fuckin' line, dude,' the prick finally offers up after a long silence.

He'd been staring at me all that time. I sigh. I don't want another line. I just want to get the fuck out of this mess. The prick grabs at the magazine lying on the glass table with the mound of coke and the old five-euro note sitting on top of it.

'Me first this time,' he says while rolling the note back together.

I don't have time for this.

10:55

Vincent

THE CHURCH STREET BUILDING IS SIMILAR TO THE ONE ON CAMDEN. IT'S A modern slice of Dublin architecture, right next to St Michan's Church. But it's nicer. It's fully clear glass. No dimmed black pointless windows here. I don't visit this branch that often, at least not anymore. The further I stay away from Noah, the better for everybody involved. Nobody notices as I come through the first door. By the time I'm buzzed through the second, Kelly at the first Customer Service desk is smiling at me. She waves out from behind her glass-protected window. I mouth the name 'Noah' to her in return and she points me towards his office. I rattle on the door before letting myself in.

'Noah,' I say, fake grinning as he reaches for his mouse to click a button.

What the fuck is he hiding?

'Ah, Mr Butler,' he says, flashing both his gums and his teeth.

Are some people just not aware that they do that? Nobody wants to see anybody's fuckin' gums. I really hate this prick.

'I thought you were coming at ten-thirty, sir?'

'No – I said ten-thirty*ish*, Noah and I've been held up. So if you don't mind I'd like to collect the funds as quickly as possible.'

'Yes, Mr Butler, of course, sir,' he says before walking towards me, holding my stare.

He's an awful-looking asshole. I initially thought he was coming to hug me, but he rests his left arm on my shoulder and shouts past me.

'Gary!' he calls out.

His spotty junior member of staff screeches back, 'Yeah, Noah?'

'The paperwork for Mr Butler, please.'

'Yeah, I got it.'

'Okay then, will you bring it to me, please?'

'Yeah, in a minute, Noah.'

This is why I don't like Voss. Nobody has any respect for him.

'Excuse me, Gary!' I shout so loudly that everybody in the branch takes notice, including the queue of customers. Gary must have leapt to the sound of my voice. He sprints towards Noah's office, his stupid haircut flopping on top of his head.

'Gary, do you think it's okay to talk to your boss the way you just have?' I ask, flippantly.

'What way, Mr Butler?' he answers, looking puzzled. I don't have the energy for this shit. Not this morning. I swipe the paperwork out of his hands while offering him an evil stare.

'That is Mr Voss, do you hear me?' I say, pointing the paperwork in Noah's direction.

'But eh … but … He told us not to call him Mr Voss, Mr Butler. He … he said it's too formal.'

I breathe heavily in the direction of Gary, thinking about what to say next. I then look at Noah who offers no support, just that ugly gummy smile of his.

'Well I'm telling you formal is what we do round here. He's Mr Voss, got it?'

'Yes, Mr Voss, Mr Butler, sorry,' Gary replies as his head sinks lower into his shoulders. What a mess of a branch this is.

'I'm sorry, Mr Butler,' Noah says as Gary makes his way back to his desk. 'I just thought I would change things up a little. It's no problem keeping it formal. I understand your decision on that, sir.'

I don't respond. Instead I try to think what lurks behind Noah's fake politeness. This fucker is dark. I need to know what he's hiding.

Noah told the interview panel that he rose from bank clerk at Barclays in London to eventually managing his own branch within three years.

'They really liked me and rated me. I got promoted seven times in my first two years,' he boasted, flashing his gums at everyone.

My nose pinched itself as I recoiled in my seat, but I was the only one. Each of the other three board members who bothered to turn up for the interview were grinning back at him, nodding in approval. They'd clearly hired him in their heads already. I was devastated. I didn't want to be working with this prick. On his first day in the job he told me God was looking down on him that day in the interview and that he has since prayed for each of us that were in that room. My mouth opened and closed in a swift second as a response. I was about to screech something in return but managed to stop myself.

Don't you fuckin' dare pray for me!

I wish I had followed through and said it. I should have nipped this religion bullshit in the bud, right from the start. He hasn't told me he's prayed for me since, but if he does today he's getting a fuckin' reality check. I really shouldn't allow myself to get wound up by him. I need to get in and out of here as quickly as I possibly can. It's hard for the blood not to boil in here though. There's a pathetic looking figurine on his desk of baby Jesus being swaddled by his whore of a mother. There's a framed picture of an older Jesus with a halo above his head eyeballing me on the wall behind Noah. It's creepy as fuck. I saw Noah hang that on his first day in the office – the day he told me he had prayed for me.

'I looked at the specifications of the withdrawal procedure,' Noah says, flipping over the paperwork on his desk. 'You know it doesn't specify an amount you can personally withdraw, Mr Butler. I think two million euros is a lot of money—'

'Of course it's a lot of fuckin' money, Voss,' I shoot back. It stuns him. I've never sworn in his company before.

'I … I'm sorry, Mr Butler. Yes, of course it is a lot of money,' he stutters with his African accent weighing more than his put-on posh English tone for a change.

'Listen, Noah. I don't have time for this box-ticking nonsense today. I'm under stress from the board members to take two mill from here this morning and deliver it to Mayor Street, okay? That's what I've been ordered to do and it's what I am ordering you to do, so can we just please get to it? I've a hundred and one other matters, more urgent than this, to get to today and I really need this out of the way.'

'The board asked you to do this?' he asks, looking up at me.

'Yes.'

'It's just I mentioned it to Mr Sneyd this morning and he didn't know anything of it.'

I feel my face flush with rage. If I was to touch it, I'm sure I would burn my fingers.

'Clyde Sneyd?' I ask in a firm tone.

'Yes. But it's okay, Mr Butler.' Noah is panicking. 'He said you're the boss. He said he doesn't know anything about bank transfers and that you know what you're doing, so all is … all is …' he stutters again.

'Listen you, Voss,' I say as I rise to my feet. 'You ever fuckin' go behind my back again and I'll—' I don't get to finish.

Noah stands up, matching me for height. 'Sir, sir, please, please. I'm sorry. I'm sorry.' He keeps repeating himself. He knows he fucked up. 'Please sit down, sit down. Relax, Mr Butler.'

I tug at my tie, loosening it from the collar and perch back slowly onto the chair, keeping eye contact with Noah.

'I am sorry, Mr Butler,' he offers once more. 'I just wanted to know the amount allowed to be taken in one lump. That's all. I couldn't reach you by phone, so I contacted Mr Sneyd.'

I allow a silence to wash over us both as I take all this information in. It's a good job he contacted Sneyd and not any of the others on the board. Sneyd is the least interested. I bet he's forgotten all about Noah's call by now anyway. It would have been too much trouble for him having to field such an enquiry. I'm surprised he even answered, to be honest. It must have been midnight in New York when Noah called him. He doesn't answer any of my calls when I ring him at a reasonable hour. He never has.

'Let's just get this done, Noah, shall we?' I suggest, trying to defuse any tension between us.

'Yes, Mr Butler,' he agrees, picking up a pen from his desk. Even his fuckin' pen has a picture of Jesus's face on it.

10:55

Darragh

I MAY HAVE GONE OVER THE TOP JUMPING FOR JOY WHEN PAUL POGBA scored that penalty kick. I don't mind. Only this fag saw me anyway. I take a moment to think this through. United are now two–one up in this game but three–two up in total over the two legs. Even if Bayern Munich score a goal here, they won't go through due to the away goals rule. It's complicated but cock breath here explained it to me earlier and I think I've got it right. Bayern need two goals in the remaining five minutes and they're not gonna get them. Game over. I fist pump the air and make a silent vow to follow United's fortunes from now on. They remind me of home, even though home isn't Manchester. The fag is staying pretty silent. He's obviously not a United fan. I grab at the kitchen chair close by and drag it right in front of him. He shits himself, I'm sure of it, as I sit down on it and eyeball him from close range. Our kneecaps are almost touching. I decide to play nice cop to start off with, but only because I still haven't figured out what to do yet. We talk football again. He thinks Real Madrid will make it to the final to play United, but I think Juventus will do it. I've seen them play before, years ago. They're an Italian team and very good as far as I remember. This little fag doesn't know what he's talking about. Fags really don't have a clue when it comes to sport. He doesn't seem to be in the mood for talkin'. He's just shitting himself, not knowing what I'm gonna do next. I guess neither of us do. I pause to take a look around the room. I'm looking for inspiration.

'Let's do another fuckin line,' I say, grabbing the sports magazine from the glass table.

I don't need him to test this shit for me anymore, so I'm going first this time. I use my library card to separate enough for two decent lines before rolling up the five-euro note. This coke burns the edges of the nose before it's even in the system. I love this stuff. The little fag cunt ain't getting his bag of coke back. It's coming with me.

'Here ya go,' I say, handing him the note. I haven't forgot that his right arm is free. I'm not stupid. He sucks up his line in less than a second before staring up at me with his eyes watering.

'That's some fuckin shit, dude,' I say, laughing into his face. He doesn't respond. Fine by me. I just wanna have some fun. I am a gangster after all.

JR's kind eyes reflect his personality. They kinda sparkle a bit. That was the first thing that struck me about him. It's probably because his eyes are the only feature you can actually see on his face. He told me his work at the paint factory was a front for his real job. He used to work for one the hottest gangs in Dublin but had given up on a life of crime years ago to go straight. But after losing his family he turned back to crime. He thought life was too short for pussyfooting around with a regular nine-to-five job. He needed that adrenaline buzz again. He told me he was on the lookout for an apprentice who could handle the sort of shit he wanted to get involved in. It was like music to my ears. He knew I'd been involved with The Boss before and had been told I was very trustworthy. He had a lot of information on me. JR is a perfectionist. It's why I love working with him.

'I'm not interested in any drama,' he would say to me repeatedly. 'I just want a guy who can get the job done.'

'No better man than me, JR,' I would tell him over and over again.

He liked the fact that I had a clean record and decided to take me on after meeting me a couple of times. I couldn't believe my luck. I still can't. I've gone from earning ten euros a day for selling two bags of weed to, today, earning four million for five hours' work. From day one, JR has been open and honest with me. He told me how he made his way up the ranks of the criminal underworld in Dublin, from being a junior member of a protection racket right through to aiming to become the number one bank thief in the whole of Ireland. We would meet up in the Deer's Head and he would amaze me with stories of his past. He told me from the outset that if we were going into business together he would only consider it fair that we split everything down the middle. He said that's how his boss operated with him when he first started. I insisted it wasn't about the money. For me it was about the work. I think that's what ultimately won him over. He liked me right from the start and I adored him. I owe him so much. He's my knight in shining armour, really.

I'm not sure what real-life gangsters do in these situations. I flick through the movie library in my head for inspiration. *Reservoir Dogs* springs to the forefront of my brain for some reason. Probably because Ryan is tied to a chair. Yes, of course! The fuckin ear cut-off scene. Brilliant! I leap for the TV remote and push at buttons to find the music channels. How many fuckin channels do these fags have?

'What number's the MTVs?' I have to ask.

'They start on 701.'

I continue switching through the music channels until I see something I like. Eminem. I notice the title of a show currently on called *Eminem's Top 10*. Fuck yeah! The channel's on a commercial break at the moment. I look over at Ryan. He has no idea what's coming. Poor fag. While the ads play I head towards the bathroom mirror. I noticed a razor in there earlier. I clip the head off to give me access to the blades. The final ad is playing on the TV when I return. I know it's the final one because it's for the channel itself. They always advertise themselves each side of a programme. You get to know this kind of shit when all you do is watch TV all day. Then I hear the beat kick in. 'Cleaning Out my Closet'. Probably me favourite Eminem track. Well it's in my top three anyway. I hold up a pretend mic to my mouth and dance towards Ryan.

'Have you ever been hated or dis-sumtin-ated against?
I have, I've been protested and demonstrated against
Spicky signs for my rhyme-y rhymes, look at the times
Sick as the mind of the motherfuckin' skin skanny skind
Dosy ocean techosim um dip oceans explodin'
Tempers flaring from parents just blow ee owe ee o-opin ...'

I know this spit so well. I nailed the lyrics years ago. Well, I know most of them. If you don't know a particular line in a rap song, then it's easy to just flow over it. Just make similar sounds to the rapper. Everyone does it, it's simple. I sway in front of Ryan, moving my arms to the beat of the track, spitting out the lyrics. It's such a good fuckin tune. I try to think what the dance is like in the *Reservoir Dogs* scene. I think I know it. It doesn't really suit this beat, but I make up my own version. I pace my moves to and from Ryan, just to freak him the fuck out. That's the way the guy does it in the movie. I feel sinister cool right now. This is the feeling I've been chasing all me life. I palm the blade in my right hand. I bet Ryan is shitting himself. He must think I'm a fuckin psycho.

11:00

Ryan

MY NOSE IS STILL STINGING FROM THAT LINE OF COKE. I REALLY DIDN'T want it. At least he's left me alone now. He's too busy changing channels on the TV. He wants to know where the music channels are. He eventually settles for a channel with adverts on and then walks out of the room. He's unpredictable, I'll give him that. His departure gives me time to really tug away at the tape around my left wrist. It's tough to get a good grip on it to free myself. I have to give up when I hear him strolling back into the room. He appears in front of me, his arms flapping.

What the fuck is he doing?

He begins mouthing away to the Eminem song that's started playing on the TV. *Holy shit, he's seriously rapping this shit to me.* He doesn't even know the words. I feel like laughing but for the absurdity of it all.

Is he dancing? Is that supposed to be dancing? This guy's a fuckin' psycho! He swings his hips trusting towards me and then back to the TV. *Seriously. Is that dancing? What is going on?*

It's 'Sick as the mind of a motherfuckin' kid that's behind' not 'Sick as the mind of the motherfuckin' skin skanny skind' for fuck's sake. I'm beginning to think I'm on a hidden camera TV show right now. I actually look up into the two corners of the room facing me to see if there are cameras bearing down on us. That's how long it takes me to take that delusion away from the realm of possibilities. I'm snapping right back to reality when the prick sits on my lap facing me, still rapping made-up lyrics. This is getting so much fuckin' weirder with every passing second.

177

I'm not sure if he's grinding on me or whether he's continuing the dance that led him here. I feel frozen. Stunned. Then he produces a razor blade in his hand and holds it right in front of my stare. A ton of thoughts float through my mind, but at the forefront is the dreaded feeling that this guy is going to cut my fucking balls off. His grinding continues as he lifts the blade with one hand while grabbing at my left ear with the other.

Holy fuck. This kid thinks he's in Reservoir Dogs. *He can't be for real. Can he?* I react like any man would, even though it will give my game away. I jab my knee right up into his bollocks. It goes deep, as hard as I can muster. He squeals like a cat, and slumps to the floor. The squealing lasts long enough, but the silence that follows is going on way too long. He remains curled up in front of me. I think about making a jump for the gun but pause just as he stirs. I'm an idiot. I wasted valuable seconds there when I should have jumped. Even with the chair tied to my left arm I would have had a big advantage over him. I didn't think his pain was going to take that long to recede. He finally manages to shift himself into a sitting position on the floor, pinning the top of his back up against the edge of the glass table.

'I was only fuckin' messin' with ya, fag. I wasn't going to cut your ear off. Who do you think I am?' he snaps back at me.

'A murderer, a kidnapper. Isn't that what you told me you were?' I reply like a hero. But I need to shut the fuck up. I need to get him back focused on something else, anything but me. I'm almost free. How has he not noticed that my legs are no longer taped? How does he think I managed to knee him so hard in the balls?

'Listen, dude,' I say, cringing. I hate the word 'dude' but he said it earlier on and it's stuck at the forefront of my mind. 'There's an hour left till the deadline. Can we both just wait it out? Go back to watching TV or somethin'?'

'I'm in charge here, fag,' he replies, lifting himself slowly to a standing position. 'I'll decide what we'll do. You ever knee me in the bollocks like that again and I *will* cut your fuckin' ear off, boy, d'ye hear me?'

'Understood,' I say, nodding my head while he waves the razor blade in my face.

'Right,' he says, limping back to the couch. 'What's normally on this time of the day? Do you watch *Jeopardy?*'

Brady won my heart in the short elevator ride we took to the sixth floor of the Travelodge. He was adorable. He kept asking how Nicole was and if I thought they could ever be husband and wife one day. Guilt welled up inside me. I could feel it as I stared down at him. He chatted away without removing the smile from his face. I bet his parents were really proud of him. He was super cute. He bounced up on the bed like any ten-year-old would when we entered the room. He was still asking questions about Nicole. It would break his heart if I told him I was really Nicole and that I'd been the person Facebook messaging him for the past eight weeks. But I couldn't tell him. It was all part of the act. I needed to persuade him that Nicole had insisted he was sexually active before she met him. I'd been told that once I was in this situation, showing him the porn movies and telling him what the girl wanted from him, I'd be able to close the deal one hundred per cent of the time. I practically had little Brady by the balls.

'What videos does Nicole want me to watch?' he spat out. It was about the hundredth question he'd asked, but it was one I took time to answer. I rubbed my face in frustration.

'She ... eh ... she – you know what?' I said, kneeling down to touch his face as he sat on the edge of the bed. 'I forgot the tapes.'

'Oh no,' he said, appearing really disappointed in me. 'How could you?'

'I ... I'll tell you what. Next time I'll bring Nicole with me, huh? And you two can watch the tapes together. I just need to tell her if I think you are a good guy.'

'And do you?'

'Do I what?' I asked.

'Think I'm a good guy?'

'I think you're adorable,' I said, kissing him on the forehead.

He beamed a wide grin at me as an awkward silence filled the room. I took the time to think, rubbing at my face again.

'Go on. Go. I'll tell Nicole you'd be the perfect boyfriend. I promise.'

11:10

Jack

DINAH HAS THE AIR CONDITIONING TURNED ON. I FIND HER OFFICE perfectly cool. It helps me breathe. I am certain I'm coming across as normal to her. I'll miss Dinah. She knows our meetings are coming to an end anyway. It's been a couple of months since I last met with her. Before that, I hadn't seen her since before Christmas. We used to meet every week, at the same time of the same day – nine a.m. Thursdays. We'd sit and talk for over an hour about my grieving. Well, that's not strictly true. We would talk about anything. Sports, politics, Dublin, my family, her family – or lack of it – and anything else that popped up. We talked like friends talk but I always knew that the conversation would eventually swing around to how I had been handling my losses. Dinah didn't have to assist with my feelings of guilt. That's a bullshit feeling to have after somebody's died. It's supposed to be a natural part of the grieving process but I leapfrogged it. It's a waste of time. You can never go back, so stewing on feelings such as guilt is a hundred per cent pointless. I began to really understand that soon after Karyn passed. Denial and bargaining are two further features of the grieving process that I didn't need counselling for. Again, they're a total waste of time. Of course, you should accept what's happened to you. It's happened. Deal with it. But I needed Dinah to help me with the anger I felt – not with Karyn's passing, but with Frank's.

It's been eighteen months since I first met with her. I feel slightly sad that I'm going to give her my usual goodbye hug in about five minutes' time, never to see her again. She doesn't know for certain that I'll never visit, but she's aware that I feel I no longer need her. I'm one of her best clients. I guess it helps when you can be open-minded enough to skip most of the processes she has to help you get through. I smile and nod at her as she tells me about the holiday she's just returned from. She and her husband have just been to Oslo. She'd always wanted to go but couldn't afford it. Bereavement counsellors mustn't be paid an awful lot. They should be. I'm not sure what her husband Tom does but I know this is the first time they've holidayed together outside Ireland since they met. She's not suffering from post-vacation blues. She's still smiling from the delights of the Norwegian capital.

'You need to visit,' she insists, staring at me over the top of her retro-style glasses frames.

'I will, I promise,' I say, lying to her. It's such a shame to lie to Dinah.

'So you just wanted to drop by to let me know everything is okay?'

'That's all. I figured I hadn't seen you in too long, so wanted to say hi,' I lie again.

'You look great.'

'I hope I look half as good as you,' I return. 'I guess I need ten days in Oslo, huh?'

Dinah tries to bring up Frank but I bat it away politely. She probably noticed, but she won't be surprised. I don't mind talking about Frank. I'd talk about Frank to anybody. But I don't want to talk about the whys or the hows; why Frank died, how Frank died. I just don't. My mind has to move forward.

I stayed with the Ritchies for eight long days after we lost Frank. I had nowhere else to turn. I think I was depressed, but I mostly remember feeling shocked. Or stunned. It was certainly surreal. I felt like I was walking around in another world. Harry was devastated. He cried for seven of those eight days. As soon as he started talking about revenge I decided to go back to my own place. That was tough. Walking into Frank's bedroom for the first time since I lost him was heart-breaking. I fell onto his bed and allowed it to swallow me up as I forced out some tears. I only cried because I felt I should. I'm not sure it did me any good. His room didn't feel right. The cops had been in days ago, searching through all his belongings and, although they did their best to restore everything, it didn't look the same to me.

The sight of a cop standing at the front of your house, pursing their lips in sorrow, is something that tattoos the brain. I'll always remember Declan O'Reilly's face even though I have tried my best to forget it. He was only a young Garda, maybe in his late twenties. I've often wondered if I was the first person he ever had to bring such heart-breaking news to. His pale face told me Frank was dead. I didn't even have to listen to his words. I stumbled back into the hallway before flopping myself on the bottom step of our staircase. I was always conscious, always aware of what was happening, always aware of what I'd just been told. The surreality kicked in two days later, when I was being smothered by the entire Ritchie clan. They did help in some ways, I guess. I needed people around me. I distinctly remember the pain of Frank's death as being physical. My bones and my muscles genuinely throbbed with pain. And I never thought that pain would ease. I believed I was destined for a lifetime of hurt. Bizarrely I'm fulfilled now; happier than I've ever been. My life is exciting, more exciting than I ever thought possible.

'You know I'd still like to see you on a regular basis,' Dinah says.

She mentions this every time I see her. She's proud of how I've recovered, but I'm pretty sure deep down she feels I got over my losses way too quickly. She thinks I will wake up one morning and a grief explosion will go off inside my stomach. She sees contentment in me, but she has no idea that I'm actually filled with joy. That my life without Frank has actually been largely exciting. I came up with this plan a couple of months after I lost my son and I'm buzzing with anticipation. My new life is going to be perfect. Our new life is going to be perfect.

'I'll come a-calling any time I feel like I need a Dinah hug,' I reply.

'I know you will, Jack. You'll always be my favourite.' She says this every time too. She doesn't precede it with 'I really shouldn't say this, but …' anymore.

When I stand up to embrace her I know I've nailed it. This meeting went as swift and as normal as any of our last few meetings. A drop by. A catch-up. I've been the exact same person I have always been when I'm in this little office. Dinah would have no idea that I am masterminding the greatest bank robbery Ireland has ever seen at this very moment. If – and it's a big if – I ever need an alibi for this morning, I've just perfected one. I haven't looked at the time since getting to the help centre. I didn't want to look at a clock any time I was there, consciously. Dinah couldn't say I was preoccupied in our short meeting. She could genuinely just say I was focused on her. But I guess it must be around eleven-fifteen now. Maybe eleven-twenty. I pace towards my car trying not to get noticed by Trevor. He's still sitting in his own car, about ten or fifteen minutes after meeting with Dinah. Poor fella. He winds his window down as I pass by.

'That was quick,' he calls over to me.

Ah, shit, he's getting out of the car. He purses his lips at me again. This guy is desperate for consolation. I have nothing to say to him. I could rant on and on about him having to deal with the hand that he's been dealt, that his story is his story and he needs to just continue it, that his wife's passing was just a big blemish in the narrative of his life. But I don't have the time for that. I also don't have the personality for it either. I'm too nice a guy to be that blunt to a stranger.

'I … I just see Dinah every now and then for a quick catch-up. She's been very good to me,' I reply.

'Me too.' He smiles. 'She's a huge help.'

I think about patting him on the shoulder and walking away in the immediate silence that follows, but his mouth beats me to it.

'Liver cancer, it was,' he says, looking at his feet.

Jesus, do we really need to do this?

'I'm … I'm really sorry, Trevor. You know … keep seeing Dinah. Tell her everything. She will get you through this. I promise.'

'She's already helping,' he says, trying to sound upbeat. But he's failing. This guy is miserable. 'And you … your wife?' he asks, looking back up at me.

'Skin cancer. Thirteen years ago now. She was gone within six months of diagnosis. Went right through her.'

He looks a little puzzled. 'Same as your son? Was it cancer too?'

'No. No,' I say almost laughing. I don't know why I almost laugh. I think it's the manner in which he seems obsessed with cancer. 'He was killed. Got into a fight one night … y'know.' I shrug. 'One punch and … he was gone.'

11:10

Vincent

'And the last one, Mr Butler,' Noah says, sliding the paperwork towards me.

I'm eyeballing him, not the paperwork. Why has he been so quick reading this? He basically skim-read through the pages, far from as thorough as Chelle or Jonathan were. I should have stopped him, insisted he read every word clearly for me. But I really need to get the fuck out of here. I feel a little disappointed with myself because I let Noah get away with something. I suck my teeth signing the last page. Noah must think I'm still upset with him over his staff not calling him 'Mister'. Then again, perhaps he thinks I'm always upset with him over something. I've never been nice to Noah. I've never been polite to him. It's odd. I'm a really nice person. I'm certain I'm not the only one who thinks that. All my colleagues would consider me fair. Stern, but fair. I wouldn't say people would have reasons to dislike me. Noah would, though. He's probably the only one. Which is why it annoys me that he's always really nice and polite to me. He's got to be fake. He's got to be a fraud.

'Ready, Mr Butler? Three, two—'

I interrupt. 'Hold on, Noah. I'll do the countdown. Okay? Three, two and one.'

We both swipe our keys to enter the first door of the vault. *Fuck you, Voss*, I think, before realising that really was a petty little victory. I shouldn't let this fucker get to me. I need to stay in character. Stay in control. I need to get this job done. Ryan's dimples flash through my mind. He's still kinda cute.

We started to clash when he was home all the time. I didn't have my respite after work. I just wanted an hour to myself to tune out. I always had that when he was working evenings at Wow. But I started to miss that luxury from my day. It irritated me. Ryan didn't irritate me, the circumstance did. But I still took it out on him. I'd casually ask about his novel in the first couple of months, not really caring about the answer. His response was always vague. I just thought I should ask. We began to fuck a lot more then. I think he was bored all day and sex crossed his mind more often. Besides, he wasn't fucking anybody else behind my back for the first time in a while. All his erections were for me. I understood he was most likely living out another fantasy in his head when we were fucking, but I actually appreciated and enjoyed the sex. It was a workout. Besides, most people imagine anybody but the person they're fucking when they're having sex, don't they? I do.

Our relationship was in the 'okay' status, I would have thought. I loved him and hated him in about equal measure and I think he felt the same way about me at that stage. I guess being in an 'okay' relationship is about the average for any couple. But what really bothered me most was that my professional life had sunk to 'okay' status too. I was always a high-flyer. I was always somebody. I felt like somebody when I walked around Dublin. I had control over important matters in this city. But I felt I was starting to become less significant. I could feel it. My walk even changed. There was less of a bounce to it. I knew I was lucky after the redundancies were handed down in early 2009. The board told me they wanted me to stay on as overseer of the four remaining banks. It was a huge responsibility. But there are some days when I think I was actually the unlucky one. Soon after the restructure of the branches, the elderly board members started to wilt away. Slightly earlier-than-they-thought retirement decisions were made and I was left with a naïve board who didn't involve me in any decision-making. It's such a shame. If I had been operating in this position under the previous board I think we'd be back to a similar situation to the one we were in before the recession. As it stands now, we're making slow progress. The progress because of me, the slow because of them. I didn't have a midlife crisis, I had a midlife settlement with myself. I remember sitting down one evening while watching a Bill Maher clip on YouTube and realising I was okay with 'okay'. I was too lazy for anything other than 'okay'. I was beginning to distance myself from social occasions and even reduced Chelle to just a colleague. I was content getting up for work at seven o'clock every morning and arriving home at six-thirty in the evening to crash on the couch with Ryan. I couldn't claim to be the happiest man in the world, but given that the experts were saying one in three people will suffer with depression at some point in their lives and I happened to steer clear of it all my life, being 'okay' was okay by me.

I stand parallel to Noah, intently glaring at his face out of the corner of my eyes. I don't even blink. I really don't understand this guy.

Why did he race through the paperwork? Why does he seem in as much of a rush as I am?

Maybe it's just that I'm such a great boss that when I suggest I'm in a hurry, you are too. It's not even Noah's rushing that's bothering me about him. It's just his face, his bullshit-believing face. I hate it. Even the breaths he's breathing in between each count of ten bundles are annoying me.

'Stop fuckin' breathing,' I spit out of my mouth as if I've got Tourette's. I said what I was thinking. He looks up at me in disbelief. A silence fills the vault and I know it's totally my responsibility to put an end to it.

'Eh … so loudly. Sorry. It's echoing in here and I can't concentrate on counting along with you.' He's still staring at me, his mouth slightly ajar. So he should. What a ridiculous thing to say to somebody. *Stop breathing.* Fuckin' hell!

'I'm sorry, I'm sorry. That was a really rude thing to say, Noah,' I continue, filling the second silence.

I touch him on the shoulder. I'm sure a vision has flashed past his eyes where he saw himself punching my lights out. I wonder if Noah has a really dark side. I'm sure he does. Most of these Jesus freaks are fronting for a secret life of darkness.

'That's okay, Mr Butler,' he finally says, flashing me his bright pink gums again. They're revolting.

'No, no. I am sorry. Please forget I said that. Please. I'm just under a lot of stress.'

I cringe when he takes his eyes off me. I can feel the embarrassment shudder through my insides. I have never been that rude to anybody in my entire life. I'm just feeling so stressed. I look at my watch. It's almost twenty past eleven. Fuck me. I've forty minutes left.

'Come on, Noah. Let's finish counting these notes, pal.'

11:20

Jack

I FIND IT DIFFICULT TO GET TREVOR'S SAD FACE OUT OF MY HEAD. BUT I need to refocus. His puppy-dog eyes made me want to hug him and then slap him across the face. 'Move. The. Hell. On.' I felt like screaming at him. Poor sod. My heart went out to him, but I had to make an excuse to get away. I'm glad I bumped into him, though. He gifted me another witness, just in case. After I get to the car and put my wig and beard back on, I hit the standby button on my cheap mobile phone and when the light finally flashes on, I call Darragh. I'm not sure whether I should make my way to Church Street to catch Vincent coming out, or whether I should go straight to the IFSC to watch him enter the fourth and final bank. Either way, I know where I'm driving to now.

'Hey,' Darragh says, answering quickly. He mustn't be letting that phone out of his sight.

'No word from Vincent about Church Street?'

'Not yet. Probably be another ten minutes, I reckon. Time is really tight, JR. Are you sure you don't—'

'Darragh!' I snap down the line at him. 'Me and you, buddy. This is our plan.'

'You're right,' he says. 'I'll call you as soon as he's out of Church Street. Shouldn't be long.'

'How's Ryan?' I ask. It's for a reason. I want to make sure he hasn't been getting into Darragh's head. It's always been imperative that Darragh keeps Ryan under control.

'Grand,' he replies. I don't know what the hell Cork people mean when they say 'grand'. They use it all the time.

'What d'ye mean, grand? He's keeping quiet, yeah? You still have him taped up, around his mouth?

'Yes, JR,' he almost moans back at me. He hates being told anything twice. The problem is, he needs to be told things multiple times. I drilled every aspect of this morning into his head every day for months.

'Good man,' I say before tapping the red button on the phone and starting the car's ignition again.

I'm off to Parnell Street. That's where this car's being left. It'll probably be discovered as having not moved in about a week's time, but it won't link back to me. None of the three cars I'm driving today will. I learned from the best. A walk to Church Street to see Vincent come out of there or to Mayor Street to watch him enter is about eight to ten minutes either way. That's why I chose Parnell Street as the place to leave the first car. Just in case I was caught in this decision. I've thought of everything.

I pleaded with Harry to allow me to handle the hunt for Frank's killer. Even before we'd buried my son, Harry and the lads had been doing their own investigation. Revenge is their reaction to anything, let alone murder. They were ahead of the cops from day one. Sinead, the girl Frankie had picked up in a bar that night, somehow led the police in the wrong direction. She was certain the three lads who encroached on them had come from the opposite side of Tallaght to the one they actually had. That tiny bit of misinformation, innocent to the core, set the cops off on the wrong track. From there, Harry was steps ahead and, within a week or two, the cops allowed him to take control. They continued on their phony investigation, knowing Harry was steering them in the wrong direction. They were happy to do this. The cops in Ireland are like that. They're happy for gangland feuds to play themselves out without having to get in the middle of them. The closer Harry got to finding out who killed Frankie, the more anxious I was getting. I didn't want Frank's death to begin another gangland feud. So I stepped in. I almost got down on my hands and knees to beg Harry to let me take control. I had, unbeknown to him, been led to believe that the killer was part of the Alan Keating gang. If Harry had ever found that out, and he wasn't far off learning it, it would have begun a turf war in the city. I wanted no part in that. Dublin had had enough of that shit for way too long. Frank wasn't involved in that sort of nonsense when he was alive and he certainly wasn't going to be part of it in his death.

'I trust you to do the right thing, Jack,' Harry said, staring into my eyes.

I could see it was paining him to not be directly involved in the revenge on Frank's killer. But he understood my need to see this through for myself.

'I promise I will, Harry. For Frank, for Karyn. I'll make this right.' I had no idea what I was going to do. But I knew if I was the only person who knew who Frank's killer was, then I could buy myself some time to think it all through. Harry had given me great experience on how to investigate without leaving a trace. I'd seen it all before when I used to work for him. His expertise as a gangster really lies in keeping his hands clean. After about a month of chopping my own way through the maze Harry had set me out on, I finally found out who killed Frank.

I feel the phone buzz just as I'm parking up in Parnell Street.

'He's out,' Darragh says.

'That was quick,' I reply, looking at my watch. It's just shy of eleven-thirty.

'He said he got in and out of Church Street within twenty minutes because the manager there is a good friend of his.'

That doesn't sound right to me. Noah Voss is manager of Church Street. Odd.

'And he's all good? He has all two mill?'

'Yeah. It went great. He's made back some time. Just over half an hour to go to the IFSC and out. He's gonna do this, JR. He's gonna do it!'

I can sense the excitement in Darragh's voice. This is not about the money for him. I genuinely believe that. He is excited because of the thrill of the robbery alone. All he's ever wanted to be is a gangster.

'Okay, calm it down, Darragh. Keep cool in front of Ryan. Maybe you're right. We could have all eight mill pretty soon. As I've always said, stick to the plan. You're doing a great job, buddy.' Then I hang up.

Vincent's swiftness in Church Street makes me pause for thought but I really shouldn't let it stop me in my tracks. I need to get out of this car. I shouldn't be noticed in it. The phone call has made my next decision for me. I didn't get to see Vincent walk out of Church Street so I've got to head to Mayor Street at the IFSC. I might get there before him.

11:25

Vincent

EVEN WALKING OUT OF THE CHURCH STREET BRANCH WITH THE TWO CASES cuffed to me, I'm trying to figure Noah out. I guess I never will. I got in and out of there within twenty minutes. And I thought that would be the difficult branch. I can't get the 'stop breathing' line out of my head. I'm laughing about it while I pace towards the car. Imagine telling somebody to stop breathing? For fuck's sake. I look up to see John smiling back at me. I shouldn't be seen smiling today, surely. Reality hits. Ryan has only about a half an hour left to live.

'Quick as you can, John,' I say, holding the briefcases up. As I uncuff them, John throws them on top of the others in the back of the boot. That's odd. He's normally so careful. I really am a good boss. If I'm in a hurry, so are you.

'Mayor Street, John boy,' I say, hopping back into the cool air. 'As quick as you can.'

I immediately call Ryan's captor.

'All done in Church Street,' I tell him and hang up.

Fuck him. He'll probably ring back. I allow myself to come out of character listening to Tchaikovsky while I wait. At least I think it's still Tchaikovsky playing. I imagine what the outcome of this robbery will mean for ACB. The board will hardly bat an eyelid, I bet. I wonder if this could cause one of the branches to close. I hope they choose Church Street if they have to choose any of them. But the reality is, it might not mean a whole lot for the company. Eight million euros is really a drop in the ocean and it will be covered by our insurance companies. It'll be a complicated mess, but it should be swept over in time. ACB branches have been robbed on six occasions in the time I've worked for them. Only once has a bank ever been robbed that I've been in. It was in my early days as a junior employee at ACB, when I was trying to work my way up through the ranks. Two guys entered in masks and held one of my colleagues at gunpoint while insisting the cash tills were emptied into a black plastic bag. I watched on with my fear diminishing into nothingness within seconds. The notes kept falling out of the black plastic bag and the two thieves were forced to scramble around the floor picking them up. We all eyeballed each other awkwardly. They managed to get out of the bank within seven minutes with €110,000, never to be caught. It's not that easy to rob a bank these days. The double door buzz system has killed any attempts at a quick in-and-out cash-till theft. I've always been at the forefront of any advances in security. I think that's why the branches I've worked at since becoming a manager have never been robbed. ACB was one of the first banks in the whole of Ireland to use the double door buzz system and I was the one who pushed for it. The unique thing about this theft is that nobody knows this is happening, so no lives are at risk in the branches. Nobody has a gun pointed at them. Except Ryan, of course. Poor Ryan. I sneak a look over John's shoulder to check the time. 11:28. Half an hour left. I need to get back into character. I need to look like this is an ordinary day. Ken Lockhart won't be much of a problem. He may be over-thorough with the paperwork, but I'll be able to hurry him up.

Ken joined ACB a couple of years after me. He wasn't as good as me initially, but he's learned from the best by now. He's a mini-me. In work mode, not looks. Ken is short and fat; I'm just a little podgy. Ken has round chubby cheeks and a constantly smiling face that makes him endearing to people. But I know the Ken behind that smile. He has a dark side. Not too dark. He's just moody. I think he tries so hard to be nice in public that when he crashes down from that, he crashes hard. As it turned out, most of Ken's crashes coincided with him drinking alcohol. It didn't matter what it was: beer, whisky, spirits, wine. Ken would turn into a totally different person when he had a drink. He threw a punch at me one night. He blamed me for bitching behind his back, but what Ken came to finally realise was he harboured bizarre paranoia traits when he drank. He would just make stuff up off the top of his head and believe it to be true. It sounds so strange, yet it's so common. Everybody knows somebody with this affliction. I've been told it goes undiagnosed in up to ninety per cent of people. But Ken was one of the lucky ones. Thanks to me, he visited a psychiatrist who detailed exactly what was happening to him. He stopped drinking about seven years ago, but he still has mood swings every now and then. He's capable of turning from the happiest man on the planet to depressed in a split second. He manages to keep it under control in work. That saddens me. I know Ken is all smiles all day in the bank and then goes home to feel depressed. And he has nobody to go home to. He owns a beautiful terraced home in Donnybrook but it's wasted on him. He tells me he has good neighbours and a circle of friends that he hangs out with at the weekends. I have to believe him. I spend a lot of my thinking time hoping it's true. I just felt like I couldn't do any more for him. I led him to the psychiatrist and I ensured he got one of the assistant manager positions when the bank restructured. That's surely enough. He runs a decent branch too. He's always done as I suggested, which was why I wanted him as one of the assistant managers. He better do as I suggest today. And quickly.

As John turns onto the quay, I look at my watch. It's just gone half past. This is going to be so tight. We're a couple of minutes from the branch. I need to get in and out of there in less than twenty-five minutes. It's doable.

Stay in character. Don't be anything other than regular Vincent. Stern but fair. One more branch and I am done.

Ryan's dimples flash through my mind again. I'm trying not to think of him. I reach for my iPhone and decide to turn it on again. It takes ages to load up. I notice John turn into the IFSC as my voicemail robot tells me I have two new messages. I sure as hell hope Jonathan isn't one of them.

'Hello, Mr Butler, this is Gareth calling from Vodafone, we'd just like to ask how you are …' I hang up. Fuck off, Vodafone. There's a longer pause than normal before the next message. At least it seems that way. I'd like to listen to it before John pulls over. Shit! It's Jonathan again. Fuckin' meddling asshole.

'Vincent …' he stumbles. 'What's going on? I'm here with Belinda, she says … I've, eh … I've also been onto Michelle.'

Shit!

'She says you've taken two million from her branch this morning as well. I'm sure you know what you're … doing, and it's for good cause, but can you … Tell you what, gimme a call back when you're ready.'

I hit five to listen to the message again. I want to find out what time it was left at. Eleven twenty-six. About seven minutes ago. This is fucked up. The car has pulled over on Mayor Street right outside the branch and

John is making his way around to me to open the door. I didn't even notice us stop. I take these seconds to think about what to do. I have to ring Jonathan back. I have to quench that fire. The little cunt is in my office, drooling over Belinda's tits, I bet. I'm about to dial when Ken pops his fat head into the car, scooting John out of his way.

'What's going on, Vincent?' he asks. 'Jonathan's just been onto me.'

11:30

Darragh

ME GUT IS JUST SETTLING AFTER THAT KNEE TO THE BOLLIX. I'VE NEVER felt pain like that in me life. I wanted to get up and shoot the cunt in the head there and then. But while I was flaked out in pain, I kept hearin' JR's voice.

Stick to the plan.

I shouldn't even be tryna fuck with this fag's head anyway. I just need to wait it out until I'm instructed to leave or shoot. There's not long to go now. I stare at the phone in my hand.

Should I just ring that fucker back?

'All done in Church Street.' Cheeky cunt.

'What is the capital city of Poland?' I shout out.

I'm good at *Jeopardy*. Ah shit. I'm wrong. I'm having a bad game today. I thought Ascunsion was in Poland. Paraguay? At least it begins with P. I was on the right track. The fag hasn't answered one question yet. Dope. I love a bit of *Jeopardy*. I love the cheesy ass American TV game shows ye get on during the day. I look at the phone again. Fuck Vincent. If he's done, he's done. We've six million guaranteed now. I'll just get onto JR to give him the good news.

JR and me started out lightly. He used to order me to rob some shops of their tills just to test me nerves, I think. He didn't need convincing for long. He put his trust in me early. He proved it by sticking to his word and splittin' everything down the middle. We weren't makin' much money but he told me that would come with time. He let me in on his big

194

plan and said it could involve a murder and wondered if I'd be okay to follow through if it came down to that. I told him about the murder I'd committed before. If I couldn't trust JR, who could I trust? He's the closest friend I've ever had. I told him that first murder was just an accident but I let him know it gave me the appetite to kill again. JR knows what I mean by appetite to kill. He's been there, done it all, even before I was born. His master plan sounded fuckin deadly the moment he first told me it. He kept the fine details away from me at first, but I knew the big picture. I knew it involved a bank heist and a possible murder. That fuckin excited me. I couldn't wait. We'd meet once or twice a week in the Deer's Head, talkin' shit. JR wasn't just interested in my future, he was keen on my past too. I'd open up to him about how me family left me oul fella behind in Cork to fuck off to Dublin. I even told him how I fell out with me sisters after me ma died and that I was left with nothing until The Boss took me on. I'd never told anyone that before. I don't know if I should look at JR as, like, a da or a brother. I guess he's just me best mate. He's always had me best interests at heart. I didn't need to tell him much about The Boss. He knew him well. It's a small old world, the underworld. JR was aware of what level I'd been able to get to with The Boss. He also knew I was hungry for more. When he sat me down and told me the story of how his former boss had tracked down some scum rapist just outside of Mayo, he got me excited. He wanted me to rob him, then kill him. He used to spike women's drinks before dragging them into his car and rapin' 'em. I couldn't wait to kill the fucker. Throughout the entire four-hour drive to Mayo, I imagined blowing his brains out. Killing somebody is every bit as powerful as you would think it would be. Ever since I knocked that poor fucker's head off the step, I've wanted to kill again. But this time for real. To mean it. I can still hear the rapist cunt denying what I was saying to him.

It wasn't me, you have the wrong man.

'Any last requests?' Bang! Fuck you.

Remembering the high of that killing makes me itch to do it again. I allow meself a little look at Ryan. He's still glued to the TV. He still hasn't answered a question on *Jeopardy* yet. It's mad to think I could be blowin' his brains out in less than half an hour.

'Who is, eh … who is – what's 'is name?' I rush out of my mouth after turning me attention back to the telly.

'Richard Hawkins,' says Ryan.

'Yeah … yeah … yeah, Richard Hawkins,' I shout at the TV.

Correct! That's four I've got right today, now. Maybe it's not been such a bad game for me. I have a *Jeopardy* app on my phone; I'm good at it. But I don't have me phone with me, of course. It's at home. I'll have a game of it when I get back. I need to head straight home after this. I have to follow through on the alibi JR made for me. Me laptop's been pinging all morning. I can't believe the next time I'll have a game of *Jeopardy* on me phone, I'll be a multi-fuckin-millionaire. Holy shit! A wave of adrenaline runs up me stomach, just where the pain was a few minutes ago. I breathe deeply and try to refocus on *Jeopardy* when I notice Ryan leap out of his chair.

11:35

Vincent

COMING CLEAN IS CROSSING MY MIND. I'M ALWAYS HONEST TO KEN. I THINK about telling him the truth: telling him Ryan is being held hostage in our apartment until I return with eight million euros. Tell him to keep fucking quiet about it though until I'm finished. That it will save my boyfriend's life. But my gut's fighting coming clean.

'I'm taking two mill from each branch,' I say to Ken as I wrap my arm around him and head towards the bank's entrance. I'm bluffing. I have no idea where I'm going with this.

'It's a test,' I continue slowly. I'm trying to buy myself time. Time to think. 'The … the board have asked me to test security at each bank. They want me to … to see if each manager will hand out two million.'

'What?' he says, a smile beginning to show on his face. He looks as if his day just got a whole lot more interesting. 'So … what do I—'

'Just get me the money,' I say, smiling back at him.

'What, is it good to give you the money? I don't …'

'No. No it's not. Not really,' I reply. 'But that's what I want. I want them to beef up security. I need this to fail. Michelle, Jonathan and Noah have handed it over and I need you to also.' Ken will do anything for me. I'm sure of it.

'But won't that put me in a bad light with the board? I mean, if … if it's not right to give you two mill … Hang on a minute. It is okay to give you two million though, right? There is no limit we can transfer between banks. So this doesn't add up.'

197

'They're just testing everybody. Me, you, the other assistant managers. Let's just get this over with and see what they're looking for from all of us. I guess they're testing timescales and … I don't know. I genuinely don't know,' I say, creasing my brow at him as we're buzzed through the second door. 'There's a meeting tomorrow that all of us need to attend. That's all I know. I haven't told you about this, okay?'

'Okay. No problem, Vincent,' he says. His smile still hasn't faded, even though he's as confused as he possibly could be. My improvisation wasn't great. My story is filled with holes. But I did the best I could, thinking on my feet. Ken is leading me into his office when my iPhone buzzes. It's Noah. Holy fuck!

My 'okay' life stayed okay for a number of months, but it started to wane. I'd only have to hear Ryan rustling around in our kitchen for me to get pissed off with him. Everything he did seemed to annoy me. So, I started to annoy him, purposely. I'd ask him about the progress he was making on the book with more regularity.

'It's a work in progress,' he would repeat.

I didn't buy it. I also didn't care. I was just irritating him for the sake of irritating him. I wasn't even snooping when I opened his laptop one Saturday afternoon when he was out. He said he was off doing some research for his book. Maybe he was. I didn't give it much thought, to be honest. I was happy he was doing something different and out of my way for a couple of hours. My laptop was on our bed and Ryan's was nearer to me as I slobbed on our couch, so I picked his up out of pure laziness. There was fuck all on the TV and I wanted to pass a boring afternoon watching shit videos on YouTube.

I searched for the Google Chrome browser but it was nowhere to be seen. I know Ryan likes to use Safari, but I've always found it a weak search browser. It was only when I tried to download Chrome that I realised he already had it. Weird. A search through the desktop led me to it in a hidden folder. It kept getting weirder. The browser history was totally blank. There was only one reason for that. He'd been deleting it. I'm not very tech savvy, but I know that much. As it turned out, I certainly knew more than Ryan. Deleting the history only deletes it from the history section of the browser but not from the entire hard drive. I had to Google how to relocate his activity, but it didn't take long for thousands of URLs to flash up before me. I sat upright on the couch. Ryan had clearly been addicted to a forum called honeypotcommunity. I had to have a snoop. I was gobsmacked. There was an ongoing chat sitting at the top of the first page I opened by two scumbags who called themselves

ItalianoStalliano and TeenCum069. They were sharing sick videos of kiddy porn. I could see that from the still screen of one of the videos before even pressing play. Waves of nausea echoed through my body. I couldn't watch. Instead, I read the discussion these two sick fucks were having. One of them was telling the other how to lure kids through Facebook. I knew Ryan's novel was supposed to be dark, but I racked my brain to remember if he had mentioned any paedophile subplots in it. I couldn't think straight. There was a constant pinging sound in my ear. I couldn't shake it off. Why the fuck would Ryan be reading these forums? What would he get from it? He'd been through thousands of pages of this stuff. So many questions ran through my mind, so much so that I couldn't answer any of them. I figured Ryan must be trying to get into the mindset of a paedophile for his book. That was the only logical explanation for this sick shit. He must have been reading these forums to understand how these scumbags work, how they operate. I remember feeling certain that Ryan wouldn't have pressed play on any of the videos. The two cunts exchanging tips on the forum made my blood boil. The discussion was really sick. I scrolled to the top of the page to take note of the home URL of the website. I figured I'd have to ask Ryan about it. That was when I noticed the login details in the top corner. They read: 'ItalianoStalliano signed in'.

Holy fuck. Ryan was one of these sick cunts!

'Mr Butler, Jonathan just rang and said you are taking two million euros from every branch today. Did you lie to—' Noah attempts to ask sternly. I don't let him finish.

'Noah,' I sigh. 'You're sticking your nose in where it doesn't belong. You are actually ruining a very good security examination.'

'I'm sorry, Mr Butler. I don't understand.' Neither do I.

'I'll, eh ... I'll call you back in two minutes, Noah. Bear with me. Do not speak to anyone. Not to any of your staff or to any of the board. I will explain everything in two minutes.' This is a mess. I take a look at the screen of the phone after I hang up. 11:41. Holy shit.

'Ken,' I demand like a sergeant in the army. 'Get the paperwork signed. Bring it out to me to sign and then let's get to your vaults as soon as possible, okay?'

'Okay,' he replies. He looks perplexed. I don't have much time to think my way out of this mess.

11:35

Ryan

IT'S HARDER TO PICK AWAY AT THE TAPE ON MY WRIST. BUT I'M DOING THE best I can. I think the best way to get this off is to loosen it upwards and slide my arm out. Easier said than done. Each tug painfully plucks a hair from my hand. It's like mini torture. I could probably be more aggressive in my approach but I don't want to stir the prick, especially when I'm so close to getting free. If I needed any confirmation that this fucker is as stupid as I felt he was, then having *Jeopardy* on the TV has nailed it. He's swept away by the quiz show, not paying any attention to me as he embarrassingly gets each question wrong. He's a fuckin' retard.

'He is author of *The God Delusion* and *The Greatest Show on Earth?*' asks the host. It's the first question I've genuinely listened to. *The God Delusion* caught my attention. Vincent has a copy. I know he's never read it, but he tells people he has.

'Who is, eh … who is – what's 'is name?' the prick spits. He keeps pretending he has the knowledge to play along.

'Richard Dawkins,' falls out of my mouth. I don't know why I even bothered. I shouldn't be engaging with him.

'Yeah … yeah … yeah, Richard Hawkins,' he shouts at the TV.

Fuckin' idiot. Hawkins. This cunt makes me laugh inside, he really does. He'd make a great character for a book. If only I had the balls to write one. He punches the air with delight when the answer is confirmed. He didn't even get the answer right when given the correct answer. As he's steadying himself for the next question, I manage to force the thumb of my right hand underneath most of the tape wrapped around my left wrist. It's the first time I've managed to get in this far. I stretch it upwards as far as I can and try to squeeze my arm out slowly. It's plucking out every remaining hair on my hand, but I'm making progress.

It's coming out! It's coming out!

I'm not sure if it's relief or nervousness that fills me when I finally find myself free from the chair. It's probably a bit of both. I'd just been concentrating on getting free for the past couple of hours, but now the real test begins. I stare over at the glass table. The gun is about five feet from him, maybe ten feet from me. But he's slouched into the corner of the couch. If I move first, I'll be at the gun before he even notices me. I'm sure of it. I take a moment to play the possibilities out in my head.

When I get to the gun, I'll shoot at his kneecap.

I don't want to kill this cunt. I don't want the mess of a murder charge on my hands. I'm sure I'd be cleared in self-defence, but I'll just down this fucker and let the cops deal with him from there. I allow myself a deep, silent breath before rubbing my thumbs across the palms of my hands to remove the excess sweat. It's now or never. Two more breaths and then I'll leap.

Teencum069 bullied me into believing I was a pussy for not taking advantage of Brady. I knew it was ironic. Somebody who rapes kids calling another guy a 'pussy'. It reminded me of school. And just like school, I gave in to the bully. My obsession with trying to be liked has always got me into trouble. It makes me gullible. It wasn't just Teencum069's taunts that lured me back, it was my fascination with wanting to finally play around with a kid. I watched a hundred different videos of other guys abusing all sorts of kids: fat ones, skinny ones, ugly ones, cute ones, boys, girls. They kept playing in my mind over and over again. I wanted to create my own memory. I couldn't dampen the urge. I continued to message Brady, as Nicole. But I never arranged another meeting with him. I haven't arranged a meeting with any kid since then. An alarm seems to go off in my head every time I get to that point. My fascination with kiddie porn lies in just watching it. I haven't had the balls to rape a child … not yet anyway. I don't trust myself to not follow through with my urges. I've thought about killing myself to end the pain of admitting to myself that I may be a paedophile. I've even written a suicide note.

I don't know why I screech as I leap; it stirs the prick. But he stands no chance. I'm at the gun before him. I end up on my arse, facing him, pointing the gun towards his knees as he tries to get up off the couch. But it won't fire. I pull the trigger twice before he's on top of me, punching at my head.

Have I been held hostage by a fuckin' fake gun?

I know his punches are landing on me, but I don't feel a thing. I'm numbing to the eventuality of being battered to death. I don't want to die. At least I don't want to die today. The cunt pins my shoulders to the ground, using his knees as he straddles my chest. He's shouting at me as blows continue to rain down on my face and chest. I don't know what he's saying. I've become deaf. When he releases his grip to get off me I assume he's done. That's until I see his large boot come straight towards my face.

11:40

Darragh

I STAND OVER HIS BODY, ONE FOOT EITHER SIDE OF HIM, AND CLICK THE safety off on the gun. I don't know why I make a point of doing that as loudly as I can. He can't hear me. He's knocked the fuck out. That was some kick to the face. It was like Paul Pogba. I want to shoot him right now. But I can't. I need to wait on JR's instruction. Not long now. Twenty minutes left. I'm out of breath after that. That came outta the fuckin blue, like.

Why the fuck did I leave his right hand untaped?

He musta peeled off all the tape round his ankles and wrist. I duck me head to take a look under the chair he was tied to and see loadsa torn strips of the stuff.

'You're a fuckin idiot, Darragh, a fuckin idiot,' I repeat over and over, stabbing my temple with the barrel of the gun.

I might be goin' mad. Maybe it's the coke. I knew I shoulda stayed sober this morning. At least I have everything under control now. I better get this cunt tied back up to that chair. He's a heavy little fuck. It's not easy liftin' a bare body. His skin's all slippery. Thank fuck he still has his boxer shorts on.

The feeling in the air was quite dead when I returned to JR after killing that rapist. He didn't greet me like The Boss did after I'd got away with the delivery to Limerick. There was no party thrown in me honour. JR takes his business much more seriously. He had exciting news for me when I returned though. He told me he could fully trust me after I'd

203

carried out the hit, and told me about the most exciting plan I could ever dream of. He wanted me to go fifty–fifty with him on the biggest bank robbery in the history of Ireland. And it was genius. He had been looking into this one for over a year. He was researching Bank of Ireland's staff first to see how he could pull off a tiger kidnapping theft through them. But he couldn't find anyone. I didn't know what a tiger kidnapping was. I thought it was fuckin genius when it was explained to me. He told he wanted to kidnap a bank manager's wife and instruct the manager himself to rob the bank. But he said the process of taking money out of the Bank of Ireland was complicated and would have taken a longer period of time. That was when he stumbled onto ACB. Being a smaller bank is exactly what made them perfect for this heist. They had only four branches left in Dublin and we were going to take two million out of each of them. He said he even found some pussy-ass gay couple who we could use for the robbery. 'As easy as taking candy from a baby,' was how JR explained it to me. I couldn't see how it could go wrong. I still can't. Once I keep this fucker tied up, of course. I nearly fucked everything up.

JR has done his research on every aspect of the morning. He followed Vincent and Ryan for weeks, trying to understand their patterns. He even knows the patterns of all the four other bank managers. He's a fuckin legend. Right now, ACB is being robbed of eight million euros and nobody in this whole city has one fuckin clue about it. In the earlier plan, JR was going to do the kidnapping while I followed Vincent around the banks, just to keep an eye on him. But he was so impressed with how I carried out the murder of the rapist that he felt I was the best man for the more forceful job. He could see it in me that I really wanted to do this part of the job. I told him hundreds of times that I wanted to get me hands as dirty as I possibly could. An eight-million-euro theft, a kidnapping and a possible murder. Me hands can't get much dirtier than that. I couldn't wait for this day to come. It was four months ago when JR first said it to me. I've read every note JR has taken ahead of this mornin'. We've studied every possible scenario. Someday, in the future, I'm going to be just like JR. I'm gonna have me own little apprentice and I'm gonna teach him the genius ways of being a gangster. After all, I'm learning from the best. The Boss was pretty good, I could never deny that, but JR is on a different level. I bleedin' love the guy.

I've eventually got this greasy fuck's body into a sitting position but not even severe slaps across his face are waking him up. I need his head to stop flopping down towards me. I manage to wrap more tape around his wrists, but it's difficult to get his legs steady without his body slouching to one side of the chair and falling towards me. His legs are pointing out and forming a stand for himself. That's the only thing keeping him upright on the chair. I couldn't give a fuck anymore. I wrap the tape around his mouth to the back of his head once again. I never should have removed that this mornin'. I take a look at the microwave as I'm done. 11:45. Fuckin hell. Fifteen minutes left. I wonder where Vincent is. This is getting too close now. I grab at the phone and dial one.

'He's not out yet,' JR whispers into the phone. He knows. He's waiting outside the bank.

'No, I, eh … I'm just wonderin', ye know, it's like eleven forty-five. It's …'

'Darragh,' he says sternly. 'What am I gonna say next to you?'

'Stick to the plan.'

'Exactly. Listen, Vincent will be coming out of here soon, but if he doesn't, you need to get ready to shoot that fuck you have there, okay?'

'No problem,' I say.

'It would take Vincent ten minutes to drive back to you from here, so if he's not out of here in the next five or so minutes, Ryan's fate is decided. You need to be strong.'

'I am strong. I will be strong. I've got it all under control here, JR.'

'I know you have,' he says. 'I trust you to complete the plan, Darragh. Get yourself ready.'

When JR hangs up I let a spray shoot through my lips, causing them to make a fart sound. That's what finally stirs Ryan. That's how much this cunt loves asshole.

'You're about to be fuckin killed, lover boy,' I whisper at him as I reach for the gun.

11:45

Jack

DAMN! I MISSED VINCENT GOING INTO MAYOR STREET. I CAN SEE HIS CAR parked on the opposite side of the Luas tracks. Mayor Street can be a busy-ass street. There's a Luas stop just a hundred yards away and there are thousands of offices around here. My plan was to stand outside the wine bar across from the branch smoking a vaporiser in an attempt to not look suspicious. So many people smoke outside bars and go unnoticed. But there are too many people already here smoking this morning that I almost get into a conversation. I don't know why there are half a dozen guys smoking here already. It's not even midday. They must do a popular lunch inside. I never thought of that as part of the plan. I assumed it would be a quiet bar around this time. I thought they only served alcohol. The last thing I want to do is to get into a conversation with somebody – especially after the Antoinette mess. I ain't taking any chances. The less I'm seen, and especially heard from, the better. I decide to pace up and down Mayor Street very slowly, with the phone to my ear. I don't need to call anybody so I just pretend to talk again. I need to steer clear of the CCTV at the Luas stop. I'm waffling some nonsense down the phone when it surprises me by ringing. It's Darragh. He's fretting about the deadline again, but I put him straight. I know he'll shoot Ryan at midday.

I'm starting to get a bit nervy now that I'm not standing where I assumed I would be. I wonder how long Vincent will be in that bank. I need to know. It's a pivotal part of the plan. I look at my watch. It's between a quarter to and ten to twelve. Jaysus, this is so tight. I guess he'll be another ten minutes at least. I already know he'll miss the deadline. There's no way he'll get in and out of there and back to his apartment before midday. But that's fine. That was always part of the plan. Vincent was never meant to make it back home. The wine bar was the ideal spot to stare over at the bank's exit but it's not going to work today. The only option I have to see Vincent come out is to stand on the other corner of Mayor Square. It's busy with pedestrians over there but at least I won't have others standing around me like I had outside the bar. It's not ideal, but there's not long to go. Christ! This is all about to go down in the next few minutes.

I had a few pints on a couple of different occasions in the Deer's Head before arranging to meet Darragh. I knew the barman was aware he sold a bit of weed out of his pub. When I asked him if he knew where I could buy a twenty-euro bag he didn't hesitate in telling me a guy came in around two o'clock almost every day that could fix me up. I wanted to smash my son's killer square in the jaw when I first met him, but I'd already worked on keeping my cool. It wasn't easy. In fact, that's been the hardest part out of this whole process. He thought I was a cop at first, but I soon quashed that idea in his head. I knew straight away he was as thick as horseshit but I had to pretend to like him. I had to befriend him. He was fascinated with my plan to use him as my apprentice. We'd meet up once every couple of weeks in the pub but I made sure to leave no trace. I told him he could call me JR on our very first meeting and he never questioned what the initials stood for. He still hasn't asked. In fact, this idiot has been robbing and murdering for me and he has absolutely no idea who I am. He hasn't even questioned it. He's just been caught up, living his dream. That's what he told me I had done for him – made his dreams come true. He thinks he's Henry Hill in *Goodfellas*. He didn't hesitate in taking money from tills when I ordered him to. We'd split it all down the middle. The money I was getting was being put towards this whole plan. The first wad of cash I spent was on petrol. I sent Darragh off on a road trip to Mayo to test his nerve. He arrived back high as a kite after killing Bob Nugent, a bloke I had researched meticulously to find. He got a thrill from the killing. He told me, 'It was much better than the first time.' That really tested my cool. But I just about managed to pass the test. I've seen Darragh every week for about a year now and I've wanted to knock his lights out each time. I should be rewarded with a medal for remaining so calm and patient. I sat him down one day, soon after he returned from Mayo, and read through the plan for today. He was like a five-year-old on Christmas morning. Giddy with excitement.

'Eight million euro,' he kept repeating over and over again.

Quite odd for somebody who always insisted it wasn't about the money. I bluffed and told him I'd carry out the kidnapping and possible murder while he would shadow Vincent to each bank. I always knew that wasn't going to be the case, but I just wanted Darragh to feel like it wasn't a set-up. I let him naturally tell me he would like to work the apartment. It made it feel like he was plotting and planning with me. He wasn't, of course. I played him.

I don't like where I'm standing but it's either here or outside the wine bar. This street is just way too busy for my liking. I check my watch again. Only three minutes have passed since I last looked at it. I'm sweating. And it's not just because of the sun. I'm not supposed to go over to the car until I see Vincent come out, but I have to bring that part of the plan forward. There are just too many people passing me by. The car's about five hundred yards from where I'm standing now, but I decide to walk around the short block and come back to it from the other angle. That way nobody will see me starting from a standing position and heading straight to the car. If anybody does see me get into it, I want it to look like I'm getting into it because it's mine. Maybe I'm getting too paranoid. I don't like changing my plan, even if it is just bringing something forward by two minutes. It's only a short walk around the back of Sheriff Street. I feel at the back of my trousers pocket to confirm I have what I need. As I approach the car from the pathway I keep my fingers crossed that the doors are unlocked. They should be. John never locks them. Releasing my crossed fingers just ten yards from the car I reach into my back pocket for the taser. John turns around and almost smiles at me when I open the passenger door. He thinks I'm Vincent. His smile turns to confusion just before I stretch my arm towards him and taser his ribcage. He's out cold as soon as I do it, but I follow up with a second blast just to make sure. The car is freezing. He must have had the air conditioning on its coldest setting all morning. Suits me. I've been sweatin'. I turn off the terrible classical music playing on the radio and notice the digital clock as I'm doing so. 11:53. I grip the taser tighter in my hand and sigh loudly. Not long now.

11:50

Vincent

I TAKE A DEEP BREATH AS I SIT DOWN NEXT TO KEN. WE'VE ORDERED TWO of his staff to count out the bundles of cash. They looked at us as if we'd just landed from another planet. Ken's assistant manager, Chloe Brannigan, genuinely thought we were joking. She's only allowed inside the vault with Ken. They know something odd is going on but they didn't question us. I press the button on Ken's office phone to dial out and take the time while the tone rings to wipe my face with the palm of my hand. I haven't been this panicky since I collapsed on all fours this morning on Nassau Street. Ken must be starting to feel my fear. His excitement of minutes ago seems to have waned. He looks up at me before being distracted by Noah's voice.

'Hello, Mr Butler,' he booms out. I stretch to the phone to lower the volume.

'Hi, Noah,' I say, trying to sound calm. 'I've Ken here with me.'

'Hi, Ken.'

'Hi, Noah.'

'Hello,' another voice screeches.

'Hi, Jonathan,' I answer. 'Bear with us one second.' That's literally all it takes for Chelle to add her voice to the conference call.

'Okay,' I start. 'We're all here. Listen, I have ten minutes to get out of Mayor Street with two million euros or the board are gonna be pretty pissed.'

I've been thinking about what I'm going to say for the past few minutes. I haven't had much time. There are still holes in my story.

'They spoke to me last night after work and said they were going to test each bank's security measures …'

'It doesn't make sense,' interrupts Jonathan.

'Didn't I say listen?' I ask. Nobody answers. I fill the silence with a soft tut before carrying on.

'They are trying to test the withdrawal times. They are claiming withdrawals are taking way too long from both internal and external sources. They want to test internal today and maybe external next week. I don't know …' I stumble. 'I don't know what they're up to. You know yourselves, they probably don't even know what they're up to themselves. It's … it's …'

Noah takes my stuttering as a signal to chime in.

'But, Mr Butler,' he starts, sounding annoying as always. 'I spoke with Mr Sneyd this morning and he had no knowledge of the withdrawal from my branch.' Fuck! Ken stares at me. It elongates my silence.

'You know Clyde,' I say, pushing out a fake snigger. 'He doesn't even know what day of the week it is.'

No response follows. I notice Ken's eyebrows raise. My spine falls back into the leather chair. My mind is lost.

'Vincent …' calls out Chelle.

'Boss …' says Ken into my face, following up after a further silence.

I can't answer them. I'm stumped. My improvisation skills are normally so good. As they talk over each other, trying to get to grips with what's happened so far this morning, I peel my spine, vertebrae by vertebrae, from the back of the chair.

'We're being robbed,' I sob.

I still couldn't genuinely believe Ryan had been watching kiddie porn even when reading his sick forum discussions with Teencum069. I figured there'd have to be an explanation. Maybe he was trying to get information out of a paedophile for his book? Maybe he was trying to get into the head of a paedophile for his book? But the ringing in my ears wouldn't stop. I clicked on almost every URL link he had hidden in his folder as I tried to come to terms with it all. That was when I remembered there was a Word document called 'note' hidden in the folder too when I first opened it. I clicked out of Chrome, my stomach still turning, and opened the document.

'Dear world,' it started. The ringing in my ears grew louder. 'Today is the day I end my time with you all.' It was a fucking suicide note. I slammed the lid of the laptop down and sprinted for the door of our apartment. I wasn't even dressed. I had an old T-shirt and a pair of boxer shorts on. That was it. I remember a bizarre moment as I stood at the elevator doors waiting for them to open, not knowing what I'd do if another resident appeared in front of me. Luckily the lift was empty. I stood inside staring at myself from all angles in the mirrors that surrounded me. I didn't press any button. I just stood inside for what seemed like ten minutes until the ringing in my ears stopped. Then I strolled back into my apartment and read his suicide note word for word. He left it until the end to mention me, but he did so in glowing terms. He thanked me for all I had done for him, for the life he'd enjoyed with me before he got depressed and turned into a sick man. Tears rolled down my face. But I couldn't sympathise. I couldn't get to grips with what I'd found out over the past hour. My boyfriend was a fuckin' paedophile. The ringing in my ears started again after I'd finished reading the note. It didn't go away until the exact moment Ryan arrived back home that night.

Ken rushes from his chair to grab at me, holding my arms in a hug that confirms he really cares for me. Noah is first to speak.

'I knew it,' he says before the others join in, making the noise from the speaker inaudible.

'Calm down, calm down!' shouts Ken into the phone as he loosens his grip on me. 'Let the boss speak.'

'Ryan is going to die,' I continue sobbing. 'They have Ryan.'

'Who has Ryan?' asks Chelle. Everyone else seems stunned into silence.

'Some asshole broke into my penthouse this morning and told me to come back with eight million in used notes by midday or else he'd shoot Ryan in the head.'

'Call the police,' offers Ken. I look at him as if he's stupid.

'Don't you think I've thought about that?'

'Sorry, Vincent, sorry. I'm just … I'm just …'

'No, I'm sorry, Ken. It's me who should be apologising. To everyone. To all of you.'

The line has gone silent again. The other three had been offering something to the conversation but they all spoke over each other. I didn't hear any points or questions they raised.

'Listen,' I say. 'I just need to get back with all the money and Ryan will be safe, okay? I want you guys to ring the cops after twelve o'clock. But only after twelve o'clock, d'ye hear me?'

'It's almost twelve now, Vincent,' Noah pipes up.

'Vincent, are you alright?' asks Chelle, butting in with what I hope is genuine concern.

'I'm fine,' I exhale.

'I knew you weren't right this morning when—' Chelle's sentence is cut off by Jonathan and Noah trying to have a say. The sound grows inaudible again.

'ENOUGH!' screams Ken. He's still on his knees next to me. 'For fuck's sake – Ryan's life is at stake here. There's only about seven minutes left. Vincent,' he says, removing my own hand from my face to look at me. 'Do you have the other six million?' I nod in reply. 'Okay, well let me get the other two mill for you and get you outta here.'

I can hear the panic on the other end of the line but I try not to listen to it as Ken leaves me alone in his office.

'Guys,' I say, shutting the three of them up after a few moments. 'Call the cops. But only after midday, okay? Wait until Ryan is safe. Promise me you'll wait until after midday.'

Chelle is the first to answer. 'We will, Vincent,' she says. 'We promise.'

Noah is still adding to the conversation but I speak over him.

'Please, Chelle. I'm leaving this with you. I trust you so much. Leave it another ten to fifteen minutes until I can get back to him and then call the cops.' I hang up and sit stunned in the silence. The noise of Ken's wall clock brings me crashing back to reality after a few seconds. *Tick, tock, tick, tock.* I look at the screen of my iPhone. 11:54. Fuck me! I have to ring the fucker holding Ryan hostage.

'Here you are, boss,' Ken says in one breath, swinging the two briefcases towards me before I lift the phone to my ear. 'Go get Ryan!'

I don't know why I'm wasting time hugging him and trying to justify all that's gone on this morning. Ken wipes the tears from my eyes before shoving me towards the door.

'Go on, boss, go!'

I can barely see the phone through my moist eyes, but I know I only have to press one to reach the greasy prick.

'I have it, I have it,' I say down the line as I race through the floor of the bank.

'Wow, good man,' he replies. 'With just a few minutes to go. You kept it tight, fag, huh? I bet you like it tight.'

'I'll be back to you in ten minutes. I'm getting into the car now,' I pant down the line as I'm buzzed out of the bank door. He hangs up. I don't have time to care.

I put the phone back into my pocket and race across the tram tracks and into the back seat of the car with the cases. John wasn't by the boot to meet me this time. It doesn't matter.

'My apartment, John, quick as you can.'

11:55

Ryan

FUCK ME. MY HEAD FEELS LIKE IT'S SPINNING IN A WASHING MACHINE. IT doesn't take long for reality to set in. When it does, my stomach spins quicker than my head. The blur in front of me focuses after a few seconds tick by. The prick is standing staring at me, smiling behind a pointed gun.

Holy shit.

My plan clearly didn't go well. The last thing I remember was this exact scenario happening the other way around. I was pointing that gun at him. Then I remember. It's a fuckin' fake gun.

I turn my head towards the microwave even though it really hurts to do so. It's just ticked to 11:56.

Four minutes.

I try to ask if he knows where Vincent is but only a muffled sound comes out of my mouth. I've been taped back up. Fucking hell. I won't be able to talk myself out of this. I can't tell this smarmy little cunt that he's left his DNA all over my TV screen, that he's fucked either way. My mind tries to focus, but it can't. I can't remember where Vincent was when I pounced for the gun, so I've no idea where he could be now. My mumbling is making this prick laugh. He only stops when his phone rings. I know it's Vincent. It's typical Vincent. The hero at the last second.

'Wow, good man,' says the prick down the line.

Vincent has done it! Jesus Christ. This is like something from one of Tom Cruise's shit action movies. The clock stopping with just seconds remaining before the world blows up. I can't believe this is real life. The prick doesn't even bother to look at me after he hangs up. Instead, he dials out. He must be letting his partner know everything is complete. I wonder how Vincent is. He must be in pieces. I try to breathe in a relaxing manner, imagining I'm back at yoga when the prick begins fretting on the phone. Something's not right.

'Sorry?' he asks, puzzled.

Pause.

'But he'll be … Vincent is … he'll be here in a few minutes with all the money.'

Pause.

'But I … Really?'

Pause.

'Of course, JR. I'll do it now.'

What the fuck is going on here?

I thought about suicide for forty-eight hours straight without any sleep breaking up my nightmare. I wondered how I could kill myself in the most painless way. I assumed an overdose of painkillers would be the way to go, but a quick Google search led me to believe that slitting my wrists might be the most sudden ending. Fuck that. That sounded way too dramatic for me. It also sounded tough to do. I wasn't sure where I would kill myself either. Doing it at the penthouse never crossed my mind. That would've been too much for Vincent to bear. He would have had to deal with losing the love of his life, as well as finding his body, and possibly having to move out of his dream home if that was the case. He surely couldn't go on living here if it was where I topped myself. And Vincent has worked so hard to own this home. He loves his penthouse.

After two days, I began to think myself out of it. Maybe I was too much of a coward to go ahead with killing myself. When I finally managed a decent stretch of sleep, I woke up a new man. Why should I give up my apartment, my boyfriend, my life? I had so much to offer the world. I wrote the first two chapters of my novel that morning. It was great work too. A real gripping opening; Chad Sutcliffe was an amateur photographer turned paparazzo who began to obsess about one Hollywood star in particular. I thought about using real Hollywood stars for the story but when I realised I'd have to kill a couple of them off, I figured I'd have to make 'em up. Denise Knight was the name I concocted for my leading lady – a cross between Denise Richards and Kiera Knightly. I envisaged a smiling face with big, beautiful eyes and that was the name I came up with. I wanted my readers to fall in love with her so that when she's killed late on, it's a real shock twist. But it's hard to use the laptop for an extended period of time without surfing the web. And when I go surfing, I inevitably end up in choppy waters. Before I'd even started chapter three the very next day, I was already looking at kiddie porn. I was determined to not enter the chatrooms to converse with TeenCum069, but I only staved that off until lunchtime. The sick fuck kept at me to meet kids. He wanted me to film myself with them. He was beginning to repulse me but then again, so did cocaine the first time I tried it. Now I'm addicted to both. We chat for hours, talking about what strategy we would use for our victims. But there's never been a victim my end. I just can't bring myself to do it. I guess that probably makes me a coward. No matter what I do, I end up being a fuckin' coward.

He seems to have a grin on his face as he points the gun at me. I'm pretty certain, even though I didn't hear, that his partner in crime has just ordered him to kill me. I think about screaming and shouting but for some reason I'm quiet. I believe he isn't really going to do it. He can't do it.

That's a fake gun, right?

'Any last requests?' he asks.

12:00

Jack

HERE HE IS! HE HAS THE PHONE TO HIS EAR AS HE RUSHES TOWARDS THE car, hugging the final two cases with his other hand. They're not even cuffed to his wrists. He's obviously pleading with Darragh. He jumps into the back of the car without noticing John slumped in the passenger seat.

'My apartment, John, quick as you can,' he says before realising it's not John he aimed that demand at.

I don't hesitate. I dig the taser under his arm and squeeze the trigger. He falls flat into the gap between the front and back seats. Perfect! I turn the key in the ignition and pull away slowly, noticing that nobody has followed Vincent out of the bank.

I've done it! I've fuckin' done it!

The rush feels insane. As I'm pulling away, Darragh calls.

'JR, he's out, he's out. We've done it,' he yelps. 'He said he'll be back here in less than ten minutes.'

'Game over, Darragh,' I say. 'It's midday now and he's not back. Do your job.'

'Sorry?' he asks, puzzled.

I didn't think he'd be. I figured he couldn't wait to blow Ryan's head off.

'I'll look after Vincent from here. I'll get the money. But kill Ryan. Vincent missed the deadline. We stick to our plan.'

'But he'll be … Vincent is … he'll be here in a few minutes with all the money.'

217

'It's midday and he's not back at the apartment. Do your job.'

'But I … Really?'

'Stick to the plan!' I say, raising my voice a little.

'Of course, JR. I'll do it now.' I know he'll do it. But I'm not taking any risks.

'I'll stay on the line. Let me hear you do it,' I say.

I've always trusted Darragh to carry out the murder. His eyes lit up when I first told him about this whole plan. He kept telling me I was a genius over and over again. Maybe he's right. It is a pretty smart plan. I told him as much as I possibly could. He knows I have two getaway cars parked up in different areas of Dublin. I wanted to sound legitimate to him at every opportunity. I certainly achieved that. He never guessed for one minute that I was setting him up. As soon as I hang up from Darragh, I call the cops.

'There's something huge going down at the penthouse of Arbour Building on Horse Fair. A man is holding another man at gunpoint. He's probably already killed him. You need to get there as soon as possible,' I say in one long breath.

'Okay, sir, please calm down. Can you stay on the line?' It's unbelievable how cool these emergency operators remain in circumstances like these. But I know this woman has already ordered a police car to arrive at Vincent and Ryan's penthouse through the push of a button.

'No, I can't stay on the line. This is very real, ma'am,' I say. 'You need to be quick.'

'A police car is on its way right now, sir,' she says. 'But if you can stay on the line to give me—' I don't let her finish. I hang up. I have to call Darragh back. It's an important part of the plan. I wait two minutes before making the call.

'Darragh,' I say, deliberately sounding panicked.

'Yeah, JR?'

'Where are ya, buddy?'

'I'm just headin' out of the apartment now. Everythin' alrigh'? What's wrong…'

'The cops are coming. I think Vincent, the fag bastard, had somebody call the cops. You need to get out of there as soon as possible.'

'Wha' the fuck? Comin' here, ya mean?'

'Yeah. On their way to the penthouse. You should be fine. Get out as quickly as you can. Darragh, listen to me. Best of luck, buddy, okay. And remember, whatever happens, stick to the plan.'

I can't keep the smile off my face as I drive down Sherriff Street to head towards East Wall. That's where I have my second car parked up. That's my job done. I've no more calls to make. All I have to do is slot this car in behind the grey Toyota Corolla that I have waiting for me and transfer the money into the boot. The cops should be arriving at the apartment any minute now. It's touch and go whether Darragh will make it out before they come. But even if he does, they'll catch up with him within minutes. I've spent a large amount of time wondering whether he'll try to shoot himself out of this situation or just hold his hands up. I'd prefer he spent the rest of his life in prison over a quick death. But I made my peace with both possibilities a long time ago.

As I turn onto East Road, I look at the clock on the dashboard. 12:08. I'm so good with time. I think I have a natural clock in my head. This morning couldn't have gone any more perfectly. I slowly roll the BMW into the space behind the Corolla and take the first two cases Vincent dropped in the back of this car with me as I get out. I take a good look around the street as I do this, but I know nobody will be lurking here. It's too remote. It takes me two more trips from car to car before I have all eight cases flung into the Corolla. Vincent and John are still out cold in their car. They will probably start to come round in another fifteen minutes or so. A flutter of relief runs through my body when I drive away. It's not that I didn't think the car would start, it's just that driving away in this car confirms the robbery went as planned. There's no way I'll be caught from here. Even when the cops are on this case they won't be looking for a grey Toyota Corolla in Dublin. I smile at myself in the rear-view mirror as I pull out onto Alfie Byrne Road and head north. I've one more car stop to do before heading for Belfast.

12:00

Darragh

I SHOULDN'T BE SURPRISED THAT JR STILL ORDERED ME TO KILL RYAN. I guess he's right. Vincent's instructions were to be back here by midday, not to be coming out of the last bank at that time. I gotta stick to the plan. I don't think Ryan knows what's comin'. He's very quiet for someone who's about to have their brains blown out. I screw the silencer onto the barrel of the gun after I place the phone on the arm of the sofa with JR listening in. Then I point the silencer between Ryan's eyes.

'Any lasts requests?' I say, really cool, before firing a bullet through his head.

His chin just rests on his chest after the shot. I'm amazed at the lack of blood. It was the same with the sick rapist I killed a few months ago. The small amount of blood from a headshot is really surprising. I always assumed it'd be a mess. That's not the case. Maybe that's the difference between movies and real life. I grab a fistful of his hair to lift his head up, just so I can make sure there are no signs of life.

'Rest in peace, fag,' I whisper into his ear before dropping his head back down.

'Job done, JR,' I say into the phone.

'Excellent, Darragh. I'll see you tomorrow as planned, okay?'

'You got it.'

I feel high as a kite as I begin to pack my bag to leave. I notice the broken tape on the chair under Ryan and tut. That was me only mistake of the day. It's disappointing but I'll learn from it. At least I sorted out the mess. The morning has gone almost perfectly for me. I got the job done. Here I am. It's midday and I'm a multi-fuckin'-millionaire, just as JR promised I would be. I'm almost skippin' out the door with pride when the phone buzzes.

'Darragh,' JR says in such a way that it frightens me.

'Yeah, JR?'

'Where are ya, buddy?'

'I'm just headin' out of the apartment now. Everythin' alrigh'? What's wrong...'

'The cops are coming.'

I can't believe what he's saying to me. I'm so stunned that it almost stops me in me tracks but I gotta keep moving. I need to get the fuck outta here.

'You should be fine,' says JR, tryna keep me calm. 'Get out as quickly as you can. Darragh, listen to me. Best of luck, buddy, okay. And remember, whatever happens, stick to the plan.'

Holy fuck!

I can't help but take a look at Ryan's body hanging off the chair before I slam the front door of their apartment behind me. I can't take the lift. At least getting down the stairs will be easier than comin' up. With me bag thrown over me shoulder I bounce as quickly as I can down each step. I bet it was that Noah what's-'is-name that rang the cops. JR always said he'd be the troublesome one. I started the day feeling a mix of nerves and excitement. That's certainly how I'm feeling now. I've just killed another man. That's three on me list now. But this is the closest I've been to gettin' caught. I have no idea how long it will take the cops to get here.

I'm almost on the ground floor when I get me answer. The sirens ring through me ear. It's the scariest sound I've ever heard. I've been frightened before but this is proper fuckin scary. It's a really, really strange feeling to be properly frightened. Your stomach turns. I can feel fear inside me body. I hold me hand out in front of me to see how much it's shaking. Quite a lot. I'm normally cool. I manage to get meself into the cramped staff area I broke into this morning when I hear the cops screech outside and make their way into the lobby. I don't fuckin' believe this. I'm literally trapped. I have to think my way out of this mess. My only option is to sneak back up the stairs to break into another apartment. I could probably hide out there until the cops go. But surely they'll check each apartment. Staying here is probably me best bet. At least I can hear them from here if I press me ear up against the door.

'Everything okay?' I hear one booming cop's voice say.

The receptionist is quite quiet. I can't hear her response but I get the feelin' she's surprised by all this. So am I. Everything had gone perfectly right up until the last minute, literally. Now I'm about ten feet away from bein' arrested for murder. I stare at the gun in my hand. I know I've five bullets left in the round. That should be enough to get rid of a couple of cops. But I know that's the stupid decision to make. I wonder what JR would do in this situation. He gave me strict instructions to get away from the rapist's house a few months ago but I have no instructions for leaving this place. We never thought it would get to this. I'm just supposed to return home now. I'm conscious of the mobile phone in me pocket but I can't ring JR. If I can hear them talking in the reception area then they would surely hear me.

I'm lookin' for ways of hiding in this small room when I hear another cop car pull up outside. I'm really fucked now. I've gone from being high as a kite to practically shittin' meself. I feel me stomach again. I genuinely need to shite right now. I notice the empty bucket I tripped over this morning. Shitting shouldn't be at the forefront of me mind, but I can't hold it in. Maybe it will relieve some of the tension. Sometimes I do me best thinkin' on the jacks. I hear the ping of the elevator arriving on the ground floor and I know the cops are on their way up to the fags' apartment. They're gonna find Ryan's body and call for more backup. They're bound to search every inch of this place. I loosen me belt, pull down me jeans and squat over the bucket. Me stomach rumbles as my ass practically pukes. I really am sick with worry. Me hole seems to think I'm finished but me stomach has other ideas. It's still rumbling. The shitting isn't helping me relax. It's not doin' the job I hoped it would. I can't think straight. I find meself eyeballing a rack of towels and decide that they'll be great to wipe me hole with. How can I be thinkin' about that right now? Then I notice a janitor's uniform hanging behind the towels. That seems to stop the shitting.

Yes, Darragh! You fuckin' genius.

I kick me shoes off and pull the waistband of me jeans over me feet. The uniform is way too big on me. The sleeves look like a fuckin elephant trunk hanging over my arms. But at least it looks like I work here. I should be able to walk out unnoticed. I'm thinkin' 'bout whether to take the direction of the stairs or whether to brave it and walk out onto the lobby floor and straight through the exit. I can't hear any cops in the reception but I'm sure there's one or two out on the street waiting to see if someone comes out. I'll have to bide me time. I decide I should head upstairs. I'm about to make me way to the stairwell when me stomach rolls again. This has only ever happened to me once before when I got food poisoning. Fear genuinely does seem to make you shit yourself.

I zip down the top half of the uniform towards me knees and squat over the bucket again. Me shit is still wet. It slaps against the rest of the shit in the bottom of the bucket at the exact same time the door slams open.

'Stay where you are,' a fat cop shouts at me before yellin' out for backup.

I pat me hand around to feel for the gun but I don't know what way I've pulled this uniform down. It seems to be inside out. The realisation that I'm fucked makes my stomach roar again. The two of us hear the shite spray outta me hole as we stare into each other's eyes awkwardly. He holds his gun in one hand and his nose in the other as he makes his way towards me. I'm fuckin done for.

SIX MONTHS LATER

12:00

Jack

I DON'T FEEL FRANK'S PRESENCE THAT MUCH AROUND HERE ANYMORE. Especially not on these rooftop terrace bars. We didn't come up to one of these when we visited together. I did feel his presence the first few times I returned after his death. But ever since I moved here permanently, his shadow seems to have disappeared from every street corner. It's probably the clearest sign that I've started a new life. He's still very much in my heart, of course. My memories of Frank are my most treasured thoughts. They're worth a lot more to me than the millions I possess.

I split the money between sixteen different banks throughout Europe. Four of those are here in Rome. I'm so rich. I'm rich in more than just monetary terms. I couldn't be happier. Which is some achievement given how much of my life has been filled with heartache. I've been living in Rome for over four months now.

I drove to Belfast straight after the robbery, only stopping in Drogheda for another car change. I stayed in the Radisson Blu Hotel for ten days. My flight to London was always booked for May the third. I spent two weeks there, setting up four accounts with two different banks. I don't like London. There's a real lack of warmth on the streets of that city. I've travelled through France, Belgium and Switzerland on the way to my new life and, while they all have many beautiful traits, spending time in them has reassured me that Rome is the most idyllic place in the world to live in. My travels went perfectly well except for patches of boredom. But I got everything done that I needed to without any hitches.

It went almost as perfectly as the morning of the robbery itself. I was always certain Darragh would do as instructed. His commitment was never really an issue for me. The little prick was so gullible – gullible and stupid. It was his stupidity that made the whole plan possible. I almost felt sorry for him on occasions. He'd make me laugh. He was so dumb that he became the comedy in my life for seven months. But there was never a moment where I forgot he murdered my son. I was intent on screwing him over, more so than getting the money. I often wonder what he's up to. I know he was brought to Portlaoise prison initially. I'm not sure if he's still there now. They sent him there the day after he was arrested. That's what I read in the *Irish Daily Star,* crashed out on the bed of my hotel room a couple of days after the robbery. His trial can't be far off. He's most likely racking his brain trying to figure out who the hell I am. Then again, he might not be. He probably still thinks we're best pals. Maybe he's still sticking to the plan. The cops must be leaning heavily on him for any nugget of information about his accomplice. He knows nothing. I covered every track I made. I went through everything with a fine-tooth comb countless times and couldn't find any holes in the plan. We executed everything perfectly. The only time I felt worried through the whole ordeal was when I bumped into Antoinette. I often think about her. I never used to. But she became a central figure in my most memorable morning ever. When I was shacked up in Belfast, I worried that I would see a picture of myself in the newspapers. But I knew in my heart that Antoinette had no idea who she was talking to that morning. I was totally unrecognisable. There was another small instance when a police car siren almost made my heart jump out of my mouth after I'd picked up the third car just outside Clogherhead. I had literally just transferred the cases into it and had driven only twenty metres when I heard a blaze of sirens. The cops flew by me, much to my relief. I laughed out loud, banging on the steering wheel.

I'm certainly safe now. There's no catching up with me here. I adore Rome so much. There's character on every street. But it's been slightly lonely, living here for seventeen weeks without much company. I made friends with a Dutch couple, who were staying in the first hotel I was living in, but ever since they went home I've had nobody to share a drink with. That's all about to change. I look at my watch and release an excited puff of my cheeks. Two minutes past twelve. I'm so excited about our new life. My favourite thing about Rome is these rooftop terraced bars. There is no better place on the planet to be on a bright day. It's not hot, but the glare of the sun is making me squint. My eyes take in as much as they possibly can from this height. The Hotel Forum overlooks the Colosseum and the grounds of the Roman Forum. In the distance you can just about make out the steeples of Vatican City. That's a country all to itself. The smallest country in the world. I've walked through it twice now, laughing at the hypocrisy of Christianity. Religion is a joke, but it's a funny joke – ye gotta give them that. The big tourist attractions aren't the reason we've hungered to live here. It's the tiny nuances of this ancient city that made us crave living here. My stroll down Via Margutta and Via Gregoriana this morning still had the same effect on me that it had the very first time I walked it ten years ago. I love the effortlessness of the architecture. Nothing's flashy, but it's all beautiful. It makes Dublin seem really ugly. Rome makes every city unimpressive by comparison, in fairness. I take another sip of Château Petrus as I breathe in the excitement of today through my nose. That's the sort of wine I can drink now. I just paid almost two thousand euros for this bottle. I guess that's what multi-millionaires do. As I place my glass back down onto the table I hear a faint shuffle of footsteps brush the patio ground behind me. My stomach flips over.

12:00

Darragh

PRISON ISN'T BAD. WE'VE A GAMES ROOM HERE. THERE'S AN XBOX 360 AND a PlayStation 3 in it. I've been masterin' FIFA over the past few months. Nobody can beat me Man United team.

Prison's a bit like a boys' club. It's fine once your cell door is open, but when you're locked up it can get a lil boring. All you have for company is your own mind and that often plays tricks on itself. I look at the clock on the wall of the meeting room. It's just ticked by midday. Jennifer is always late. I bet she's not here for at least another ten minutes. I'm not bothered. It'll be more of the same. She'll try to get me to plead guilty again. I left so much DNA at the fags' apartment that she feels I've got no chance in me trial. They found me fuckin cum all over the television. Fuck it. I never thought of that. I don't know what I was thinkin'. The cops are tryna get me to rat JR out but I ain't givin' in. I'm sticking to our plan.

This prison doesn't look like anything I've seen on the telly before. It's actually a bit modern. It's clean. It's certainly cleaner than my bedsit. The bed's a bit uncomfortable, but that's me only real complaint. The mattress is so thin it's like sleeping on an ironing board. But I'm slowly getting used to it. The screws are fine. Most of them are keen to get along with the prisoners. They just want to get through a work shift without any drama. There's a couple of dicks, but most of them really couldn't give a shit. I haven't had a run in with any of them. In fact, I haven't had a run in with anyone. The prisoners seem okay to me too. I just keep meself to meself. There are a few guys that I play computer games with but that's about it. It's winner stays on down in the games room so my company can change every ten minutes. I'd like to be known as The FIFA King but that nickname hasn't really caught on. I guess you don't get to come up with your own name in prison. I'm not bitter about gettin' caught. I think we were just unlucky. Me lawyer says there were three phone calls made to the cops at around twelve o'clock on the day of the murder. They know who two of them are. Michelle and Noah from the banks. Vincent caved at the last minute, tryin' to save Ryan's life, and told them everything. But he fucked up. He got his pussy-ass boyfriend killed. I hope he's carrying that guilt around with him. The cops seem to think it was my partner who made the third call. I don't believe them. JR would never have ratted me out. We're too close. They keep tellin' me I can halve the amount of time I'll have to spend in prison if I give him up, but that's just not gonna happen. I'm going to get through this on me own. My trial's supposed to be only two months away but me lawyer seems to think it will be delayed past that. She's not happy with me. I can sense it. She really wants me to rat JR out. She doesn't understand the rules of bein' a gangster.

When I'm alone in me cell I think through the morning of the murder again and again. Sometimes I get a little paranoid about JR's involvement. It often flashes through me mind that he wanted to keep all that money to himself. But why did he give me fifty per cent of every other robbery we carried out? It doesn't make any sense. I've added up in my head that he musta made me over eighty grand in the short few months that we worked together. And why did he set my computer up on the day to make it look like I was home all morning? He gave me an alibi. He gave me the disguise. Besides, JR rang me to warn that the cops were on the way. Why would he do that if he was trying to frame me? None of it adds up. He's hardly an enemy. He's a good friend. A great friend. Probably the best friend I've ever had. In fact, he's definitely the best friend I've ever had. My lawyer and the cops have a different twist on it though. They haven't a fuckin clue. They just want to put an end to this whole thing. One prisoner told me they have quotas to reach anyway. My lawyer would benefit from me taking a plea deal and reducing my sentence. She has a reputation for plea deals and that's how she gets so much business. I like her though. Jennifer must be over fifty but she's hot. Her face ain't great. She's got a few scars dotted around her cheeks. I'm not sure if it's from acne or a knife. But she has that Latino body all men drool over. Big ass, big hips. I like spending time with her even if she does try to bully me a bit. She complains that I don't say enough in our meetings, but that's because all I'm ever thinkin' is how much I'd love to bend her over and fuck her South American brains out. Besides, even if I did want to give JR up, I don't really know that much about him. I know his name, that's about it. In fact, I don't really know his name. I know his initials. Billy, the barman who introduced me to JR, told me once that he thought his name was Jack somethin'-or-other. I think it began with a B or a D. He says JR looked like a guy a mate of his used to play golf with years back. He wasn't a hundred per cent sure though. But even if I went down that road, I have no idea where Billy is now. The last I heard he was moving to Galway to become a barman at some jazz club. I don't even know Billy's surname. I could look into it, I suppose. Maybe I will in the future. But I'm certain JR will contact me at some point. We can hardly talk now. These cunts are trackin' everything I do. JR will have to wait it out, probably for another couple of years. That's a shame. I miss him. We spent so much time together. I certainly have the time on my hands to be patient. I have to shut out the bullying from Jennifer and the cops. I can't let it play on repeat in me head while I'm in me cell alone. I'd probably ask for a less annoyin' lawyer if Jennifer's ass wasn't making me dick hard.

I guess the good thing about prison is me urges to kill seem to have gone away. I still think of the faces of the three men I've murdered. I can only remember the first two from the photographs that appeared in the newspapers over the days after their deaths. But Ryan's face is very clear to me. I can even hear him talkin' to me sometimes. I feel a sense of success over the cops that they think I've only murdered one man. I may have to spend the rest of me life in prison, but I still got away with murder – twice! I'm a proper fuckin gangster. I'm gutted I got caught but I'm fine with how my life's gone. If I had the chance to go back in time to meet JR in the Deer's Head, I'd do it all over again.

12:00

Vincent

I NEVER RETURNED TO THE PENTHOUSE. I COULDN'T.

Chelle and her husband Jake organised the collection of my furniture and all my possessions. I've never set foot in any of the banks again either. My colleagues understood. I told them I was moving to Sydney to live out the rest of my life where Ryan always wanted to live; that I was dedicating the rest of my existence to his memory.

The bank sorted me out with a very handsome redundancy package. They rushed it through as quickly as they could. Half a million euros. Thank you very much. That added to the €890,000 profit I ended up with for the sale of the penthouse. I couldn't leave Dublin until the police finished their investigation, though. There was a period of two weeks where I was under serious consideration of being involved in the crime. Nobody at the bank thought I had any part in it but one of the detectives came down very hard on me. Even my tears of self-guilt didn't give him reason to sympathise with the fact that my boyfriend had just been murdered. I suppose he was just doing his job. The other detective looking into the case was always on my side. Maybe they were just playing the good-cop, bad-cop card. It seemed that way to me. But after a couple weeks of intense scrutiny and uncertainty, they relieved me of any involvement.

They're still on the lookout for whoever escaped with the cash. Darragh Galligan isn't giving up his partner in crime. That freak wasted no time putting a bullet through Ryan's head. My ex-boyfriend died instantly. I imagined Ryan's face every minute of every day for the next three months. I couldn't get what he would have gone through that morning out of my mind. But I was keen to put that whole life behind me.

The glare of the low sun makes me blink as I push through the glass door. It reminds me of the morning of the killing. A waiter greets me with a friendly smile but I don't need his assistance. I know who I'm looking for. There's no mistaking the back of that head. It's always had more hair on it than mine. He feels my presence and spins around just before I get to him; then grabs me in tight.

'We did it,' he whispers into my ear. I've missed his voice. I've missed his face. I've missed those lips. Jack is the best kisser I've ever kissed. I guess that's down to the years he spent kissing girls before he realised he was gay. I don't know why it took him so long. He's so obviously camp. Much camper than me.

'Yes we did!' I reply before leaning off him so I can stare into his blue eyes. I love every inch of him.

I never felt our plan would fail. Jack had new passports and identifications set up for us through his contacts with his old mates and I set out a plan to spread the money without any suspicion. We're both Canadians now. Stanley Lam and Roy Gagnon.

Fucking Stanley! I've actually become quite fond of it ever since Jack first told me what my new name would be. It's grown on me over the past few months. The paperwork is official. The guys Jack knew from his gangland days know all the tricks with that sort of shit. The real Stanley Lam and Roy Gagnon are dead, but their deaths have never officially been recorded in Canada. We are them now.

I taught Jack how to spread the money throughout Europe. The main bulk of the eight million is dotted around four different banks in Switzerland, but we've bank accounts in London, Brussels and here in Rome. Between us, we possessed the expertise to pull this off. We just needed to make sure the execution of the morning went without a hitch. I knew what the rough tiger kidnapping plan was, but Jack purposely didn't tell me when or exactly how we were going to pull it off. We planned it that way so that my fear would be very much real on the day.

We talked about living in Rome on the very first date we ever went on almost two years ago. Now here we are, multi-millionaires in our favourite place in the world, living out the rest of our days. Hopefully there's a lot of days to come. We're both classed as middle aged, but at almost 50, the chances are we're both over the half-way line.

It was Jack who raised the idea of me robbing my old bank pretty early on. But he was genuinely only joking. We laughed at the thought. We were two genuinely nice guys whose lives got turned upside down at the very same time we started to fall in love. Not long after I'd found out Ryan was fucking kids — and as a result was suicidal — Jack's investigation into the killing of his son Frank was tying itself together. He discussed his search for Frank's killer with me over pillow talk even in our early days of dating and we had long discussions on what he should do when he finally caught up with him. A light bulb went on in Jack's head one day when he revealed the rough plan to me. I thought he was crazy. But the more we talked about it, the more it seemed to make perfect sense. It actually became a no-brainer. We were shocked we could both be so dark.

We figured out a way to get rid of both Ryan and Darragh in one genius swoop while helping ourselves to our dream life. We both genuinely felt that we deserved our dream life. We'd both been served shitty hands up until that point. I try not to think about Ryan at all. I don't feel a huge amount of guilt. He wanted to die. I'm not sure if Bob Nugent wanted to die, but he deserved to. The shit I saw that sick fuck doing to young kids in videos he posted to Ryan as TeenCum069 was vomit-inducing. He left a few hints in the forums about who he was and where he was based. It didn't take long for Jack to track him down and use him as the ultimate test for Darragh. We had to know if he could kill. It all fell into place for us. The serendipity of it all would almost make you believe in fate. Jack and I had always arranged to meet up here on the rooftop of the Forum Hotel at midday exactly six months from the day of the robbery.

Darragh's upcoming trial gave me a big problem though. I was due to be a key witness for the prosecution. My lawyer fought hard to keep me away from the courts. The police weren't happy but I was finally pardoned on the grounds of personal grief. The detective who had come down hard on me during the investigation turned out to be my hero. He told the courts they had more than enough evidence to put Darragh away for life without me needing to take the stand. The little fucker had actually wanked all over our apartment during that morning, spraying his juice all over our TV. You couldn't make it up.

Besides that, there's a mountain of evidence stacked against him. He even had the gun he killed Ryan with in his pocket when he was arrested. He's clearly not a bright little prick at all. Jack nailed it. He got everything spot on. So did I. I was brilliant. Not only during the morning of the robbery, but in the months that followed. I had to play the victim to perfection and I fucking nailed it. Everybody was smothering me with sympathy. Even the board members went out of their way to fawn over me after flying over from America. They have a plaque dedicated to Ryan in each of their Irish branches now. That makes me laugh. The only time I almost came out of character was when Clyde Sneyd snuffled under my arm at Ryan's funeral to cry into me like a little baby. I should've been given an award for the straight face I kept as I patted the top of his head.

And to think somebody once told me I couldn't act!

THE END.

WANT TO KNOW...

- what Jack and Vincent got up to next?
- how Darragh is getting on in prison?
- how Jack and Vincent concocted their plan?
- how David B. Lyons came up with the idea for this novel?

Well, you can watch this exclusive interview with the author right here where he will answer all of the above questions as well as many others.

www.subscribepage.com/middayq&a

BOOK II

WHATEVER HAPPENED TO BETSY BLAKE?

By David B. Lyons.

For Lola

10:00

Gordon

I DON'T KNOW WHY I'M SMILING WHEN I'VE JUST BEEN TOLD I HAVE A FIFTY per cent chance of dying today. But I am smiling. I can feel it; my cheeks high and wide on my face. It must be the shock. Or perhaps the prospect of death is appealing to me; the thought of my mind finally shutting the fuck up.

'Do you understand, Gordon?' Mr Douglas asks.

I feel my cheeks fall back down to their resting position, then let out a little sigh and nod my head.

'I understand, Mr Douglas.'

'Well, we're going to prep the theatre as soon as it's free. In the meantime, Elaine here,' he says pointing to a young nurse dressed in purple scrubs, 'will be available for you to talk to anytime you want. She'll be positioned outside at the nurses' station. Just press this button and she'll be with you in no time.'

He hands me what looks like a Nintendo games controller from the early nineties; one red button in the middle of it. Then he purses his lips at me before spinning on his heels. They all follow in unison, like a synchronised swimming team. I count them as they head towards the door. Seven. I'm waiting on them all to leave so I can sink the back of my head firmly into the pillow and yell obscenities. But Elaine turns back, walks towards me.

'Mr Blake, are you sure there's nobody I can call… nobody who can come up to see you?'

'It's Gordon, please,' I tell her, my forearms propping me up on the bed. 'And eh... no, there's nobody. Not yet anyway. I may call my wife a little later.'

'Your wife?' she says, her eyebrows twitching.

'Ex wife.' Elaine makes an 'O' shape with her mouth. 'There's a few things I need to iron out in my head before I call her.'

Elaine places the palm of her hand on top of mine and then purses her lips before turning around and walking out the door to catch up with the rest of her team. They must master that in medical college; how to purse your lips before spinning on your heels. As soon as she has closed the door I push my head firmly into the pillow.

'Fuuuuuck!' I screech, clenching my fists; my fingernails stabbing into the palms of my hands. I allow the reality of the situation to wash over me as much as it possibly can. A fifty-fifty chance of survival. That's what Douglas said. Fuckin hell. I reach out to grab my phone and hold my finger against the screen so I can check the time. 10:03. Douglas told me the theatre would be ready at three p.m. I twitch the top of each finger on one hand to count upwards. Five hours. Jesus Christ. I might only have five hours left to live.

'Fuuuck!' I don't screech it this time. I scream it. I tilt my head; stare over at the door handle in anticipation of it being pushed downwards. But it remains upright. Nobody's coming to soothe me.

My breathing grows heavier. Flashes of Betsy's pretty little face consume me. At first she's smiling. Then crying. Gagged. Suffocating. I shake my head to get rid of her. This is nothing new. I've been doing this almost daily for the past seventeen years. I consciously try to slow my breathing, then rest my head back on to the pillow.

I remember a college lecturer – many years ago - asking me a question that relates to the situation I seem to have found myself in right now.

'If you had just hours left to live, what would you do?'

I think I answered by saying 'sex' or 'bungee jump' or some other adrenaline-filled piece-of-shit activity. She was trying to get across the concept of bucket lists and positive thinking. But that's a load of bollocks. I've never had a bucket list. Unless finding your daughter is applicable to being on a bucket list. That's the only thing I want in life. To see her face again. To hold her. To apologise to her.

A tear squeezes itself out of my left eye. I shake my head again. Not to remove the tear, but to remove the image of Betsy from my mind. Then I grip my mobile phone; scroll into my contacts list until I see the name Ray De Brun and stare at it. I picture his chubby little face; bet he's all fat and old now. Useless prick. I touch his name and then hold the phone to my ear. That annoying high-pitched tone you get when a number is out of use pierces through me. I grip the phone firmer in frustration, let an audible sigh force its way out of both nostrils. I scroll through the screen of my phone again, into my Internet browser and search for 'Kilmainham Garda Station'. The phone number appears instantly. I press at it, bring the phone back to my ear.

'Hello, Kilmainham Garda Station.'

'I need to talk to detective Ray De Brun.'

'Just one second, Sir.'

I chew my bottom lip while I'm on hold. What I've been told this morning is too mammoth to fully comprehend. But I've just realised I'm not my greatest concern. Betsy is. And always has been. My greatest fear may play out today; I may very well die without ever knowing what happened to my daughter.

'I'm sorry, Sir, Detective De Brun is not on duty today. Is there anybody else who can assist you?'

I speak slowly.

'My name is Gordon Blake. Betsy Blake's father. De Brun knows who I am. I have his mobile number but it seems out of action – has he changed it?'

'Oh, I'm not aware of that, Mr Blake. Detective De Brun is in semi-retirement now. Our lead detective is Detective Marshall, shall I see if she is available to talk to you?'

I fall silent. Marshall. Never heard of her.

'It's an emergency. I need to talk to De Brun right now. Please pass me on his mobile number. He won't mind. I'm dying... may only have hours to live.'

'Eh... hold on just one second, Mr Blake.'

A tipple of piano music plays. Doesn't last long.

'Hello, Mr Blake – this is detective Marshall. How can I help you?'

'Marshall... De Brun was the lead detective in the case of my missing daughter over seventeen years ago. You may be familiar with it.'

'I am indeed, Mr Blake. But you are fully aware that case is closed, right?'

I turn my face away from the phone and gurn. Nothing annoys me more than being told the case is closed. It's not fucking closed! It won't be closed until I'm holding my daughter again.

'Mr Blake, the case was closed in 2009. Elizabeth was announced deceased and—'

'Listen, Marshall,' I shout, my patience already stretched. 'Firstly, her name isn't Elizabeth okay, it's Betsy. And secondly, she's not fuckin dead. How can she be announced deceased when you and your colleagues never found a body?'

'Mr Blake, I can call up the files for you later and—'

'I don't have *later*, Marshall!' I snap. 'Listen, can you please just get me in touch with De Brun. I need to speak with him as urgently as possible. I'm in Tallaght hospital. I have to undergo emergency surgery in a few hours time and there's a huge chance I won't wake up from it.'

The line falls silent. All I can hear is my own breathing reverberating back at me.

'Please,' I say, sounding desperate.

'Mr Blake, Detective De Brun is in Galway – he's semi-retired, has a home out on the west coast and spends an awful lot of his time there. He—'

'Please.' I say it even more desperately this time.

'Tell you what. I'll give him a call and let him know you are looking for him. I can see your number here on the screen. I'll ask him to ring you as soon as possible. But… I must inform you, Mr Blake, Detective De Brun goes to the west coast to get away from phones, to get away from work. He may not have it switched on. There's no guarantee I can reach him imminently.'

My eyes twitch, flickering from side to side. Maybe I'm going mad. I've been seventeen years searching for Betsy, with possibly only five hours left. What makes me think I can get to the bottom of this today? I allow a long sigh to force its way out of my nostrils.

'Just ask him to ring me as soon as he can. It's an emergency.' I hear my voice crack as I say that. Then I hang up. The tear that dropped out of my left eye is now hanging from my chin. I swipe it off with the palm of my hand, almost cutting my fingertip against my sharp stubble. Then I lie flat back down on the pillow.

Maybe I should ring Michelle. Tell her my terrible news. Though I'm not quite sure what that would achieve. Douglas said it's imperative I relax ahead of my surgeries, says that having a positive mind-set could be key to success. Having Michelle come up to me will only cause me stress. *Us* stress. She gets more worked up than I do. She can't stand the fact that I can't let go; that I haven't accepted that Betsy is gone. And I can't stand that she gave up; that she's happy to accept the cops' theory.

And that's all it is; a fuckin theory.

No. Fuck her. There's nothing I can achieve by ringing Michelle.

But I can't lie here and do nothing. I pick up my phone, scroll into the Internet search browser again.

10:00

Lenny

LENNY CAN FEEL CLAIRE'S KNEES VIBRATE AGAINST HIS. IT ISN'T A shivering of her knees that is causing the vibration. It's the constant swiping of her palms against her thighs. She's trying to rid them of sweat; is all too aware that she's about to receive an answer to the mystery that has engulfed her for the past six months.

They're both sitting at Lenny's tiny desk, inside his tiny office. Calling it a desk is exaggerating; it's no bigger than the type of table you would find on a train. And calling it an office is probably exaggerating too; it's no bigger than a laundry room in a modest home. But it's all he can afford. The office just about has enough space for the desk, two chairs and one tall, skinny filing cabinet, which can't fully shut due to the amount of paperwork desperate to jump out of it. Most of the paperwork is redundant, but sorting it out isn't high on the list of Lenny's priorities. It's not as if the day doesn't afford him ample time to sort it out, he just couldn't be bothered. He's more interested in finding new assignments than pouring over the contents of old ones.

He finally stops typing, then turns his laptop screen to face Claire. She sucks in a sharp breath, then holds a finger to the tip of her nose; her attempt to halt the tears from loosening their grip from the tips of her eyelashes.

'He's… he's my line manager at work,' she whispers into her finger.

'Have you any idea why he would be doing this to you?' Lenny asks.

Claire begins to drum the tip of her finger against her lips as she sinks into her thoughts. Then she shakes her head slowly.

'I mean... he tried it on with me at our Christmas party last year,' she says, finding volume. 'But... that's about it. I can't think why... Derek! Derek Murray. I don't believe it.'

Lenny closes the lid of his laptop and looks up sympathetically at Claire. He's been in this position many times before; not really knowing what to say next. The job she offered him had reached its conclusion, yet he understands Claire will have a thousand questions racing around her head right now.

'Do you know why... why he is doing this to me?' she asks.

Lenny scratches at his temple. He always feels awkward when he has the opportunity to upsell.

'Well that's another job. If you would like me to confront Derek, get those kind of answers for you, I can indeed do that but...' Lenny shrugs his left shoulder.

'I eh... I eh,' Claire stutters, 'I don't really know what to do next.'

'Tell you what. Now that we've found out the who, why don't you take a step back and think it all through. If you want to find out the why, get in touch. I'll be here for you. For now, I recommend going home, having a nice hot cup of tea and thinking all this through before contacting me again. I'm at the end of this phone anytime you need me,' he says, picking up his clunky mobile from his desk. 'Y'know, perhaps you have enough information now to see if the cops would be interested – now that you know who has been stalking you they may look at it differently.'

Claire throws her eyes towards the stained ceiling, then stares back down to her fidgeting fingers on her lap. She'd taken that road before. The cops didn't want to know; they didn't even hide the fact that such a complaint was beneath them either.

'I'll think it through, Lenny. I'll go home, have that cup of tea, and eh... thank you so much for all of your help.'

Both Claire and Lenny stand up at the same time. Lenny holds his hand out for his client to shake, but she squashes it between them both as she drags him in for a hug.

'Allow me,' Lenny says after they release. He pulls his door open, then steps aside so Claire can squeeze her way out.

'I'll send my report on to you by email, but eh... just so you know, there'll be no H in the report. This old thing,' he says, slapping the lid of his laptop, 'it's getting old. The H key came off and...'

Claire offers Lenny a thin smile and then nods her head once before turning around. She's still in a sterile state of shock as she slumps down the corridor, her head bowed. Lenny doesn't watch her leave. He's too bothered chasing the sheet of paper that has floated into his office. He tuts, picks it up and then paces down the corridor himself, turning left before he reaches the stairs Claire is now making her way down. He walks past two doors, all equally battered as his, then knocks on the third one he comes to.

'Sorry, Joe,' he says, after opening the door himself. 'Any Blu Tack?'

'Again?'

Lenny holds the sheet of paper towards Joe as an answer.

'Fuck sake, mate… can you not get a proper sign? Won't cost much.'

'I keep meaning to, it's just…' Lenny shrugs his shoulder again, then blinks his eyes rapidly.

'Didn't you have a client in with you just there? She was alright lookin' wasn't she?'

'Yeah, nice girl really – job's all done.'

'She paying you?'

Lenny nods.

'Well then buy a fuckin sign,' Joe says as he lobs a marble-sized blob of Blu Tack towards Lenny. 'Or at least buy some of your own fuckin Blu Tack.'

Lenny looks around Joe's office space. It's not much bigger than his; probably longer. It's more rectangular in shape, but still only fits a small desk, two chairs and one filing cabinet – though Joe's filing cabinet is a little chunkier than Lenny's.

'Thanks, man,' Lenny says before closing Joe's door and plodding back down the corridor. He grips the sheet of paper between his teeth while pulling at the blob of Blu Tack, dividing it into four separate smaller blobs. Then he removes the sheet from his teeth, stabs a blob onto each corner and slaps the paper to his door before rubbing his thumb repeatedly over each corner firmly. He knows that no matter how many times he rubs his thumb over the corners, the sign is still going to fly away again. But he might at least try. He stands back, stares at the sign as if it's the first time he's ever read it.

Lenny Moon – Private Investigator.

It's written in black felt-tip pen on a blank A4 sheet of white paper.

Pathetic.

He closes the door behind him and sinks back down into his Ikea office chair. Aside from the laptop, the chair is the most expensive thing in the room. A hell of a lot cheaper than the chair on the other side of the desk; a fold-out seat his mother used to use in their old home to help her reach the top shelf in the kitchen.

Lenny opens a Word document on his laptop labelled 'Claire Jennings' and types the word 'complete' at the bottom of it, all in capital letters. Then he highlights what he has just typed and changes the font colour to red before slapping his laptop shut and resting the back of his head on to the top of his chair. He always pictures his wife when he does this. Imagines her staring at him; her lips turned down. It's almost impossible for him to picture her smiling anymore. When he's intent on picturing her smiling, he has to close his eyes even firmer. By the time the lips in his imagination have turned upwards, Sally's face will have turned into something else. Somebody else. He barely tries to imagine her smiling anymore anyway. He's just content to picture her. To know she's still around. Still alive.

The noise of the phone vibrating on his desk brings him back to the real world. But he knows it's not a massive deviation. The person ringing is most likely the person he has just been thinking about. Either that, or someone is ringing about work. The chances of that are slim, though – about twenty-five per cent. Only one in four phone calls are work related; the rest of the time it's Sally calling. She rings three times a day.

'Hey, sweetie,' he says.

'Busy?' she asks. She always asks this. He always answers the same way; by sniffing a short laugh out of his nose.

A silence rests from both ends of the line. This is not unusual. Sally mostly calls for no reason, other than routine.

'You okay?' Lenny asks.

'Yeah – today's a good day. I think. Been cleaning the house; put another load of washing on. Jesus, Leonard, do you have to change your boxer shorts so regularly?'

Lenny sniffs again, but then stays silent. She's often asked this question. It's best he doesn't answer, best he doesn't try to justify that he changes his underwear every morning like most people do. Like most people should. Because if he did try to justify it, he'd get barked at. It would turn Sally's 'good day' into a 'bad day.' And that's the last thing he wants.

'Spoke with Jared's teacher this morning when I dropped them off… says he's been doing well in class lately.'

'Oh… good, good,' Lenny replies. 'Was that the classroom teacher or the SEN one?'

'Eh… the short one.'

'Yeah – Ms Moriarty,' he says, 'it's Mrs Morrissey we need to get information from. She's the one who keeps track of him on a daily basis. We must arrange a meeting with her soon.'

'You're always saying that.'

Lenny nods his head. He's well aware that he's always saying that.

'Okay – just thought I'd see how you were doing,' Sally says.

'Thanks, sweetie, talk to you later.'

Sally hangs up after repeating the word 'bye' seven times, like most Irish women do when finishing a phone call.

Rather than rest his head onto the top of the chair Lenny opens his laptop, scrolls down to the Solitaire icon at the bottom of his screen and opens up a game he had begun playing when he first entered the office just before nine o'clock this morning. He's good at Solitaire is Lenny; gets lots of practice at it. But his meeting with Claire Jennings consumed his mind this morning and he didn't get a good enough start at the game. And getting a good start at Solitaire is everything. He checks the clock ticking away at the bottom corner of the screen. Thirty-eight minutes.

'Pathetic,' he whispers. And he's right. It is pathetic. Especially for someone who plays the game almost every day. His meeting distracted him. He wasn't sure how Claire would react when he revealed to her that it was her line manager at work – Derek Murray – who had set up two fake online accounts to stalk her. The poor girl has been on edge for the past three months, even left home to live with her sister because of the fear it was causing. She turned to the cheapest Private Investigator she could find after the Gardaí told her there was nothing they could do about the fact somebody was bullying her online. Lenny liked Claire, felt sorry for her. He'd be intrigued to follow up the investigation, to confront Derek, ask him why he was reducing himself to such juvenile behaviour. But he won't follow it up until Claire instructs him to do so. He needs the upsell. Needs the money.

The phone vibrates again.

Fuck sake.

'Yes, sweetie,' he answers.

'Sorry?' a man says.

'Oh… no, no, I'm the one who's sorry.'

Lenny sits upright, resting both of his elbows on his tiny desk. 'I thought you were my wife. Eh… Lenny Moon, Private Investigator – how can I help?'

'Is this Lenny?'

'It is, Sir.'

'Oh, good. I thought I'd get your secretary.'

Lenny's head pivots around his pokey room, wondering where a secretary would even sit. Atop the filing cabinet perhaps.

'My name is Gordon Blake. My daughter went missing seventeen years ago. I'm dying. May not have long to live. How soon could you get to Tallaght Hospital?'

Lenny squints his entire face; his eyes, his nose, his lips. When he started up his Private Investigating business, he had wishfully thought he would be inundated with calls such as this one. But none had ever come. Not one in the past six years. This is such an unusual call that Lenny immediately feels he is being played. Having a Private Investigating business listed in the Yellow Pages opens you up to a whole world of prank calls.

'Eh… Gordon Blake, that's B. L. A. K. E. – am I right?' Lenny asks, tapping the name into a fresh Word document.

'Yes… my daughter's name was – is – sorry, is, Betsy Blake. She went missing in 2002. Was snatched from our street.'

Lenny sits even more upright, his mouth slightly ajar.

'Betsy Blake. I remember,' he says.

'Yeah – she's my daughter. Please tell me you have time to give me today. I can give you one thousand euro for the next five hours of your life. If you can give me some answers, there's more on offer. A hell of a lot more.'

Lenny stares over his computer screen at nothing in particular. He's trying to soak in the surreality of the call.

'Let me, eh… let me just check my schedule, Mr Blake… it seems… eh…' Lenny slaps away at his keyboard, just randomly typing nonsense into the Word document in an effort to sound busy. 'I can push some things aside. And eh… that's cash is it – the one thousand?'

'I can transfer it into your bank account as soon as you get here. I'm in St Bernard's Ward, Tallaght Hospital. Are you in your office? It's close by right? You're in Tallaght village…'

Lenny takes the phone from his ear. Checks the time on the top of the screen. 10:19. Then he lets out a long, silent breath that almost whistles through his lips.

'I'll be with you just gone half past,' he says.

SEVENTEEN YEARS AGO

Betsy

Daddy turns around and looks at me.

'Don't go far, Betsy.'

Then he smiles. I like when he smiles. It means he is happy. When he is happy we play games. When we get back to our house we can play hide and seek or football. I like hide and seek best but most times I play football because I know Daddy will play that for longer with me. Football lasts longer than hide and seek. A lot longer. Sometimes we play until dinnertime. But that's only on days when Daddy is happy. Like today. We'll probably play football until Mummy calls us in for some stew or pasta. Today is Wednesday. It might be pasta.

I smile back at Daddy and then he turns away. That is okay. Maybe he is busy thinking about work. When he can't play with me he says it is because he is working. But normally when he is working he is on the phone or on his computer. But now he is just looking out onto the road. I don't know what he is doing. I do some dancing while I wait. I'm a good dancer. There is no music. But sometimes I don't need music. Then a man puts his hand towards Daddy and Daddy puts his hand in his. I don't know who the man is. It is somebody Daddy works with I think. They just stand there talking. And talking. And talking even more. I'm bored. Too bored to even dance anymore.

I see a little wall at the end of the road and skip towards it. I am good at walking on walls. Mummy and Daddy say I should hold their hand if I'm ever walking on walls but sometimes I do it when they are not looking. I'm a big girl now. I don't like holding Mummy and Daddy's hands. Not all the time. My cousin Ceri doesn't hold her Mummy's hands anymore and she is five. I can't wait to be five. But June seems a long way away. Even though Ceri is a bigger girl than me, I don't think she is happier than I am. She doesn't have a Daddy. I would hate to not have a Daddy. It would make me sad. Really, really sad. I would cry. A lot.

I put one foot in front of the other and spread my arms out. I have seen somebody do this on the TV when they were walking on a rope. I don't know how you can walk on just a rope. But this man did it. Way up high. Almost in the sky. He walked on a rope from the roof of a building all the way across to the roof of a other building. Mummy says the man must have gone to school for lots and lots of years to learn how to do that. That seems like a fun thing to do at school. I wonder when I am going to start learning how to walk on ropes at school.

I put the other foot in front and then the other. Slow. I try not to look down because when I look down I feel a bit dizzy. The wall is big. It is about the same size as me. Mummy measured me with a measuring tape before. I think it was in the summertime. She said I was three foot, three inches. She said I was going to be a big girl soon. That made me happy. I can't wait to be a big girl.

I put the other foot in front. Then the other. I am getting close to the end of the wall. I turn back to see if Daddy can see me. I want him to smile at me again. But he is too far away. He is just like a small spot at the end of the road. There are two small spots. He must still be talking to the man that works with him.

'Daddy, Daddy.' I wave.

He doesn't look. I am too far away. I should shout loud.

'Da—'

A man's hand is on my face. He picks me up off the wall and then down behind it. He has one hand across my mouth. His other hand is around my legs. He's holding me really hard. It hurts.

'Don't scream, Betsy.'

I don't scream because I am scared. But I want to.

10:20

Lenny

LENNY SNATCHES HIS BUNCH OF KEYS FROM HIS DESK, THEN PAUSES IN THE doorway. He's trying to work out whether or not it's appropriate for him to drive to Tallaght Hospital from here.

It's one of those in-between decisions most of us have to make on an irregular basis; take a fifteen-minute walk or be a lazy bollocks and take the car for a three-minute drive. The hospital is less than a mile away from Lenny's office, at the far end of Tallaght.

It's a shared office block Lenny works from; nine small business all renting space within it. There is an array of 'entrepreneurs' operating here; two start-up tech guys, two freelance graphic designers, a photographer, a jeweller whose sewing machine can be heard stuttering throughout the building, a stationary designer, a copywriter – which is what Joe does when he isn't being distracted by Lenny asking for Blu Tack – and, of course, a private investigator.

Each of the office spaces are cramped; though cramped in different ways. Some of the rooms are square – like Lenny's – some more rectangular – like Joe's. But they're all dingy, echoey and almost always cold – whatever the season. They are solitary though; allowing those who rent the spaces the opportunity to work undisturbed for most of the day and – more importantly – they are as cheap as chips to rent. Lenny pays two hundred and fifty euro every month for his space. A pittance in Dublin, even if it is for a room the size of an under-the-stairs bathroom. It's fine for Lenny though, because aside from his advertising costs –

which consist of an annual fee for his appearance in the Yellow Pages – Lenny's overheads are minimal. He just has to make sure he brings in at least one-thousand four hundred euro every month to cover his outgoings; two hundred and fifty euro to pay for his office space, eight hundred and fifty to pay the mortgage on the family home along with utility bills, plus the three hundred he and Sally calculate they need for groceries each month to feed all four Moons.

For the most part he just about manages to sneak in the required amount, but there are months when the family have to live on reheated stews and coddles for days on end when he comes up a little short.

Lenny has tied himself to two insurance companies who use him on a regular basis to find out whether or not they are being scammed by people making claims from them. The money from these jobs is decent enough – about two hundred euro a go. But Lenny needs to ensure he picks up at least seven of those gigs a month. Sometimes he does, sometimes he doesn't. There's no projecting it. Though a new wave of clients seems to have evolved for Lenny over the past year; those who hire him to find out who's anonymously bullying them online. This type of 'crime' is a growing concern in the modern world; but it's not much of a concern for Lenny – it puts an extra few quid in his coffers. He likes this type of job, it's less boring than sitting outside somebody's house, waiting on them to come out so he can take a photograph of them that may prove their back injury isn't as bad as they are claiming.

Though neither of these gigs have anything to do with the reason Lenny became a Private Investigator in the first place. He assumed he would be playing detective; solving proper crimes; murders, kidnappings, thefts, larceny. But that was slight delusion, borne from reading too many crime fiction thrillers over the years. He never got a call asking him to solve such a crime… until three minutes ago.

He nods his head, decision made. He'll drive over to the hospital. That way if he needs to get on with the job immediately, he'll have his wheels close by. Lenny grabs at his yellow puffer jacket and Sherpa hat, then pulls the office door behind him and sets off down the rickety stairs.

During the months of October through March Lenny always wears a Sherpa hat; he needs the fur inside to protect his bald head from the elements. Lenny lost his hair in his early twenties. Aside from the fact his head is always freezing during these months, losing his hair has never bothered him. He has the right shaped head to carry it off. He offset the baldness by growing out some stubble on his face. The stubble irritates Sally – she finds it discomforting to kiss her husband – but they both agree that a full beard doesn't suit him; it hides his jaw line, while a fully-shaved face makes him look like a twelve-year-old. And that's not a good look for somebody who wants to be taken seriously as an investigator. So they both decided stubble was the best option for him. Even with the stubble, Lenny still looks much younger than his thirty-three years, but at least he has the maturity to pass himself off as a man in the middle stages of life.

He thumbs his dated mobile phone as he paces his way to the car, trying to remember the images of Betsy Blake that were plastered all over the media many years ago. The most prominent picture used was a school portrait; her beaming a gummy grin at the camera dressed in her navy-blue uniform. The nation was obsessed with the story of Betsy Blake. Lenny was only a mid-teen when the story blew up. Over half his life-time ago. His memory is letting him down. If he had a smart phone, he'd be able to recall that image now. But what would it matter? Betsy isn't four-years-old anymore; she'd be twenty-one now. A woman. Lenny shakes his head and puffs out his cheeks as this reality hits him.

He throws his phone on to the passenger seat of his car, turns the key in the ignition and pulls out of his parking space without hesitating. He sings along to the Little Mix song that blasts from his stereo. This is always a tell for Lenny that he's in a good mood. He's excited about this job. The one thousand euro on offer from Gordon Blake is definitely playing a part in dictating Lenny's positivity, but it's more the job that has him buzzing. Trying to find a girl who's been missing for seventeen years. That sure as hell beats filling in paperwork for an insurance company.

He drums at the steering wheel, imagining the press he would receive if he were to somehow make a breakthrough in the Betsy Blake case. Though Lenny's not stupid; he's aware he's day-dreaming. He's a decent private investigator – more often than not his clients are pleased with his work – but he has never achieved anything of note that would suggest he's capable of making even the smallest of dents in the highest-profile missing person's case the country's ever known. Anyway, he assumed Betsy was dead. Was certain the Gardaí closed the case about ten years ago.

Soon he's turning right into the hospital grounds and circling the parking lot. When he finally finds a space he can fit his tiny Nissan Micra in to, he leaps out of his car, trudges down the brick staircase and finally across the zebra crossing that leads to the hospital entrance.

He takes in the stench of antibacterial soap immediately, can almost taste it on his tongue.

'St Bernard's Ward?' he asks the man sitting at a rounded reception desk.

'Floor three.'

Lenny sprint-walks towards the elevators and then pauses after pushing at the button. He watches the digital numbers above the doors click upwards, from three to four, then eyeballs the staircase behind him. He knows he would get to Gordon quicker if he used them. But he can be a stubborn fucker sometimes, can Lenny. So he stares back at the digits, taking seconds to will them to count downwards. But they don't. Both lifts are now on floor five. He huffs, spins on his heels and makes his way to the stairs, striding up them two at a time. He's almost out of breath by the time he reaches a sign that reads St Bernard's Ward. The hospital corridors are overly bright, the yellow glare constant, regardless of the time of day. Lenny knows the hospital quite well. Has spent many hours in here, sitting next to Sally.

'Gordon Blake?' he asks a young nurse dressed in purple scrubs.

'Oh... Mr Blake is in room number thirty-two,' she replies. She stares at Lenny after answering, but he doesn't say anything. He just nods a 'thank you' at her and then paces in the direction she had pointed, staring at the numbers on the ward doors as he goes. When he arrives outside number thirty-two he pauses to catch his breath. Gordon Blake had asked him to be as quick as he could possibly be. Lenny removes his mobile phone from the inside pocket of his coat, notices it's 10:36. Fourteen minutes since Gordon Blake called him. Not bad. Then he blinks and pushes at the door.

A pale face turns towards him, then the man in the bed sits up, pushing his back against the railed bed post.

'Lenny Moon?'

'Yes, Mr Blake. I got here as quickly as I could.'

Lenny stares at the man. He looks as if his death is imminent alright; the face gaunt, the veins in his neck trying to poke their way out of the skin that covers them. All of his limbs are thin and long; even his fingers. Strands of his balding black hair are matted to his forehead.

'Lenny. I may only have a few hours left to live. I need you to find out who took my daughter.'

Lenny nods his head as he walks closer to the bed.

'I've been trying to recall Betsy's case on the way over here,' he says. 'What is it you would like me to find out for you, Mr Blake?'

'Gordon... please. And eh... I need you to find out who took her.'

Lenny sniffs out of his nostrils, then points his hand towards a blue plastic chair. When Gordon nods an invite for him to sit in it, Lenny takes off his hat and coat, hangs them on the back of the chair and then sits in it, crossing his right ankle over his left thigh. He reaches into the back pocket of his trousers, pulls out a small note pad that has a pen attached to it, and opens it up to a blank page.

'Okay, Gordon,' he says, clicking down on the top of the pen, 'what makes you think I can find out what happened to your daughter in the next few hours?'

SEVENTEEN YEARS AGO

Betsy

IT'S DARK. DARK FOR A LONG TIME. A LONG, LONG TIME. EVER SINCE THE man put me in the back of his car. I don't know how long I've been in the back of his car but I don't like it. I'm hungry. And thirsty. And tired. Really, really tired. But I can't go asleep. Even though I want to. It's been too bumpy and wavy. I lifted up the flap that is under me earlier. There's a big wheel underneath it. That's why I can't lie down nice and go asleep. I'm really scared. But I'm not crying. I stopped crying a long time ago. I don't have any tears left inside my eyes probably. I just want to go home. I want my dinner. Want my Mummy. My Daddy.

It smells really bad in the back of the car. A bit like Daddy's old socks. But maybe the smell is my wee wee. I did two wee wees in my Dora the Explorer pants. My pants aren't wet anymore. But it still smells. He opened the door one time. He threw me in a apple and a bottle of water. But that was a long time ago. It's gone really cold. It's not as cold when he's driving. But when he stops driving it is really cold. Really, really cold. And he has been stopped driving for a long time now. I wonder what Mummy and Daddy are doing. They have probably called the police. The police might be looking for me. But maybe the man will let me go soon. If he does, I'll stop a man or woman on the street. Tell them my name. Who I am. Who my Mummy and Daddy is. I don't know the name of where I live. But if Mummy and Daddy have called the police then they can come and take me home.

Daddy will be crying. I'm not sure if Mummy will. I've never seen her cry before. Daddy cries all the time. Even when he is watching telly. I saw him cry watching Coronation Street one time. I sometimes think I love Daddy more than Mummy. But then other times I think the other way round. Sometimes Mummy is my favourite. It can be different. But I know they love me because the two of them buy me sweets sometimes. And the two of them play games with me. Wish I was playing a game now. Maybe next time I play hide and seek with Daddy I will hide in the back of his car. Because it would be a good place to hide. Nobody can find me in here. Oh. Nobody can find me in here. My eyes do still have tears inside them. I can feel one come down my cheek. Then another one. I wipe them away. But my nose is making tears too and I can't stop it. I don't want to cry. But I'm making the crying noises now and I can't stop it. My body is shaking. I'm scared again. I had forgot I was scared.

> 'Twinkle, twinkle little star,
> How I wonder what you are.
> Up above the world so high,
> Like a diamond in the sky.'

Daddy sings that to me when I cry at sleep-time. It helps me stop crying. But it's not helping now when I sing it to myself. My nose still has tears coming out. I should keep singing anyway. It might work. Might help me stop if I keep singing it. I haven't sung Twinkle, Twinkle Little Star in a long time. I told Daddy I was becoming a big girl and didn't need that song anymore. I told Daddy I didn't like it. But I do. I wish he was singing it to me now. If he was singing it to me now I would stop crying. I know I would. I miss my Daddy singing. I miss hearing my Daddy's voice.

> Twinkle, twinkle little star,
> How I wonder—

I hear him. He is close by me. Maybe he is going to give me another apple. Another bottle of water. He is definitely going to open the door. I can hear the keys. The door lifts up. But I can't see him. It's too dark.

'Shhh.' I think he is holding his finger to his mouth. I blink my eyes loads of times to try to see him. I think it's getting brighter. I can see him a little bit now. He reaches in to me and grabs me around the shoulders and around the legs. A bit like when he carried me off the wall earlier. I think that was yesterday or maybe today. I don't know. But I do know it's night time now. I can see the light on the other side of the street on. That's the only light I can see. Everything else is dark. Really, really dark.

'It's okay, Betsy.' He drops me to my feet. Then he reaches up and puts a key in the door. I think it's a purple door. Or maybe it's black. After he opens it, he picks me up again. I don't want to go into his house. Maybe I should scream. But I don't want him to hurt me.

He carries me past two rooms. I try to look inside. But don't see anybody. I don't see anything. Then he kicks open another door and carries me down some steps.

'There ye go, Betsy.' His voice is all funny. He has a different voice. It sounds funny. Not like my Mummy's or Daddy's. Not like Ceri's Mummy or anybody I know. I think he is from a different country. I saw somebody on the television one time from a different country and he had a voice like this man. But his skin was brown. This man's skin isn't brown. He has the same kind of skin as me and Mummy and Daddy.

He walks back up the steps. He opens the door then walks out. It's dark in here too. But not as dark as in the back of the car. I can see a few things. I can see walls. Can see the floor. It's all very hard. Like stones. I try to walk around but my legs are tired I think. They won't let me walk. So I sit down on the cold floor. I wonder why I'm here. What the man wants me to do. I just want to go home. Maybe I should scream. My lips shake a little bit. Scream. I want to scream but my voice won't let me. Scream, Betsy. Go on.

'Ahhhhh.'

The door opens. He runs down the steps.

'Didn't I tell you to be quiet, Betsy?'

I think he looks angry. It's the first time I can see his face. It got lighter in here. Because the door up the steps is open. And it's really bright up there. He is about the same age as Daddy. But more scary looking. 'You scream out loud again, Betsy, and I will hurt you. Do you understand?'

I look down at the stone ground. Then I nod my head. I don't want to make him angry.

'Good girl.' He puts his finger under my face.

'Look.' He takes a teddy bear from behind his back. It's brown. 'You like teddy bears don't you, Betsy? This is yours. It's called Bozy.'

I look at the bear. That is an odd name. I nod my head again because I don't want the man to hurt me. Then he holds Bozy to me and I take it. The man runs up the steps again. I just look at the bear. I used to have a teddy bear in my bed with me. But it wasn't brown. It was white. And I didn't give him a name. Just teddy bear. But I better call this one Bozy, because the man might hurt me if I just call it teddy bear. Then the man comes back down the steps. Not running this time. Slowly. Real slowly. He is carrying something big. He throws it down in front of me.

'This is your bed tonight.'

I look down at it. Then I look at him. I don't want to cry. But I can't stop it. Another tear comes out of my eye.

'Why do I need a bed?'

10:40

Gordon

HE DOESN'T LOOK LIKE A PRIVATE INVESTIGATOR. HE'S TOO SHORT. AND HIS beard – if anyone would call it that – is a mess, like he just hasn't bothered to shave for the past week. Not that I'm in any position to judge someone's appearance. It's just… I assumed a private investigator would look more like… more like… well… I'm actually not sure what I expected a private investigator to look like. Maybe I've watched too many movies down the years; expected this guy to turn up in a trench coat and fedora hat, not a fuckin plastic yellow jacket that makes him look like the Michelin man and a stupid furry-muff hat.

He points towards the blue plastic chair by my bedside and I nod to welcome him to sit in it. Though he shouldn't be sitting for long. He needs to be out there; out there finding Betsy.

He sits, removes a pad and a pen from his pocket, and then crosses his legs as if he's getting comfortable.

'Okay, Gordon,' he says. 'What makes you think I can find out what happened to your daughter in the next few hours?'

That's a hell of a question. A question I don't have an answer to. I've been looking for her for seventeen years. I don't expect this guy to find anything in the next few hours, but I have to at least try. I can't lie here and do nothing.

'The police have never done a good enough job,' I say, not wanting to pause too long, in case he realises I don't have an actual answer to his question. It's the first thing that came into my head. But it's also the truth. They didn't. They fucked up the investigation on day one. They took too long to ignite their search – concentrating on me as if I had something to do with it. It meant whoever took my daughter had time to get away; time to get Betsy hidden in whatever place he wanted to hide her.

'They questioned a few suspects, but not intricately enough. I know she's out there, Lenny. And I—'

'But what makes you think *I* can find her in the next few hours if nobody has found her in the past seventeen years?' he says, interrupting me.

I take a deep breath as I push myself back into the steel bedpost to sit more upright.

'There're a few things that have niggled at me for years, things I couldn't push too far because the cops wouldn't let me. But now that I'm dying… or probably about to die, I need a new perspective on this. I can't lie here in the final hours of my life and not… and not…' A tear drops from my eye. Lenny stands up, turns towards the bedside cabinet and pulls two tissues from their box.

'Here,' he says. I fold the tissues in half, dab at my face.

Then I turn to him.

'One thousand euro to try your very best over the next few hours, but,' I say, pausing. 'If you make any breakthrough I'll make you a rich man.' Lenny blinks. Repeatedly. About four little twitches. He looks like a fuckin idiot. But I know he's totally tuned in. He's intrigued. 'Listen; I have no family, no friends. Not anymore. I've got nothing. My life is my home. It's all I have,' I tell him. 'If I don't make it through the day and you do your very best for me in my final hours… I'll leave you my house. I have a lovely home on the South Circular Road. Y'know those red brick Victorian houses?' Lenny nods, but he looks perplexed. As if he doesn't know what to make of me. 'They're worth close to a million,' I say. 'A neighbour sold his at the tail end of last year for nine-hundred and forty grand. And he didn't have the kitchen extension I have.'

Lenny squints his eyes, circles his tongue around his mouth.

'Gordon, let's start with the one thousand promised. Can you – as you suggested – transfer that into my account? I think we're both keen for me to get started. Then I'd like to talk to you about the leads you said you had.'

I take my phone up from my lap, log into my online banking app and within seconds I'm punching digits into the screen.

'What are your bank details?' I ask him. He scoots one bum cheek up off the chair and removes his wallet from his back pocket. Then he slips out a debit card and hands it to me.

'Account number and sort code are on the bottom,' he says. I type them into my screen, then turn the phone to face him.

'Press transfer,' I say. And he does. Without hesitation. Maybe he's desperate for the money. Maybe I've chosen the wrong private investigator. If he's not very rich, he mustn't be very successful. I just plumped for the nearest private investigator I could find on the Yellow Pages website. I was surprised to even find one based in Tallaght. I needed someone here as quickly as possible.

'Transfer complete,' I say, turning the screen back to Lenny.

He blinks rapidly again. It's really weird.

'Thank you, Gordon.'

He sits back in his seat, reopens his notepad and re-crosses his legs. He has the same tics every time. He's meticulous. Perhaps he is a good investigator after all. I guess we'll find out.

'In terms of leads—'

'You only have until three p.m.' I interrupt him. 'I'm having emergency heart surgery then. May not wake up from the procedure.'

He flicks his eyes up from his notepad to stare into mine.

'My heart's a mess. The hiatus hernia I've had as far back as my late twenties has grown and torn my main aorta. I have to have an open aortic valve replacement as well as some other procedure… a eh… triple-A something. I can't pronounce it. The two surgeries have to be done at the same time. If they're not carried out as quickly as possible, I'll have an unrecoverable major heart attack. My heart's basically a ticking time bomb, Lenny. Doctors said if I hadn't come into the hospital last night, I'd already be dead. They're just waiting on a couple more members of the surgical team to get here, and for the theatre to be cleared and set up. Said everything will be ready for three o'clock.'

Lenny gets up from the chair, walks slowly towards the foot of my bed.

'Do you mind?' he says, nodding towards the clipboard hanging on the bed rail.

I shake my head.

'An abdominal aortic aneurysm repair,' he says, his eyes squinting.

'That's the one.'

'So this could literally be your last roll of the dice. You want to throw everything into your final hours to find Betsy and you're hiring me to do it?'

'Ah – you *are* a good detective, huh?' I say. I laugh as I say it. But the laugh isn't reciprocated. Probably because it wasn't funny.

He hangs the clipboard back onto the rail, then paces to the blue plastic chair and sits in it again. But he doesn't cross his legs this time; instead he leans forward, eyeballs me.

'Gordon. It's admirable that after seventeen years of looking for Betsy and all that you've been through that you would dedicated the final hours of your life to continue looking for her... but...' he pauses, then blinks rapidly again. 'What, eh... what do you think I can actually achieve in such a small amount of time?'

Monkeys see as monkeys do. I blink too, mirroring him.

'Barry Ward,' I say. 'Police interviewed him. Dismissed him too early for my liking. I've spent a lifetime digging around, following him, getting information on him—'

'So you think he took Betsy?'

'Him or Alan Keating.'

'Hold on,' Lenny says, scribbling down the two names I gave him on his pad. 'Just so I can be clear now... you are paying me one thousand euro to speak to a Barry Ward and an Alan Keating to see what they know about Betsy's disappearance? Is that what you're hiring me to do?'

'I'm hiring you for more than that. I'm hiring you to find Betsy,' I say. I know it sounds ridiculous. I know I sound like a madman; like the madman Michelle has often told me I am. But what else am I supposed to do? Lie here and die without giving it one last go?

Lenny's eyebrow twitches, as if he is trying not to blink. I swing my legs over the side of the bed, wait for him to look up at me, to meet my eyes.

'You make a breakthrough in this case today, Lenny, my house is your house. While you're out investigating, I'm going to write a new draft of my will. It'll include you getting my house if I die today. I'll leave it in an envelope there on that cabinet with your name on it. I'll send a picture of it to my lawyer. But you'll have to make a breakthrough for that will to be sanctioned.' I grip the top of his hand; the one he has resting on his notepad. 'It means everything to me that you try your hardest to find Betsy; that you give it your all. You have until three o'clock.'

I take my hand off his, reach it under my pillow and take out the note I spent the last fifteen minutes writing.

'Here you go. Everything you need to know is on here.'

SIXTEEN YEARS AGO

Betsy

I LIKE LOOKING AT THE PICTURES ON MY WALL. DOD LET ME HANG THE pictures with something called Blu Tack. They are pictures from the magazines he buys me. Some pictures are of girls. Some pictures are of boys. I like the picture of a girl called Christina Aguilera the most. She looks pretty. She has yellow hair and orange skin. I put that picture over my bed. I look at it when I wake up in the morning and then look at it before Dod puts the light out at night and I have to go asleep. My bed is nice. I remember the first night I slept here. I only slept on a small bed with a cushion and a blanket. It was really cold. I cried all that night. I don't cry so much anymore. Sometimes if I can picture Mummy and Daddy in my head and they almost become real I will cry. But it's hard for me to picture them as if they are real anymore. When I close my eyes I want to see them. I want them to become real. But it is not easy. Most times when I close my eyes I see the people who I read about in my books. Dod brings me lots of magazines and books.

I have fourteen books now. I counted them yesterday. One book I have teached me how to count. One book teached me all about shapes. One book teached me all about the farm. One book teached me all about the park. I used to go to a park with Mummy and Daddy. It had swings and a slide in it. Just like the park in my book. But I haven't been to a park since I got here. I haven't been outside at all. Haven't been out of the house. Haven't been out of this room. I did go up the steps once when Dod left the door open but when I got in to another room he just rushed me back down the steps. It was bright up there.

Sometimes people come to Dod's house. He says I have to be very quiet when they come. He says if I'm not quiet he will hurt me real bad. So I just read my books. Sometimes Dod reads them to me. He hugs me on the bed and puts his fingers in my hair and reads to me. I like that. Sometimes I am scared of him. Sometimes he is really nice. I always know when he is coming. There is a small light that I can see under the door. And when he comes to the door the light goes away a bit. It's gone away now. He's coming.

'Happy birthday to you.
Happy birthday to you.
Happy birthday, dear Betsy.
Happy birthday to you.'

He has a cake and there are light sticks on it. He brings it over to my bed. Then he sits on the bed and smiles at me. He is being nice today.

'Blow out the candles.'

I look at him.

'What is candles?'

He makes a blow on the light sticks and the light almost goes away.

'Go on, blow.'

I do the same. I blow really strong and two of the lights go out. Then I do it again and the other three go out.

'Happy birthday, Betsy.' He kisses me on the cheek and then puts the big cake on the bed. I read the cake. It says 'Betsy'. And then a big number five. Dod walks back up the steps and then comes back down carrying a box.

'Am I five?'

'Yes, Betsy. You are five today. It's your birthday.'

'Am I a big girl now?'

'Yes, Betsy. You are a big girl now.'

'Does it mean I don't have to hold Mummy and Daddy's hands anymore?

Dod doesn't say anything. He just hands me the box. It has red paper all over it. I should be happy. But I am thinking about holding Mummy and Daddy's hands instead. I told them before that I didn't like holding their hands. But I want to be holding their hands now.

'Open it.'

I look at Dod.

'Rip the paper off… here, let me help you.'

Dod begins to rip the red paper and then I help him. The box has pictures of a slide on it. It is a yellow slide. With a blue ladder. Dod is smiling. He must really like this slide. I smile too.

'A slide?'

'Yes. A slide that you can have in here. You can pretend it is like being in the park in your book.'

Dod pulls the box open and then takes out the big yellow slidey bit. Then he takes out the blue ladder bit and gets down on the stone floor. He tries to put them together so I can climb up the three blue steps and slide down the yellow slide. I should be looking at him and being really happy. But I am looking up at the door. Dod has left it open.

'Don't look up there, Betsy.'

I look back at Dod. He is not smiling anymore. He is just trying to put the slide together. Maybe I should be happy that it is my birthday and Dod bought me a cake and a slide. But I am not happy. I am thinking about Mummy and Daddy. I am thinking about what presents they would get me for my birthday.

'Ah for fuck sake!' Dod seems really angry. He throws one of the blue steps against the wall. 'My fucking thumb.' He kicks the slidey part. 'Stop fucking looking up there. Didn't I tell you, Betsy? Never look up those steps when the door is open. You little shit.'

Dod picks me up and throws me on to the bed. The cake falls off.

'I'll hurt you, Betsy. You do as I say.'

Dod puts his thumb in his mouth and sucks it. Then he turns around and runs up the steps really fast and closes the door. It gets all dark again. I put my hands all around the bed until I find Bozy. Then I lie back under the covers with Bozy and we hug each other. This is what I do when Dod is angry. Hug Bozy. Bozy is my best friend. When we are scared, we sing.

'Twinkle, twinkle little star…'

10:50

Lenny

LENNY STABS AT THE BUTTON. SIX TIMES. AS IF IT'S GOING TO MAKE THE lift come any sooner. He doesn't eyeball the stairs behind him this time. He just waits; transfixed on the sheet of paper he's just unfolded. Gordon rushed him out of the ward; told him to concentrate on the note he'd written and to call him when he needed to ask any questions.

Suspects
  Alan Keating. Keating is a well-known criminal, nicknamed The Boss in the newspapers. I had some dealings with him before Betsy went missing. Underhand dealings. Illegal. I'm sure he had something to do with Betsy's disappearance. But Keating keeps his hands clean. Knows he is always being watched by the cops. He's now living up in Rathcoole. His seventh house in the last seventeen years. He has a sidekick freak who does all the dirty work for him…

Barry Ward. Keating's sidekick freak. I think he was a traveller. Certainly sounds like one. Would do anything for Keating – including killing people for him. He's more than capable of kidnapping a four-year-old. I've no doubt about that. He's a scumbag. Lives in Drimnagh still. Be careful with him.

Jake Dewey. Slippery fucker. Thinks he's ex IRA – but he's not. He's

273

deluded. Lies for a living. Came into my wife's life just as Betsy went missing. Never trusted him. Cops sounded him out but didn't dig far enough. Has a restraining order against me, so I can't go near him. Need you to dig deep today.

You make an impact today, Lenny, my house is yours. This is literally a million euro job for you if you get it right.

Lenny takes a deep inhale as the lift door pings opens into the hospital lobby. He hadn't even realised he had gotten into the lift. Then he paces out the door, over the zebra crossing and towards the car park. He stares upwards just before he enters the archway, after the first drop of what looks like many today drips onto his shoulder. The clouds turned from off-white to dark grey in the fifteen minutes Lenny had been inside the hospital.

'The fucking Boss,' Lenny whispers to himself as he slides his parking ticket into the machine. He's lost in thought as he waves his debit card over the reader, not even noticing that he's paying ten euro for leaving his car here for just a quarter of an hour. If he noticed, he'd be furious. Ten euro can go a long way in the Moon household. Goose pimples begin to bubble up on his arms; and not because the temperature has dropped. He smiles to himself as he paces up the steps and towards his car.

'Fuck it!' he says as he swings his legs inside. 'This is why you became a private investigator, Lenny boy.'

He turns the key in the ignition only to be met by a loud hissing of white noise. The radio doesn't work in here. He reaches for the standby button, knocks it off. Then he stares at his own eyeballs in the rear-view mirror and winks to himself.

'You can do this.'

His orange Nissan Micra pulls out of the car park and over the speed bumps. It's a 2005 Micra Lenny has. He can't afford anything more modern. With the temperature dropping, and the car heaters not working, Lenny flicks the collar of his yellow puffer jacket up to cover his bare neck, then reaches for his Sherpa hat and pulls it on. A small part of him – the conservative, weak side of him – is beginning to wish he was back in his pokey office, playing Solitaire, waiting on one of the insurance companies to ring him with another boring job. But another part of him – the adventurous life-is-too-short side that he used to be filled with until he married Sally – is excited about what lies in store. He became a private investigator because he wanted to solve crimes. And it's pretty impossible to solve crimes if you don't deal with criminals. Though, he must admit, criminals don't come more notorious in Dublin than Alan Keating. The whole of the country knows Keating's the head of one of the biggest crime gangs in Dublin – but the cops can't do anything about it. He keeps his nose too clean; controls his men from the comfort of his own homes.

Lenny knows titbits about Keating – like most people in Ireland do. It's no secret Keating was involved in the attempted murder of crime journalist Frank Keville back in 2003. Keville was shot in the back outside his child's classroom during a routine school pick up one Friday afternoon. The Guards still haven't found the man who pulled the trigger, but they know the instruction came from Keating. They just can't prove it. Keating was on holiday in Portugal when Keville was shot. He always hid himself well. It was actually Keville who first coined the nickname 'The Boss' for Keating. He was obsessed with Keating; wrote about him at least once a month in his weekly column for the *Irish News of the World*.

Lenny squelches up his mouth, then sucks his teeth. While he's aware just how dangerous Keating can be; he can't see a reason why he would have abducted Betsy without there being financial gain for him and his gang. It doesn't make sense. He drums his fingers against the steering wheel as questions whizz around his mind.

'Where'll I even start?' he says, eyeballing himself in the mirror again.

He reaches into his pocket, pulls out his phone and when the traffic halts his progress, he presses at buttons on his cheap mobile phone and goes into his call history, straight to the last dialled number. Lenny can't quite afford a hands free kit for his car, but he's mastered the art of gripping the phone between his thighs with the phone's loud speaker turned on. A horn beeps from behind just as the tone begins to ring and Lenny steps on the accelerator and pulls off with his wheels spinning.

'Hello.'

'Gordon, it's Lenny Moon.'

'Good. Where are you now?'

'I'm on the N7. Heading to Rathcoole to see if I can have words with Alan Keating. You wrote on the note 'Peyton Avenue' – where is that exactly?'

'It's up off the village, a left turn before The Baurnafea House pub. You can't miss the estate.'

'Estate? What number does he live in?'

'I have that information at home. I can't think of it. You'll have to ask somebody when you get there. I think it's on the second row of houses.'

Lenny rolls his eyes, then blinks them. The surreality of the whole job begins to consume him.

I'm off to question The fuckin' Boss about the Betsy Blake disappearance.

Lenny stares at his eyes again in the rear-view mirror as he pulls off the N7 at the Rathcoole exit.

'Lenny,' Gordon says, startling him back to the call.

'Yeah.'

'What are you gonna ask him?'

Lenny blows out his cheeks.

'I'll just start off as if I'm interviewing him for a routine investigation. I certainly won't be accusatory. I'll just say that as an associate of Gordon Blake at the time I'd just like to ask you a few questions.'

'Lenny…' Gordon says, then pauses. 'Ye have to tell him I'm dying. We used to be mates once; ask him… please, if he knows *anything* about Betsy. Anything at all. I don't have much time. No pussy-footing around. If you're happy with one-thousand for your day's work, fine, pussy-foot. But if you want serious money – and I mean if you want to become almost a millionaire in the next few hours – you gotta get me some answers. Answers I've never heard before. Please. I'm almost convinced that fucker has something to do with Betsy's disappearance. He's gotta know something. I'm begging you to figure it out!'

'Hang on, Gordon.'

Lenny scratches at the stubble under his chin, then pulls into a parking spot outside a bungalow at the entrance to Rathcoole Village.

'You wrote on the note that you had illegal dealings with Keating. You're gonna have to give me the details.'

Lenny hears the sigh on the other end of the line.

'I was his accountant. He practically forced me to handle his books; ran all his dealings through me. In simple terms I cooked his books… what can I say? I was doing it for about five years. I was probably a bit afraid of the fucker… but I… y'know… I was earning great money doing it and then… And then we just had a falling out. He kept wanting to push it too far… I was wary of getting caught. At one point I told him 'no'. And he… he threatened me.'

'Threatened you how?'

'Y'know… he just held me up against the wall, said I'd regret fucking with him.'

'Did he ever threaten Betsy?'

The line goes silent. Then Lenny hears a woman's voice in the background.

Gordon's tone turns different. More mature. More pronounced.

'Sure, Elaine. That is no problem. Whatever if it is you need to do, my love… Lenny,' he says, returning to the call. 'I'll have to ring you back. A nurse is here to run some tests.'

Lenny stares at the phone in his hand after Gordon's hung up.

'What the fuck am I doing?' he says. He laughs after he says it too, then shakes his head.

I'm off to question The fuckin Boss about the Betsy Blake disappearance.

The million pound house on South Circular Road crosses his mind. Not because he's dreaming about living in it – nor is he even considering the possibility – but because it's added to the craziness of his morning. He then runs back through the moment he held Gordon's medical chart in the ward; just to remove the possibility of being bullshitted to. He's been pranked well before, but this'd be some world-class award-winning pranking. He picks the phone up from his lap and presses in to his call history before pressing at the button beside 'home'. It was at moments like this, when he had to ring Sally to check something on the internet, that Lenny wished he had a smart phone.

'Hello.'

'Sweetie, sorry to bother you, But could you just check the online banking? I wanna see if money was put in this morning. Somebody was supposed to pay me today for a job.'

Sally hid her sigh well, but Lenny still caught a hint of it. It didn't bother him. He wouldn't have expected anything less. The fact that her sigh was so subtle was actually a sign that she was having a good day. The slight humming of a tune from her lips while she typed away at the home computer confirmed it. Today was a good day for Sally Moon. Normally that'd be enough to make Lenny content, but he's still staring down into his lap, scratching at his bald head with confusion when Sally sucks her lips; signalling she's about to talk.

'Yep. One thousand euro exactly. About half an hour ago. Who's that from – that's a big payment?'

'Oh a client I did a couple of jobs for a while back. He's owed me that for quite a while.'

'Gordon Blake?'

'Yeah – he's a guy I met through one of the insurance companies… asked me to look into a number of old clients of his he thought was scamming from them. I had to look into each of them. Turned out to be very little in it, but eh… yeah, he said he'd pay today, so I can scratch that off my list.'

Lenny wasn't concerned Sally would take the conversation much further. She'd been bored by his job for quite some time. Nothing exciting ever happen to her husband.

'Okay,' she says. 'Nice few quid. We need that coming up to Christmas. How is your—'

'I'm so sorry, sweetie. I'm gonna have to go. I got a spate of calls from insurance companies this morning and… eh… give me a call at, y'know, the usual time. Love you.'

Lenny hung up. It was unusual he'd hang up on Sally, but her feelings, unusually, aren't at the forefront his mind right now.

'A grand,' he says to himself. He's chewing on the edge of his rubber mobile phone cover when it buzzes in his hand.

'Yes love.'

'Sorry?'

'Oh sorry. Eh… Lenny Moon – Private Investigator.'

'Lenny… it's Gloria Proudfoot, Excel Insurance.'

'Gloria – how are you? Sorry… miles away.'

'Listen, I have a job for you. A Delaney Griffith. Claims she injured her back in a car crash back in August. But we've just had somebody tell us she's off down the gym lifting weights this morning. Can you get out to Coolock now, get confirmation and a photograph for us?'

'Now?'

'Yeah.'

Lenny brings the phone back towards his mouth to bite on the edge of his rubber case.

He normally jumps on anything an insurance company offers him. In fact he lives for it. But he never had the option of comparing the taking of a standard photograph of somebody in a gym over the interviewing of Dublin's biggest gangster about the most intriguing missing persons case to ever hit Ireland.

'Can't, Gloria. I'm sorry. I'm on a job at the moment.'

'Ah… okay, no probs, Lenny. I'll hit you up next time.'

'Sorry, Gloria,' he offers once more before the line goes dead. Then he stares at his eyes through the rear-view mirror again and laughs; his laugh fogging up part of the mirror.

He rolls down his window and points his index finger towards an elderly lady pushing her trolley along the narrow pathway.

'Can you tell me how to get to Peyton Avenue?' he asks.

The lady twists her body, to look in the opposite direction.

'That's one of the new estates,' she says, rolling her eyes, as if new estates are bothersome to her. 'Next left, then you'll see it when you get to the first roundabout. Sure, ye can't miss it.'

Lenny winks a thank you back at the lady, then winds his window back up and pulls out from the curb.

The woman was right. You couldn't miss it. Even before Lenny got to the roundabout he could see a massive sign reading 'Welcome to Peyton'. It was like one of the signs you'd see in America for a new housing estate; he even had to drive through a pointless archway to enter it. He blows out his cheeks while driving towards the first row of houses.

'There must be a hundred gaffs in here,' he mumbles to himself. He rounds the first bend, to get to the second row of homes just as Gordon instructed, then pulls over to stare at the front doors. They're big enough gaffs. Red brick, three storeys. The homes of people who make comfortable money. He couldn't quite work out why Alan Keating, who must rake in millions a year, was living here.

Lenny pulls the zip on his puffer jacket all the way up to his chin and yanks at the two strings of his hat, as if those actions are going to protect him from the rain. Then, without hesitating, he walks up the pathway of the house he pulled up outside and rings the doorbell.

A middle aged woman greets him with a confused smile.

'I'm looking for the Keating house. Do you know what number they live in?'

The woman drops her smile, narrows the gap in the door so just half of her face is showing.

'Number forty-nine,' she says. 'You'll know he's in if his black Merc is in the driveway.'

The door is fully closed before Lenny has finished his thank you. He walks back down the pathway, begins to stroll past the row of houses, counting the numbers on the doors as he goes. Then he stops dead, stares at the front of a black Mercedes that's taking up way too much space on the driveway of number 49. He takes the mobile phone from his pocket and then brings it to his mouth; not to ring anybody, just to chew on the rubber case; the rain falling around him.

Go on, Lenny Boy – grow some fucking balls!

He swivels, stares up and down the estate for no reason and then, almost as if somebody pushes him, he paces confidently, as if he isn't intimidated one iota by the infamous figure who lives behind the door.

It's only when he holds his thumb against the bell that his stomach flips itself over.

11:05

Gordon

THERE'S A FUMBLE AT MY DOOR, A CLANGING. THEN ELAINE WALKS IN, wheeling a small machine in front of her; leading it towards me. She purses her lips at me again, but I don't mind this constant sympathy gesture coming from her. She's nice looking. Not good looking. There's a distinct difference. And I'd take nice looking over good looking all day long.

She notices I'm on the phone, mouths the words 'heart rate'. I stretch the phone away from my mouth.

'Sure, Elaine,' I say. 'That is no problem. Whatever it is you need to do, my love.' Then I bring the phone to my mouth again. 'Lenny. I'll have to ring you back. A nurse is here to run some tests.'

Elaine opens the Velcro strapping on a small rubber tube and then releases two blue suction tabs. She motions towards my T-shirt and without hesitating, I lift it over my head. Then she places the two tabs on my chest and turns to twizzle at some nozzles on her machine.

'Sorry to disturb your call. Won't keep you long,' she says. 'We just need to keep checking your rate.'

I'm about to tell her the call wasn't that important when Elaine makes a strange sound; almost as if she's sucking her own tongue.

'Heart rate's gone up significantly, Gordon,' she says staring at me.

'I'm not surprised. After the news I was told an hour ago.'

'Have you been resting as we suggested?' she asks, while walking to the end of my bed to pick up the clipboard. She scribbles some notes on it while I try to find the words to phrase my lie.

'Yes. Just as you said. Haven't really done anything… Was just ringing a friend of mine there to—'

'That the same friend who was in with you half-an-hour ago?' she asks, staring at me over the clipboard.

'Yeah – an old friend. My best friend. The only person I could think of to call on to be honest.'

Elaine purses her lips again. She hangs the clipboard back on to the rail at the foot of my bed and then walks around to sit her pert bum on the edge of my mattress.

'Gordon… Mr Douglas spoke to you about the need for relaxation today. I can't stress how important that is.'

I roll my eyes. She catches me. It wasn't difficult – my eyes are about two feet from hers.

'I can't fully understand how difficult it is to digest the news you've been given, Gordon,' she says, 'but your best chance of surviving these procedures is to keep your heart rate steady.'

Douglas had already mentioned this to me; he told me my ability to keep my mind-set consistent over the next few hours would be just as important to my success as his steady hands during the procedures. The medical team are mostly afraid of blood clots; there's a high risk that multiple clots will form during my operations that can swiftly make their way to my lungs, to my brain. If that is the case; I'll never wake up. That's why Douglas – and now Elaine – are keen for me to relax – they want my heart rate to remain consistent. The more relaxed I am, the less chance there'll be of blood clots forming. But blood clots aren't their only concern. My heart's a ticking time bomb. I could have a massive heart attack while I'm cut open, could even have it before then, which is why they're trying to get me to the theatre as quickly as they possibly can. Two more of Douglas' surgical team are flying in from London as I lie here and the theatre will be prepped after the surgery that is going on in it right now is complete. It's why they've been very specific about my surgery time; three p.m. I pick up my phone just to make the screen light go on so I can check the time. 11:11. Jesus fuckin Christ. Less than four hours. While the phone is in my hand I imagine what Lenny is up to right now. He's probably knocking on Alan Keating's door. What the fuck is he going to ask Keating? How can he get any more information out of him that the police didn't get in their investigations? I know it's an impossible ask. But

I can't lie here, with death's door opening up to me, and not do all I can to find Betsy.

My head is melting. I'm torn between relaxing ahead of these surgeries and doing all I can for my daughter. Fuck! I allow a massive sigh to rasp itself up from the pit of my lungs and all the way through my open mouth.

Elaine reaches her hand and places it on top of mine. Then she smiles at me; not a purse of the lips this time, an upturn of the lips.

'It's why I keep asking you if there's anybody who can come up to visit you, Gordon. Company will help you relax. Are you sure you don't want me to ring your ex wife for you?'

'I thought you want me to relax,' I say, offering her a smile of my own.

'No other friends I can call?'

I shake my head.

'What about the friend who you've been on the phone to and who was up earlier… can he come back to you? Keep you company?'

I blow from my lips, making a bit of a motorboat sound, and then shake my head.

'He's out doing a job for me; don't worry, it's all being taken care of.'

Elaine looks at me the way a teacher looks at a cheeky student; her face stern, trying to hide the hint of a smile that's threatening to force its way through.

'Surely you have other friends who can be here for you. Who was best man at your wedding?'

'Guus Meyer,' I say.

'Well let's call Guus. I'm sure he would—'

'We haven't spoken in years,' I tell her. 'We blurred the lines of business and friendship. It's true what they say; don't mix business with pleasure.'

'I'm sure given the circumstances…' Elaine says, but I shrug my shoulders at her, allow another tear to drop from my eye. My head is spinning. I don't know how to feel; how I'm supposed to react to the news I've been given this morning. And I'm torn; I don't know who my main concern should be right now; me or Betsy. Maybe she's been my concern for way too long. Probably why my heart's fucked.

Elaine stands up, fixes my sheet so it's nice and snug under both of my arms. I stare into her face as she's doing it. I like her freckles. She's not unlike Michelle. They don't necessarily look alike, but there's a similar energy they both give off. I mean the Michelle I knew when we first met, not the bitchy Michelle who exists now. As I'm staring at Elaine I figure she must be the same age Michelle was when I first met her.

'How old are you?'

'Twenty-six.'

Yep. That's the age Michelle was when I sat beside her on a bus one day coming home from town. I'm pretty sure I fell in love with her before we both got off that bus half-an-hour later. I never thought, not for one millisecond back then, that I would ever hate her. But I do. She fucked me over. I feel another tear drop from my eye. Elaine notices, reaches for the tissues on my bedside cabinet.

'Thank you.'

I breathe in heavily, try to soak the surreality of the morning up my nose and deep into my lungs. Who do I love more? Me or Betsy? It has to be Betsy. Of course it's Betsy. It's always been Betsy. Fuck relaxing. Fuck my heart rate. I reach for my phone; tap into my call history and hover my finger over Lenny's number. I need to know where he is; what he's doing.

'Y'know... if you don't have anyone to come up to see you, how about I sit here with you for a while? We can watch some TV together... just relax?'

I haven't had anybody offer anything quite like that to me in years. Company.

'That'd be lovely,' I say, placing the phone back down onto my lap.

I can't make up my fucking mind.

FIFTEEN YEARS AGO

Betsy

SOMETIMES IT IS REALLY HOT IN MY ROOM. SOMETIMES IT IS REALLY COLD. It has been cold for a lot of days now. Every morning I wake up I feel the cold. I stay in my bed, under my blankets all day, most days. Once I have my books – and Bozy – that is okay. I read my books to Bozy all the time. He likes them as much as I do. His favourite is *Pirates in Pyjamas*. My favourite is *The Enormous Crocodile*.

I have thirty-three books. Eight of them are by a man called Roald Dahl. I would like to be a writer like him one day. I am going to write a book called *Bozy's Adventures*. I have asked Dod to bring me some paper to write a book on but he hasn't brought it to me. He keeps forgetting. But he is kind. Sometimes. He brings me lots of different books. I love books. I am thinking about going over to get *The Enormous Crocodile* to read it again but I don't want to get out of the bed. It's too cold. Then the door opens and Dod walks down the steps. I know if he is going to be good Dod or angry Dod from how he comes down the steps. I think he is good Dod today. He is walking properly. He is not falling against the walls.

'Everything okay, Betsy?'

'It's cold, Dod.'

He makes a noise but I don't know if he said anything. I don't know if I should say something back. Sometimes he gets angry if I don't talk back to him. But I don't think he wants me to talk back to him this time. He is just looking around my room. He rubs his hands together.

'I'll get you another blanket or maybe a duvet if I can find the time to buy one.'

'What is a duvet?'

'It's just a heavier blanket for your bed.'

He is definitely being good Dod today. I see him put his arms around himself and shake a little bit. That's what I do when I'm cold too.

'Come in.'

I open up the blankets on the bed. He looks at me. Then walks over and gets into my bed. I put the blankets over him and high up to his chin. He laughs a little bit. I really like it when Dod laughs. He doesn't laugh many times.

'Would you like to read me a story?'

He looks at me and then he nods his head. That means yes.

I reach under the blankets and pull out the first book I can feel.

'This one.'

It is a Peppa Pig book called *Daddy Pig's Big Chair*. I used to like it but I think I am a big girl now and don't need to read Peppa Pig books anymore. But it is okay. Because reading is fun all the time. And if Dod is reading, then it is even more fun.

'Daddy Pig's Big Chair.' Dod laughs again when he opens the book.

Before he starts to read I say something. I only say it because Dod is happy and I like it when Dod is happy.

'My Daddy had a big chair too. I miss my Mummy and my Daddy sometimes.'

He closes the book and then gets out of the blankets and off the bed. Oh no. I think he is angry Dod now.

'What have I fucking told you, Betsy? They're gone. They're not your parents anymore.'

He throws *Daddy Pig's Big Chair* against the wall and it makes a big noise.

I go under my blankets. Dod has never said that before. He never said they're not my parents anymore. Why is he saying this?

'You fucking mention Mummy and Daddy again and I'll hurt you, you little bitch. Do you hear me? Do you fucking hear me?'

I can't see him. My face is under the blankets. But he takes the blankets off the bed. His face is really red. This is bad. When his face is red he is really, really angry Dod. I am frightened. Frightened and cold. I am shaking so much.

Dod lifts me up. He holds me in the air. He is shouting but I can't hear what he is saying. He throws me against the wall. I land on top of *Daddy*

Pig's Big Chair. My back and bum hurt. Really, really hurt. I don't want to cry but I can not stop it. I start to cry really loud. Dod picks me up again.

'Shut the fuck up crying, Betsy, or I swear to God I'll fucking kill you.'

I stop crying. Well, I stop making crying noises. But tears are still falling down my face. I wipe them away and then he throws me again. But this time it doesn't hurt. He throws me on the bed. Then he bends down. He takes my hands away from my face and looks at me.

'Are you okay, Betsy?'

I shake my head. And then rub my hands against my back.

'Show me.'

He turns me around and pulls up my top. It's really sore.

Then he runs up the steps. I want to cry again but I don't. I hold up Bozy and give him a hug. That makes the pain go away a little bit.

Dod runs back down the steps. He has a bag with him. He turns me around and then lifts my top again. He puts the bag on my back and it is really cold. Really, really cold. It makes me laugh. Then Dod laughs.

'I'm so sorry, Betsy.'

He lies me down in the bed and then gets into the bed too. He puts the blankets over the two of us.

'Betsy. I have something to tell you. Do you know what heaven is? Has heaven come up in any of your books?'

I shake my head.

'Heaven is a place you go after you die. When people stop being alive they die.'

'And then they go to heaven?'

'Yes. And that's where your Mummy and Daddy are, Betsy. They are in heaven.'

I turn my head to look at Dod. I'm shaking again. Even though I'm under the blankets.

'My Mummy and Daddy are not living anymore?'

Dod kisses me on the nose.

'You're so clever, Betsy. Yes – your Mummy and Daddy are not living anymore.'

11:10

Lenny

LENNY'S BOTTOM LIP HANGS OUT, HIS EYES WIDE. HE ASSUMED KEATING would intimidatingly tower over him. But here he was, standing two feet from Ireland's most notorious gangster; Keating's nose at Lenny's nose's height. And Lenny's only five foot seven.

Keating's infamy has painted him as a bigger presence than he actually is. In fact, Keating – in the flesh – reminds Lenny of his late uncle Arthur. And Arthur was the most gentle of souls Lenny had ever known. Keating doesn't look like a gangster at all; not with the cute little side parting in his thinning hair and his bulbous purpling nose. He's wearing a pale blue shirt with grey trousers that are pulled up way too high over the waist; above his belly button. Ol' uncle Arthur used to do the exact same thing. Most men in the later years of life do; they lose their hips and their trousers don't have much to cling on to, so the roundest part of the gut has to do.

'I'm eh…' Lenny hesitates, his eyes blinking. 'I'm Lenny Moon. Private Investigator.'

Keating's eyebrows arch, then he breaks out a little smile. Or is it a grin? Lenny's unsure. He's watched a lot of gangster movies over the years; is a big fan of Guy Ritchie flicks and knows gangsters mostly smiled when they were being menacing. Yet Keating didn't look menacing. He just looked like good ol' uncle Arthur. Harmless.

Keating doesn't speak. He just keeps the grin on his face; inviting

Lenny to continue talking. The rain's falling heavily now, but Keating's certainly not offering Lenny the chance to stand inside his doorway.

'I'm investigating the disappearance of Betsy Blake.'

Keating laughs. Then stares at Lenny, still not saying anything; still waiting to learn why this weird looking fella with the kiddish Sherpa hat and God-awful yellow jacket has had the audacity to ring this doorbell.

Lenny jumps backwards as the roaring barks of Keating's dogs echo from behind their owner. They both sound as if they're eager to get outside, eager to confront Lenny on their owner's behalf. Lenny glances down, sees one of them through Keating's legs; foam dripping from its mouth.

Keating stays still; doesn't even blink at the sound of the barking. He just stares straight ahead, eyeballing Lenny and welcoming him to keep talking.

'I eh... have been hired by Gordon Blake to eh... to see if... are they Rottweilers?'

Keating nods his head, squats down to his hunkers, grabs each dog by the collar.

'This is Bernie,' he says, speaking for the first time. 'And this one here, this is Barbara.'

Being held by their owner hasn't calmed Bernie and Barbara down; they're still barking, still foaming at the mouth.

Lenny holds the tips of his fingers to Keating's car as he stands back, anticipating he may have to leap upon it should one of the Rottweilers break free from their owner's grasp.

'Get your fuckin' hand off my car,' Keating snaps, standing back up.

Lenny swipes his hand away, places it inside the pocket of his puffer jacket and then stands still, as if he's frozen. Keating yells 'release' and the dogs shut up barking, swivel and go back down the hallway.

Lenny gulps, then almost mouths a 'thank you' to Keating, such is his relief.

Keating steps outside, the heavy rain not a bother to him.

'Betsy Blake... you were saying...'

Lenny gulps again, then holds a blink closed for a few seconds, taking the time to remind himself that he should grow some balls, man the fuck up, be an investigator.

'Gordon Blake is dying. Could be dead by the evening. He's in Tallaght Hospital right now. He's hired me as his last chance to find out what happened to his daughter.'

'Shit. Poor ol' Gordy. What's wrong with him?' Keating says, looking genuinely concerned.

'Heart problems. He has to have emergency surgery this afternoon at three o'clock. Doctors are only giving him a fifty per cent chance of making it through.'

Keating bites his bottom lip, shakes his head.

'He's only young. Must be twenty years younger than me... What's he – fifty?'

'I'm not entirely sure of Gordon's age, Alan. But—'

'The poor fucker.'

Keating seems ashen-faced by the news Lenny has just shared with him, even though he hasn't worked with Gordon Blake for seventeen years – not since Betsy went missing.

'As an associate of Gordon's at the time of Betsy's disappearance, I wouldn't mind asking you some questions, Alan.'

Keating looks behind him, stares at his door as if that was going to remind him of what happened when Betsy Blake disappeared.

'Gis a sec,' he says, before pushing at the door and walking back inside.

Lenny's eyes flick from left to right, his pulse quickening. He holds his blink closed again, reminding himself that he is an investigator; that there is no need for him to be intimidated; that he's only doing his job. But he's finding it difficult to convince himself. He leaps when a high-pitch beep sounds behind him; the lights of Keating's Merc flashing on, then off.

'Get in,' Keating says, walking back out the door and banging it shut behind him.

Lenny turns, stares down the row of houses, contemplating whether or not he needs this job, whether or not it's all worth it. He blinks repeatedly again, for so long that Keating is already inside the car before he has re-adjusted his eyes. Then he grabs at the handle of the passenger door and pulls it wide open. As soon as he gets in, he removes his hat. He stares at it, realises immediately what Keating must have been thinking when he saw him; that he looks like a kid with this blue and black chequered tartan piece of shit atop his head. It has the same pattern of an eighties' Christmas jumper. It's okay for going incognito to spy on unsuspecting insurance claimants, but not ideal for confronting the country's biggest criminals.

'I don't deal with pigs,' Keating says, taking Lenny's gaze away from his hat.

It takes a couple of seconds for Lenny to realise what Keating's saying.

'Oh no; I'm not a cop. I'm—'

'You're investigating, aren't you? You're questioning me over the disappearance of a little girl, right?' Keating sniffs sharply in through his nose three times. 'Well that means I smell bacon.'

'Alan – I'm not investigating you. I'm just... it's just... you were a close associate of Gordon Blake at the time of Betsy's disappearance and I'd just like to ask you if you were aware of anything out of the ordinary that was happening in or around the Blake family in 2002. Anything at all. Lenny has asked me to beg you – it's his last chance.' Lenny says all of this so quickly that his intimidation is blatantly obvious.

'Lenny Moon, that your name, yeah?'

Lenny nods.

'Well, Lenny Moon. Let me finish this investigation for you in the next two seconds, huh? Betsy Blake is dead. She was hit by a car and whoever hit her with the car disposed of her body.'

Lenny coughs into his hand. Clears his throat. He doesn't want to sound intimidated, doesn't want his voice to crack.

'Gordon Blake doesn't believe the findings of the Gardaí. He's certain somebody kidnapped his daughter,' he says, slowing down his pace.

'Lemme guess... he thinks Barry Ward kidnapped his daughter on my orders?'

Lenny coughs again. Then blinks; not one long blink, repeated blinks, as if he's readjusting his eyes to a bright light. He'd love nothing more than to chew on the rubber case of his mobile phone right now, but is already aware he has come across as inexperienced to Alan Keating in the four minutes they've been talking.

'This isn't news to me,' Keating says before Lenny has a chance to reply. 'Sure that's what he told the cops in 2002. And sure poor ol' Gordy has even been hanging around outside Barry's house over the years; as if one day Barry's gonna walk out holding his daughter's hand. He's a brave man, doing that to Barry. But Barry doesn't mind. Neither of us do. We feel sorry for Gordy.' Keating uses his hands as he talks; it's another reminder to Lenny of ol' uncle Arthur. But he shakes his head of his thoughts, tunes backs into Keating's words. 'Listen, Lenny Moon; there are two truths you need to face up to. One; Betsy Blake is dead. And two; Gordon Blake is as deluded as a flat-earther. He went mad. Listen, it's understandable,' Keating says, shifting in his seat to face Lenny. 'I've two daughters. If one of them was killed and I never got answers, I'd go fuckin mental meself.'

Lenny shifts in his seat too, mirroring exactly what Keating had done moments prior, but not to talk, just to listen.

'I liked Gordon Blake. As I said, I feel sorry for him. Always have. In fact, I sent my lads out to help look for Betsy. We put sounders out, came back with nothing. I tried to help Gordy. My heart has always gone out to him and his wife. It's the only reason I'm sitting here talking to you now. Otherwise, any fuckin pig knocks on my door, I don't hold the dogs back, ye get me?'

Lenny nods. Then he blinks again, repeatedly, until he finds – somewhere deep within his blinking – an ounce of courage.

'It's just Gordon insists you threatened him just before Betsy went miss… he said you guys fell out.'

Keating laughs. Again, Lenny isn't sure if it's a sinister laugh or whether or not he actually found what was said funny.

'What did he say exactly?' Keating grunts as the rain falls heavier on the car.

Lenny allows a silent exhale to seep through his nose.

'Nothing much. Just that you were pushing him to do things with the money he was handling for you. And when he refused, you held him up against a wall; told him he shouldn't be fucking with you.'

Keating laughs again.

'That's not how I threaten people, Lenny Moon,' Keating says, the laughter disappearing from his face abruptly. 'That's just how I deal with people who work for me. I just wanted to get as much out of Gordy as I could. And I did. He was great for me. Y'know… I actually haven't had somebody cook my books quite like him ever since I lost him.'

Lenny nods at Keating, then forces his lips into a sterile smile.

'Thank you for your time, Alan. I eh…'

'Ah don't go. Is that it? You come knockin' on my door telling me ol' Gordy Blake is on death's door and desperately wants to find out what happened to his daughter before he dies and now… and now, what, you're just leaving me?'

Keating stretches his finger towards his door, clicks a button. Lenny instantly feels panicked at the sound of all car doors locking simultaneously. He reels back in the passenger seat, holding his hands up as if he's being robbed at gunpoint; the strings of the Sherpa hat he's holding dangling over his face.

'Alan, I don't know anything more than you do at this—'

'What did Gordy Blake say about me; tell me!' Keating says, the creases on his forehead wedging deeper, the tone of his voice demanding. It's striking to Lenny just how instantaneously ol' uncle Arthur can turn into Scarface and vice versa.

Lenny's breaths grow sharp, not just with fright, but with uncertainty.

He doesn't know what to tell Keating, doesn't know how he's going to get himself out of this situation.

'I only spoke to Gordon for five minutes. He rushed me out of his ward… told me to get on with the investigation. To do what I could in the few hours he has left. He gave me a thousand quid up front, told me if I found anything new – anything he hadn't heard before – that he'd leave me his house in his will.'

Keating relaxes his brow, but his eyes still burn through Lenny.

'His house?' He clenches his jaw as he says it. Then continues. 'He musta said more than that. Why are you here? He obviously told you to pay me a visit.'

'He… he… gave me a list. A list of people he suspected might've had something to do with Betsy's disappearance.'

Keating sits back in his chair, rests both his hands on the steering wheel, then laughs to himself. Lenny sits upright too, just to stare through the windscreen at the image of the houses blurred by the rain. He's well aware of Keating in his peripheral vision, anticipating any movement. Then it comes. Movement. Keating holds his hand out, palm up. Lenny gulps, then reaches inside his jacket pocket and takes out the note. Keating eyeballs Lenny as he places the paper atop his palm and then, almost in slow motion, he holds it up in front of him and begins to read; his laugh growing louder as each second passes.

He crumples the note up and throws it back at Lenny.

'I've been called worse,' says Keating. Then he turns his key in the ignition and rolls the car out of his driveway and down the street past Lenny's little Micra.

'Where we going?' Lenny asks, not bothering to hide the fear in his voice.

'Do you believe everything I said to you, Lenny Moon?'

Lenny nods his head. 'Yes, yes, Alan – everything. I believe you. I don't think you had anything to do with Betsy Blake's disappearance.'

'Good. Then you can scratch me off the list.' Keating drives under the archway, back out of his estate and turns left at the roundabout. 'So open up your note again there, Lenny Moon.'

Lenny picks the note up from his lap, uncrumples the paper and then stares back at Keating.

'Who's the next name on the list?'

'Eh… Barry. Barry Ward.'

Keating turns to Lenny, winks.

'Good – let's go have a word with him then, shall we?'

11:30

Gordon

I KNOW DAYTIME TV SO WELL THAT I CAN CALL THE BEATS.

I always know which items are going to sell for a profit on this show. Dickinson records his little voice overs after the scenes are shot, so there's always little clues in there as to whether or not the antique will do well when it comes to auction. I knew that little ornament would sell for more than the thirty-eight quid they bought it for because Dickinson suggested it was a bargain when they got it. It's so fuckin predictable. Had it not have ended up with such a heavy profit, Dickinson's voice over would have been a lot more negative.

'Told ya,' I say to Elaine. She smiles up at me.

'That you did! You must know your antiques, huh?'

'Nope. I just know my tele,' I say.

I look at her as she returns her gaze to the screen; even the way she's sitting reminds me of Michelle.

I am certain I fell in love with Michelle during that first bus ride, but it took her a lot longer to love me. I'm pretty sure she ended up falling for me only after she got wind of how much money I had. I've often felt she fell in love with the idea of being married to a rich business man, not the businessman himself. But we had good times, did me and Michelle. We travelled the world together. I was only too delighted to bring her to places she had only ever wished to go to before she met me. The first six years were dream-like really. It's difficult to explain what it's like being in love; I've often measured it as being the opposite of being depressed.

Depression is difficult to explain, it's just a sour feeling, a negativity that resides in both the bottom of your gut and in the centre of your mind. Being in love is the total opposite in every way. I know. I've felt both.

We got married in St Michael's Church in Inchicore in 1994; reception in the K Club, overlooking the eighteenth green. We were both high as a kite; had no idea what bizarre fates lay in front of us. It took us almost four years to get pregnant. My balls were the problem, we found out. I had become a little infatuated with the laptop I had bought, holding it too close to my balls as I was working. When I resisted using the laptop for its exact purpose – typing on the lap – my little swimmers woke the fuck up. Michelle held a white stick with a blue cross on it in front of me one Saturday morning and we celebrated as if Ireland had won the World Cup. Over the next few months we both felt as if all of our stresses and strains had packed up and fucked off thanks to the little bump. We'd no idea that bump would one day deliver the biggest nightmare any parent could ever possibly fathom.

'Okay... that's it,' Elaine says as the shite end title music to Dickinson's Real Deal begins. 'I gotta go do some work. Just press this if you need me.'

'Elaine,' I say, unsure of what I'm going to say next.

She turns, purses her lips at me, then smiles again when she realises exactly what I called her for – no reason.

'Stay relaxed,' she says. Then she leaves.

I push the butt of both my palms as far as I can into my eye sockets and twist them. Then I let out a yawn that sounds more like a deep sigh than anything. Maybe it was a sigh. I pick up the TV remote, begin switching through the channels; skipping by *This Morning* because Holly Willoughby's not on it, skipping by an old episode of *The Ellen Show*, skipping by *Morning Ireland* and by *Jeremy Kyle*. I stall at Sky News just to read the scroll banner. As soon as I see the word 'Brexit' I click on, only to be met by white noise. That's it. Six fucking channels. What a load of me bollocks. I grasp the remote control firmer and swing my arm back, but rather than throw it across the room like I want to, I just let it drop onto my bed.

I twist my body, grab my mobile phone from the bedside cabinet and deliberately don't even look at my call log button.

I scroll into the Sky Sports app instead, try to catch up with any football news. But there's fuck all new on there. Nothing's been added since I looked at it just before Douglas and his team came in to give me a harsh reality check over an hour or so ago. Then I click into the WGT Golf app, decide I'll have a game. It might pass some time. It's the only game I've ever played on a mobile phone. It can get quite addictive. I play it on the loo mostly. A shite these days isn't enjoyable for me unless I'm putting for birdies at the same time. The load icon appears, scrolling from twenty per cent to thirty per cent to forty per cent to… Betsy. Betsy.

Fuck it. I tap out, straight into my call log. I've gotta get onto Lenny; find out what he's up to. I can't be playing bleedin' golf games when I've only a few hours left to live. I tap at his number, hold the phone to my ear.

'Heya, Gordy,' comes a voice. I sit up straight in my bed, instantly know it's not Lenny on the other end of the line. Only one person's ever called me Gordy.

11:30

Lenny

LENNY CONTINUES TO STARE STRAIGHT AHEAD; NO PART OF HIS BODY – except for his eyeballs – have even twitched over the course of the twenty-minute drive. He's just sat upright the whole time and listened to Keating sing along to Frank Sinatra's greatest hits. The gangster crooned to *My Way*, *Got You Under My Skin*, *Come Fly With Me*, *Witchcraft* and was at the crescendo of *Lady is a Tramp* when he began backing the car into a parallel parking position outside a row of terraced houses.

Lenny was actually impressed by Keating's vocal, but stayed mute all the way, not even nodding in compliment for fear of disrupting him. He was practically scared stiff, though the score was keeping his heart rate quite consistent. It is, after all, almost impossible to be scared while a big band are providing the backdrop. But he now understood for certain that Keating's smiles weren't smiles at all; they were gangster grins. The man is a living parody of a Hollywood gangster. A sociopath.

As Keating takes the keys out of the ignition, ending his duet session, Lenny turns his head for the first time.

'That's Barry's house there, number thirteen,' Keating says. He then gets out of the car, waits for Lenny on the footpath, still oblivious to the rain. Lenny thinks about putting his hat back on his head, but instead crumples it up and stuffs it inside his jacket pocket, making it look as if he has one of those bulbous hernias bursting from his gut.

'This'll be fun,' Keating says, holding the gate open for Lenny to walk through.

'Thanks, Alan,' Lenny says. He was unsure what tone to talk to Keating in; wondered was thanking him for holding the gate open even applicable conversation to have with a gangster. Keating hadn't explained anything on the drive over and Lenny was still wondering why they had both made the journey; whether Keating was genuinely trying to help him with his investigation or whether he was just taking the piss and trying to intimidate him. He took his mobile phone from his pocket, just to check the time as they waited on Barry to open his door after Keating repeatedly rapped his knuckles against the window panes on it. 11:37. He's wasting time here; is certain Keating and Barry have fuck all to do with Betsy Blake's disappearance. Poor Gordon's time is ticking away; no impact is going to be made on his final wish; not today.

'Whatsup, boss!' Barry says holding his hand for Keating to grab. They greet like gangsters do, a grasp of hands that helps them lean in for a half-a-hug.

'Who this?'

'Barry, meet Lenny Moon. Lenny Moon's a PI.'

Barry looks Lenny up and down, then stares at Keating, his eyes squinting, his mouth almost forming a smile.

'A PI? Ye don't look like a PI. Ye look like the fuckin' shit member of a shit boy band.'

Keating laughs as he enters Barry's hallway. 'You rolling?'

'I'm awake amn't I?' says Barry.

Barry swings his hand, welcoming Lenny inside his home, the whiff of cannabis in the hallway alone enough to get anybody stoned. They all enter the square living-room, Barry making his way straight to a glass decanter in the far corner. He picks it up, shows it to his guests.

'Jesus no, too early for me,' says Keating.

Barry stares at Lenny, awaits his response.

'Eh... too early for me, too,' he says.

Barry and Keating take a seat on the dated furniture, leaving Lenny standing. He stares around the room, takes in the impressive artwork on the walls. They look so out of place in the tiny gaff; probably just as valuable as the gaff itself.

'Sit down, PI,' says Barry. Lenny does as he's told, plonks himself on the couch next to Keating. He becomes aware of his left knee bouncing up and down, so places his hand over it, holds it in place.

'Wait till ye hear this,' Keating says, turning to Lenny. 'Go on... tell Barry why you're here.'

Lenny takes in a breath, then blinks rapidly.

'I'm investigating the Betsy Blake disappearance on behalf of her father Gordon Blake. He—'

Lenny is interrupted by Barry's laughter. Then it stops abruptly, almost as if he was half-way through his laugh when a sniper aimed a dart into his neck.

'Well, you've come to the right place, PI. She's under the stairs.'

Lenny swivels his head to peak out the sitting-room at the door leading under the bannisters and is then met with an even bigger laugh. This time Keating joins in; bringing Lenny back to school, back to the days he used to be picked on for being the oddest boy in the classroom. But back then it was only harmless insecure teenagers picking on him – not Ireland's most notorious gangster and his psycho sidekick.

'Ye know what?' Lenny says, standing up. 'I have decided to stand down from this job. I will be notifying Gordon Blake of my resignation and – gentlemen – I am so sorry to have disturbed your mornings.'

'Sit down, Lenny Moon,' Keating orders. Lenny does as he's told, his eyes blinking. 'Barry – are you just gonna let that J sit in the ashtray or are you gonna offer your guest a welcome puff?'

Barry bends down to his glass ashtray, picks up the joint he had started to smoke when the knocks came at the door. He holds it in front of him, ignites the flame on a lighter with his other hand, then holds the flame to the joint until it catches. Lenny squints. He had smoked weed before, back when he was studying for a pointless certificate in media at college, but had never seen this technique for lighting a joint before, didn't think it was possible to light one without inhaling.

'No thank you,' he says when Barry holds the joint towards him. 'Too early for me.'

Barry laughs again.

'I understand it being too early for whiskey, but no such clock exists for this shit.'

Lenny turns to look at Keating beside him, hoping ol' uncle Arthur would appear; pat him on the back, tell him to get home if he wants to. But Keating holds Lenny's gaze, again staying mute, allowing Lenny to do the talking. Lenny reaches out, takes the joint, assumes being on friendly terms with these two is probably his quickest route to getting the fuck out of here.

He inhales slowly, making sure the smoke isn't too harsh on his throat. The last thing he needs right now is these two laughing at him for coughing up a storm.

'Gordy Blake's dying,' Keating speaks up as Lenny exhales. 'Lenny

Moon here has told me he may only have a few hours left to live. Has to have a massive heart operation later today that he might not wake from. He's hired Lenny as his one last shot at finding little Betsy. And… guess who he came to investigate first?'

Barry arches his right eyebrow, breaks out a tiny smile and then shakes his head.

'Poor Gordy. I'll miss him. Y'know,' he says, turning to Lenny, 'he's hung out a few times on this street, stalking me. Haven't seen him in a long, long time… but Jesus yeah, I'll miss the poor fucker. We've always felt sorry for him, haven't we, boss?'

Keating nods his head then pinches the joint out of Lenny's hand as Barry continues.

'I did my best to look for that little girl. Even held a lot of fuckers heads under water trying to get answers. Nobody knows anything. She wasn't taken, wasn't kidnapped. She died, didn't she? Hit by a car.'

Lenny clears his throat, his attempt at ridding his mouth of the stale taste of tobacco. It's been so long since he's inhaled smoke, inhaled weed. Can already feel his head spin a little.

'I believe so yeah… Gardaí closed the case in absentia.'

'Are you talking fuckin Latin now, PI?'

'Without a body,' Keating says while exhaling a huge cloud of smoke. 'They closed the case and announced her dead without finding a body.'

'Well they're hardly gonna find her body if she's living under my stairs, are they?' Barry says.

Keating coughs out a laugh.

'I'm just… I'm just trying to carry out Gordon's last wish; trying to give the investigation one last roll of the dice,' Lenny says. 'That's all. I'm just doing what I was hired to do.'

Keating leans forward in his chair, passes the joint to Barry.

'Here, show Barry the note.'

Lenny rolls his eyes sideways – almost in slow motion – to stare at Keating. Then he reaches inside his pocket, flattens out the crumpled paper and holds it between his fingers, stretching it towards Barry. Barry takes it, squints at it. Laughs. Takes a drag of the joint. Laughs again.

'Freak he calls me?' he says, 'That's rich coming from that nut job. Listen, PI… it's no surprise Gordy thinks me and Keating are top of this list; he's hung onto that theory for… I don't know how many years it's been.'

'Seventeen,' says Keating.

'Is it that long? Fuck! Listen, PI; Gordy Blake's a nut job. He goes around believing his daughter's still alive, when it's been proven she died. His daughter disappearing didn't just break his heart, it broke his head too. The man's sick. We had nothing to do with his daughter's death. Pigs initially thought it was Gordy himself, then when they cleared him, they came straight to us. Gordy told them he'd been working with us. But the cops knew we didn't have anything to do with it. What the fuck would we want with a bleedin' four-year-old girl? That's twelve years below the age I like.' Barry laughs, then takes another quick drag of his joint before passing it to Lenny.

'If you wanna get honest answers for Gordy Blake before he dies; go to the cops, get them to give you the proof that Betsy is dead… Tell him and make him believe it. Because if he wants closure, he has to believe the truth.'

Lenny smiles a thank you, hands the joint towards Keating without taking another drag and then stands back up.

'Gentlemen, thank you very much for your time.'

'Where d'ye think you're going?'

'To eh… the cops, as you said. I wanna get confirmation of what really happened, to stop messing around following up the false leads on that note.' Lenny takes his hat out of his pocket, then holds a hand out towards Barry. Barry remains sitting, hands still flat on the arms of the chair.

'Who the fuck is the Jake Dewey fella on the note?'

'I eh… I know only what's on that note,' Lenny says, blinking. 'Gordon was keen for me to get out and interview all three men named on there and kinda just rushed me out of the hospital, telling me to get on with it, that time was ticking.'

'It's Michelle Blake's new husband isn't it?' Keating says.

Lenny nods his head. 'I assume so, judging by what's written there.'

'You're not a very good private investigator, are ye, kid?… Here.' Keating says, handing Lenny the joint back. 'Take a couple of drags, calm yourself down.'

Lenny pinches the joint, looks at both men and then sits back down.

'How did you become a PI?' Barry asks.

'Had to leave the force.'

'Ah… so you were a pig. Knew I could smell it on ye.'

Lenny looks at Keating, then back at Barry. He feels like he isn't in his own head; can't quite fathom the reality he's finding himself in: about to open up to The Boss and his main henchman about his ambitions for a career in serving out justice.

'I didn't last long as a cop. Was looking to go down the detective route… made good progress in my first eighteen months but eh… then… then… We have twins, me and my wife. She suffered with post-natal depression from the day they were born. It's been…' Lenny stops, swallows back the emotion that threatened to run to the back of his eyes. 'It's been a testing five years for us. She tried to commit suicide a couple of times. So I quit as a cop; decided to start my own PI business so that I could be close by at all times, case she needs me. I rent a little work space five minutes from where we live. It's tiny. Quarter the size of this room.'

Barry moves his eyes to look at Keating.

'So you've been a PI how long?'

'Almost six years.'

'How come I've never seen you sniffing round us before today then?'

Lenny sucks in a tiny inhale of the joint, passes it to Barry. He's starting to feel slightly relaxed; feels as if sharing his truth about Sally has endeared him to the gangsters. He doesn't feel as intimidated.

'I only really work for bloody insurance companies. I'm not an investigator really… I'm eh… I don't know what you'd call it. I find out if people claiming from insurance companies are telling lies or not. Today's the first day I've ever been asked to investigate a criminal case.'

Lenny's phone buzzes. He slides it out of his jacket pocket, stares at the screen.

'That's him ringing now. Gordon Blake.'

Keating takes the phone from Lenny's hand, stabs his finger at the answer button.

'Heya, Gordy,' he says.

There's a silence on the other end of the line. Barry, Lenny and Keating all inch their ears closer to the phone.

'Alan Keating!' Gordon says.

'Long time no speak, Gordy. Y'know… I still wish you were running my books. I've never quite replaced you; isn't that right, Barry. Don't I say that often?'

'He does, Gordy,' Barry says.

'Jesus Christ. Lenny must be a good investigator after all. He found both of you in the same room, huh?' Gordon says.

'Don't get carried away with compliments for Lenny. He didn't orchestrate this – I did,' Keating replies.

A gulp can be heard coming down the line, followed by a distant beeping sound.

'So, it's true is it, Gordy. You're in hospital, fifty-fifty chance of ending the day alive?'

'Let Lenny go,' Gordon says.' He's an innocent man. Is only carrying out what I paid him to do.'

'You just worry about yourself, Gordy, yeah? We'll look after Lenny for ya.'

Lenny double takes; stares at Keating, then at Barry, then back to Keating, his eyes blinking as he does so. He can't read what's going on.

There's a long silence, Keating stretches the phone outward a bit; insisting he's not going to talk next. Lenny cops it; Keating had been playing this game with him since he met him; staying silent. He waits on information, he doesn't offer information.

'Look, lads… I just asked Lenny to put my mind at rest before I die,' Gordon says. 'The only people I'd fallen out with around the time of Betsy's disappearance was you guys. It's all I've had to go on all these years… Just you two and that fuckin smug asshole my wife shacked up with. I just want to cross you off my list once and for all.'

'What do you think we did, Gordy; kept Betsy chained up in Barry's gaff all these years?'

The line falls silent again.

'Tell ye what,' Lenny pipes up. 'We're in Barry's house now. I know you've hung outside here over the years. Would it eh… would you be willing for me to cross this theory off your list for good? What if I was to just call out Betsy's name while I'm here – so you will know with absolute certainty before you go for your surgeries that these guys had nothing to do with this? That she's certainly not shacked up in Barry's home.'

Barry snarls up at Lenny, his confusion made obvious by the deep vertical line that has just formed above the bridge of his nose. Then he looks at Keating wondering how the fuck he should react to this. Keating doesn't move, doesn't say a word. Lenny realises what he's just said is quite risky. He hadn't thought it was as he was saying it. He was genuinely thinking of the best way he could move on, get the fuck out of the situation he was finding himself in. Perhaps it was the weed talking for him.

'I don't really know whether or not Alan and Barry had anything to do with this, but yeah… yeah… anything to get something off my mind. If you can confirm for me that Betsy isn't in that house, I guess that's something.'

Lenny's heart begins to rise again. Not out of fear – out of excitement. Gordon told him earlier that if he got an answer for him that Gordon hadn't got before, he'd leave him his house in his will. Or maybe he's just getting carried away, getting high. He looks at Barry, then at Keating. Keating shrugs his shoulders.

'Just because we feel a real sympathy for you,' Keating says. 'So you can put this theory to bed.' Keating licks his lips, looks agonisingly at Barry. Barry's been unusually silent; probably caught off guard.

'Ye might as well start here,' Keating says, brushing past Lenny and into the hallway. He twists at the knob on the door under the stairs, pulls it open. Lenny walks towards it, stares into the darkness, then at Keating.

FOURTEEN YEARS AGO

Betsy

Dod drops four new books on my bed. I crawl out from under my sheets and give him a hug. I wrap my arms around the top of his legs. Squeeze him tight. Then I pick up the books and smell them. It's the first thing I do every time he gets me a new book. My favourite smell in the whole world is books.

The first of my new books that I look at is called *The Letter for the King*. It says on the back that it is 'suitable for eight-year-olds'. I'm only seven but I know I can read it. I'm so good at reading. That makes me lucky. Because I am good at my favourite thing to do. I look at the other books. *A Series of Unfortunate Events*. That looks good. *The Wind and the Willows* and then… yes! – another Roald Dahl Book. *Matilda*. I turn around and squeeze Dod's legs again.

'Thank you.'

He doesn't say anything. Just smiles. He has been smiling so many times when he comes to see me these days. I haven't seen angry Dod in a long time.

'Ah for fuck sake.'

I stand still when I hear him say that. I wonder what I did wrong. Then I turn around slowly.

'Not you. Not you, Betsy. Just this… fuckin…'

He likes to say the word fuck or fucking a lot but I don't really know what they mean. They're never in any of my books. I guess it just means

Dod is angry. I turn around. He is looking into my basin. Into where I wash and pee. And poo.

'You're filling this a lot lately.'

He lifts it up. It looks heavy. Heavier than the other times he has had to lift it up before. Then he walks up the steps.

When I first came to this room I had to pee and poo on the floor. Then Dod brought me a box to go toilet in. Then he brought the basin. I think that was two years ago now. Yeah – when I was about five, I think. I've been living here for about three years. A little bit more. Sometimes I wish I lived in a place like the one Charlie Bucket from one of my favourite books lives in. It says in the book that he is poor and his family don't have many things. But I think he has everything anybody would ever need. He has his Mummy and Daddy. And he has his granddads and grandmothers. I only had grandmothers in the outside world. I think both my granddads were dead. They must be in heaven now with my Mummy and Daddy. I hope they are having fun. Sometimes I wish I could go to heaven to be with them. But I have to wait until I die. I don't know how long that will be.

'Betsy.'

I look up. Up the steps.

'Betsy.'

Dod is calling me from the top of the steps. He has never done this before. I can't really see him because the light behind him is too bright. He is like a shadow. Then he takes one step down and I notice his hand. It is waving me to come up the steps. I take one step forward. Then I stop. I'm afraid. Dod gets really angry when I go near the steps. I don't want him to be angry. Even if he is calling me. I don't know what to do. I turn around. I grab Bozy.

'C'mon, Betsy. Come up. It's okay.'

I squeeze Bozy and then walk onto the first step. I look up and wait for Dod to shout at me. But he doesn't. He is just waiting for me at the top. Then I walk onto the second step. Then the third. And fourth. Dod is still quiet. I close my eyes. That way, he won't get angry if I see anything. I don't think I'm allowed to see what's up the steps. I walk up the rest of them. All thirteen. I know there are thirteen. I count them every day.

Dod puts his hands on my shoulders when I reach the top.

'It's okay, Betsy. Open your eyes.'

I do. I open them wide. But it's too bright. It hurts my eyes a bit. It smells different up here. In my room it is mostly the smell of poo. Except for when I smell my books. Then the poo smell goes away for a few seconds. But up here smells like… I don't know. Different. Nice.

Dod keeps his hands on my shoulders and walks me down a room that has a brown wood floor. It's nice. It looks a lot nicer than my stone floor. More flat. Then he makes me turn around. I still can't see much. The light is too bright.

'This is my downstairs toilet.'

I blink my eyes until I can see more clear. Then I see white walls with a big white bowl. It makes me think of my Mummy and Daddy's house. We had a big white bowl like that too.

'You can do your pee and poo in here.'

Dod opens a lid on the big white bowl and I look into it. There is a little bit of water in it.

'What do you mean?'

'If you need to poo or pee just knock on the door and I will let you come here to do it.'

I look up at Dod. I am a little bit scared.

'Am I okay to walk up the steps and knock on the door?'

Dod laughs a little bit.

'Yeah.'

'And you won't get angry. Won't turn into angry Dod?'

Dod laughs again. This time louder.

'You're becoming a big girl now. I can't be carrying that basin up and down the steps all the time. You can pee and poo in this, and see here…' He points at another white bowl. It's like the first one. Just a bit smaller and a bit higher up. 'You can wash yourself some mornings in this one.' He turns the shiny bit on top and water comes out. I think of my old house again. Mummy and Daddy's house. I think they had the same bowl too.

I smile a big smile. But I am also a bit scared. I'm afraid of being up the steps and inside the light rooms. I turn around and look at Dod. He is smiling too. I notice another bright room behind him. It has a big blue chair in it. I wish I had a chair like that in my room.

'No looking in there.'

Dod says that a bit angry. But then he smiles again. I don't know what to do. So I just squeeze Dod's legs.

'You're welcome.'

He bends down towards me so that his nose is close to my nose. There's always a bad smell when his face is close to me.

'But there's one condition. Anytime you're up here, you need to be really quiet okay?'

I nod my head.

'And I mean really fucking quiet. If you ever raise your voice or make any noise up here at all, I won't just hurt you. I will kill you.'

11:55

Lenny

LENNY FEELS A TSUNAMI OF RELIEF WASH THROUGH HIM AS THE HALL DOOR closes and he finds himself outside. Never before has rain felt so good. Keating and Barry almost folded over with laughter as soon as Lenny called out Betsy's name. Then the light switched on under the stairs. He was staring into a space a human could barely stand up in, let alone be held captive in.

He thought Barry was going to throw up, so heavy was his convulsion of laughter. He looked at both of them, then headed for the door.

He removes his phone from his pocket as he paces down Barry's tiny garden path and then begins to jog down Carrow Road. He fidgets with his phone, is keen to ring Gordon back, ask him if getting into Barry's home and concluding with absolute certainty that Betsy isn't there constitutes triggering the gentlemen's agreement they made earlier.

But he also knows Gordon heard the men laughing, that it was all a joke and he isn't quite sure how he's going to take it. Maybe it won't constitute enough to activate the will.

He turns around to walk backwards, such is the force of the wind driving down the canal. When he reaches the junction that the old Black Horse pub used to sit on he squints into the distance, into the greyness of the day in hope of seeing a taxi light approach.

It doesn't take long; just five minutes, though those five minutes felt a lot longer than five minutes to Lenny. He's soaked by the time the taxi pulls up alongside him; his hat weighing heavy on his head. On numerous occasions during his short jog he had wished the phone call from Gloria Proudfoot at Excel Insurance had come before his phone call from Gordon Blake – that way he'd be most likely snug and warm in some gym taking sneaky pictures with his dated film camera instead of feeling like a drowned rat in the back of a taxi going in search of somebody he knew he couldn't possibly find. But that house, that big old house on South Circular Road won't leave his mind. What if Gordon Blake is telling the truth; what if he genuinely left it in his will to Lenny, Sally and the twins? Soaked to the bone or not, chasing a lost cause or not, Lenny had to admit to himself that this was one hell of an interesting morning.

'Fuck the warmth of a gym,' he mutters to himself in the back of the taxi. As the driver is turning on to the Naas Road, Lenny's phone vibrates in his jacket pocket. He knows who it is; it's midday.

'Hey, sweetie,' he says.

'I know you rang me since our last call, but I still thought I should ring you at twelve.'

'Of course.'

Lenny had made a pact with Sally that she would ring at ten a.m., midday and then again at two p.m. every day just so Lenny could rest assured that the day was going well for his wife. The story he'd shared with Keating and Barry was true. Every word of it. Sally is suicidal. Has suffered with high levels of depression ever since the twins were born. In fact, she'd shown signs of depression even in pregnancy; her levels of anxiety rising so much she had to be kept in hospital on occasions. Lenny assumed post natal depression was inevitable for Sally, yet he never quite knew how awful it would be. He found her one morning standing atop their toilet seat trying to put her neck in a noose she had tied using the belt of her woollen bathrobe. The twins were only eight weeks old then. On his first day back in work – three months later – he got a phone call from Sally who told him he had to get home quick before she started to slice at her wrists with a Stanley knife. She was sitting in a corner of their sitting room with the blade in her hand when he arrived home, the twins both crying upstairs. There were no cuts on her skin, but Lenny has never been entirely convinced of what would have happened had he not been fortunate enough to have his phone in his possession when she rang that day. As a police officer, he was supposed to have it turned off.

His station chief offered him six months leave after Sally's second suicide attempt, but Lenny knew it wasn't enough; that he could never return to a job in which he had no control over his time, over his phone. It was a shame; Lenny had always wanted to be a Garda, had ambitions to be a detective from quite a young age. Sally hasn't made any suicide attempt since, but her moods have still not evened out or even become consistent day-to-day. Every morning he wakes up, he doesn't know how Sally is going to be feeling.

'Any more work today?' Sally asks. She sounds okay, monotone but alert.

Lenny pauses; the hesitation even obvious to the taxi man.

'Leonard,' Sally says re-prompting her husband.

'Sorry, love, phone is playing up a bit. Eh… yeah. I've to go to some gym in Coolock now; usual stuff. Got to take a photo of a girl who—'

'Think you'll be home to go meet the teacher today?' Sally interrupts, clearly not interested in the answer to the initial question she'd asked. This wasn't unusual. Their phone calls weren't about anything, merely routine.

'Yeah… yeah,' Lenny says, his eyes blinking. It was unusual he'd blink when speaking to his wife. But that's because it was also unusual he would lie to her. He didn't want to tell her about the Betsy Blake case, didn't want to raise her anxiousness levels in any way. 'Yeah – I'll be there if you can get a three o'clock meeting.'

'Good. I'll make an appointment so,' Sally says.

Lenny thanks her and after the phone call ends he bites at the cover of his phone, disappointed with himself. He knows there's a chance he won't make that meeting; hates that he might let not only his wife down, but his sons too. Particularly Jared. He's having an awful time of it at school. Not only is he being bullied, but he's being drowned in the politics of the education system. The school don't know what to do with him; so low is his comprehension. Lenny's only concerned about the bullying, not bothered about the latter. He genuinely feels institutional education is vastly overrated. Though he is keen to stay on top of things if only for Sally's sake. If she's worried, then Lenny is worried too. He lets out a little sigh. The meeting he just agreed to attend is supposed to take place straight after the kids leave school at three p.m., exactly when his case with Gordon Blake is due for conclusion too.

Lenny shakes his head as the taxi man pulls into Peyton estates, ridding his mind of the worry.

'If you can pull over at the orange car there please…'

Lenny almost tuts as he hands the taxi man a twenty euro note. He hates spending money, unless it's on something that would cheer either his wife or the twins up.

He runs the five yards to his car door, wrestles with the lock and then jumps in. It was pointless trying to be quick; he really couldn't get any wetter than he already is.

He starts the engine, begins to pull out of Peyton estate when he hears an unusual sound. His car slogs, even though he's pressing hard on the accelerator. He squints at himself in the rear-view mirror, then his eyes widen. He begins to slap at the steering wheel; the penny finally dropping. He doesn't stop slapping, not until the palms of his hands sting unbearably.

Then he gets out of his car and looks up and down the driver's side, walks to the other side of the car and does the same thing. He clenches both fists, tilts his head back – eyes open, mouth open – and lets the rain shower down on his face.

'Fuck sake!' he roars into the sky.

12:10

Gordon

I FINISH WRITING UP THE LETTER AND WILL; TUCK THE FLAP OF THE envelope inside itself and then push it under my pillow. I want Lenny to know I'm deadly serious; that I will leave him my house if he can somehow get me some answers today. I may have come across like a right twat having him call out Betsy's name in Barry Ward's gaff, but I don't mind looking like a twat. I'd do anything to find some answers. Her disappearance plagues me every day; her loss from my life eats at me. But it's the guilt that makes the most impact. It resides in both my stomach and my head, and it won't go away. It was my fault she went missing. It was on my watch.

I wasn't a lazy dad; I was just like any other dad – unfocused. Mothers are great at paying their children every nuance of attention. But dads? Fuck no. We're easily distracted. I was busy working. Guus had managed to bring in two massive clients to our company just before Betsy went missing; they were million euro deals. I was finalising one at home while I was supposed to be looking after my daughter. I think she got bored, walked away from me, walked away from our home. One of the main reasons I feel guilt is because I'm genuinely not sure how long she was gone before I realised she was missing. May have been just ten minutes, could've been two hours. I was too consumed with work.

I went into shock when I realised she was gone; ran into the streets shouting her name. I stopped people, asked if they'd seen a four-year-old with mousy brown hair. Nobody'd seen anything. I thought I was going mad. I remember running back into the house and checking everywhere for her; under the beds, in the closets, the washing machine. I even checked the fuckin microwave. I don't know why. I think I was beginning to lose it. I rang the police before I rang Michelle; knew it'd be a much easier call to make.

'My child's gone missing,' I said matter-of-factly down the line. I know I said it matter-of-factly because it was played back to me about eight times when I was being questioned by Detective De Brun a few days later. I was their first suspect; they assumed I had something to do with her disappearance. By that stage I was convinced it was Keating who'd taken my girl. I told the police about my dealings with him; spilt the beans. But they were still convinced I knew something. I didn't. I hadn't one fucking clue what happened to Betsy. I still don't. I still don't have one iota of an idea what happened to her that day, or what has happened to her any day since. But I know she's alive. I know deep down in my gut she's out there somewhere. If only the cops had acted sooner, instead of wasting time questioning me, I'm pretty certain they could've found her. But now – just over seventeen years later – there's probably no chance whatsoever that I'll ever see her pretty little face again. I can't give up though. I've told anyone who's ever listened to me over those years that I will fight until my dying day to find Betsy. Well, today may well be my dying day, and I ain't stopping. I guess I just have to put all of my hope in little Lenny Moon. Not that I've given him much to go on; same old leads I've looked into hundreds of times – all of them producing sweet fuck all over the years. But fair play to him, he got into Barry's house within an hour or so of starting his investigation. That's some going. It took me four years to get inside that gaff.

'That time again, Gordon,' Elaine says, opening up the door to my ward. I twist my head on the pillow, crease my mouth into a slight smile.

'You look more relaxed anyway,' she says.

I just maintain the smile, pull my T-shirt over my head again and wait for her to attach the blue tabs to my chest.

'The theatre will definitely be ready for three p.m., Gordon. Everything's running on time. Dr Johnson and Mr Broadstein are due to land at one p.m. and should arrive here at the hospital around two-ish. The surgery that's going on in the theatre right now is expected to be finished in a couple more hours. Half an hour clean up and prep after that, then we'll get you down there.'

I'm listening to what Elaine is saying, but I don't react, except for nodding my head out of politeness.

'Okay… heart rate is still high,' she says,' but it's come down a good bit. Keep that head back on your pillow and just relax, Gordon. It's your best chance of beating this.'

I just nod again.

'You okay… You've gone very quiet on me?'

I look up at her, meeting her eyes for the first time since she re-entered the ward.

'Just letting it all sink in,' I say. 'Y'know what's upsetting me the most?'

She doesn't finish wrapping the rubber tube around her hand, instead she puts it aside, squints at me, then perches on the bed.

'Ever hear of Betsy Blake?' I ask her.

She squints again. The name didn't immediately register with her.

'Girl that went missing seventeen years ago, was taken outside her home?'

'Oh yeah,' Elaine says. 'South Circular Road. I was too young to remember at the time, but I've heard about it since.'

'My daughter,' I say. Her mouth opens a little, then she places her hand on top of mine again.

'Oh I'm so sorry, Gordon.'

'It's okay, Elaine… you didn't take her.' I sit more upright in the bed again. 'It's just, the thought of dying without ever finding out what happened to her is… It's…' I pinch my thumb and forefinger into the corner of my eye sockets.

'Gordon… we'll get you through this,' Elaine says, rubbing her fingers across the top of my hand. 'I thought… I thought…' she hesitates. 'I thought they concluded Betsy's investigation… wasn't she supposed to have been found to have been knocked down… they found a car or something with her DNA in?'

'That was all baloney,' I say, removing my fingers from my eyes. 'That was the cops trying to close off a case many years later because it was costing them too much money, costing them too much time. They've always been embarrassed by the fact they never found out who took Betsy… So they made that shit up.'

Elaine's brow creases.

'Are you serious?' she asks.

'Dead serious.' Then I breathe out a long, drawn out sigh. I haven't opened up about Betsy in years.

'I had no idea,' Elaine says, still rubbing at my hand. 'Listen. I have to go downstairs to Mr Douglas' office for a consultation about your surgeries. I'll be half-an-hour, forty minutes at most. When I'm back, I'll

314

pop in to you. You can tell me what you want… we can keep quiet… we can watch more TV; whatever it is you would like to do.'

She's so lovely. Very genuine. Very natural. I wonder if Betsy would have grown up to be just as impressive.

'She'd be only five years younger than you are now, y'know?'

'Really?' Elaine says as she scribbles a note on the clipboard. 'I'm so sorry for your loss, Gordon. I don't know what to say. Y'know I thought about you and your whole family a number of times over the years… I guess most people have. Everybody's hearts went out to you.'

I smile my eyes at her and then wave my hand.

'Go on, go to your meeting and… yes please, drop in when you're done. I'd love the company.'

She takes a step towards me, rubs at my hand again, and then pinches each of the tabs off my chest.

'You just relax for the next half-an-hour, Gordon. Put the back of your head on that pillow and close those eyes.'

As soon as the door's closed, I do exactly as Elaine suggested. Closing my eyes relieves some of the throbbing in my temples. I breathe in and out really slowly, allow the whole mess my life has turned into to float away from my mind. Rather than thinking about my surgeries and rather than thinking about Betsy, I reminisce… I go back over my life. I remember when I was the age Betsy was when she went missing; my first day at school was fun, adventurous. I remember the holidays my mam and dad used to take me on to Blackpool; the donkey rides on the beach, the rollercoasters on Pleasure Beach, the pinging sounds of the arcades. I remember my first girlfriend; Linda Tillesly – she was so pretty. I was thirteen when we shared our first kiss; round the back of Goldenbridge School. Neither me nor Linda had a clue what we were doing, we both just went with it until it felt right. I allow myself my first genuine heartfelt smile of the day; then the ward door opens, taking me out of my daydream.

'Jaysus, Gordy; ye certainly look as if yer dyin' anyway.'

I open my eyes, notice the waistband of his trousers pulled up over his belly button and then mouth the word 'bollocks' to myself.

FOURTEEN YEARS AGO

Betsy

'Do you think I should do it, Bozy?'

I always make up what Bozy says to me and say it back to myself in a silly voice, but this time I can't think of what he would say. I'm scared. My hands are shaking. A bit like when Jim Hawkins is hiding in the boat in *Treasure Island*. That's a book Dod bought me a few months ago. I've read it three times now. It's really good. Probably my new favourite.

I stare up the steps. Maybe I shouldn't do it. It could hurt. A lot. My breathing gets bigger. And quicker. Then I take one big, big breath in and hold it. I look at Bozy. Then I let the breath out.

'Fuck it, Bozy. I'm going to do it.'

I walk up the steps. Slowly. Really, really slowly. I stop at the top, then look at Bozy again. But he still doesn't know what to say to me. I give him a big squeeze and a kiss. 'I love you, Bozy. You have been my best friend.'

Then I place him down on the top step and close my hand tight. I knock at the door. Sometimes I have to knock a few times. Sometimes Dod doesn't answer at all. He might not answer now. He has been angry Dod for a long time. He's always shouting. He hasn't smiled for ages. Sometimes I wonder what makes him sad. Maybe he is sad for the same reason I get sad. Maybe he doesn't have a mummy and a daddy either. Maybe they're in heaven too.

No answer. Not yet. I close my hand. Knock again. Then I hear him. His footsteps getting close.

'Need to do a poo.' I say it from behind the door. I hear him make that breath sound that he makes when he is being angry Dod. This is probably the wrong time to do this. But I am doing it because he always seems to be angry Dod these days. He hasn't let me out to wash in a long, long time. Hasn't bought me any books in lots of weeks. Maybe months. He just comes into my room two times a day and leaves some food and water. Sometimes he doesn't say anything. Then he leaves. The only other times I see him is when I need to do a pee or a poo.

He unlocks the door and doesn't say anything. He just pulls it open and I put my hands up to my eyes stop the bright light from hurting them. I always do this. He sometimes says something like 'hurry up' or 'don't be long' but he says nothing today. I walk down the wooden floor and then turn in to the toilet room and close the door behind me. The door has a small lock on it. Dod told me to never go near it. But I do. I slide it really slowly so that he can't hear it. When I turn around a tear drops from my eye. I wipe it with my hand even though there is toilet paper in front of me. I sit up on top of the toilet with the lid shut. I remember what Dod said to me the very first time I was ever in this room. I keep hearing him saying it. Like I'm hearing it in my head.

If you make any noise up here at all, I won't just hurt you. I will kill you.

I know what 'kill you' means. It means I will be dead.

I hold in another big breath and then I just do it. I scream. Really loud. Really, really loud. I don't stop. I stand up on top of the toilet seat and just scream. I hear Dod at the door, banging away at it. But I don't stop screaming.

'Shut the fuck up. Betsy, I swear to you I'm gonna fuckin rip you to pieces when I get in there.'

I stop. Rip me to pieces? Probably he's not going to kill me. I want to die. I want to go to heaven. I want to see Mummy and Daddy. Probably he's just going to hurt me. I sit back down. My body begins to shake. My legs shake. My arms shake. I am so scared. The door is banging. Really loud. So is my chest. Dod isn't saying anything. He is just banging on the door. I think it is with his foot. Then there's a big hole in the door. Dod puts his face in the hole. I can see his eyes and his nose.

'I'm gonna fuckin hurt you, Betsy.'

Then his arm comes through the hole and his hand goes to the lock and he slides it back.

When the door opens, he stands there. His face is all red. His hands are closed tight.

'You little fuckin bitch. You better hope nobody heard all that.'

Then he grabs me.

12:15

Lenny

'ANSWER YOUR FUCKING PHONE!' LENNY SCREAMS INTO HIS MOBILE. THE taxi man eyeballs him in the rear-view mirror. Lenny notices; holds his hand up in apology.

'Excuse my language. Some bastards just slashed all four tyres of my car.'

'Jaysus, yer jokin', says the taxi man. 'Why'd anyone do that?'

Lenny sighs.

'Long story.'

The taxi man opens his mouth to ask more questions, but manages to bite his tongue. Instead, he just stares at Lenny through the mirror, noticing the passenger's irritation pour from every nuance of his body language; the constant blinking, the scratching at the back of his neck, the sharp breathing. He wants to advise him to call the cops but is beginning to think Lenny might be caught up in something he doesn't want to get involved in, so he remains mute. He doesn't have far to drive, another few minutes and he'll be dropping this drenched passenger off at the entrance to Tallaght Hospital.

Lenny presses buttons on his phone again, brings it to his ear. He can sense the tone ringing in sync with the throbbing in his head.

Still no answer.

He doesn't overreact this time. He just brings the butt of his phone back to his mouth and begins to chew.

'Fuckin Jesus bleedin Christ,' he mumbles to himself.

The taxi man flicks his eyes back up to the rear-view mirror, doesn't say anything.

Lenny fumbles with his phone again. He doesn't like sending text messages – they take him too long to type out – but he feels he's been left with no choice. His phone is so dated that he has to punch a couple of times at each number to produce even one letter of text. After a couple of minutes he's done.

`Answer your phone. Please.`

He wanted to add an exclamation mark after 'please' but didn't know how to. He's also wary of Gordon's delicate situation and doesn't feel as if it's fair to vent his frustrations at him specifically.

'Ye want the A&E or will I drop you at the main reception?'

Lenny looks up, realises they're already inside the hospital grounds.

'Main reception.'

Lenny stares at the meter. That's another twelve euro spent. He hands over a tenner and a fiver; waits for his change.

The rain has tempered somewhat, it's just lightly spitting now, but Lenny is still kicking up puddles as he races across the zebra crossing. He allows his breathing to slow down once he's inside and then rolls his eyes back into his head. He's trying to think through how he should play this with Gordon. Should he go in all guns blazing, demanding that he is paid his expenses so far? Should he be angry at Gordon for getting him in this mess in the first place? Or should he forget his misfortune, start talking about his fortunes instead? After all, Lenny found out for definite that Betsy wasn't in Barry Ward's house. Surely that was enough for them to trigger their agreement; that Gordon's home would be left to Lenny in his will should he not make it through his surgeries. By the time he's reached St Bernard's Ward, his mind is made up. He needs to be fair to Gordon, fair but firm.

'Sir,' a female voice calls out, just as Lenny reaches a hand to push at Gordon's door.

He spins around to be met by the pretty nurse – the same pretty nurse who showed him to Gordon's room earlier this morning.

He smiles at her, waiting on her to explain why she called out to him.

'Are you visiting Mr Blake again?'

Lenny nods his head, then mutters a 'huh-huh'.

'Would you mind if I gave you a small note?'

Lenny squints, takes a step towards the young woman.

'It's just – as you likely know – Mr Blake's situation is very delicate. He would largely benefit from relaxing ahead of his surgeries. Any…

any sort of rise in heart rate this morning could prove fatal to him later.'

'I'm not here to cause Gordon any stress,' Lenny says. 'Just here to support him.'

Elaine smiles.

'Good... it's just that—' Elaine stops talking; Lenny has already turned away from her, is entering Gordon's ward. Gordon is sitting up in the bed, almost as if he had anticipated Lenny's arrival.

'Gordon, Jesus Christ, I know you're not having the best day of it yourself, but those fuckin savages just slashed every tyre in my car. I've had to get a taxi here to see you.'

Gordon holds a finger to his lips.

'Who?' he then asks, raising his voice.

'Fuckin' Keating and that Barry Ward fella.'

Gordon stares at Lenny, can see the confusion stretching across his brow.

'Well, at least I think it was them. Can't have been anyone else surely. Listen...' Lenny says, then pauses as he whips off his hat and puffer jacket before sitting back down on the blue plastic chair. 'You're gonna have to pay me some expenses. I've already paid out thirty-two quid on taxis and... Gordon, I just don't have the money to be splashing out left, right and centre. Unless...' Lenny pauses again, stares up at Gordon, his eyes tense. 'Unless... you said if I found out something brand new for you today that you would leave me your house in your will.'

Gordon nods his forehead forward once.

'Well... I confirmed for you that your Betsy isn't in Barry Ward's home. He isn't holding her captive.'

'That's not really new to me,' Gordon says as he reaches for a book on his bedside cabinet. Then he clicks at a pen and continues talking as he scribbles on a blank page.

'Keating and Ward are just two gangsters who happened to be in my life when Betsy went missing, so it was always obvious that they would be suspects. After all, I didn't hang around or know anybody capable of crimes... but they're not so bad, Keating and Ward. Not really. I never really believed they had taken my Betsy.' Gordon continues to scribble away as he talks. Lenny pivots his head, so he can try to make out what Gordon is writing.

Keating's hiding in my toilet cubicle.

Lenny turns back, stares at the bathroom door.

'Keating may be interested in controlling street affairs and drug distribution in Dublin but he's harmless really when it comes to hurting people. I don't think he's capable of hurting a four-year-old girl. I really don't...'

I was getting your calls and your text messages, but didn't want to answer while he was here. I knew Betsy wasn't in Barry's because I've been in Barry's house before. I broke in. A couple of times. Went looking for any trace of Betsy, but there was none.

'...I just wanted you to rule them out once and for all. Given what you've told me, that they welcomed you into Barry's home to help you with the investigation, I am content that they haven't had anything to do with Betsy's disappearance.'

Lenny keeps twisting his head from Gordon's scribbles, to the door handle of the toilet cubicle. He's not even listening to a word Gordon is saying, he knows he doesn't have to; that Gordon is just talking for the sake of appeasing a listening Keating.

'...What else was I supposed to do, just lie here and die? I hired you to...'

If you clear Jake Dewey, I will leave you the house. I promise.

'...look again at the suspicious people who were around me, around my family at the time of Betsy's disappearance. I'm sorry you have had to pay out some expenses but I can't afford to pay you any more. I don't really have much more money.'

Gordon underlines – with emphasis – the last line he wrote. Then he looks up at Lenny, meets his eyes and winks.

'I promise,' he whispers really softly.

Lenny's eyes almost water. He genuinely believes Gordon. As Lenny is imagining his twins running around a much bigger home, Gordon twists in the bed and removes an envelope from under his pillow.

'I think it's probably best if we call an end to the job, Lenny, but I am very grateful for your time. I need to relax ahead of my surgeries and the nurse is getting all antsy because my heart rate's been high since I hired you...'

As Gordon continues to talk, he removes a letter from the envelope, pivots it so that Lenny can read it.

This is the will and testament of Gordon James Blake.

I hereby wish to leave the home, addressed 166 South Circular Road, Inchicore, Dublin 8, Ireland to Leonard Moon.

Signature 1

Signature 2

Signature 3

Lenny eyeballs Gordon again, then blinks rapidly.

'My signature plus two witnesses,' Gordon whispers. 'I promise that I will have two nurses sign this here today and then I'm gonna leave this will there.' He nods at his bedside cabinet.

Lenny stands up, places his hand on top of Gordon's and then gives an affirmative nod.

'I am so sorry I couldn't do much more for you, Mr Blake. I'll get going back to my office. I wish you all the very best with your surgeries this afternoon. I'll be thinking of you.'

Then he bends down close to Gordon's ear.

'Jake Dewey's address?' he whispers.

'I'll text it to you,' Gordon whispers back.

'Goodbye, Mr Blake.'

Lenny never could act. He can't even lie. And you have to be able to lie convincingly to be an actor.

Although Gordon seemed to cringe a little at Lenny's acting attempts, they both feel as if they did a good enough job. Lenny picks up his yellow jacket and hat, then strolls out of the ward and heads straight towards the lift. After the lift doors close, Lenny produces a little dance – the type of dance a fourteen-year-old girl would do if the boy she'd had a crush on for months text her to ask her out on a date. He believes Gordon, genuinely believes that if he can eliminate Jake Dewey from having any involvement in the Betsy Blake disappearance then he truly will be left a million euro house.

'Who else is he gonna leave it to?' he says to himself in the mirror of the lift after finishing his dance. When the lift doors ping open, he heads straight to the shop next to reception.

'It says ATM on the window?' he says to the young girl behind the counter.

She doesn't answer verbally, she just points. Lenny paces down the back of the shop, takes his debit card from his wallet and places it in the machine. He then taps in his pin number and selects 'View Balance'.

€1,166.

The grand Gordon transferred into his account this morning would keep the Moon's heads above water this month; but in a more pressing way, it would allow Lenny to take taxis for the rest of the day, would help him get to Jake Dewey's home, help him eliminate him from Betsy's disappearance and – ultimately – help Lenny come into possession of a million euro gaff.

Lenny removes the three twenty euro notes at the same time his phone pings. He checks the screen. A text message from Gordon Blake's number.

`Jake's address: 49 Woodville Road, Terenure, D 6.`

Lenny smiles to himself. Then tucks the notes and his phone inside his jeans pocket and heads straight towards the rain.

FOURTEEN YEARS AGO

Betsy

I ROLL BACK OVER IN MY BED. ONTO THE OTHER SIDE. I'M TRYING TO MAKE my back feel better. But nothing is working. I stare at the floor. The pages of my books are all ripped. Every time I look at it, it makes my belly sore. It means every part of me is sore. My head, my face, my belly, my back, my legs.

I see the cover of my book *Fantastic Mr Fox*. It's silver. Shiny bright silver. I can see my face in the cover. I saw it for the first time a few months ago. It was scary a bit. But now I like seeing my face in the cover. I'm pretty. I think. I have brown hair and brown eyes. And a little nose. A really small nose. I crawl really slowly out of the bed and try to grab at the book but it's too far away. So I crawl a bit more. My back is really hurting me doing the crawling. But I get the book and then crawl back to the bed. I pull the sheets across me again. Then I look at the book cover. I twist it until I can see my face. I don't look pretty anymore. My whole face is red. There is a really dark red ball at the side of my eye. I cry again. But even crying is making my back hurt.

I shouldn't have done that. I shouldn't have screamed. I was silly. I look at Bozy lying on my pillow. I am so glad Dod didn't rip him up. Just the books. But I'm still really sad. Really, really sad. Sad like the first night I came to this room when I was only four years old. I know Dod is angry Dod and has been angry Dod for a long time. But I think I have been angry and bad too. Bad Betsy. Dod told me to be quiet when I am up the steps. I should do what he says all the time.

Then I hear the door opening. I throw the sheets over my head.

'No. No. No. Not again.' I say it really quietly. So just me and Bozy can hear.

'Betsy.'

Dod says my name nicely. Like he's not angry Dod anymore.

I take the sheet down from my face a little bit and see him standing by my bed. His face isn't as red anymore. His hands aren't closed as if he is going to hit me again.

'Why did you do that, sweetheart?'

He only calls me sweetheart when he is being good Dod. Maybe he is good Dod again. Good Dod hasn't been here in a long time.

'Why did I scream?'

Dod nods his head. I look at Bozy and then back at Dod. I don't know if I should tell him the real truth. But maybe I should be telling the truth all the time. Maybe I won't get hurt if I tell the truth all the time. I wipe my eyes and then look up at Dod.

'I wanted to go to heaven.'

Dod's eyes get bigger. I think he is going to hit me again. But he just sits down. He puts his back against my wall and then puts his hands on his face. I think he is crying. I look at Bozy. Then back at Dod. Dod's shoulders are going up and down. I take my sheets away and put one foot out of the bed. Then I put the other foot out of bed even though it really hurts my back. I take one step to be beside Dod and then put my arms around his shoulders to stop them going up and down. It's like a hug. He *is* crying. I can hear him now. His cry is getting louder.

'Don't be sad, Dod.'

He grabs me. Puts his arms around me and we hug really tight. Really, really tight and for a long time. The hugging is hurting my back a lot. But I feel a bit happier. I am less scared.

'I am sorry.'

Dod takes his arms away from around me and then he wipes his face with his two hands. He looks at me. There are more tears in his eyes. But they are not coming out.

'No. I'm sorry.'

He grabs me for another hug. Another really tight hug. It hurts. But I don't say anything. I just hug him back.

'I will never, never do anything like that to you again.' He says it really quietly into my ear. 'I love you.'

'I love you, Dod.'

I think I do. I read about love in my books. You love people who are your family and your friends and your wife and your husband. I don't think Dod is any of those things to me. But I must love him. Because him and Bozy are the only people I know. Bozy is not even a person. But I definitely know I love Bozy.

'I'm gonna buy all those books again. And more new ones. I promise.' Dod is on his knees now. Staring at my face. 'And you just need to promise that you will never do anything like that again. The neighbours could have heard you. It's very dangerous.'

I've been really bad Betsy. Screaming was very dangerous. Very stupid.

'I promise. I won't make any noises again, Dod.'

He blows out through his mouth. His lips shake as he does it. It makes a silly noise. Like a fart.

'Look at your eye.' He rubs his thumb against my face. Up and down slowly.

'Where hurts you the most?'

I turn away from him. Then I pick up the back of my T-shirt as far as I can. He helps by pulling it up a bit more. Then he sucks in a really big breath through his teeth.

12:35

Gordon

'You can come out now, Keating.'

The door handle of the toilet cubicle clicks and his fat belly makes its way back to the ward first, followed by the rest of him; his sleazy fuckin grin stretched wide across his face. He wears that grin when he feels he needs to. He was wearing it the very first day I met him.

Our business was doing well. Guus and I had grown it into something really special; turning over a couple a million a year. It didn't start out that way. When I first began as a freelance accountant, I was only really interested in making enough money to get a roof over my head. After I'd left University, I started to work for a big accountancy firm – Fullams. Three years later I realised for certain that working for somebody else wasn't for me. So, using just eight loyal clients, I set up on my own. After a couple of years of continued growth, I decided I needed a partner. Guus was the first person I'd thought of, in fact I'd thought of him as a business partner long before I even realised I actually needed a business partner. We'd worked together at Fullams, sparked up not only a great friendship but a perfect working relationship too. His strengths paper over my weaknesses and my strengths paper over his. With my attention to detail on the numbers combined with Guus's ability to sell our vision to new clients, we were the perfect cocktail. And we thrived. The zeros in our business accounts stretched month on month as soon as we partnered up. But of course, I got greedy. When Alan Keating arranged a meeting with me one Friday afternoon about twenty years ago, I was fascinated by his plan. He was turning over a few mill a year – and we'd get ten per cent if we were willing to cook his books for him. It felt like a no-brainer at the time; easy money. But I was being cocky; I was being a fuckin idiot. Had I not seen the dollar signs in front of my eyeballs and accepted Keating's proposal that day I'm pretty certain that not only would I still be running my business, but I'd also still have my daughter, still have my wife. Still have my life. This fucker grinning in front of me right now ruined me.

'So you've called off little Lenny Moon, yeah?'

I just nod, still unsure how or even why I'm letting this prick talk to me again.

He opened the door to my ward about twenty minutes ago, began to tell me that he was the one person who could fulfil my dying wish. Then we heard Elaine outside talking to Lenny. Keating said I shouldn't mention that he's here, to just get rid of Lenny and that he'd oversee the investigation for me. He hid in the toilet cubicle. I didn't know what to do, what to say. I still don't.

'As I was saying, Gordy, I did my own investigation at the time; it didn't pull up anything. But let me have another dig around for you today. Who d'ye think's more likely to get you answers in what could be your final few hours: Alan Keating or little Lenny Moon? He's not even an investigator, he's a fucking insurance pussy. He rats out people who are making scam insurance claims. He has no chance of finding answers for you about Betsy.'

I nod my head, melt my face into a soft look. I felt, for years, that this cunt was responsible for Betsy's disappearance, yet I've never been able to join up all the dots.

'I know you've always suspected me and Barry, but – trust me, Gordy – we had nothin' to do with Betsy goin' missin'. And I know you know that deep down. You've always known it.'

I shift in my bed a little. It's funny that he thinks I'd trust him to find answers for me. I wouldn't trust him with a bucket of water if my balls were on fire. I suck in a breath through my nostrils, but remain silent. I just tilt my head to look at him, wait for him to talk.

'I'll get on to the cops; I have a few of them in my pocket. I'll get all of the information they have on the investigation into Betsy's disappearance and I'll act on it for you, how about that?'

I shift again in the bed. I really don't want to give this prick the satisfaction of my forgiveness. But what else can I do? I may be dead in a few hours time. The more people out there looking for my Betsy, the better, even if I do get a huge sense that he's bullshitting. I know Keating definitely has some cops on his payroll, but not high-ranking detectives; not cops who'll give him classified information about a seventeen-year-old case.

'But sure the cops think she's dead,' I say, finally speaking up.

'You know as well as I do that that was just a theory because they couldn't close off the investigation, right?'

He looks up at me with puppy dog eyes, as if him going all coy will bridge my forgiveness. He can do that, can Alan Keating; transform from looking like Ireland's most notorious gangster into looking like a cute old granddad. He has the most persuasive forms of seduction; the fucker can get anybody on his side. It's why I was intrigued by his business proposition twenty years ago. But I don't trust the fucker. I wonder what he's after. Alan Keating doesn't do anything unless there's something in it for himself.

'Why would you do this for me... after all the years I've insisted you had something to do with Betsy's disappearance?' I ask him.

'I've always felt sorry for you, Gordy. For you and Michelle. I helped at the time, had my men look for Betsy. And I would've offered to help a lot more over the years only you went really cold on me. You made some outrageous claims to the cops about our dealings; almost got me into a lot of trouble.'

I shift again in the bed. I can't get comfortable, not with this gurning prick in my room. But he's right. I did rat him out; revealed all about his money funnels to Ray De Brun. I'm still not quite sure why it didn't go much further. Keating covers his tracks too well, I guess. The small businesses he had set up under different names to filter his money through saved his bacon. That and the fact that I refused to become a witness for the state. I didn't care about Keating's money laundering then; the only thing that consumed my mind was finding Betsy.

'Yeah... well I'm sorry about that, Keating, but y'know, I still don't know who took Betsy and you were the only person at the time who had a problem with me... So I went on auto pilot, told the cops everything. I'd have done anything to find my daughter... still would.'

He places his hand on mine, much like Elaine did about half an hour ago.

'I understand why you told the cops everything and I understand why you initially suspected me and Barry. But c'mon... still suspecting us today and having your little PI hang around our homes is crazy, Gordy. You need to believe me; I had nothing to do with Betsy going missing. I'm not that kinda gangster. You know that.'

He sits back down, his puppy dog eyes still on show. I don't get why he's being so nice to me. The fucker has always had intrigue pouring out of him.

'Listen, our slate is clean. Let me help you investigate. What've you got to lose?'

I stare up at the stained ceiling of the ward, my mind racing in a million different directions.

'You don't do anything for nothing,' I say.

His silence makes me turn to face him again. Then he shakes his head, removing the puppy-dog eyes; transforming from the cute old granddad back into the grinning gangster.

'Just put the same offer you made to Lenny Moon on the table for me.'

I laugh. Should've known.

'Ah, so you got out of Lenny just what I was offering him. You want my house.'

'It's a grand oul house,' Keating says. He sucks his teeth as he says it too.

Then he takes a step towards me again. He doesn't place his hand on top of mine this time. Instead he reaches for the pen on the bedside cabinet and then holds it towards me.

'Rewrite your will, make me the benefactor of that house.'

FOURTEEN YEARS AGO

Betsy

'It's nice that, isn't it?'

I don't answer by talking. My mouth is too full. So I just rub my belly and smile at Dod. He smiles back at me.

'I've more up in the kitchen. Think I'll have one myself later.'

Dod's sitting on the edge of my bed while I sit on my new chair. I love it. It's all squishy and comfortable to sit in. I do a lot of my reading in this now, not in my bed like I used to. Though my bed is more comfortable than it's ever been. Dod bought me loads of new things – a chair, a bed, shelves for all my books, lots of new books including loads of my favourites that he ripped up during that really angry night, magazines, colouring books, wallpaper. I forgot what wallpaper even was. When Dod put it up in my room I remembered I had some back in my Mummy and Daddy's house. I had pink wallpaper then with my name Betsy written across it in white.

I tried not to feel bad when I thought about my old bedroom back at Mummy and Daddy's house because Dod was being so nice to me and trying to make my bedroom all nice and fresh. The wallpaper he put up in here is yellow. Bright yellow. Yellow isn't my favourite colour, but I still like it. Even though Dod has put loads of new things in my room, the room looks bigger. I have sixty-one books now. Amazing. My new favourite books are called *Chronicles of Narnia*. It's seven different books all in a little box that Dod bought me.

He has been really nice ever since the angry night. I think that when I said I wanted to go to heaven that Dod felt really sad. That's why he made my room more bright and beautiful and why he bought me loads of things. He buys me new things every day now. Today I got an ice cream. I'd never heard of an ice cream before, but it is delicious. It said on the wrapper that it was called Orange Split. I lick at the little stick, taking all of the cream off and then breathe. I think I ate all the ice cream without breathing.

'Jaysus, ye milled all that.'

'Milled?'

'Yeah... like you ate it really fast, really quickly.'

'Oh.'

I grab at my notebook and pen and write down the word 'milled' and then beside it write 'to eat something really fast'.

I do this all the time if I am reading and don't know a word. I'll try to work it out for myself and if I can't I'll ask Dod when he pays me a visit. I love learning new words.

'Can you get me another notebook, Dod, please?'

'Ye running out of room on that one already?'

I flick through my notebook.

'Not yet... but I want this one to be for new words but in a new notebook I would like to write my own story.'

'A story? What's your story going to be about?'

I look up at my ceiling. Even though the stone walls are now covered with wallpaper and my stone floor is mostly covered with an orange rug, the ceiling is still stone. It's still cold.

'I might write it about you.'

''Bout me?'

'Yes. I think I might call it Dod's Adventures.' He smiles a little bit at me. 'It would be about what you do when you are not in my room. What you do when you are up there.'

I just point up the steps, I don't look up them. Dod hasn't been angry Dod in ages – not since the really angry night – but I still don't want to make him turn into angry Dod, so I don't look up the steps.

Dod laughs a little bit.

'And what do you think I get up to up there?'

I stare up at the cold ceiling again. I don't want to mention my Mummy and Daddy because I know that is how good Dod can turn into angry Dod.

'Eh... I remember from before I came here that there was a thing called television. I used to watch a show called *Thomas the Tank Engine*. It was about trains. I think you probably watch television when you are not here with me.'

I close my eyes a bit because I'm not sure if talking about what happened before I came here will turn him into angry Dod. He moves off the bed and comes near me. He gets down on his knees right beside me.

'And what do you think I watch on the television?'

I can smell his breath. It's the same all the time. It smells warm. Every time I smell it, it reminds me of the day he stole me away from Daddy.

I open my eyes and look at him. He is smiling. That is good.

'Do you watch *Thomas the Tank Engine?*'

He laughs. Then he shakes his head.

'I eh... don't know. How many things are on television?'

'Too many things.'

I laugh this time.

'I don't know, Betsy... I watch the news.'

'The news?'

'Yeah – it's a television programme where somebody reads out what happened around the world every day.'

'Wow.'

That sounds really good. Really, really good. I would love to watch the news. But I don't say anything else to Dod. I can't ask if I can go up there anymore. He's afraid I will scream again even though I never would. My back hurt for so many weeks after that last time. I still don't think my back is as good as it used to be. I read in a book once that somebody broke their bones. I think I might have broke a bone in my back. But Dod doesn't let me see doctors or let doctors see me. Dod doesn't let me see anyone. See anything.

'You were on the news lots of times.'

I look at Dod.

'Me?'

'Yeah – lots of times. For lots of years.'

Dod stands up, puts his hand on my head and messes my hair like he does sometimes. Then he walks back up the steps.

'I'm gonna go get me one of those Orange Splits.'

I turn around and watch as he goes up the steps and closes the door. Then I get out of my chair and crawl under my bed sheets to find my best friend.

'Did you hear that, Bozy. We were on the television lots of times.'

12:40

Lenny

LENNY ASKED THE TAXI MAN TO TURN THE RADIO OFF AS SOON AS HE GOT IN the back seat. He needed all the headspace he has to think through his morning and is a typical man when it comes to multitasking; if Lenny needs to think, he needs to do so in silence. Right now, the only thing playing in his head is the vision of the will Gordon showed him when he was back at the hospital twenty minutes ago.

He stares at his phone.

'I'm buyin' a fuckin good phone from that grand,' he mumbles, before eyeballing the rear-view mirror to see if the taxi man heard him.

'Sorry?' the taxi man says.

'Ah nothing. Just this piece of shit phone. I need one of those with some internet on it. All it's good for is making and taking calls.'

Lenny blinks rapidly, then his eyes widen. He clicks into his call history, sees the name 'home' and taps at it.

'Hello.'

'Sweetie, I need you to do me another favour,' he says.

'Go on.' There was no sigh this time. Sally must be having a really good day.

'Can you eh… can you check on Google what the requirement is for a will in Ireland?'

'A will?'

'Yeah – as in a will somebody leaves behind when they die.'

The line goes silent for a few seconds.

'You planning on dying on me, Lenny?'

There's a small hint of humour in Sally's response; on any other day hearing his wife crack a tiny joke would overjoy Lenny, but he's too distracted today.

'Course not. Just a client of mine was asking and my phone is a piece of shit. I can't get the information I need.'

'Okay... lemme see,' Sally says. Lenny can hear her tap away at the keyboard of their home computer. He eyeballs the rear-view mirror again, wonders what the poor taxi man must be thinking.

'Jaysus, I'm just getting pictures of men called Will,' Sally says.

Lenny fake laughs awkwardly, then rolls his eyes.

'Ye know what, Sally, I have to get myself a good smart phone, I get caught out too many times when I need to find certain information.'

Lenny winces a little as he says this, his shoulders slumping in anticipation of his wife's moan. But she doesn't say anything at all, almost as if she didn't hear what he'd just said.

'Ah... hold on a second,' she says. 'Got it... ye ready?'

'Uh-huh.'

'For your will to be valid in Ireland it needs to be handwritten and signed by you yourself, plus two witnesses.'

'Okay... and?'

'And that's it... that's all it says.'

'Really?'

'Well... it says that the witnesses must witness you signing it and that's it.'

Lenny blows out his lips, allows himself a little smile. Gordon was right. The will he has written up in hospital would be valid.

He slows his breathing, doesn't want to get over-excited, certainly not on the phone; he doesn't want to disclose anything to Sally. Not yet anyway. If she got carried away by the hope of getting that house, she would crash hard if it didn't come to fruition. And if she crashes hard, the unthinkable could happen. Lenny's tried to rid their home of items Sally could use to kill herself, but it's impossible for a home not to have knifes, not to have belts.

'Okay, sweetie, thank you so much.'

'That it?'

'Yep, that'll do for now. I'm so sorry I've had to bother you a couple of times today to do things for me.'

'I don't mind,' Sally says. 'I like hearing your voice. But Lenny...'

'Yeah?'

'Y'are in your shite getting one of those expensive smart phones. We just don't have the money.'

Lenny rolls his eyes again, then blinks them rapidly.

'Okay, sweetie,' he says. 'I love you. Speak soon.'

Lenny brings his cheap phone to his mouth after he has hung up, begins to gnaw on the edge of the rubber case again.

'Fuckin hell,' he mumbles. 'A bleedin' massive gaff for a few hours work.'

He tries to stem his excitement by wondering if he's being played. Maybe this is all just one huge hoax. But he knows it's not. It can't be.

'Y'know… that's right. I only did my will there at the beginning of this year,' says the taxi man. 'I turned sixty-six in February – felt it was about time I finally put it all down on paper. I just went into a solicitor, wrote it all down and had him and his assistant sign it.'

'It's that easy?'

'Yep… was surprised how easy it was meself. It doesn't even have to be signed by a solicitor… anyone can do it.'

Lenny's nose stiffens; his attempt at holding back the smile that's threatening to spread across his face. Then he throws his head back to rest on the top of the seat and allows himself the daydream of living in a much bigger home. He wonders if a bigger place would take Sally out of her depression; perhaps being cooped up in their tiny terraced house in Springfield plays its part in dampening her mood. Or maybe he could sell the house, pocket the million so he doesn't have to work. He lets the smile spread across his face and it remains that way until the satnav calls out to him; informing him he has arrived at his destination.

He sits upright, takes in the house they have pulled up outside. A bright yellow door, hanging baskets of flowers either side of it, the latest BMW 3 Series in the driveway. Michelle must've married well the second time round.

'Nine euro, mate,' the taxi man says.

Lenny continues to stare at the big house as he hands a ten euro note over the shoulder of the driver. As usual, he waits for the change before getting out of the car and strolling up the driveway.

He hasn't yet decided how he's going to approach this. The will occupied way too much of his thinking on the way over here. But the will is redundant should Lenny not get any original information out of Jake Dewey. He already assumes Jake has had nothing to do with Betsy's disappearance, much like he felt that Keating and Barry didn't have anything to do with it either. But maybe if he can get confirmation of that, it might be enough for Gordon to trigger their agreement.

As the taxi man pulls away, Lenny bides himself some thinking time by checking out the BMW. Maybe he could afford a car like this if he sells the million euro gaff. He nods, impressed by the cream leather interior. Just as he places both of his palms either side of his face to get closer to the driver's window, a voice calls out.

'Excuse me,' she says.

Lenny, startled, places both of his hands towards the woman in apology. He instantly recognises her. Whereas Gordon looked different to the man who appeared at press conferences and in newspapers following Betsy's disappearance, Michelle has barely changed. There are a few more lines round her eyes, but there's no mistaking who she is.

'I'm so sorry,' he says. 'But I'm looking to speak to Jake Dewey.'

'And did you think you were gonna find him in the car?'

Lenny shakes his head and smiles.

'Sorry – I'm just a big fan. Thinking of buying one for myself actually. Does Jake enjoy driving it yeah?'

'Jake's never driven it. That's my car.'

Lenny's mouth makes an 'O' shape, then he slightly gurns with embarrassment.

'It's Michelle, isn't it? Michelle Blake?'

Michelle's stare turns inquisitive.

'Dewey. I haven't been called Blake for fifteen years.'

'I'm so sorry... of course. Dewey. Mrs Dewey.'

'Ye know, I've been talking to you for one whole minute and you've apologised to me three times already... whaddya want?'

'I'm sorry eh...' Lenny scratches at his forehead, blinks rapidly. 'I need to speak with Jake as a matter of urgency. Would it be okay if I came inside?'

Michelle tilts her chin into her neck, then opens her eyes wide.

'Lookin' like that?'

Lenny stares down at himself, realises he looks like a drenched rat.

'I got caught in the rain and...' he shrugs his shoulders.

'Well, Jake's not in; he's away in Belfast working.'

Lenny squelches up his mouth, wants to swear; feels as if the possibility of him earning a million euro gaff may have just evaporated.

'Who'll I tell him was looking for him?' Michelle asks.

Lenny pauses, looks back down the garden path, then at Michelle again.

'I'm Lenny Moon – Private Investigator.'

Michelle takes three steps closer to him, folds her arms.

'Oh yeah – what are ye investigating? How to piss people off by staring into their cars?'

Lenny huffs out a small laugh, rubs his hands together back and forth as he blinks his eyes.

'I'm eh… I'm eh…'

'Go on, spit it out,' Michelle says, now resting both of her hands on her hips.

'I'm investigating the disappearance of your daughter.'

12:55

Gordon

HE STANDS UP TO WATCH OVER ME AS I SCRIBBLE ON ANOTHER TORN PAGE from my novel.

This is the will and testament of Gordon James Blake.

His big belly inches closer to me, almost resting on the edge of my bed. I feel nervous writing this, as if I'm back at school doing an exam. Don't know why I'm nervous; I stopped being intimidated by this asshole years ago.

I hereby wish to leave the home, addressed 166 South Circular Road, Inchicore, Dublin 8, Ireland to Alan Keating.

I draw three lines to fit the necessary signatures and then smile up at him.

'Good man, Gordy. I promise I will get you some information on Betsy's disappearance. Something that will give you peace of mind going into your surgeries.'

He scratches at his nose as he says this, a sure sign he's lying. Then he removes his coat from the back of the chair he'd been sitting on and throws it on.

'So you'll just leave that there,' he says, pointing at my bedside cabinet, 'and if I do find you something original you'll activate that will, yeah?'

I nod my head.

'Sure thing, Keating.'

He takes a step closer to me again, his face turning back into the kind old granddad he can inhabit any time he wants to.

'I'm really sorry about everything that's happened to you, Gordy. Not just Betsy, but this… this situation you find yourself in today. You were always a good man; you haven't deserved any of the shite you've been served in life.'

I offer him another of my fake smiles and then mouth the word 'thanks'.

'I'll be back with you before three… and I'll have something. I promise I'll do my very best. And if I do have something for you, I'll look after that house, Gordy. I'll treasure it.'

He winks, strolls away from me and out of the ward. Before he's three steps down the corridor I pick up the will I had just written for him and rip it into tiny pieces, then toss it on the floor.

It was weird talking to that cunt again. I've blamed him for all that's gone wrong in my life. But I'm as certain as I've ever been that he had nothing to do with Betsy's disappearance. Though just because I can rule him and Barry out, it doesn't make me feel any better.

Not only did I lose Betsy in 2002, I lost my wife as well. I knew even before Betsy disappeared that I was losing Michelle anyway. I was aware she was having an affair. I didn't catch her or anything, I could just tell. Not only had we stopped having sex, but we'd stop communicating with each other. She was beginning to 'work late' at the bank and basically showed me every sign I needed to see that she was fucking somebody behind my back. I didn't know who it was until months after Betsy went missing. Michelle had the audacity to stamp on my heart when my heart was already broken. She said she was falling out of love with me anyway, but the fact that I looked after Betsy so carelessly – to the extent that she went missing on my watch – ensured she didn't just no longer love me, but hated me.

That's what she said to me three months after Betsy went missing. She screamed it at me in the most explicit of terms. 'I fucking hate you, Gordon… properly hate you. I'll never forgive you for this.'

It's still never been made clear to me, because she never looked me in the eye and suggested such a thing, but I think deep inside me that she felt as if I had something to do with Betsy's disappearance initially, especially around the time the cops were questioning me. But she did stick up for me in some respects; she told the police I had always cared for Betsy, even if I was never likely to be named 'father of the year'. But soon after I was cleared as a suspect, Michelle broke the news that she was leaving.

I found out about a month later that she was seeing this Jake Dewey bloke. I needed to find out about him; wondered from very early on if he had something to do with Betsy going missing. Perhaps he snatched her so that me and Michelle would split up. I haven't found anything on the fucker, aside from the fact that he's a smug cunt. But I still haven't ruled him out, probably because I've got nothing else to go on. If Lenny can give me something... anything today that clears Dewey, then I will genuinely leave him my house. I've got no one else to leave it to.

'Hey,' she says, offering me a big smile.

'Hey yourself.' She sidles towards me, takes a seat. 'How did your meeting go?'

'All good. We have everything in place to be set up. You're going to be in great hands with Mr Douglas – he's the best heart surgeon in Ireland. Once you do your part – staying relaxed – we're very hopeful we can get you through all this.'

It's either the tone of her voice or the delivery of what she says that reminds me of a young Michelle. I'm not quite sure what it is. I just know that I feel comfortable in Elaine's company.

'So... eh...' she says, 'would you like to continue what we were talking about... or d'you want to talk about something else or just watch tele... whaddya think?'

She crosses her legs, gets as comfortable as anyone possibly can in those horrible plastic chairs.

'Sorry?' I say, scratching at my head. 'What was it we were talking about?'

'Betsy. You just informed me Betsy Blake was your daughter before I had to go.'

'Oh... I could talk about Betsy all day, every day.'

Elaine smiles again, but it's not a happy smile, more sorrowful than anything.

'Are you sure you want to talk about her today... if... y'know... if you're supposed to be staying calm, keeping relaxed?'

I sigh a little, scoot down in the bed a bit and let the back of my head sink into the pillow. So much has happened this morning that I can't get my head straight. I remember talking to Elaine now, just before she headed out for her meeting. She knew of Betsy, was totally shocked when I told her she was my daughter. I stare up at the stains on the ceiling.

'She was only four years old... would be twenty-one now,' I find myself saying. I hadn't even decided in my own head that I was going to continue talking about my daughter. 'I was supposed to be looking after her while Michelle – my wife at the time – went shopping for the afternoon. It's all my fault. All my fault.' I pinch my forefinger and thumb into my eyes. I feel Elaine reach out a hand and rest it on my knee. 'It wasn't the first time… I once left Betsy alone in the kitchen and didn't she split her head open, falling off a chair and onto the tiles. I loved her, still love every inch of her, but I wasn't a great dad. I was too easily distracted.'

'Gordon,' Elaine says, now standing up. 'You don't have to… not if you don't want to. We can talk this all through tomorrow if you want… after you recover from your surgeries.'

I take my fingers away from my eyes, open them. She's staring down at me, that sorrowful smile still etched on her pretty face.

'Why don't we turn on the tele, watch some crappy daytime TV, huh?' she says. 'It'll help you relax.'

I sit back up, dry my eyes by sweeping the palm of my hand across my face, then smile back at Elaine.

'Anything but *Loose Women*,' I say.

Elaine laughs as she reaches for the remote control. After a few clicks of a button, she stops on an old episode of *Top Gear*.

'I like this,' she says, 'my dad got me into cars.'

I look over at her, wonder how much more perfect her dad was to her than I was to Betsy. I bet Elaine's dad never left her alone while he was working, I bet he never left her alone in the kitchen to split her head open.

'Perfect,' I say.

I try to get as comfortable as I can in my bed, then watch Jeremy Clarkson make a tit of himself by interviewing an A-list celebrity. The guy's such a buffoon. Though the buffoon seems to be having a positive effect on me. It's either him or Elaine's company. She's right, watching tele does allow me to escape from my own head. Suddenly I'm matching Elaine's little giggles. Never in my life did I think I'd ever laugh at something Jeremy fucking Clarkson said.

'That you?' Elaine says turning to me.

'Huh?'

'The buzzing.'

I look down to my lap. My phone's alight. I pick it up, the number ringing unfamiliar, then press at the green button.

'Hello.'

'Is this Gordon Blake?'

'Yes… who's this?'

'Gordon, I just heard your terrible news, it's me – Ray De Brun.'

ELEVEN YEARS AGO

Betsy

'Double figures, huh?'

Dod pushes his shoulder against mine as he says that and smiles at me.

I never thought of it like that. Double figures.

I suck in a big breath and then let it out as hard as I can. I miss just one of the candles. But Dod blows it out for me, then looks up at me and laughs. I laugh too. I love when it's my birthday.

Dod didn't just bring a cake down the steps with him, he brought three presents too. I really hope they're all books – every one of them. But I know one present looks too small to be a book.

'Go on then.'

I reach for the rectangular present first, rip the paper off it and bring it close to my eyes. It's a box-set of books: called Harry Potter. Six of them. Brilliant. I think I read the name Harry Potter in one of my magazines before. Didn't know who it was. But I will soon. I hug Dod really tight. Really, really tight.

'Supposed to be the best books ever written.'

'Really?'

'So they say.'

I stare at him. He looks just as excited and as happy as I am. I don't know why. It's my birthday, not his.

'Has Harry Potter been on the television as much as I have?'

Now he looks confused. He turns his head and stares at me as if he doesn't know what I'm saying.

'Remember you told me I was on the television a lot?' I say.

He still looks confused.

'You said that to me a few years ago. That I was on television lots of times.'

'Did I?'

It makes me sad that he's forgotten. It's one thing I will never forget. It has actually made me happy ever since Dod told me I was on television and now he's just forgotten all about it. I really like Dod. He buys me lots of things and makes my room really beautiful and bright. But sometimes he hurts my insides a little bit. I don't think he means it. Not in the way he used to hurt my outsides; like the time he dragged me down the steps by my hair because I screamed in the upsteps toilet, or the time he threw me against the wall. But my insides seem to hurt when he has forgotten something he's said to me or the way he doesn't let me talk about the memories I had before I came to this room. I wish he would let me talk about my memories because it helps me remember Mummy and Daddy and my old house. The memories seem to be getting smaller and smaller. That's why I talk to Bozy about them when I can. I talk to Bozy about my Mummy's smile and about playing football with my Daddy.

'Go on... open this.'

I take the present from him and rip the paper really quickly. It's not more books. It's a box with a really bright yellow coloured blob on it.

'What is it?'

'It's a lava lamp.'

'A lava lamp?'

'Yeah – you can put it in the corner here.' He points over to the corner near the steps. 'It'll help brighten that area up and look...' He opens the box, takes out the lamp. 'The colours all change and go in different directions.'

Dod looks more happy about this lamp than I am.

'Ye don't like it huh?'

'I do. I do. Thank you, Dod.' I wrap my hands around him again for another hug.

'You wished it was more books, didn't you?'

I lean off him. I don't want to hurt his insides, but I remember that I should always tell the truth to Dod.

'I love books the most.'

He doesn't get angry. He hasn't been angry Dod for years now. I think angry Dod is gone forever. I hope he is.

'Well, I think you'll like this present more than books.'

He picks up the small present and hands it to me. I shake it and wonder if I can get any clues from how it sounds. But it doesn't make any noise. Not really.

Then I open it quickly. It's weird; black with loads of buttons on it.

'What is it?'

Dod smiles. It's a big smile.

'Come with me.'

I follow him up the steps. Even though he hasn't been angry Dod for years I still feel frightened when I'm up the steps with him, just in case I make a noise or something. When we are at the top he walks into the room I am not allowed to look into. I just wait outside and close my eyes.

'C'mon.'

'What?'

'Come in.'

I open my eyes.

'Come into that room?'

'Yep.'

I feel really frightened now. But I walk in only because Dod asked me to. It's beautiful. It has three really big brown chairs in it. One with room for three people and the other two have room for one person. There is carpet. I haven't seen carpet since Mummy and Daddy's house. And there are big white curtains. I feel like I'm going to cry. I'm not sure if I'm excited or frightened. Dod kneels down beside me, holds up my hand that's gripping the strange present I just opened.

'Here... press this red button at the top.'

I do press it and then the big black box in front of me shines a big light... it's a television. Dod's television. I see the first person I have seen that isn't Dod in six years. She is beautiful. All smiley with blonde hair. Tears come out of both of my eyes.

'Told you you'd love it.'

Dod grabs me and holds me really tight to him.

'One hour every day I'm going to let you watch television with me. You're a big girl now. Happy birthday, Betsy.'

13:00

Lenny

MICHELLE HOLDS HER HAND OUT TO TRY TO STEADY HER BALANCE BEFORE giving in and slumping down into an armchair. Lenny has never met the woman before but he already knows that she's more pale in the face than she is on any normal day. She fidgets with her fingers, then begins to pull her wedding ring on and off rapidly.

Lenny remains quiet, was oblivious to how Michelle would react to such news. His assumption led him to believe she hated her ex husband, that she really didn't give two shits about him. Certainly not to the extent that all of the blood would drain from her face.

'When you say fifty per cent, what do you mean exactly?' she says, staring at nothing.

Lenny shifts his balance from his left foot to his right foot.

'I don't know the ins and outs specifically, but eh…' he says. Michelle stares up at him, awaits an answer to the question she posed, 'his surgeries are so complicated that there is a major risk of him not waking up.'

'I can't believe it. I probably should believe it. He's not even capable of looking after himself… but I… I…'

Lenny sits down without being invited to do so on the couch across from Michelle. She doesn't react, continues to stare into space.

Lenny squelches his mouth with unease. He genuinely didn't give himself time to think this through.

'Which hospital is he in?'

'Tallaght,' Lenny says.

'I can't… I mean… I can't get up to see him. I've got to wait for the twins to come home from school.'

'Twins?' Lenny asks.

Michelle stares at him. Then looks towards a family portrait in a glass frame that's sitting on the mantelpiece.

'I'm sorry,' she says, her eyes refocusing, almost as if she has been turned back on after being on standby for the past two minutes. 'You're a PI did you say… did Gordon send you to tell me this news? That why you're here?'

Lenny blinks. Sometimes his blinking sorts his mind out for him, bides him vital seconds to think things through. But he's stumped. He only came here with one goal: securing Gordon's big house by eliminating Jake Dewey as a suspect. But he didn't realise the full complications of his call to this home.

'Michelle, your ex husband didn't want to spend what could be his last few hours lying in a bed and doing nothing. He wanted to spend that time at least trying to find out what happened to Betsy.'

Lenny watches as the blood returns to Michelle's face; her cheeks turning from faded pink to a roaring red. Her jaw swings. Then she holds her eyes closed, takes a big sigh and sucks a long, slow breath in through the gaps in her teeth. Lenny can sense she is doing her best to refrain from saying exactly what she wants to say. Michelle then places her hands on her knees, stands up and walks to the doorway of the sitting room. She swings it open, takes one step aside.

'Thank you, Mr Moon, you can leave now,' she says.

Lenny stands up, ringing his Sherpa hat through his hands. His mood has changed from excited to gloom over the past few minutes. If Jake Dewey is up in Belfast on business; the chances of Lenny ruling him out as Betsy's abductor are limited. The million euro house is locking its doors on him.

'Michelle – listen; I don't believe at all that he had anything to do with it. But can you give me something concrete that Jake was not involved in Betsy's disappearance?'

Michelle's face stiffens; her nose, her chin, her lips. She reaches a hand towards her sitting room door again and ensures it's as wide open as it can be.

'Out!'

Lenny shuffles his feet towards her, pauses to say something when he's as close to Michelle as he can possibly be.'

'Mich—'

'Out!' she shouts without even opening her mouth. It roars from the back of her throat.

Lenny feels bad. He didn't want to upset Michelle; she'd been through enough in life. His trainers squelch down her hallway, towards the hall door. He fumbles with the latch before opening it. Then he stalls in the door frame, looks back.

'I'm so sorry for upsetting you, Michelle,' he says. He steps out and pulls the door closed behind him.

He covers his face with his hat on her doorstep.

'Fuckety fuck!' he says into it as he strolls down the garden path, kicking up rain spray as he does so. Then comes to rest against a lamppost outside the next-door neighbour's drive. He looks up to the clouds to feel the sprinkles of rain fall on his face. It's only light rain, but the greyness of the clouds suggests it won't be light for long.

He breathes in his thoughts. All he has to do is to close Jake Dewey off as a suspect, then the house is his. But how can he do that? How can he get closure for Gordon?

He removes the phone from his jacket pocket, begins to nibble on the rubber case once again. Instead of thinking about the Blake family, he thinks about his own. He's barely noticed Sally is in great form today; when he imagines her, she's normally mute, downbeat. He wonders what she's up to now; probably carrying another heavy basket of clothes towards the washing machine, getting down on her knees and sighing as she carries out another boring, routine daily task. Then he imagines Jared and Jacob; the two of them sitting in class wondering what the fuck their teacher is rambling on about. He blinks rapidly into the rain, then turns on his heels.

'Fuck this,' he says to no one. 'If you're gonna be a good PI, be a good fucking PI.'

He paces up Michelle's drive again, doesn't even take a split second to look at her beautiful car this time. He heads straight for the door, his finger stretching for the doorbell.

Michelle's eyes look heavy when she answers; as if she's been twisting the palms of her hands firmly into them. Lenny doesn't give her time to snap at him.

'Michelle, I'm just trying to carry out Gordon's dying wish. He's been living with so much guilt for so many years and—'

Michelle shoots a laugh out her mouth.

'Guilt? Gordon doesn't even know what the word means.'

Lenny tilts his head back to look up at the dark clouds again, then pivots his chin back down to stare into Michelle's eyes.

'If I could step in for just five minutes… I can explain everything to you.'

Michelle pushes the door open wider, giving Lenny the space to pass her. He walks up her wooden-floored hallway again and this time enters the living room without even being invited to. The first time he walked into this room – not more than ten minutes ago – he was struck by the size of it; the richness of it. But this time, all he's drawn to is the tiny family portrait encased in a glass frame atop the mantelpiece.

'Got twins myself. Boys – Jared and Jacob. We tried for four years, couldn't get pregnant. Had to spend almost fourteen grand on IVF before we finally got a positive result.'

He looks back at Michelle, offers a sterile smile. But she doesn't react. She's mute, her arms folded under her breasts.

'We thought it would be the start of a great life when they were born; a life we've always wanted. But it's been traumatic. My wife's had post-natal depression; has tried to kill herself twice.'

This makes Michelle squint a little. She unfolds her arms, allows them to hang by her side.

'We're taking it each day as it comes. I used to be a cop, y'see. I always wanted to be a detective; but the circumstances meant… I just… I had to be close to my wife at all times, couldn't risk not being on call for her if she needed me. That's why I opened up my own private investigating business.'

Michelle stiffens her mouth, nods.

'I'm just trying to do my job here, Michelle, much like Jake is in Belfast today. We're just trying to provide for our… for our twins, for our wives, right?'

Michelle plonks herself on the sofa. Lenny's not sure if she's listening to the words he's saying now, wonders if she's still in shock with the news he gave to her earlier.

'Your ex-husband needs to go into his surgeries with a clear mind. He just asked me to rid his mind of all of the evil thoughts he's had over the years. Of course he doesn't believe Jake had anything to do with Betsy's disappearance.' Michelle's head stays still, but her eyes look up, her tongue swirling in her mouth. 'In the same way that Gordon felt Alan Keating and Barry Ward didn't have anything to do with Betsy's disappearance, but he asked me to talk to them this morning, just to clear his mind of any small doubt.'

'You spoke with Alan Keating today?' Michelle asks, her face contorting.

Lenny sniffles his nose, then nods his head.

'He was very helpful… Gave me—'

'Alan Keating is a fucking scumbag. Of course he didn't have anything to do with Betsy's death, but that doesn't stop him being a scumbag.'

Lenny pauses, tilts his head and then walks tentatively towards Michelle and sits beside her on the sofa.

'Betsy's death?'

Michelle turns her head, stares at his face from about ten inches away.

'Oh for fuck sake, I can't deal with this right now. Please. Please.' She holds her hands to her face, her fingers gripping at the top of her crown. Her shoulders shake, a sobbing sound purring from somewhere deep within her.

Lenny winces in his seat. He holds out a hand to place around Michelle's shoulders, then pauses, unsure whether to follow through or not with his embrace, his arm remaining stretched and hovering behind Michelle's head. He holds his eyes firmly shut, wondering what to do next. The buzzing inside his jacket pocket makes his mind up for him.

He relents, takes his arm back and then fumbles inside his pocket and removes his phone. A strange number. Michelle continues to cry, continues to break down right beside him, but Lenny – unsure how to react – stands up, presses the answer button and holds the phone to his ear.

'Hello,' he whispers.

'Lenny Moon?'

'Yeah.'

'I'm Detective Ray De Brun; Gordon Blake has asked me to call you.'

'Oh.'

'Listen, I don't have a lot of time; large pike are prime for catching this time of year, so I'm gonna clear the case you're working on in the next five seconds. Betsy Blake is dead. Was killed when she was hit by a car on the day she was reported missing. Was put into the boot of that car and driven away. Body's never been found, but she wasn't kidnapped, wasn't taken by some psychopath, isn't trapped in somebody's basement. She's gone, Lenny – dead. Has been for seventeen years.' Lenny stands in silence. Doesn't know how to respond to De Brun's bluntness. 'Listen, I feel really sorry for Gordon Blake; I always have done. That's why I told him I'd take two minutes out of my day to ring you… so, I've rung you and, well… that's that.'

'No wait... Hold on, De Brun,' Lenny says, sounding desperate, panicky.

Michelle removes her hands from her soaked face and an in almost slow-motion rises from the sofa.

'Is that Ray fucking De Brun?' she asks, both of her fists clenched.

Lenny inches the phone from his ear, nods his head once.

'Arghhh!' Michelle roars. She takes two large strides towards her mantelpiece, holds out her arms and with one large sweep, she cleans the marble top of all that was sitting on it; the candle sticks, the glass picture frame, the glass clock. They all come crashing down on to the designer floorboards, smashing into an array of shards; the noise echoing through the room.

'What the hell's going on?' De Brun squeaks down the line. 'Lenny... Lenny...'

13:15

Gordon

'GORDON, WHAT IS GOING ON?' ELAINE ASKS WITH GENUINE CONCERN IN her eyes. I place the phone back down on my lap, then swallow hard as I realise, inside my head, that there's no way I can lie my way out of this.

'That was Ray De Brun,' I say, nodding towards my phone. 'He was the lead detective in Betsy's case. I rang him this morning after you and the whole surgical team came in to give me my news. I just didn't want to... I didn't want to...'

I try to not sob, but I can't stop my shoulders from jittering. Elaine holds a hand towards my left bicep, rubs at it gently. I look up at her. Her body language is screaming sympathy, but the look on her face is in total contrast; she looks stern, disappointed. She doesn't say anything, just continues to gently rub at the top of my arm as she waits on me to finish what I'd started to say.

'I don't want to die without knowing the truth. My worst nightmare is coming true.'

As soon as I say that my shoulders do more than jitter; they shake uncontrollably. The tears jump from my eyes, from my nose too. I cover my face with my hand, then feel one of Elaine's hands at the back of my head. What a fucking mess I am. Surely there can't be anything more pathetic than this.

'Oh, Gordon,' she says. 'We'll do our best to get your through this, to make sure you still have an opportunity to find out what happened to Betsy once you recover from your surgeries.'

I'd love to answer her back, tell her that there's just as much chance of me dying on the operating table as there is of me recovering fully, but I can't... the crying has totally consumed me, rendered me speechless.

'I understand the news we gave you this morning is a massive shock... and I also understand that your mind would have gone straight to Betsy and to the fact that you haven't had the answers to questions that must have eaten at you for years. But... but your best chance of getting answers is by living longer. I'm sorry to say, but it's highly unlikely you'll get answers in the next couple of hours anyway, is it?'

I suck up my tears as soon as she's finished. It's not as if I haven't been thinking along those lines all morning, but hearing somebody else say it really highlights how deluded I've been. I feel lost inside my own mind, trapped in a bizarre swirl of confusion. I've been confused and heartbroken for the past seventeen years, but I don't recall being this discombobulated since the time Betsy actually went missing. I guess hearing you may only have a few hours left to live will do that to a man.

I've been a mess in different ways ever since Betsy went missing, but that first ten or twelve months was a total headfuck. I was so pissed off with De Brun once he relieved Keating and Barry Ward of any involvement in the case. I was convinced at the time that they had something to do with it; but then my suspicions turned to Jake Dewey, probably out of sheer jealousy and heartbreak. The cops wouldn't entertain my opinion; so I took it upon myself to look into him. I began to stalk the fucker. Two months later I was told I had to stay away from him for twenty years; that he'd filed a restraining order, using one hell of a lawyer to pull it off. I couldn't cope; decided to fuck off on a break around Europe to get away from it all. The cops cleared me, said I could go. I took the car on a ferry to the UK and then to France, drove all through central Europe; Belgium, Holland, Germany, then back around through Austria and Northern Italy before coming home. I was away for seven weeks in total, and there were times on that trip that I felt I'd sorted my head out. But when I arrived home, my mind became more discombobulated than ever before. I was a changed man, but not for the better.

I know I'll never get over Betsy's disappearance, not until I have answers. But I really don't know how to get them. Don't know what the fuck I'm doing. I could curse De Brun forever for closing the case with his made-up theory that Betsy died; it means nobody is out there looking for my daughter. Except of course little Lenny Moon this morning. That's so fucking pathetic. I know I'm going to die today, I can feel it deep in the pit of my stomach, and with that, I know I'll never find out what happened to Betsy.

My shoulders begin to shake again, my hands going directly back up towards my face in an effort to stem more tears from falling. But Elaine grabs at my wrists.

'Gordon, let's get you out of this room for a few minutes, huh? Will we go for a little walk, try to get you into a more positive mind-set?' I shake my head. I can't, I can't face real life. Not now. 'Because, Gordon, I have to say, that if things continue the way they are, I'm going to have to inform Mr Douglas that you're not mentally fit enough to go through with the surgeries and… and… well, if you don't have surgery on that heart as soon as possible, Gordon, well, we both know an unrecoverable heart attack is inevitable.'

I look up at her, blinking the wet away from my eyes.

'I either get into a positive mind-set and give myself a chance of living… or I die?'

Elaine nods her head slowly.

'It's what we've been saying all morning. It's your only chance.'

I throw my legs over the side of the bed.

'Okay, take me for a walk. Let's try and calm my mind down.'

Elaine gathers my sneakers at the foot of the bed and I slip my feet into them. I look a right state, but why am I even bothering to give a fuck about what I look like? Just as Elaine holds my right arm to lead me out of the ward, my phone buzzes. I reach back towards the bed for it, but Elaine snatches at it before me.

'Ah, ah,' she says. She holds down the standby button, then scrolls across the screen to turn the phone completely off. 'The investigation is over for you for today. I'll turn your phone back on for you in the morning when you recover and you can take it from there. How about that?'

I don't say anything. I just watch Elaine place my phone in the drawer of the bedside cabinet and then allow her to link my right arm and lead me out of the ward.

TEN YEARS AGO

Betsy

THE SIMPSONS IS MY FAVOURITE. IT ALWAYS SEEMS TO BE ON WHEN DOD LETS me up the steps to watch television at six o'clock. It's funny. Bart is funny, Homer is funny. But watching television isn't better than reading a book. No way. It is nice to be up the steps and out of my room for an hour every day though. It's different.

We normally watch *The Simpsons* and then a show called *The Weakest Link*. A woman asks loads of questions but I never know the answers. Dod knows some of them some of the time. I think he is clever. He reads lots of things, but not books. Just normally loads of pages with loads of words and numbers on them. I'm not sure what they are.

I always feel a bit sad when I have to go back down the steps but today it has gone past seven o'clock and Dod hasn't told me to go down yet. He is in the room next to me. I can hear him with plates and stuff. It's the first time he has ever left me alone in this room. I click at the buttons of the remote control to see if there are any other cartoons on but I can't find any.

'Betsy.'

'Yes.'

'Come in to me here.'

I walk out of the television room and then stop at the door of the kitchen where Dod is.

'Come on – you can come in.'

I step inside. I've never been in the kitchen before. It is all white. The table in the middle is white, all the little doors around the walls are white, the walls are white.

The smell is delicious. It makes me lick my lips.

'I'm cooking a stir fry.'

Dod tilts the pan he is holding towards me and I see loads of different colours in it. I think they're all different types of peppers; red, green and yellow ones. I take a step forward and breathe in the smell again. The closer you are to it, the nicer it is.

'I've decided I'm going to teach you how to cook with me after we watch television every evening. How about that?'

I don't answer him by talking. I just throw my arms around him and squeeze him tight. Really, really tight. Like I do when he buys me books. I'm really happy. It means I get to spend more time out of my room and up the steps with Dod. I'm becoming a big girl now. I squeeze him even tighter.

'Whoa, whoa; careful, I'm holding the pan.'

'Thank you, Dod.'

I smile a big huge smile.

'Okay, sit up here.'

Dod puts down the pan then grabs me and sits me up on the counter where all the food is.

'I really trust you now.'

I smile again.

'I think you are getting old enough to be able to do things around the house, so you don't have to spend too much time down in your basement, what do you think about that?'

I feel really excited. My belly has that fuzzy feeling it can get sometimes when things are good.

'What would you like me to do?'

'Well, has cooking come up in any of your books?'

I nod my head.

'Sometimes. Some books talk about making breakfasts and dinners but I don't know how to do it. It doesn't say how to cook in the books, just that dinners are cooked. That's all... I think.'

Dod laughs a little at what I'm trying to say. I feel a bit embarrassed.

'Well, see these books here?'

Dod reaches past me and to four really big books. They're huge. Really thick. There must be a million words in them.

'Well, I know you like reading, so maybe you can read some of these and they'll teach you how to cook.'

I take the first book off him. It says *Gordon Ramsay: Easy* on it. I flick through it then nod my head.

'I can read this. Thank you, Dod.'

'Great. Soon you'll be like my little housewife.'

I look at Dod and am not sure whether to laugh or not. I'm not sure if he was making a joke. Then he leans towards me and kisses me on the lips. That's weird. He hasn't done that before.

'I think you're old enough to be a little housewife now,' he says.

13:20

Lenny

LENNY GRASPS MICHELLE BY BOTH WRISTS. HE WANTS TO STARE INTO HER eyes, but can't really make out her face, not with her hair strewn over it.

'Michelle, it's okay. It's okay.'

He helps her to an upright position and walks her to the sofa where she sits. She parts her hair from her face and then covers it with her hands.

'Michelle, we are only looking after Gordon's last wish,' Lenny says. 'I didn't mean to bring back so many horrible memories for you, I'm sorry.'

Michelle blows out a sigh, then wipes her hand across her nose, sniffing as she does so.

'It's not you I'm angry with. It's bloody Gordon. I haven't heard from him for years… and now this… *this*.' She stretches her arms outwards as if she's preaching at a ceremony.

'Just gimme one sec,' Lenny says before spinning on his heels and making his way to his mobile phone he'd left resting on the arm of the chair.

'Ray…' he says.

'What the hell is going on there, Lenny?'

'I'm eh… I'm with Betsy's mother Michelle right now; she's obviously and rightly upset by all of this. Can I please ring you back in ten minutes? I'd love to talk to you.'

There's an obvious and awkward hesitation on the other end of the line.

'Okay – but don't leave it longer than ten minutes. I'm all set to go back out onto the lake.'

Lenny thanks Ray, hangs up and then moves slowly towards Michelle again. She's removed her hands, is now staring into space, oblivious to the mess of broken glass on the floor.

'Michelle, can I make you a cup of tea or get you a water or anything?'

Lenny's question is met with silence.

'Michelle... Michelle.' He inches closer to her. Then her eyes refocus and her head snaps to face Lenny.

'So he's probably gonna die today huh?'

Lenny stiffens his nose, then nods.

'It's not definite, he still has a fighting chance, but...' Lenny plonks himself on the sofa next to Michelle and holds out his hands as if he's finishing his sentence through body language.

'I feel sorry for him, but this... bringing all this shit to my door again. Lenny – it's not fair. I've never done anything wrong in my life. And I've just lost my job as well. Why does he always—'

'He just wants closure before his operations,' Lenny says, interrupting Michelle in an effort to stop her from flying into a rage again.

She turns her soaked face towards him.

'We got closure twelve years ago. Betsy's gone. She's dead.'

Lenny swallows hard, then taps his hands against his knees, unsure what way to continue the conversation with the devastated woman next to him. Even when Lenny had dreamt of investigating real crimes, he never quite concocted a case in his head that would involve such complicated conversation. When he was training to be a policeman, his tutors touched upon the communications required with family members of deceased persons, but nothing could have prepared him for this. He subtly presses at a button on his phone so he can see the time on his screen. 13:24. He only has an hour and a half to ensure Gordon activates the will. Lenny clenches his teeth, then speaks up.

'Are you absolutely certain in your heart that Betsy is deceased?' he asks.

Michelle turns her head slowly to face him again.

'You're as bloody deluded as he is. Aren't you supposed to be an investigator? Some investigator you are. It's on record... go, go on, ring De Brun back, he'll tell ye. Then you can give up the ghost. You can go back to Gordon and tell him his dying wish is not achievable. That Betsy is gone. And it's all his fucking fault for never being mature enough to be responsible for somebody else.'

Lenny cringes a little inside. He knows he fucked up. It wasn't his place to ruin poor Michelle's day. The woman had been through enough over the years. Last thing she needed was him dragging all of her miserableness back into her home. He reaches out to her, places the palm of his hand on her shoulder.

'Get your hands off me,' she snaps. Then she stands, her arm stretched towards her door. 'Get out of my house. Out you go. And don't come back this time.'

'But Michelle—'

'Out!' she screams, so loudly that Lenny immediately takes a step back.

He places his phone back in his pocket, picks up his hat and heads for the door without saying another word. He'd like to offer Michelle more apologies but feels every time he opens his mouth to her he says the wrong thing.

When he gets outside the rain is falling harder than it has at any point so far today. He wonders if he should call a taxi or Ray De Brun first. As he's thinking it through, he strolls down Michelle's drive, plonking his hat atop his head, then comes to rest against the lamppost outside the neighbour's house – much like he had done fifteen minutes ago. It's a bit like Groundhog Day – one of Lenny's favourite movies – only Lenny's mind was swirling too much for him to entertain such a notion.

'You're a fucking idiot, Lenny,' he says to himself as he bumps the side of his head against the lamppost. Then he holds the phone to his ear and awaits an answer.

'Yep.'

'Ray, it's Lenny Moon. Thanks for taking my call. So sorry to disturb your day, but as you know, Gordon Blake is in a very bad state, may well be dead in the next couple of hours—'

'Lenny – let me stop you there so we can end this conversation quickly and get back to our day. As I said, Betsy Blake is dead. If Gordon wants finality or closure or whatever it is he's looking for; that's closure right there. She's gone. She was killed the night she was reported missing… there's no investigating needed anymore. Case is closed.'

Lenny sucks cold air through his nostrils. He knows this information is likely true, given that not only Betsy's mother, but the lead detective in the case has confirmed it for him in the past ten minutes. But he's also aware that going back to Gordon with this information most likely won't be good enough reason for him to activate the will. Lenny needs something, something Gordon hasn't heard before.

'Is there anything… anything about the case that Gordon and Michelle won't have known?' Lenny asks, almost cringing as he does so; his eyes shutting, his neck hunching under his raised shoulders.

'What do you mean?'

'I just want to find out as much information about the investigation as possible.'

A snort of laughter comes down the line.

'Lenny... Please.'

'I'm sorry, it's just...' Lenny doesn't know what to say.

'What happened with Michelle; is she okay?' De Brun asks.

'Yeah – she just got upset at me dragging back up her past. I'm an idiot. I should've handled it more sensitively. Gordon sent me to her house. He says Jake Dewey might've had something to do with Betsy's disappearance.'

'Well... I've mishandled things many times as a detective when it comes to dealing with families, so you have my sympathy. As does Michelle... and Gordon. They've always had my sympathy. But listen, Jake Dewey had absolutely nothing to do with Betsy's death.'

'What about Alan Keating and Barry Ward?'

'Lenny, you sound like Gordon. Listen to me, it wasn't Jake Dewey, wasn't Keating or Ward, it wasn't Gordon Blake himself and it wasn't... Look, Betsy is dead.'

'Hold on – it wasn't who... who was the other suspect you were gonna name there?'

'Lenny, Betsy is dead. We found a car many years later that had her DNA in it. And that DNA pointed to her dying. We believe the driver of that car that night hit Betsy when she ran out onto the road and, rather than face the music, he scooped her up, put her in the boot and dumped or hid her body somewhere... She's gone, Lenny. Betsy died. She's not being held captive anywhere. Case is closed.'

'But who was the other suspect you were about to name there? Please.'

'Listen, all suspects were cleared, okay... cleared because they didn't have anything to do with Betsy. Lenny, I gotta go. I can't give you specific details of any suspects and you know it, or you should know it.'

Lenny slouches against the lamppost, breathes out a cloud of a sigh, then holds his hands together as if in prayer, the phone sandwiched between them.

'I am begging you, Ray. Just for something. I'm a poor guy... I have nothing, my family has nothing. Gordon Blake promised me some riches if I could find anything out today. If I don't find anything—'

'Don't believe anything Gordon Blake tells you, Lenny. I'm sorry... goodbye.'

Lenny kicks at the lamppost when he hears the dead tone whistle through his phone. Then he stares back at Michelle's house and pictures the poor woman inside balled up on her sofa crying. It makes him kick the lamppost again. This time harder.

'She's dead. Course she's dead! What was I even thinking?'

Lenny opens his hand, stares at his phone and then begins to dial for a taxi. He's half way through punching in the number when the phone begins to vibrate.

'Hello.'

'Lenny; listen,' says De Brun. 'This is only because you pleaded... I can't give you any inside info from our side, but if you want to know what happened in the Betsy Blake investigation off the record, then perhaps you should speak to Frank Keville. D'ye know who he is?'

'Frank Keville? The journalist fella who's in a wheelchair?'

'Yep – he covered the case for years, knows it inside out. Perhaps he'd be willing to share information with you that I can't.'

TEN YEARS AGO

Betsy

MAKING CURRY IS MY FAVOURITE. ME AND DOD BOTH REALLY LIKE CHICKEN Madras. I cut up the chicken breasts so they are really small, like little Lego blocks, and then I cut some onions and green peppers. After I fry them in the pan for six minutes, I add the sauce. I love the smell of the sauce. I am so happy Dod lets me cook. I have learned so much from the Gordon Ramsay books. Me and Dod have curries every Tuesday and Thursday. On Monday, I cook a stir-fry and Dod cooks the other days. He doesn't let me up the steps to eat every day, but I come up most days.

It depends on how he is feeling. He's not always happy, but he is definitely never angry Dod anymore. He doesn't hurt me. He doesn't pick me up and throw me around. He hasn't done that for years. I feel happy when I am around him. Not scared like I used to be. The only weird thing now is that he keeps kissing me on the lips, not on the cheek like he used to. It doesn't taste nice.

'How long?' Dod asks. He is on the sofa watching the television.

I check the time on the top of the oven.

'Two minutes,' I say.

He says something else. I can't really hear him that well. The curry is sizzling too loudly. I step down off my little step that Dod set up for me in the kitchen and then go see what he was saying. I walk into the television room.

'I couldn't hear you. What did you say, Dod?'

'I said hurry up, I'm bleedin' starving.'

I feel sad. Dod is not good Dod today. I walk a little closer to him.

'Are you okay, Dod?'

He stares at me. He has that angry look in his eye. I hate it when he has that look.

'Are you a fuckin doctor now?'

I shake my head. I don't know what to say. He is still looking at me. Then I hear a loud beep sound.

'Ye little shit,' Dod says. He runs by me and into the kitchen.

'Look, you fuckin idiot.' He shows me the pan. The food has gone a little bit black. It's not much. But Dod is angry. He presses a button that turns the beep off and then throws the pan against the wall.

'Clean that shit up and start the dinner again.'

He walks out of the kitchen. I think if I was younger I would cry. But now that I am eleven and nearly a grownup I don't cry. I just get down on my hands and knees and begin to clean up. I like to think about story ideas when I am doing things I don't like.

I have a story idea about a girl who becomes a magician and goes to a magic school. It's a bit like Harry Potter but I want it to be different. Except anytime I sit down to write I get confused. My writing is not good and it takes me ages to write even one sentence. I wish I had have gone to school like the characters in my books do. If I did, I bet I could write much better and much quicker. Reading books has taught me a lot about words and I can talk really well. But when it comes to writing words, it takes me ages to spell them out. It has taken me nearly three months to write two pages of my story. The Harry Potter books have two-hundred and fifty pages in them. It will take me years to write a book that size. But there isn't really anything else for me to do when I'm in my basement. So maybe I will finish my book one day. I think it's going to be called *Magical Mabel*. That's the name of the girl: Mabel. She is seven years old in it, has red hair and loads of freckles. Then she gets kidnapped and taken to a big school with lots of other children who have the same magic powers as she has. But she doesn't like the school and wants to escape. Sometimes I think I would like to escape from here. But I can't. If Dod caught me he would really hurt me. I don't want to be hurt again. My back still gets sore from the last time. And that was years ago.

'Here, let me help you,' Dod says. He gets down on his hands and knees too and helps me put the dinner back into the pan. Then he brings the pan to the bin and tips the food into it. 'I'm sorry for being so... so snappy,' he says. 'I'm just not feeling well.'

'Did you call a doctor?'

'I was at the doctors last week.'

'Oh, that's where you went that time you locked me in the room?' I ask.

He nods his head.

'Yeah, the doctor says I need to take some tablets and get some rest. But none of that seems to be working. I'm sorry I shouted at you and threw the pan against the wall. I'm gonna order us some take-away instead. You like pizza?'

'Pizza?' I never heard of it.

Dod laughs.

'C'mon, come in and watch television with me. You can stay up here late tonight.'

We walk into the television room and I go to sit in the chair I sit on all the time.

'Nah, Betsy. Come over here with me.'

Dod lifts the blanket he is lying under and I get in it with him. He throws his arm around me and hugs me as we both look at the television.

'This is nice, huh?' he says. I just nod my head. But I don't think it's nice. I would be more comfortable sitting on the chair I like. On my own. Then Dod kisses the back of my neck. Yuck.

13:25

Gordon

WALKING THE CORRIDORS OF A HOSPITAL IS HARDLY A RECIPE FOR relaxation. Every ward door that's open offers me a view to another grey-skinned person lying in a bed, much like I had been minutes ago. Still, Elaine – god love her – is doing her very best to soothe me. She keeps talking about football, has assumed that because I said I like the sport that I know as much about it as she does. She's been rabbiting on for the past couple of minutes, ranting about how much her beloved Manchester United have damaged their reputation ever since Sir Alex Ferguson retired. The amount of statistics she has thrown at me in the past three minutes is, I'm sure, quite impressive. But it all sounds like gobbledygook to me.

She stops talking, then turns to face me.

'You're not really that big a fan of football are you?'

It didn't take her long to realise that. I laugh, my first laugh of the day, then shake my head.

'Certainly not as much as you are. No, I mean – I might watch the odd game if it's on tele, but no... maybe I exaggerated a bit. I'm not that big a football fan.'

She giggles.

'Okay – then what do you like, what can we talk about that will help you relax?'

I shrug both shoulders.

'Don't know really.'

'What hobbies have you got? What do you do when you're not working?'

'I don't work. Not anymore. Got paid off by the company I founded less than a year after Betsy went missing. I understood why. I couldn't focus. But it was tough. Y'know... I lost my daughter, my wife and my business all in the space of ten months.'

Elaine does that pursed lips thing again, then reaches her left arm around my shoulders as we continue to walk.

'I'm so sorry, Gordon.'

She doesn't know what else to say other than apologise for something that isn't even remotely close to her fault. I wrap my arm around the small of her back and suddenly we are strolling as if we're a happily married couple. I know it feels a little awkward for both of us, but I'm gonna take the slight intimacy while I can get it. After a few seconds, she relents, takes her arm from around me so that we're just linking arms again.

'So what do you do with your spare time?' she asks.

I don't have an answer. Not really.

'I watch some TV and I eh... obsess about Betsy. Y'know... talking about Betsy is probably the only thing that would relax me.'

Elaine makes a slight pop sound with her mouth, then stops walking.

'Okay, well... tell me all about Betsy.'

I raise my eyebrows, then let out a steady breath as we stand facing each other in the middle of a corridor.

'She was the cutest little thing, y'know. Brown hair, a splash of freckles across her face. She had the smallest little nose too. Tiny it was.'

I already feel my shoulders relax.

'I bet you doted on her, huh?' Elaine says.

'Yeah,' I reply smiling. But my smile is disingenuous. I was a shit dad. And I know it. I was just too obsessed with work at the time to care for the little person who was turning our house upside down. Ironically, back then Betsy was second in my thoughts. Now I can't stop obsessing about her. 'I'd give anything to go back in time.'

Elaine takes a step closer to me, then places a curled knuckle under my chin and lifts my head slightly.

'You're supposed to be relaxing now, okay? Not evoking feelings of guilt. You shouldn't feel guilt anyway. You are not the one who took her.'

That's the first time anyone has agreed with me in years; that Betsy was taken... abducted.

'Y'know the police don't believe somebody took her. They think somebody knocked her down, killed her, then hid her body. All seems a bit convenient to me, that. It took them seven years to come up with that theory.'

Elaine stares into my eyes, intensely.

'Gordon—'

'It's fine. I'm relaxed talking about her. Honestly.'

'Okay,' Elaine says, relenting. She links my arm again and we continue on our mission to walk up and down every corridor of floor three.

'Y'know they all think I'm mad when I say she was taken. But I'm not mad, Elaine. I'm not crazy. I just have a feeling deep in the pit of my stomach that somebody took her and that she's still out there... out there somewhere. I just hope wherever she is, she's happy; that she's being taken care of.'

Elaine seems to have fallen silent, is either happy to just listen, or perhaps she agrees with the rest of them. That my theory is the one that's wrong. I place my hand across her, stop her from walking and then stare into her eyes.

'You don't think I'm mad, do you, Elaine?'

She squints a smile at me, the tiny lines on the edge of her eyes creasing.

'I think you're being a great dad. You're not giving up on your daughter. I know that if I was Betsy, I'd hope I had a dad like you who would never give up trying to find me.'

I step into Elaine, give her a hug and breathe in her hair. It feels so good to have somebody who'll listen to me.

'That's why I have a private investigator looking for her now,' I whisper into her ear. 'I just couldn't lie there on that bed after being told I may only have five hours left to live and not do anything.'

Elaine nods her head slowly on my shoulder. I know from a personal point of view she agrees with me, but I also know she's conflicted; from a professional point of view she thinks I'm doing the worst thing I could possibly do given my situation. I hold her off me a little, so that we are facing each other.

'Don't answer this question as a nurse,' I say. 'Answer it as the beautiful human being you are, okay?'

She nods her head, then squints her eyes at me again.

'I'm doing the right thing amn't I?'

Elaine glances down at her feet, then back up at my face.

'If I was your best friend, not your nurse, I would be giving you this advice, Gordon. Your best chance of finding out what happened to your daughter is by staying alive and giving yourself more time to look for her. Surviving the surgeries is everything to you right now. It's all you've got. I'm sorry to say this, because I know it's not the answer you want to hear, but... relaxing right now, not obsessing over finding Betsy, is genuinely the best thing for you to do.'

I look up to the ceiling. Then rub my thumb firmly across my forehead, as if I'm erasing what I've just heard from my memory.

'It's just the detective who looked after the case is currently talking with the private investigator I hired this morning. What if... what if somehow—'

'Gordon,' Elaine says, just like a school teacher would say to a student who's rambling on too much about nothing. 'It's been seventeen years. The fact of the matter is, Betsy is not going to be found in the next hour or two. I mean, what more can I say? You have to agree with me on that.'

I look back down at her, stare at her entire face.

'I do agree – of course I do. It's just... if I do die today... I wanna give it my all until my last breath. Like you said, if you were Betsy, you wouldn't want your dad to stop looking for you, would you?'

I can spot a moistness form in her eyes. I'm not the only one close to tears. She removes her old-school pocket watch from the top of her scrubs and sucks at her own lips.

'You're going for make or break surgery in the next hour and a half. I'm going to be straight and honest with you. You're not going to get any information in the next ninety minutes that you couldn't find in the past seventeen years. I'm sorry if that's a hard truth for you to take; but I owe it you to be totally honest.'

I thumb the tear that has just fallen out of her eye away from her cheek, then grab her close. The two of us sob in unison in the middle of the corridor; her sobbing with pity for me, me sobbing because I'm being pitied. Again. Surely there can't be anything more pathetic than strangers pitying you a couple of hours after they've just met you for the first time? But everyone pities me. I am the living, breathing definition of a loser. I literally lost everything I ever had.

13:25

Lenny

'INDEPENDENT HOUSE, HOW CAN I HELP YOU?'

'I need to talk with Frank Keville please?'

'Frank Keville – and which newspaper does he write for?'

'Ah... I don't know, doesn't he write for them all? Surely you know Frank Keville, the guy in the wheelchair, does all the crime stuff?'

'Hold on one moment, Sir.'

Lenny tenses his jaw, his eyes focused and controlled by his deep thoughts. He can't even feel the rain anymore; the weather a concern deep beneath him now. He continues to walk towards the main Terenure Road where he told the taxi company he would be waiting.

'I'm afraid Mr Keville is busy right now; is there anybody else you can speak to?'

Lenny takes the phone away from his mouth and exhales a disappointed grunt.

'I need to speak to Keville urgently. It's an emergency. Can you ask him to ring this number as soon as he can? My name is Lenny Moon; I'm a private investigator and I need to talk to him about a story he spent years working on.'

Lenny listens in as the receptionist mumbles back his name and number, then politely says goodbye before hanging up.

A small ball of excitement has resurrected itself within him. He knows quite well that he's not going to solve the case of Betsy Blake's disappearance, but that's not his task. All he has to do is bring something different to the table, then Gordon Blake will sign off on the will.

Lenny bites his bottom lip as his selfishness calls out to him. It's becoming more and more apparent to him that he may be an hour away from hoping a man dies; a man that has already given him a thousand euro. A man who's had an awful life. Poor Gordon Blake.

But Lenny can't allow sentiment to get in the way; there's fuck all he can do about Gordon's chances of surviving the surgeries. All Lenny has to focus on is the task in hand: speak to Frank Keville, find out who the other suspect was that Ray De Brun had alluded to. Gordon mustn't be aware there was another suspect. Otherwise he would have named him in the note earlier. If Lenny finds out who the other suspect is, then that's brand new information. That should be enough.

Lenny picks up his phone, dials Gordon's number and waits. But the tone is dead. He tries again. Same result. He's gurning and tutting to himself when he hears a car horn. A maroon-coloured taxi has just pulled up outside the Centra and is awaiting his fare.

Lenny opens the back door, slides into the seat.

'Thanks. Independent House, ye know it? On Talbot Street?'

'That's where all the newspapers are, mate?'

'That's the one.'

Lenny chews on the butt of his mobile phone as the taxi man pulls away. He's cursing, under his breath. The fact that Sally has always dismissed his need for a smart phone is grating on him now more than ever and it's always grated on him in some way.

Lenny looks up, realises the taxi man's smart phone – resting in the small cradle on the dashboard – is not currently in use.

'Guess you don't need the satnav to get to Talbot Street, huh?' he says.

The taxi man looks in the rear-view mirror, offers a polite laugh.

'Course not,' he says.

Lenny grinds his teeth together, blinks rapidly.

'Any chance I could take a look at your phone. I don't need to call anyone, but I need to check something online. My phone's a piece of shit and… look, you can add an extra fiver to the journey fare.'

The taxi man sniffs.

'Make it an extra tenner and I'll give it you, but I'm locking the doors.'

'Perfect,' Lenny says, shifting in the back seat. He reaches forward, takes the phone from the taxi man.

He immediately presses at the internet browser and then hesitates, biting his lip.

He types the words 'Betsy Blake Dead' into the search bar. The first option that pops up is an article from the *Irish Independent*. Lenny speed reads it, finds out little information than he had already been given. Ray De Brun closed the case in 2009 after a Toyota Corolla that had been used in multiple robberies over the years had been found with Betsy's DNA inside it. Lenny shakes his head, realises it was ridiculously farfetched to conclude that the cops made all this up just to close the case. It has to be true. Betsy must be dead. He continues his internet search, desperate to find out why the owner of the car hadn't been charged or even arrested over the findings, but the report was void of these details. He swipes out of that story, into the next one. Ironically, it was written by the man he was hoping to meet in the next few minutes: Frank Keville.

This article included more detail. It suggested the car wasn't specifically registered to anyone on the date Betsy was supposedly killed, and that it had been swapped between many different arms of criminal gangs over the years. It had once been owned by a woman called Sandra Wilson who had reported it stolen in 2000, but since then it was off the grid until the cops found it abandoned almost eight years later. It was suspected of being involved in a post office heist and when the cops carried out tests on it they – rather surprisingly – answered the question a whole nation had been asking for years: whatever happened to Betsy Blake?

'Fuckin hell,' Lenny mutters to himself.

The taxi man twists in his chair.

'Y'okay, mate?'

'Sorry – yeah. Just having one of those days.'

Lenny tilts his head down, gets back into the information on the taxi man's phone. He decides to Google 'Frank Keville'.

Like most people in the country, he's aware of what Keville looks like. Aside from writing the news, Keville had also become the news. He often appears on TV chat shows and has a picture by-line in the newspaper that's ridiculously oversized. It's Keville's professional mission to rid the streets of gangland crime. And he's good at his job; so good in fact that a gangland member tried to assassinate him. Lenny was aware – as was most of the country – that it was most likely Alan Keating who ordered the failed hit on him – but trying to prove that was an impossibility.

Lenny smirks to himself at the craziness of the underworld he has somehow found himself entangled in today; mucking around with The Boss and now Ireland's best crime reporter all in the space of a couple of hours. He's still smirking when the taxi man spins around to him again.

'Can't get fully down Talbot Street, mate; I'll leave ya here. Independent House is that one there on the left-hand side, can ye see it? The one with the glass shelter outside it.'

Lenny looks up, can just about see the building the taxi man is pointing at through the greyness of the rain, then hands the phone back to the driver.

'You're a legend,' Lenny says, tapping him on the shoulder.

'Well that's eighteen euro for the ride, plus the tenner you owe me for using the phone.'

Lenny fumbles in his pocket, takes out a few of the notes he had withdrawn from the ATM at the hospital, separates a twenty and a ten and then hands them over to the taxi man.

'Here, take thirty – and cheers for lending me your phone. It's been very helpful.'

The taxi man unlocks the doors and Lenny pops out, then runs towards the building with the glass shelter. He's not running to get out of the rain – Lenny's already drenched to the bone. He's running because he's in such a hurry. He's aware, because he looked at the taxi's dashboard before he got out, that it's just gone half one. Time isn't on his side. Gordon Blake will be going under the knife in less than an hour and half.

Lenny tries to push at the door at the entrance to Independent House but is stopped in his tracks, his face almost squashing up against the glass. He then waves at the security man inside and, after being eyeballed, the security man reaches for a button under his desk and presses at it to release the door.

'Thanks,' Lenny says, as he scoops the drenched hat off his head and steps inside the marble reception area. 'I need to speak with Frank Keville as a matter of urgency.'

'Ah – you were the man on the phone to me about fifteen minutes ago, huh?'

'Yep, that's me,' Lenny says, almost dancing due to his lack of patience. 'I'm in a real hurry and need to speak with Keville straight away.'

The security man picks up a large black phone receiver and then dials three buttons.

Lenny stares around the reception area, notices the list of newspaper brands encased in glass frames on the wall. Six national newspapers are all produced from this one building in the heart of Dublin's city centre.

'Sorry, no answer from his phone,' the security man says, placing the receiver back down.

Lenny takes a moment to stare at the nametag on the security man's navy jumper.

'Gerry... please, I need to speak with him as a matter of urgency. I don't have time to waste.'

Gerry stands up, showing not only his height, but his weight; his belly hanging over the waist of his trousers as if it's eager to touch the floor. Then he shrugs his shoulders and places a red lollipop in his mouth.

'Sorry – there's not much else I can do if he's not answering his phone,' he mumbles, before popping the lollipop out of his mouth. 'Would you like to take a seat over there?'

Lenny glances over his shoulder at the green sofa in the corner of the reception area, next to a glass table adorned by a helping of the day's national newspapers.

'Please keep trying his number,' Lenny says after sighing. Then he solemnly walks towards the sofa, ringing the hat through his hands with impatience. He sits, observes Gerry picking up the phone receiver, holding it to his ear, then placing it back down again. He watches as staff come in and then out of the elevator. When one stands at reception, blocking his view of Gerry, Lenny walks slowly to the elevator and waits on the doors to slide open. When they do, he steps inside, stares at all of the buttons and shrugs his head before deciding to start by pressing number one. But even after pressing the button the doors remain open, the lift not interested in taking him anywhere.

'Fuck sake,' he mumbles to himself.

'Sorry?' a woman asks, entering the lift.

'Oh – was just talking to myself. One of those days,' Lenny replies.

The woman laughs, then lifts her security pass to a reader above the number pad on the elevator and presses at the number three. The lift doors close at the same time Lenny's eyes close. He mumbles a quiet thank you under his breath and when the doors open he steps out with the woman.

'I'm sorry,' he says, offering his gentlest smile. 'I might have got off on the wrong floor. I'm looking for Frank Keville. I have a meeting scheduled with him and I'm running a tad late.'

'No,' says the woman. 'You didn't get off on the wrong floor. His desk is through that door, on the left side.'

Lenny bows as a thank you, turns on his heels, then presses at the door release and walks through to be met by a young woman sitting behind a large mahogany desk.

'I'm looking to speak to Frank Keville,' he says. The young woman smiles back at him, then stands up and tries to peer over the top of a tall fake plant by the side of her desk.

'He should be just behind that,' she says, pointing her pen.

Lenny thanks her, walks around the plant to find an empty desk. He lets out a dissatisfied sigh and then rings his wet hat in his hands again, his knuckles turning white with frustration.

'Can't catch a fucking break,' he snarls to himself. He then peers down the length of the newsroom, takes it all in. He'd never been in a newsroom before, often wondered what one looked like. It's just like any other office; though the walls aren't painted a neutral bland colour like most offices are, they're bright red – the colour of the branding of almost every tabloid newspaper in the country. Then he spots what he's looking for: wheels. They're parked up in amongst a group of people who seem deep in conversation. As he moves closer he makes out the familiar profile of Keville.

'Frank, Frank,' Lenny calls out. Everybody in the office turns to face him. 'I need to speak to you urgently.'

Keville scowls up at the man approaching in an awful-looking yellow puffer jacket.

'Sorry, but we're in a very important meet—'

'I have a story for you,' Lenny shouts out, interrupting Keville. 'Remember Gordon Blake – Betsy Blake's father? He's dying. May well be dead by this evening. I've lots to tell you.'

NINE YEARS AGO

Betsy

I'M STRUGGLING TO READ. NO. I'M NOT STRUGGLING TO READ. I'M struggling to find books as good as the Harry Potter books. I've read all six of them three times since I got them. That was about nine months ago now. They are brilliant. But no other book has been as good since. I wish I could write like JK Rowling. He is so clever. I wonder how long it took him to write all of those books. I'd love to meet him. I have a million questions I would like to ask.

I'd like to meet anybody. Me and Dod are great now. He is never really angry Dod anymore. We watch TV together. We cook together sometimes. We always eat together. And he never shouts at me. Not anymore. But I would just like to meet another person. To have another friend. I wish I had a friend like Hermione. That would be cool. So many of the characters in the books I read go to a school. But none of the schools seem to be any better than Hogwarts. Sometimes when I am in bed and before I fall asleep I imagine I am in Hogwarts. I think I'd be really good at Quidditch. Sometimes I try to play it. I use Bozy as the Quaffle, and my bin as the basket. Bozy doesn't mind. It's fun. But it would be great to have somebody to play it with.

When I am upstairs watching TV, sometimes I see people walking by the house. They just look like shadows from where I sit, but my heart always gets a little faster when somebody does walk by. Sometimes I make up who they are in my head. As if they're characters from a book.

I keep trying to write a book. But I'm not really good at it. I keep getting words wrong. I can read. But I can't really write good. That makes me sad. Hopefully one day my writing will get good enough to write a big book. If I went to a school, I bet I could learn to write much better.

I close *The Golden Compass* and leave it on my bed. It's a good book. It's just not Harry. Then I let out a big breath. I always seem to do that when I'm bored. I take a few steps towards the end of the steps and wait. And wait. I know Dod will open the door soon and call me up to watch TV with him. I never know what time it is. I don't have a watch. Or a clock. But I always know when he is going to open the door. I think it is because I know the sounds of him upstairs so well.

I am not waiting too long when I hear the key in the door. And when it opens the light shines down the steps and I walk up towards it.

'Hey, Dod,' I say.

'Hey, Betsy.'

We both walk into the TV room. He doesn't stare at me all the time now. I think he trusts me more. I get up into the big sofa and then Dod comes and sits beside me. He looks at me then gives me a big kiss on the lips. I don't really like it. But he seems to do it every day now.

'Here,' he says. He gives me the remote control.

I press at the buttons until *The Simpsons* comes on. It's so funny. The only thing better than watching *The Simpsons* is reading a book. Even a bad book is better than anything on the TV. I think my favourite thing about *The Simpsons* is that it makes Dod laugh. I like to hear him laughing. It makes me feel good. It makes me feel safe.

As soon as it starts I know I've already seen this one before. It's the one where Mr Bergstrom becomes Lisa's favourite teacher in school.

I look at Dod and watch him smile. He laughs again. And again.

'What's with you?' he says. He looks at me.

'What do you mean?'

'Why aren't you laughing?'

'Oh.'

'I eh… I'm just thinking instead of watching,' I say.

'Thinking about what?'

I wiggle my feet. Maybe I shouldn't say it to him. He might turn into angry Dod.

'Thinking about what, Betsy?' he says. He sounds nice. He's not angry. I don't think so anyway. Maybe I can say what I want to say.

'Thinking about what it would be like if I went to school.'

I look away from him as I say it because I don't want to see if his eyes go that funny way they go when he is turning into angry Dod.

'Children hate school,' he says. 'I hated school when I was your age.' I look up at him and then blink. 'I love you, Betsy. But it's not right for you to go to school. Not all children go. You are one of the luckiest ones. You get to spend all of your time at home… with your books. And with me and with Bozy.'

He puts his arm around me and hugs me in close.

We just continue to watch *The Simpsons*. None of us talking anymore. None of us laughing anymore.

'I love you too,' I say after ages. 'And I love Bozy. And all of my books. But it would be just nice to see other people.'

I hold my eyes closed after I say it. I know that that's bad. I know that saying that will turn Dod into angry Dod. But he doesn't do anything. He doesn't even say anything. He just keeps watching *The Simpsons*. And so do I.

Lisa hates it when Mr Bergstrom leaves the school. She thought he was a great teacher. It actually makes me sad a little bit. Even though I know everything works out well in the end.

I turn my eyes a little bit and try to look at Dod. I think that maybe a tear is falling down his cheek. I turn my head fully and stare at him. It *is* a tear.

'What's wrong, Dod?'

He wipes the tear and then smiles a big wide smile.

'Nothing. Nothing,' he says.

I don't believe him. He can't be crying because Mr Bergstrom left the school. Dod's already watched this one with me. He knows everything works out well in the end. I wonder why he's crying. I snuggle my head into him. He wraps his hand around me and holds me while we watch the end of *The Simpsons*.

When it's over, Dod stands up.

'Come here with me,' he says. He holds his hand out for me and I grab it. We walk towards the edge of the stairs. Not the steps that go down to my room. But the stairs that lead up to the room Dod says he sleeps in. I've never been up there before. But Dod takes a step up while he is holding my hand. So I do the same. And then we go up the next one, up the next one and all the next ones until we are at the top of the house. It looks magical up here. The walls are like a purple colour.

Dod opens a door and then turns back to me.

'You have to get down on your hands and knees okay?'

I smile a little but only because I think I'm a bit afraid. I'm not sure what is happening. I get down on my hands and knees, like a dog, and then follow Dod into the room. I can't see much. Just a really big bed. A much bigger bed than mine. Dod walks around it and then stops. I look up. He has stopped near a really big window.

He holds his finger to his mouth. It means I should try and be as quiet as I can be.

'You ready?' he says.

I look at him funny because I don't know what he means, but then I just nod my head.

'Okay, put your hands here and pull yourself up a bit.'

I do. And then I see it. A magical place. Just like in one of my books. There are lots of houses. Some with blue doors, some with green. One has a black door. One has a red one. There're lots of cars parked outside the houses. All different colours too. I rest my head against the window and then my breathing makes it go all funny. Dod laughs and then wipes it all away. And then I see one. A person. She is beautiful. She has long brown hair and a red coat on. And a really pretty face. Very pretty. More prettier than mine.

I look up at Dod. I know my eyes are bigger than normal because I can feel it. He rubs at my hair, then bends down and kisses me on the top of my head.

'I'm so sorry, Betsy. I can't let you go outside because... well... because I love you so much. I can't lose you.'

13:40

Gordon

I'VE OPENED AND SHUT THE BEDSIDE CABINET DRAWER THREE TIMES SINCE Elaine left me alone. On each occasion that I've done that I've hovered my hand over my phone, then pulled it away. I hugged her before she left me, promised her I would just lie back and relax.

I really like Elaine, but I can't allow my smittinness to control me. Lenny's out there – somewhere – trying to find Betsy. Surely I should turn my phone back on, see what he's up to. I let out a frustrated sigh. My mind keeps changing. I can't get a fucking grip on my thoughts. I can't get them in order.

I pull at the drawer again, and this time I grab at the phone without pausing for thought. I take it into my chest, hold down the standby button and wait for the screen to blink on. Then the ward door swings open.

'Gordon,' Mr Douglas calls out like a teacher. He's got one eyebrow slightly raised as he strides towards me. It's only when I hear tiny footsteps behind him that I notice Elaine has followed him in.

'I stressed to you this morning the importance of keeping your mind positive and your bloods even, isn't that correct?'

I just nod my head once, stare up at him in anticipation of being barked at. I can't believe Elaine ratted me out. Especially after I'd totally opened up to her on our little walk.

'You may shrug at me, Gordon, but the truth is you haven't been adhering to that advice have you?'

Douglas scowls at me. It's almost laughable how serious he is taking all this; as if it's his life at stake.

I don't say anything. I just switch my glance from Douglas's scowl to Elaine's guilty eyes. She can barely look at me.

'Well if you don't want to talk, I will,' Douglas says as he plants his hands onto his hips. 'It has been brought to my attention that you have had quite the morning. Look at this,' he says, turning his clipboard to face me. He jabs his fat finger at a line of digits. 'Your heart rate has gone from 122 this morning at eight a.m., to 152 at ten a.m., back down to 130 at just gone eleven a.m. And when Elaine last checked your heart fifteen minutes ago you were back up to 155. I can *not* stress to you how dangerous it is for us to operate with your heart rate fluctuating.'

I take the clipboard from him, squint at it as if I can comprehend in any way what I'm staring at.

'Gordon, the risk of you forming blood clots during the procedure is enormously high. Even in the 120s these procedures are a big risk, but the 150 range makes your chances of survival minimal at best.'

I shake my head slowly, still nothing coming from my mouth. I need to speak up. Need to justify myself.

'I eh… I'm sure Elaine has told you. I have a fear of dying without ever knowing what happened to my daughter and I just wanted to—'

'I understand your situation,' Douglas interrupts. 'But what is most important is that you understand everything we have advised you. Your best chance of finding out what happened to your daughter is to survive these procedures. Then you can live your life thereafter, in any way you please.'

I look down at the foot of my bed, feeling like a teenage kid being told off.

'Gordon, I'm not sure we can continue with these procedures,' Douglas says, his voice shifting to a more direct tone.

My head shoots up to stare at him.

'But then I'll just die.'

Douglas arches his eyebrow again, then offers me a tilt of his head. The cheeky fucker. I swirl my jaw towards him.

'How the fuck does that make sense? If I'm going to die anyway, isn't it best that you at least give me the opportunity of surviving the surgeries?'

'Gordon, if you don't mind curtailing your language,' Douglas says as he takes his clipboard from my hands. 'There's something you don't get.' He looks back at Elaine, then returns his gaze to me. 'As a surgical team we are measured on our abilities to oversee successful procedures. The last thing a surgeon wants is his patient dying under the knife. My – our,' he says returning to Elaine before looking back at me, 'our reputation is at stake every time we hold a scalpel to somebody's skin. It's why we weigh up all of the risks before we give the green light for any surgery.' Douglas inches closer to me, rests the tip of his fingers on my mattress. 'Gordon, even when we weighed up the option of surgery for you this morning, we knew we were playing with fire... but now this,' he says, jabbing his finger at the notes on his clipboard, 'this makes our job all the more difficult. You have left us with little choice.'

I stare over his shoulder at Elaine. She meets my eyes for the first time since she returned to the ward. I open my mouth to call out to her, but nothing comes out... I remain silent, my lips slightly ajar.

'Gordon, your heart rate is fluctuating too much. I warned you time and—' she says taking a step forward.

'So you're just gonna let me die?'

Elaine places a hand on Douglas's shoulder and stares at me, her pity eyes wide.

'I'm going to measure your rate at two p.m. again, Gordon. But... I mean, I don't know what to say... if it's not at a respectable level, it wouldn't be wise for us to continue with the procedures. And this,' she says, removing the phone from my lap, 'isn't going to help you maintain a consistent heart level, now is it?'

I swallow hard, then throw my head back onto the steel bedpost making a clang reverberate through the ward.

'What is a respectable heart rate level?' I ask in a sulky tone.

'Well, in truth, Gordon, you haven't been at a respectable level all morning, which is understandable given the circumstances,' Douglas says. 'Ideally your blood rate should be well below 100, but given the complications your heart is currently going through I would expect it to be about ten or twenty points higher – 120s maybe. Hitting the 150s is just not acceptable for me to carry out surgery on you.'

I turn my head to face him.

'So what you're telling me is...' I crease my brow at him, prompting that he should finish my sentence.

'Gordon, your bloods have got to be lowered significantly,' Elaine butts in.

'Gimme a number,' I say.

Elaine and Douglas stare at each other.

'If you maintain a level inside the 130s, we're still taking a risk, but it'd be a risk we'd be willing to take for you,' Douglas says.

I nod my head.

'Okay, okay. I hear you. So what do you want me to do…? I'll do whatever it is you suggest. I want to live. I've so much to live for. I can't die not knowing what happened to Betsy.'

Douglas reaches out a hand to me, places it on my chest.

'I know you will never forget your daughter, Gordon. But I need you to forget about the investigation into finding her today. The theatre is just emptying now and after it's cleaned up it will be prepped for your surgeries. I'll need you down there at three p.m., but only if you're surgery-ready. Lie back in that bed, breathe deeply and consistently, all the while focusing on a positive outcome.'

He pushes firmer against my chest, guiding me to scoot down in the bed until my head is resting on the pillow again.

'As I said to you countless time this morning, Gordon,' Elaine says, stepping closer. 'All you have to do is relax.'

She presses at the standby button of my phone again and then opens up my bedside drawer and places it inside.

'And keep that phone turned off, huh?'

I stare up at them both, nod my head and offer a thin smile.

'Whatever you say, guys. Honestly. I'm sorry. I don't know what I was thinking this morning. Just – Jesus, Mr Douglas, Elaine – save my life. I beg you.'

Douglas almost sighs, as if my begging for life has burdened him somewhat. Then he places his hand back on my chest.

'Elaine will check your rate in twenty minutes. If the results are in the 130s then I swear to you, not just on your life, but on mine too, that I will do all I can to keep you alive.'

13:40

Lenny

LENNY WRINGS HIS HAT BETWEEN BOTH HANDS AS HE WAITS. HE TRIES TO rehearse in his mind what he's going to say. He needs his story to have clarity, but he also needs to be swift. Time isn't on his side. He stares at the large clock above the reception desk again. 13:40.

He's muttering a 'fuck sake' to himself when he sees the group of journalists he's been staring at flitter away from the huddle. Then he sighs with satisfaction when he notices the large spokes on the wheels turn. They're coming his way.

'Frank, I'm so grateful,' Lenny says, pacing towards the wheelchair.

'Over there,' Frank nods, his voice gravelly and instantly intimidating.

Lenny points to a messy desk.

'Here?'

Frank wheels by Lenny, positions himself into the desk and then points to an office chair sitting behind the large plant pot.

'Grab that. You've got five minutes.'

Lenny wheels the chair towards the desk Frank is at, squelching his nose up at the untidiness of it. He thinks about mentioning the amount of paperwork piled up, just to break the ice, but doesn't have time for small talk. Not today.

He parks his butt on the office chair, then stares at the back of the famous journalist's head. He's unsure whether Frank is ready to hear his story yet, but decides to offer it up nonetheless.

'My name is Lenny Moon. I'm a Private Investigator. I got a call from

Gordon Blake at about ten a.m. this morning. He's in Tallaght Hospital; has to have make or break heart surgery at three this afternoon. Doctors are only giving him a fifty-fifty chance of making it out alive. He contacted me, begged me to do my very best to find out new information on Betsy before he goes under the knife. He doesn't wanna die without doing all he can.'

'Betsy Blake is dead.' Frank's voice sounds as if there are rusty cogs working it in the back of his throat; either that or he's smoked thirty cigarettes a day for the past hundred years.

Lenny gulps.

'Gordon Blake doesn't think she is,' he says, almost whispering.

Frank stretches his arm to reach for his mouse and then taps away at it. Lenny waits silently. And then waits some more.

'That it?' Frank says, turning to him.

'Oh,' Lenny says, shifting uncomfortably in the chair. 'I eh… thought you were looking for something on the computer for me.'

Frank shakes his head. 'Listen, I'm very busy today – is there anything else you have to add to your story?'

Lenny shifts again in the chair, lifting his left butt cheek before placing it back down, then does the same on his right side.

'I spoke with Detective Ray De Brun today, he says—'

'Ah, how is De Brun, haven't spoken to him in years?' Frank interrupts.

'Eh… fine, yeah, fine,' Lenny stutters, his eyes beginning to blink.

'You okay, kid, want me to get you a glass of water?'

'Fine, yeah I'm fine… the eh… oh the blinking, nah it's just a tic I have. Have had it since the very first day I was bullied at secondary school.'

Frank kisses his own lips, then returns his focus to his computer screen. Lenny looks around the office, uncomfortable. He's not sure whether or not to continue talking. He stares at the clock behind the receptionist and realises he just needs to get on with it.

'Gordon has to have a eh… an abdominal aortic aneurysm and aortic valve replacement. His ticker is fucked, almost ripped apart.'

Frank reaches both hands to his wheels and manoeuvres his chair back, and then to the side, so that he's face on with Lenny.

'Thanks for the info, kid, but to be honest; it's not much of a story. If he passes away, I'll get in contact with the hospital and we'll run a piece but y'know, we've got much more important matters to—'

'Who were all of the suspects in the disappearance of Betsy Blake?' Lenny bursts out, not giving Frank time to finish his dismissive sentence.

'Huh?' Frank grunts.

'De Brun said there were initially four suspects. He questioned and then ruled out Gordon himself, then he questioned both Alan Keating and Barry Ward before ruling them out. Gordon himself thinks Jake Dewey may have had something to do with Betsy disappearing, but the cops were never interested in him. However, when I spoke to De Brun this morning, he alluded there was another suspect. I wanna know who it was.'

Frank clears the phlegm at the back of his throat, then slaps both palms of his hands onto his knees.

'Kid, nobody took Betsy Blake. Cops found a car seven years later that had Betsy's DNA in it… and that DNA proved she was dead. I know the media – me in particular – reported that she was abducted for many years but the truth came out eventually. Ireland's biggest ever kidnapping case was never even a kidnapping case to begin with. Now, I'm really sorry, but if you don't have a story for me I'm gonna have to get back to stories I do have.'

Lenny stands, rings his hat in his hands again, visibly agitated.

'Gordon Blake said he will pay me by leaving me his home in his will if I can make any breakthrough in Betsy's case before he goes under the knife…' Frank's eyes flick upwards, meeting Lenny's. 'Gordon never knew there was any other suspects other than Keating and Ward. If you can tell me who the other suspect was I'll give you all of the information on my investigation this morning, of all of my talks with Gordon. I'll go on the record and you can write about it in your next column. Gordon Blake tried to find Betsy right up until his death, ended up leaving the PI who last worked on it his million euro home in his will – it's a good story. And it's exclusive to you.'

Keville holds a balled fist to his mouth, coughs twice into it; the sound of his raw chest almost grotesque.

'He's going to leave you his house?'

Lenny nods his head, almost too frantically.

'Sit back down, kid,' Frank says.

He spins his wheelchair back into his desk, reaches for his mouse again, rolls it around an oversized mouse mat and clicks on it repeatedly.

'Jesus, is it that many?' he mumbles to himself. 'Wow, I wrote eighty-three stories on the Betsy Blake case over an eight-year period. Crazy.'

The excitement in Lenny's stomach turns up a notch, adrenaline slowly pumping its way towards his heart. Frank's playing along. He may well get the keys to that big house.

'Lemme ask you this question for starters,' Frank says. 'Do you believe

Betsy is dead, or are you singing from the same conspiracy hymn sheet as Gordon Blake?'

'I eh…' Lenny pauses. He wipes his brow with his hat. 'If De Brun says she's dead, I guess she's dead. But I eh… my job is to just try to look into this a little further. If I can get information Gordon's never heard before, it would mean the world to him.'

'To you, you mean.'

'And to me.' Lenny nods his head. 'Yep.'

Frank leans his head back, stares up at the ceiling of the open office. Then he interlocks his fingers and rests them on top of his rotund belly.

'Betsy Blake was reported missing on the twenty-first of January 2002,' he says. 'I assumed, as soon as I found out that Gordon Blake had dodgy dealings with Alan Keating, that that scumbag had something to do with it. But as the days passed, I realised it couldn't have been him. Keating's a prick. A prick of the highest order – he's the reason I'm in this wheelchair. But he's no kidnapper. Gordon Blake didn't realise that his falling out with Keating was insignificant to Keating. Keating had bigger fish to fry. Just because Gordon refused to launder parts of Keating's cash was in no way reason for Keating to kidnap his daughter. So after the cops hit a roadblock, they looked into similar cases, see if they could form any link.'

Lenny's eyes light up. He removes his left bum cheek from the seat, takes out his notebook from his back pocket, folds his legs and then rests the notebook on his left inner thigh. He pops his pen, begins to scribble as Frank, still looking up at the ceiling, continues.

'There were zero other cases in Ireland. Young girls just don't go missing, do they? Not on our little island. But there were two other cases that intrigued De Brun – both in Britain; one girl who went missing in England, one who went missing in Wales. Eh… lemme see…'

Frank looks down, repositions his wheelchair back into his desk and reaches for his mouse again. He hums as he clicks away.

'Yeah – this case; a three-year-old, Sarah McClaire. She went missing from a park in Kings Heath, Birmingham in the summer of 2002, about five months after Betsy. The police were interested in that case because there was an associate of Gordon Blake who happened to be in both Birmingham when Sarah went missing and in Dublin when Betsy went missing.'

'Who?' Lenny snaps.

Frank turns around, offers a scowl to Lenny.

'Hold on, I'm telling you about the two cases…. the other one was only of interest to De Brun because the names were similar. Elizabeth Taylor. Or Betsy Taylor as her parents called her. Same name, similar profile to Betsy Blake, but nothing in it.'

'I think I remember that case,' Lenny says.

'Yeah, that got a lot of exposure because of her name. If you share the same name as a Hollywood celebrity, then you're bound to stick in the mind of people. Sub editors had a field day making up headlines for Elizabeth Taylor.'

'So, the only reason that was of interest to De Brun was because the name was the same?'

'Yep,' Frank says. 'There was nothing in it, only the name coincidence. Turns out, it seems Tommy Saunders was responsible for Elizabeth Taylor's abduction. No link to our Betsy at all.'

'Tommy Saunders, the serial killer?'

'That's the one,' Frank says, clicking at his mouse.

'But what about the link with Sarah McClaire, who was the associate of Gordon's who was also in Birmingham at the time she went missing?'

'It's not only that,' Frank says. 'This guy was also questioned in 1999 for possession of child pornography.'

Lenny's mouth falls open. His eyes widen too.

'No need to get too excited, Lenny. De Brun looked into him, all was innocent. Lots of people visit Birmingham and Dublin regularly; the two cities have major links. It's hardly a coincidence.'

'Who is it?'

'Listen to what I'm saying to you, Lenny. This guy didn't do it. Nobody did it. Betsy was knocked down by a car, was killed by accident and then—'

'Who?' Lenny says, his volume rising.

Frank shakes his head.

'Guus Meyer – Gordon's business partner.'

'Woah – Guus Meyer is a paedophile and they just let him go?'

Frank closes his eyes shut, the lines on his face deepening.

'You haven't listened to a word I've said, Lenny. I didn't say anybody was a paedophile, did I? I said he was caught in possession of child pornography on his computer. The cops looked into it and let him go, so I assume it was very minimal at worst.'

'I don't believe this,' Lenny says, standing up. He lightly curls his fist into a ball and punches dead air, adrenaline rising in his stomach. He's done it!

'And Gordon won't have known this?' he asks, shuffling his feet.

Frank shakes his head.

'Because of the sensitive nature of the findings, what-with the kiddie porn and all, it wasn't shared with anyone that Guus was a suspect in the Betsy Blake case. Listen, they brought him in, questioned him and let him go. So don't go getting your hopes up that you are about to solve anything. You're not gonna solve jack shit. I'm just letting you know who the fourth suspect was because your running around might make a good story on a slow news week.'

Lenny punches dead air again, in celebration. He really has done it. He's managed to get information Gordon would never have known about. The million euro gaff is going to be his. Well... if Gordon doesn't make it through his surgeries. Lenny spins in a circle, his mind racing.

'So Guus Meyer is not only somebody who views child porn, but he happened to be in Birmingham when Sarah McClaire went missing and was in Dublin when Betsy Blake went missing?'

Frank holds a long blink... irritation evident on his face. He says nothing.

'Where does Guus Meyer live?' Lenny asks when he finally stops fidgeting.

'Lenny, I told you our little chat was off the record. You can't go around accusing any—'

'And I agreed. I won't say you told me anything. I just want to speak to him.'

'Well, the answer to your question is: I don't know where Guus Meyer lives.'

Lenny sucks the dryness of the office air conditioning in as Frank turns back to his computer. He clicks at his mouse again, then types away.

'I'm going to write this story, the story of Gordon's investigation from his death bed, do you hear me?' Frank says. 'But I want to emphasise, I did not give you this information so you could go around accusing innocent people, I gave it to you because it will suit my story.'

'Yeah, yeah, of course.'

'Clontarf,' Frank says.

Lenny's eyes light up. He inches forward, to see what Frank has called up on his computer screen. Then reads it out loud over the journalist's shoulder.

'Number one Avery Place, just off the main Clontarf Road.'

He grips both sets of fingers around Frank's shoulders.

'You're a legend, Keville.'

EIGHT YEARS AGO

Betsy

I HAVE TWO NEW HOBBIES NOW. TWO NEW FAVOURITE THINGS TO DO. I STILL read. Lots. But I don't read what Dod told me are called fiction books much anymore. I read non-fiction most of the time now. But my new favourite hobby is to look out the window in Dod's bedroom. I see different things all the time. I ask him if we can look out the window instead of watching the TV. He agrees most of the time. Sometimes he lets me watch TV and look out the window afterwards. I like looking out the window because it gives me ideas to write my own books. Although, because I now like to read non-fiction I have started to write a book all about myself. I'm going to call it *Betsy's Basement*. And it will have me, Dod and Bozy in it. I will write about what I do every day down here. It will be a bit like the books I read now.

I think my favourite non-fiction book so far has been the one called *I Know Why the Caged Bird Sings*. I have learned lots of new words because of that book. It's about a young girl like me called Maya who felt she was trapped but then became a really good writer. She wasn't a good writer when she was younger and then she became really good because she read lots and lots. I hope the same thing happens to me. She had brown skin. I'd like to see somebody with brown skin. People with brown skin sound as if they'd be beautiful.

Another girl who I have read a non-fiction book about also has brown skin. Serena Williams. She is another woman who wasn't really happy when she was younger but then became really happy when she got older.

She thinks women are the best. Better than men. So do I. She plays a sport called tennis. And is the best person to ever play it. I asked Dod if he could show me some tennis on the TV but we can never find it on any of the channels. We have tried to look for it a few times. He keeps buying me new non-fiction books because I ask for them now. I think he feels just as happy as I do when he gives me a new book. He buys me a new book almost every week. I read so fast.

My room is mostly taken up by the big shelf I have against the wall. It is filled with books. I counted a few weeks ago. I had ninety-five. And Dod has bought me four more since then. So the next one I get will be my hundredth book. I wonder what it's going to be. I hope it is about another strong woman. A woman who has a bad childhood but then becomes really, really happy. Because I think that is what is going to happen in my life. I will be happier when I'm older. I want to be a happy writer when I am an adult. Just like Maya Angelou.

I have started to write *Betsy's Basement* but it is not easy. It takes too long for me to spell out the words correctly.

I hop up onto my bed and pick up Bozy. Then I place him so he is sitting up against my pillow and say: 'Are you ready, Bozy?' I make him nod at me by using my fingers to push at the back of his head.

'This is the start of Betsy's Basement.'

I flick open my copybook.

'I was playing on my street one day while Daddy was talking to somebody from work. It was a long time ago now so I don't really remember everything. I was four years old. I know that. Now I am thirteen years old. So it was nine years ago when it happened. But I was walking on a wall and then Dod just took me. He put his hands around my mouth and around my legs and just took me. He told me to be quiet. Then he put me in a car and he drove for ages and ages and ages. I was really scared. And I was really hungry. And then after ages he took me out of the car and into my basement.'

I look up at Bozy.

'What do you think so far?'

I think he likes it.

I just wish I could write much faster. That much has taken me two weeks to write. I keep spelling words wrong and then changing them. Maybe when I am older I will be able to write much quicker. I want to write loads of books. *Betsy's Basement* is just my first.

13:50

Gordon

I TOOK A MINDFULNESS CLASS ONCE. WASN'T FOR ME. BUT I REMEMBER ONE instruction quite clearly; the five breaths per minute technique. Breathe in for six seconds, breathe out for six seconds. I've been trying to apply this since Douglas and Elaine left me a few minutes ago, but it's a difficult technique to maintain; especially when you have a multitude of stuff whizzing through your mind. I've tried leaning fully flat out on the bed, tried half sitting up with the pillow behind the arch of my back, tried fully sitting up while resting my head against the steel bed frame. But nothing seems to be helping me calm down.

I keep seeing Betsy's little face. I always imagine her as she was – four years of age; mousy brown hair, a dash of freckles across the bridge of her nose. I can never quite imagine what she would look like now. She'd have turned twenty-one last August. A bona fide adult. I'm pretty certain she would have ended up being something special. Guess I'll never know.

I press both shoulder blades firm against the bedpost, then close my eyes and attempt to concentrate on my six-second breaths. I'm refusing to even look at the bedside cabinet my phone is currently resting in. Poor old Lenny Moon out there running around for me when I don't even need him to anymore. But fuck it; he got a grand for his morning's work and, given his appearance, I'm guessing that's quite a lot of dosh for him. He'll be fine. Last thing I heard from him he was on his way to Jake and Michelle's house. I'd love to know how that went... but I can't turn on my phone, can't ring him. It'll only raise my heart rate again.

Six seconds in through the nose… six seconds out through the nose.

I can't stop my mind from swirling. It's too quiet. Maybe I need a little background noise to help me focus. I pick up the TV remote control, hold down the standby button.

Loose Women. Fuck that! Jesus, if there's anything that will raise my heart rate it's watching that shite. News. No! More news. No! Ah… a music channel. Maybe. But it's blaring out some awful hip-hop song that can barely be filed under the medium of music as far as I'm concerned. No! A crappy, dated American sitcom. No! Fuck it. I tap at the standby button again. The screen blinks off.

Six seconds in through the nose… six seconds out through the nose.

Christ, this is difficult. Not the breathing. The shutting off of my thoughts. I've always been a deep thinker. Have never been able to shake off my guilt. Even when I'm not directly thinking about Betsy, there's always a grey cloud circling my every moment.

I wonder what time it is. Without my phone I can't tell, but it's got to be coming up to two o'clock. That's when Elaine said she'd be back in to measure my bloods. Jesus… I may have only one hour left to live. And here I am, lying in an uncomfortable bed, doing my best to focus on six-second inhales and exhales. I blow out through my lips, making a rasping sound. The thought of what happens when you die flipping over in my head. I wonder what the fuck a God would say to me if I was to somehow find myself at the gates of Heaven this evening.

'Why did you never have faith in me, Gordon Blake?'

'Because you made it fucking impossible for anybody with half a brain to have faith in you, you long-bearded twat!'

I make myself laugh a little with that thought. The first time I've produced a moment of giddiness all morning. But the giddiness doesn't last long; the thought of dying and ceasing to be begins to hit me hard. I've never really been afraid of death itself; I've only ever been afraid of dying without knowing what happened to Betsy. It looks very likely that my biggest fear may become a reality in just a few hours time. I let out the saddest sigh I've let out in years. I can hear the self-pity within it.

Six seconds in through the nose… six seconds out through the nose.

The ward door opens while I'm finishing my long exhale. I stiffen my lips, look over at Elaine strolling towards me. She stares at me sympathetically, unsure of what to say. We've been quite open with each other throughout the morning, but right now she knows she's about to give me a quick test that will determine whether or not I'm guaranteed to die today. That's hardly an easy topic to raise. So, instead of talking to me, she nods slowly, then clenches her lips tight.

'So this is it?' I say.

Elaine remains silent. She almost looks as if she'd cry if she spoke. I think that's why she hasn't said a word. It's either that or the guilt she has felt for ratting me out to Douglas is eating at her. She holds up the blue tabs, presses them into my chest. Then she turns to her machine, presses at a couple of buttons and glances at me, her eyes blinking.

'Very best of luck, Gordon,' she says.

I reach out my hand, grab a strand of her hair and brush my fingers gently through it.

'Thank you, Elaine.'

She breathes deeply, presses another button and then holds her eyes firmly shut. She must be willing the digits to blink to something in the 130s as much as I am. I bend forward to stare at the small screen when it beeps and as I do, Elaine opens her eyes.

Bollocks. 142.

Elaine holds her eyes closed again, then opens them and tilts her head to stare at me. I fall back onto the bedpost, hold my hand to my forehead and for some reason begin to breathe in for six seconds, then out for six seconds. By the time I'm finished one breath Elaine is at the foot of my bed, unhooking the clipboard from the rail.

'One thirty-nine,' she says, scribbling. I remove my hand from my forehead, then smile up at her.

She walks towards me without saying another word, removes the tabs from my chest and then folds them neatly before hooking them to the machine.

'You are an angel sent from heaven,' I say, aware that such a statement totally contradicts the thoughts I had been stewing around my head just minutes ago.

She doesn't even look at me. She just swirls on her heels and heads for the door.

'I'll let Mr Douglas know he should begin to prep the theatre. We'll be going down in an hour, Gordon. You just continue to relax.'

14:00

Lenny

LENNY TOUCHES A BUTTON ON HIS PHONE, JUST SO THE SCREEN BLINKS ON and he can see the time. Bang on two o'clock. One hour left. He clicks into call history, brings up Gordon's name and presses at it.

'Ah for fuck sake,' he says as he pushes at the glass doors of Independent House and walks out into the rain.

He stops, fidgets at his phone to recall Gordon, then looks up to the grey sky upon hearing the dead tone again.

'Please tell me they haven't taken him down to surgery already,' he says to the clouds.

He stands in against the wall of a newsagents as if that's going to protect him from the rain as he contemplates his next move. He knows he's taking a taxi to Clontarf, but he needs to let Gordon know what's going on. The whole point of finding out something new is so he can secure the million euro house. He tries calling one more time. Same frustration – dead tone.

He places the phone back inside his jacket pocket, zips it up and then paces towards Amien Street in search of a taxi. He bounces shoulders with one young woman, holds a hand up in apology as he walks away, then slaloms through two umbrellas coming towards his face.

'Ah for crying out loud,' he yells out as a woman stops in front of him, causing him to walk around her. The woman stares at him, shock at his over-the-top outburst evident on her face. Lenny doesn't react, doesn't apologise. He just continues to walk at a swift pace, head down, sheltering his face from the rain.

His mood has changed swiftly in the past three minutes. He had ran down the three flights of stairs of Independent House feeling elated at the thought of giving Gordon something new in the investigation. But now his blood was slowly coming to the boil; the thought he may never be able to communicate this news with Gordon settling in his mind as a high probability. He can't bear the thought of being that close to earning a million quid and losing it all.

'Taxi,' Lenny shouts out, holding his hand up as if he just leaped off a pavement in New York City. A silver Ford Focus screeches to a stop and Lenny – his clothes soaked right through, his woollen Sherpa hat heavy on his head – jumps in.

'Head for the Clontarf Road,' he says.

The taxi man eyeballs Lenny in the rear-view mirror as he resets his meter, then pulls out and sets off.

Lenny removes his hat, unzips his puffer jacket to allow him space to breathe, then lays his head back on the rest. He chews on his bottom lip, stewing. Blinks his eyes rapidly, stewing. Then brings the phone to his mouth and begins to chew on the butt of the cover, stewing. He remains in the same position, head back, as the taxi man finally drives out of the city centre and towards the coastal road.

'What's the number when you don't know a number,' Lenny says, shooting himself back into an upright seating position.

'Huh?' the taxi man says.

'Y'know when you don't know a phone number and there's a number you can ring that'll give it to you?'

'Jaysus,' says the taxi man. 'Who uses that shite anymore, sure can't you just search for any number on your phone?'

'Don't have Wi-Fi on this,' Lenny says shaking his mobile in the air. Then he leans forward. 'Can I eh... any chance you'd give me a loan of your phone for a minute? Need to get the number for Tallaght Hospital.'

The taxi man eyeballs his passenger in the rear-view mirror again, then removes his phone from the cradle and hands it back. As soon as Lenny has the phone in his hand, the sound of the doors locking sounds out.

'You're a star, thank you.'

Lenny scrolls through the phone, into the internet browser and types 'Tallaght Hospital' into the search bar.

The hospital's information flashes up straight away; address, phone number, fax number, an About Us page, visitor information.

'Gotta get me one of these,' Lenny whispers to himself. Then he picks up his own phone and begins to punch in the number.

As he's handing the phone back over the shoulder of the taxi man a friendly voice answers his call.

'Tallaght Hospital, how may I help you?'

Lenny double taps the bicep of the taxi man after handing back the phone, his way of thanking him.

'Yeah, I eh… I need to speak with a patient please. A Gordon Blake. He was taken in last night, has to have heart surgery today and eh… yeah, can I speak to him?'

'Sir, patients don't have phones in their rooms.'

Lenny falls silent, then blinks rapidly.

'How can I get a message to him?' he asks.

'Let me see… do you know what ward he's in?'

'Floor three eh… what is it, oh yeah – St Bernard's Ward.'

'Hold on one moment, Sir.'

Lenny clenches his fist, gives the air a little jab as the sound of elevator music pierces down the line. He stares out the window as he waits, taking in the greyness of the day. The taxi is splashing up rain spray, pedestrians are wobbling around with either umbrellas held high or hoods clenched tight. He begins to whistle along to the elevator music, his mood suddenly shifting. He's certain Gordon doesn't know that Guus Meyer was another suspect in Betsy's disappearance; feels confident that this information is enough to trigger the will he had been shown back at the hospital. He begins to imagine Sally's face when he finally tells her they have the keys to a new million euro gaff. Then he sits upright, chuffed with himself for picturing his wife smiling for the first time in God knows how long. He offers the air an uppercut this time, not just a jab, then beams a huge smile of his own, stretching it right across his face.

'I'm sorry, Sir, nobody seems to be answering up at St Bernard's Ward. Is there anything else I can help you with?'

Lenny lies back in the chair, his smile disappearing.

'I need to get a message to Gordon Blake, can you deliver it for me?'

The man on the other end of the line offers a subtle laugh.

'I'm sorry, Sir, but there is no way I would be able to do such a thing; the front desk here at the hospital is constantly busy. I can eh… can keep trying St Bernard's Ward for you… I do know the staff up there are extremely busy, but when a nurse finally sits at the nurses' station they will answer.'

'Yeah, yeah… keep trying,' Lenny says, bowing forward out of frustration, his head hanging through the gap between his knees.

The elevator music sounds again and Lenny lets out a deep sigh.

'Rough day?' the taxi man asks. Lenny looks up, meets the eye of his driver through the rear-view mirror.

'I'm not sure,' he says. 'Odd is the word I'd use for it. Could turn out to be rough, could turn out to be one of the best days of my life.'

The taxi man creases his brow in confusion.

'How's that then?' he asks, tilting his head.

'Putting you through now, Sir,' the man on the other end of the line says. Lenny raises his index finger, holding it up for the driver to signal that he will return an answer in time.

'St Bernard's Ward,' a woman says.

'Hey, I'm looking to speak to a patient there – a Mr Gordon Blake. I'm a eh… an associate… a friend of his.'

'We don't have phones in the rooms themselves, I'm afraid. But if you are looking for updates on Mr Blake's health, I can see if I can find his nurse – Elaine Reddy – to speak to you about his current condition.'

Lenny sits up straight in the back seat, reaches a calming thumb to massage his temple.

'He hasn't gone down for his surgeries yet, has he? Please don't tell me they've taken him down.'

'No… not yet. But soon. I think he's due to go down at three p.m. Again, Elaine would be the one to give you all of the details of Mr Bl—'

'Can you please enter his room, let him know Lenny Moon is on the line for him and that I'd like him to call me back on his mobile as soon as possible. Tell him I have news for him.'

'Eh… hold on one minute.'

There's no elevator music this time. No sound at all except for distant murmurs of a functioning hospital; muffled footsteps down hollow corridors, the odd beep.

He looks back up at the taxi man while he waits.

'I'm eh… I'm holding out for news on a house,' he says. 'I've either got it or I haven't… Still hasn't been made clear to me.'

The taxi man's brow creases again. He looks totally miffed.

'It's kinda complicated,' Lenny says, his attempt at straightening his driver's brow lines. He knows how ridiculous that sounds, especially as the taxi man is well aware that he is on hold at a hospital. Lenny turns his face, stares out at the greyness of Dublin again. He takes in the big terraced Victorian houses on the Fairview Road, imagines the faces of the happy families that must live in such comfort within them.

'I'm sorry, Sir, but Mr Blake said he's not able to make or take any more phone calls today, he's preparing himself for surgery,' the woman's voice says down the line.

Lenny feels his heart pinch a little. He hangs his mouth open, then folds himself right over – his head hanging well below his knees this time.

'Fuck sake!' he yells.

14:05

Gordon

I PICK UP THE PEN I'D LEFT RESTING AT THE SIDE OF MY BED, BRUSHING THE envelope I have addressed to Lenny aside. I wonder what he's up to now; how he's handling Michelle and Jake. It won't be easy. It always infuriated me that the cops wouldn't look into Jake for me. It's hardly just a coincidence that he came into our lives just as Betsy was taken. But it still doesn't add up that he took her. The only motive I've ever been able to come up with is that he would have wanted me and Michelle to split up... but why would he go to such lengths? I don't know. I've fuck all to go on. I'm pretty sure Jake had nothing to do with Betsy's disappearance, but what was I supposed to do... lie here in my last hours of life and do nothing? I bet Lenny's been trying to get hold of me. I'd love to turn my phone back on, see what he's up to. But I guess it's gonna be a case of him saying he questioned Jake and came to a conclusion that he had nothing to do with Betsy's disappearance.

I stare over at the envelope again, suck at my own lips. I don't know who I'm going to leave the house to if I die today. Probably nobody at this stage. The state will take it, do with it whatever the hell they please. Anyway, I'm not planning on dying. I'm going to get through these surgeries. I'm so grateful to Elaine... lying to Douglas for me; knocking a couple of digits off my actual heart rate. I owe it to her to just lie here and relax.

I grab at my book, rip out another blank page and without even thinking of how I'm going to construct this letter, I begin writing.

Dear Michelle,

Then I bring the pen to my mouth and begin to nibble on the top of it. I've so much to say to this woman. Half of it in an irate tone, half of it filled with adoration. How the fuck do I even begin to sum up what she's meant to me? Fuck it!

I know you and I have had our differences, but I don't want this letter to come across in a negative way.

If you're reading this, it's because I'm dead – that I didn't make it through my surgeries.

I guess I'm writing to you because I want to apologise for all of my faults. I know I was never the perfect husband. And it's pretty clear to everyone – you especially – that I was never a perfect father either. But I need you to understand that, while I have lived with the guilt of our dear Betsy going missing on my watch, I genuinely feel as if

As if... as if what? I lay my head back against the rail. What the fuck am I trying to say to her? I'm sorry, but it's not my fault? I don't know. I gurn in frustration, then come to the realisation that the process of writing a goodbye letter to Michelle is not going to be as cathartic as I'd hoped it might be. It's only going to raise my heart rate even more. This wasn't a good idea. I place the pen back down on the bedside cabinet, then rub at my face with both hands, rubbing them up and down until the frustration I have running through my mind disappears.

The door opening causes me to take my hands down and when I do I immediately feel better. She's smiling at me. It seems as if we're friends again.

'Thank you so much, Elaine,' I say, as she makes her way towards me. She has both hands held aloft, palms out. I hold both my hands out to her too and we high ten.

'All sorted, Gordon,' she says. 'The team are going to operate. The theatre has been cleared of its last surgery and it's being prepped for yours now. Mr Douglas was deadly serious about not operating, but when I told him your bloods had just crept below the one-forties and that you were now being as restful as you possibly could be, he agreed to go ahead.'

I stare at her wide eyes. My little heroine.

'I may literally owe you my whole life by tonight,' I tell her.

She waves my compliment away, then points a finger at me.

'You can't tell anybody I fudged the numbers, you hear me? Even when you do survive, this has to be our little secret. I'd totally lose my job if that ever became known.'

I grab the hand that is pointing at me, turn it over and then bring it to my mouth to lightly kiss it.

'I promise I will never tell a soul.'

Elaine creases her lips into a friendly smile, then looks at the sheet of paper on my chest.

'Writing letters?' she asks.

I rub at my face; the reminder of me trying to justify myself to Michelle making its way to the forefront of my mind again.

'The ex wife,' I tell Elaine. 'Problem is, I don't know what to say.'

'You never asked her to come up to see you, no?'

I shake my head. Can't bring myself to explain an answer. It's just way too complicated.

Elaine lets out a deep breath, her hand still being held by mine, and then eyeballs me.

'It's probably for the best,' she says. 'Let's just keep you relaxed, there isn't long to go.' She lets go of my hand, removes her pocket watch and then raises her eyebrows. 'A little less than an hour. I have to say, Gordon, you are in the best hands and—'

She looks behind at the door opening. Another nurse, dressed in a slightly different shade of purple scrubs, steps inside.

'Sorry, Elaine,' she says, 'but Mr Blake, I have a Lenny Moon on the line. He said he has something to tell you and wondered if you could call him back.'

I feel my heart rate instantly rise. What the fuck has he found out about Jake Dewey? I need to know.

'That's okay,' Elaine says, staring over her shoulder at the nurse. 'Mr Blake won't be taking or making any phone calls until he's come out of his surgeries, isn't that right, Gordon?'

She squeezes my hand. I look up to her, offer a thin smile.

'Eh... yes, I eh... I'm prepping for the surgeries now. I won't be talking to anybody.'

The nurse steps backwards towards the door.

'Of course, Mr Blake, sorry to have disturbed you.'

Elaine continues to squeeze my hand, then offers me a little wink.

'We're a good team me and you, huh?' she says.

I gulp as I offer her a fake laugh.

'You're the best,' I say.

'That's Saoirse; Saoirse Guinness – a new nurse. She'll put Lenny straight. You can speak to him after you wake up from the surgeries... okay? So, will we turn the TV back on?' she suggests casually, as if news from Lenny is insignificant.

I nod my head slowly, reach for the remote control under my sheets and hand it to her. She sits in the blue plastic chair, presses at the standby button and proceeds to click through the channels, asking me at every turn whether or not what's showing on the TV is something that interests me. I continue to just shake my head, even though I don't know what's on. I'm staring through the TV, not at it; my mind racing.

'Oh... that's all the channels,' she says eventually. 'Will I just leave something on? Pick a number.'

I smile with my eyes, wave my hand.

'I don't know... number three,' I say.

We both stare at the screen, a cheesy toothpaste advert showing images of an annoying-looking boy grinning from ear to ear comes on.

'Is Colgate going to help you relax?' Elaine says, looking to me.

I sniff a small laugh out of my nostrils, then tilt my head back as a thought comes to me.

'You know what would help me relax?' I ask.

'Go on.'

'Fruit Pastels.'

'Fruit Past— sure you're supposed to be fasting.'

'I won't swallow them, just the taste... they'd, I don't know. I just really fancy some. I have some change here,' I say, reaching for my bedside cabinet. I open the drawer, shovel some loose change into the palm of my hand then hold it towards Elaine. 'Please,' I say, sounding a little bit like a pleading Oliver Twist.

Elaine twitches an eyebrow.

'If it'll help you relax.' She scoops the coins from my hand, then hands me the remote control. 'You find us something to watch. I'll be five minutes.'

I click at the buttons of the remote, not looking at the screen but at her as she leaves the ward. When she closes the door, I reach for the drawer of the cabinet again and grab at my phone. I hold down the standby button and wait for the screen to blink on.

'C'mon, for fuck sake,' I hiss at it. It seems to take an age for the phone to load up. When it does, I immediately click into my call history, then hold my finger against Lenny's number.

'Jesus, Gordon, what took you so long ringing me back?' he says.

'Never mind that; what's the news you have for me?'

SEVEN YEARS AGO

Betsy

MY WRIST CAN GET SORE FROM WRITING. I TWIST IT ROUND AND ROUND IN circles until the pain goes away. Then I lift up my pen again and keep going.

I think my spelling is getting better. I am writing words a little bit quicker. I've been nearly a whole year writing *Betsy's Basement* and I am on chapter five. This morning I've been writing about the time I screamed when I was in the toilet upstairs. That was silly of me.

I wanted to die that day because I thought I would go to see Mummy and Daddy in heaven. Whatever heaven is. A lot of the books I read don't mention heaven. Maybe it's not even real. It makes me sad to think that I will never see Mummy and Daddy again. But I can't talk about it with Dod. Talking about Mummy or Daddy is one way to make sure Dod definitely turns into angry Dod. So instead of talking about it, I write about it in my story. Chapter one was all about me being taken by Dod. Chapter two is about how I used to keep really quiet in the basement when all of the people used to come visit Dod's house. Not so many people visit anymore. Chapter three is about me and Bozy and how we became best friends. Chapter four is about Dod letting me go upstairs for the first time. And now chapter five is about how I got beaten up by Dod for screaming when I was upstairs. I think my back is still not the same since that beating. It's sore when I wake up every morning. But even though all of my chapters are about me being here, in the basement, they always have a bit of Mummy and Daddy in them. Not that I can

406

remember much about that time. But writing helps me remember. Or what it does is make sure I don't forget.

I can't wait to write the chapters about how me and Dod became really good friends again though. About him buying me lots and lots of books. About him letting me go upstairs to watch TV. And about him letting me look out the window from his bedroom. When I get to those chapters, I'm going to have lots of stories. Lots of stories about all of the different characters I see when I look out the window. There is a woman who lives across the street, in the house with the red door. I call her Mrs Witchety and she is a secret witch. She has fifteen cats and twelve brooms in her house. She is really funny. But scary too. I have so much fun when I am looking out the window and making characters up.

When Dod opens the door, I rest my pen down inside my book, then fold it over. I walk up the steps and hope Dod will let me look out the window today and not watch TV.

'Whatcha wanna do?' he asks when I get to the top of the steps.

I just look up at him.

'You wanna go upstairs, huh?' He makes a funny shape with his mouth and then nods his head towards the stairs. 'Okay, c'mon.'

We both walk up and as soon as I am outside his bedroom, I get down on my hands and knees and crawl around his bed until I am at the window ledge, Then I place my hands on the ledge and bring myself up so I can see out the window. I look straight away to Mrs Witchety's house but she's not outside, not today. Then I look up and down the street. Nobody's walking. This happens sometimes. Sometimes I can spend a long time looking out the window and not see anybody. Maybe today is going to be one of those days.

I look around Dod's bedroom again. There isn't much in it. A big bed and two really big wardrobes. I often wonder what's in the wardrobes. But I have never asked.

'Dod.' I say his name really slowly.

'Yes, Betsy?'

'Do you not have lots of books in your room like I do in my basement? Are they in these wardrobes?'

He laughs a little. That makes me feel good. I was worried he might turn into angry Dod for asking him about his wardrobes. He walks over to the far side of his bed and then opens a drawer.

'Here are all my books,' he says.

I'm not sure what he is showing me. It looks like just one book, but it's grey and skinny. When he brings it closer I notice that it isn't a book at all. There are no pages. I make a funny face at him and he laughs again.

'It's called a Kindle,' he says.

I keep the funny look on my face.

'I have over a hundred books on here. He presses at a button. A light comes on and makes it look like a really small TV. He turns it around so I can watch. 'See all these,' he says, 'they are all the books I have on here and I can choose to read one anytime I want.'

I'm a bit confused. But when I point my finger at one of the books, it opens. Chapter one appears on the screen.

'That's magic,' I say.

But I'm still confused.

'I buy books and they just download on to here.'

I give him my funny face again.

'Tell you what, you take a look at this. The books I read are a little old for you, but take a look through the Kindle. I've a tiny bit of work to do. So I'm going to go downstairs. I'll give you twenty minutes up here, okay? Keep your head down, Betsy.'

I look up at him and then nod my head slowly.

'Okay, Dod.'

He's never left me up here on my own. I think he thinks that I'm becoming a big girl now. A bit like a grown up. I'll be fourteen next month. I smile to myself when he leaves the room. I feel really happy that he thinks I can be left alone up here.

I take the Kindle from him and begin to press at the screen. Into one book called *War and Peace* and then another one called *Anna Karenina*. There are lots of big words in these books. Dod is right. I don't think I'd be able to read these. But this is so much fun. I can't believe all of his books are in here. Mine take up so much room in my basement.

I crawl back towards Dod's wardrobe so I can sit with my back leaned up against it and continue to play with his Kindle. I would love one of these. Except I think I would miss the smell of the paper from books. One of the first things I do when I get a new book is to flick the pages under my nose and breathe in the smell. I bring the Kindle to my nose, try to smell it. Nothing. It smells like nothing.

I stare over at the drawer Dod took the Kindle from. Wonder what other magical things he has in there. But I shouldn't look. I'd get myself into so much trouble. If I don't keep my head down, Dod will definitely turn into angry Dod. And that's the last thing I want. I look towards the window, then towards the drawer again. Then the window. Then the drawer.

I place the Kindle on top of Dod's bed and then crawl. I do it really, really slowly. When I reach his drawer I pull it open and then place my hand on his bed so I can pull myself up a little bit. I look inside. There are some pills that look like sweets and an old watch. I hold up the watch and stare at it. The hands aren't moving. It must be broken. I put it back inside, then close the drawer really slowly, making sure there is no noise. Then I crawl back over to the wardrobe I'd been sitting against. My heart thumps a little bit. That was naughty. I probably shouldn't have done that. But I can't help myself. I pull open his wardrobe. See lots and lots of clothes. There are lots of shoes in the bottom of it, lots of shirts hanging at the top. Then I pull open the drawer at the bottom of his wardrobe. Lots of papers. I flick through them to see what they are all about. But there's too many of them. I lift the top one off and then sit with my back to the wardrobe and begin to read it.

In big black writing at the top, it says "DNA confirms Betsy Blake is Dead".

14:15

Lenny

A SLITHER OF ORANGE IS THREATENING TO RID THE SKY OF ITS GREYNESS BY the time Lenny steps out of the taxi, but the sun has a lot of work to do if it wants to make itself known over Dublin today. The rain is still falling, but only lightly now. Lenny stands outside the uneven wooden railing of Guus's house and just stares at it. It's a big detached house, yet it's unkempt; the grass in the garden overly long and peppered with litter, the windows dusty and smeared. Lenny stiffens his nose at the contrast of what he's seeing. In order to live in this house – especially around here – you'd have to be worth a good few quid. Why couldn't a rich man afford somebody to at least make their home look good?

When he finally takes his eyes from the garden, Lenny feels his phone vibrate in his pocket. He flips it over to see who's trying to reach him.

'Ah for fuck sake!' he rages, stamping on the pavement. He sighs deeply, then presses the answer button.

'Hey, sweetie,' he says.

'How's work?'

'Eh... grand. Y'know, the usual.'

'You seemed quite busier than usual earlier when I rang you.'

'It's been a bit of a different day alright, sweetie. I'll tell you all about it when I get home.'

Sally makes an interested huff sound down the line.

'Okay cool. Will you be coming by the house to pick me up before the meeting or will I see you at the school?'

Lenny opens his eyes wide, then squelches his entire face in to an ugly gurn. He places both hands over the phone, holding it away from his face, them mouths a quiet 'bollocks' to himself. He lifts one hand from the phone, stares at the screen to catch the time. 14:17.

'I eh…' he stutters as he blinks rapidly. 'I eh… got caught up in a job. I don't think I can get to the boys' school for three p.m.'

He winces in anticipation of Sally's response. But he doesn't get one; both ends of the line deathly silent.

'Sweetie,' he says eventually.

'You've let me down. No, no… hold it: you've let us all down. Me, Jacob, Jared.'

Then a dead tone sounds.

Lenny kicks the pavement again. He immediately begins to fumble with his phone, then holds it back to his ear, a ringing tone sounding.

'Go on… explain yourself then,' Sally says upon answering.

'Sweetie… I can't tell you exactly what is going on right now. I will when I get home, but I'm on a very delicate job that I can't discuss over the phone.' Silence. Again. 'It's good news, baby. I got big money for this gig. A guy gave me a grand just to do a tiny bit of snooping but it's ended up with me out in Clontarf now and I'm just not going to get back in time for the school meeting. I'm sorry. I really am.'

'The grand that was transferred into the account this morning?'

'Yeah… yeah, that's it,' Lenny says.

'You told me that was for some older job.'

The line goes dead.

Lenny thumbs his phone, calls the home number again. No answer. Tries again. Same result. He stares at the big old house in front of him and then tips his head back, all the way back so that the light rain begins to fall against his mouth. He's unsure what to do; whether to take a taxi back home or to follow through on his investigation. Sally has always been his priority, always will be. He should go home, give up the ghost. He spins around, faces the coastal road and begins to nibble on the butt of his phone. He thinks about his wife, about his two sons. About their sad existence.

'Fuck it,' he says, bringing his phone down to thumb at it again.

Sweetie I'm really sorry. Please don't do anything stupid. I'm doing this job for us… for the whole family. Trust me. Call me back when you can. I love you. x

Then he spins on his heels and heads straight for the rickety wooden gate in front of him. He's beyond intrigued now, the thought of making an impact in Ireland's biggest ever missing person's case overriding the concerns he has for his wife. He can barely bring himself to imagine what kind of attention he would get if he solved – in the space of a few hours – a mystery that has plagued the country for seventeen years.

Instead of heading for the front door, he walks to the side of the house, towards an old Volkswagen Beetle, the grass growing thick around all of its deflated tyres. He cups his hands to stare in through the window but sees nothing but darkness. Then he paces around the back of the house, notices that it's even more unkempt than the front. The grass must be at least three foot in height, going all the way up to Lenny's waist.

'Jesus, this place could be so fucking gorgeous,' he whispers to himself.

He walks further into the back garden, wading through the blades of grass and then peers in through the back window from a distance, noticing a massive, modern kitchen. He squints again – not sure what to make of the place. But he's enjoying playing detective; his heart rate working at a pace he seems to revel in. He rummages through the long blades, picks up some litter, examines it as if he's doing something worthwhile and then releases it from his fingers. He picks up dirty ice pop wrappers, empty plastic bottles, a broken picture frame with no photo inside it, an old oil-stained T-shirt and then the arm of a doll.

'What the fuck?' he says, staring back at the house. His pulse quickens. He wants to examine further, to go deeper into the mass of land at the back garden, but decides he needs to get inside. He's not going to find Betsy out here. If Guus Meyer has her, he has her locked up inside his home. Lenny puts the doll arm in his jacket pocket, creeps back through the grass, past the Beetle and then finds himself at the large front door. He looks for a bell, can't find one. The only thing noticeable on or around the door is a sign reading: 'No unsolicited mail.' Then he clenches his fist and rattles on one of the door panels. Nothing. He knocks again. Nothing. Lenny paces backwards to take in every window of the front of the home, to see if any curtains are twitching. But the house seems dead.

'Bollocks,' he says to himself. He contemplates ringing De Brun back, letting him know he's outside Guus Meyer's house and that he is growing in certainty that she may be inside; the arm of a doll enough evidence to suggest Betsy wasn't killed by a car on the day she went missing; that she's been holed up in this gaff all that time. But he knows he'd be laughed at. De Brun would have to be here in person to comprehend the creepiness of it all. It's only when Lenny looks up to allow more rain to fall on his face that he realises it has stopped raining.

Then his jacket pocket begins to vibrate. He parts his lips, sighs a little and then reaches for his phone, mindfully preparing himself for his apology to Sally. But it's not Sally ringing. Lenny's eyebrows rise as he jabs at the answer button.

'Jesus, Gordon, what took you so long ringing me back?' he says.

'Never mind that; what's the news you have for me?'

Lenny pauses, takes a deep breath and then composes himself.

'There was another suspect in Betsy's disappearance – somebody De Brun never told you about.'

Lenny can hear the shuffling of bed clothes, assumes Gordon has got out of bed and is now on his feet anticipating news he has waited seventeen years to hear.

'Who?' he says.

'Now hold on, Gordon... I want to know that you will abide by the deal we made a few hours ago. If I am to give you information on Betsy's disappearance that you've never heard before, you will leave me your home in your will.'

'Who?'

'Gordon, do we have a deal?'

'Who the fuck is it?' Gordon says, his voice rising in both volume and frustration.

'Gordon – I need you to—'

'Of course you can have my fucking home if I die... tell me who the other suspect was. It's Jake Dewey, isn't it? The cops always told me they didn't look into him, but they did, didn't they? The dirty fucking—'

'Gordon, it's not Jake Dewey. Dewey didn't have anything to do with Betsy's disappearance. I spoke with De Brun and then to Frank Keville, do you know who he is?'

'Frank Keville, the journalist guy?'

'Yep... he told me there were four initial suspects in the case. You were one. Keating and Barry Ward the others.'

'And?'

Lenny pauses, and for the first time imagines how Gordon is going to take this news; that his best friend and business partner for many years looks likely to be the person who abducted his daughter. Then the green door creaks open and a man, dressed in a crisp white shirt, peers through the crack.

'Who, Lenny?' Gordon continues to bark down the line.

Lenny holds the phone down by his side, stares at the stranger.

'Who?' Gordon continues to yell.

'What'sh going on – why are you shnooping round my property?' the stranger asks with a broad accent.

Lenny holds the phone back up to his ear, just in time to hear Gordon speak.

'Guus… Guus… Is that Guus Meyer?'

SIX YEARS AGO

Betsy

'HMMMM. THAT WAS GOOD,' I SAY TO BOZY AS I PUT DOWN MY COPY OF A book called *Agatha Christie: An Autobiography.* She was an incredible woman. I must read some of her books sometime. I don't really read too much fiction these days, but I'd love to read some of hers.

Some of the words in her autobiography were a bit difficult for me. But I managed to read it all and thought it was really good. I just wish I could write as many books as her.

I climb down off my bed and sit against the wall and pick up my copybook. I flick it open to where my pen is – right at the start of chapter 21. Chapter 20 was all about me seeing out of Dod's window for the first time. Chapter 21 was supposed to be about the stories of the people I see when I look out the window. But I was thinking last night that I should begin to write about the newspaper articles I find up in Dod's bedroom instead.

I look up at the crack beneath the door at the top of the steps and when I am sure that Dod is nowhere near, I go over to my shelf, pick up my *Harry Potter and the Philosopher's Stone* book and open it. Then I pull out the newspaper article I took from Dod's room two nights ago. I read it again. It's an article about how a detective called Ray De Brun has been under pressure to find me. At the top of the newspaper page it says the date was sixth of September, 2006. I went missing in January 2002 according to another article. This isn't the best one I've read. And it doesn't have any pictures of me either. It's just a small bit of writing down the side of the page with a headline that says: De Brun Feeling the Heat.

It is weird when I see pictures of myself in the newspaper pages. I never think they look like me. But I guess it is difficult for me to remember what I looked like when I was four years old. It always seems to be the same picture; me with a little smile on my face wearing a navy jumper. I don't remember that jumper at all. I don't remember much about who I was or what I did before Dod took me. I just know that he took me and that there is a big detective out there looking for me. I really want to read all of the newspaper pages Dod has in his room. But it is not often that he leaves me alone up there. When he does, I open that drawer under his wardrobe, take one of the newspaper articles out and shove it down my pants. This is the fourth newspaper article I've taken and I think I found them for the first time nearly a year ago. I like reading them, even though they scare me a little bit. They also make me hate Dod a little bit because he took me from Mummy and Daddy. But then he will just walk into my basement and hand me a brand new book. And suddenly I don't hate him anymore.

He can be so good. And yet he is so bad. I guess that's why there is a good Dod and an angry Dod.

I hear the key turn in the door and then it swings open. Oh no. I put the newspaper article inside the Harry Potter book and snap it closed really quickly. This is the first time Dod's come down to the basement without me having a newspaper article I've stolen from him hidden safely. I hear my heart thump louder than it normally does. I stay silent, don't even look up at Dod when he comes down the steps. I don't know where to look or what to do.

'Hey – what's wrong with you, moody pants?' he says. I finally look up at him and then shrug my shoulders. He probably has a little present for me. I should be feeling excited about it. But I don't. I feel really scared. I stare down at the Harry Potter book, then back up at him.

'I've got you a little something,' he says.

I get to my feet, walk over towards him.

'Close your eyes, put out your hands.'

I do.

'No peeking.'

And then he puts something into my hands. It feels a little cold. Hard and cold.

'Okay, and open.'

A Kindle. A Kindle!

'Is this for me?' I ask.

He laughs.

'You betcha.'

I wrap my arms around his waist and hug him really hard.

'Thank you so much, Dod.'

He laughs again, tosses my hair with his hands.

I look up into his eyes and smile a really, really big smile.

'Well, I figured we wouldn't have much room for many more books down here.'

He turns around and points at my shelves.

'How many do you have now?'

'A hundred and thirty-three,' I say.

'Well a hundred and thirty-three in this,' he says, touching the Kindle I have snuggled into my chest, 'won't take up a whole wall of your basement, huh?'

I laugh.

'Ah… and this one still is one of your favourites out of all one hundred and thirty-three, isn't it?' he says.

'Huh?'

My heart thumps when I look to him.

He bends down and picks up my *Harry Potter and the Philosopher's Stone*.

'Y'know – I know I'm an old man at this stage, but I really should try these out.'

He smiles, looks at me. Then his smile goes away.

'What's wrong with you, Betsy? Looks like you've seen a ghost.'

I hug my Kindle, step back a few steps and just nod my head. My heart sounds like a train. Ka-chunk, ka-chunk, ka-chunk.

'Betsy. Betsy.'

He calls out my name as he takes a step towards me. I try not to look at the Harry Potter book in his hands. But I can't help it. He holds a hand to my forehead.

'Your temperature seems fine. Why don't you just hop into bed? Take some rest today. Maybe you can read your Kindle. I have two books loaded up on it for you. I can teach you how to download newer ones too. I've set up an account for you.'

I sit on the edge of my bed. Dod then lifts my feet, turns me into the bed and pulls the sheet up over me.

'Do you not like the Kindle?' he says. 'Hold on – you just want books, huh? You prefer paper.'

I don't say anything. I just stare straight ahead.

'What's wrong, Betsy? Why have you gone really quiet?'

I'm not quiet. My heart is being really loud. Really, really loud. Ka-chunk, ka-chunk, ka-chunk.

'You'd rather read a paper one like this, huh?' he says wiggling my Harry Potter book.

Then I see it fall out. The newspaper article floating slowly from my Harry Potter book, and sailing in the air until it finally reaches the ground. I stay still.

Dod crouches down, picks it up and opens it. Then he stares right at me. As if he wants to kill me.

14:15

Gordon

I sit up sharply, whip the sheets away from me and throw my legs over the side of the bed.

'Who?' I say.

'Gordon, do we have a deal?'

My palms begin to sweat. I suck a sharp breath in through my grinding teeth.

'Who the fuck is it?'

'Gordon – I need you to—'

'Of course you can have my fucking home if I die! Tell me who the other suspect was. It's Jake Dewey isn't it? The cops always told me they didn't look into him, but they did, didn't they? The dirty fucking—'

'Gordon, it's not Jake Dewey,' Lenny says and then my world seems to almost stand still. 'Dewey didn't have anything to do with Betsy's disappearance. I spoke with De Brun and then to Frank Keville, do you know who he is?'

My eyes flicker around the ward.

'Frank Keville, the journalist guy?'

'Yep… he told me there were four initial suspects in the case. You were one. Alan Keating and Barry Ward the others.'

'And?'

The line pauses. For way too long.

'Who, Lenny?' I bark.

Silence again.

'Who?'

Then I hear a quiet voice. A voice I haven't heard in years. The Dutch lisp still strong.

'Guus... Guus... Is that Guus Meyer?'

My eyes widen. I pace around the room, my feet slapping against the cold floor.

'Yes, Gordon. I'm at Guus Meyer's home. I'll ring you back in a few—'

'You will in your bollocks ring me back... I wanna know exactly what's going on.'

For some reason I find myself in the toilet cubicle, then outside it. I perch on the end of my bed, then pace over to the far wall. I can't stay still. My whole body is sprinting just as quickly as my mind is.

'Gordon, I know this has come as a major shock to you. But please just calm down. I am going to get answers and then I am going to ring you straight back.' I hyperventilate down the line, can actually hear my heavy breaths reverberate back into my own ear. 'Gordon, just get that will signed and I will deliver on my promise. I am about to have news for you that you have never heard before.' The line goes dead.

I lean back against the wall, slide down it until my ass is sitting on the cold floor. I don't think it takes long for my head to snap out the spin it's been in. My eyes focus on the bed rail in front of me. I lift the phone back up to my face and press at Lenny's number. I remain focused on the bed rail, my eyes in no way interested in even blinking. Bollocks! The phone rings out. I get to my feet, try again.

'Answer the fucking phone, Lenny,' I pant just as my ward door opens and Elaine walks in. Her face contorts seeing me strolling around with the phone to my ear.

'Gordon!' She paces over to my bedside cabinet, drops a tube of fruit pastels on top of it, then folds her arms under her tiny breasts and sighs at me.

I hold the phone down by my side, hold her stare before I finally speak up.

'Elaine, my PI found something new. My best friend, can you believe it? He thinks my best friend took Betsy.'

Elaine doesn't react; she stands still, her arms still folded. The silence is almost deafening, both of us deep in thought.

'I need to ring him back. I need to ring him back.'

I bring the phone to my face to redial and just as I go to press on Lenny's number Elaine finally makes a move, stepping towards me and grabbing my wrist.

'Mr Douglas will not go through with your surgeries if you make that call,' she says. She's gripping so hard it actually hurts. 'You promised me you would keep that phone turned off, promised me you would relax. I'm trying to keep you alive, Gordon Blake. Whatever your PI has to say to you, he can say it to you after you recover from your surgeries.'

I hold my eyes tightly closed. And as I do, I sense Elaine leading me over to my bed. Without questioning her, I arch my bum cheeks on top of the mattress and then lie down.

'I need you to witness me signing something,' I say.

She doesn't reply.

'In fact I need you and some other person to witness me signing something, can you do that?'

She stands back after draping the sheets over me.

'Elaine?' I say, turning to her, opening my eyes.

'Gordon, I need you to relax. There is barely any time left until you are taken down for surgery.'

I close my eyes again, then shift down in the bed until my head is resting on the pillow.

Guus. Fucking Guus. No. Couldn't be. I can't get my head straight. My thoughts keep jumping. Is this why the cunt hasn't spoken to me in years? Jesus, Gordon, get your act together. Think, for fuck's sake!

I feel Elaine grab at my left hand as I continue to stew in thought. She feels for my pulse. I don't pull away. I just let her do what she needs to do as I think this through. Guus Meyer took by Betsy?

'Just breathe, Gordon,' Elaine says, her thumb pressed against my wrist. Then I feel her face near mine; she breathes in deeply, then out deeply.

'Follow my breaths,' she whispers.

I do. I sync my breathing with hers. It slows my thinking.

'In just over half-an-hour, you are going down for major surgery. You need to survive these surgeries.' Elaine sounds like one of those meditation tapes. 'In order to survive those surgeries, you need to be calm. Your heart rate needs to be consistent. Keep breathing.'

I imagine myself on the surgical table, Douglas slicing his scalpel into me, ripping my chest open. Fucking hell. I'm going to die. I'm going to die in the next couple of hours. My eyes open wide. I whip the sheets off me again and jump out of bed, almost pushing Elaine aside. I still have the phone gripped in my hand. I tap at it, call Lenny's number. It rings. And rings. And rings. Then cuts off.

'Gordon Blake, I swear if you don't lie down right now I am going to advise Mr Douglas to cancel your procedures.'

I don't answer Elaine; I just pace around the room, look at the phone's screen and press again at Lenny's number. I know I look like a madman, almost running around, but I don't give a fuck.

'Gordon please!' Elaine shouts. She stops me from pacing in circles and grabs me around the waist. I can hear the tone ringing out again as she tries to wrestle the phone from my hand. We end up in a scrum in the middle of the ward, both of us tumbling to the floor.

Then the door opens. I look up, under Elaine's armpit, and expect to see Mr Douglas standing there with his clipboard, shaking his head. But it's not him. I relent, release the grip on my phone and allow Elaine to take it. Then I scramble to a standing position.

'Michelle,' I say, stretching a big smile across my face. I wipe both of my hands down the front of my T-shirt and walk towards her, leaving Elaine sitting on the floor. 'What are you doing here?'

FIVE YEARS AGO

Betsy

THIS IS THE WORST CHRISTMAS EVER. DOD JUST PUT EXTRA MONEY ON MY Kindle account as a present. That was it. No box to unwrap. No funny hats to wear. No silly songs to sing. I've been down in the basement all day. Dod upstairs. We barely speak to each other these days. Not since he beat me up back in February. He threw me against the wall. Slapped my arms, my stomach, my back, my legs. He was really angry. Really, really angry. His face was purple.

He doesn't let me upstairs to watch TV anymore. Doesn't let me go to his bedroom to stare out the window. I miss staring out the window the most. I loved to see other people.

But I know it's all my fault. I shouldn't have been stealing newspaper articles out of his drawer. Even if they were newspaper articles about me.

The worst thing about it all is that Dod feels really disappointed in me. I don't think he loves me anymore. I don't even know if he likes me. He probably wishes I was dead.

The other times he beat me up, he always felt bad about it. He would come back down to my basement the next day and tell me how sorry he was. But ten months on from the last beating he gave me, he still hasn't said sorry. And I think that's because he is not sorry. He feels I deserved the beating. And so do I. I'm the one who should be saying sorry. I have tried to say sorry lots of times since, but Dod doesn't say anything back.

The only time I really see him these days is when he lets me upstairs to wash in the toilet room and then on some days I go to the kitchen to cook dinner for us. But I don't eat with him in the TV room. I have to take my dinner down here and eat it all by myself. I thought he would have let me upstairs to eat today of all days. But no. I'm here doing nothing. He's up there doing nothing. This is the saddest Christmas I've ever had.

The thing that I'm most sad about is that I will never get to see the rest of those newspaper articles. I wanted to find out so much about them for my book. I only ever got to read four of them. I found out things I never even knew about myself. I didn't know my second name. But now I know that. I didn't know the date I was taken. Now I know that. I didn't know that I had a big detective looking for me. Now I know that. I wonder if he is still looking for me. The first article I stole said that I was dead. So maybe they've given up.

I've written all of this into my book. *Betsy's Basement* now has thirty-three chapters. The last seven chapters have all been about characters I made up that I saw when I was looking out of Dod's bedroom window. So the book has changed. It has turned from a non-fiction book to a fiction one. Some days I think it's all just rubbish and other days I think it is good. I've been writing it for three years. But the problem is, I don't know how to end it. I don't know what way the story should finish.

I pick up my copybook and wonder what I should write about today. But I'm not really in the mood. I'm bored. Or tired. Maybe both. I stretch my arms way above my head and then let out a big yawn.

Worst Christmas ever.

Bozy has the right idea. He's all snuggled up under my sheets on the bed. I yawn again. Fuck it, I'll join him. There's nothing else to do.

I lift up the sheets, grab at my Kindle which is lying under them and then snuggle into Bozy.

'This is a bad Christmas, Bozy,' I say. I use my two fingers to make him nod back at me. Then I give him a big kiss.

I roll back over, turn on my Kindle and go straight into the bookstore. I have twenty-five euro in my account now. I click into non-fiction books and scroll through the list. I've read most of the ones I want to read. Nothing else really interests me. So I click out and into the fiction list. Nothing really on this list interests me either. I think this year has been my worst year for reading. I just haven't been interested in reading too much. I haven't really been interested in anything.

Ever since Dod beat me up, I've just wanted to do nothing but lie on this bed. I feel really sad. Really, really sad. So sad, I'd rather not be alive. Being alive and having all these sad thoughts makes me wish I didn't have any thoughts at all. Being asleep is now my favouritist hobby. It would probably be better if I was always asleep.

I press the home button on my Kindle. Only because I don't know what else to do. A little box flashes up that I've never seen before.

Software update required.

I click on it and then loads of writing comes up. It says 'Terms and Conditions' up the top, but when I try to read it I get confused. I don't know what any of it means.

By the time I get to the bottom of the page it asks if I would like to continue. I am about to press 'Yes' when I see another box below.

Chat with one of our representatives now.

So I click that. And then a blank box appears. I don't know what to do. I try to find something that will let me click away from it, but I can't find anything. Then some writing appears.

Hi, my name is Sana. How may I help you today?

I stare at the message. Then a little keyboard appears. I hit at one of the keys and it shows up in the box.

My heart begins to get faster. Wow. This is amazing. I can talk back to Sana. This will be the first time I've spoken to anybody other than Dod since I was four years old. That'll be a whole thirteen years next month. I breathe in and out really fast. Then in and out really slowly.

I wiggle my fingers in front of my face and then begin to type back to Sana. Slowly. Really, really slowly.

Hello, my name is Betsy Blake.

14:20

Lenny

LENNY BLINKS RAPIDLY AFTER HANGING UP THE CALL.

'I'm so sorry about that,' he says to the man in the doorway. 'That was eh... that was your old mate on the phone – Gordon Blake.'

'Gordon? What the hell were you two talking about?' Guus says, looking dumbfounded, his eyebrows almost coming together above his narrow eyes.

'Guus, would you mind if I came in to speak to you for a few minutes?'

Guus looks behind him, into his hallway, then back out at Lenny.

'I'm a busy man. What'sh going on?'

Lenny stares at Guus, assumes he certainly doesn't look the type to kidnap a kid, though he's under no doubt that his home looks exactly like the type of house a missing kid would be kept in. It's eerie. Creepy. Something's not right about this place. He can't quite work out why Guus would be so well refined in his appearance, yet his home is a total mess.

'I just need ten minutes of your time. I have some bad news about Gordon.'

Guus's eyebrows are still narrowing when he steps out from his front door and stands aside.

'Ten minutesh,' he says, pointing his hand towards his dark hallway. Lenny inches forward, then stalls to look Guus square in the eye. He nods a silent thank you before walking past him. As he does, his phone begins to ring. He looks at the screen, sees Gordon's number, then hits a button that silences the call and places it back inside his jacket pocket. He sucks

426

on his own lips as he takes five steps down Guus's floorboarded hallway, sparks of adrenaline beginning to rise from the pit of his stomach. This is the rush he's been chasing his entire career. This is proper fucking investigating.

Lenny stops and looks back at Guus closing the front door. When it's fully closed, the hallway falls into total darkness. Lenny's knees almost buckle as Guus's slow footsteps edge closer to him. Then he flinches slightly when he feels Guus raise an arm. Click. The entire hallway lights up. Lenny straightens his neck, lifting his head away from his shoulders and then takes in his surroundings. He's immediately drawn to a door at the end of the hallway. A door that must lead downstairs. A basement. The perfect place to hide somebody.

'I eh... I'm sorry to say,' Lenny croaks, 'that Gordon Blake may only have hours left to live.'

Guus's eyebrows straighten and his pupils grow wide.

'You're fooking kidding me.'

'I'm afraid not, Guus. He has to undergo major heart surgery that he may not wake up from.'

'Jeshus fookin Christ,' Guus says, bringing his hand to his mouth. 'All the fooking shtress and strain he's been under for so many years... I'm not surprised.'

The hallway falls silent but for the buzzing inside Lenny's jacket pocket. He ignores it while staring into Guus's face just inches away from his own. Lenny taps Guus on the shoulder, offering condolences in an attempt to come across as initially supportive. He figures it may be best to endear himself to his suspect before finally pushing at his buttons.

Guus turns his wrist over, checks the time.

'Please,' he says. 'Let'sh go in here... would you like a cup of tea?'

Guus leads Lenny through a doorway before turning on another light. The kitchen is a beautiful white; modern and bright. Lenny creases his brow, confused by the contrast of the interior of the home compared to the exterior.

'Please. Two sugars, drop of milk.'

As Guus makes his way towards the kettle, Lenny paces the kitchen, taking in all of his new surroundings. He stares at the framed abstract artwork on the walls, then picks up the salt and pepper shakers from the table as if inspecting them. He's acting how he assumes a detective should act in these circumstances.

'So... what'sh wrong with Gordon exactly?' Guus asks.

Lenny places the pepper shaker back on the table, then looks up sheepishly at his suspect.

'He has to have abdominal aortic aneurysm surgery at three p.m. today. The procedures he has to undergo carry major risks... surgeons are only giving him a fifty-fifty chance of making it out alive.'

Guus shakes his head and then blows out through his lips, making a raspberry sound that stops just as the kettle comes to the boil.

'That man never caught a break his entire life. Do you know him well?' Guus asks as he begins to pour.

'I eh... only met him for the first time this morning.'

Guus stares back over his shoulder at Lenny, his eyebrows creasing inwards again. He makes his way to the fridge, pulls out a bottle of milk and when he realises Lenny isn't following up, he asks another question.

'You just met him today? Are you from the hoshpital or something?'

Lenny clears his throat.

'No, Guus. I'm a private investigator.'

Lenny maintains his stare after he says that, he doesn't even blink. It's his attempt at acting cool, composed, calm. He thinks back to Alan Keating and how brilliantly the gangster handled confrontation earlier this morning. He's trying to act nonchalant, as if he's in control of both the pace and the tone of the dialogue.

'A private inveshtigator?'

Lenny just nods but then loses his cool persona when Guus walks towards him with a hot mug.

'Oh, oh, oh fuck that's hot,' he says as he takes the mug from Guus.

'I'm shorry. Let me cool that down for you,' Guus says, turning around and then grabbing at the bottle of milk.

He pours some into Lenny's mug, then sits at the table opposite and begins to sip his own brew.

Lenny pulls out a chair of his own, sits on it and then stares across at Guus, wondering how he should approach the conversation. He takes a deep breath, then dives straight in.

'I'm investigating the disappearance of Betsy Blake.' He stares at Guus's face as he says this, determined to find a glimmer of guilt. All Guus does is tip his head back in surprise, then forward again.

'Betsy's disappearance? Does Gordon still think Betsy is alive?'

Lenny clears his throat again. He's finding acting like a cool investigator particularly difficult. It just doesn't seem to come naturally to him.

'You don't think she is?' he asks, before sipping on his tea.

Guus offers half-a-laugh, a tiny snigger that sneaks out of the side of his mouth.

'Nobody believesh she is alive, surely,' he says. He stares over the rim of his mug at Lenny. His eyes change; his pupils growing large. He swallows, then gasps. 'Hold on, does Gordon genuinely shtill think Betsy is alive?'

'Yep,' Lenny replies. 'Gordon is convinced she is; that somebody abducted her.'

Another laugh sneaks out of the side of Guus's mouth. Lenny swirls his jaw; the laugh grating on him.

'Well... he must be the only person on the planet to think tha—'

'He's not,' Lenny says placing his mug back down on to the table. 'I think it too.'

Guus opens his mouth ajar.

'But I thought the cops concluded Betsy was killed in a car accident. The DNA in the back of a car they found shuggested she was dead, no?'

Lenny coughs again, then shifts uncomfortably in his chair.

'That's one theory, yes,' he says. He flickers his eyes up to the ceiling, reminds himself that he should stay cool, stay composed, stay in control.

'I don't believe it,' Guus says, shaking his head. 'You're telling me the cops got it wrong, made it up?'

'It's possible the cops came to a conclusion under pressure to close the case. They never found anybody or anything relating to Betsy. There was a lot of heat on them.'

Guus pushes back his chair a little, then leans more forward, his elbows resting on the table.

'Cops don't do that kind of shtuff in Ireland,' he says. 'That doesn't make any sense at all.'

'Well, we've looked at the evidence of the car theory and none of it adds up,' Lenny lies. 'So we are looking again at all of the original suspects. We feel something went under the radar.'

Guus laughs; not with humour, with discomfort. He stands up, spins around and then grips the back of the chair he had been sitting on.

'This doesn't make any... I mean... I eh... I don't know what to say.'

Lenny stands up, almost matching his suspect for height.

'Well, you can start by telling me where you were when Betsy Blake was abducted.' He lifts his mug from the table, stares over the rim at Guus as he sips from it. He notices Guus's face crumble, his eyes darting left and right.

'Not this shit again,' Guus says. 'I told the cops when they questioned me that I was here, working from home, ash I normally am, when Betsy was taken.'

'And do you have any witnesses that can confirm that for you?' Lenny asks.

Guus washes the palm of his right hand over his entire face; swiping it right, then left.

'Listen, the cops have been through all this. I didn't take Betsy... of course I didn't. What would I be doing taking a four-year-old girl?'

Lenny shrugs his shoulders.

'Well... you tell me,' he says.

Guus squints, then shakes his head.

'What does that even mean?'

Lenny falls silent, stares up to the ceiling in search of an answer to the question posed. He realises he may be taking his cool detective persona past a place of no return. Guus's right; that question doesn't make any sense. If he keeps acting ambiguously, he's either going to be run out of the house, or run out of time. He tilts his head back upright, places his mug back down on the table and then eyeballs his suspect.

'I'm intrigued,' he says, 'why is the inside of your home so immaculate yet the outside is eh...'

'Unkempt?'

Lenny nods his head once, then awaits an answer.

'I don't like people coming to my home. Shimple as that.'

'Hold on. You own this massive house that you must have spent an awful lot of money on, have it looking supreme inside, but on the outside you make it look...'

'Unwelcome.'

Lenny squelches up his nose. 'Why?'

'I mostly work from home, like to be left alone. I don't like attention. Lotsh of different reasons. I don't live in the garden, I live inside the house. This ish where I'd rather spend my money, my time, my efforts.'

Lenny squints.

'You got something to hide?' he asks.

'You mean apart from the young girl I have hidden in the basement?'

Lenny blinks rapidly. His cool persona dissipating. He doesn't know how to react to what's just been said. He wonders why Guus kept such a straight face as he said it. He tries to shield his eyes with his hand, to hide his blinking tic, but he's aware Guus has already sensed that the investigator has been stumped.

'Lenny, if that's all the questions for now, I'd like to get back to work.

430

Tell Gordon I'm shorry to hear of his condition and that I hope he makes a full recovery.'

Guus walks towards the kitchen door, holds it open, readies himself for Lenny to move. But Lenny remains where he is.

'I have another question for you, Guus.'

Guus brushes his hand through the air, signalling that Lenny should fire away.

'When is the last time you maintained your garden... gave it a good clean up?'

'Holy shit – are you a PI or a horticulturisht?' Guus says, a creepy laugh seeping out of the side of his mouth again.

'I'm a PI, and I'd like you to answer the question.'

Guus sniggers.

'Probably seven or eight years ago. When I first moved in, I looked after it. It was messy when I moved in, I gave it a good going over and then decided I preferred it looking dilapidated because nobody used to call to the house when it was dilapidated, so I've let it grow out since.'

Lenny sits down, stares right through the man standing across from him.

'So you cleaned up the whole garden when you moved in?'

Guus shrugs his shoulder.

'As best I could, yesh,' he says.

Lenny smirks, adrenaline starting to rise in his stomach again. It was moments like these he'd had ambitions of experiencing for years – ever since he was a teenager. He reaches inside his jacket pocket while eyeballing Guus.

'So if you cleaned up your garden, why did I find this in it today?' he says, sliding the doll's arm across the table.

Guus stares down at the plastic arm, squints to work out what it is, then looks back up at Lenny before creasing into laughter.

'Sure you could find anything out there. There's lotsh of shit in my garden.'

Lenny sucks in both of his cheeks, then nods his head slowly.

'But you said you cleaned up the garden after you moved in.'

Guus sighs, then strolls back to the kitchen table and sits down. He rubs his hand over his face.

'I really don't have time for this shit,' he says. 'Lishten, I gave the garden a once over when I moved in. My once over is fooking nothing. I cut down some bushes, trimmed parts of the garden. There is a whole load of shit out there that is probably lying there years. I don't fooking know. What are you suggeshtin? You're going to have me arrested because you found an old toy in my garden? Is this all you've got?'

Lenny stops himself from blinking; consciously stretching his eyes wide open. But he goes quiet, moot, as he tries to think of where he can go to from here. He thinks about the door in the hallway that leads down to the basement, then flicks his entire face when his next question pops into his head.

'No, that's not all I've got, Guus,' he says.

Guus hangs out his bottom lip, shakes his head a little.

'What… you've got a teddy bear in the other pocket?' The volume of his laughter goes up five notches after he says this. Lenny doesn't wince though. He doesn't feel intimidated. He knows what's coming next.

'No – no more toys. Just records.'

'Records?' says Guus, still laughing.

'Yep. Records of your online activity – records of your fascination with kiddie porn.'

14:25

Gordon

MICHELLE DOESN'T ANSWER MY QUESTION. SHE JUST LOOKS AT ME, THEN shifts her gaze to Elaine on the floor. Shit. Elaine. I turn around, offer her my hand. She allows me to help her to her feet.

'I am so sorry, Elaine,' I say. She keeps her gaze away from me as she steadies herself. What the fuck have I done? This young woman has done nothing but help me all morning.

'What's going on?' Michelle finally pipes up. She removes her handbag from her shoulder, stares at me with wide eyes.

I hold my eyes tight closed for a few seconds, try to let everything wash over me.

'Myself and Elaine here just had a little disagreement about how much time I've been spending on my phone; it's nothing to worry about, Michelle.'

Elaine walks by me, heading for the doorway Michelle is standing in.

'No, no... wait,' I call out, holding a hand across her. 'Please.'

She stands frozen. Then stares at my ex wife.

'Gordon, let the nurse go,' Michelle says.

I take my arm away, then clasp both of my palms together, as if I'm in prayer.

'Elaine, Michelle... please,' I beg. 'Listen to me, both of you – I have something astonishing to tell you.'

Neither of them look at me, they're too invested in each other's faces; both of them wondering what the fuck I'm rambling on about.

'Please,' I beg again, 'hear me out for two minutes.'

Michelle walks by both of us, places her handbag on the blue plastic chair and then sighs.

'What have you got to tell us, Gordon?' she says.

I look at Elaine, wait on her to turn around. She does. Slowly. I reach for the door, slap it closed, then make my way back towards my bed.

'Just give me a sec,' I say scratching at my temple. I want to get this out right but I have to let it all sink in. I perch on the side of my bed, then look up at both women. Michelle is a little drenched, her hair slightly matted to her shoulders, but she still looks good, still attractive. Even if there is strain splashed across her eye set. Elaine looks pained, disappointed. Disappointed in me, I guess. I need to speak up.

'You'll never guess what I've just heard,' I say, then stop to gulp. 'Guus Meyer – he took Betsy.'

I look down on the floor, afraid to witness the reaction of Michelle. I can sense her looking over at Elaine and rolling her eyes. But there's silence. A very strange silence. As if I didn't say anything at all.

'I had a private investigator dig deep into Betsy's disappearance and he found out that Guus was involved. He's out in his house interviewing him now. I couldn't just lie here and die without... without...' I hold my hand up to my face, try to stop the tears from spilling out of my eyes, but it's a hopeless task.

Elaine's the first to react. She takes three steps towards me, places her hand on my shoulder and helps me to lie down flat on the bed. I use my feet to scoot myself backwards, so that I'm sitting up, my back against the bed rail.

I know Michelle is silent, but I can hear her thoughts. She thinks I'm a fucking madman. That I'm making this all up.

'Gordon,' Elaine whispers towards me, 'I have to go now to speak with Mr Douglas about your surg—'

'No, no,' I say, panicking. I pinch at Elaine's scrubs, hold her sleeve between my clenched fingers. 'Please – you can't do that. These surgeries have to go ahead. You can't just let me die.'

She stares at me, her pity eyes larger than ever. She looks as if she's going to cry too.

'We had a deal, Gordon. You said you would relax and now—'

'Can somebody tell me what the hell is going on?' Michelle screeches out from behind Elaine.

I swallow down some tears, hold both of my palms out to face the two women.

'Elaine,' I say slowly, 'this is Michelle – my ex-wife.'

Elaine purses her lips at Michelle, then nods before turning back to me.

'Gordon is in need of emergency surgeries on his heart. He is due to go down for these surgeries in about twenty minutes, but that's totally dependent on his heart rate remaining stable.'

Michelle folds her arms, stares at Elaine, not at me.

'Is it true that he only has a fifty per cent chance of surviving these surgeries?' she asks.

Elaine sticks out her bottom lip and then nods her head slowly.

'I'm afraid that's the ratio,' she says. 'The more stable his heart rate going into these surgeries, the more his chances of survival rise. But… but…' she stutters.

'But he hasn't been able to remain stable because he's been cooking up conspiracy theories about our daughter's disappearance,' Michelle says.

Elaine confirms Michelle's assumption with a slight sigh and a shrug of her shoulder.

I hold my hand to my face again, my head thumping from all angles; both temples, the crown, the tops of my eyes. I have to stop Elaine from ratting me out to Douglas. I have to tell my wife that our daughter might be found today. I have to get on to Lenny, see what the fuck he's found. Jesus Christ. Where do I even begin? I swing my legs over the side of the bed again and attempt to stand. But Michelle steps between me and Elaine, holds her hand to my chest.

'You're going nowhere,' she says, bossing me about just like she used to. 'Are these surgeries at three o'clock?' she asks Elaine.

'They were supposed to be, but…' Elaine purses her lips again. I'm fucking sick of her pursing her lips.

'Please,' Michelle says rubbing at the side of Elaine's arm with her other hand, 'make sure the surgeries go ahead. He's too young to die. I'll see to it that he relaxes now and when he makes it out of the surgeries I'll make sure he's looked after.'

I actually feel my heart almost mend. Nobody has said anything nice to me in years. Jesus, I miss Michelle so much. I place my hand on top of the one she has resting on my chest.

'Thank you,' I say. She doesn't respond. She's more interested in what Elaine has to say than what I have to say.

Elaine pinches the bridge of her nose with her index finger and thumb, stares down at her feet.

'I'll give you two five minutes alone. If you can do your best, Michelle, to steady him ahead of surgery, that'll at least give him a fighting chance.'

She looks at me, says nothing, then heads for the door.

I take Michelle's hand, place it aside before planting my feet on the floor.

'Elaine,' I say, walking towards her. She turns around. I take two steps then throw my arms around her and breathe in her hair. 'I'm so sorry.'

She leans off me, purses her lips right in my face, then spins around and walks out the door.

Michelle reaches out for my elbow, helps me back to my bed.

'Chelle,' I say, settling my back comfortably against the bed rail again, 'I hired a PI called Lenny Moon – he's—'

I stop talking when Michelle holds her eyes shut and sighs through her nostrils. I've already pissed her off and I haven't even finished my first sentence.

'I know,' she says, opening her eyes. 'He paid me a visit. Gordon, you need to listen to me now. You have to calm down, your life depends on it.'

'But he has informa—'

'Gordon, stop!' she raises her voice.

'Michelle, look, it makes sense. Guus fucking Meyer. Of course he took Betsy; it meant I would lose interest in the business, that he would be able to take it over.'

Michelle places her hand over my mouth.

'Gordon, honestly, you need to stop. You need to let it all go.'

I try to talk but only a mumble comes out, so hard is Michelle's hand pressed against my lips.

'Listen to me, and listen to me carefully, okay?' she says, craning her neck so she can stare straight down into my eyes. She places her cold hands either side of my face, holding my head still. 'Betsy. Is. Dead.'

FIVE YEARS AGO

Betsy

I FEEL REALLY SAD WHEN I STARE BACK AT SANA'S MESSAGE.

How may I assist you, Betsy Blake? Do you need help downloading the latest software update?

I thought she might know who I am. Thought she might know the girl who has been in the newspapers and on the news on the TV. It takes me ages to type back to her.

Do you know me?

I stare at the screen. I can't wait to see what she says back. I tap my fingers against the back of the kindle until her reply comes up on the screen.

I'm sorry. Would you like help downloading the latest software update?

Ah fuck, no, no, no!

'I don't think everybody watches the TV and the newspapers,' I say to Bozy. Bozy just stares back at me. I'm not sure what I should type back to Sana. I hang my fingers over the letters for ages. Hitting buttons and then deleting them.

Betsy; are you still available to chat? Here are the details for the software update.

I try to read everything Sana has sent me but it doesn't make sense. It is really long. Really, really long.

Betsy, you haven't answered in a long time. Please

437

get in touch with our representatives on 1800 852
852 should you need further assistance.

'No, no, no,' I shout as I type at the keyboard and hit send.

Hkjsuy sihkh

I just wanted to type something. Anything to let her know I'm still
here. 'Oh, Bozy,' I say, climbing back up to my bed beside him. I keep the
Kindle on my lap.

Betsy - please call the helpline. Goodbye. And
Happy Christmas.

The Kindle screen goes blank. I let out a big, big breath and then
cuddle into Bozy. I feel really sad that Sana has gone. But I also feel really
excited. That was the first time I've spoken to anybody other than Dod
since I was four. I decide I must practice how to type, in case that message
thingy ever comes up again. Next time, I'll be ready.

I press at the screen of my Kindle. The box that Sana's words were on
is gone. There are just words saying:

Software update needed.

It won't let me go to the page where all my books are. This Christmas
is getting worse and worse. I have nothing to do. I crawl out of bed, walk
over to my book shelves and look at all the books on there.

'No. Too baby-ish. No. Too baby-ish. No. No. No. No. Hmmmmm.
No.'

I keep saying no at every book I see. Then I let out a really big yawn
and when it is finished I feel tears in my eyes. I fall down onto my knees
and let the tears pour out. Then I bang my hands onto the floor. I just
want to get all of the sadness out. Maybe if I get it all out, I might feel
happy again. I was stupid robbing Dod's newspaper articles. Because I
was the happiest girl I ever was when he used to let me upstairs to look
out his window. And now here I am, in my basement doing nothing all
the time. If I'm not sleeping, I'm yawning. Every day seems to go really,
really slowly.

My crying gets louder and louder as I lie on the floor. I can feel my
whole body shake as I cry. Then the key rattles in the door.

'Betsy, Betsy, what's wrong?' Dod walks down the steps quickly. I
don't raise my head to look at him. I'm still bent over on my knees with
my head on the floor.

His arms lift me up.

'What's wrong, sweetheart?' he says.

He takes my hands away from my face. Then he rubs his fingers under
my eyes, wipes up some of the tears.

'This,' I say, then cry again. 'Is. The. Worst. Christmas. Ever.' I sob in between each word until my sentence comes out.

He holds me close and suddenly I don't feel so sad anymore. This is the first time he has hugged me in ten months, since he beat me up for finding the newspaper article.

After a really, really long hug, Dod lifts me up a bit and puts me on the edge of the bed. Then he sits beside me.

'It's been a pretty shit Christmas for me too,' he says.

I look up at him.

'I'm so sorry, Dod. I am sorry for everything. I shouldn't have taken your newspaper articles. I was really bad. You were right to get really angry and beat me up. I will never do anything like that again. I promise. I promise. I promise. I just want us to be friends. I hate it when we don't talk.'

Dod puts his arm around me and drags me into him. Then he kisses the top of my head.

'Those articles weren't about you,' he says. 'That's another little girl. And... I hate it when we don't talk too. I want us to be friends.'

I get away from his arm and look at him.

'The newspapers weren't about me?'

He laughs a little bit.

'Betsy; I've told you this before. You weren't the little girl taken. Your Mummy and Daddy died, so I had to look after you. You know this. I told you this before.'

I don't think I believe him. I remember him taking me. I remember being on the wall and walking and then Dod putting his hand on my mouth and around my legs. He took me when I was looking at my Daddy. My Mummy and Daddy weren't dead when he took me. But I really don't care. I hold up both my arms and then wrap them around Dod. I need him to be my friend. I hate living if I'm not friends with Dod. The days are really, really bad when we aren't friends.

'I love you, Dod,' I say.

He kisses the top of my head again.

'I love you too, Betsy.'

We hug for ages. Then after he lets me go, he picks up the Kindle.

'Ah, you need a system update,' he says. 'Let me sort this out for you. Why don't you come upstairs with me. There's a Christmas film on the TV, you can watch that while I fix your Kindle, huh?'

I smile at him. Then I grab his hand and we both walk up the steps. This is the happiest I've felt in a long, long time.

'Happy Christmas, Dod.'

14:40

Lenny

'WHAT THE FOOK ARE YOU TALKING ABOUT. KIDDIE PORN?' GUUS SNAPS, narrowing his eyes again.

Lenny clasps his hands together atop the table, then nods his head slowly.

'Don't just sit there nodding,' Guus says. 'Tell me what you mean by kiddie porn?'

Lenny's cool demeanour begins to wear away again. He just can't stay consistent with it; it keeps coming and going. He begins to blink rapidly, then shifts uncomfortably in his chair. He didn't get enough information from Frank Keville to follow through on his claims; he was in too much of a rush. Is not sure where to take the conversation from here. He coughs lightly into his hand.

'Yes. I have it on good authority that you were charged with possession of child pornography.'

'This ish unbelievable,' Guus says. He stands up again, spins in his kitchen, his hands on his hips. 'Not this shit again.' He pauses, facing away from Lenny and takes in three long breaths. 'I've been through this with the cops. I have never had any interest in child pornography. And this was all proven. I was just checking on paedophilia, to see what is classed as paedophilia exactly... because I myshelf was sexually abused as a child. I was doing research for my own sanity.' Guus spins back around, faces Lenny. 'I put my laptop in to be repaired one day, next day I know the cops are at my door wanting to talk to me.'

Lenny looks sheepishly up at Guus.

'And?'

'What do you mean 'and'?' They fooking let me go because it was nothing. They looked at the computer – nothing. I wasn't watching child porn, I was researching paedophilia. That'sh it. Then when Betsy went missing, they dragged all this shit up again because they had nothing elshe to go on… they questioned me about Betsy for four hours in Kilmainham Station before they realised I had nothing to do with it. They said they'd never tell anyone I was a shuspect because the links to my paedophilia search were so sensitive and so innocent… Now, here you are, dragging all this shit up again.'

Lenny rubs at his own temple, still unsure whether or not to believe everything he's just heard.

'How did you find out that I was questioned about Betsy?' Guus asks, his face turning stone cold.

Lenny shifts in his seat again.

'I can't divulge that information.'

Guus paces towards him, crouches down so he is face on with the investigator, their noses just centimetres apart. Lenny can taste his stale breath.

'You have fooking nothing on me.'

Lenny holds his eyes wide open, determined not to produce his tic with his suspect in such close proximity. They eyeball each other, seconds passing without either of them blinking. Then Lenny's jacket buzzes, causing them to break the standoff. Guus leans back to an upright position. Lenny gulps, then removes his phone from his pocket. Gordon. When the ringing stops, he checks the time on his screen. 14:49. Jesus – Gordon only has eleven minutes. Lenny stares down at his own feet resting under Guus's table and tries to think everything through. The end goal is securing the house. He's got to call Gordon back before his surgeries.

'Guus, let's take a time out. Two minutes for us each to calm down. Then I have one more question for you and once that's answered I'll be out of your hair.' Guus doesn't say anything, he's too busy circling his kitchen floor, his anxiety evident. 'I just wanna make a quick phone call, get all my ducks in order and then we can rule you out of our investigation. Am I clear?'

Guus shifts his eyes sideways, to look at Lenny. Then he nods his head.

'As long as it'sh to rule me out,' he says.

Lenny stands up, nods his head at Guus as he passes him and then makes his way out of the kitchen. He looks right, takes in the door of the basement again, wonders what's behind it, before turning left towards the front door. When he's outside, he palms his phone, presses at Gordon's number. The call is answered before he even hears a dial tone.

'Lenny, what the hell's going on?' Gordon snaps down the line, though he sounds as if he's whispering it, as if somebody might be in earshot that he doesn't want listening in.

'I'm at Guus Meyer's house,' Lenny says, almost in a whisper himself. 'Guus was a suspect for De Brun back in the day, Gordon. They never told you about him because of some sensitive information relating to the cop's interest in him. But I'm questioning him about all of that now and I'll have answers for you in the next few minutes. I'm going in to search his house now.'

'Are you telling me Guus took Betsy?'

Lenny stares back at the house.

'That's what I intend finding out.'

'They're coming to get me for my surgery in a few minutes. I don't have much time, minutes...'

'Gordon, I promise you I will ring you back before three o'clock. Guus's house is odd. *Very* odd. There's something not quite right about it. He has a basement that I wanna get inside. After I check it all out, I promise I will ring you back. And I'll have answers for you. Now... are you keeping your promise to me?'

Lenny bites softly down on his bottom lip in anticipation.

'Lenny, I gotta go. Ring me back!'

The line goes dead.

Lenny stares at the phone in his hand, then takes a long, deep inhale. He clicks into his text messages, re-reads what he sent to his wife earlier. Then he taps at his buttons again.

Please get back to me. I'm so sorry, sweetie. I'll be back home soon and will tell you everything about my crazy day. Don't do anything stupid. I love you. x

After the text is sent, he eyes the hall door again, then walks towards it and pushes it open. When he closes it behind him, the whole hallway falls into darkness again. He walks slowly, his shoes tip-tapping against the floorboards, then calls out.

'Guus.'

No answer.

'Guus.'

Lenny steps backwards, his heart thumping when the light switches on.

'Lishten,' Guus says appearing right beside him. 'I don't know where you got your information from, but it'sh not on, you coming here to my house and opening up old wounds. I'm shorry Gordon's health is in a bad way, but I would like to be left alone now.'

Lenny holds a palm out, to signal to Guus that they need to calm tensions down.

'I promised Gordon I would give this my best shot. I told you before I went to make a call outside that I had one last question for you – do you mind?'

Guus stiffens up his nostrils, then turns around and walks towards the kitchen again. He opens the door, flicks on the light and awaits Lenny.

Lenny turns his head left, stares at the basement, then follows Guus into the kitchen. Guus has his arms folded, is leaning the arch of his back against his kitchen countertop.

'Go on,' he says.

Lenny blinks, and as his eyes refocus he notices the time on Guus's microwave oven. 14:53. He's gotta get a move on.

'The cops weren't only interested in you because somebody had once reported that you searched for... paedophilia, I guess, on your laptop, there was another coincidence.'

Guus shrugs his shoulder towards Lenny.

'Sarah McClaire,' Lenny says, and as he says it, Guus's eyes close. And stay closed.

'Same shit, Lenny,' he says, his fists closing into a tight ball.

Lenny doesn't let up. He knows he doesn't have the time.

'You happened to be in Birmingham when Sarah McClaire went missing, you happened to be in Dublin when Betsy Blake went missing. There were searches of paedophilia on your laptop—' he spits all of this out of his mouth like a rap verse.

Guus finally opens his eyes, takes a step forward, stopping Lenny's flow.

'The fooking cops have been through all this with me. I am in Birmingham about six or seven times a year. My business requires it. This is nothing new. You have nothing new. You are just dragging up old shit. I was cleared. The cops cleared me. How fooking dare you come back in to my home and drag all this shit up again.'

Lenny holds his hand across his own face as he blinks in rapid succession. He tries to reassure himself he's doing the right thing, that he is conducting a huge investigation just as he always dreamed he would. He's got his suspect rattled. Surely that's a good thing. He's doing a stellar job. He pays himself a compliment inside his own head, reminds himself to stop blinking, that he's winning here.

'I wanna check your basement,' he spits out.

Guus baulks his head backwards. He looks as if he's aged ten years since Lenny first saw him twenty minutes ago.

'The fook you will.'

Lenny blinks again.

'Well if you want me to remove you from the investigation, you will let me see what's down there.'

'I'll tell you what's down there. A fooking washing machine and boxes of files from work. Who the fuck do you think you are coming into my home and demanding to look around? You will do no such thing.' Guus walks towards Lenny, his index finger pointed. He jabs it back and forth at Lenny's chest. 'I think I'm a better investigator than you, Lenny, you know why? Because I've learned more about you in the past twenty minutes than you've learned about me. You know fooking nothing about me, nothing that the cops haven't already questioned me on. But y'know what I've learned about you?' Lenny starts to shake a little. He takes steps backwards, driven by Guus's jabbing finger, finds himself in the hallway, up against the wall. 'I've learned that you don't have a fooking clue what you're doing. You came to my home acting like some kind of big shot inveshtigator. Please. You're not an inveshtigator. You are a fooking bluffer. You thought you could catch me out by bringing up my old Google searches, by bringing up Betsy, by bringing up Sarah McClaire. Hey... why not ask me about Elizabeth Taylor too? The cops asked me about that one back in the day as well. Ooops, did you forget about that one? Or did you just not know that bit of information? You're embarrassing. You're not an investigator, you're a clown. I'm sure Gordon only hired you becaushe you were the cheapest option. Are you really that shtoopid that you thought you could solve the Betsy Blake case in just a few fooking hours?' Guus laughs out of the side of his mouth again.

'I... I,' Lenny stutters, his bottom lip shaking. Guus has him practically pinned up against the wall, his finger digging into the centre of his chest. 'I just want to clear you from my investigation, that's all. Quickest way is for you to let me see what's in the basement, then I'll be on my way. On to the next suspect.'

Guus looks away from Lenny, stares towards the basement door.

'No.'

'Guus, listen to me. Gordon doesn't have long left. Minutes. He just wanted one last sweep of the investigation so he could clear his mind before his surgeries. Don't let him go down for his surgeries thinking you had something to do with Betsy's disappearance. What if he dies thinking you took his little girl?'

Guus removes his finger from Lenny's chest, then reaches his hand around the back of his own neck and starts to rub at it.

'Well that's all your fooking fault isn't it? Gordon didn't know I was a sushpect until you somehow found out today and told him.'

Lenny gulps. He doesn't know what to think. Maybe he did fuck up. Maybe he shouldn't have told Gordon that Guus was once a suspect. It probably wasn't his place. What if Guus is totally innocent; that he really was just researching his own abuse as a child, that he really does visit Birmingham six times a year. But what if... what if he isn't innocent? What if Gordon's best mate took Betsy in 2002; has been hiding her in his basement ever since?

'Guus,' he says, holding the stare of his suspect. 'Let me see the basement, then I'm outta here.'

'Uuugh,' Guus rages, punching the wall just behind Lenny's head. He snarls, breathes deeply right into Lenny's face. 'You know what; fook you.'

Guus walks away from Lenny, allowing him to breathe properly for the first time in minutes. He'd felt smothered.

He straightens the collar of his yellow jacket, then watches as Guus walks up the hallway, towards the basement door. He stretches up, on his tip toes, takes a key that had been resting atop the door frame, then places it into the keyhole and turns it. The door creaks open. Lenny walks slowly towards him, notices Guus's hands are clenched tightly.

'You first, hot shot,' Guus says.

THREE YEARS AGO

Betsy

I TAKE DOD'S PLATE OFF HIS TRAY, PUT IT ON TO MINE, THEN PLACE MY TRAY on top of his empty one and make my way to the kitchen.

'Thanks, Betsy, that was lovely,' Dod says.

I made a chicken stir fry in sweet and sour sauce. It was a recipe I got from a cookbook by a chef called Jamie Oliver. I liked it too. I just think next time I can make it even nicer. I can add a bit more spice. I read the four cookbooks Dod has bought me over the past year or so and pick out ingredients that Dod will go and buy from the shops. He calls us a 'team' now. I agree. We're a really good team. Dod hasn't been angry in nearly two years – not since we made up on that great Christmas day.

I get cookbooks and other nonfiction in actual paper books. But I use my Kindle for all fiction stuff. Dod always has money in my account. I just download some great books with the push of a button and get reading. I am really happy that I am back reading fiction these days. It makes me sad to think that I didn't really read fiction for a few years. I hope everybody reads fiction; reading a book like that takes you away from real life. It makes you have adventures.

'I'll wash up,' Dod says, following me into the kitchen. 'You go and watch the TV. You like that cooking programme.'

I smile back at him, hand him over the dirty plate I was about to dunk in the sink.

'Thanks, Dod.'

The show he's talking about is called US Masterchef. Loads of different people cook dinners and desserts to try to win their own restaurant. I love it. As I'm walking out of the kitchen I notice the back door on the other side is slightly open. Dod opens it sometimes if I'm cooking to let the steam out. Looks like he forgot to close it today.

I decide I better not go near it. I don't want to upset Dod. So I just continue to the TV room, pick up the remote control and turn the volume up.

I really like the chef Gordon Ramsay. He shouts at the cooks all the time. But he knows what he is talking about. I have four of his cookbooks. Dod says he is going to buy me his latest one when it comes out in November.

I read non-fiction during the day and fiction at night. Last year, I asked Dod to buy me a copy of The Bible because religion and God kept appearing in my books. Some of the characters in my books prayed a lot and I wanted to know what God was all about.

The Bible's a big book. A really, really big book. And the way it is written means it is tough to read. But I got through it all in the space of one month. I wasn't sure whether it was a fiction book or a non-fiction book when I asked Dod to buy it for me. But I know now. It's definitely fiction. It has a talking snake at the start of it and then after that it is all about a man called Jesus who grew up in a place called Nazareth. In the story it says his mother, Mary, got a visit from an angel who made her pregnant from God. Then when Jesus grew up he was able to perform magic. A bit like Harry Potter. I still can't understand why some people think it is a non-fiction book. They must be really stupid.

It's the same with my book; Betsy's Basement. Some people might think it is fiction, some people might think it is non-fiction. But I'm not sure who is ever going to read it. Maybe people will only read it after I'm dead. It is still in my copy book, in the bottom drawer of the cabinet beside my bed. I have often thought about asking Dod if he would like to read it. But that's not a great idea. He is likely to get upset, or angry. I have only written the truth in it about Dod. Most of the things I write about him are nice things. But he might get angry about me writing about the beatings he has given me in the past. And about the newspaper articles. It makes me a bit sad that I won't be able to share it with anyone. Especially him.

I laugh when Gordon Ramsay spits out one of the cook's dinners into a bin.

'Christ, that's raw chicken,' Gordon says. 'It's redder than your cheeks.'

I giggle so loudly that Dod pops his head around the door.

'Gordon cracking you up again?' he says as he dries his hands with a tea-towel.

'He always does,' I reply.

'Okay… Betsy. I'm just gonna run upstairs to hang up some of my clothes. Are you okay staying here, or should I put you back down in the basement?'

I'm sure my eyes are really wide. I can't see them of course, but I think I can actually feel them getting bigger. Dod has never given me this option before. Ever. Anytime he's not with me, he puts me back down in the basement and locks the door. I even wonder if he is messing with me, testing me. I decide to take the test.

'I'd like to watch the end of this,' I say nodding over at the TV.

'Thought you might,' he says coming over to me. He kisses me on the top of the head. 'I trust you, Betsy, okay? Don't do anything silly.'

I look at him.

'Course I won't.'

Dod winks at me then turns around and I hear him run up the stairs.

I lie back on the sofa and watch as Gordon calls more cooks up to him at the top of the room before he samples their dinners. He high fives the next cook and tells him that his chicken is cooked to perfection. But just as he is about to put the next cook's dinner in his mouth, the silly voice over man says 'next time on Masterchef'. Uuuugh. I hate when it does that. I'll have to wait till tomorrow to find out what happens. I pick up the remote and begin to press at the buttons to see what is on the other channels. I don't see anything that I'd like to watch. Then I remember. The back door is open a bit.

I put the remote down and walk slowly into the hall. Really, really slowly. I don't want Dod to hear me. If he sees me, he will go crazy. I tip-toe towards the back door and when I get there, I push at it gently. It doesn't creak. It just opens up silently.

The brightness of the outside almost blinds me. I have to close my eyes. When I open them I am amazed. I've never seen the back garden before. The grass is really long. Really, really long. It's probably up to my waist. At least. But it's beautiful. Really green and beautiful. Birds are chirping in the big tree over in the next garden. The sun is really high in the sky, and there is a little breeze that is making the grass look as if it is waving at me. The wind feels so nice on my face. It makes me stand still. I would love to stay out here for the rest of the day. I breathe in some of the wind up my nose, then let it out really slowly. I can taste it at the back of my mouth. It's so nice. The nicest breath I have ever taken.

As I breathe in again I stare at the fence that separates our house from the next door neighbour. I bet it's about my height. I wonder if I could climb over it.

I let my breath out really slowly again. These breaths taste so nice. While I am tasting it at the back of my mouth I hear Dod speaking to me. 'I trust you, Betsy.' He says it three times. I open my eyes, turn around and step back inside. I close the door as slowly as I can without making a noise and then tip-toe straight to the basement and back down the steps.

14:45

Gordon

'SHE'S NOT FUCKING DEAD!' I SCREAM. BUT ONLY INSIDE MY HEAD. I REMAIN still, until Michelle removes her hands from either side of my face. Then I open my eyes, stare up at her. She's almost in tears, her eyes glazed over. I wanna hold her, whisper sweet nothings in her ear – tell her how much I miss her, how much I miss Betsy, how much I miss us. But I don't. I just lie flat on my back and let my mind wander in a million different directions. Guus? Guus? The fucker won the lottery after Betsy was kidnapped. He took over the company, bought a massive big house out in Clontarf. The cunt had motive. It all makes sense. I want to grab at my phone, ring Lenny back. But I remain still, Michelle towering over me. She wipes a tear from the corner of her eye, then takes one step back, removes her coat and hangs it across the back of the blue plastic chair.

'I'm really sorry you are going through this, Gordon, I really am,' she says. I continue to stare up at the ceiling, not sure whether I should be listening to Michelle's voice or the one inside my head. 'I sincerely hope you get through this, get yourself together.' She sits in the blue plastic chair, scoots it a little bit closer to me and then grabs at my left hand, gripping it between both of hers.

It's been years since Michelle and I have sat in the same room, let alone held hands. I feel so grateful that she's come up to see me just before my surgeries, but she's hardly going to tell me all is forgiven; she's hardly going to say all of this wasn't my fault. I curl my fingers, gripping her hands in a sign of gratitude.

I wouldn't mind talking it all out with her; tell her she's a fool for buying De Brun's theory; tell her she was a fool for leaving me at my most vulnerable time; tell her that my failing heart is most likely all down to her. But there's no value in me spending my final ten minutes on earth arguing with my ex wife. My mind shifts again. Guus? I begin to hear his smarmy little face scream out to me. 'I took your daughter. *And* your fucking business.' He keeps saying it, over and over again before he produces that horrible, snidey fucking laugh he has. 'I took your daughter. *And* your fucking business.' He's still repeating it as I solemnly stare over at Michelle. He's still repeating it as I decide to strike up small talk with her.

'How's life?'

She offers a vacant huff of a laugh.

'We don't need to talk about me,' she says.

'No... no I want to,' I offer up. 'I need the voices in my head to stop. Let's just talk... like adults. Honestly. How have you been?'

'Shit,' she says, producing a short snort of laughter out of her nose. Jesus, how much I've missed that laugh. 'I mean, the banks have let us all go, I've no job for the first time in my adult life. The twins are causing trouble in school. I mean...' she stops. 'I mean... I guess it's nothing compared to... compared to being sick. But... life's just... well life's just shit, I guess.'

Wow. Michelle hasn't opened up to me in years.

'I'm sorry to hear that,' I say. 'Y'know when I found out ACB were closing down, I was going to call you, tell you how sorry I was to hear you'd lost your job, but...' I shrug my shoulder and nod my head. She knows what I mean.

'Thank you,' she pouts at me.

She lets out a small sigh, then releases her hands from mine.

'I eh... need to visit the rest room. I need to wipe my eyes, freshen up,' she says.

She points to the door inside my room and I nod to confirm to her that it is indeed a toilet cubicle. Then, as she disappears behind the door, I grab at my mobile phone, press at Lenny's number as quickly as I can.

Fuck! It rings out. I begin to type a text; to get him to ring me back straight away. While I'm typing, I notice the time. 14:49. Fucking hell. I might only have eleven minutes left to live. I'm re-reading my text and am about to send it when the phone begins to buzz in my hand.

'Lenny, what the hell's going on?' I snap down the line, though I snap it as quietly as I possibly can.

'I'm at Guus Meyer's house,' he says. He's whispering too. 'Guus was a suspect for De Brun back in the day, Gordon. They never told you about him because of some sensitive information relating to the cop's interest in him. But I'm questioning him about all of that now and I'll have answers for you in the next few minutes. I'm going in to search his house now.'

'Are you telling me Guus took Betsy?' I can actually physically feel my heart rate rise, but at this stage I really don't give a shit.

'That's what I intend finding out.'

'They're coming to get me for my surgery in a few minutes. I don't have much time.'

'Gordon, I promise you I will ring you back before three o'clock. Guus's house is odd. *Very* odd. There's something not quite right about it. He has a basement that I wanna get inside. After I check it all out, I promise I will ring you back. And I'll have answers for you. Now... are you keeping your promise to me?'

I stare over at the envelope resting on my bedside cabinet, then hear somebody outside my room. They begin to wrestle with the handle of the ward door.

'Lenny, I gotta go. Ring me back!'

I manage to hang up and then hide the phone under my sheets before the door fully opens. Bollocks!

'Gordy, Gordy, I found her. I fuckin found her. I know where Betsy is!'

I stare up at him as if I'm staring at a ghost.

He moves closer to me, right to the edge of my bed, then leans over and stares into my eyes.

'Have you got that copy of your will – leaving your house to me? If you have it signed, I'll tell you where she is.'

I remain schtum, stunned. Then my eyes go wide when I hear a rustling in the cubicle. Oh fuck. Michelle. The door snaps open and out she strides. Straight towards him.

'You fucking scumbag bastard,' she screams, clawing at his face. I can actually see rows of cuts form under his eyes.

'Fuck you. Fuck you. Fuck you, Alan Keating,' she howls. She's on top of him, slapping, punching, scraping.

I throw my legs over the side of the bed, and ready myself to pounce on Michelle; to take her off Keating. But then the ward door opens wide. It seems as if the whole of the bloody surgery team are there. Each of them open-mouthed at what they're witnessing, Elaine front and centre of the group. She looks up at me, then back down at the two wrestlers on the floor.

14:50

Lenny

LENNY FEELS HIS WRIST BEGIN TO SHAKE A LITTLE, WHICH IN TURN MAKES his entire hand, even his fingers, shake. He takes the first step down, more wary of what's going on behind him as opposed to what may lie in front of him. He takes another step down, then another – walking towards the darkness. The light from the hallway behind him is all that guides his next step. He inches an ear towards the dark, the deathly silence making his heart sink a little.

As he reaches the bottom of the steps, he flinches upon hearing Guus's arm shoot up behind him. He turns around, elbows up, ready to defend himself.

Click.

Guus has pulled at a hanging light switch. Lenny doesn't take the time to sigh a relieved breath; he just swings his head back around, takes in the basement. Boxes. More boxes. An old washing machine. More boxes. Shelves with boxes on them. He swallows hard, then holds his hands up, palms out, as if to signify some sort of an apology. Or maybe it's just disappointment. He's beginning to think Guus isn't involved at all. Yet why does he always produce that snidey laugh that screams 'guilty'? Lenny looks back and sees Guus shrug a shoulder, a sly grin on his face.

'Wanna check she's not inside any of the boxes?' he says, then delivers that horrible laugh out of the side of his mouth again.

Lenny holds two fingers to the centre of his forehead and bows his head a little. Heat rises within him, as if his blood is coming to boiling point.

'Betsy! Betsy!' he shouts from the top of his voice.

He brushes Guus aside, runs past him and back up the steps.

'Betsy Blake. I'm here to save you. To bring you home!'

He sprints in to the living room opposite the kitchen. Then darts back into the hallway and into a large dining room. Back out into the hallway. Up the stairs.

'Betsy! Betsy!'

Into one bedroom. Then another. A bathroom. Another bedroom.

'Betsy!' he ends up in the middle of the square landing; his voice echoing off the walls and back into his own ears. As he hears himself calling Betsy's name, his face cringes. He takes two steps backwards until his back leans against the wall. Then he slides down it slowly into a seated position, and sinks his eyeballs into the caps of his knees.

'What the fuck am I doing?' he whispers into his crotch.

Then footsteps sound out. Slowly coming up the stairs towards him. He doesn't look up. He feels too ashamed, too embarrassed.

Guus shuffles towards him, then slips down into a seated position, their shoulders almost touching. Nobody says anything; Lenny's frustrated breathing the only sound between them.

'I'm so sorry,' he finally mumbles.

Guus lets out a soft sigh.

'I think old Gordon has made you jusht as deluded as he is,' he says.

Lenny almost edges to peel his eyes up from his knee caps, but stops himself. He can't bring himself to look at Guus. He's never been more mortified at any point in his whole life.

'You didn't really think I took her, did you?'

Lenny doesn't answer. He can't find the words to justify his madness. He just closes his eyes firmer, forces them deeper into his knee caps. He begins to question whether or not he genuinely believed Betsy was here. He actually can't remember. The past ten minutes have been a bit of a blur. A cringe runs down his spine, making him shudder.

Guus nudges his shoulder against Lenny's.

'Look, maybe you got carried away, but it's not all your fault. You were just doing a job.'

There's a hint of sympathy in Guus's voice. Lenny can't understand why he'd be sympathetic, certainly doesn't think he himself would be that sympathetic if somebody ran around his house calling out for a missing girl.

Lenny lets out a grunt; a real frustrated ugly yelp. Then he shakes his head as he wonders why the hell he thought he could solve a seventeen-year-old mystery in just five hours.

'Cops questioned me seventeen years ago and let me go within a few hours,' Guus says, interrupting Lenny's swirling mind. 'I was in Birmingham alright when Sarah McClaire was taken, but I was in a meeting with twenty-five other people. I wasn't anywhere near the area that poor girl went misshing from. And when Betsy went misshing, I was on a phone call here to a client of mine. The cops know all this, I had alibis that were proven to be correct within minutes of me being questioned. I don't know what elshe to say to you... it wasn't me who took Betsy. In fact, nobody took her, well nobody abducted her. She was killed when a car hit her, her body taken and disposed of somewhere. I thought everybody in the country knew that. Well, everybody except Gordon. It'sh kinda why we had to buy him out of the company. Gordon went... well, Gordon went a bit mad. The guy's nuts, Lenny.'

Lenny shakes his head one more time, then finally peels each of his eyes from his knee caps. He raises his left hand a little, rests it on Guus's knee.

'I'm sorry.'

Then he rises up, manages to get himself safely to his feet without stumbling despite his head still spinning. He rests his palm against the wall for balance, takes a deep breath, then he reaches down to Guus, pats him on top of the head and apologises again. He staggers towards the stairs, trudges down each step as if he's got major back problems and then finds himself out in the hallway.

'Listen, when you talk to Gordon, pass on my best wishes, and tell him I mean that genuinely,' Guus shouts down the stairs.

Lenny doesn't answer. He wrestles with the zip of his jacket pocket, then whips out his mobile phone and checks the time on the top of his screen. 14:58. He told Gordon he'd ring him back before three; told his wife he'd be at the school for a meeting at three. He thumbs the buttons on his phone.

'Priorities. Priorities,' he mumbles to himself as he opens Guus's front door and steps out, finding himself in the messy garden once again. He looks up as the tone rings. And rings. The sun is starting to dominate the sky, a light blue winning out against the grey.

'Bollocks,' he says when the tone rings out. 'Please answer, sweetie.'

He rings again; breathes in some fresh air through his nostrils as he waits. It rings out. He thumbs his way into his text messages.

Sweetie. I'm getting a taxi home right now. I'll
be with you soon. I'm so sorry about today. I'll
tell you all about it when I get home. Love you. X

Then he scrolls into his contacts list, presses at another number as he
walks up Avery Street towards the main Clontarf Road.

'Hello, Lynck Cabs.'

'Hi, I need another taxi please. I'm on the Clontarf Road, I'll be waiting
just outside The Yacht pub.'

'No problem, Sir, we'll have one with you in less than ten minutes.'

After Lenny hangs up, he edges the phone closer to his mouth, begins
to nibble on the rubber cover as he tries to straighten his thought process.
He can't put this phone call off much longer. He tilts the screen towards
his eyes. Checks the time. 15:00. Then he looks up to the sky, squints at
the brightness.

'Fuck it,' he says, then thumbs at his phone again, holds it to his ear. It
rings. And rings. Until finally a click confirms the call has been answered.

'Thank fuck, Lenny,' Gordon says, almost panting down the line.
'They're bringing me down to theatre now, what have you got for me?'

ONE YEAR AGO

Betsy

DOD TURNS OFF THE LIGHT IN THE BACK HALLWAY AND THEN INCHES towards the door. When he opens it, he steps out, looks around at the back of the houses behind us, his head turning left, then right. Then left, then right again. He turns to me and curls his finger to let me know I can follow him. He does the same thing every time.

I pull at the door really carefully to step out and immediately breathe in through my nose to taste the fresh air in the back of my throat. It's the first thing I do every time Dod lets me out the back. He's been letting me do this for nearly a year now. I couldn't stop thinking about that time I sneaked out and really, really wanted to ask him to let me outside. But I didn't know how I could ask him without letting him know that I had sneaked outside once while he was upstairs. So when he asked me what I wanted for my nineteenth birthday last year, I told him I would love nothing more than to breathe in some fresh air. He really didn't want to do it, but after he turned out all of the lights in the back of the house, he realised nobody would be able to see us. We just have to stay quiet, that way nobody will ever know we are here.

He lets me out here every Saturday night. Just as a treat. He always stares at me as I take long breaths up through my nose. We stay here until Dod feels as if it's too cold, then we go back inside. Saturdays are always fun. There's always something good on the TV whatever time of the year. We like to watch *Strictly Come Dancing*. And when that's not on, there might be *Britain's Got Talent*. Or *Saturday Night Takeaway*. Ant and Dec are

458

really funny. I think I might fancy Dec. He has a really pretty smile and everything he does makes me laugh. He doesn't have to do much. He might just look down the camera or something like that and it makes me giggle.

I don't have to cook on a Saturday. Dod orders Pizza. We get pepperoni, chicken tikka and green peppers on our pizza. It's so yummy. It'll probably arrive in about ten minutes' time.

It's cold tonight. I put my arms around Dod's waist and lean my ear in to his chest as I breathe in the air.

Every time I'm outside here I think about the first time I sneaked out. I often imagine what I would have done if I had have jumped over the fence. I could have screamed at the neighbours and started to bang on their back door or windows. But I'm so glad I didn't. Life is good now. I am a really happy girl. Or woman, seeing as I'm going to be twenty soon. That'll mean I've been here for sixteen years. Some of those years were really bad. Some of them really good. Like this year. The best year I've ever had.

I squeeze Dod a little tighter.

I read – once – in a book called *Dear Octopus*: *'the family, that dear octopus from whose tentacles we never quite escape, nor in our innermost hearts never quite wish to.'* That really made so much sense to me when I read it. It made me think of Dod. He is my family. My entire family. The most important person in the world to me. I'd be lost without him. I don't want the neighbours. I don't want Mrs Witchety across the street. I don't want anything or anyone anymore. I just want Dod.

'Come on, Betsy, let's go inside,' Dod says as he releases his arms. I smile up at him, then follow him in.

Dod heads straight for the kitchen after he's locked the back door. I can hear him get the pizza slicer from the drawer. I go into the TV room, pick up the remote control, switch the channels until I find BBC.

'Come on, Dod, it's almost starting.'

He arrives with the pizza slicer just in time. The catchy title music begins to play and Dod shakes his shoulders at me. I laugh really loud at him trying to dance. I can actually hear myself laugh and it fills me with a real happiness. Then he holds his hand out to me.

'No,' I say, giggling.

'Come on!'

So I do. I grab his hand. And as the professional dancers begin their routine on the TV – as they do at the start of every *Strictly Come Dancing* show – me and Dod join them on the dance floor. He spins me around as we both laugh. Then he tries to pick me up to do a lift. But I seem to be a bit too heavy for him. We fall into a heap on the floor and can't get up because we are laughing so much. In fact I'm laughing so much that I feel tears come out of my eyes.

There's no better feeling then tears of laughter. Laughing seems to be the only reason I produce tears these days. I'm so lucky.

14:55

Gordon

I'M NOT SURE MICHELLE HAS EVEN NOTICED THE PRESENCE OF FIVE OTHER people in the ward as she continues to claw and slap at Keating. I sit on the edge of the bed and just watch as two male members of Douglas's surgical team grab at my ex wife's armpits, lifting her off the old prick. Keating staggers to a standing position, his face already swollen, scrape marks visible under his left eye.

Elaine, still in the doorway, removes her hand from her face and stares at me, her lips ajar.

'That woman is a psychopath,' Keating calls out.

'Me? *You're* the fuckin psycho,' Michelle shouts.

They're both hushed; one man in a white coat standing between both of them, his arms outstretched.

'This patient,' he says pointing at me, 'is due to undergo major heart surgery now. The last thing he needs is his heart rate rising prior to these procedures. How dare the two of you act in such a manner.'

'She just fucking hopped on me, started—'

'Shut up!' the man in the white coat screams. The whole ward falls silent, no more squabbling, no more murmuring from those standing in the doorway.

'Mr Blake, what has been going on here?'

As he asks that question, three security men arrive in the ward, shuffling their way past the surgical team.

'He,' I say, pointing at Keating, 'just powered into this ward making up all sorts of false accusations about my missing daughter. My wife – ex wife – was only protecting herself, protecting us. Take him away.'

Two of the security men step towards Keating and force his hands behind his back.

Keating just snarls at me, shrugs his shoulders.

'Worth a try, wasn't it?' he laughs as he's led away.

'And, miss,' the other security man says, 'you'll have to come with me too.' He places his hand on her shoulder, moves her around so she's facing the door.'

'Hold on, hold on,' Michelle says, turning back to face me.

The security man looks at me. I nod. But as he lets go of Michelle's shoulder to allow her to come to me, Elaine walks into the centre of the room, between me and my ex wife.

'Wait!' she says, then gulps. 'It's not clear if Gordon will be going for his surgeries now.'

Out of the corner of my eye I can sense the rest of the surgical team cringe in the doorway.

'Elaine,' I call out. She doesn't react. 'Elaine!'

She walks towards the rest of her team, and as she's about to leave the room with them, she turns back. 'Give us two minutes,' she says.

The security man remains with Michelle and me; my ex-wife looking like she's about to throw up, her face paling more and more with every passing second.

'I'm so sorry, Gordon,' she says. 'I'm so sorry.'

She drapes herself over me. I breathe her in. It's been so long since I've done that.

'It's not your fault,' I whisper into her ear. 'I've been causing drama in this ward all morning.'

She leans off me, sucks wet droplets of watery snot back up her nose, then wipes at her soaked face.

'Hey, you really beat the shit out of him, huh?' I say laughing. She tries to laugh too, but it just causes her snot to fall back out of her nose.

I swallow hard, then I stare at the closed door, wondering what the fuck is going on outside. The team are literally discussing whether or not my life is worth saving. I guess it's bizarre that that isn't even at the forefront of my mind right now. I look at the phone in my hand, will it to ring. Come on, Lenny. What the fuck have you found?

The door bursts open, Elaine leading the other five people in to my ward.

'Okay, Gordon, we're going to take you down now. Mr Douglas has the theatre set up; he's awaiting your arrival.'

Two of the team approach the rail behind my head, one of them kicking out at something under the bed. Then I feel myself floating, being wheeled towards the door.

'Gordon, Gordon,' Michelle calls out. She grabs my hand. 'You're going to make it through, I know you will.' She leans in to me, kisses my forehead. My mind begins to spin, swirl, do backflips. I'm going for make-or-break surgery. My ex wife is fucking kissing me. Guus Meyer took Betsy. What the fuck has gone on this morning? It feels as if I've woken up in the middle of the most surreal nightmare fathomable.

'You won't be needing this,' Elaine says, grabbing the phone from my hand.

I shout out but she doesn't care. She hands it back to Michelle who is now sobbing in the doorway of my ward as I am wheeled away from her. I turn over on to my belly, stare backwards and watch Michelle. It almost feels as if I'm being wheeled away in slow motion.

Then Michelle begins to wave at me. She's running. Getting closer.

'It's ringing,' she says. 'It's ringing.'

Elaine tries to stop her from giving me the phone, but I swipe at it.

'Thank fuck, Lenny,' I say as I hold Elaine at arm's length. 'They're bringing me down to theatre now, what have you got for me?'

The silence between me asking that question and Lenny answering is almost torturous. I can actually hear my failing heart beat loudly in my ears.

'Gordon, Guus didn't take Betsy,' he says. The sound of my heart thumping suddenly stops. As if it no longer wants to beat. As if it no longer feels a necessity to keep me alive.

'What do you mean?'

'Gordon, she's not there. Guus had nothing to do with her disappearance.'

Elaine grabs at my wrist.

'Gordon, you need to hang up that call now.'

The surgical team push me into a large elevator. I don't even hang up on Lenny, I just hand the phone over to Elaine and lay my head back on the pillow, my mind splintering in a thousand different directions.

Bollocks. Lenny didn't get me any answers. Why the fuck did I get my hopes up? I think about the envelope I left back in my ward. Fuck it. It doesn't matter anyway. I'm going to survive these surgeries. I *have* to survive these surgeries. I need to know what happened to my Betsy.

I grab at the sleeve of Elaine's scrubs.

'I need to get through this,' I say. She sighs quietly, then purses her lips at me. 'Please tell me Douglas is going to carry out the surgeries. Please!' I'm almost crying through my begging when the lift door opens and I'm wheeled out. Elaine doesn't answer me, she just stares straight ahead.

I'm wheeled down a long corridor and then around a corner towards another long corridor. The colour has disappeared from the hospital. No greens or blues or yellows. Everything is just white here; either white or clear glass. As the team and I are buzzed through a double doorway, I see him. Douglas.

'What took you all so long?' he asks.

The surgical team look at each other. Except Elaine. She's too busy staring at me.

'Sorry, Mr Douglas, but we had an issue with the bed, it wouldn't wheel. We had to find another one.'

Douglas tuts loudly, then motions, with curled fingers, for the team to wheel me into his theatre.

'We're all ready here,' he says. 'We need to do this asap.'

When I'm wheeled through, a member of the team places his hand around my back, moves me up into a sitting position. Then the T-shirt I'm wearing is taken from me, my arms reaching up so it slips up over my head. I stare around the room, almost blinded by the brightness of it all.

'Ready, move,' somebody says beside me. Suddenly I find my whole body being lifted and then placed down on another bed. Possibly my deathbed. Douglas is dictating orders to his team, but I can't really make out what he's saying. My mind is racing too much. My whole life seems to be flashing before my eyes. My parents, my school friends, my horrible fucking teachers, my first job, meeting Michelle. Betsy. Betsy. Betsy.

'Gordon, Gordon?' Douglas says, removing me from my thoughts.

'Huh?'

'Do you understand everything I've just said to you?'

I arch my head back a little, strain my eyeballs to look up at him. I've no idea what he's just said to me, but I just nod anyway.

'Okay, so take one deep inhale.'

I do. And as my lungs are filling, he places a mask over my mouth and nose.

'I'm going to ask you to count backwards from ten. By the time you do, you'll be asleep, okay?' I nod again. Then Douglas nods at me, prompting me to start. I look around, find Elaine, then hold a hand out towards her. She grabs on to it, squeezes my fingers.

I take in another deep breath as I close my eyes. Then I begin to count. 'Ten… nine… eight… seven… si—'

YESTERDAY

Betsy

ANOTHER BLOODY SOFTWARE UPDATE. THIS SEEMS TO HAPPEN ABOUT EVERY three months now. A box flashes up offering me the chance to:

Chat with one of our representatives now.

I just click the tiny 'x' on the corner of that box and then continue to download the new software update. I don't need to 'chat' with anyone. Downloading the latest Kindle update is easy. Dod showed me how to do it.

I couldn't live without my Kindle. It's one of the best inventions ever. I have nearly two hundred and twenty books inside this skinny little machine. There's no way I'd be able to fit all of those books in this basement. Not unless I slept on top of them. Dod still buys me my non-fiction books in paperback form. I'm currently reading about a president of America called Barack Obama. He was the first ever president of America with black skin. I don't know why I always seem to relate to people with black skin. I think it might have to do with the fact that they were held as slaves for so long until they fought their way to a better life. Maybe I can relate to that in some way. Obama seems to be a real modern-day hero. I'd like to say that it would be great to meet him but I really don't have much interest in meeting people anymore. It used to be my dream to meet somebody... anybody, but I've learned to love my life. It might be restricted; I don't ever leave this house, except to breathe in some air out the back garden, but I have everything I could ever want. I have all my books. I have Bozy. And I have Dod. What more do I need?

I love Dod so much. He is so many different things to me; a best friend, a parent, a partner, a cook, a hairdresser, a TV critic, a book critic. Sometimes we read the same books and then discuss them afterwards. We both read *Dreams From My Father* at the same time, although he finished it way before me. Then afterwards, over dinner, we discussed what we both love the most about Barack Obama. We also both read *The Hunger Games* books at the same time and then discussed them. I think Dod liked them more than I did. We've also watched the movies. They're crap in comparison to the books.

The software update finishes and I click back into the book I was reading: *The Fault in Our Stars*. It's very sad. Very, very sad. But it is so gripping. I only downloaded it yesterday morning. Am nearly finished it already.

'You should read this one, Dod,' I say.

He looks at me, then squidges his nose.

'Doesn't seem like my cup of tea.'

A small laugh comes out of my nose.

'You're just afraid you'll cry.'

He makes a face at me, then continues to paint the wall of my basement. He's so good at looking after me and my little room. I asked him to paint it light blue, so that it looks like the sky. He bought some paint yesterday and began the job today. The smell is a bit strong, but I don't mind. It will look great when it is all done.

Dod's going to buy me two plants as well that I can put in the corner of the basement, just so I can bring a bit of the outside into my inside. We still go out the back, with the lights turned off, every Saturday evening before our Pizza arrives. The smell of fresh air is still a joy for me. We whisper when we're out there; about anything and everything. It's normally the best twenty minutes of my week. But anytime spent talking with Dod is always great. He is so clever.

I stare at him as he runs a paint brush up and down the far wall. I think he has lost some weight in the past months. I asked him if he was doing more exercise.

'No. Apart from running around seeing to your demands!' he said to me laughing. He says I have him under my thumb, that I totally control him. He might be right. I don't know. I just know that we love each other. And that neither of us would change a thing. We don't even hold any secrets from each other.

Well, apart from *Betsy's Basement*. I still haven't told him about it. I'm not sure how he would react to reading it. I think it's a great book. I really do. It's a hundred per cent non-fiction now. I got rid of all of the fictional stuff about neighbours who I made up. The whole book now is about my time spent here. It's like a memoir; a bit like the Obama book in a way, a bit like the brilliant book I read last year: *Angela's Ashes*. That kinda thing. Somebody in the future will find it. Somebody will read it and know the full truth about my life in this house. And I will continue to add to it. My life is far from over. I'm only twenty-one. Have lots of years left. My spelling and my writing improves all the time, but it's still not perfect. I'm sure there are still lots of mistakes in it, but I really like *Betsy's Basement* and think whoever does find it in the future will really enjoy reading it. I might even become famous. Only I won't know. Because I will be dead.

I sniffle up a tear that almost falls out of my eye as I continue reading *The Fault in Our Stars*. I always know if a book is good or a bad depending on how it makes me feel. Once it makes me feel anything – happy, sad, angry, afraid – then I know it's good. It's the writer's responsibility to make the reader feel... feel something. This book is definitely making me feel something: sad. But that's a good thing. The writer has done her job. I hope whoever reads *Betsy's Basement* feels something. But I don't want them to just feel sad even though there are sad bits in it. I want them to feel happy too. And angry. And afraid. Because they are all the feelings I have had while I've been writing it.

'Ohhh,' I need a glass of water,' Dod says as he scrambles back to a standing position.

'I can get one for you,' I say.

He shakes his head.

'Don't worry about it. I wanna take a little break. I don't feel too good. I'm a little light-headed from the fumes, I think. I'll be back in ten minutes. You just keep on reading.'

I smile back at him and watch as he makes his way up the steps. He doesn't seem to be walking like he normally does. He's holding on to the wall for balance as he makes his way towards the light in the hallway.

Then he just drops; his whole body slapping against the floorboards in the hallway.

FIVE HOURS LATER

20:00

Lenny

LENNY CRUNCHES ANOTHER PLASTIC CUP IN HIS GRIP, TOSSES IT INTO THE bin and then interlocks the fingers from each of his hands around the back of his head. He lets out another sigh and then begins to pace the corridors. Again. Slowly. Really slowly. He's not going anywhere, but he's sick to death of sitting in the waiting room. He can't fathom why the plastic seats in these waiting rooms are always so uncomfortable, as if they're designed to itch people's arse cheeks. He has studied each face he's come across during his repeated walks, but none has matched the pretty girl's in scrubs he'd seen in Gordon's ward this morning.

He grinds his teeth again, the day's events constantly nagging away at him, then squirms. He's furious with himself that he spent much of his day running around strangers' homes shouting out Betsy Blake's name – as if she was just gonna magically poke her head out from behind a curtain after seventeen years.

'I'm a fuckin idiot,' he whispers to himself as he continues to walk, his hands still interlocked behind his bald head. It's not the first time he's mumbled that sentence in the past couple of hours.

He's frustrated with himself over a number of things, but none more so than the fact that he put Sally on the backburner. He'd never done that before. He got so wrapped up in his job that he let Sally down. He's promised himself – and her –countless times over the past hours that he will never do that again.

Still, despite the cringe-worthiness of his day, it may all work out wonderfully for him in the end. As far as he's aware, Gordon said he was leaving his home to him in his will; it was practically the last thing he said as he was being taken down for surgery. Wasn't it? The day's been such a blur, Lenny isn't entirely sure what was said. Though, if he learned anything since he arrived home and researched the Betsy Blake case, it's that it wouldn't be particularly wise to trust anything Gordon Blake says. Yet, despite that, here he is – back at the hospital, desperate to find out if that will Gordon wrote in front of him was left on his bedside cabinet before he was wheeled down for his surgeries.

The first thing Lenny did when he arrived back at the hospital was to go up to St Bernard's Ward; into the room Gordon had been lying in all morning. But there was nothing in it; nobody in the bed, nothing in or on the bedside cabinet. Lenny has begun to wonder if he's being equally as deluded as he was earlier in the day, thinking Gordon would leave him his house. But he couldn't just sit at home not knowing for sure. He felt he had to be here, he had to find out. Intrigue was controlling him.

He told Sally everything. It took quite a while for it all to sink in and for her to understand what had gone on during his morning, but once the penny dropped that Lenny was doing everything for his family – for her and the boys – she held her arms out, invited him in for a hug. They held each other for about half an hour, until the boys finally asked why dinner was taking so long.

When Sally released him from their long embrace, Lenny made his way to their pokey dining-room and wiggled the mouse of the home computer, making the screen blink on. He researched the Betsy Blake case as thoroughly as he possibly could. Every minute of reading made him squirm even further into his seat. He never thought he could be so gullible.

Everybody he spoke to during his investigation; from Alan Keating and Barry Ward to Michelle Dewey – Betsy's own mother – to Ray De Brun, the lead detective on the case, Frank Keville who reported on the case for a decade and even Gordon's former best mate Guus Meyer – they all told him Betsy was dead. And yet he still raced around thinking he could find her. The internet informed him there's no doubt about it: Betsy Blake's DNA was found inside that car back in 2009. And that DNA did indeed confirm she was deceased. Unless the cops are unfathomably dirty and had somebody in the lab ensure their findings matched up to the theory, then there's absolutely no doubt about it: Betsy Blake is dead.

The penny dropped within Lenny that Gordon Blake must have just gone crazy after he lost his daughter, and couldn't bring himself to admit that she was gone forever. But that's exactly why Lenny is here – because Gordon Blake *is* crazy. Maybe, just maybe he was crazy enough to leave a small-time investigator he barely knew a million euro house in his will.

Lenny lets out another deep sigh as he turns another corner, into another corridor that looks identical to the other thirty he's strolled down over the past hour and a half. He spots another water cooler, decides to fill another plastic cup just to break the monotony of his corridor walking. He holds down the small white tap, and when the cup is only half-filled, he stops and tilts his head sideways. He can hear a familiar voice; a voice he was talking to earlier today. He takes one large step back, just so he can peer around the corner. Michelle. She's nodding her head, in conversation with a nurse. Michelle's eyes look heavy, as if she's been crying. Maybe Gordon didn't make it. Though maybe she's been crying because Gordon *did* make it. Their relationship is so toxic, Lenny's not quite sure what way Michelle would react to any result of Gordon's surgeries.

Lenny's eyes stretch wide and he instinctively takes a step forward, out of her sight, when Michelle glances her eyes towards him.

'Bollocks,' he mutters to himself. The conversation around the corner stops dead. Then the sound of heels stamping their way towards him echoes against the walls.

She doesn't say anything when she's directly behind him, but he can feel her eyes burn into the back of his head. After blinking rapidly, he finally spins around, widening his eyes in mock surprise.

'Michelle, how did Gordon get on?'

She holds his stare, snarls up the butt of her nose at him.

'You should be fucking ashamed of yourself,' she says. Then she trots away, her heels clapping against the tiled floor again. Lenny tucks his chin into his chest and waits for the cringing to stop running down his spine.

'Eh... Mr Moon, am I right?'

He lifts his chin, sees the nurse Michelle had just been speaking to approach him slowly. She holds a hand out to his bicep and pats it gently.

'I'm really sorry to tell you that Gordon Blake passed away during his procedures this afternoon. His... his heart rate was too high, making the surgeries all the more complex. Plus he produced about six massive blood clots after the procedure had begun; a couple of which entered one of his lungs. I know it's no consolation right now but he slipped away under heavy anaesthetic, so wouldn't have felt any pain.'

The nurse continues to pat at Lenny's bicep, continues to try to console him but he's barely listening anymore. All he wants to know

now is whether or not Gordon left behind an envelope with his name on it; whether or not he is now the owner of a million euro gaff. He nods solemnly towards the nurse, trying to act as if he's desperately saddened.

'If you would like to meet with any of our grief counsellors, I can put you in touch with them…'

Lenny stiffens his face, then blinks before composing himself.

'Did he eh… did he leave anything for me?'

The nurse purses her lips, then shakes her head really slowly.

Shit!

'Not that I'm aware of,' she says, 'But I didn't clear Gordon's ward. I know all of his possessions were brought to our family storage room – would you like me to check them for you?'

Lenny nods. Probably a little too eagerly. But before he's even stopped nodding, the nurse slips her hand around to the top of his back and begins to guide him back down the corridor.

Lenny can sense that the nurse is interested in talking, perhaps she's intrigued by the life of Gordon Blake – she must be if she found out he was the father of Betsy Blake. But they don't talk as they take a lift down to the ground floor, and don't talk as they stroll down a long corridor to reach a small reception area.

'Hi, Tanya,' the nurse says, 'Gordon Blake, the patient we lost on the table today, his belongings were taken down here a couple of hours ago…'

'Oh yeah,' Tanya says, turning her back and entering a pokey room to the side of her reception desk.

The nurse reaches out another hand to Lenny's bicep, pats at it. But he can't bring himself to look at her, he's afraid he has guilt written all over his face. She thinks he's saddened by the news she's shared with him, she has no idea he is bubbling up inside with excitement.

'It's not much,' Tanya says, standing in the doorway. She holds the door open, nods for Lenny to enter.

'I'll leave you to it,' the nurse says. 'I'll be back up on floor three if you feel you need to come talk to me, okay?'

Lenny barely reacts, he's too busy staring inside the pokey room. He paces forwards, bypasses Tanya in the doorway and stares at a plastic bag resting on a small white fold-down table.

'That's everything we took from Mr Blake's ward,' says Tanya. 'I'll leave you to it.'

When she closes the door, Lenny looks to the ceiling first, as if he's praying to a God he doesn't believe in. Then he takes one deep breath, still staring up at the ceiling, and steps forward to spread the bag wide open.

He removes a T-shirt and a pair of shorts before spotting a small brown envelope. He snatches at it, spins it around in his hands.

Fuck yeah!

For the attention of Lenny Moon.

He rips the envelope open with his thumb, and unfolds the paper inside it. There are two sheets of paper. But it's the very first sheet that makes his heart thump loudly. It *is* the will. And it's made out to him.

This is the will and testament of Gordon James Blake.
I hereby wish to leave the home, addressed 166 South Circular Road, Inchicore, Dublin 8, Ireland to Leonard Moon.

It's signed by Gordon and signed by two girls – one named Elaine Reddy, the other Saoirse Guinness. Lenny's eyes almost glaze over with joy. The guilt he had been feeling has dissipated, the cringes that were flittering up and down his spine all afternoon forgotten. He and his family are now rich. In bricks and mortar at least.

He places the first sheet aside, sniffles up the tears that threaten to fall, then continues to read.

Lenny, if you are reading this it is because I have passed away.
Yes – I did, as promised, leave you my house.
I hope you enjoy living in 166 South Circular Road. I certainly didn't. Too many dark memories.
You'll find a girl in there when you go in. Elizabeth Taylor. Betsy Taylor. I took her when I was travelling around Europe ten months after my Betsy was taken. Even on this day – my dying day, I guess – I'm not sure what possessed me to snatch her. I guess I just wanted to replace my daughter.
I stopped for lunch in a small town in Wales during one of the last days of my travelling and was amazed when I heard a man call out the name 'Betsy'. I stared at her. Couldn't keep my eyes off her. She didn't look exactly like my Betsy – not in the face – but she had the same brown hair. Was a similar height. Similar age. I followed her and her family for hours, staring from behind bushes, around corners. Suddenly she started walking on the wall I was hiding behind while I was trying to

look at her. And I don't know what came over me. I just wanted her. I thought my pain would disappear. I stood up and grabbed her.

But she was never my Betsy. I didn't know what to do with her. Whether to treat her like a daughter, like a friend, like a partner. I tried all of those hats on, none seemed to fit. Not until the final few years when we both realised we couldn't live without each other. But she'll have to live without me now, I guess.

I love her very much. I looked after her; she's well nourished, well read. I guess that's the best I could do.

I must have apologised to Betsy a thousand times over the years. Guilt kept eating away at me. Give her one last hug and one last apology from me before she's sent back to her real home. And tell her I'm going to miss her. Just as much as I've missed my own Betsy.

Sincerely,

Gordon Blake

TODAY

Betsy

I'M WORRIED. REALLY, REALLY WORRIED. I HAVEN'T BEEN ABLE TO READ FOR the past twenty-four hours. I can't concentrate. I keep seeing Dod with his eyes rolled into the back of his head. He was breathing funny. And his tongue was hanging out of his mouth. I kept calling his name, louder and louder each time. Right into his face, right into his ear. It was working. A bit. He would respond by making funny noises, but I wasn't sure what he was trying to say to me. So I rooted through his pockets, took out his phone and fumbled with it until I could find some numbers. Then I dialled 999 and waited.

'I need an ambulance,' I said. 'Dod needs to go to hospital.'

The girl on the other line asked me for the address. I ran to the door.

'Number one-six-six,' I said.

'One-six-six where?' she asked.

My eyes went wide.

'Dod... Dod,' I screamed. I slapped him across the face. Did whatever I could to wake him up. To make him talk. 'One-six-six. One-six-six.' I repeated the number into his face over and over again. Then I watched him swallow hard and his eyes turned more normal.

'South Circular Road.' he squeaked out of his mouth. Then his eyes rolled back again.

I keep playing it over and over in my head. Him looking like he was about to die; me making the phone call; me letting the ambulance man and woman come into the hallway; me watching as Dod was put on a stretcher and wheeled out of the house.

I feel so alone. And very, very sad. I cried most of last night. And this morning. I've had to creep outside the back door; just to breathe in some fresh air. I know Dod would be angry that I did that during the daytime, when a neighbour could see me. But I needed the fresh air. Desperately needed it.

I'm back in the basement now, under my covers with Bozy on my chest just waiting to hear Dod come back through the front door. I wipe my hand over my face and let out a big sigh. I think all of my tears have dried up. The crying has stopped.

I sit up in the bed and look at my Kindle. I'm really not in the humour of reading. My brain won't let me concentrate on the story. All I can think about is Dod. About how he collapsed when he reached the top of the stairs yesterday. The noise of his body slapping on the wooden floor.

Then I look to my right, to my bedside cabinet, whip the duvet off me and pull it open. I reach inside and take out my copybook. Betsy's Basement. If I can't read because I keep thinking of Dod, then maybe I can write, because I'll be writing about Dod. I click at my pen and then begin to scribble a new chapter. Chapter 115. I chew on the top of the pen, wonder what to call this chapter.

Dod goes to hospital.

And then I begin to write it. I write about him painting my room, then needing a glass of water, then falling onto the floor at the top of the stairs. Sometimes when I write the name Dod, my 'o' looks like a small 'a'. He told me once, not that long ago, that he asked me to call him Dod because it sounded like the word Dad. But then he said he was only messing. I'm actually not sure if he was or not though. Then I write about me calling the ambulance and about the ambulance man and woman coming into the house. I write about how odd that was for me. I hadn't spoken to anybody but Dod for seventeen years. The woman asked if I'd like to go in the ambulance with them. I looked out the door, stared at the big bright yellow ambulance with blue lights flashing on its roof, and then shook my head.

'I shouldn't go out,' I said. Then I asked her to look after him as best she could. I write about that too. And about me crying all night.

This is the fastest I've ever written. And the longest. I've probably been writing for the past two hours. Maybe three. Then I stop suddenly. I think I hear a key in the hall door.

I slap Betsy's Basement shut and look up the steps. The hall door creeps open and my heart thumps really fast with relief. Ka-chunk, ka-chunk, ka-chunk. A big smile stretches right across my face. Dod. Dod is okay. He's safe. He's home.

I place Betsy's Basement and my pen on top of my cabinet, grab Bozy, and we both make our way to my steps. But I stop suddenly because I get confused. I think Dod's brought somebody home with him. I'm sure I can hear people talking up there. I stand at the bottom of the steps and try to listen. Then the basement door opens and I see a shadow of a man. It's not Dod. Then a woman appears. Then another man. He's not Dod either.

All three of them walk slowly down the steps, one of them shining a torch towards me. I squeeze Bozy tight. Really, really tight.

THE END

DID YOU SPOT ANY OF THE CLUES TO THE END TWIST?

WELL, AUTHOR DAVID B. LYONS GOES THROUGH THEM DURING THIS exclusive Q&A.

You can watch it in the link below. Get ready to kick yourself!

www.subscribepage.com/betsyblakeq&a

.

BOOK III

THE SUICIDE PACT

By David B. Lyons.

For me mam

Our Suicide Pact

1. The decision has been made. Neither of us can ask the other if we want to change our minds anymore.

2. Spend our last day at home, saying goodbye to family (without them knowing we are saying goodbye for the last time).

3. Meet up at 7:30, visit the people we love the most to say goodbye (without them knowing we are saying goodbye for the last time).

4. Get back to Rathmines at Midnight.

5. End our lives.

19:00

Ciara

WHAT ARE YOU SUPPOSED TO SAY TO YOUR MAM WHEN ONLY YOU KNOW IT'LL be the last time you ever speak to her?

I mean... she doesn't know it's the last time. She doesn't know anything. She's an idiot. But I know when I leave this house in twenty-minutes time that I will never come back; that I will never sit in this squeaky leather sofa again, that I'll never see my mam's nose get any redder than it's already gotten, that I will never hear my dad tut at me again.

I thought he'd be here today. But it's no surprise that he's not. In fact, it's appropriate that he's not here, I guess... because he's never been here for me anyway.

I place my glass of Coke down on the side table and wonder what I can say to her that won't give the game away. She's shuffling round in the kitchen, probably wondering who my dad is out with this evening. A lot of their shouting seems to be about him not telling her where he's going and who he's going to be out with. They make being an adult look really difficult. I can't bear the thought of growing up.

I stare at the back of her as her shaking hand lifts the glass to her mouth. Any time I think about my mam, I imagine her in this *exact* position; sat up on one of the uncomfortable high stools at our kitchen island with a bottle of red wine open in front of her. Sometimes there're two bottles. And she's either swirling the wine glass around in her hand or she's lifting it to her mouth.

I tried it once. Wine. Yuck. I don't know how she does it. Every day. I heard her telling Auntie Sue one time that it helps calm her down. That made me laugh a little. I don't think my mam knows what calm means exactly. I've never seen her calm. Ever.

I walk towards her, tiptoeing across the tiles of our kitchen and when I get close she spins around, holding her hand to her chest.

'Jesus Christ, Ciara, you frightened the shite outta me. Don't sneak up on me like that!'

I hold my eyes closed and hear my own breaths as she swivels back around on her stool, back to her wine. She holds that glass much tighter than she's ever held me.

'Sorry,' I whisper as I stare down at my feet.

She doesn't react; doesn't turn back around to accept my apology. She just stays on her stool, swirling her glass, staring out the double-doors at nothing. I wonder what she thinks about every time she stares out there. I'd love to know what goes on inside her head.

I fidget with my hands a bit, each of my fingers taking turns to tap against my thumb and then I curl my bottom lip downwards. I'm stuck. I really don't know what to say to her. And I've had all day to come up with something.

'Where's Dad?' I ask.

I don't know why I call him Dad... or her Mam. I should just call them Michael and Vivian. They don't deserve to be called parents.

'You still there?' she says without turning around. Then she lets out that deep bloody sigh she always lets out. I've heard this sound a million times before. I hear it a hundred times every day. 'I don't know where he is. Working late again, I s'pose.'

I know that's a lie. Everything's a lie. He's lying to her. She's lying to me. Our whole family lives in a house full of lies. And I'd know. Because I'm about to lie to her right now.

I clench my hands so that all of my fingers are in a ball and no longer fidgeting. Then I look around the kitchen, as if the words I want to say will be written somewhere for me to read from.

'I'm gonna stay in Ingrid's tonight, Mam. We're studying for our exam. Mrs Murphy said it's okay.'

She holds the hand that's not gripped to her glass up and swirls it in the air.

I almost laugh; a short snort shooting out of my nose. What a bitch! Maybe I should just go... go now... head out the door. That way when they find my body in the morning, this moment will haunt my mam forever: the time she had the chance to say goodbye to her only child and she couldn't even bring herself to turn around. So I do. I spin on my heels, grab at my tracksuit top and then look back at her and realise I have to do this. There's no way I can risk ending up like her.

There was a tiny part of me that hoped this evening would give me some sort of relief. When I thought about the final goodbye to my parents, somewhere in the back of my mind I hoped they would see right through me. That they'd know what I was up to. That my dad would sweep me into his arms and cry. And tell me that he's sorry. That he knows he's been a terrible dad. That he won't be a terrible dad ever again. Then my mam would join in; a big family group hug that we'd hold for ten minutes before my mam would make her way to the kitchen to pour every one of her bottles of wine down the sink.

I stare at the back of her head. Then check the clock. It's not even ten-past seven. I told Ingrid I'd knock for her at half-past. I'm way too early.

But there's not much else for me to do. Dad's not here; Mam's too busy cradling her wine to even turn around and look at me, let alone talk to me. I slip on my tracksuit top and, without even thinking, I pace across the kitchen tiles again, wrap my arms around my mam's waist and snuggle my head into the lower part of her back. I couldn't help it. I couldn't let a swirl of her hand be the last conversation we ever have. But maybe I should have. Because as soon as my hands are around her, I hear that bloody sigh again.

'Jesus, Ciara, I nearly spilt me wine. What are ye doing?' She unwraps my hands from her waist then turns around on her stool. 'What do you want from me?'

I just laugh. A full, proper laugh that seems to roar through my nose. And my mouth. I literally laugh in her face. Take that! Let that be the last conversation we ever have. Me laughing at you. I tried to hug you; I tried to say goodbye, but you were more worried about your bloody wine than me.

I zip my tracksuit top all the way up, so it's tight under my chin, then turn on my heels and — as I'm walking away from her — I raise my hand in the air and swirl a goodbye.

19:05

Ingrid

I STAND ON MY BED, STRETCH ONTO MY TIP TOES AND KISS GARY BARLOW'S face. I'll miss Take That the most. People always say that early Take That were the best; that when they had Robbie Williams in the band they had better songs. But I like the Take That now more. Then I kiss Howard. Then Jason. Then Mark. I touch at Mark's lips as I sink back down to my heels… I guess I'm not going to grow up and marry him after all.

I hop off my bed and look around my room. I'll miss my teddy bears, even though I haven't played with any of them in years. I haven't even touched one of them in years. But it's always been nice to know that they were there if I ever needed a hug.

I guess I need one now.

I walk towards them, grab them all up in to a bunch and hold them against me.

'I'm gonna tell you a secret,' I whisper. 'Me and Ciara, we're gonna die tonight. We hate our lives.'

Then I smile. And drop them all back down on the chair they normally sit on. I'm going mad; talking to stuffed animals as if I'm three years old again.

I spin my head round my bedroom to stare at it for the last time and then decide I've gotta leave before some memory in here makes me change my mind.

My bedroom kinda lies. It doesn't look as if I'm a sad girl at all. It's filled with magazines and posters and books and toys. Lots of things my

490

parents bought for me. But that's exactly one of my problems. They think it's *things* that'll make me happy. They've no idea things mean nothing. Not to me anyway.

'Bye room,' I whisper through the crack in my door as I close it and walk out. I find myself on the landing, my eyes shut, my hands sweating.

I open my eyes, stare at my digital watch. 19:09. Ciara will be here in about twenty minutes. I need to do this now. I need to say my last goodbyes.

I edge closer to the stairs and stop at the top of them. I really don't want to go down there. How am I supposed to say goodbye for the last time without actually saying goodbye for the last time? I'm a terrible liar, too. I'm worried all three of them will see right through me. That they'll know where I'm going. What I plan on doing.

I take one step down and move my ear closer, to hear if they're saying anything about me. All I can hear is *Heartbeat*. Of course. *Heartbeat*. Mum watches reruns and reruns of that every Sunday night. Not sure why she watches that stuff. Anytime I see bits of those soaps she likes to watch there's normally somebody looking miserable in it. When I watch TV it's to get away from real life. Not to drown myself in it. Though I get the feeling Mum doesn't realise her life is just like those in the soaps. She thinks she's bigger and better than them. She doesn't realise she has drama in her life. She'll know better in the morning.

None of them look at me when I get inside the living room. Mum's glued to the TV, Dad is looking over his notes for his show tomorrow. He'll be going to bed soon. Around eight o'clock. He's got to be up early; early enough to talk to Dublin as they make their way to work. I used to think his job was really cool. But it's not. He just talks into a microphone for four hours and that's it. I remember a time thinking I'd like to be a radio DJ when I'm older. But I'm not quite sure I can think of a more boring job. It doesn't matter anyway. I'm not going to be older. So thinking about stuff like that is kinda pointless.

I don't know what to do. I look at the back of my dad's head, then the side of my mum's face. A lot of people tell me I'll be just as beautiful as her when I grow up. I don't think so. Then I look at Sven curled up on the floor with his action figures. So I sit down beside him and pick one up.

'Who's this?' I ask. He snatches it from me, then gets back to his make-believe without talking. I don't know what to do next. How do I say goodbye to my little brother? I rub the back of his head and he shakes it and groans until I take my hand away. Then he continues to pretend he's GI Joe or whoever it is he's playing with. I can't blame him not wanting me to join in. I never join in. I haven't been a great older sister. Not since we were really young. When he was a baby, I used to help look after him; I'd hold him, cuddle him, kiss him. But I'm not sure when I last cuddled him, when I last kissed him. Years ago, maybe. What relationship is a thirteen-year-old girl supposed to have with her eight-year-old brother anyway? How am I supposed to know that? It's not something they teach at school.

I stare around at my parents again. Neither of them have moved. Then I look back to Sven and blow him a quiet kiss before I get to my feet. I walk, slowly, to the sofa and plonk myself beside Mum. She looks at me, gives me a tiny smile and then gets back to *Heartbeat*. I place my hand on her knee and she places her hand on top of mine. We sit in silence for ages; her staring at the TV, me staring at the big clock above the mantelpiece. Ciara will be here in fifteen minutes. I don't have long to say my goodbyes.

I snuggle into Mum; resting my ear on her chest. Her boobies are really hard. Much harder than they've ever been. They've been that way since she came home from hospital last year after spending a day in there.

'Hey, what's with you?' she says.

'Just fancy a hug.'

She grips me tighter.

'Well, I'll take that,' she says. 'I remember hugging you so tightly on this sofa when you were a baby. I never wanted to let you out of my sight. Now look at you… feels like you're out of my sight way too often.'

I look up at her and feel a bit of pain in my belly. I think it's guilt. I bet it's guilt. Then the stupid music to *Heartbeat* plays.

'Fancy an ice-cream and a wafer?' she says.

I smile that half-smile thing I do when I want someone to think I'm happy but am really feeling sad inside.

'Me, me, me,' says Sven, throwing his action figures behind him.

'Terry?' Mum says.

Dad removes his head from his notes.

'Huh?'

'Fancy an ice-cream and a wafer?'

'Sorry,' he says, shaking his head. 'I'm just too busy here.'

Mum unwraps her hands from around me and gets up off the sofa.

'Not for me, Mum,' I say. 'Ciara's coming soon, we're gonna go back to her house to study for that exam.'

'Oh yes,' she says. 'Big one, huh?'

I nod my head. And as she leaves for the kitchen, I realise I will never hug her again. And it makes me sad. Really sad. I can feel the sadness in my belly. I turn to Dad and swallow.

I'm not sure I'll miss Dad so much. He's not the worst dad in the world. He's not as bad as Ciara's. None of my family are. But he's not a great dad either. I bet if I asked him what my birthdate was right now he wouldn't know the answer. He's too into his work. Actually, it's not work he's that into. It's fame. He used to be more famous; used to have his own show on TV. But now he just does radio. His days as a proper celebrity are gone, though I know he'd do anything to get them back.

'Busy show tomorrow?' I ask him.

He looks up at me, over his glasses and nods. Then gets back to his notes.

Fair enough.

I move towards him... not sure what to do. I can't just hug him like I hugged Mum. He'd definitely know something was up. So I just place my hand on his elbow.

'You okay, Ingrid?' he says to me, staring over his glasses again. I open my mouth to answer, but nothing comes out. Then the doorbell rings.

'Ingrid, Ciara's here,' Mum calls out.

Ciara? Already? She's early. That's not like her. Maybe she's changed her mind. I hope she's changed her mind.

Twenty-two years on, it still infuriates Helen when she isn't privy to the discussions being held in Eddie's office. They're all in there now... well the important ones anyway: Neil, Cyril, June, Patricia.

Helen can tell something major's going on. She'll just have to wait to find out what it is though. A lot of years have passed since she was among the first in line to be handed the juicy information. And waiting can be tortuous for somebody as impatient and nosey as Helen Brennan.

She folds the sheet of paper on her desk into thirds, slots it into a brown envelope and then licks the flap before running her thumb over it. If she was given a euro for every envelope she licks on a daily basis, she'd almost be earning the same money as Eddie. The same money she was destined to be on had her life not come to an earth-shattering stutter over two decades ago.

When she first started working here, way back in November of 1982, Helen had eyed that pokey office. She wanted to lead this station, not fucking stuff envelopes at the front desk. Sometimes, on days like this — when all around her is buzzing, yet she is sat still — Helen blames Scott for the mess her life has turned into. Then she stops herself and mumbles into her chest, as if she's asking somebody for forgiveness. Who she's asking for forgiveness would be news to her, though. She doesn't believe in any spiritual being. Fuck that shit. There ain't no spirit guiding her life. Unless that spirit's some sort of sick sociopath.

'Wonder what's going on in there,' she says to Leo as he passes her desk. He just shrugs his shoulder, takes another sip of his plastic cup of tea and then strolls on by.

Helen doesn't much care for Leo. The little prick has only been here for less than six months and already has the audacity to treat her as if she's insignificant. The only saving grace he has, as far as Helen can see, is that he looks mighty fine in uniform — as if it was bespokenly stitched around his muscular frame.

Helen looks around herself, to see if anyone else in the station noticed Leo's abruptness with her. Nobody. So she tucks her chin back into her chest and begins to fold another sheet of paper, mumbling to herself as she does so.

When she finally hears Eddie's office door open, she swings around in her chair so quickly that her eyes have to take a moment to focus before she can make out the individual faces. She eyeballs Cyril. Nothing. Patricia. Nothing. June. Nothing. She doesn't bother to look at Neil as he makes his way towards his messy desk. That gobshite doesn't share any information with her anyway. Never has. She chews on the nail of her thumb, wondering who she can infiltrate the quickest. Cyril's already talking to Leo. He must be filling the uniform in. So Helen stands up, flattens down the creases on the front of her grey trousers and then casually walks towards the two men. She always walks as if she's on stilts, does Helen; her entire five foot eleven inch frame as stiff and as straight as it can possibly be. She damaged the herniated disc in her lower back as a teenager; has been walking like a robot ever since.

Cyril is talking in hushed tones as Helen approaches but she hears mention of the name Alan Keating and already knows the matter is serious. Keating's been running the streets of Dublin for years. The cops can do fuck all about it, though. The clever bastard keeps his nose way too clean.

'What about Keating?' she says, leaning her face over Leo's shoulder to stare at Cyril.

Cyril looks left and then right before answering.

'He's up to something. We've just had an anonymous call that's trying to put us off the scent.'

'Content of the call?' Helen asks, tipping her chin up and then down, as if she's ordering Cyril to fill her in.

Cyril looks left, then right again. But even when his head has stopped moving, he doesn't answer. He just sucks on his teeth.

'Some kid saying two girls have agreed to commit suicide tonight. They've made a pact,' Leo says turning around.

Helen watches as Cyril stares at Leo, his eyes widening, his teeth clenching.

'Jaysus, it's alright, Cyril,' she says, tutting. 'It was twenty-two years ago. You think I can't ever hear that word the rest of my life?'

Then she spins on her heels, paces as quickly as she can and then snatches at the handle to Eddie's office door.

He looks up when she enters, his forefinger and thumb immediately stretching to the bridge of his nose.

'What makes you think it's Keating?' Helen says.

Eddie sighs.

'Jesus, Hel, you never did lose any of your Detective skills huh? You can get information out of anyone in seconds. They've only just left my bloody office.'

Helen takes one step back, pushes the door closed, then strides forward, leaning her fingertips on to the edge of Eddie's desk.

Eddie arches an eyebrow, then leans back in his chair.

'It's one of Keating's hoax phone calls to get us chasing red herrings. I've just been on to Terenure Garda station, they've had the same phone call made to them. We've looked into it; it's Keating alright. He wants our officers concentrating on something else tonight. Wants us distracted. You know how he operates.'

Helen takes one of her hands from the desk and swipes at her nose.

'What did the phone call say?'

Eddie holds his eyes shut and then sighs out of his nostrils. He uses the same tics every time Helen sticks her nose into something that shouldn't concern her at work. He uses the same tics the odd time at home too... when she infuriates him by talking while he's trying to watch television.

'Helen, c'mon... you know you're not supposed to be privy to investigative insight—'

'What did the call say?' Helen interrupts.

Eddie peers through the blinds, into the open station at his officers and Detectives beavering away, then turns back to his wife.

'It's... it's an awkward one for me to say to you,' he says, sighing deeply out of his nostrils again. 'Some young guy, maybe a boy, rang in to say two girls have made a pact to die by suicide tonight.' Eddie swallows. 'I'm sorry, Hel.'

'Whatcha sorry for?'

Eddie looks down at his lap. He doesn't answer. He can't answer.

'Anyway,' he says, 'I must get on with this investigation. I've got to organise some uniforms to call out to Keating's house. We need to get a whiff of what's going on. So if you don't mind...' Eddie points his whole hand towards his office door.

Helen looks back at it, then towards her husband again.

'What about the two girls?' she asks. 'I assume somebody is looking into that?'

'Helen, if you don't mind... I'll be running this investigation. We have every reason to believe this is a Keating distraction call. I've got information I just can't share with you. You already know much more than you are supposed to. Anyway...' Eddie says twisting his left wrist towards his face, 'it's almost half seven, you should be heading home now. Relaxing. Forgetting about work.'

Helen squints at Eddie as her breaths begin to grow in sharpness. Then she spins on her heels, snatches at the door handle and marches out of his office.

'Who's been put in charge of looking into the girls?' she says as she approaches Cyril, interrupting him as he was about to instruct two members of his team.

'What girls?' he asks. Cyril often feels uneasy around Helen; especially when she's trying to extract information out of him about work. The lines between them have always been blurred. She used to be *his* boss. Now he's many ranks above her.

'The girls who are planning to die by suicide.'

Cyril stares over his shoulder, towards Eddie's office, and when he realises he's not going to get any support, he holds his palm to Helen's shoulder.

'We don't believe anybody is going to commit suicide. It's a hoax call; Keating trying to distract us.'

Helen brushes Cyril's hand away from her shoulder.

'So nobody is looking into the girls, nobody's going to at least investigate that angle?'

Cyril re-shuffles his standing position, so he is face on with Helen.

'Helen, there are no girls, it's just a—'

'A hoax fucking phone call,' Helen says slowly into his face. Then she storms off to her front desk, grabbing at the top sheet of paper from her pile, folding it into thirds and then stuffing it into an envelope.

She looks at the digits on her phone. 19:27. *Coronation Street* will be starting in three minutes. She hates missing *Coronation Street*. But she ain't leaving yet. Not until Eddie delivers the team briefing.

'Okay, okay,' Eddie shouts out as he claps his hands twice.

Helen spins in her chair and watches as everybody in the station stands to attention; the ritual they normally go through when the Superintendent shouts and claps. There was a time Helen used to stand for briefings too.

'We've had a phone call saying two unnamed girls are planning to die by suicide in the local area tonight. Terenure have had the *exact* same call. We have it on good authority these were hoax calls, the type of call Alan Keating has used in the past as a red herring. Patricia… I want your team to tail Keating's closest confidants, find out where they are this evening and keep your nose up their asses. Cyril, ring around our grasses, find out anything you can — and keep me informed of your progress. June, can you rally some uniforms in the city and put them on red alert? I'll fill you in later on what they should be looking out for. Neil, as I mentioned to you in our meeting, I want to see your patterns on Keating again, can you give me all the paperwork you have and—'

'What about the girls?' Helen shouts over everybody's head.

All in front of her twist their necks to stare at her. She has her legs spread, is swivelling side to side slowly in her chair.

Eddie holds his eyes closed in irritation, then sighs out of his nostrils. Again.

'Hel, thank you for your input but I can assure you all is under control.'

Helen hisses a tiny laugh through the gaps in her teeth.

'I'm sure they are, Eddie. I'm sure you all believe this is a hoax call and that Keating is up to something — and if that's the case, no better station in the country to have that investigation under control.' Helen holds both of her hands up, her palms facing the team of people staring at her. 'But just in case — *just in case* — the call isn't a hoax, who is out there looking for these two girls?'

Murmurs ripple from the team. She knows what they're whispering about. She's aware that they'll all be thinking this subject is far too sensitive for her to handle.

'Hel, I've been assured by Terenure Garda station that they have somebody treating the phone call as legitimate and will be looking into that line of enquiry.' Eddie claps his hands again. 'Now, if everybody else can—'

'Who?' Helen shouts, interrupting her husband again.

Eddie holds his hands together, as if in prayer, then creases his face into a sterile smile.

'I eh…' he says, 'I don't know who exactly, but I've been assured all is in order in that regard. Now, if you don't mind, Hel, we have some investigating to do. It's half-past seven, shouldn't you be thinking of lying flat out on the couch, watching your soaps by now?'

Helen stands up, stares at Eddie long enough to make everybody in the office cringe a little, and then turns back around to swipe her leather coat from the back of the chair. She folds it over her arm, stares again at her husband, and then storms towards the exit.

19:25

Ingrid

I don't want to look at them. Any of them.

Ciara hasn't stopped talking; about her mam, about school, about me. As if her life is all rosy. It's mad how well she's hiding it all. Though I shouldn't be surprised. Ciara's always hidden her sadness well. She hid it from me for years.

'You're hilarious,' my mum says, laughing at something Ciara said that I didn't listen to because I was thinking... thinking about leaving this house for the last time ever. I'm standing in the middle of the room, staring at my shoes, making a small laughing sound every now and then just to pretend I'm listening.

'You right then?' Ciara says, nudging me. I stare up at her, offer my best half smile and then nod my head. I decide not to look at *them*. Dad won't notice anyway, he's too busy studying his notes.

'Okay, you two, enjoy yourselves. And don't come back too late, Ingrid. School in the morning,' Mum says as she holds her hand to my shoulder. I pause, just for a second, and place my hand on top of hers. And then it's gone. I don't say anything. I just zip up my tracksuit top up and head towards the door, passing Sven without looking at him. We were supposed to spend our last day at home with our family. But I just stayed up in my bedroom for most of the day.

I close the door slowly, still only half-believing that I'll never set foot back in that house again; that I'll never see my mum. My dad. Sven. But I know deep inside my own heart that this is for the best. They don't want a mopey, depressed teenager living with them. Once they're over the shock, they'll be okay. They might even be happier without me. I'm pretty sure I'm a burden to them all anyway.

'What did you say to your parents?' I whisper to Ciara as we walk down my garden path.

She puffs a small laugh out of her nose.

'Nothing. My dad wasn't in all day — surprise, surprise. My mam was... go on have a guess, where was she?'

'Sitting at the kitchen island drinking a glass of wine.'

'A bottle. That's what we say, Ingrid. A bottle!'

I sniff a laugh out of my nose this time. It's so weird knowing what we are up to and still feeling as if I want to laugh. Maybe I feel relaxed enough to laugh because I know we've made the right decision. Or maybe I'm laughing because I don't think we'll actually go through with our pact. I've been changing my mind all day. Though most of the time I've been thinking the right thing to do is to end it all. I don't enjoy living. I really don't. It's my thoughts. They keep getting on top of me. Dad. Mam. Sven. Stitch. Ciara. Every time I'm alone and thinking, I realise my life is really sad. Too sad to continue with.

'So what did you say to her?'

'I hugged her.'

'You wha'?' I say, hearing the thick Dublin in my accent. I never sound thick Dublin. My family are way too posh. They kicked all of the Dublin out of me.

'Don't know what I was thinking. I just told her I was going to your house and she didn't even turn around to look at me. She just threw her hand in the air and kinda waved it. Bitch. I shudda just left then and there, but I couldn't. So I stood in the doorway of the kitchen, staring at the back of her head as she drank her wine. Then I just ran towards her, threw my arms around her waist.'

My mouth opens. I can feel my bottom lip hang out.

'Sure, you're not supposed to give it away. No suspicion, that's what we agreed to.'

'Don't worry. She didn't have any suspicion. She doesn't think about anyone but herself.'

'What did she say when you hugged her?'

'She gave out that I nearly spilt her wine.'

I laugh. There it is again. Me laughing... as if everything is normal.

'Then what?'

'I walked away from her, threw my hand in the air and waved. Two minutes later I was ringing your doorbell.'

'You were early. Thought you were coming to change your mind.'

'None of that!' Ciara says, giving me an angry look. 'We don't talk about changing our minds. It's part of the pact.'

I hold my hands up, purse my lips and then stop walking.

'Ciara. I'm one hundred per cent in,' I say. 'I can't... I don't... I don't want to live anymore. It's... it's...' I shake. Not just my head, my whole body.

Ciara steps towards me, wraps both her arms around my shoulders and drags me in close. Our noses are touching. As if we're about to kiss.

'I know, I know,' she says.

Of course she knows. We talked about nothing else all last night.

One thing's for certain, Ciara won't change her mind. She's been suicidal a lot longer than me. In fact, I think she's just been waiting on my sadness to catch up with hers so we could do this together. I didn't say that to her last night. But I've thought about it a lot today. It doesn't change anything, though. I think I still want to do it. I really want my mind to turn off. I know now how Ciara has been feeling for the past couple years. It's horrible. Really, really horrible. It feels like such a heavy weight on top of your head. There's only one way to lift that weight off. Stop the mind from working. Stop thinking altogether.

'Ready for the last supper?' I say.

Ciara's eyebrows twitch. Then she laughs.

'Been looking forward to it all day,' she says.

She throws her arm through mine, swivelling into me and we link as we turn from Castlewood Avenue onto Rathmines' Main Road.

'It's going to be really tough isn't it?' I say. 'The whole saying goodbye without saying goodbye thing.'

Ciara turns to me, then shrugs her shoulder.

'Once we know that we visited them for the last time and kinda gave them all one last hug, that's enough. It's why we're doing it, isn't it? So they know that they meant something to us. We just need to act cool, as if we're just... y'know... dropping by. We're the only ones who'll know it's our last goodbye. They won't know a thing.'

'Just dropping by to Miss Moriarty's house?' I say. Then we both laugh again. This is mad.

'We discussed last night what we'd say at Miss Moriarty's house. Y'know... that we happened to be in the area she lives in so thought we'd knock on her door.'

I poke out my chin.

'Guess so,' I say. 'Gonna miss her the most probably.'

'Yeah, I kinda love Miss Moriarty. That's why she's on our list of last goodbyes though, isn't it? I'll miss either her or Debbie the most. Or you.'

We stop walking to stare at each other and hold hands. Both of them. I can feel tears come up behind my eyes. I've no idea if Ciara is feeling the same. She doesn't cry. Ever. I've done enough crying for both of us over the years.

'I'm gonna miss you too. So much.'

Then we hug. Really tightly. I know we'll hug again before we finally do it. But this feels quite final. We've been walking and talking for ten minutes now. Neither of us are backing out. Neither of us have let the day change our minds. This hug tells us everything. We're both ready for this. Our pact won't be broken.

'Tell ye what I'm also gonna really miss,' Ciara says.

I laugh before I answer. Because I know the answer.

'Macari's chilli chips.'

She drags me in close, kisses my forehead and spins me so that we're both linking each other again. Then we head straight towards the chipper; towards our last supper.

19:35

Greta

'THAT WAS WEIRD.'

'What was, love?' he says, squinting over his glasses at me.

'They're up to something.'

'Who, love?'

'What d'ye mean *who*? Those two. Ingrid and Ciara.'

He just pushes back his glasses on the bridge of his nose and looks back down at his paperwork. Course he does.

I sit back in to the sofa, pick up the wafer I'd left on the side table and lick at a melting drop of ice cream as I sink into my thoughts.

'She couldn't look at us going out that door. Lying, she is. Saying she's going over to Ciara's house.'

Terry looks over the rim of his glasses at me again, then back down at his notes.

It's not like Ingrid to lie. I knew she would eventually. I guess turning thirteen is the ideal time for little girls to start lying to their parents. I used to lie to my parents all the time as a teen. Couldn't let them know I was off doing modelling shoots. They'd have killed me. Swedish households are much stricter than here in Ireland. Certainly much more strict than our house. Terry's way too laid back as a father. Especially in comparison to mine. Even had he known I'd grow up to be a successful model, my father still wouldn't have let me do the shoots back then. He was way too conservative.

That could be what Ingrid's doing. Modelling shoots. Same lie as I had when I was a teenager. She certainly has the looks for it. Not sure why Ciara'd be going along though. Maybe for some moral support.

Nah.

That can't be it. I bet they have boyfriends. It's probably boyfriends. Ingrid would be starting to attract boys now. They'd love her long golden hair and golden eyebrows. She certainly got a lot more of my Swedish genes than the Irish genes of her father. Both our kids did. Sven's hair is practically snow white.

I wonder if Ciara's got a boyfriend too. I love Ciara. She's a great character and I'm delighted Ingrid has such a close bond with a girl who only lives down the end of our avenue, but she's not the prettiest. She's slightly overweight and I'm not sure the sharp bob haircut does much to hide that. If anything, it makes her face look even plumper.

'Bet it's boyfriends,' I say, before licking at my ice cream again.

Terry stares over the rim of his glasses.

'Better fuckin not be,' he says. That's about the extent of his parenting. Laying down the odd opinion without so much as doing anything about it. I guess he's used to it; giving opinions and then doing sweet fuck all about them. It's what he does for a living.

'Who's on the show tomorrow?' I ask.

He removes his glasses this time. That's the only way I can ever get real engagement from him; ask him about his job.

'We've got the transport minister on. Have to try and catch him out over these plans for the M50 upgrade,' he says.

'No better man,' I reply, then take another lick.

'Yeah — I want to get him to admit live on air that he's blown the budget, that he's overspent. Just trying to think of the best way to go about it.'

I'm not really that interested. Terry thinks he has the most important job in the world. So I play along. Would never admit that I don't think he's as much of a major player in society as he thinks he is. I used to love that he was a famous broadcaster. If he wasn't, we never would have bumped into each other. We met at the Eurovision Song contest in Sweden seventeen years ago. He was doing a backstage broadcast for RTE. I was there as a guest of the promoters. Jaysus, I used to be on the guest list for everything back then. I don't miss it. Not really.

Terry's still talking interview tactics with me when I tune back into his words. When he stops talking, I nod my head.

'Yeah good idea,' I say.

That usually works; telling him that his plans are A-Okay.

I twist my neck and look over my shoulder at Sven playing with his action figures on the floor. Where else would he be?

'Ten more minutes, Sven,' I say to him. He doesn't look around. Poor thing. I don't know what he hears and what he doesn't hear. I've researched his condition so many times but still can't find definite answers to the questions I need answering.

'Do you hear me, Sven? Ten more minutes.'

Nothing.

So I lick my ice cream again and think about my daughter. I wonder who her boyfriend is. She was at a birthday party last night. I bet she met somebody. That's why they're snooping around. Ah, sure I shouldn't be worrying. I'll leave them to it. Didn't we all snoop around at that age?

HELEN DRUMS HER THUMBS REPEATEDLY ON THE TOP OF THE STEERING wheel any time she's impatient. Which is somewhere close to always when she's driving. She automatically hates the stranger in the car in front of her, no matter who they are. She'll find a reason readily; perhaps because they're driving too slow, or maybe they forgot to indicate properly at a roundabout. Sometimes she'll decide to hate them simply because she doesn't like the colour of their car. No matter the reason, if you happen to be driving in front of Helen Brennan, you're bound to hear her car horn blast every couple minutes.

'Fuck sake,' she mutters under her breath as she stops at another red light. She picks up her handbag, roots inside and pulls out a small tub. She's staring up at the Rathmines Clock Tower, snarling at it as she always does, as she tries to pop open the lid. But the light turns green before she can, so she just throws the tub back into her bag, the pills rattling, and then steps on the accelerator. She wheel spins the car, turns on to the canal road and makes her way to Terenure Garda Station.

She's still mumbling to herself in frustration when she steps out and paces — in her own unique robotic way — to the entrance, not hiding the sigh she produces when she steps inside to see a young woman struggling to contain her two children at the front desk. The young woman's trying to get information on a boyfriend. Something about a raid at their flat this morning and his subsequent "unfair" arrest.

Helen shuffles her feet from side to side, her attempt to get the

507

attention of the officer dealing with the woman — and her two snotty little brats.

One of the kids turns around, drops his bottom lip open when he stares at the vision behind him. Helen sure does look intimidating to a child. To anyone really. Her upright posture makes her stand out, but more so because she always tries to hide it under a long leather overcoat. The coat falls all the way down to her ankles; just her red Converse sneakers on show under it today. And her hair doesn't help blend her into the crowd either. She doesn't have the patience to allow her brown hair dye to soak into her greying strands for the full hour as is recommended on the bottle. It means her short bob is a streaky shade of rusty oranges.

She stares back at the kid, his face smudged with stickiness, and then scoffs.

'Sorry,' she says eventually, taking one large stride forward. 'I'm Helen Brennan; Detective from Rathmines Garda station,' she lies. 'I'm here to talk with the Detective looking into the phone call that was made about two eh...' she stops herself, looks at the young woman and her two snotty little brats, then leans forward to the officer behind the desk and whispers, 'the eh... hoax suicide call.'

The officer raises his eyebrow.

'Let me buzz you through, Detective Brennan,' he says, reaching under his desk. Helen hears the double doors to her left release and then pushes through them without even turning to thank the officer who opened them for her.

When she steps inside, she gasps. Terenure Garda station is a helluva lot more modern than Rathmines. Rathmines has barely changed in the thirty-seven years she's known it. Aside from maybe the office chairs. They needed to be updated to comply with modern health and safety requirements a few years ago, but the desks are still the same old-school oak desks she sat at on her very first day.

Here, though — in Terenure — the desks are a modern white. As are the walls. They look as if they've just been painted. She can't remember the last time anyone painted the walls at Rathmines Garda station. They're supposed to be magnolia, but time has turned them dirty yellow.

She stops a young plain-clothed officer who was about to walk past by holding up a hand.

'Detective Helen Brennan from Rathmines,' she lies again. 'I need to speak with the Detective who's looking into the two girls reported to be planning suicide tonight.'

'The hoax call?' the woman says.

'No, well… I want to find the Detective looking into the two girls. As if the call is legitimate.'

'Oh,' the young woman says, tugging at her ear. 'It's not a Detective looking into that. This is definitely a hoax call. So eh… Charlie, I think… yeah Charlie Guilfoyle is taking care of that.'

Helen raises both eyebrows and then shrugs her shoulders.

'Who?' she says.

'Oh, he's eh…' the woman looks around the room. 'That guy there; the spikey hair.'

'The uniform?' Helen says, all high-pitched.

The woman huffs out a small snigger as she nods her head, then walks on.

Helen sucks her lips, making a pop sound before she strides towards the spikey hair. She can't believe her eyes as she nears; the face below the spikes is way too fresh. Way too young. There isn't a trace of even light stubble on it. Plenty of acne, but no hair.

'Charlie Guilfoyle,' she says standing over him. 'I'm Detective Helen Brennan from Rathmines Garda station. Believe you are looking into the phone call.'

Charlie swallows a lump down his throat when he sees the woman hovering behind him, then he coughs into his hand.

'Yeah… well, kinda… yeah.'

'Kind of?' Helen hisses.

'Well, I'm just, well eh…' he looks down at his lap, then back up, 'all the intel leads us to believe this is a hoax call, right? Alan Keating.'

'Intel?' Helen says, nodding her head sarcastically.

'Well, Keating's done this before, hasn't he?' Charlie says. 'Besides, who would report a suicide attempt and then just hang up without giving us any names? It don't make no sense.'

Helen wipes her face with her hand and then she squints at the young man sitting in front of her. His ears stick out below his black spikey hair, his nose slightly upturned and pointy at the nub end, making him look like some sort of human-rodent hybrid.

'How old are you, Charlie?' Helen asks.

He creases his brow. 'Twenty-three.'

'Twenty-three? You look ten years younger than that.'

Charlie's brow creases even more. He's not sure if what he's just heard was a compliment or not. It wasn't.

'Well,' Helen says, pulling at a chair from the desk beside Charlie's and wheeling it behind her so she can drop into it. 'I've been asked to look into the suicide angle for Rathmines station. What have you got for me so far?'

Charlie coughs into his hand again, then turns back around to his desk and begins to fidget with his mouse. After a couple silent seconds, he turns to Helen again, the palms of his hands facing upwards.

'I eh... don't really have anything yet. Telephone network can't tell us where the phone call was made from. It was too short... only lasted eighteen seconds.'

'The two of em?' Helen asks.

'Sorry?'

'Did both phone calls last eighteen seconds?'

'Both calls?'

'Yes, Charlie. Two calls were made. One here, one to Rathmines.'

Charlie makes an 'O' shape with his mouth and as he does so, Helen tuts.

'Listen, if two girls commit suicide tonight, you're gonna take a serious amount of time getting over it, d'ye hear me?' she says. 'You and I both. We're gonna find them, we're gonna save them.'

Charlie creases his brow again.

'Do you... eh... do you really think the phone call is legit?' he asks.

Helen looks around herself, swivelling ever so slightly on the chair.

'It's *your* job — *and mine*,' she says, pointing at her own chest, 'to take this phone call as legit. Everybody else, here, and at Rathmines, is treating it as a hoax and getting their knickers in a twist about Alan Keating. But me and you; we're the ones who owe it to these girls to save them. If the call is legit, we can be heroes. If it's not... well, fuck it, there's enough of the force looking into what it might be.'

Charlie offers Helen a smile that makes him look even younger. He stands up, readjusts his navy tie into his sky-blue shirt by repositioning his tiepin and then holds his palm towards Helen.

'You wait here a second, Detective Brennan. I'll go find out what the latest is with tracking the call.'

'It's eh...' Helen says holding her hand out in front of him, 'it's Helen, call me Helen. And,' she looks around again, 'don't tell *anybody* I'm looking into this with you. I'm off duty, but I can't live with the guilt of two girls dying by suicide. I need to be looking into this, whether it's legit or not. Besides, you can use a helping hand, right?'

Charlie smiles again, then winks before pacing to the back of the station. Helen stretches her legs wide apart and swivels side-to-side in the chair again, her fingers forming a diamond shape just above her naval.

She's popping her lips with impatience when the pocket of her coat begins to vibrate. She reaches inside, grabs her mobile phone and then winces when she notices who's calling.

'Hello.'

'Hel, listen, I'm so sorry. I shouldn't have talked to you like that. It was...' Eddie doesn't want to finish his sentence, but Helen's silence forces him to continue. 'It's just, we're pretty certain this is Keating. Fucker's done this to us before, had us running around all night looking for two missing girls when... well... you know. I just wanted to ring you to apologise for being... for being short with you.'

Helen sighs.

'Apology accepted,' she says. 'How's the investigation going?'

There's a slight pause on the other end of the line before Eddie finally speaks up.

'We've got guys all over Keating and his cronies, but God knows what's going on. Chances are they aren't going to be the ones carrying anything out, ye know how Keating operates. So, I guess all we can do is gauge things as we go.'

'But what about the calls that were made... any progress tracking them?'

Another pause.

'Yeah... one phone network gave us an approximate area — somewhere along the Grand Canal between Inchicore and Drimnagh, but no specific number. Anyway...' he says, 'nothing for you to worry about. I'll fill you in in the morning. How about I treat you to breakfast — Bark about ten-ish in the morning?' Helen nods her head. She loves a breakfast at Bark. Best Poached Eggs in Dublin.

'Okay,' she says.

'Good. So... did you get home safe?' Eddie asks.

Helen looks around herself, taking in the cleanliness of Terenure Garda station, noting it in comparison to the one she and her husband work in.

'Yep, all curled up on the sofa... watching *Coronation Street.*'

The line falls silent. For way too long.

'Good... good,' Eddie eventually says. 'So I'll see you, okay? I guess you'll be asleep by the time I get back tonight... we'll do that breakfast when we wake up, huh?'

Helen doesn't answer, she just takes the phone from her ear and presses at the red button. Then she clicks into her news feed; just to see if there have been any oddities reported by the national media recently;

something that might offer her some sort of lead. It's rare that the media would be a step ahead of the cops… but it still doesn't stop Helen from checking. She scrolls. And scrolls. Nothing. The media are just running with the same story they've been running with all day: the two Dublin guys who've been arrested in Rome for stealing from American Central Banks last year. She clicks out of her news feed and places her phone back into her pocket. Then she stands and peers down at Charlie's desk. A framed picture of a pretty girl, way too pretty for Charlie, smiles back at her. She picks it up, puts it back down. Then she picks up a bunch of keys and turns them over in her hand before placing them down. Then an open bottle of Coke. Then a notepad. She's flicking through it when she hears him breathing behind her.

'Charlie,' she says, turning around and dropping his pad back on to his desk, 'whatcha got for me?'

'Don't think anybody's been able to determine where the call was made,' he says, sitting back into his chair. Helen rolls her eyes. 'But I do know it was made — to this station anyway — at six forty-nine p.m.'

'That it?' Helen says.

'Nope,' Charlie responds, shuffling his chair back into his desk. 'I have it here.' He slips a USB stick into the side of his computer screen, then fiddles with his mouse. Helen reaches for the chair she had been sitting in earlier, wheels it closer and plonks herself in it.

'Terenure Garda station, how can I help you?'

'Two girls from my school are going to commit suicide tonight…' the voice sounds panicky. 'I heard them talking about it. They've made a pact. Please help them. They're good girls. Just misunderstood.'

'Thank you for your call, Sir,' a female voice says. 'Can you give me your name to begin with and then I can—'

A dead tone pierces through Charlie's computer.

He turns around and stares at Helen.

'Can't be legit. Who'd ring in a suicide warning without giving us the names—'

'Replay that,' Helen says, interrupting him, 'the bit where he says "please help them".'

Charlie's brow creases, but he turns back to his computer and drags at his mouse again.

'They've made a pact. Please help them.'

'There, hear it?' Helen says.

'Hear what?'

'The Luas. The chiming of a Luas tram.'

Charlie drags at his mouse again.

'Oh yeah,' he says listening to the same two lines over and over. 'The call musta been made somewhere close to the Luas tracks. But sure that could be anywhere.'

'Red Line, between Inchicore and Drimnagh,' Helen says standing up. 'Let's go.'

'Huh?' Charlie puffs out of his mouth, before turning back. He swigs from his bottle of Coke then throws his navy Garda jacket on and follows Helen towards the exit.

'How the hell can you tell the call was made between Drimnagh and Inchicore?' he asks.

Helen doesn't answer.

19:40

Ciara

I LOOK UP INTO THE CORNER OF THE CHIPPER AND NOTICE THE CCTV camera staring down at us. Then it hits me. I bet this footage is going to be shown on the news over the next few days. Our last movements. How the two girls who committed suicide in Rathmines looked happy and were laughing in the local chipper just a few of hours before they ended it all. But I don't mention it to Ingrid. I don't want to take her out of her thoughts. She's more likely to change her mind than I am. In fact, I'm one hundred per cent certain I won't change my mind. I'm going to do this. *We're* going to do this.

I've thought about this day so much over the past two years. I'd have done it two years ago if it wasn't for Ingrid; if it wasn't for the beautiful friend she is. I have the best mate in the whole world. She'd do anything for me. Including kill herself.

'What you staring at?' she says, twisting to look over her shoulder.

'Nothing, nothing. Just thinking.'

'Here ye go, you two,' Marjorie says as she plonks our fries in front of us. 'Enjoy.'

We don't waste time even thanking Marjorie. We just pick up our wooden forks and dive straight in.

This has been our favourite meal for years. We pop in here every Friday after school for chilli chips. I think the secret is in how they melt the cheese on top of the chips before they pour the chilli over. Ingrid thinks it's all in the sauce. It doesn't really matter. Every mouthful is bleedin' delicious.

'I'm gonna miss this,' Ingrid says, her mouth full. She half smiles, then drops the smile. I know how she's feeling. She's excited because she knows her suffering is almost over. But then the suffering hits again. It's a roller coaster of feelings. Up and down. Up and then deeper down. Up and then really, really low down. So low down you can't even be bothered going up again. Just keep me down, get me down. Six foot down. Inside a wooden box.

I've thought about my funeral lots of times. My mam will be sobbing; will probably have to have two people either side of her to hold her up in the church. She'll make it all about her, of course. How my suicide was *her* loss. How my suicide affected *her*. I think my dad'll keep a straight face as usual. He'll pretend to be holding it all together. Or maybe he will be holding it all together. I'm not sure my death will be a huge loss to him. Perhaps it'll be a weight off. Something less for him to care about. I don't think he likes caring. About anyone.

'Penny for em?' Ingrid says.

'Huh?' I refocus my eyes and realise that as I was thinking about my funeral I almost finished my chilli chips.

'Penny for your thoughts.'

I dig my fork into the last of my chips, leave it standing there and then suck at my lips.

'Was thinking about my funeral. How much my mam will be sobbing. She'll probably roar the church down.'

Ingrid's eyes roll upwards. Then she leans back in her chair and folds her arms.

'Bet they'll play a Take That song for me. Probably *Pray*, whatcha think?'

'Defo. A hundred per cent. It'd be madness if they don't play *Pray* at your funeral.'

'Think I'd kinda like to be there… at my own funeral. I want to see who turns up.'

I laugh a little, then pick up my fork again and take another bite.

'Ohhh,' Ingrid purrs.

I look up; my heart beating a little faster. I really don't want her to change her mind. She can't change her mind.

'What's wrong, Ingrid?'

'My last bite. Ever.'

I smile. I think it's from relief more than anything.

'Hold on,' I say. 'My last bite too. Let's do it together, okay?'

We both scrape the bottom of the tin tray our chilli chips came in, so that we have all of the mince, all of the sauce, all of the cheese and all of the chips that are left and then hold the fork up.

'Let's do it,' Ingrid says. And we do. We stuff our mouths with Macari's chilli chips for the final time; both of us holding our eyes closed so we can suck down the deliciousness of our last supper.

'It's fucking delicious,' Ingrid says after she swallows. It always makes me laugh when Ingrid swears. She's so posh that any time she says 'fuck' it sounds as if she uses an 'o' instead of a 'u'.

I rub my belly and then tilt my head sideways. I don't enjoy much in life. That's why I want to end it. But I do enjoy these chilli chips. And now I know I'll never have those tastes in my mouth again. But I genuinely don't mind. We're doing this. Life is not worth living just for a ten-minute taste thrill at Macari's chipper every Friday evening.

'Don't be sad, Ciara,' Ingrid says, placing her hand on top of mine. I'm not sad. In fact I'm happy; happy that she's encouraging me as much as I'm encouraging her.

'I'm not sad,' I reply. 'I'm ready to do this.'

'What do you think it's gonna feel like?' she whispers over the table to me, her fingers tapping on top of mine.

I blow out my cheeks.

'Oh — it won't hurt. We'll be dead before we even know it,' I whisper back.

'Nah, not the actual suicide itself... death. What do you think death feels like?'

I squint at her. How can she be asking such a stupid question? She knows dead means dead. Neither of us are that thick. Even if we are only thirteen. We're not dumb enough to believe we go anywhere after we die. We don't *want* to go anywhere anyway. We don't *want* another life. We want to die because we want to stop all of the horrible thoughts that we have. We spoke about this before we wrote out our suicide pact on the park bench last night.

I place my other hand on top of hers, so her hand is sandwiched between my two.

'Y'know what it feels like before you were born?' I ask.

She looks at me funny.

'Before I was born? Course I don't. I didn't feel anything. How could I?'

'Exactly,' I say.

Her brow points down. Then her eyes widen.

'So, we won't feel anything? Just like before we were born. We only feel when we are alive?'

I nod my head slowly at her. I thought she knew all this. Maybe she just needed reminding. Confirmation. Isn't that the word?

'And that's why we're doing it, isn't it? So we don't need to feel again,' I say, clapping her one hand between my two. She nods back at me, then holds her other hand into our little hand huddle and we both sit there, gripping each other as tightly as we can.

It makes sense she'd have all these questions. I've thought all this through over the course of two years. She's only been suicidal for less than a day.

'I'm not gonna change my mind,' she says shaking her head. And I believe her. She won't. She has never lied to me. I don't think Ingrid is capable of lying. 'Okay, so we're visiting who first? What's the timetable again?' she asks.

I purse a tiny smile back at her and then release one of my hands to hold my finger to my bottom lip.

'So it's Debbie's house first, then Harriet's, then Miss Moriarty's.'

Ingrid nods her head.

'Then what?'

'Then... then we do it.'

She bends a little backwards in her chair so she can see the clock in the middle of the menu behind the counter.

'So we'll be dead around midnight, right?'

I nod my head slowly.

'About that time, yeah.'

IT'S A SORRY SIGHT. I KNOW.

I know because I stare at it every night.

My reflection.

In the windows of the double doors that lead out to our back garden.

I'm fuckin sick of this. Yet it's all I do. Sit here, a glass of wine swirling in my hand, staring at a blurry image of myself.

I take another sip. Taking in my reflection as I do so.

What a loser.

Yet, I know tomorrow evening I'll be doing the exact same thing. And the evening after that. And the one after that. Probably be doing this for all the evenings I have left. Another forty years of sipping wine. That'll take me into my early eighties. Isn't that what they say the average age to die is? Seems like a long way off to me.

I pick up the bottle of wine, pour it into my glass, shaking every last drop out of it, and then huff because it didn't fill my glass enough. So I place both forearms across the kitchen island and lay my forehead on top of them.

'Fuck sake!' I grunt into my elbow. I lift my head slowly, swivel on my stool and slide off it. I drag my slippers as I walk across the tiles and reach up into the cupboard to grab at another bottle of Chateaneuf-du-Pape. Then I drag my slippers over to the slide drawer for the corkscrew and wrestle with the horrible red wrap of film that covers the top of the bottle. I've opened two bottles of this shit every night for the past seven years and I still struggle with the process every time. Opening the second bottle is always more difficult than the first. It'd probably make sense for me to open the two of them when I'm sober and leave them in front of me. But making sense has never really been my thing.

'Fuck!' I say when the sharp point of the corkscrew pinches at the top of my thumb. Then I finally release the film, and am faced with the task of popping the cork itself. I've let one or two bottles slip out of my hands over the years during this part of the process. It should be a helluva lot fuckin easier than this in this day and age to open a bottle of wine. How have they not come up with something better than a bleedin' corkscrew? Sometimes I can nail this in one go. But most times I have to spoon out lumps of cork from my glass after I've poured it.

'Come on, you bitch,' I say to the corkscrew as I yank at it. Pop. Done. Decent job.

I fill my glass, then sit back into my stool and stare at the blurry image of myself again. I often wonder if I stare at this reflection because it hides the lines in my face and makes me look younger. Then I turn my face to notice the time on the oven. 19:50.

What a prick. Why can't he be home with his family? Then I realise his family aren't actually here. Ciara's out too. Where'd she say she was going? I can't remember. Didn't she try to hug me? What the hell was all that about? Silly child. She *is* gone out, isn't she?

'Ciara. Ciara.' I shout it so that I can be heard as far up as the loft. Sometimes she likes to hang out up there. I don't know what she does be doing.

No answer.

She must be gone out. Probably in Ingrid's house.

She'd rather be there than here. I don't blame her.

I envy the Murphys. They've got it all together. A proper family, they are. Terry's as successful professionally as my Michael, but at least he's man enough to stay loyal to his wife and kids. Even if one of the kids is a bit retarded. I'm not sure what his condition is. I keep forgetting. Some new-age made up mental illness that begins with an 'A'. I'm sure it begins with an 'A'.

Maybe it's easier for Terry to stay at home with his family because he has a mental son. Or perhaps it's just easier because his wife's an ex-model. She's beautiful, is Greta. Tall. Slim. Blonde. I'll never be tall. Never be slim. I tried blonde once. Just to see if Michael would like it. He tutted. Said I looked like a tart.

The Murphys have invited us to have dinner in their house loads of times over the past few years. They want us to be closer because our girls are best friends. But we've never taken them up on their offer. That'd be Michael's worst nightmare. A double date with the neighbours. Jesus, could you imagine?

Besides, I'm not that keen myself. Even if by some miracle Michael did agree, I can't really be relied on to do socialising. I'm too... what's the word... too nervy, too anxious. I'd be over-conscious of my dependence on wine. They probably wouldn't want Ciara to pal around with Ingrid anymore if they found out I was a borderline alcoholic. And she needs that friendship more than anything. It's Ingrid who looks after my Ciara. Especially now that Debbie has gone.

I stare at my reflection again and take another sip. Sometimes I swirl the wine around in my mouth to get a sense of whether or not I can taste it anymore. I'm numb to it by now, I think. But I'm not numb to the effect. I need it. I need the alcohol to take the edge off. Couldn't live without it.

I turn my face to look at the oven again. 19:54.

Where is this prick?

I place one foot down, then the other, holding a hand to the edge of the kitchen island for balance, then I drag my slippers across the tiles again, the swish-swash of them irritating me as if my hangover has settled in already. I find myself in the hallway, picking up the telephone and dialling one; the quick dial for Michael's office. He has one of those new fancy mobile phones, but the bloody thing is never switched on.

The tone rings. And rings. Then cuts off.

I blink my eyes so I can become more conscious to my thoughts. What time was it when I looked at the oven clock again? Jesus. I can't remember. I shuffle my way back down the hallway, down the one step that leads to the kitchen tiles and then cock my head so I can see the microwave. 19:56. Yeah. Almost eight o'clock. That's what I thought. I'm sure he's still in the office. He's normally there till ten-ish, even later sometimes. So I shuffle my way back up the hallway and pick up the phone again, dial one and hold the receiver to my ear.

It rings out.

'Fuck sake!' I yell, slamming the phone back down on its receiver.

Then I remember.

'It's a fucking Sunday, isn't it?'

I blow out my cheeks and shuffle my way back to the kitchen. Back to the island. Back to my stool. Back to my wine. And back to my blurry reflection.

THERE WAS A STRANGE SILENCE IN THE CAR, EVEN THOUGH ENERGIES HAD somewhat heightened.

Charlie had already felt as if he'd asked too many questions before they even started the engine. Or at least the same question too many times. So he just concentrated on his driving while Helen stared out the side window of the passenger seat as they made their way towards Davitt Road.

There was no doubt Charlie was intimidated by the lanky woman he thought was a Detective from Rathmines Garda station. Yet he seemed somewhat excited. When he was offered the task of looking into the phone calls as if they were legitimate, he assumed he was put in charge of an insignificant case again; the type nobody else in the station could be bothered looking into. It'd be nothing new for Charlie to be doing a whole lot of nothing for his entire shift. But now that he'd been partnered with a Detective from another station, his mood seemed to be shifting. Adrenaline was threatening to pump inside of him.

'How long you been a cop?' Helen asks, just as they reach their destination.

Charlie indicates left, slots his car into one of the tiny parking spaces outside the Marble Arch pub and then pulls up the handbrake before answering.

'Eighteen months.'

Helen stiffens her nostrils.

'Enjoy it?'

'I will.'

'What ye mean you will?'

'Soon as I'm outta this,' he says, lifting up the flap of his tie and letting it fall back down.

Helen opens her door, stretches her long legs out, and by the time she has walked around the other side of the car, Charlie has done the same. He's zipping up his navy Garda jacket when Helen places a hand on his shoulder.

'What... you want out of uniform already? Wanna be a Detective?'

Charlie nods, then stares down at his clunky black shoes, his jaw clenching. Perhaps he's said too much already.

'You got balls, Charlie? You willing to play the game, not the system?'

Charlie's brow creases. Every time he does this, Helen notices that his nose gets even stubbier.

'Whatcha mean by that?' he asks, looking back up at Helen.

Helen doesn't answer. She steps off the path and, in her own unique stiff way, strides across the road towards the tram stop.

Charlie waits, hands in his pockets, his mind swirling, before he jogs after her.

He observes Helen as she stands still at the tram stop. He's intrigued, not just by how she seems to be going about her job, but by every nuance of her character. Her coat looks, to him, as if she is trying to dress for a role in a cheesy TV series. And her hair? Well... Charlie could barely keep his eyes off it. Is itching to ask her what colour it is. But there isn't a chance that question will ever come out of his mouth. He knows that odd face would offer him a strange stare. And no answer.

'Whatcha looking for?' he asks, his rural accent thick.

'See that?'

'What?'

Charlie's gaze follows Helen's. Right up into the corner of the shelter of the tram stop.

'CCTV.'

Charlie holds his eyes closed, then grinds his teeth. He feels like an idiot. He should have known that's what she was staring at.

'Lights are on. It's working. All along the stop the CCTV seems to be working.' She flicks her wrist, stares at her watch. 'It's eight o'clock. Call was made at six forty-nine you said... over an hour ago.'

Helen huffs out a sigh from her nostrils, then pivots her head left and right, all the way up and down the straight stretch of the Grand Canal.

'No point in us being here, then,' she says. 'We need to go up to the Luas HQ, up to the Red Cow roundabout.'

'To get the CCTV footage from six forty-nine?' Charlie asks.

'Good boy, Charlie.'

He creases his brow again. Then realises Helen is already halfway across the road, heading back to the car. He jogs again to catch up with her.

'Do you mind if I ask you a question, Detective Brennan?' he says.

She doesn't answer as she opens the passenger door and swoops her way inside the car.

When Charlie gets in to the driver's seat, buckles up his belt and ignites the engine, he turns to her.

'How did you know the call came from here, from somewhere along the tram tracks between Drimnagh and Inchicore?'

Helen stares straight out the windscreen.

'You've already asked me that... five times.'

Charlie squirms a little before he shoves the gear stick into reverse and pulls out of the parking space.

'Sirens,' Helen says.

'Really?' Charlie's brow creases again.

When he doesn't get an answer, he flicks the button next to the steering wheel that allows a loud blare to sound from the car and suddenly the speedometer jumps from twenty miles an hour to sixty in the space of five seconds.

'It's just... if I wanna be a Detective, I'd love to learn from you,' he shouts over the sirens.

Helen turns her face and looks him up and down before taking her gaze back through the windscreen. 'You will,' she shouts back.

Charlie smiles to himself. His first smile of the day. He's been frustrated with life. Had become an insurance broker straight from school; working at a small brokers called Fullams before realising he hadn't one Goddamn care about insurance in any capacity. It took two-and-a-half years for him to realise that. When he noticed the Gardaí advertising for new recruits, he assumed a life solving crime would take him out of the boredom of office work. But after landing a job in Terenure Garda station straight after his graduation, he was longing to be back helping people renew their car insurance policies. He hates being a cop, is sick of every colleague at his station talking down to him. The egos he has come across as a Garda stagger him. He can't comprehend why those trusted the most to be as impartial as possible in society possess such vanity. But perhaps he was about to catch a break. If he were to assist Helen in solving a case everybody else was poo-pooing, he might buy himself some credibility. Maybe he could become one of them; somebody who didn't have to wear a fucking tie.

When the siren dies down, so too does Charlie's smile. He leaps out of the car, fixes his hat to his odd-shaped head and makes his way to the front office of the Luas headquarters without even looking back at Helen. He's feeling determined now; transfixed on earning that credibility.

He holds the door open for Helen who scoots by him without thanking him. Then she holds an open palm towards the young woman at the front desk.

'Detective Brennan and Officer…' she turns around, stares at Charlie.

'Guilfoyle,' he says.

'We need to speak with the person in charge of your CCTV.'

The young woman gulps, eyeballs Charlie's uniform and then picks up her phone.

'Can you tell Larry I have two police officers in the reception please.'

'He's coming straight away,' she says to Helen after placing the receiver back down.

Helen takes one step backwards and stands straight and tall as she waits, her arms shovelled deep into her coat pockets. Charlie looks around the pokey reception area and begins to read the work notices on the board. He feels he should look busy, as if he is investigating. He wants to impress Helen. Though he hasn't one darn clue what he's looking for. He's hardly going to solve the mystery of the anonymous phone call by reading staff notices about a new training initiative for tram drivers. After cringing a little, he steps back towards Helen and stands as straight as he can to at least try to match her for height.

'What the fuck were you doing?' Helen whispers.

Charlie turns his head sideways, stares at the unusual face beside him and then shrugs his shoulders. The door flying open saves him from his discomfort.

'Officers, I'm Larry Hanrahan, how can I help you?' says a tall, skinny bald chap in a purple shirt.

'We need to view the CCTV footage of your Drimnagh and Goldenbridge stops between six thirty and seven o'clock this evening,' Helen says.

Larry nods his head once, then holds the door he had just come through open, waving both Helen and Charlie through.

As the three of them pace down an overly warm corridor, Helen taps Larry on the shoulder of his purple shirt.

'I assume, Mr Hanrahan, judging by the fact that you haven't said anything, no other officers have come to you today to view this footage?'

Larry's eyes widen a little.

'No,' he says shaking his head. 'Why, what's going on?'

'Police inquiries, Mr Hanrahan. The case is confidential right now, but there are two separate teams looking into the same case today — two different lines of enquiries. So I assume we won't be the only team calling by this evening.'

Larry purses his thin lips.

'Whatever you guys need,' he says. Then he pushes down on the handle of a heavy door and heaves his way through to a tiny room packed with computer screens.

'Kristine,' this is eh... this is...'

'Officer Guilfoyle and Detective Brennan from eh... well, I am from Terenure Garda station, Detective Brennan here is from Rathmines,' Charlie says.

Kristine stands and stares at Helen as if she was staring a creature from another planet.

'They need to view footage from the Red line, the CCTV from Drimnagh and Goldenbridge stops please,' Larry says.

He approaches Kristine's desk, scribbles some notes on her yellow post-it pad and then stands back a little. Helen strides forward, standing beside Larry and watches as Kristine stabs her chunky fingers at her keyboard.

'Kay, so between six thirty and seven, hmmm...' Kristine mumbles to herself. 'Right, this screen here,' she says slapping a monitor to her left, 'is footage from the Drimnagh stop from six thirty onwards and this one here,' she slaps at the monitor to her right, 'that's Goldenbridge from the same time.'

Helen eyeballs Charlie, then nods her head towards the screen on the right. Charlie steps forward and stares at it. And then Helen does the same on the other side.

'S'what we looking for, Detective Brennan?' Charlie asks.

Helen stares at him almost cross-eyed, making him feel like an idiot again.

'What do you think, Charlie? C'mon, you said you wanted to be a Detective when you grow up. What do you think we're looking for?'

Charlie's shoulders shrink. He looks down, straightens his tie, even though it doesn't need straightening, and then gulps.

'A eh... a young man making a phone call from a mobile phone?'

'Bingo,' Helen says.

19:55

Ingrid

'I SN'T IT MAD TO THINK NOBODY KNOWS WHERE WE ARE, THAT NOBODY'S looking for us? I almost feel... what's-the-word?'

'Free?' Ciara says.

I nod my head. Yeah. I think that's the word I mean. *Free*. In control. As if we don't have to answer to anybody for the first time ever. I'm actually enjoying this. But I know I only feel free because of what we're about to do. If we weren't gonna kill ourselves in a few hours time then I wouldn't feel like this. If I had to go back home and wake up and go to school tomorrow then there's no way I'd be feeling this... what's-the-word... content. Yeah, that's it. I feel content. Maybe it's because I know we've made the right decision. I bet that's why we've been laughing and joking a lot. We're happy with the decision we made.

I turn my face back around and look out the window as the bus shakes its way down the canal road. Ciara just seems to be staring into her lap. She's gone a little quiet. In fact we've both been quiet since we left the chipper about fifteen minutes ago.

'I feel free too,' she whispers. I turn to look at her, grab her hand and clench it really tight. Then I bring her knuckles towards my face and kiss them.

'I love you, Ciara Joyce,' I say.

She smiles at me.

'I love you Ingrid Murphy, ye mad thing,' she says.

We both laugh. And then both sigh after we're done laughing.

527

I return my stare out the window and look into the darkness. Stitch keeps coming into my mind, but I don't want to let him in there. He's been in there way too long and doesn't deserve it. The words he said to me last night keep repeating over and over and over. I need to stop thinking. Maybe I should continue talking to Ciara. The silences will just drive me mad. Even if I do only have about four hours left of the madness.

'It's only two more stops, isn't it?' I ask.

'Yup,' she pops out of her mouth,

'So, do you know what you're going to say to her?'

Ciara sticks out her bottom lip, then shakes her head.

'It's just about... y'know... her realising that I called by to say goodbye, even if I don't—'

'Actually say goodbye!'

She huffs out a small laugh, then looks up at me again and smiles. I'm used to this; Ciara's moods being up and down. I'm never really certain when I knock for Ciara in the mornings before we go to school just what Ciara I'll be walking to school with. Some days she's buzzing; laughing and joking all the way there. Other days she just has her chin resting into her chest, staring down at her clunky shoes as she walks. She's been like that for years. Is never going to change. Some days she's a cross between both moods; can be buzzing one minute, staring at her shoes the next. I've tried to work out what it would feel like to be depressed, but only last night did it really sink in. Then I think of Stitch again and I have to shake my head to get rid of his words.

'What you shaking for?' Ciara asks.

'Nothing. Just eh... just looking out the window here, staring at all these houses.'

'A lot smaller than our gaffs aren't they?' she says.

I nod.

'Yeah. Imagine living in one of them. They're tiny.'

'Bet they have better lives though. I bet the kids in those houses aren't going to kill themselves tonight are they?'

I stare at Ciara and hold my lips tight together. She's right. Dead right. I mean, we have everything we could possibly want. Both of us live on a lovely street, in massive big houses. Ciara's gaff has six bedrooms, ours has five. And we don't even need them. Neither of our families do. There are literally rooms in our homes that we never walk into; that we never use. Ciara's dad is stinking rich. He owns about ten different accountancy and insurance businesses. My parents aren't poor either. My dad's been a big name in broadcasting for about twenty years. I don't know whether

I'd call him rich, but we're certainly not poor. Dad drives a brand new Mercedes. Black it is. Mam has a red Mini Cooper. He's got to be doing well. Having your own show on RTE radio must pay good money, I guess.

We're lucky, Ciara and I. Or at least we should be lucky. But I guess our lives prove it: money can't make you happy. There are kids at our school who go around in ripped runners and who live in tiny little gaffs like these and they're a hundred times happier than me and Ciara. It's always annoyed me when people at school say they want to be surgeons or lawyers when they grow up because they want to be rich. Having a big job that pays lots of money isn't a good ambition. My dad barely listens to me because he's too busy planning for his show. Ciara's dad doesn't listen to her because he's never home. If I was going to grow up I wouldn't want a big job. My ambition would be to pay my children as much attention as I possibly can. That's being a proper parent. A proper adult. I wouldn't care if I was earning a hundred pound a week or a thousand. I'd only care that I was loving my children. Anyway. It doesn't matter. I'll never be a parent. Will never need a career. And that's all fine by me. Cos I don't want any of that stuff.

'Here we are,' Ciara says standing up. She presses at the bell and suddenly the bus is pulling in for us.

'Thanks, mister,' Ciara says to the driver. I just nod my head at him and offer a half smile.

We both leap off the step and then turn left, towards Debbie's. I've never called to her house before but Ciara has pointed it out to me. It's a tiny little gaff; the type of house happy people live in. Debbie is really nice. She practically raised Ciara until sometime last year when, because Ciara was going to secondary school, her mum felt she no longer needed a nanny. Debbie minds three other children now, in Rialto I think it is. That hurts Ciara. I know it does.

'It's that one there with the blue door isn't it?' I say.

Ciara nods her head and then pushes at the gate that leads us into Debbie's tiny garden. It's no bigger than the small room under our stairs that mum keeps all the cleaning stuff in.

Then Ciara holds her finger to the doorbell and we wait until we see Debbie's figure through the frosted glass.

'What the hell are you two doing here?' she says when she answers.

20:05

Ciara

I SKIP FROM ONE FOOT TO THE OTHER AS I WAIT FOR HER TO ANSWER THE door. Haven't seen her in ages. I'm a little excited. I think I am anyway. I've never really been able to tell exactly how I'm feeling. I've always been like that.

'What the hell are you two doing here?' she says when she finally answers. My heart sinks. I thought she'd be delighted to see me.

I look at Ingrid then back up at Debbie.

'I eh... I...'

She opens her door further and stands to the side.

'C'min, girls. But you can't really stay long. I have a friend coming soon. Thought you were him.'

She shuts the door, and I stare at her. She's barely dressed. She only has a black bra and a pair of matching knickers on. They're pretty knickers; they have a little pink bow on the front of them. She must have been getting dressed when we knocked. Maybe that's why she was a little bit upset at first.

Then she holds her arms wide for me and I walk into them. I smell her perfume as we hug, then I rest my chin on her shoulder and try to stop myself from crying.

'Long time no see,' she whispers into my ear.

'Hey, Ingrid,' she says as she releases me. She offers Ingrid a high five and then takes a step back, her hands on her hips. She looks... pretty. *Really* pretty. Like one of those girls you see in magazines. I've never thought of Debbie as pretty before. When she used to mind me she'd wear some oversized jumpers in different colours; normally dark colours like grey or black. Or navy. Mostly navy, I think. And she never wore make up. She seems to have lots on today.

'S'wot you two doing here?'

'We eh… we…' I look at Ingrid.

'We were just in the neighbourhood. I have a friend who lives close by and Ciara said she'd love to pop by to see you… as a little surprise,' Ingrid says.

Debbie takes one step to the side and leans to look through to her sitting room.

'Well, it's lovely to see you. I eh—'

'We won't stay long,' I say. 'Just wanted to say hi and that I miss you.'

Debbie smiles. I miss that smile. I used to see it every day. Now some other snotty little kids get to see it every day.

'I miss you too. Course I do. I think about you all the time.'

Then I smile. At Debbie first. Then at Ingrid. Ingrid will know just how much it means to me that Debbie told me she thinks about me all the time.

The three of us stand smiling at each other in Debbie's hallway. Then the silence goes on a little bit too long. I don't know what to say. I'm here to say goodbye without saying goodbye. Where do I even begin?

'How about a quick glass of squash, then?' Debbie says. 'I'm sorry, but yis can't stay long.'

'Have you blackcurrant squash?' Ingrid asks.

Debbie turns around and walks into her kitchen. We both follow. It's tiny in here. You wouldn't even fit the island we have in our kitchen in this entire room.

'Don't you eh… want to finish getting dressed?' I say as Debbie roots around in a cabinet.

'Yes!' she says turning around. 'I do have blackcurrant.' She holds it up and then looks down at herself. 'Yeah… tell you what, the glasses are there drying by the sink. Fill one for yourselves and I'll be back in a second.'

Ingrid reaches for a glass and begins to run the tap.

'She seems different,' I whisper when Debbie has left.

Ingrid looks back at me, nods her head once. Then she picks up the bottle of squash and pours some into her glass before downing it all in one go.

'Those chilli chips sure are salty,' she says. 'You having a glass?'

I shake my head.

'Nah, I'm alright.'

I feel weird. Really weird. Though maybe I'm supposed to feel weird, seeing as me and my best friend are going to kill ourselves tonight… but I didn't feel this weird on the bus coming out here. There's something odd about Debbie.

I turn and head towards the sitting room to wait for her. Ingrid follows me.

'We shouldn't stay long, not if she has a friend coming over,' Ingrid says to me.

Then I gulp. That's why I feel weird. I know I'm going to say goodbye to Debbie in just a couple minutes for the last time ever. I love Debbie. *Of course* that's why it feels weird… I think. I didn't feel weird saying goodbye to my mam because I really don't care about her. But Debbie… Debbie's different. I love her. She's always been good to me. Like a mother. Like a mother should be. I'm so jealous of the kids she minds these days. Jammy bastards.

Ingrid's eyes widen. As if she's just seen a ghost.

'What?' I ask. But she doesn't answer because we hear Debbie run down the stairs.

'Did yis get a drink?' she says, tightening the belt of her bathrobe around her waist.

'Thought you were getting dressed?' I say.

She puffs out her cheeks.

'I eh… I'm waiting on my friend, then we're gonna decide what to do.'

Ingrid shuffles her way in front of me, her eyes still wide.

'We need to go,' she says, grabbing at my hand.

Debbie gasps a little, as if she choked on her breath.

'Well, out of this room anyway,' she says sweeping both of her arms towards the hallway.

I feel bad again. Weird. It really seems as if Debbie doesn't want us here. As if she is done with me; has moved on to other kids and would rather forget that she ever helped raise me. I'm old to her now. Too old for her to care about. It's only kids she likes.

Then the doorbell rings and Debbie looks at us as if she's annoyed; as if we've done something wrong on her.

'I just wanted to say goodbye,' I say, wrapping my arms around her. She pats me on the back.

'Hey, why don't we meet up soon? I can take you to that park you like in Harold's Cross. We can buy ice-cream, hang out for the day.'

She's said that to me a few times over the past year. We still haven't done it. Then she releases me from my hug and walks towards her hall door and opens it.

'C'min, Gerry,' she says. 'Don't mind the girls. They're just leaving.'

An old man walks in and stares at me and Ingrid. He looks older than my dad. How the hell is he friends with Debbie?

'Okay, girls, out ye go,' Debbie says, almost shoving at the two of us.

My heart sinks. I can't believe this is the last time I'll ever see her and she doesn't even want to know. She doesn't have time for me anymore. Fine. She'll miss me in the morning.

'Goodbye then,' I say.

'Bye,' Debbie calls out without even looking at us. Then the door bangs shut and we're out in the tiny garden, standing right next to the stinky bins.

'What the hell was all that about?' I say.

Ingrid doesn't answer, so I turn to her. Her eyes are still wide.

'Ingrid!'

'Oh my God,' she says holding her hand to her forehead, 'did you see what I saw... in the living room?'

LARRY CONTINUES TO BREATHE HEAVILY BEHIND HELEN. SHE'S TURNED HER cheek in his direction three times now, just to let him know she'd rather he fucked off. But the poor fella hasn't copped her irritation.

'Nothing yet?' Charlie asks.

Helen stares over at him, one of her eyebrows raised.

'Don't you think I'd tell you if I saw something?'

Charlie swallows, then returns his gaze to the screen in front of him, his nose just inches from it.

'If we're gonna see anything we'll see it now, right?' he then says. 'According to this screen it's 6:48. The call to Terenure will be made in one minute. Fingers crossed it's caught on camera.'

Helen doesn't answer. She moves her face nearer to the screen, stretching and then blinking her eyes to relieve some of the strain.

'How old you reckon he is?' she asks.

Charlie takes one step to his left, stares at the figure Helen's pointing at.

'About fifteen,' Larry says.

Both Helen and Charlie look over their shoulder at the bald head behind them. Larry takes one tiny step backwards and sinks his neck into his shoulders a little, finally becoming aware of his insignificance.

'Yeah, about fifteen, I s'pose,' Charlie says as he and Helen return their gaze to the screen. 'Think it's him?'

Then the figure on the screen lifts the phone he had been holding in the palm of his hand towards his ear.

Charlie stares at Helen; his stubby nose a little too close for her comfort. She balks away a bit, all the while staring at the black and white image. She watches as the figure hangs up the phone, before he flips it in the air and catches it.

'It *is* him, isn't it?' Charlie says a little high-pitched. He's beginning to let his excitement pour out of his mouth.

'Well... that call was made at bang on 6:49 and it must've lasted the same eighteen seconds as the call you played for me earlier,' Helen says. She rolls her tongue around her mouth. 'The direction this figure is walking to,' she says turning to Larry, 'he's going towards the next stop, what is it?'

'Suir Road,' Larry says. 'You want me to call up that footage?'

Helen nods her head, then places her hands in to the deep pockets of her leather coat.

'This is so cool,' Charlie says.

Helen stares at him, until he realises what he had just said was rather *uncool*.

''Kay, here we go,' Larry says, tilting another screen towards both Charlie and Helen. 'This is the Suir Road stop from 6:49 onwards.'

'How long does it take to walk from Goldenbridge stop to Suir Road?'

'Two, three minutes. Straight down the canal,' Larry says.

The three of them stare at the screen while Kristine, who had been tapping away at the keyboard on her desk, stops and turns to look at them. She watches their faces, waiting on a moment of realisation to drop on one of them. But it doesn't come.

'It says 6:53 now on the screen, he hasn't walked this way, he'd be here by now.'

Helen spreads both of her lips open, so that her clenched teeth are showing. Then she slams the palm of her hand against the top of the screen.

'Bollocks,' she says.

'What's it matter?' Charlie says. 'We got a shot of him. Isn't that enough to go on?'

Helen holds her eyes closed in annoyance and then lets a sigh slowly exhale its way out of her nostrils.

'I wanted to see what direction he was walking in next, Charlie. It might help us catch up with him.' She nods her head and stretches her brow sarcastically as she says this. Charlie sinks his neck into his shoulders. Helen has an incredible ability to make men do this. It's why she initially fell in love with Eddie; because he never shied away from her. He was her perfect match. Always has been.

'He could have gone anywhere after the Goldenbridge stop, right? Over Goldenbridge itself into Inchicore. Across to Drimnagh past the Marble Arch pub? Onwards down the other side of the canal towards... Jesus, he could have splintered off in any direction after that, right?'

'Yup, on towards the hospital or perhaps Kilmainham. Could have even headed up towards Rialto.'

Helen allows another sigh to shoot through her nostrils. Then she chews on her bottom lip as Kristen answers a ringing phone.

'Larry, two more police officers at the front desk looking to view CCTV,' she says.

'Ah, must be the friends you were telling me about,' Larry says to Helen as he makes his way towards the door.

'Hold on, hold on, Larry,' Helen shouts out, 'Charlie, take out your mobile phone, get a clear picture of the best still of that young boy we have. Kristine,' she says as if she's an army major barking out orders, 'can we make this image any clearer?'

Kristine rises from her desk, begins to tap away at a keyboard right next to Charlie.

'Shall I go get your colleagues—'

'No, hold on!' Helens says, holding the palm of her hand towards Larry.

He creases his brow, begins to wonder what the hell is going on.

'That's as clear as I can get it,' Kristine says.

Helen nods towards Charlie, ordering him to take a picture with his phone.

'Kay let's go,' Helen then says, cupping his shoulder.

'Larry you can go get the other officers... is there a eh... Ladies room you can show me to on the way?'

Larry nods slowly. 'Yeah, there's one just here, down this corridor.'

Charlie and Helen leave with Larry, forgetting to thank the only person who was actually helpful to them while they were in the control room. Kristine doesn't mind. Is used to not receiving praise for the mundane tasks she carries out.

'Through there,' Larry says pointing at a door.

'You come with me, Charlie,' Helen says.

Charlie stops walking. 'What? Sorry? You want me to go to the Ladies with you?'

Larry stops walking too, but when Helen turns to face him, he gets the gist and then heads towards reception to allow the other offices through. Helen strides to the door and holds it open to allow Charlie to enter before her. He scratches at his forehead, wondering what the fuck Helen is up to, inviting him into this pokey, smelly cubicle.

'Let me see the photo?' she says, still holding the door ajar. She peeks through the crack of the door, then back at Charlie. After he's handed her the phone, she peeks through the crack again, notices Cyril and Leo from her own station being led to the CCTV control room.

When they're inside, the door closed behind them, Helen pulls at the toilet door and walks out. Charlie doesn't know what to do; whether or not he should follow her. So he stands still, waits on instruction.

Helen brings his phone closer to her nose, refocuses her eyes to the image of the boy. He looks blond, though it could be brown hair. His face isn't really clear. Could be anybody, really.

'Fuck sake,' she mumbles to herself. Then she pivots her head left to right. 'What the fuck?' she says. She turns around, strides in her own unique way towards the toilet and pushes the door wide open.

'What the hell are you doing? Will ye come on?' she says.

Charlie opens his mouth to respond, then thinks better of it, so he just follows Helen like a trained puppy dog back down the corridor, past the reception and out towards his own police car. He's still wondering what the hell just happened when he presses at a button on his key ring, allowing Helen — who is still a couple yards ahead of him — to swing the passenger door open and sweep her tall frame inside.

He scratches at his head again, then opens the driver's door and gets in himself.

'Eh... sorry, Helen, but eh... what was all that about?' he says.

'What was what about?' she says as she reaches for her seatbelt.

'Why eh... why did you invite me into the toilet?'

'Oh, that?' Helen responds. She sniffs her nose. 'Normally lights in toilets are more clinical.... to stop people from shooting up in them. You can't find a vein if the light is clinical. Did you not know that?'

Charlie creases his brow at her, making himself look as young as the boy he took a photograph of just a few minutes ago.

'Public toilets in bars and restaurants maybe, but not a bloody office toilet,' he says. Then he shrinks into his chair a little, in fear of what way Helen will react to him questioning her.

She swipes a sleeve across her mouth, wiping up some of the moisture under her nose.

'Yeah, you're right. There was no clinical light. Just thought we should give it a go,' she says.

Charlie's brow hasn't uncreased and his silence makes Helen look at him for the first time since they returned to the car.

'I just wanted to see what other Detectives were looking into the CCTV footage, wanna know who's on the job, okay?' she says, relenting.

'Why?'

Helen shrugs her shoulders.

'See who we might need to lean on later if we need anything.'

Charlie scratches at his head again, the lines in his brow still wedged deep.

'But why the secrecy, why didn't we just tell them we had a visual of the boy who made the phone call?'

Helen whistles, a slow piercing whistle. 'Wow, young Charlie, you've a lot to learn about this Detective business,' she says. 'Now; given the information we have, where d'ye think we should go next? If you were leading this investigation, where would your next port of call be?' she asks, changing the direction of the conversation.

Charlie sits more upright, grabbing the steering wheel with both hands, then makes repeated bop sounds with his lips as he thinks through Helen's question.

'Well,' he says, 'we don't really have anything, do we? A grainy picture of a boy who looks to be in his mid-teens. We don't know where he went after the call... so eh...' he scratches his forehead again, 'I actually don't know.'

Helen allows a small snigger to creep its way from the corner of her mouth.

'You're right,' she says. 'That *is* all we have. One grainy picture of a boy. A boy whose friends are going to commit suicide in about four hours. It's not much to go on. But we can't sit here and wait for those two girls to tie nooses for themselves. We have to act. *Think*. Where could we possibly get information from about the boy in this image?'

Charlie brings his fingers to his mouth and begins to tap away at his bottom lip.

'Sorry, Detective Brennan. But I actually don't know. Walk the streets, show young people the image, ask if they know who he is?'

Helen nods.

'Not bad, Charlie,' she says. 'We could do that. But that'd take an awful lot of time. Time we don't have. What about the school next to that Luas stop, the one on the Drimnagh side of the canal.'

'Yeah, Mourne Road school. What about it?' Charlie asks.

'That'd be the place to start wouldn't it? Rather than ask a hundred teenagers on the streets of Inchicore and Drimnagh if they know this youngfella, we can ask the Head of the school. He's bound to know every teenager in that whole area.'

'Ahhh,' Charlie says as he places the key in the ignition.

Then he pulls the car out of its parking spot and heads towards the Naas Road.

'But hold on a minute,' he says, 'the school'll be closed now. It's half eight in the evening.'

Helen flicks her eyes towards him.

'Jesus, Charlie… you do have a lot to learn.'

She takes her mobile phone out of her pocket and begins to flick her fingers across its screen.

20:25

Ingrid

THE DOORBELL RINGING FRIGHTENS ME, TAKES ME OUT OF THE SHOCK I'M in. I can't believe it. Debbie?

My eyes are wide when an old man walks in, wearing a suit. He must be fifty, sixty even? I don't know. I'm not good with ages.

He stares at me and Ciara as if he's never seen two teenage girls before.

'Kay girls, out ye go,' Debbie says. She holds both of her arms out, almost pushing us to the door. That's fine by me. I want to get out.

'What the hell was all that about?' Ciara says when we're standing in Debbie's tiny front garden.

I don't answer her. I'm too busy thinking about Debbie. I think I'm in shock.

'Ingrid!' Ciara says.

'Oh my God,' I reply. I still haven't decided if I want to tell Ciara. It'll break her heart. 'Did you see that... in the living room?' I ask. Ciara's face goes all scrunchy. She does that when she's confused. 'Cocaine,' I whisper. 'Loads of it on a little mirror. I know. I've seen cocaine in films.'

Ciara's face is no longer scrunchy. She's making an 'O' shape with her mouth. Her eyes are kinda making the same shape too. She knows I'm not making this up. I've never lied to Ciara. I've never lied to anyone. Not until tonight. Not until I told my mum I was going to Ciara's to study.

Then Ciara swallows really hard.

'Debbie? Drugs?' she says. 'That doesn't make any sense.'

Ciara blinks then twists her head left and right. I know Ciara inside and out. I know she wants to go back in there. She'll have to know the truth. So I hold my hands to the back of both her shoulders and try to lead her out of Debbie's gate, back to the bus stop.

'C'mon,' I say. 'We've got to go say our goodbyes to Harriet and Miss Moriarty.'

But Ciara bends forward a little, places her hands on both of her knees and begins to breathe a bit heavier.

'C'mon, Ciara, let's go. You've said goodbye to Debbie. Two more stops. Then we can finally get ourselves away from all these thoughts. Please. C'mon… let's go.'

She stands up straight, blows a large breath through her lips and then heads straight for Debbie's door, pressing her finger against the bell and holding it there until Debbie snatches the door open.

'Whatcha playing at, Ciara?' she says. She seems to have lost her bathrobe; is back in just her bra and knickers again.

Ciara storms by her, heads straight for the living room. I don't want to follow her in. But I kind of have to. I have to be by my friend's side.

When I get to the living room I see the old man with his shirt all open, lipstick marks on his chest. Ciara is pacing around the living room, looking for the mirror I told her had cocaine on it. When she looks up at me I nod my head to the corner of the room, where a nest of tables sit. Ciara walks over to it, picks up the small mirror and then stares at Debbie.

'Ciara Joyce, that is none of your—' but before Debbie can get her full sentence out, Ciara holds the mirror above her head and throws it as hard as she can against the wall. She walks over to Debbie and I can see her jaw moving in circles, like it does when she gets really angry. I blink my eyes, because I think I know what's going to happen next. Ciara raises her hand, slaps Debbie across the cheek and then turns to me.

'Let's go, Ingrid,' she says. And we do. We run out of the house, out the garden gate and down the avenue. After a while we are both out of breath. Both hunched over, holding on to our knees.

'Whew,' Ciara says, before she starts laughing. 'That was mad.'

I look at her in shock. Though I don't know why I'm in shock. I know Ciara better than anyone. I know she can be really angry one minute, laughing her head off the next.

'What did you do that for?' I say.

She stops laughing and looks up at me.

'That bitch is doing drugs,' she says, pointing back to the avenue

Debbie lives on. 'She was supposed to be one of my best friends. Like a parent to me. The only adult I thought cared for me.'

Ciara takes steps closer, waving a finger at me as if it's all my fault. But I catch her as she continues to rant, and wrap both my arms around her. I let her cry on my shoulder. Again. This is nothing new. Though it was quite the opposite last night.

'But... but Debbie has her own life outside of being your nanny,' I say, as if I'm protecting Debbie. I don't know why, though. I'm as shocked and as disappointed as Ciara is.

'Debbie? Drugs?' she says, wiping at her nose after she's lifted her head from my shoulder.

I just shake my head a little. I want to tell Ciara that I think she overreacted; that she didn't need to smash Debbie's mirror; that she didn't need to slap her across the face. But I won't. I'll just keep her close by me, my arms wrapped around her waist until she stops crying.

'This will all be over soon,' I say, stooping my head a little to catch her eyes. I want her to stare at me. 'We want out of this life, right? Look, we can't even say goodbye to the people closest to us without getting upset. We're just... we're just not right for this life. Time to do this, Ciara. Let's just do it!'

Ciara swipes at her nose again as her eyes stare into mine. She offers me a tiny smile, then nods her head once.

'Okay, let's just do it. Let's do it now!'

'Ciara Joyce. You come over to me right now!'

I look over my shoulder. It's Debbie. She's tightening the belt of her bathrobe around her waist again.

Ciara turns, runs as fast as she can and I sprint after her.

'Ciara! Ingrid!' We can hear Debbie shout, but her shouts are getting further and further away.

'Here's the bus, here's the bus,' Ciara says. We both stop running. Then I see that look in Ciara's eye. She's changed moods again. The tears have stopped.

'Let's run out in front of it, ye ready?' she says, grabbing both of my hands. 'On three. One, two—'

'No! Wait!' I scream. 'I'm not ready. I'm not ready.'

20:25

Michael

I FUCKIN LOVE THIS STUFF. I PINCH AT MY NOSE, MAKING SURE NONE OF IT falls back out, then duck my head down again, grab at the rolled up note and sniff.

'Fuck yeah,' I say.

Claudia laughs, then sits up and kisses me, her tongue filling my mouth.

'C'mon, fuck me,' she begs, lying back down on my desk.

She looks fuckin deadly with her blonde hair all sprayed out over my work notes. I hired her because she reminds me of that filthy lookin' bitch who lives up the street from us. The Swedish one. Ingrid's mam. Jesus, I'd love to fuck her brains out. That jammy bastard Terry Murphy gets to bang her every night. That's good snatch he gets to play with for someone who's such a known bore.

I squint my eyes a little, just so Claudia's face turns into Ingrid's mam's and then I slap both of her thighs wide open and shove my dick inside.

I've had tighter pussy. But I didn't know what I was hiring, did I? I could hardly have a go on her before she started working here. That's not how it goes down.

It's the power these chicks are into. You have to exert the power before they'll let you inside them. Once they figure they have opportunity to better themselves in the workplace, they'll do anything. Filthy bitches. I'm riding three birds from the office at the minute. This time last year I had five on the go. That's how it works round here. It's my thanks to myself for building this place up from scratch.

'Yeah, ye filthy slut,' I say grabbing a fistful of her hair. I continue to thrust in and out of her, enjoying each and every one of her little squeals. Then the fucking phone rings. Again.

Claudia lifts her head to stare at it. As if she's never seen a phone ringing before. I yank at her hair and pull her back into position.

'Ignore it,' I say. 'It'll be just my wife.'

HELEN PUFFS OUT HER CHEEKS, PLACES THE PHONE IN THE DRINKS HOLDER next to the gear stick and then turns to face Charlie.

'He lives in Walkinstown. A Mr Patrick Tobin. Balfe Road.'

'Okay,' Charlie replies, swinging the car around. 'D'ye think he'll know the boy in the image?'

Charlie can see Helen staring at him in his peripheral vision and, in that moment, realises the question he asked was quite stupid. How could she possibly know that? 'Sorry,' he says.

Helen looks away, back through the windscreen.

'No need to apologise, Charlie. He's more likely to know the teenagers in this area than anyone. He works with them all day every day. So... there's more chance of him knowing who the boy is in the image than anyone.'

Charlie nods his head. He's glad, more than anything, that Helen didn't snap at him. Maybe she's beginning to warm to his company.

He shifts his ass cheeks, leaning from one to the other, as he drives, wondering whether or not he should ask her a question that's been burning his mind ever since she first walked up to his desk about an hour ago. He scratches at his forehead, then sucks in a cold breath through his teeth.

'Mind me asking you a question?' he says. He tenses his eyeballs as he awaits the response.

Helen turns to face him again.

'Go on.'

'It's just eh... it's just...' he pulls at his ear lobe, 'every other member of the teams, at Rathmines and at Terenure stations, are eh... well they don't believe the call is legit, do they? They're out trying to stop something major from happening. Why do you eh... why do you think the calls *are* genuine? Do you really believe two girls really are out there somewhere wanting to kill themselves tonight?'

Helen arches an eyebrow, then returns her gaze through the windscreen to allow a silence to settle.

'It's personal,' she says.

'*Personal?*' The pitch in Charlie voice rises.

'Listen,' Helen says, pulling at the strap of her seatbelt and turning side on so she can face Charlie. 'What did they teach you in Temple Moor when you were training as a cop about dealing with phone calls to the station?'

Charlie nods his head once. 'To treat every call as seriously as the caller themselves.'

Helen doesn't say anything, she just opens both of her palms and then closes them.

Charlie shifts in his seat again.

'It's just... it's just, the caller wasn't really serious was he? The youngfella didn't give any names... any location. It just screams as a hoax call to get us out here looking for something that probably isn't happening. Meanwhile, something else is going down—'

'Charlie shut the fuck up!' Helen spits out of her mouth. 'Listen to me, and listen to me carefully. There are enough Detectives and officers out there looking into the possibility that this was a hoax call. Too many if you ask me. I'm actually furious with how this phone call is being considered by both of our stations. A suicide concern is not... *not*... to be taken lightly.'

Charlie glances over at Helen, the emotion in her voice offering the first slither of evidence that there's a heart beating somewhere beyond that leather coat.

He wants to ask more, is repeatedly lifting his bum cheeks from side to side in anticipation of asking more. But he stops himself.

'Sirens,' Helen then says.

Charlie doesn't even look at her to question the instruction. They're not attending an emergency, but he knows matters need to be dealt with as soon as possible. He's not fully convinced, as much as Helen seems to be, that there are two girls out there planning to commit suicide. But if they are, the clock is ticking.

He steps on the gas, overtaking cars with his sirens blaring and heads past Crumlin shopping centre towards Walkinstown; towards the home of the local school's Headteacher.

'If we find the boy, we'll know everything,' Helen shouts over the siren.

Charlie nods his head. He knows she's right. Regardless of whether or not there are two girls out there wanting to end their lives, or whether it's just Alan fucking Keating playing games with the cops, they need to track down the boy who made the phone calls. This is a proper investigation, no matter what way Charlie looks at it; his first proper investigation. Normally he's dealing with domestic disturbance calls, or calls from annoyed elderly neighbours giving out that boys are using their gates as goalposts for their little street football matches. Life as a rookie cop really hadn't lived up to the dramatic hype painted in a lot of TV shows Charlie used to watch.

'D'ye think the other cops will be coming out to this Headteacher's house as well? Think they'll be just behind us?' he asks.

Helen shakes her head.

'Doubt they'd have thought of it this way. They'll be wasting time trying to view other CCTV footage of where they think that boy would have gone to next. They'll be trying to trace his movements. But sure, that was almost two hours ago now since he made that call. He could be anywhere. They're trying to find *where* he is... me and you, we're gonna find out *who* he is. That's because we're better investigators,' she says. She then winks at Charlie. He's not sure how to feel about the wink. It sure looked weird. And came at the end of a very weird comment. But it's more confirmation that she's warming to him; that she's happy to teach him as they go.

Despite his growing confusion, he doesn't say another word as he races the car up Balfe Road, before turning sharply — causing Helen to grip the handle of the passenger door as her body leans towards Charlie.

'What number we looking for?' he asks as he reaches for a small switch that turns off the siren.

'It's that one there,' Helen says pointing, 'look, he's outside waiting for us already.'

As Charlie is pulling in, to park his car across the drive of the man they've come to visit, Patrick Tobin strides towards them.

'Hi, officers,' he says. 'I got your call. I do hope none of my students are in trouble.'

Helen waits until she is fully out of the car, standing upright and towering over the short, balding man, before answering.

'We believe two of them may be in quite a bit of danger,' she says. 'May we?' She points towards his open front door.

'Please,' he says. He leads them up his modest garden path, into his modest home before closing the door and holding a hand to his forehead. 'Which two students is it?' he asks.

'Well, that was the information we were hoping you could help *us* with, Mr Tobin,' Helen says. 'We have a picture to show you. Can you name this individual? We believe he may be a student of yours...'

Helen looks behind her, her hand outstretched. Charlie's eyes widen.

'Shit,' he says, 'left me phone in the car. Gimme one sec.' He rushes back out the door.

Helen sighs. A deep, frustrated sigh.

'What is it? What's wrong?' Tobin asks, tilting his head. He had initially been annoyed, thinking students had been up to no good. But he's sensed a haunting mood since the police entered his home. This news is bad. Really bad.

'We've had a call saying two young girls are planning to die by suicide locally tonight. At midnight. We don't have much time to save them. A young boy rang in to give us that information, but he didn't leave any names, any locations.' Tobin scrunches up his nose, then squints at Helen. 'We don't know why,' Helen says, answering the question before it could come out of Tobin's mouth.

'Here,' Charlie says, racing back in the door, holding his phone out.

'We are hoping you can give us the name of the individual in this image,' Helen says.

Tobin takes the phone and stares at the screen as he walks towards his green sofa and sits in it. Helen winces a little as she watches his head begin to sway from left to right.

'No, I'm sorry. I mean the image is not very clear but I don't think I know this face. I'm pretty certain he's not a student in my school.'

Helen runs her hand up and down the back of her neck, tossing her orange hair into a mess. She's gutted; genuinely felt she was going to leap yards in front of the other investigation.

'Are you sure, Mr Tobin? Take another look.'

Tobin shakes his head again.

'Sorry,' he says, handing the phone back to Charlie. 'Is there anything else I can help with? I'm willing to help, as much as I can. Course I am. I care for every one of my students. I can't believe... I can't believe two of them are planning on committing suicide. You have to stop them... you just have to stop—'

'We will, Mr Tobin. Rest assured we are doing all we can. We just need to know who they are. If we knew who this young man was, we could get to the girls.'

Helen washes her hand over her face this time, giving herself a quiet moment to think.

'Are there any girls in your school suffering with depression that you know about?' she asks.

Tobin blows out his cheeks.

'Well... yes, we have so many issues with so many students. Depression?' He blows his cheeks again. 'You'd really need to speak with Sana Patel. She's our safeguarding and student welfare officer. Bloody good at her job, she is. Knows every student inside out.'

'Can you get her on the phone for me?' Helen asks.

Tobin stands up, reaches for the mobile phone on his mantle piece and begins to scroll through it.

'Hey, ring her on Facetime... you got Facetime?' Charlie asks. Tobin looks at him as if he has two heads. 'Sana Patel, you said, yes?' Charlie says, taking the phone from Tobin. He scrolls through it, then scrolls through his own phone with his other hand.

'Got her,' he says,' holding his own phone in front of his face as a gurgling tone rings.

'Hello,' a woman answers.

'Ms Patel, my name is Charlie Guilfoyle, I'm a Garda at Terenure station, this here,' he says turning the screen to face Helen, 'is Detective Helen Brennan from Rathmines station and I'm sure you know who this man is.' He turns the screen towards Tobin who holds his hand up to say hello to his colleague.

'Oh my,' she says, with a subtle Indian accent, 'what is going on? Are you okay, Patrick?'

'I'm fine, I'm fine,' he says.

'It's a couple of your students we are worried about,' Charlie says. 'I want to show you a photograph of a young boy. I need you to tell me if you recognise him.'

Charlie fumbles with both phones, mumbling to himself as he does so, then turns the image of the boy on his phone towards Tobin's screen.

'Take your time, Ms Patel, don't come to a conclusion straight away, allow the image to sink in,' Helen says. As she's saying this, she holds her eyes closed in anticipation, her fists clenched inside her coat pockets.

'No. No, sorry. He's not one of our students. I know the picture isn't clear, but I could tell if he was one of ours.'

Helen shows her teeth; her hands tightening into a firmer ball inside her pockets. Then she lets out a huge grunt.

'Okay, Ms Patel. We have one more question for you,' she then says, trying to compose herself. 'Can you tell us of any girls who have come to you with any suicidal tendencies recently.'

'Oh my,' she says 'what is going on?'

'We just need answers to the questions, Ms Patel,' Helen says.

'Okay, okay. Let me compose myself. You have me so worried. Suicidal tendencies. No!' she says, matter of factly.

Helen holds her eyes closed.

'What about depression? Any female students talk to you about feeling depressed?'

'Oh yes, oh yes,' Sana says.

Helen's eyes widen. And when Charlie glances towards her, she winks at him.

'Can you give me the names of those girls?' Helen says.

'Of course. But we'd obviously have to go through the proper procedure in order to—'

Helen snatches the phone from Charlie, pointing the screen towards her own face. She notices Sana balk backwards at the sight of her. Helen's aware she's odd looking. Is used to this kind of reaction.

'Excuse my French here, Ms Patel. But *fuck* procedure. Two students of yours are planning on killing themselves tonight. Two girls. I need access to the list of female students who have ever confided in you about depression.'

Sana's mouth falls open. She doesn't answer. Is too shocked to talk.

'Sana, you have my permission to share the information with these Guards,' Tobin says. 'This is an emergency. We'll deal with all of the red tape tomorrow. Just let these officers do their job as quickly as they can.'

Sana nods her head.

'Wait there,' she says. 'I need to access my computer.'

Helen winks a thank you towards Patrick, then holds a hand on Charlie's shoulder. A breakthrough at last. She's gonna find out who these two girls are. Is gonna save their lives. It'll make up for the fact, somewhat, that she couldn't save Scott's.

'Okay,' Sana says down the line. 'I have my notes here. What do you want me to do, read out the names?'

'Yes. Please,' says Helen.

Sana clears her throat.

'Okay. Jacinta Archer.'

Helen nods at Charlie.

'Elaine Bailly. Anna Barnes. Nicole Casey. Elizabeth Clarence. Sarah Dunne...'

Helen's eyes squint.

'Are you... are you reading these names in alphabetical order?' she asks, bringing the screen to her face again.

'Yes, officer,' Sana says.

'How many girls have you had come to you to talk to you about their depression?'

'This year, officer?'

Helen nods slowly.

'Yes.'

'Eh... lemme see...'

Helen watches as Sana's lips mumble her counting. She looks up at Charlie. Then at Tobin.

'Modern times,' Tobin says, shrugging his shoulders.

Helen holds her eyes closed, gripping the phone as firmly as she can, her knuckles whitening.

'One hundred and sixty-four,' Sana says.

'Ah for fuck sake!' Helen roars.

20:35

Ciara

I'M BREATHING REALLY HEAVILY. I'M NOT USED TO RUNNING SO MUCH. Ingrid's fitter than me. Always has been. She could probably keep on running. But I can't. I stop. And bend over. I can't get the slap out of my head. Jees, that was probably bad. But she deserved it.

Debbie. Drugs.

I can't believe it. But I have to. Because I saw it with my own eyes.

I have my hands on my knees, breathing as heavily as I can to try and get rid of the sharp pain in my chest. Then I hear it. A bus. It's coming down the road quite fast. I can end it all right here. Right now.

I grab both of Ingrid's hands and stare into her eyes.

'Let's run out in front of it, ye ready?' I breathe in and out really heavily. 'On three. One, two—'

'No! Wait!' Ingrid shouts in my face. 'I'm not ready. I'm not ready.'

She releases both of her hands from mine and wraps her arms around my waist, pulling me back as I try to step out onto the road. The bus whizzes by. Beeping its horn.

Wow. I nearly did it then. I nearly killed myself. After years of telling myself I would do it and chickening out every time, I nearly did it just then. It seems a little bit... I don't know... exciting.

'Jesus Christ, Ciara,' Ingrid says, releasing her grip on me and then holding a hand to each side of my face. 'Let's calm down a bit. We have a pact. We have to stick to the pact.'

She's right. We discussed this last night. Then we wrote out a pact that we swore we'd stick to.

She uses her weight to push me back a little until I'm sitting on a small wall outside somebody's house. Then she sits beside me and throws her arm around my shoulder.

'Ciara, how stupid would that have been?'

I nod my head, then look up to the sky and suck up the wet snot that's running down my nose. What was I thinking?

'I know. I know,' I say, blinking away some tears.

'Jesus, we could have ended up in hospital, like vegetables forever.' I nod my head again, swipe my sleeve under my nostrils and then look at my best mate. 'You talked me through this,' she says. 'We spent two hours talking through this last night. There are ways to do it and ways not to do it. Running out in front of a bus is not a way to do it.'

I lean my head onto the top of her shoulder.

'It's just... Debbie. Drugs,' I say.

I hear Ingrid swallow.

'I can't believe it,' she says.

Me neither. I really can't. I've a lot going on in my mind right now. But the shock of Debbie doing drugs is taking over.

'And what the hell was that guy doing there?' I say, taking my head up off Ingrid's shoulder and turning to face her.

Her eyes are all wet. She shakes her head, sticks out her bottom lip.

'Were they... were they having sex?' I ask.

Her lip stretches out further and then she shrugs her shoulders.

'What a bitch!' I say.

'Hey,' she says. 'It's Debbie. There must be some... some... what's-the-word?'

'Explanation?'

'Yeah... explanation, there has to be.'

I shake my head slowly. I really can't think straight.

'There was cocaine on the mirror and she was in only her bra and knickers. That old man's shirt was all open... uuuugh,' I say as an image of the grey hairs on his chest come into my mind. 'He was older than our dads.'

Ingrid closes her eyes. Tight. She's remembering the chest hair too. Some of it had lipstick marks on it.

I rub at my face with both hands. Then Ingrid leaps from the small wall, wraps her hands around my waist and leans into me. I place my cheek on top of her head and just look down the street at nothing. The road is totally silent. As are we. Except for the thoughts that are going around in our heads non-stop. We need to shut them up. Shut them up once and for all.

I'm glad Ingrid stopped me running in front of the bus. Glad we're going to do this right. Just as we had planned. It won't be long. Two more bus rides. Two more houses to visit. Then we're done. For good.

I suck up my nose again, to stop snot from dropping onto Ingrid's beautiful hair. I've always loved her hair. Never been jealous of it though. Ingrid is too nice to ever be jealous of. I've only ever been jealous of her once; when she told me that Stitch asked her to be his girlfriend. I fancied him first.

'If anything, tonight has proved we've made the right decision,' she says, lifting her head. 'Think about it. You tried to say goodbye to your mum, she didn't want to know. You tried to say goodbye to Debbie, she didn't want to know. I know some people love us but…' Ingrid shrugs her shoulder as tears start to fall down her cheeks. She wipes one of them with her baby finger, then smiles up at me. Not a real smile. A fake smile. A pity smile.

'No need for us to cry,' I say, leaping off the wall. 'We've made a decision. There's not long to go, Ingrid. Couple more stops. Soon all this pain will be gone.'

We hug each other, knowing there's probably going to be another fifty hugs like this before we finally do it.

'So… off to Harriet's, then. You know what you're going to say to her?'

Ingrid almost laughs. Then she shakes her head.

'Same problem isn't it? Got to say goodbye without letting anybody know we're saying goodbye,' she says.

I think of my mam again; imagining her crashing to her knees when the police call to the house after our bodies are found. Sobbing her heart out. But she'll only be crying because of herself. Not because of me. Then I think of my dad; wondering how he'll take the news. He'll be put out. He'll have a funeral to arrange. A drunk wife he'll have to try to keep sober until the funeral is all done. He'll be so relieved when it's all out of the way. Then he can get back to doing… whatever the hell it is he does.

'Think your dad will do a show about us?' I say as Ingrid's parents come into my mind.

Ingrid nods her head.

'Definitely,' she says. 'He'll even begin some sort of suicide charity, won't he?'

We stand in silence thinking about that. She's right. That's exactly what Terry Murphy will do. He'll be on every chat show in Ireland talking about us over the next few months. Pity we won't be around to see that. I've thought about that kinda thing a lot over the years. It's quite annoying that I'll never be around to see the aftermath of my suicide. My mam crashing to her knees. My dad rolling his eyes during the funeral as my mam cries into his chest like a baby. The students at our school being given the news at assembly in the morning. The look on the faces of those who will feel most of the guilt.

Jaysus, if only we could turn into ghosts straight after we die and come back and watch all of the carnage we've left behind. That'd be ace.

'Will we go then?' Ingrid says, shivering a little. We've been standing in the cold too long, thinking about stuff we've thought about way too many times already.

'C'mon then, let's catch the bus to Harriet's. I promise I won't try to jump in front of it this time.'

Ingrid puffs another one of those laughs out of her nose, then throws her arm around me as we walk towards the bus stop on the far end of the road. We're strolling, very slowly, when flashing blue lights flicker in the sky.

'Girls,' a voice calls out. 'Stop right there!'

20:40
Debbie

I HOLD MY HAND TO MY CHEEK. JESUS FUCKIN CHRIST DID THAT HURT. NOT just the slap. But her running away, the disappointment on her chubby little face. I haven't seen Ciara's face that purple since she used to struggle to poo into her nappy when I first started minding her. I feel so bad. So guilty.

I shiver as I walk back towards my house, holding my bathrobe closed around my waist. I'm not sure if most of my shivering is down to the cold, maybe it's the guilt; the embarrassment. I pivot my head up and down my street as I walk, hoping none of the neighbours come strolling by.

But I'm not really that concerned about myself. I'm only concerned about Ciara. How the hell would she even know what cocaine is? Surely it just looks like bloody salt or sugar to her. I hold my eyes closed and allow a loud groan to force its way from the back of my throat and all the way out through my mouth. Then I stop walking.

'Oh my God, she's going to tell her folks isn't she?'

I look up to the darkening sky and try to think it all through.

I know she also saw Gerry with his shirt undone and me back in my lingerie. But what could she deduce from that? She's too young. Or am I just being a fuckin idiot; assuming Ciara is and always will be a baby?

I hold my hand to my cheek again to try to rid it of the stinging. Jesus, she gave me a fair oul whack. Come on — get your thoughts together, Debbie. Try to think straight. Ciara and Ingrid came into the house for whatever reason. I rushed them out. Then Ciara came back and saw the coke. Threw the mirror against the wall. Saw a man on my couch with his shirt undone, me back in my lingerie. Shit... this doesn't look good.

She's probably off home right now, to tell Michael and Vivian that I do Class A drugs.

I let out another groan. Then squelch up my nose and shake my head.

Fuck Vivian and Michael. Sure they probably do coke themselves. I'm certain Michael has always had the glazed eyeballs of a coke user. And Viv, well, I'm not sure Viv does coke. She wouldn't take her nose away from her glasses of wine long enough to sniff a line. They probably won't give a shit if Ciara runs home and tells them. Sure, why am I even worrying about Michael and Vivian Joyce? It's not them I give a shit about. It's Ciara. I wanted her to be a part of my life forever. I know I haven't seen her much lately, but I just assumed she'd always be there; like a little sister to me. I fuckin raised her. I can't just let her go out of my life.

I head towards my garden gate and as I do so, I decide I'll ring their house in the morning. To make sure I explain myself. Tell her I wouldn't even dream of doing drugs. That it's not my thing. I'll take her out somewhere nice next weekend. Treat her. I've been meaning to spend more time with her anyway. I've missed her.

I push at my door and walk into the living room to see Gerry man spreading on my couch.

'What the fuck is going on?' he says.

'Sorry, Gerry... that little girl, the chubby one, I helped raise her. She's like a little sister to me. I feel awful that she saw the coke.'

'What t'hell did ye have them in here for, anyway? Ye know I booked this time with you.'

I eyeball him. All of him. His horrible saggy neck, the matted grey hairs on his chest, his huge belly hanging over his yellowing Y-fronts. What the fuck am I doing with my life?

I've asked myself that question loads of times over the past year or so. But I need this. It's only one hour. One hour every Sunday night for a hundred quid. It increases my income by twenty-five per cent. I'd barely be able to afford food for myself if I didn't do this. The Joyces paid well... the Franklins just don't pay the same. I need the extra income. So I signed on to be an escort. It's not as if I'm out on the streets every night waiting on anyone to ride me for a few quid. I'm part of an elite escort agency that sends a man — mostly fat fuckin Gerry — to my house every Sunday night for one hour. They pay one-hundred and fifty quid for that hour and I ship fifty of it to the agency.

'They just knocked on the door, Gerry. I thought it was you. I couldn't just throw them back on the street, I invited them in for a drink until you came, and when you did, I kicked them out. What more do you want me to do?'

'I'll tell you what I want ye to do,' he says, opening his legs even wider. Jesus, the fuckin state of him. 'Do a line.'

I huff, then tut.

'I don't do fuckin drugs, Gerry, how many times do I have to tell ye? It's your fuckin coke. And that's the last time you leave it in my house, d'ye hear me?'

I unwrap my bathrobe, sit beside him on the couch and then sigh. 'You do a line yourself,' I say. 'Then do me. Let's get this over with.'

HELEN IS STILL PACING UP AND DOWN PATRICK TOBIN'S TINY SITTING ROOM, her jaw clenching, when Charlie stands up and winks at her.

'Okay, got it,' he says.

Helen nods her head, then strolls over to Tobin.

'Think it through, Patrick,' she says. 'And ring us if anything comes to mind.'

Tobin mumbles a worried 'yes' to her, then Helen cocks her head sideways to motion to Charlie that it's time for them to leave. As they're heading for the door Charlie scrolls his finger down the screen of his phone.

'There's a hundred and sixty-bloody-four names here, Helen. How the hell are we gonna find out which two are the girls we're looking for?'

Helen makes a sucking noise with her mouth, then pops her lips.

'We'll find em.'

They both pace towards the police car; Helen still stewing their next move. They have a list of girls' names that's been emailed to Charlie's phone, all of whom have been noted by the school as having symptoms of depression. And — of course — they have an image of the teenage boy who made the phone calls that started this whole investigation. It wasn't a bad start, not by any means — and Helen was secretly quite chuffed that she hadn't lost any of her investigative nous — but it was only a good start if they had time to investigate. With the clock ticking towards midnight, Helen and Charlie had it all to do. They didn't have the time to trawl through the list of girls' names; didn't have time to go door-to-door asking the community if they knew who the young boy in the grainy CCTV image was.

'Sirens?' Charlie asks while both of them are pulling at their seatbelts.

Helen narrows her eyes then sucks her mouth again.

'What would you do, Charlie? If you were the lead Detective in this case, what would your next move be?'

Charlie gently drums his two index fingers against the steering wheel as he stews his answer.

'Ye think the two girls are on this list?' he says, nodding his head towards the phone he dropped in the cup holder beside the gear stick.

Helen scrunches up her face.

'Can't be sure of it,' she says. 'I just... ugh... we just need more time.'

'Let's ask the local teenagers about the boy in our image,' Charlie says, there's a football club who play their games around the corner here. St John Bosco they're called, there's always lads hanging around that clubhouse.'

Helen swallows, then nods her head.

'Okay. Let's do it.'

'Sirens?' Charlie asks.

Helen shakes her head this time.

'Not if you still want the teenage boys to be hanging around when we get there.'

Charlie holds his eyes firmly closed as he cringes a little. He should have known. That was quite an amateur question.

He drives off, rounds the first bend and by the time he's approached the roundabout, both he and Helen can see a group of lads sitting on a small wall next to the dressing-rooms of the football club. Some of them stand, bracing themselves to run as the police car edges up beside them. But when Helen gets out, her hands held in the air as if to call for peace, they all seem to relax.

'We're only looking for a bit of help,' she says as she inches towards them; her hands now back in her pockets, the leather coat open, making her look like a character from *The Matrix*.

'Need you to identify a boy of your age. He's not in trouble, we just need to find him.' She looks behind her at Charlie fumbling with his phone, then rolls her eyes because he's not prepared. He was supposed to show the image bang on cue. Now she thinks he's made her look uncool to the boys. As if her leather overcoat and orange hair hadn't already done that.

'C'mon, piglet, hurry up,' one of the boys shouts to a ripple of laughter. Helen offers the boy who yelled a stern gaze. He just stares back.

Then Charlie holds his phone towards the pack and they circle in.

'Ah yeah — that's Mike Hunt,' one lad says.

An ounce of excitement forms in Helen's stomach, until she hears the rest of the boys laughing again. Mike Hunt. My cunt. She should have copped it; had been fed that fake name a few times when she used to do routine beat work back in the day.

'Boys, lemme ask you this,' Helen says, stepping in to the middle of the group. 'Any of you got sisters?'

One boy cocks his head up, a couple others mumble a 'yes'.

'You,' she says talking to the boy who cocked his head. 'Your sister younger or older than you?'

He swallows.

'Younger.'

'So about… twelve, thirteen?' Helen asks.

The boy cocks his head again.

'Well let me tell you this.' Helen takes her hands out of her pockets. 'Two thirteen-year-old girls are planning to die by suicide tonight, somewhere in this area. We don't know who they are or where they are. We just know they are alone, and they want to end their lives. The boy in this photograph is the only person who can lead us to the girls. Guys… they're only young. Same age your sister. Please,' she says, holding her palms out, 'no more messing; we need you to be serious. Do you know who the boy in this image is?'

Charlie stretches the phone closer to the boys and they shuffle their way for a closer look.

Helen winces when she notices the beginning of a Mexican wave of heads shaking from side to side.

'Sorry,' the boy who had called Charlie a piglet says, 'we don't know him. He's not from round here anyway; we'd know.'

Helen spins on her heels, pivots her head backwards and offers a silent grunt towards the sky.

'Thank you, boys,' Charlie says, before he trudges after Helen and into the car.

Helen is snarling as they both reach for their seatbelts again.

'We've enough information to find these girls, don't we?' Charlie says as he repeatedly knocks the butt of his phone off his bottom lip. 'It's just we don't have enough to find them before midnight tonight. We'd need a team of officers, wouldn't we? Calling around houses, showing neighbours this image. Calling around each of the girls' homes that are on our list.'

Helen nods her head slowly as she stares out of her passenger window.

'Yep,' she says. 'If we were to take the time to ring each girl's home on that list, and spent just two minutes on each call, that'd take us over five hours.'

Charlie digs the phone into his lip, then looks over at Helen.

'It's stupid that it's just the two of us out looking for these girls. The rest of em are all obsessed with tracking down whatever it is they think Alan Keating is up to.'

'Uh-huh,' Helen says, still staring out the passenger window.

The evening has turned to darkness; the moon forming full in the navy sky. Not a good sign for Helen. She believes in all that quirky shit; is convinced bad things are more likely to happen when a fuller moon makes an appearance. She's also one of those who believe that the horoscopes printed in the *Irish Daily Star* every day are genuinely accurate. This morning's horoscope suggested she should be looking at taking every opportunity by the scruff of its neck as it will lead to a brighter future. She's now wondering whether the horoscope meant she could get back on the force if she were to save these girls' lives. That'd certainly offer a brighter future for her. Though maybe the future the horoscope was referring to was the future of these two girls. If Helen can stop them, she can turn their lives right around. And that'd mean more to Helen than getting her job back. Saving people from the brink of suicide would be a lottery win for Helen Brennan. A goal she wishes she could have achieved twenty-two years ago.

She moves her head for the first time in a couple minutes to snatch Charlie's phone out of his hand and then presses at the screen to view the time.

'It's almost nine o'clock,' she says. 'We need to get a move on.' Charlie looks at her, his eyes squinting. 'You're gonna have to ring your SI; tell him that you need more men to carry out door-to-door enquiries,' Helen says.

She hands the phone back to Charlie and notices him swallow hard as he grips it.

'He'll just laugh at me, Helen. I'm just... I'm just—'

'You are a police officer doing his job properly,' Helen says. 'Put him on speaker phone. And remember... don't mention you're with me. I'm supposed to be off duty.'

Charlie holds his eyes closed in frustration before he scrolls at his screen.

A ringing tone eventually sounds and both of them cock their ears towards the phone Charlie has held between them.

'Yello,' a voice says.

'Superintendent Newell it's eh... Charlie, Charlie Guilfoyle.'

'Ah, howaya, young Charlie, Everything alright?'

'Yeah... it's just, I was asked to look into the possibility that the anonymous phone call made earlier about the suicides was well... well...' he pauses, looks at Helen. Helen nods her head, then waves her hand in a motion that suggests he should just get the fuck on with whatever it is he's trying to say. 'Eh... well, I've been asked to look into the phone call as if it was legitimate and I've found something interesting.'

A snuff of a laugh crackles down the line.

'Y'know the call's not legitimate, young Charlie, yes? It's that fecker Keating playing games with us.'

'Yeah... yeah, I know,' Charlie says, looking at Helen again. 'It's just... my job was to look into the call as if it *was* legitimate and well... I have a list, a list of girls in the vicinity who suffer with symptoms of depression. I got them from the local school's Headteacher.'

Charlie stops talking, then squints his entire face in anticipation of a response. But no sound comes down the line.

'Sir,' he says, reprompting Newell.

'Well, I'm glad you are taking your work very seriously, Charlie. And that is... that is fine investigating indeed. Really impressive outside-the-box thinking. But ye know... this *is* Keating. We're one hundred per cent certain of it. I've got five Detectives sniffing their noses around — so do Rathmines station — and we really need to get back to the invest—'

'Sir, I need help. I need more manpower to try to locate the two girls from this list. I'm sure the two girls who are planning to die by suicide are on it.'

As the line cackles with laughter Helen grinds her teeth, itching to get in on the conversation. But she manages to bite her tongue. If her husband found out she was investigating behind his back, that could spell the end of their marriage. It's surviving on such tenterhooks as it is. They've been sleeping in separate bedrooms for the past fifteen years; Eddie accepting that they will stay with each other forever, but their marriage — in a traditional sense — well and truly ended the day Scott died. Helen's been waiting on Eddie to retire, so that they can move to Canada. He promised her — on the evening before Scott's funeral — that they'd both retire to Toronto when the time was right. That dream is the only thing that's kept Helen going over the years. She's desperate to move away from Dublin; desperate to move on from Scott's death. She nags Eddie about his retirement on a regular basis; but has a horrible feeling the move will never happen. She thinks Eddie loves his job a little more than he loves his wife. She couldn't be more wrong.

'Listen, young Charlie, you keep following up your leads, I'm glad you are taking the role you've been given as seriously as you can, but... I've gotta go.'

Charlie stares at Helen as a dead tone echoes through the car.

'The cunt!' Helen yells. 'Why are all Superintendents a bunch of fucking cunts?'

She clicks at the buckle of her seat belt, then opens her car door.

Charlie inches forward in his seat and watches as Helen screams into the sky.

'Did the two girls kill themselves missus?' one of the boys they had been speaking to a few minutes ago shouts over.

Helen doesn't answer him; she pinches at the bridge of her nose, then tucks her chin into the collar of her leather coat. After forcing in and out three deep breaths, she takes her own mobile phone out of her pocket.

'Guess I'll have to make a call,' she says to herself. She presses at the screen a couple times, then brings the phone to her ear and, as she does so, she walks slowly away from the car.

'Hey,' Eddie says. 'We're crazy busy here at the minute, what's up?'

20:50

Ingrid

'C'MON THEN, LET'S CATCH THE BUS TO HARRIET'S. I PROMISE I WON'T JUMP out in front of it as it's coming,' she says, smiling. Typical Ciara. Running out in front of a bus one minute, joking the next.

So I smile too, pretending I'm not scared. And then we both walk, arms wrapped around each other, towards the end of the road where the bus that'll take us to Harriet's house stops.

Harriet is the only one I really want to say goodbye to. Apart from Ciara, she's the one person who speaks to me like I'm me... not as if I'm somebody she wants me to be. My parents talk to me as if I'm another person altogether; like a daughter they wished they had instead of me. I feel like I'm bothering them anytime I have to ask a question.

My teachers don't talk to me at all. Most of them don't even know my name. I'm just another face in a room full of faces to them. In primary school, our teachers were great. I love Miss Moriarty with all my heart. But in secondary school it seems as if they don't care. A little part of me was excited when we were getting old enough to go to secondary school. But I've felt so sad ever since we've gone there. I never wake up happy in the mornings. Secondary school has been such a let down.

We're walking in silence when blue lights flash off the windows of the houses in front of us. Then I hear a car pull up slowly and I turn around to see a policeman with his head sticking out of his window.

'Girls — stop right there!'

I look at Ciara's face; wondering if she's going to make a run for it and thoughts of whether or not I should run with her go through my mind. Running from Debbie is one thing, but running from the police… well… But Ciara doesn't run, she just stands still beside me as the policeman approaches us.

'Girls, a bus driver has just stopped me up the street there and said two girls fitting your description almost ran out in from of him.'

He frowns his forehead. His wrinkles are really deep. Like an old man's. Only he isn't really that old.

'No… don't be silly,' Ciara says laughing. 'I just nearly walked out in front of the bus by accident… my friend here pulled me back. I just wasn't looking where I was going.'

He looks at my face, back at Ciara's, then at mine again.

'This true?' he asks me.

I nod my head. This isn't good. I'm lying to policemen now. He reaches into his back pocket and takes out a small notepad.

'You two girls from around here?' he asks.

Ciara nods her head before I have a chance to speak. Which is fine by me. I don't even know what to say. I'm half scared, half-relieved that a policeman has come to save us.

'Well, not far from here. We'd need to get a bus home,' she says.

'What're your names?' He clicks on the top of his pen and rests it against his pad.

'Emma Brown,' she says as quickly as she can, 'and eh… Mel Bunton.'

I hold my eyes closed. The last thing I want to do is laugh. But I know exactly where she plucked those names from… it's a mix up of two of the Spice Girls. Typical Ciara. Thinking on her feet. Making everything up as she's going along.

The policeman looks at me when he's finished scribbling.

'Are you okay, Mel?' he says. 'You look a bit eh… ashen-faced, if you don't mind me saying.'

I slowly nod my head, unsure what ashen-faced means exactly.

'She's not ashen faced. She's just pale. Always has been. Has Swedish blood, don'tcha, Mel?'

Ciara nudges me.

'Yes… yes, Sir.' I say. I can hear the fright in my voice. I try to swallow it down, deep in to my stomach before I speak again. 'Yes. My mother is Swedish. I got her pale skin, her blonde hair.'

The policeman doesn't react; no words, no nodding of his head, no scribbling of his pen. He just shifts his eyes from my face to Ciara's and then back to mine again.

He clicks at his pen, then stuffs his notepad into his back trousers pocket.

'I'm concerned that the bus driver had to stop me. He got a big fright, said he had to swerve to miss you and he has about twenty passengers on that bus. Nobody was hurt, thankfully.'

Ciara reaches her arm around my shoulder and gives it a squeeze.

'We're sorry, officer. It was an innocent mistake. I just didn't look where I was going. We wanted to cross the road and — silly me — I tried to cross it without using the Green Cross Code and then... last second, Mel here dragged me back. She saved my life.'

Ciara squeezes me tighter.

I don't do anything, except stare at the ground in front of me. I want to stare at the policeman's face. I'd love to know what's going on inside his head. But I can't bring myself to look up.

'And you can get home safely now, yes?' he asks.

He's going to leave us alone. I'm not sure if I feel relief or fear go through me.

'Yes, officer,' Ciara says. 'We're just walking to the bus stop now. Heading straight home. Promise.'

He nods his head once.

'Kay, look after yourselves, girls. And watch what you're doing when you're crossing the road, young Emma, yes?'

Ciara giggles.

'Course I will, officer. I won't make that mistake again.'

He looks at her face, then at mine. I don't think he's buying all of this. But he seems done with us. Is almost turning to go.

'One thing I don't get,' he says, holding a finger to his lips. 'If you were crossing the road, why haven't you crossed it since?'

I feel my mouth fall open. I look at Ciara. She seems lost for words... for once.

'Well?' the policeman says.

'Changed our minds,' Ciara says.

He stares at both of our faces again, shifting his eyes back and forth as if he's watching a bloody tennis match.

'Girls... I'd like you to come with me,' he says. 'Into the car please.'

20:55

Greta

I'm popping another Malteser into my mouth when I realise the second episode of *Heartbeat* is about to end. That flew in quick. I look up at the clock. Almost nine.

My two men are in bed. No idea where my little girl is.

I chomp on the Malteser, wait on the stupidly addictive *Heartbeat* theme tune to play over the credits and then sit up straight on the couch. She was only here a couple hours ago, cuddling into me. It's not unusual she'd be in Ciara's house, but — I don't know whether it's mother's intuition or what it is — I just have a feeling all is not right. It was something about the way she held her face as she was leaving. She didn't want to look at me. She was holding something back.

I shuffle my feet into my slippers and make my way to the hallway. Then I flick my way through our little phone book until I see the Joyce's number and I proceed to dial it.

'Hello.'

'Vivian, it's me... Greta. The girls at your house, yes?'

There's a silence.

'Oh, sorry. I thought you were going to be Michael. I'm expecting him to call.'

Another silence.

'Vivian... the girls with you? Ingrid said they were going to your house to study.'

I hear her sniff her nose.

'No. Eh… I'm sure Ciara said they were going to your house.'

Shit. Something *is* up. I bloody knew it!

'Little rascals are up to something. Y'know, I knew it as soon as they left the house. Ingrid looked… she looked as if she was hiding from me.'

Vivian sniffs again.

'They're probably down in Macari's eating chips,' she says.

I sigh. I can't imagine that's what they're doing. They only go to Macari's on a Friday evening. Nah… something else is going on.

'It's just they were at that party last night. I'm wondering if something happened at it.'

'Ah… they'll be fine. They'll be fine,' she says; almost as if she doesn't care.

'Well eh… if they come back to yours, tell Ingrid she has to come straight home. She's in trouble. They shouldn't be lying to us.'

'Ah, we all lied to our parents when we were teenagers,' Vivian says. I hold the phone away from my ear and stare at it as if I'm staring at Vivian, my eyes narrowing. 'But yeah… I'll send Ingrid back when they get here.'

Then she hangs up.

She really is a crap mother. Always has been. So bad, she had to hire a nanny even though she didn't even work herself. I know it must be nine o'clock, but I still look up at the clock over the fireplace when I stroll back into our living room to make sure. Maybe they did sneak out for some Macari's chips. But it seems too much of a coincidence that they've gone AWOL the night after they've been to a party. I bet they're meeting boys. I get it. We all start fancying boys at that age… it's just, I can't stand the thought of Ingrid lying to me. I love Ciara, but her character is probably becoming too influential on Ingrid. I don't want Ingrid to grow up. Not yet anyway. I love that she's quiet. Love that she's shy. Because it means she'll never really get herself into trouble. Though that may be wishful thinking. I read a book once that said parents never truly know their own children, because children act differently at home than they do outside the house. But I always assumed that was a bullshit theory when it came to my two. At least I know Sven will never lie to me. He's not capable.

I suck on my lips and then find myself taking our stairs two at a time, clinging on to the banister as I go. I peak around the door of Sven's room and stare at his face; his mouth open, his nostrils whistling a little snore like they always do.

I walk, almost on my tiptoes, into my own bedroom. Terry's not snoring, but I can tell by his heavy breathing that he's already fast asleep. He'd hate it if I woke him. He's got to get up at five a.m., needs to get into the radio station for six. But maybe I *should* wake him; our daughter's a hell of a lot more important than his little show.

I tip-toe back towards the bedroom door, and shut it behind me. Tight. Fast. Then I hear him... shuffling under the duvet before he lets out a groan.

'For Christ sake, Greta,' he says, 'you've just fuckin' woken me.'

I blink my eyes and feel a little relief wash itself through my body.

'Sorry, dear,' I say, turning around to re-enter the bedroom. 'Door slipped out of my hand as I was closing it. I eh... I'm glad you're awake though. I'm eh... worried. About Ingrid. And Ciara. They've gone missing.'

20:55

Ciara

HE PRESSES AT THE TOP OF MY HEAD AS I GET INTO THE BACK OF HIS CAR, then does the same with Ingrid.

I feel frightened. Though I'm not sure why. He's hardly arresting us for walking out in front of a bus, is he? He's just worried for us. Is doing his job to protect us. But he won't. There's nothing he can do that'll save our lives. Even if he delays it by an hour or two, even if he calls our parents to come pick us up from some police station, me and Ingrid will eventually get around to doing what we want to do. I try to slow my breaths, reminding myself that there's no need to be frightened.

When he shuffles his way into the driver's seat, he reaches for a button that turns off the blue lights. Then he turns around to us, his hand resting on the top of the passenger seat.

'No need for you to take the bus, I'll get ye home,' he says. 'Where is it ye live?'

I feel Ingrid about to speak up, about to rattle off her address, so I place my hand on her knee; my sign to her that she should leave the speaking to me.

'Connolly Gardens, in Inchicore,' I say. 'Number fifty-one.'

The officer winks at me, then turns around and starts the car.

I feel Ingrid turn to face me. I'd bet any money her eyes are wide. But I don't look at her. I don't want to give the officer any clues that we have lied our asses off to him ever since he started asking us questions. So I just stretch my fingers towards hers and grip on to her. I can feel the sweat on her palm. Bet she can feel the sweat on mine too.

'How old are you girls?' the officer asks, staring back at us through his mirror.

I cough before I answer.

'Eh... thirteen, both of us.' That's the first answer I've given him that isn't a lie.

'Does eh...' he says nodding his head in the mirror, 'does Mel not talk, no? Cat got your tongue?'

I squeeze Ingrid's fingers.

'She's just quiet is all,' I say.

'That right?'

We don't answer and the car falls silent as we turn onto the canal road.

The officer made me forget what happened back at Debbie's house for a few minutes. It starts to play at my mind again. That slap. But to hell with it! I can't let what Debbie does affect me. I thought she was bigger and better than doing bleedin' drugs though. But I guess I don't really know her as well as I thought I did. I can hear the slap over and over in my head as I stare out the car window and every time I do I feel the sting of it inside my hand. She deserved it though, I s'pose. And besides, that's only a tiny bit of pain compared to how she'll be feeling in the morning when she's told the news. I don't really wanna hurt Debbie by dying, though. I don't want to hurt Miss Moriarty either and Ingrid sure as hell doesn't want to hurt Harriet. That's why we were visiting them this evening, to let them know that we called by to say our final goodbyes. We wanted those three to know they meant something to us. But instead of a long hug to say goodbye to Debbie, I ended up slapping her across the cheek. And now here we are — both of us — in the back of a bleedin' police car.

I squeeze Ingrid's fingers again and then we both turn to face each other. I wink an 'it's all okay' at her and she gives me that half smile thing she does. She seems to be taking being in the back of a police car better than I ever thought she would. She's not crying, anyway. Unlike last night. Jesus, she could have filled a swimming pool with the amount of tears that came out of her eyes.

I twist her wrist a little so I can look at her digital watch. 20:59. Just a few hours until all of her pain is gone away. And mine. We're almost there. As soon as this officer drops us off, we'll be back on track.

'I love you,' I mouth to her. And as she does the same we squeeze each other's fingers even tighter.

'What school do you go to, girls?' the officer asks.

I think quickly.

'Goldenbridge.' I'm so good at lying. It's almost as if the lie comes to my mind before the truth does. That seems to be how my brain works. I'm sure I got that skill from my dad. I knew I had to say the name of a school that was close to the wrong address I gave him. I know Harriet goes to Goldenbridge. She's actually in her last year this year. Is doing her Leaving Cert in June.

'Ah… I know it well. I went to Junior Infants in Goldenbridge. Grew up in Inchicore until I was seven meself,' he says.

Neither me or Ingrid say anything back to him. We both just turn our heads to look back out of the side windows.

Hopefully he gets the message. We don't wanna talk. We just want you to drop us off.

The streets are too dark. I can't quite make out where we are, though this area is a bit unfamiliar to me. Ingrid would know it better than me. She hung around here a bit when she was younger. I assume we're in Inchicore by now. It shouldn't have been that long a drive.

'Okay, so which one is Connolly Gardens?' he asks, eyeballing me in the mirror.

I turn to Ingrid. She coughs.

'Eh… next turn right and then it's the eh… I think it's the second turn after that,' she says.

I look at him in the mirror, notice his brow go all wrinkly again. Shit. I hope he isn't getting suspicious.

'Yeah, this turn here,' Ingrid says.

Now I know where we are. I've been here a few times with Ingrid. It's a quiet little cul de sac. The type, I'm sure, no drama happens in. Not like the road we live on.

'That house there,' I say. And then I unclick my seatbelt.

He turns around to us after he stops the car.

'Ye want me to walk ye up to the house?'

'Oh… no thank you,' I say. 'I don't want to give my dad a fright. It'd be his worst nightmare if I showed up at the door with a policeman.' I reach my hand towards his shoulder and pat it gently. 'Thank you, officer.'

Then I open the door and hop out.

I can sense him watching us as we stroll towards the house and push at the gate that leads us into the tiny garden.

He's pulling away slowly as we knock at the door. I know he's waiting to see if anybody answers. It doesn't take long until he gets what he wants.

'Wha' you two doin' here?'

'Ah, Uncle Brendan. We just wanted to see Harriet. Is she in?'

Ingrid's uncle pushes his door wider to allow us to walk in to his hallway. And as we do, I turn back and offer a wave of my hand to the police officer.

'She's inside watchin' the tele. Your mother know you're here, Ingrid?' Brendan says.

Ingrid turns to face her uncle and then nods her head slowly.

'Course she does,' she says, her cute little smile wide on her face. But I know that will have hurt Ingrid a bit. She hates lying.

21:00

Terry

So I'll just cut to the chase, Terry. The reason we called you in here was not to marvel at your successes so far, and not to meet you and see that big, handsome smile of yours. We asked you here for a very specific reason. We need a new Saturday night prime time entertainment show on RTE television, something that'll get the entire nation tuning in. And, we know of no better man to front that show than the great Terry Murph—

My eyes shoot open. I let out a groan.

'For Christ sake, Greta, you've just fuckin woken me.'

It's not like her. She's normally very careful when I'm sleeping. So I know she closed that door with a bang on purpose.

I turn my face to look at the clock. 21:01. Jesus, I've only been asleep an hour.

She pushes the door open and looks around it sheepishly at me.

'Sorry, dear. I'm glad you're awake though. I eh... I'm worried. About Ingrid. And Ciara. They've gone missing.'

I try to clear my mind of the annoyance by squeezing my eyes closed. I fuckin hate being woken. Then I rub a hand over my face.

'What do you mean missing?'

She perches her butt on the end of the bed and looks over her shoulder at me, her arms crossed.

'Ingrid said she was going around to Ciara's house to do some studying for that exam they have coming up. But I've eh... I've just rung Vivian and they're not there.'

I rub my face again with my hand.

'What did Vivian say?'

'She eh… she said Ciara had told her they were coming around here to study.'

I sigh as loudly as I can and then sit up in the bed, leaning the back of my head onto the top of our wooden headboard.

'Something's going on, Terry. I know it. I said it to you as soon as they left the house this evening. Ingrid could barely look at me as she was going out the door. That's not like her.'

I hold each of my forefingers to my temples; not so much to think through where Ingrid might be, more to stop the annoyance of being awake from scratching through my mind.

'She'll be back soon. She knows she has school in the morning,' I say.

I scoot myself back down in the bed, until my head is resting on the pillow again.

'Call it mother's intuition or whatever Terr—'

'Jesus, Greta. She'll be home soon. And when she walks through that door you'll be annoyed with yourself that you woke me up for no fuckin reason.'

I sit up sharpish. Because I know that was a little harsh.

'Sweetie, it's Ingrid. She's incapable of doing anything wrong.'

'Except for lying.'

Greta's standing now, her hands on her hips.

'What do you mean lying?'

'Well, lying about where she was going.'

'Ah,' I say, shaking my head. 'That's a little white lie. She's thirteen now. Isn't that what teenagers do?'

'I hope it's just a boyfriend or something. They probably met boys at that party—'

'It fuckin better not be boys,' I say, sweeping the duvet off me. I take one step over to our window and pull at the curtain so I can stare up and down our street. Then I look back at my wife.

'Jaysus, I always loved that Ingrid was really pretty, but now that she's a teenager, I wish she had a face like the back of a bus.'

Greta shoots a little laugh out of the side of her mouth. That'll do me. She's obviously not as concerned as she seems to be letting on.

'Sweetie, she'll be back in a while,' I say, tossing her hair. 'Don't worry about it. I'll talk to her when she gets home from school tomorrow. If she's messing around with boys, she'll have an awful lot of explaining to do.'

I jump back into bed and pull the duvet nice and snug around me again.

'Now,' I say, turning on to my side. 'I've got a big show in the morning… Close the door gently this time.'

THE KIDS ACROSS THE STREET ALL COCK THEIR HEADS UP AGAIN AT HELEN AS she strolls away from the police car, the phone to her ear.

'I know you're crazy busy, won't keep you long, Eddie. I was just, y'know, lying here on the sofa and thought I owed it to you — owed it to our marriage — to be totally honest and up front with you.'

There's a hesitation on the other end of the line.

'Go on,' Eddie eventually says.

'You *did* hurt me earlier. So much so I've been crying. I thought what you said was really insensitive... about me needing to go home to watch the soaps. In front of everybody.'

There's silence again, but Helen is aware Eddie will be rolling his eyes.

'I'm sorry, Hel... it's just I'm under so much pressure here and... well, yeah... there's no excuse for me saying that in front of everybody. Please accept my apology once more and we'll speak in the morning, yeah?'

Helen fake-coughs down the line, is not really sure where to take the conversation from here.

'Yeah, yeah — I know you didn't mean it. It just hurt is all, and I didn't wanna just lie here getting angry with you, so thought I'd call so I can just put it all behind me. I know you're mad busy... how's the investigation going?'

'Frustrating,' Eddie says. Helen smiles to herself. Is aware her husband has fallen into her trap. 'We're certain Keating is up to something. He's keeping well away, for sure. We know he's in Spain. Again. Same place he always is when he's pulling off something big. None of his main men seem to be doing anything, but we'll get to the bottom of this. We have to before it's too late. I'm not letting this fucker give us the run around again.'

'You'll sort it. I'm sure you'll figure it out. Did you eh...' Helen looks over her shoulder, 'did you trace the caller? Y'know; if you get the caller, you'll almost solve this thing.'

'Yeah. Call was made near the Drimnagh Luas stop, we managed to get CCTV footage of the boy making the call. He looks about fourteen, maybe fifteen. The type of young recruit Keating normally uses to carry out a little bit of the dirty work for him.'

'Track him down yet?' Helen says, nibbling at the edge of her thumb. She stops walking, awaits the response.

'No. We've no name. Just an image. That and the fact we know he walked to Harold's Cross after making the call. We tracked him on CCTV all the way up the canal. He turned off at the main Harold's Cross bridge. No sight of him after that. We're closing in.'

Helen grabs some air with her fist, chuffed that her little mind game of pretending she was upset soothed Eddie into opening up to her. She spins on her heels and begins to pace back towards the car.

'Interesting... interesting,' she says. 'Eh... apology accepted. We'll do that breakfast after we wake up tomorrow, yeah?'

'Helen, you okay?' Eddie asks. But Helen barely heard; was too busy bringing the phone back down to press at the red button. She places the phone in her coat pocket and begins to quicken her pace as she gets nearer the car, wiring her finger around as if to signify to Charlie that it's time to get going.

'Here, yis aren't gonna find the two girls if you're just gonna leave that car parked there all night,' one of the teenage boys roars towards her. She doesn't pay him any attention, nor any of the other boys who decide to laugh at his silly statement. She just snatches at the door handle, folds her tall frame into the passenger seat and instructs Charlie.

'Harold's Cross.'

He stares at her, then turns the key and speeds off, staining the road with tyre marks.

'What's going on?' Charlie asks.

'The young boy, in our image... he's in the Harold's Cross area now. Walked there after making the call.'

'How do you know?' Charlie asks as he reaches for the siren switch.

As the sound blares out from the car, Helen sucks on her lips and then says nothing; as if Charlie hadn't just asked that last question. She's trying to remain mysterious; as if she's operating at a different level to Charlie. It seems to be working. He has no idea that his low rank as a recently-recruited uniformed beat officer makes him her senior.

Charlie chicanes out of the narrow streets of Drimnagh and finds his way back on to the canal road. He's a decent driver, is Charlie. Was given the share of a car with another beat officer who works a different shift pattern to him about three months ago. For the minimal admin work they do, as well as the odd walk beat they take, they barely need the wheels. But there was a car left over at the station. And Charlie was chuffed with the offer. It almost felt like a promotion to him.

'So, what we gonna do? Door-to-door?' Charlie shouts over the siren.

Helen has the nail of her thumb held between her teeth.

'Same again,' she shouts. 'Let's contact the local school Headteacher. He'll know every teenager in that area. What's the local school in Harold's Cross?' she asks.

Charlie answers by picking up his phone and handing it to her.

Helen clicks into his Internet browser history, Googles 'secondary school Harold's Cross' and finds her answer in a matter of seconds.

'St Joseph's CBS,' she says. 'The number's here.' She holds the phone to her ear; hears a tone ring twice before an answer machine kicks in.

'The school office is currently closed. We operate between the hours of eight a.m. and five p.m., Monday to Friday. Please leave a message after the tone or — alternatively — call our emergency site team on 01 5333873 in case of an emergency.'

Helen holds her eyes closed, soaking in the number just read out to her, then she swipes at the screen of Charlie's phone and punches in the digits.

Another answer machine.

'Ah for fuck sake!' she says before the beep sounds.

'This is Detective Helen Brennan from Rathmines Garda station,' she yells down the line, 'ring me back on this number as soon as you possibly can!'

Then she hangs up, places Charlie's phone back in the cup holder and screams into her hands.

'Supposed to be a fuckin emergency number that!'

Charlie continues to speed up the canal road, swerving past cars that pull over for him.

He looks at Helen, then back at the road in front. He does this numerous times. Is itching to ask her another question, but he can sense her frustration and isn't quite sure now's an appropriate time.

'Helen,' he says tentatively.

She doesn't hear him.

'Helen!' She opens the hands from around her face, looks over at Charlie. 'I eh… I can see why you are a brilliant Detective. You take things really seriously, but do you eh… do you normally get this animated during an investigation?'

Helen stares straight ahead.

'I take every case as seriously as the last one,' she says.

Charlie can just about hear her over the siren. His fingers begin to fidget on top of the steering wheel.

'It's just,' he shouts again, 'you said earlier that this one was personal…'

Helen looks over at him, arching one of her eyebrows. Then she lets out a long sigh.

'Just do lights,' she says.

Charlie reaches for a button near the ignition and clicks at it. The sound of the siren stops but the blue lights remain flashing, bouncing off the car bonnet and back into their faces.

Helen sits more upright in her seat and then fixes the seat belt around her so that it runs at a straighter diagonal across her chest.

'Somebody very close to me died by suicide,' she says.

Charlie turns his face towards her and purses his lips. But she doesn't notice. She's just staring at the light show on the bonnet.

'Sorry to hear that,' Charlie says.

'You've nothing to be sorry for.'

The car falls silent, except for the noise of tyres zooming down the canal road.

'My son,' Helen then says, still staring straight ahead. Charlie offers another purse of his lips. 'Similar age to these two girls, I suspect. He'd only just turned fourteen. Y'know… I still don't know why. What I wouldn't give to know *why*. Ye know what my husband says to me all the time? "Helen, you will *never* know why." As if it's that easy to just forget about it.'

'I'm so sorry,' Charlie says, 'I can see why you are so passionate about saving these girls. Suicide… it's … it's such a waste of life—' Charlie holds his hand up to his mouth. 'Oh, I'm so sorry. I meant… I meant, if only they could be stopped…'

'I know what you mean, Charlie,' Helen says, taking her stare away from the lights. 'And you're right. I think how much of a waste of life suicide is every single day of my life. That's been every day for twenty-two years.'

Charlie winces a little as he clicks down the gears to turn off the canal road; at the Harold's Cross junction.

'It was the same as these two girls... him and his friends, they must have made a pact.'

The vibration of Charlie's phone ringing in the cup holder halts Helen. She reaches for it and without even looking to see who's ringing, presses at the green button and brings the phone to her ear. Then she stretches across Charlie, flicking at the button that makes the sirens blare up again.

'Hello, Detective Helen Brennan speaking,' she shouts, holding one finger to her opposite ear.

'Detective Brennan, my name is Trevor Halpin, I am the site manager of St Joseph's CBS... I just received your voicemail, is everything okay at the school?'

'Trevor, I need to speak with the school's Headteacher right away, I need you to give me his contact details.'

'Brother Fitzpatrick is his name,' he says. 'Is everything okay, sounds like something bad has happened.'

'Nothing bad has happened *yet*, Trevor, and only Brother Fitzpatrick can help stop something bad from happening. We need him to identify a school student as soon as possible. Tell me, Trevor, where does Fitzpatrick live?'

'Jesus, Mary and Joseph,' Trevor says, 'I hope the student is okay. Eh... hold on for a second. He doesn't live that far from the school. I have his details in my phone... gimme a sec.'

Helen winks over at Charlie, then waves her hand up and down, signalling that Charlie should slow his driving.

'Parkview Avenue, number one-three-six,' Trevor says. 'A little cul de sac, y'know those old Victorian style houses off the main road?'

'Gotcha, Trevor. Thanks for your help.'

Helen hangs up the call, then taps into the Maps app and punches in the address that had just been read out to her.

'Do a U-turn, Charlie, then it's the second left.'

Charlie causes the wheels to smoke as he swings around.

'He's got to know him. If the kid lives around here, the Headteacher of the school *has* to know who he is. We just had the wrong area when we spoke to the first Headteacher.' Helen slaps her palm off her knee, excitement beginning to grow inside of her.

'One-three-six, one-three-six,' she repeats as Charlie inches the car down Parkview Avenue, switching the sirens off. 'There it is,' Helen says, pointing. She clicks at her seatbelt, jumps out of the car whilst it's still moving and sprints — in her own unique way — across the street. Charlie doesn't even bother parking; he leaves the car — lights show still on — in the middle of the road and paces after Helen; catching up with her just before she presses at the doorbell. No one comes to the door.

'Brother Fitzpatrick,' she shouts as she bangs at the knocker. 'I am Detective Helen Brennan, I need to speak with you as a matter of urgency.'

She stands back, takes in all of the windows.

'Bollocks,' she whispers over her shoulder to Charlie when she realises nobody's home.

Charlie rubs at the back of his head as Helen makes her way to the window, clasping her hands either side of her eyes to peer into the darkness.

'Not a sign of life. Fuck it,' she says, turning around, to be met by the face of an elderly woman, waiting at the gate.

'Ye won't find him at home, not at this time o' the evenin',' she says.

Charlie takes a step towards the woman.

'Where would we find him, ma'am?'

'Same place as always,' she says. 'The Horse and Jockey.'

'A pub?' Helen asks.

'Yep, not far from here. It's on the other side of those houses. Better off walking. If ye take the car, you've to go round the Wrekin... but there's a lane way over there ye can cut through. You'd be there in five minutes.'

Helen walks towards the woman and places the palm of her hand on her shoulder.

'Thank you, miss.' Then she turns to Charlie. 'Park the car up. We're going for a little walk.'

21:05

Ingrid

HARRIET LOOKS HAPPY. SHE *ALWAYS* LOOKS HAPPY. I REALLY DON'T KNOW why though. She's had so much pain in her life. Much more pain than I've ever had. But she seems to be able to get over it. She's got a strength I know I will never have. I've tried. I've tried to be strong like her, but it's not me. I guess everybody just has different minds, even if they do share the same blood.

'Hey, good to see you two,' she says as she hugs me. Then she hugs Ciara. She knows Ciara a bit. Not that well. But whenever Harriet has hung around in my house, Ciara is normally there. Me and Ciara often talk about Harriet; we say how cool it would be to be just like her. And we both agree that we never will.

She has a hooped nose ring that we know would look stupid on us. If we walked into school trying to dress the way Harriet does, we'd be laughed at until we raced out of the classroom with embarrassment. She wears clothes like Indians do. Not Indian people that live in India. Indians that live in America. She always seems to have a poncho on over her shoulders; a different coloured one almost every time I see her. Today it's brown with light blue stripes. And she's wearing long trousers that are so wide at the end that they cover her shoes. Mum says those type of trousers used to be big in the seventies. They have a name, but I can't remember it.

'Great to see you too,' I say. 'We just thought we'd pop in to say hello.'

Harriet gives me a big smile, then points to the sofa; right next to where Uncle Brendan is sitting.

'Take a seat,' she says. 'Can I get you anything?'

We both shake our heads and plonk ourselves on the sofa. I'm not really sure what to say. Here we are, trying to say goodbye to somebody we love without letting them know we'll never see them again. It seemed like an easier thing to do when I came up with the idea last night. It was me who added it into our pact; I felt I couldn't end it all without paying the people I love one final visit.

'Don't you two have school in the mornin'?' Uncle Brendan says taking his eyes off the tele.

I sit more forward on the sofa so I can look at him.

'Yes, we do. But we were visiting a friend of Ciara's who lives nearby and said we'd pop in to see Harriet. To see you both.' Uuugh. I hate lying. But maybe I'm getting good at it. That's about my fourth lie today.

Uncle Brendan nods, then looks back at the tele. I'm not sure what it is he's watching.

I feel sad for Uncle Brendan. Always have. Aunt Peggy died when I was just three. It must be coming up to ten years now. Cancer she had. I don't really remember her that much. If it wasn't for the photos I don't think I'd have a face in my mind for Aunt Peggy at all. Harriet was only eight when her mam died. That's why it confuses me that she's always happy.

'Where's your friend live?' Harriet asks Ciara.

'Eh...'

'Up in St Michael's Estate,' I say, jumping in. Lying again.

'Jaysus, I don't want you two up there in that estate at this time of the evening... are yis mad?' Uncle Brendan says. He doesn't look away from the tele this time. He's just sitting there, slouched into the sofa, his two hands on top of his big belly. 'Yer mammy and daddy know you were there?'

'We eh... we were with my mam. She just dropped us off here so we could say hello to Harriet,' Ciara says.

I feel a bit of relief in my body. Ciara ended Uncle Brendan's questions with one sentence. Maybe I'm not that good at lying. Certainly not better than her anyway. The last thing we need right now is Uncle Brendan ringing Mum and Dad to check up on me. Aunt Peggy was Dad's sister. Dad took ages getting over her death. Almost as if he took it personally. He ran a marathon to raise money for a cancer charity the year after she died and raised fifty-five thousand pound. That's a huge amount of money. He talks about it all the time — more than he actually talks about Aunt Peggy.

I can feel Harriet stare over at me from the chair she's sitting in. She's so clever. I wouldn't be surprised if she knows we've been lying. I turn to look at her and she nods her head towards the stairs.

'Wanna go up to my room? Three of us can have a girly talk?'

I'm off the sofa before I even say 'yes', Ciara following me.

It's a tiny house is Brendan and Harriet's. Especially compared to our homes. The hallway is barely a hallway. There's only enough room for a tiny table that the house phone sits on. The kitchen doesn't even have room for a table. It's only about the size of our downstairs toilet. That's why I often say to Ciara that poorer people are happier. If you're in my house, you can sometimes hear Mum and Dad argue. If you're in Ciara's, you're almost guaranteed to hear her mum and dad argue. That's if her dad is in. But here — in Harriet's — it's always quiet, even though the house is tiny. She's much closer with her dad than me and Ciara. It kinda makes me jealous a little bit. Only I don't mean anything bad about being jealous of Harriet. I love her too much to have any bad feelings for her. She's always been a cool cousin. The only cool cousin I have. She's five years older than me, but she has always spoken to me as if I am the same as her. Nobody else in my life does that. Cept for Ciara.

'What's up with you two?' Harriet asks as she holds the door to her bedroom open for us to walk into under her arm.

It's a super cool bedroom she has. She's into the coolest old bands. Bands I've barely even heard of. There's a picture of two crazy lookin' fellas with crazy hair cuts from a band called Oasis over her bed. And another one of a weird looking blond fella called Kurt Cobain.

'Eh... nothing much. Same stuff,' I say.

She looks at me with a funny face then shuts the door.

'Don't give me that. You can't lie to me, Ingrid. I can see right through you. It's this boy, isn't it? What-his-name again, funny name he had?'

I look at Ciara, then rub at my nose.

'Stitch,' I say.

'That's it! Stitch. Because he had one stitch in his lip one day in school that was hanging out, right? What did he do on you?'

I look at Ciara again. I'm not sure what to say. Or really, I'm not sure how much to say.

I can see Ciara tapping her shoes off the carpet. She's nervous too.

Maybe coming to say goodbye to Harriet wasn't the best idea. She might get everything out of us. She's too bloody clever.

'G'wan,' Ciara says sighing, 'tell her what happened with Stitch last night.'

21:10

Ciara

SHIT. MAYBE THIS WASN'T A GOOD IDEA. HARRIET IS TOO INTELLIGENT. SHE might make Ingrid cave in and tell her everything.

I can feel Ingrid staring at me; trying to get a hint from me about how she should answer Harriet's question. So I look back at her and before I can even stop myself, the words come out of my mouth.

'G'wan, tell her what happened with Stitch last night,' I say.

Bleedin' hell. I hope she doesn't tell her everything. Because Harriet will talk her down; will make her feel better. Ingrid will refuse to do this... refuse to kill herself with me. And we need to do it. We need to do it tonight. We can't let anyone change our minds.

'We were at a party last night. He made fun of me in front of everybody in our school year,' Ingrid says.

'The little bollix,' Harriet says. I laugh. Then hold my hand up in apology to Ingrid. It's the way Harriet says things sometimes.

Ingrid sits herself on the edge of Harriet's bed. 'Me and him, we were... we were supposed to go to the party together to let people know we were... y'know...'

'Boyfriend and girlfriend?' Harriet says.

As Ingrid nods her answer, I sit beside her.

My head is talking to me as I sit. In fact, not just talking to me. It's screaming at me. It's telling me I should interrupt Ingrid. She might say too much. I know what Stitch said last night isn't the only reason she wants to kill herself. But it is the reason she finally agreed to do it. So

588

talking about it — giving Harriet the chance to mend her broken heart — might make Ingrid change her mind about ending it all. Only I don't know what I can say to stop her.

'He wouldn't even look at me the whole night. He was too busy mucking around with all those eejits he hangs out with.' I look up at Harriet and notice she is pulling one of those faces. Like a sympathy face; her lips closed tight, her eyes squinting. 'And when I tried to talk to him, he just sort of hushed me away. He was like... I don't know... he's a different person when it's just me and him.'

'Boys,' Harriet says. 'They're all like that. It's not just when you're thirteen. Boys are different around their mates than they are their girlfriends their whole lives. All my fellas have been like that. Boys are dopes.'

'How many boyfriends you had, Harriet?' I ask. I already know the answer. She's on her fourth. She told us that before. But maybe asking this will help change the conversation.

'Four,' she says. 'Just finished with Conor there a couple weeks ago.'

'Finished?' I ask.

'Same thing. Too immature. Was always changing plans when we were to meet up and stuff. Did me head in in the end. He started crying like a baby when I dumped him. Told him it was all his own fault.' She turns to Ingrid and rubs at her knee. 'This won't be your first heartbreak, honey, trust me. Specially someone who looks like you.'

I look down at my lap. It's always awkward for me when people mention looks. I know I'm not the prettiest. Never will be. But sometimes I think the better looking you are, the more attention you get from the boys. And who would ever want that?

'Boys don't notice me,' Ingrid says.

Harriet tips her head back and laughs.

'Yeah right? Ciara, do all the boys fancy her or wha'?'

I shoot my head up and twist my neck to look at Ingrid. Then I laugh a little and nod my head.

'Course they do,' I say. But I'm lying. The boys don't fancy Ingrid. I don't know why. She's probably the prettiest in the class. Either her or Tiffany Byrne. But the boys never seem to mention Ingrid. Or notice her at all. I think it's cause she hangs out with me. We're seen as the two little quiet weirdos.

'No they don't,' Ingrid says, making a funny face at me. I just shrug my shoulder. I wasn't really sure what to say. The truth? That my fat cheeks puts all the boys off her too?

'So where were yis last night?' Harriet asks.

'A guy in our year had a free house; his mum and dad were away for the weekend,' Ingrid says. 'Mum took a lot of persuading to let us go, but she did in the end. Told her it was a normal birthday party and that his parents would be there. About fifty people from our year turned up. We weren't really invited. Stitch and his mates were, so I asked Stitch if it was cool if we went too, so me and him could kind of...'

'Come out?' Harriet says.

Ingrid nods her head.

'But it just ended up with me and Ciara standing in the corner all night, eating bloody Cheesy Puffs.'

'I love Cheesy Puffs,' I say, before I realise what I've said. Harriet looks at me and laughs a little through her nose.

'So, what happened... did you confront him?' Harriet asks, turning back to Ingrid.

'It was when the slow music came on, wasn't it?' I say.

Ingrid nods.

'Yeah, the fella whose gaff it was, he had music playing all night. Then it switched to slow songs, so that the boyfriends and girlfriends could get up and dance together. I didn't know what to do. I was really nervous. And the room was so quiet because the music was so low. I just... I just walked up to him and tried to hold his hand.' I can feel Ingrid's insides cry, she almost bends herself over in two while sitting on the edge of the bed. 'He just looked at me as if he hated me. "What the fuck are ye doing?" he said. "Get your bleedin' hands off me you... ye fuckin smell like fish fingers".'

I look up at Harriet and notice her face go all funny.

'*Fishfingers?*' she says.

'There's always been this thing,' I say, 'that Ingrid smells of fish fingers because she's half Swedish. It's been going on for years... from when we started Primary School.'

'*Fishfingers?*' Harriet says again, this time really high-pitched.

'We don't get it either. It doesn't even make any sense.'

Ingrid sniffs some wet snot back up her nose.

'And then everybody just laughed. Really loudly,' she sobs.

'Ohhh... Ingrid.'

Harriet walks over to her, kneels down and gives her a big hug.

I hope she doesn't make Ingrid feel better. Well... better enough to not want to do what we plan to do. We better not have said too much already.

CHARLIE HAS TO ALMOST JOG TO KEEP UP WITH THE WIDE-OPEN STRIDES OF Helen.

'Jaysus, I hope he knows this kid,' he says, bounding up behind her.

'If the kid is from this area, then he'll definitely know him. We just needed to find the right Headteacher is all. We had the wrong area earlier on. But now we've got it. I'm sure of it.'

They cut through a narrow side entry — squeezing up a gap between an overgrown bush and a semi-detached home — and on towards the laneway the neighbour had pointed them to.

Then Helen stops, bends over slightly and holds her hands to her knees.

'Sorry, Charlie, I'm moving too fast for a woman of my age.' She looks up at him, still bent in her own unique way, and then sucks a large breath in through her nostrils. 'How old you reckon I am?'

Charlie's eyes widen a little. He pivots on his heel, swaying one way, then the other.

'Jee, I don't know...' he says before blowing out his cheeks. 'Fifty-odd, mid fifties?'

'Ha,' Helen shouts out, almost too loudly. 'Nope. Sixty-three. Can you believe that?'

Charlie can believe it. He politely aimed low with his estimation. Her face looks every inch the face of somebody in their sixties, perhaps even in their late sixties. There are heavy lines around her mouth, two rows of bags under each eye.

'Really? Wow. You don't look it. And your... eh... movement, sure, Jaysus, I have to run to keep up with ye,' he says.

'Well, you don't have to run now, do you? I've stopped. Gimme a second to grab my breath.'

Charlie swallows, then pivots again on his heels as he waits on Helen to stand back up.

'I won't move so fast this time,' she says, holding out a hand to Charlie. He grabs it, allows his weight to help Helen to straighten up.

'People always say I look younger. I think it's the hair.'

Charlie swallows again, then stares at the back of her hair as she walks on. He still hasn't worked out what colour it's supposed to be.

'Yeah... it's cool,' he says. 'Bet you're a really cool grandmother.'

Helen balks a little, but keeps walking.

'Never got a chance to be a grandmother,' she says.

A cringe runs down Charlie's spine. He slaps himself in the forehead, then sets off after Helen, trotting again to keep up with her.

'I'm so sorry,' he says. 'I eh... I want you to know. I am just as determined as you are to find these two girls before they do the wrong thing. We'll save their lives, okay? We'll save their lives in Scott's memory.'

Helen stops walking to glance back at Charlie.

'Thank you,' she says. Then she paces again, forgetting that she said she'd slow down.

'Never in a million years would I have thought he'd do it. I mean suicide... Scott? And every parent I've talked to since, who has had a child who has done the same thing, they say exactly that. Not in a million years could they have even guessed their child would end it all. I bet... I bet you any money that the parents of these two girls haven't one darn clue what's going on tonight.'

Charlie stretches out his arm and gently pats Helen between her shoulder blades as he catches right up to her.

'You never get over it, y'know? Well, I didn't anyway,' she says.

Then she stops walking again and pinches the top of her nose.

Charlie pivots on his heels, then winces a little before wrapping his two arms around her.

Neither of them say anything as he hugs her in the middle of the dark laneway. Then Helen swipes her nose with the sleeve of her leather coat, pushes Charlie gently away and walks on.

'C'mon, let's get to this Headteacher. What time's it now?'

Charlie reaches for his phone and stabs at the screen so the light comes on.

'Just gone quarter-past nine,' he says.

'Fuck sake. Not that long to go. Right....' Helen says, blinking her eyes as she continues to walk. 'If we can get a name for this boy from this Headteacher, we'll be fine. We can get to him, get the names of the girls out of him, track them down. If he knows they are gonna kill themselves, then he'll likely know where they're planning on doing it. We're going to stop them from doing what they want to do.'

Charlie nods his head, though his instinct is telling him Helen's plan doesn't sound particularly genius. There are no guarantees to any part of what she's just said. He squelches up his face, then decides to talk.

'But, Helen, why didn't he leave all that information... the girls' names and everything else... why didn't he share everything he knew when he made the calls?'

Helen twists her head to face Charlie, still striding forward, then shrugs her shoulder.

'It's happened thousands of times before, people ringing in to the station and offering up tiny bits of information.'

She notices Charlie's face contort.

'It does, Charlie. Happens all the time. I don't know whether these guys just like to get their kicks from it... or... I don't know. He's a young kid. He's probably frightened. Maybe he's the reason they're planning on killing themselves... there might be a lot of guilt on his part, that's why he rang it in. And perhaps he's too frightened that it'll all come back on him.' She stops walking and holds a hand out towards Charlie. 'Listen; the psychologist will have a field day with this boy after we bring him in. But we're not the psychologists are we? Our job is to investigate and act. And that's what we'll do.'

Charlie swallows again, then nods his head. And they both walk on, past the last of the bush that squeezed them into the laneway and out into an open road.

'Where the fuck is this pub?' Helen says, spinning around, her palms face up.

Charlie takes a few steps forward and peers around the bush.

'Here it is,' he says.

The pub looks like a large cottage house, topped off with a hay-brush rooftop.

'Jaysus, never knew there was a pub around this neck of the woods,'

Helen says before swiping some of the bush away and forcing her way through a gap.

She puffs out her cheeks as they cross the small car park and towards a lit open porch.

'Bar or lounge?' Charlie asks.

'Locals always drink in the bar,' Helen says, pulling at the door to their left. She steps aside, allowing Charlie to enter first.

The murmuring of chatter she heard as she opened the door immediately stops.

'We are looking to talk to Brother Fitzpatrick,' she says to the dozen people sitting at low tables.

Heads pivot around the room.

'He was here a minute ago, hardly did a bleedin' runner did he?' an elderly man says.

A mumble of laughter sounds out before the man behind the bar, drying a pint glass with a stained tea towel, cocks his head at Helen.

'He's in the Gents, Guards. Be out in a minute.'

Helen and Charlie take one step backwards and then both clasp their hands in front of themselves in unison as they stand still. Nobody's eyes divert from them and only the hum of a distant hand dryer creates any sound at all.

'Can I get yis a drink?' the barman, still drying the same pint glass, asks.

Helen waves a 'no' at him, almost managing a smile in the process.

The sound of a door creaking turns everybody's heads in the opposite direction. Then the door with 'Gents' written on it swings open and a bearded man limps into the bar; suddenly stopping upon noticing all faces staring at him. Then he spots the two strangers — one in a Garda uniform — and he staggers backwards, resting his shoulder blades against the wall.

'You're in trouble, Brother,' one man calls out. Most of the other patrons laugh. But their laughter sounds cautious, non-committal.

'Brother Fitzpatrick, I assume?' Helen asks, taking a stride forward towards him, staring at the clerical collar that she can see behind thin strands of his beard.

'Oh sweet Jesus, Mary and Joseph,' Fitzpatrick says, blessing himself.

Helen squints her eyes when she gets closer to him, can tell by his glazed look that he's had a few too many already.

'We eh... we need to speak with you as a matter of urgency.'

Helen points her hand towards the door behind her.

Fitzpatrick doesn't move.

'Unless you would eh... like us to talk to you here in front of everybody, Brother?'

'Hold on, hold on,' he says, raising a palm to the air. 'Gimme a second.'

He steadies his feet, sucks in a stuttering breath, then exhales slowly before leaning off the wall and walking, one foot in front of the other, as slowly as he can — past Helen, then past Charlie and finally out the door.

He's leaning against the porch wall when Helen and Charlie get outside.

'I'm so sorry,' he says. 'I eh... it's all really innocent... it's...' he shrugs his shoulders.

'What are you sorry for?' Helen says, folding her arms.

Fitzpatrick stares at her, then eyeballs Charlie before repeatedly blinking.

'Huh?' he says. Helen looks back at Charlie and whispers a 'fuck sake'.

'What are you saying sorry for?' Charlie asks.

'I.... I... need to speak with a what's-it-called? A eh... someone who eh... a legal thing?'

'A lawyer?' Charlie steps forward so that he's shoulder-to-shoulder with Helen.

Fitzpatrick nods his head, burping quietly as he does so, then re-steadies himself against the porch wall in an effort to rid himself of the swaying motion that's going on inside his head.

'How much you had to drink?' Helen asks.

'Eh... few pints. Just a few. I'm not driving. I just live down... see that lane way over there?' he says, almost tripping over his own feet as he turns to point.

'We know where you live, Brother Fitzpatrick. We've just called by. A neighbour said we'd find you here.' Fitzpatrick turns back slowly. 'Now before we tell you why we're here, mind telling us why you feel you need a lawyer... why you are apologising to us?'

Fitzpatrick tries to focus on both faces by repeatedly blinking again.

'I think I need a lawyer,' he says.

Helen holds her fingers to her forehead and stares down at her red Converse trainers.

'We don't have time for a lawyer,' she says, 'and we don't have time to deal with, well... whatever it is you are sorry about. We believe two of your students are in grave danger tonight and we need to track them down as quickly as possible.'

She looks up to see Fitzpatrick readjust his standing position, a hint of relief causing his brow to straighten.

'Oh,' he says. 'Students? Which students?'

'That's what we need to find out,' Charlie says.

'Brother, we need you to look at this image and tell us if you know who this boy is,' Helen clicks her fingers as she's finishing her sentence. But when she looks at Charlie, she notices he has missed his cue again. He fumbles into his pocket, grabs his phone and thumbs through the screen until he comes to the fuzzy CCTV image.

Helen takes the phone from him and stretches it towards Fitzpatrick's face.

Fitzpatrick squints, then blinks, before moving even closer to the phone and blinking again.

'Shurr what am I looking at here? I just see black and white,' he says, his glazed eyes narrowing.

Helen peers around at the phone, then points her finger at the screen.

'This, here… this boy… can you make out the face? Do you know who he is?'

Fitzpatrick blinks some more, then falters his step backwards, so that he's leaning against the wall again.

Helen puffs out a sigh and hands the phone back to Charlie.

'Back in a sec,' she says. She opens the door to the bar and holds up her hand.

'Pint of tap water, please. Cold… lots of ice.'

The barman grabs at a glass, then turns to the tap.

'Actually, make it two glasses,' Helen says.

'Brother Fitzpatrick okay?' the barman asks.

'He will be in a minute.'

The barman shovels ice cubes into both glasses, then hands them over to Helen who mutters a 'thanks' before storming back outside.

'Brother Fitzpatrick?' she says approaching him quickly. When he looks up at her, she flings her wrist, drenching his face.

'Sweet Jesus, Mary and—'

'Joseph,' Helen says, finishing his blessing for him. 'Here's another glass, Brother Fitzpatrick; drink it up, sober up and take another look at this image. Two of your students are in grave danger and the clock is ticking. There's no time for messing about.'

Fitzpatrick swipes at his face, removing as much water as he can. Then he holds out his hand, takes the full pint glass from Helen and swigs on it, slowly at first, then gulping until the ice rattles back into the glass.

'Now let's try again, Brother,' Helen says, clicking her fingers. Charlie reads her cue this time. 'I need you to look closely at this image and tell me if you know the boy in it.'

Charlie stretches the phone towards Fitzpatrick who wipes at his eyebrows before inching his nose closer. Then he begins to nod his head very slowly.

'Yeah. I know him. He's one of ours,' he says. 'Tommy Smith. He has some funny nickname they all call him... can't quite remember it. All the boys have weird nicknames. But yeah... that's definitely him. Little Tommy Smith. He lives in one of those bungalows up at the Harold's Cross Bridge.'

21:20

Ingrid

I PUSH MY FINGER INTO THE CORNER OF MY EYE TO TRY TO STOP A TEAR from falling out.

Harriet kneels down, wraps her arms around me and I lean my ear on the top of her head, looking up at Ciara. She widens her eyes. I know she's feeling scared; scared that I will say too much and let Harriet change my mind.

'Boys are feckin' eejits,' Harriet says into my chest. She pulls away from me and looks into my eyes. 'Honestly, don't let this little fecker bring you down. You're better than that.'

She's right. I am better than that. I know I am. It's just... nobody else does; certainly nobody at school. And nobody at home. They all treat me as if I'm a bother to them. Or I certainly feel as if I am a bother to them. The only people who have ever treated me as I should be treated are in this little bedroom right now. These two and Miss Moriarty... that's it. One friend. One cousin. One old teacher. I realised this morning as I was lying on my bed just how sad that is.

'Y'know what I've been thinking about lately?' Harriet says, getting to her feet before she plonks down on to the bed, pushing herself back so she's lying, her legs hanging off the edge. 'Girls don't need boys; women don't need men. They just don't understand us. Never will. Besides, what the hell do boys offer the world anyway? We're the ones who do everything. We do all the housework, all the cooking, all the... we give birth. A man can't give birth, can he? All he can do is offer sperm and sure d'ye know what I read in a book once? There's loads of sperm stored in hospitals and stuff, so much so that men are useless to women. The world doesn't need 'em anymore.'

She twists the back of her neck, so that she can look up at us. I don't like the word sperm. It sounds horrible.

'Lie down, girls, let me tell yis something.'

I push out my bum, then lay my back down so that I'm lying in between Harriet and Ciara; all of us gripping our hands behind our heads and staring up at the cool posters on Harriet's ceiling. *Moseley Shoals* the one I'm staring at reads. Whatever the hell that means. I just know that it's cool. It must be if Harriet likes it.

'With me and Conor, even though it was me who dumped him, it still hurts me a lot. I'm not really sleeping that well at night; find meself thinking about him all the time. But I'll get over it. I know I will. Because the books I read… they tell me that I don't need a boy to make me happy. Here…' she says, stretching her arm towards her windowsill. She grabs one of the books and then lays it on my stomach. '*Backlash* it's called,' she says. 'Give it a good read. S'all about how women are going to take over the world. Feminism… ye know what that means?'

She lies back down after asking this, back in to the same position she was in seconds ago; her legs dangling, her fingers gripped behind her head.

'About female-something?' Ciara says, leaning up on her elbows.

'Yep,' Harriet replies. 'All about how women are better than men and that, y'know, we don't need them. Feminism… the movement for women to become king.'

'Cool,' I say, before turning my face to look at Ciara. She raises an eyebrow, then shrugs her shoulder. I turn my face, so I'm staring at the posters again. 'You're into the coolest stuff, Harriet,' I say. 'Wish I could be more like you.'

Harriet laughs out through her nose.

'No you don't. Jaysus, I wish I was like *you*. Any idea how much the boys are gonna be swarming over you when you're older? You're gonna be a model, just like yer mam.'

Ciara sits up.

'But sure, what's the advantage of being pretty and getting all the men if we don't need men?' she says.

That's actually a good question.

Harriet tilts her neck so she can stretch her eyes to meet ours.

'Exactly,' she says.

Ciara stares down at me, her eyebrow raised again. I don't think she's getting what Harriet is trying to say. I'm not sure I get it either.

'Ah, you're too intelligent for us two, Harriet,' I say.

'You'll understand when you're older. Read these kinda books. They'll open your eyes.' She pats the book that's lying on my stomach.

So I pull myself up to a seating position and look at the front cover.

'*Backlash: The Undeclared War Against American Women...* hmmm,' I say and then I begin to flick through it. It's a long book. Very long. And the writing is really small in it. I can't imagine I'd ever read a book like this.

'The first chapter is called 'Blame it on Feminism,' I say. 'What's that mean...? I thought you said feminism was a good thing?'

'Huh?' Harriet says, sitting up. She takes the book from me and begins to read through the chapter. 'Ah... it's just some women think the feminism movement goes too far.' Then she hands me the book again and lies back down. 'It's a warzone out there,' she says. 'But the truth is, we have to be strong. Everyone has to be strong. Especially women, though. Men have ruled the world for far too long and all they want from us is food and sex.'

I turn my face to look at Ciara again. She squidges up her nose. And so do I. I always feel uneasy when the word sex comes up.

'Sorry,' Harriet says. 'Some of the subject might be a little... what's-the-word... mature for your age. But the sooner you learn all about this stuff, the stronger you'll become. Do ye think you need that... *strength?*' she asks.

I look over at her. She's just staring up at the ceiling, waiting on my answer.

'I'd love more strength,' I say. I feel Ciara nudging me in the back but I ignore it. 'How do I get more strength?' I ask.

Harriet stretches her neck again to look up at me.

'Read that book... and all these kinda books,' she says nodding her head towards her windowsill. 'They'll help you understand what life is all about. And how you'll find that the small things such as some little tosser calling you Fishfingers is so insignificant.'

I sit up straighter and run my finger down the front cover of the book. That's interesting. If reading this book means it won't hurt me anymore when somebody calls me Fishfingers surely I should just try to read it.

'Do you wanna take that one home with you?' Harriet asks.

I sniff through my nose, then find myself nodding my head.

'Yeah... yes. I'd love to. Thanks, Harriet.'

21:25

Harriet

I STARE UP AT MY CRAPPY POSTERS, MY HANDS CREATING A LITTLE PILLOW for the back of my head.

'You're into the coolest stuff, Harriet,' Ingrid says. *Jaysus. Cool? Me? If only.* 'Wish I could be more like you.'

I laugh.

'No you don't. Jaysus, I wish I was like *you*,' I say. 'Any idea how much the boys are gonna be swarming over you when you're older? You're gonna be a model, just like yer ma.'

Ingrid isn't gorgeous yet. She's pretty, definitely. But it's so obvious that she *will* be stunning when she grows up. When she grows into her nose, when she develops her body shape, when her eyebrows thicken. Every bloke in school will regret the day they didn't find her attractive. Whoever this Stitch guy is; he's gonna be pulling the mickey off himself thinking about Ingrid in a few years' time. And he won't be able to touch her. She'll be way out of his league by then.

'But sure, what's the advantage of being pretty and getting all the men if we don't need men?' Ciara asks me.

I look back her.

'Exactly,' I say. My answer doesn't mean anything. But I hope it's enough to shut her up. I don't need her testing me on my beliefs. Because I don't even know what my beliefs are. I'm a bullshitter. Always have been. If I'm good at anything — and I'm not good at much — it's pretending I'm somebody I'm not. I constantly bluff. Constantly make up who I am. What I stand for. I try to be cool. But there's absolutely feck all cool about me. These books… these posters… my nose ring… my clothes… my CD collection…. it's all bollocks. I've never even listened to a full Oasis album in my life. I don't even know who Kurt Cobain is. Give me a Take That record any day of the week. But Jesus, I wouldn't let anyone know that's the kinda stuff I'm into. These posters, this whole room. It's just for show. It's just all about a person I want to be seen to be. It's not me.

'Ah — you're too intelligent for us two, Harriet,' Ingrid says.

'You'll understand when you're older. Read these kinda books. They'll open your eyes,' I lie, patting at the book I placed on her stomach. I've no idea what's inside that book. Never read it. Never read any of em.

She sits up and begins to run her finger down the front cover. It'll be fine if she asks me questions. Bullshitting to my little cousin is easy. It's the bullshitting to my mates that's difficult. I'm always paranoid that they'll see right through me; that they know I don't really know what feminism means, that they'll know I couldn't tell the difference between Liam Gallagher and Noel Gallagher if they were stood right in front of me.

'The first chapter is called 'Blame it on Feminism,' Ingrid says. 'What's that mean…? I thought you said feminism was a good thing?'

'Huh?' I say before swallowing hard. I sit up and stare at her eyes. It's always best to hold somebody's eyes when you are bluffing. I take the book from her. 'Ah… it's just that some women think the feminism movement goes too far,' I lie, then hand her the book back. 'It's a warzone out there. But the truth is, we have to be strong. Everyone has to be strong. Especially women, though. Men have ruled the world for far too long and all they want from us is food and sex.'

Shit. Maybe mentioning sex to my thirteen-year-old cousin wasn't cool. Jaysus, Aunt Greta would kill me if she knew I was talking about sex with her precious little Ingrid.

'Sorry,' I say. 'Some of the subject might be a little… what's-the-word… mature for your age. But the sooner you learn all about this stuff, the stronger you'll become. Do ye think you need that… *strength?*' I ask. It's a genuine question. Jees, I'd kill somebody for more strength. I'm so weak. Bizarrely weak. Always have been. People think I'm strong because I took over all of the women duties in the house after my mam died. All of our family and the neighbours kept telling me how strong I was. They'd no idea I was crying my little heart out every night. Still do sometimes.

Have been for the past couple weeks since Conor dumped me. Fucker was seeing somebody else behind my back. I miss him like crazy.

'I'd love more strength,' Ingrid says. 'How do I get more strength?'

Jesus, Ingrid, I wish I knew.

'Read that book... and all these kinda books,' I say tilting my head towards my windowsill. 'They'll help you understand what life is all about. And how you'll find that the small things in life such as some little tosser calling you Fishfingers is so insignificant.'

That's actually not bad advice. Jaysus, if only I could listen to my own advice.

Ingrid sits up. I think she's intrigued by the book. I must be selling it well; even though I don't even understand what the title of that one means exactly.

'Do you wanna take that home with you?' I ask her.

'Yeah... yes. I'd love to. Thanks, Harriet.'

'No bother,' I say. And then I continue to stare up at these old posters on my ceiling. I get them out of *Rolling Stone* magazine. Seven quid every month that bastarding magazine costs me — just so I can continue to lie to everybody that that's the sort of shit I'm into. I don't know why I plaster my walls and ceiling in these posters, nobody really comes up to my room anymore anyway.

'Have you decided if you're going to college?' Ingrid asks.

Yep. I have decided. And no I'm not going. Can't afford to.

'Yeah... thinking about doing a course in music in Ballyfermot College. Supposed to be a really cool course there.'

I don't know why I've lied about that. She'll find out soon enough that I'm not going to college; that I've taken a shitty shelf-stacking job in the local supermarket for the summer. I just need to keep up the pretence that I'm cool; to Ingrid more than anyone. She looks up to me. It's nice to have somebody look up to you.

I'd love to go to college. But we need money coming into the house. Dad hasn't worked for years... over a decade. Not since mam died. He's on benefits. It's all we have to live on. Which is why paying seven quid on *Rolling* fucking *Stone* magazine every month makes absolutely no sense whatsoever. I'm a fuckin loser. Always have been.

'Yeah — you should totally study music,' Ingrid says. 'That'd be so cool. Everything you do is cool.'

CHARLIE HAS THE ENGINE REVVING, THE BLUE LIGHTS FLASHING AND HIS finger resting on the switch to start the siren's wail by the time Helen has hobbled into the car. She started sprinting, as soon as she got the name of the boy from Brother Fitzpatrick but waned before she had even reached the laneway. From there, she slowed down — into a jog, then a trot — before she finally huffed and puffed herself into Charlie's passenger seat.

She twirls her hand in the air as soon as she's settled, signalling that Charlie should get going.

'Jesus; I'm wrecked,' Helen says, leaning her head back on the rest.

Charlie smiles on one side of his face then nudges the car into gear and speeds off.

'You're doing great, Detective,' he says. 'You were so right in thinking we should go to the local Headteacher first. That was genius investigating. Course the Headteacher would know all of the teenagers in the area.'

Helen nods.

'Wonder if the others have found out the name yet?' she says.

Charlie stares over at her as he nudges the stick into fifth gear, the car now speeding.

'Huh?'

'The others; the other dicks... Detectives. I wonder if they've managed to get the name yet... Tommy Smith.'

'Oh... yeah, lemme ring that in, in case we're ahead of them,' Charlie says.

He reaches for his car's radio but before he can lift the receiver, Helen's hand is on top of his.

'Let's look after our investigation first,' she says. 'We'll pass on all of our information once we've caught up with this fella.'

Charlie's eyes narrow, the nub of his nose so pronounced that it forms into a perfect square.

'Really?'

'Yeah... if they get to him before us, we'll never get a chance to speak to him. They'll be questioning him all about Keating. They'll take the wrong path. We need to get to him first and find out the name of these two girls without playing games with him. We'll pass the other dicks on any information we get after we've caught up with Smith first.'

She turns her face, to gauge Charlie's reaction. But he remains motionless and expressionless, his foot heavy on the pedal.

'Trust me,' she says, touching his shoulder.

'They might be ahead of us already, Helen,' Charlie says.

'Hopefully not.'

They both stretch their necks when they pull into the bungalows, on the lookout for any other blue flashing lights ahead.

'Nothing,' Charlie says, pulling the car over. 'Okay... where'll we start?'

Helen already has one foot out of the car by the time he's finished his question. She paces straight up to the nearest door and rattles her knuckles against it.

A middle-aged woman answers, holding a spoon in one hand and a cup-o-soup in the other.

'Jaysus, what's wrong?' she says, her eyes widening at the site of the police car in front of her home.

'Nothing, ma'am,' Helen says just as Charlie catches up with her. 'We are looking for the house Tommy Smith lives in... he's about fourteen or fifteen years old. You know that name?'

The woman tilts her chin upwards.

'Ah... not surprised you're looking for one of them,' she says. She looks up and down the street, then steps out of the house and whispers. 'They live in that one over there, the red door.' She nods her head across the narrow street.

'Thank you, ma'am,' Helen says turning back to see the woman closing her hall door without any further comment.

Charlie and Helen trot across the street, Charlie getting to the red door first. He holds the bell down and then stands back.

The door opens slowly after the person behind it has wrestled with an inordinate number of locks.

'Wha' d'yous want?' a rotund man with a strange neck tattoo asks.

'We need to speak with Tommy as soon as possible,' Helen barks.

'He's not 'ere.'

'Sir, we have reason to believe a couple of Tommy's friends are in grave danger—'

'I don't know anythin' about his friends.'

The man attempts to edge the door closed, Helen holding the palm of her hand against it to stop him.

'Sir... Mr Smith is it? Are you Tommy's father?'

The man puffs a sigh out of his nostrils.

'He's not here. What do yis want me to say?'

Charlie looks to Helen.

'Tommy! Tommy!' she roars, twisting her head so she can see beyond the man's round frame and into his home.

The man steps out.

'Will ye shut the fuck up, woman. Jesus. He's not here, I told ye. Stop causing a scene.'

Helen sighs.

'Where would he be, Sir? Two young girls' lives depend on it.'

The man squints a little.

'Wha' d'ye mean?'

'Two girls from Tommy's school are planning to die by suicide tonight. Tommy might hold the answer to where we can find them. We believe he knows them well.'

The man smiles a wide grin at Helen, then shifts his gaze to Charlie, the grin widening.

'That's a good un,' he says. 'Never had a cop use that kinda tactic before.'

'We're not making it up, Sir. We believe Tommy rang in calls to two Garda stations a couple hours ago suggesting two girls from his school were planning on killing themselves at midnight tonight. We have to find them.'

'Will ye get the fuck outta here... think I'm buyin' that shite?' The man laughs.

'Sir, we're not lying,' Charlie says as calmly as he possibly can. 'Where can we find Tommy?'

'Tommy doesn't hang around with girls... Jesus.'

'Sir, we need to find out where your son is.'

The man takes a step back, inching the door closed again. Helen holds her palm to it, but the man is unforgiving this time, forcing his body weight behind the door until it shuts tight. Helen balks back, shaking the strain from her hand.

'Fat fuck,' she whispers to Charlie. 'I knew as soon as he took an age opening all those locks that they were a dodgy family. Ye never get answers from a dodgy family. Ever.'

Helen sucks her lips, places her hands back in the pockets of her leather coat and then turns around.

'Over here,' she says.

Charlie follows her across the street, straight towards the door they had knocked on earlier.

'Jaysus, not letting me enjoy me supper this evening are yis, coppers?' the woman says, twirling her spoon in her cup-o-soup.

'You eh... you mentioned you weren't surprised when we told you we were looking for one of the Smiths. How come?' Helen asks.

The woman raises an eyebrow, then takes half a step outside her home and peers up and down the street again.

'Bunch o' weirdos,' she says. 'The oul fella's been in and out of prison I don't know how many times. The son's gonna be worse. Little scumbag he is.'

'Tommy.'

'Yeah... that's him. Comes and goes from that house at all times of the night and morning. I've heard him coming home, shouting and screaming, pissed as a fart at like four-five a.m. His parents don't give a shit.'

Helen inches closer to the woman.

'Ever seen Tommy palling around with girls?' she asks.

The woman sticks her bottom lip out, then slowly shakes her head.

'Nah... he hangs around with a load o' blokes his age. There's a big gang of em. About a dozen of em. They all hang around under the Harold's Cross bridge, swigging flagons of cider.'

Helen looks at Charlie.

'Do ye think that's where he'd be now?' she asks, turning back to the woman.

The woman sticks her bottom lip out again.

'It'd be my best guess.'

'Thank you, ma'am. You can eh... you can finish your soup now. Sorry to be a bother.'

Helen twists her neck sharply as a siren grows in the distance. Then she looks up at Charlie before pacing past him, into the middle of the road to stare up as much of it as possible. She makes out the familiar sound of the siren twirping to a stop.

'Guess we just about got here before them,' she says, turning back to Charlie. 'Now let's get to the bridge before them. We gotta talk to Tommy, we can't let them take control.'

'Really?' Charlie asks. 'Isn't it just a case of finding Tommy. Does it matter who gets there first?'

'Yes! Yes it does, c'mon?' Helen moans, pulling at the locked passenger car door. 'Charlie!'

Charlie doesn't answer her, he just stares at the cop car coming their way.

He bends down slightly as it passes; makes out a familiar figure in the driver's seat.

'A sergeant from my station. Louis Kavanagh. Know him?' he asks Helen.

Helen shakes her head.

'C'mon, Charlie. Honestly. We need to act fast.'

Charlie holds his hand up at Helen as he trots past her, towards the cop car that has pulled in.

'Charlie, how ye getting on?' Louis says, lifting his stocky frame out of the car and sticking his Garda hat over his ginger hair. All of the hair on Louis' head is ginger; his eyebrows, his eye lashes, even the loose strands that hang from his nostrils.

'Grand... grand... You here for Tommy Smith?' Charlie asks.

'Yeah... you too? You chasing down the caller?'

'Yep,' Charlie says, a touch of pride in his answer.

'How d'ye get here before me?'

'Myself and Detective Brennan over there — from Rathmines station — tracked him down. Soon as we saw the CCTV footage, we paid a visit to the local school's Headteacher.'

Louis nods his head.

'Good thinking.'

'He's not in. The father answered, wasn't willing to give us much, but a neighbour here behind us, she—'

'Evening, Sergeant,' Helen calls out, creeping up behind Charlie.

Louis stretches out a hand.

'Nice to meet you Detective Brennan,' he says. 'Good work so far. No sign of Smith at home, no?'

'We haven't laid eyes on him yet, but that's his house there. Red door.

Maybe you can have more impact on the father than we've had. Best of luck. Let's go, Charlie.'

Charlie only moves after Helen has tugged at his elbow. He follows her to the car and, as they reach it, they both notice more blue lights flashing in the distance.

'Jaysus, they're all getting here now,' Helen says as they climb into their seats.

Charlie turns the key in the ignition and, as they pull off, Helen scoots down in her seat, her eyeballs soaking in each of the figures in the two Garda cars that pass. In the second car she notices Eddie, and scoots down even further, pulling the collars of her coat over her cheeks.

'Right... come on, Charlie, let's go visit that bridge. It's not far from here.'

Charlie flicks on the lights, and edges his way out of the narrow estate.

'What's with you, Helen?' he asks.

'Whatcha mean?'

'Why are you being all secretive with the other cops? What's going on?'

Helen sits more upright, flattening down the collar of her coat.

'It's just... well, it's two separate investigations. We need clarity and full focus on our investigation, don't we? We can't get derailed by theories that the phone call was made as a hoax distraction.'

Charlie flicks his eyes to the rear-view mirror.

'It must be a hoax distraction, though,' he says, taking his hand from the gear stick so he can point his thumb backwards. 'Sure the whole bloody force is out chasing Tommy Smith because they think he has links to Alan Keating. It's only me and you that seem to think his phone calls were a suicide warning.'

Helen coughs into her clenched fist.

'Exactly,' she says. 'That's why we have to conduct our investigation separately. Let them conduct theirs and we'll keep focused on ours.'

Charlie pivots his neck from side to side, producing tiny bone cracks.

'Suppose you're right,' he says. 'It's cool though isn't it? All of them; only two of us. Yet we're always one step ahead. You'll turn me into a Detective by the end of the night, Helen.'

Helen laughs, only because she is relieved that she's managed to pull Charlie back around to her way of thinking.

'Well... it'll only be a success if we save these girls,' she says. 'Remember; focus, Charlie. I enjoyed the thrill of the chase when I first started investigating too. But you'll come to learn you are focusing your energy in the wrong places when you let the thrill get the better of you.'

Charlie turns to Helen.

'Thank you. You've been great to learn from this evening. Think you eh... think you could let me take you out for a coffee sometime. Just so I can pick your brain about how I can become a Detective? I'm bloody sick of sitting in the station filling out paperwork.'

Helen snuffs out another laugh. Not many would understand Charlie's frustration with administrative work more than her. Her career's gone in the opposite direction. From top Detective back down to envelope stuffer. She lost the run of her mind after Scott died by suicide. Could never get her head back on the job. Eddie had stronger mentality. Still does. He managed to get himself back to the station a month after Scott and his mates ended their lives. Five years later, after he became the station's superintendent — and after much nagging from his wife — he made sure she got a job as administrative assistant. Mainly because he could keep an eye on her. Helen always said it was for the short-term. Even suggested that she'd open her own private investigator practice one day; Eddie knocking her back insisting those guys don't make any money. It caused quite an awkward argument between them earlier this year when one PI managed to secure himself a million euro house for five hours work in Dublin. Still, Eddie knew she'd never carry through her threat. He knows Helen wouldn't have the know-how to run her own business.

'Course, no problem. We can do coffee anytime you want,' Helen says.

Charlie is smiling to himself when he's pulling the car over on the double yellow lines that run parallel to the canal.

They both get out as quickly as they can, trotting their way to the steps that lead to the under path of the bridge.

By the time they're at the bottom step, they can hear the giddy laughter of teenagers.

Charlie reaches for his torch, flicks it on and shines it towards the narrow pathway in front of Helen. They can both see the butts of joints being tossed into the canal as they approach.

'What the fuck do you pigs want?' one teenage boy calls out.

21:35

Ciara

ME AND HARRIET ARE STILL LYING BACK ON THE BED, OUR HANDS BEHIND our heads, staring up at posters of bands and movies I've never even heard of.

But Ingrid is sitting up now, flicking through the book Harriet handed to her a couple minutes ago. She just said she'd love to take it home with her. Bleedin' hell! She better not be serious. I knew coming to Harriet's wasn't a good idea. I'll go mad if Ingrid decides to put our pact on hold just so she can read that stupid book. It's all nonsense anyway. As if women will ever rule the world. I like Harriet and all, but sometimes the things she says don't make any sense to me at all. I think she thinks she's cleverer than she really is.

I sit up and stretch my hand towards Ingrid.

'Gis a look,' I say.

I take the book from her and flick through it myself, pretending that I'm interested. Jaysus… Ingrid won't read this. It's way too long.

'What time's it?' I ask.

'Coming up to twenty to ten,' Harriet says. 'Jee… it's almost my bedtime. I normally turn in about ten. How come you guys are out so late? Don't ye have school in the morning?'

I stay silent to see if Ingrid will answer. But she just continues to stare at the ceiling.

'Eh… yeah,' I say. 'Yeah we do. I actually didn't realise it was that late.

We better get going. Ingrid just wanted to drop by… to let you know about Stitch.'

Harriet tuts.

'Fuck Stitch,' she says, sitting up to join us. She smiles at Ingrid. 'I know Aunt Greta would go mental if she knew I was cursing to ya. But I mean it. Fuck him. He's gonna be way beneath you in a couple years time.' She places her hand on Ingrid's shoulder and rubs it. 'You sure you're okay, cuz?'

Ingrid turns her head slowly towards me.

'She's fine,' I say quickly. 'She'll be okay in the morning.'

'I don't wanna go to school,' Ingrid says, holding her hands to her face.

I reach out and rub her back.

'Everything will be okay, Ingrid,' I say.

'Course it will. Listen to Ciara. What she's saying is right,' Harriet says. I smile a tiny smile over Ingrid's shoulder at Harriet. 'You walk into that school tomorrow with your head held high and a 'fuck you Stitch' attitude, you hear me? That's what I've had to do since me and Conor finished. You just have to get on with it. You've a long life to live.'

I cough to distract the conversation. I don't like where it's going again. I don't trust Ingrid to not break down and open up to Harriet about not wanting to live any more. I nudge at her back and keep doing it until she's got to her feet.

'I guess we better go,' she says, staring at the ground.

'Here, don't forget the book,' Harriet says, stretching over to where I'd almost hidden it under her pillow. She hands it to Ingrid who grabs it into her chest. 'If you have any questions on it, let me know… won't you?'

Ingrid sniffs up her nose and then nods. I can tell she's almost in tears. This is her hardest goodbye of them all. She loves Harriet. But as I said to her last night, Harriet is not enough reason for Ingrid to stay alive. Harriet will move on soon; to college, to a job, to a husband with kids. She's not going to have time for Ingrid forever. Barely has time for her now. They used to be in each other's lives a lot more when they were younger. Now they only see each other if Ingrid ever bothers to call out here.

'You sure you're okay, cuz, you look like you're about to cry again?' Harriet says.

Then she stands up and rests both of her hands either side of Ingrid's waist. I've already inched my way towards Harriet's bedroom door. We really need to leave.

I watch as Ingrid nods her head before she nestles it onto Harriet's shoulder. Harriet looks over at me, her bottom lip turned outwards.

'I'm telling ya,' she says, 'in a couple months' time you won't care who this Stitch bloke is. It'll only hurt for a little while. It's a little bit of heartbreak… that's all. The heart mends.'

Ingrid wipes the sleeve of her tracksuit top across her face.

'It's… it's…. it's not just that,' she sobs. 'It's not just Stitch.'

Oh bleedin' hell!

'Huh?' Harriet says, removing Ingrid's arm from her face. 'Tell me… you can say anything to me… what's wrong?'

A creak sounds from outside, then a huff and a puff. It's Brendan, making his way up the stairs. He enters the room next to us, the latch on the door locking.

'Tell me, cuz, what's wrong?'

'It's nothing,' I say, walking towards them both. 'It's the whole school thing… how everybody will be calling her Fishfingers in the morning. But don't worry, Harriet… I'll look after her. I promise.'

Harriet offers me a sad smile, then she turns to face Ingrid again.

'You sure, Ingrid? Is there anything else you want to say to me?'

Ingrid opens her mouth.

Then we hear an almighty fart. As if thunder is rolling over our heads.

21:40

Ingrid

THIS IS THE HARDEST GOODBYE YET. I CAN'T STOP THE TEARS FROM POURING out of my eyes. And out of my nose. I didn't think it would be this hard.

Harriet hugs me and tells me everything will be alright. Again.

'I'm telling ya,' she says, 'in a couple months' time you won't care who this Stitch bloke is. It'll only hurt for a little while. It's a tiny bit of heartbreak... that's all. The heart mends.'

I wipe my face clear of the tears and snot and then nod my head.

'It's... it's.... it's not just that,' I say. 'It's not just Stitch.'

Maybe I shouldn't be saying this. Ciara will be hopping mad behind me. I know she will. I still want to do it... commit suicide. I think I do anyway. But I really wouldn't mind talking to Harriet, just to get a different opinion. She's so intelligent, so cool. She might understand why I hate the thought of being called Fishfingers for the next six years. She might understand that I feel like I'm bothering Mum and Dad if I tell them I feel sad.

'Huh?' Harriet says, taking my hand away from my face. 'Tell me... you can say anything to me... what's wrong?' I hold my eyes closed and nod my head, as if I'm telling myself I shouldn't say what I want to say.

'It's nothing,' Ciara interrupts. I knew she would. 'It's the whole school thing... how everybody will be calling her Fishfingers in the morning. But don't worry, Harriet... I'll look after her. I promise.'

I swallow hard. I'm not sure if I'm grateful for the interruption or not. My mind is too... too full; full of horrible thoughts; full of sadness; full of disappointment; full of fear. But that's why I want to die, isn't it? I want my mind to stop feeling all these bad things all the time.

'You sure, Ingrid? Is there anything else you want to say to me?' Harriet says.

I suck up a sob, and as I'm doing so, I decide I'll tell her; tell her that I'd rather die than feel the way I do. Then, just as I'm about to open my mouth, I hear a huge fart — like one of those crackling fireworks. It goes on and on.

I laugh, and as I do, my tears spray onto Harriet's face.

She falls back onto the bed, her hand over her mouth, doing her best to not laugh too loudly. I look behind, through my tears, and notice Ciara has slidden down the wall. She has her knees up beside her ears, her face buried behind them, her shoulders shaking. Squeals of laughter are squeaking out of all three of us. Then another fart comes; not so loud this time, more a splat. And suddenly I'm on my knees, holding my lips closed as tightly as I can so no more squeals of laughter can sneak out.

Then Uncle Brendan lets out a gasp and I am certain I am about to wet my knickers. Ciara can't hold it in anymore either. Her laughter gets loud. Harriet rises from the bed, her face purple, her eyes tightly closed, tears glistening on the edges of them and she begins to wave her hand at Ciara — trying to get her to shut up. But she can't. Ciara is flat on the floor now, on her stomach, laughter roaring from her. Then my dam bursts too; my lips ripping open and laughter pouring out. I fall flat onto my belly and begin banging my fists on the carpet.

'Bleedin' hell!' Ciara says, in between gasps.

I manage to suck in some air and fill my cheeks, to try to stop the laughter and return to normal. I look up at Harriet and see her drying her eyes with her poncho.

'He always does that!' she whispers to me. 'He doesn't know how loud he is.'

My lips blow out more laughter. I'm getting scared now, as if I'm gonna suffocate and die right here, right now. Jesus. Wouldn't that be a lovely way to go? Ciara has researched suicide for so long now that she came up with the quickest and least painful way for us to do it, but I bet she never thought about dying of laughter.

I manage to slow down my breathing and finally sit up, resting my back against the bed. Ciara does the same, then grips my elbow and when I turn to her she winks at me.

'Jesus, Harriet, why did you choose the bedroom closest to the toilet?' Ciara asks, a ripple of laughter still squeezing out of her mouth.

Harriet dabs at her eyes again.

'The house is tiny, all of the bedrooms are close to the toilet,' she answers as she steadies herself to stand. 'I'm so sorry, girls. That's so embarrassing.'

'Jesus, don't be silly,' Ciara says. 'All men are the same. I wonder if it talks about men's pooing habits in your books?'

The three of us laugh again, but a normal laugh this time; one we are certain we can recover from.

'Well there ye go,' Harriet says. 'There's your recipe for getting over Stitch, huh? Your uncle having a noisy shit. You've gone from crying to laughing in a split second. Told ye pain doesn't last long.'

I reach out and hug her again. She grips me tight.

'Here, take this,' she says, handing me the book. 'Read it and get back to me. If you ever need an ear, phone me. Or drop by. Anytime. Both of you.'

I shake my head, nuzzle it onto her shoulder and breathe in her hair.

'Love you, cuz,' I say.

She leans off me and stares into my eyes.

'Not like you to say "I love you",' she smiles. 'But I love you too. Always have, Ingrid. I'll see you soon, yeah?'

I nod my head; not sure whether I'm lying to her or not. Then I hold her book close to my chest and watch as she hugs Ciara.

'Actually, tell you what... Dad! Dad!' Harriet shouts over Ciara's shoulder.

'Gimme a sec!' he calls out from the toilet.

To stop myself from laughing again, I stroll around the room, pull at a little drawer below Harriet's CD player and flick through her CDs. She strolls over towards me and pushes it closed.

'Dad!' she shouts again.

'Jesus. I'm trying to wipe me arse!' he says. The three of us laugh again. Out loud. Not minding that he hears us this time.

'I'm just wondering if you can drop the girls home? It's late. Ten to ten. Do you mind?'

'No, no... Jesus no,' Ciara butts in.

'It's no problem. Any excuse to get him out of the house. Sure, it's only a ten minute drive... he'll be fine.'

Uncle Brendan sighs.

'Go on then,' he says. Then the toilet flushes and the bathroom door opens. 'Let me get me shoes on.'

'Uncle Brendan,' I call out, opening the door of Harriet's bedroom.

He's stopped at the top of the stars, is staring over his shoulder at me. I pause before saying anything — not because I don't know what to say, but because the stench from the toilet has just reached my nose.

'Doesn't matter… Uncle Brendan. Thank you. We'd appreciate the lift. We'll be down in a second.' I say all that in one breath, then close Harriet's bedroom door.

'Oh my God, the stink,' I whisper.

Harriet and Ciara laugh. I don't. It's hard to laugh when you're pinching your nostrils and holding your lips tight together.

Eventually I let go and puff out a breath.

'Okay — I guess we better go now,' I say. I hug Harriet again and thank her for the book.

As me and Ciara are walking down the stairs, she begins to strike up some sort of argument without saying anything. She's speaking with her hands, her face all creased up in that angry way she gets sometimes. I'm not sure if she's giving out about me for taking the book or whether she's angry that Uncle Brendan is going to give us a lift. Maybe it's both. Or maybe she feels I've changed my mind — that I'm not going to follow through on our pact.

I just hug the book a little tighter to my chest and ignore her.

HELEN STRIDES IN HER OWN UNIQUE WAY — POKER STRAIGHT, ARMS IN pockets — towards the group of teenagers as Charlie, close behind, shines his torch over her shoulder.

'Which one of you is Tommy Smith?' she asks.

She notices their heads spin and murmurs spark amongst them, echoing off the dome wall under the bridge.

'Which one of you is Tommy Smith?' she asks again, this time more direct.

'We don't talk to pigs,' a boy with bad acne says. He's a lot taller than the others around him, though Helen notes he can't be much older than them. They all look to be in their mid-teens, maybe even a year or two younger.

Helen sniffs her nose and then takes a large stride forward, so that she's only inches from the group. She isn't afraid of much. Except for water. Would go into a full blown panic if this confrontation got heated and she somehow found herself in that canal.

She takes in each face in front of her; eight boys, three girls.

'We have reason to believe two of your friends may be in grave danger. We're not looking to cause any trouble; we're only here to help save lives. You can keep drinking your cider, keep smoking that cheap weed. All I want is to speak to Tommy. Now... which one of you is Tommy?'

'He's not here,' the smallest of the girls says.

'Shurrup, Audrey,' the boy with the acne says. 'We don't talk to pigs.'

Audrey takes a step behind her friend to try to stifle her embarrassment by hiding her face.

Helen looks back at Charlie, then turns to the group again.

'Thank you, Audrey. Listen, guys, we're not here to disturb your evening. We have good reason to believe two girls, of about your age, will die tonight if we can't get to them first. Tommy knows who they are, and where they are. We need to speak with him as soon as possible.'

The boy with the acne takes a step closer to Helen, then sniffs his nose as loudly as he can before folding his arms and standing more upright.

'I get it,' Helen says, 'you don't speak to pigs.' She strains her neck, so she can peer past him. 'What about the rest of you?'

'We don't believe you,' another boy shouts.

Helen takes her hands out of her pockets and holds her palms up.

'I am not lying. I swear to you. To each of you. We just need to speak to Tommy for two minutes, then we'll be on our way.'

The boy with the acne sniffs his nose loudly again. No noise comes from the gang behind him.

Helen fidgets with her fingers, then sucks on her lips.

'Okay… let me ask you this. Do any of you know of any girls from the area or from your school who you feel might be tempted to commit suicide? It's imperative you tell us. We need to save their lives.'

The boy with the acne looks behind him. Then he turns back to Helen and sniffs his nose again.

Helen runs a hand through the back of her orange hair, scrunching it up in frustration.

'You're a funny looking pig aren'tcha?' the boy with the acne says. 'And you… you with the torch, ye look like a bleedin' rat. All that's missing is the whiskers.'

An echo of laughter sounds around them. Helen eyeballs as much of the group as she can, noticing that the cowering Audrey is the only one not finding acne boy particularly funny.

'How old are you, Audrey?' Helen asks.

Audrey's eyes go wide at the mention of her name, then she stares down at her Nike trainers.

'Well, if you're not gonna tell me, maybe I should guess,' Helen says. 'Thirteen? Fourteen? Well, the two girls who we believe are going to harm themselves tonight are your age. I don't suppose one of em is you, is it?'

Audrey looks up, then shakes her head rapidly.

'Shurrup, Audrey,' the boy with the acne says. 'Don't tell these pigs nuttin.'

Helen looks back to Charlie again and sighs. He takes a step forward, shining the torch in the boy's acne-ridden face.

'You're hardly one for judging people's looks, young man,' he says. 'Now, the rest of you listen up. Two girls' lives are in the balance here. We are not looking for any information other than where we can find Tommy Smith so he can give us the name of these girls. Which one of you is Tommy Smith?'

'He's not here,' a boy from the back calls out. 'He don't hang round here no more. Hasn't hung with us in months. He fucked off with another bunch of mates.'

Charlie nods.

'Thank you. Now, can you tell me where I *can* find him? Where does he hang out with these new mates?'

The group fall silent again. Charlie pivots his wrist, so he can shine the torch to each of their faces. Every time a face lights up, its eyes look down. They don't want to talk.

'You're only thirteen, right?' Helen says stepping in front of Charlie and staring at Audrey.

Audrey shakes her head.

'Fourteen?'

Audrey nods.

'Okay then... you are under arrest for underage drinking, you are coming with us.'

'Hold the fuck on,' the boy with the acne says, holding his hand in front of Helen.

Helen eyeballs him, the two of them having a staring competition in front of the group of teenagers, torchlight shining between them.

'You wanna be done too for assaulting a police officer?' Helen asks after the staring match has carried on for way too long.

The boy removes his hand and Helen holds hers out to Audrey.

'C'mon, Audrey, you're coming with us.'

'Why y'only pickin' on her... we're all drinking, we're all smoking joints?' one of the boys asks.

Helen coughs into her hand.

'Audrey here confirmed her age for me. You all wanna do the same? You all wanna come to the station with us?'

She looks around at the gang, hoping they all stay silent. Things would get a hell of a lot more complicated for Helen if they all admitted to being under age. If they all wanted to go to the station as a protest to support Audrey, Helen's plan would fall apart. She nods at the silence. Relieved.

'Good,' she says. 'We only need to formally address Audrey. We'll have her back with you in a few minutes.'

Helen stretches her hand further. Audrey creeps out slowly from behind her friend and then walks towards the torchlight and out from under the bridge; Charlie in front of her, Helen behind her.

'Fuckin pigs,' one of the gang shouts out.

Charlie leads both Audrey and Helen up the steps and towards his Garda car. He holds the top of Audrey's head as she bends into the back seat and then Helen walks to the other side of the car, gets into the back seat too.

'You can go back under the bridge,' she says, 'back swigging your cheap cider in a couple minutes, Audrey. I just have a couple of important questions I need to ask you.'

Audrey nods her head, and then eyeballs Helen before staring over at Charlie who has just got himself into the driver's seat. Her knees are shaking.

'Two girls' lives are in danger, so I need you to be totally honest with me. I don't care if you are drinking cider and smoking weed, I don't care if Tommy Smith is from a family of scumbags who have been in and out of prison. Honestly, whatever you or any of your mates have done in the past, I couldn't give two shits about it. All I want to do tonight is save these girls' lives.'

Audrey nods her head and swallows at the same time.

'Do you know of any girls who might want to harm themselves tonight?'

Audrey's shoulders hunch up, then down.

'No,' she says. Helen squelches her face up in disappointment. 'I'm being honest. No. I don't know any girls who would commit suicide.'

'Okay. Where can we find Tommy Smith? He holds the key to us tracking these two girls down. We need to find him.'

Audrey allows a light sigh seep its way out of her nostrils.

'Ye can't tell him I told yis where he hangs out,' she says.

Helen shakes her head.

'We won't.'

'He eh... he's started to hang around with some older blokes. I don't know who they are. But I think they mostly hang around the snooker hall in Terenure, ye know it?'

Helen looks at Charlie.

'Yeah, I know it,' Charlie says. 'It's called Cue, right?'

Audrey nods her head. She looks disappointed in herself; as if she's revealing some dark secret she swore she'd never tell.

'It's all okay, Audrey. We aren't looking to arrest Tommy for anything. Our only concern is saving the two girls,' Helen reminds her.

'Really? Yis aren't messing with me? This is really about two girls committing suicide?'

Helen places a curled finger under Audrey's chin and lifts it so that she can stare into her eyes.

'I promise,' she says. 'Now do you think Tommy will be in Cue right now?'

Audrey raises an eyebrow, then shakes her shoulder towards Helen.

'I assume so… it's where he normally is. But as I said, I don't really hang around with him anymore. He stopped hanging around with us months ago.'

'Do you go to the same school as Tommy?'

Audrey laughs through her nose.

'He doesn't go to school, are ye mad? Don't know when's the last time I saw him at school.'

'But you do go to St Joseph's School; Brother Fitzpatrick is your Headteacher, right?'

Audrey's eyes widen.

'Are the two girls from my school? Who are they?'

Helen removes her finger from underneath Audrey's chin.

'That's what we need to find out. Audrey… tell us, do you know of any girls from your school who you feel would put their lives in danger?'

Audrey holds her lips tight together, then begins to shake her head slowly.

'I'm sorry. I'd tell yis if I did. I want to help. I hope yis find these two girls, but I… I can't help ye. I can only tell ye where I think Tommy might be. Hopefully he can help yis.'

Helen squelches her face up again, then she takes out her phone to check the time. 21:56. Time is running out.

'D'you have Tommy's phone number?' she asks Audrey.

Audrey shifts her bum cheek off the seat and reaches into her back pocket. She scrolls through her screen, then turns it to face Helen. Helen reaches her finger towards it and presses at Tommy's name.

'Ah Jaysus, don't ring him from my phone,' Audrey says, 'he'll think I'm checking up on him.'

'Shush, shush,' Helen says, taking the phone and holding it to her ear.

The ring tone dials, and dials... then cuts out. She sighs, then takes out her own phone and types in Tommy's number.

'He never bloody answers his phone anyway,' Audrey says.

'What do you think, Charlie?' Helen asks, placing her hand on his shoulder.

'If you've got his number and we have a location, let's get there,' he says.

Helen offers Audrey a thin smile.

'You're good to go.'

21:55

Ciara

'WHAT THE HELL IS GOING ON HERE?' I TRY TO SAY THROUGH MY TEETH — without moving my lips — as we get into the back of Brendan's car.

Ingrid just looks at me and then shakes her head.

Bleedin' hell. This is crazy! We're supposed to be going to Miss Moriarty's house to say our final goodbye. Not getting a bloody lift home from Brendan. Ingrid better not be changing her mind. I swear to God that if we don't go through with this tonight, I'll never be her friend again. She can't write a pact with me and then not follow through on it.

'Y'okay, girls?' Brendan says, turning to us in the back. 'What yis mumbling about?'

'Nothing, Uncle Brendan,' Ingrid answers, gripping that stupid book to her chest.

I eyeball her, but she doesn't turn to look at me.

'When you gonna have time to read that?' I whisper.

She shrugs her shoulder.

'Ingrid!'

She pulls a bizarre funny face at me, then nods her head towards Brendan.

'Shhh,' she says.

This is really frustrating. We can't even talk now. We gotta get out of this car. We gotta talk this out. I knew we shouldn't have gone to Harriet's. I knew she would say things that'd make Ingrid change her mind. That bleedin' book is doing my head in; she's hugging it as if it's just saved her life.

I reach for it, take it from her and then sigh as I open the first page.

'Load of shite,' I whisper to her.

She looks over at me for the first time since we got into the car and offers me that tiny half-smile she likes to do every now and then. I'm not sure what she means by it.

'Ingrid,' I whisper without moving my lips. 'You're not planning on reading this bleedin' thing, are you?'

She gives me that funny face again, then pushes her lips together to shush me.

I twist my neck to look out the back window.

'We're going in the wrong direction, we're supposed to be going to Miss Moriarty's,' I grind through my teeth.

'Jaysus, you two like whispering, don't yis?' Brendan says, twisting at his rear-view mirror. 'What yis talkin' about?'

'Don't worry, Uncle Brendan... it's just girlie talk,' Ingrid says.

'Talking about me, are yis? Let me guess. Yis heard me in the bathroom. I forgot yis were in Harriet's room.'

I laugh. As loudly as I can. So does Ingrid.

'I bloody knew it!' Brendan says. 'Listen, a man's gotta do what a man's gotta do.'

When I stop laughing I place my hand on Ingrid's knee. Then she places her hand on top of mine.

'We all do it,' I say to Brendan. And suddenly I feel a little bit more relaxed, even though we're heading in the wrong direction.

I stare out the side window and recognise where we are. The canal road.

'Brendan... if you don't mind, can you stop at the garage here at the next bridge, I need to pick up something before we go home?'

He sighs a little, then smiles back at me through the rear-view mirror.

'Go on... don't be long,' he says, clicking his indicator. He turns into the garage and parks up in one of the small spaces around the back.

I cock my head at Ingrid, telling her to follow me and we both get out and walk slowly towards the garage's shop entrance.

'What the hell is going on?' I say when we're out of sight of Brendan's car.

'What d'ye mean?'

'I know it's part of the pact that we can't ask each other if we're changing our minds or not... but you just better not be!'

Ingrid shrugs her shoulder again... then shakes her head.

'No... no, course not,' she says.

'Well what about this bloody thing?' I say, holding up the book.

Ingrid swipes the book from my hand, then stares at the front cover.

'Ingrid!' I shout.

She widens her eyes, shakes her head again.

'No, course I'm not gonna read it. I was just being nice to Harriet. She handed it to me... what was I supposed to do?'

I breathe out a happy breath. She *hasn't* changed her mind. We're still gonna do this. I think.

'It's just... I got the feeling you were changing your mind. You were all upset and then suddenly we're all rolling around Harriet's bedroom laughing our heads off. It frightened me a little. I thought just because your uncle had a shite that suddenly your life got better. I got worried when you took the book and when you accepted a lift from Brendan.'

She reaches out and rubs her hand up and down my arm.

'It's not like that, Ciara,' she says. 'I just wanted to be polite, y'know. I didn't want to tell my uncle I wasn't accepting his lift. And I didn't want to tell my cousin I didn't want to read her book. I was just being nice. Just being me.'

I breathe a happy breath again. I'm so happy; happy that Ingrid hasn't changed her mind; happy that our lives are nearly over.

'Okay... what we gonna do now?' I ask.

Ingrid squelches up her mouth, then shrugs her shoulders again. She's always been like this; crap at making decisions. I'm pretty sure I've made most of the decisions in her life for her.

'We gotta tell Brendan we don't want a lift home from him; tell him we'll be okay from here. Then we can catch a bus back towards Miss Moriarty's house. Here... leave the book in the car with him.'

Ingrid sucks air through her teeth, then breathes out slowly through her nose.

'Okay,' she says, 'I have an idea.'

22:05

Ingrid

It wasn't the laughing at Uncle Brendan having a poo that was changing my mind. It was before that. It was Harriet talking to me, telling me we don't need men; telling me that I'd be stupid to allow Stitch to control all of my feelings; telling me that if I read her book then I might not feel stupid every time somebody calls me Fishfingers at school.

The pooing didn't change anything. All that did was make me laugh — really, really hard. Harder than I have laughed in ages.

Then, when the laughing stopped, I still had that pain in my belly; still had the dark thoughts going round and round in my head. That's the worst of it. When I return to the pain and to the dark feelings after they've gone away for a little while, that pain and those feelings always seem to be worse... deeper... heavier. It's like when I get high from laughing or something, the downer after that is so hard to take. It makes me think that I should never get high; that I should never laugh, never try to enjoy life. Because when I do, I know that coming down from that is painful. I could feel it as I was getting into Uncle Brendan's car. I was returning to sadness and heartache after laughing non-stop for two minutes. And it hurt. It hurt really bad.

That's why I agreed to commit suicide, I think. I can't even enjoy laughing for crying out loud. Why would I want to be alive?

'C'mon,' I say, dragging at Ciara's elbow. We both run into the tiny garage shop. 'Excuse me, do you have a pen I could borrow?' I ask the man behind the counter.

He stares at us, then points towards the Lotto stand at the end of the shop counter.

'Thank you,' I say. I turn to the tiny desk at the Lotto stand and open the book on top of it before snatching at a cheap pen that's attached to a small chain.

Ciara squints her eyes as I write.

I love you Harriet,

Ingrid. x

'Okay,' I say, slapping the book closed. 'Come on.'

We race each other out to the car.

'Here, Uncle Brendan, give this back to Harriet,' I say after I snatch the passenger door open. 'Tell her I'm sorry. We're eh... we're going to make our own way home from here, okay.'

'What... what are you talkin' about, girl?' he says.

'I'm sorry, Uncle Brendan; for getting you out of the house. And thank you for the lift this far. But... we're gonna go, okay?' I slam the door shut, then grip on to Ciara's hand and we leg it out of the garage courtyard as fast as we can.

'Ingrid! Ingrid!'

I hear Brendan roar after us but I just wave my hand in the air and keep running.

It's crazy that I feel happy. I've been at my happiest all day when I am certain I want to do it. And the great thing about feeling happy now — just before I kill myself — is that this time I know there's not going to be a come down. Because I'll be dead. I know that I am doing the right thing; that *we're* doing the right thing. All of this nonsense; the ups and downs, the stresses of school, the bullying, the heartache, the headaches... they'll all be gone soon. Gone forever.

'MIND IF I ASK YOU A QUESTION?' CHARLIE SHOUTS OVER THE SIREN.

Helen removes the tip of her thumb from her mouth.

'Of course.'

'You're a little bit nuts, aren't ye?' he says, his smile wide. He's starting to relax in Helen's company. Is really beginning to feel as if she's the one taking *him* for the ride... even though they're in his car. He believes she will foster him through to Detective status; help drag him from the dregs of administrative work.

Helen lifts her head, slowly — taking in what was just said to her — and then eyeballs Charlie, her stare a little hostile.

'Sorry. I mean. What I'm trying to ask is,' Charlie says, as he shifts awkwardly in his seat, 'Detectives... they have to be erratic, don't they? You have to go beyond the line in order to investigate properly, right?'

Helen squints at Charlie. He turns his face to her, then straight back out the windscreen. He's desperate to engage her in conversation, but is also juggling his concentration levels with speeding seventy miles per hour down the canal straight.

'Ye know...,' he says. 'The way you see on TV all these Detectives who go over the line to get what they want. You eh...' he takes his hand from the gearstick, scratches at his hair. 'You eh... you know the way you have kinda gone over the line; throwing the drink in Brother Fitzpatrick's face... being off duty and being a bit sneaky with your role in this investigation… and when you said to little Audrey back there that she was being arrested for underage drinking when she wasn't.'

Helen takes her eyes from Charlie and stares down at her lap.

'You gotta do what you gotta do in this job,' she says.

'So it is kinda like on TV? Like in *The Wire* or things like that; Detectives have to bend the rules?'

Helen sniffs.

'*The Wire*? Calm down, Charlie,' she says, her voice loud. 'All I did was splash a bit of water on a drunk man's face to sober him up.'

Charlie stiffens his grip on the steering wheel and holds a blink closed.

'Fuck sake, Charlie,' Helen roars.

Charlie swings the car away from a cyclist.

'Shit. Sorry. Sorry,' he says to Helen.

'Concentrate will you?' she barks.

Charlie puffs out his cheeks, then wipes at his brow, using the back of his hand.

'I was just… I was just trying to learn, that's all. I just really want to be a Detective.'

Helen wiggles her bum on the car seat into a more comfortable position and then flattens down the seatbelt over her shoulder.

'No harm asking questions, Charlie,' she says. 'You didn't need to call me nuts is all.' Charlie turns to her, his mouth ajar. 'Just concentrate on the road for now,' she says, waving his face away.

They're almost there. At Cue. Helen had been thinking about how to play it with Tommy Smith before Charlie started shouting stupid questions at her over the blare of the siren. Tommy's family and friends didn't seem like the most welcoming bunch. It's unlikely he's going to be any different. The apple very rarely falls far from the tree. She'd been wondering if he'll want to talk to them at all; she's still coming to terms with somebody ringing in a suicide warning without giving any names. She was stewing — before Charlie asked if she was a "bit nuts" — the realisation that Tommy is more likely involved with gangland crime than he is some kind of good Samaritan concerned by the welfare of two girls from his school. Still, she isn't taking any chances. She knows this is the greatest opportunity she'll ever have of ensuring Scott didn't take his life in vain. Helen's awareness of suicide — and how those who commit suicide think — is what gave her the gut instinct to follow the phone calls up as legitimate. If she's right, and the rest of the Garda force is wrong, she'll be a hero in a multitude of ways. Her face would probably be splashed all over the newspapers. Might be invited on to *The Late Late*

Show for an interview. Might even be offered her old role as a Detective back until Eddie finally decides to retire and whisk her away for her dream life in Canada.

'Here we are,' Charlie says, slowing down the car.

Helen looks out her passenger side window at graffitied shutters. Then she allows her eyes to flitter towards a red neon light above them.

'Cue', it reads, the 'e' flashing.

'Looks like a lovely place,' she says over the top of the car after they both get out. 'Kinda place I used to hang out in when I was a kid.'

Charlie puffs a laugh out.

'Told you you were nuts,' he says, before holding his hands up in mock apology.

Helen stops walking and stares at the back of Charlie's head. She's still wondering how to react to his quip when he spins to her again, his palms back up, his laugh loud.

'Cheeky bugger,' she says, mock swiping at his face. 'Jesus, you've grown in confidence over the past couple hours, huh? I couldn't get a word out of you earlier.'

Charlie's still laughing when he pushes at a door that provides entry to a narrow, steep staircase. The only light inside is coming from the top of the steps; an eerie bright red bulb that suggests there may be more than a game of snooker on offer upstairs.

'Creepy,' Charlie whispers as they take the first step. Each of the thirty-one steps creeks under their feet as they climb. When they reach the top, Helen bends down again, her hands on her knees.

'Nobody can say playing snooker isn't a work out if you're playing snooker in this kip,' she says, while trying to catch her breath.

Charlie laughs again; is really beginning to think this is the best shift of his career so far. He'll be glad of the experience, regardless of what the outcome is by midnight.

'This way,' he says to Helen when she stands back upright.

Charlie pushes at another door and the sound of nineties Brit Pop begins to crackle out of cheap speakers. He pauses at an empty bar, then rattles his knuckles against it.

'Hello?' he calls out.

Helen steps to the side, takes in the entire snooker hall. It's the first time she's been in one since she was a teenager. She does a quick calculation; two banks of eight tables. Sixteen in all. Yet only two are in use right now. Two middle-aged men playing at the one closest to them. And a group of guys in the back corner. She thinks a couple of them are only teens. But they're too far away for her to be certain. So she squints up at the black and white monitor over the bar, at live CCTV footage of them, but that gives no clarity on whether a couple of them are young enough to be Tommy Smith or not.

'The guy running the place is down there,' one of the middle-aged men says to her.

Helen tilts her chin upwards, acknowledging the heads up. Then she begins to walk, in her own unique way, between the two banks of tables and towards the group.

'This way, Charlie.'

'Oi, oi,' a man sweeping his hand up and down a snooker cue says as he watches them approach. 'How can we help you, officers?'

'I'm Detective Brennan. This here is Officer Guilfoyle. We're looking for a boy we believe hangs out around here.'

The man takes a step towards them, resting the butt of his cue into the carpet.

'Who?' he asks.

'Tommy Smith.'

The man looks back over his shoulder at the group who are all perched on a bench that runs around the back corner of the hall. When he turns back, his bottom lip is sticking out, his head shaking.

'Never heard of him,' he says.

'Sir, we believe two young girls' lives are in grave danger. Tommy Smith can lead us to them. We need to speak with him as a matter of urgency.'

The man's cheeks rise high as he produces a fake grin.

'I'm serious, Sir. I don't want to speak to Tommy about anything other than the fact that he made calls to two Garda stations a few hours ago saying two of his friends are planning on dying by suicide tonight.'

The man's eyes narrow. Then he looks back over his shoulder again. Charlie tries to track his line of vision, to see who or what he's looking at exactly. There are only two in this gang who could possibly be Tommy Smith; only two of them look to be in the appropriate age range.

'Are either of you Tommy Smith?' he asks, stepping forward.

The two boys look at each other, then back at Charlie.

'Never heard of him,' they both say, almost in unison.

The man with the cue bends over the table, misses a red to the far corner pocket.

'Bollix,' he says, standing back up. 'Yis are putting me off my game. Do yis wanna have a game of snooker? Or...' he rolls his shoulders.

Charlie swallows, then looks over to Helen for support. He notices that she probably didn't hear what was said, is too busy sticking her nose into her phone. Then she holds the phone to her ear.

A ringing sounds out; an annoying tone that sounds more like a crackling vibration than an actual ringtone. It's coming from one of the teenage boy's jeans pocket.

Helen presses at her screen, hanging up the call, then takes a stride forward.

'Tommy, we need to speak with you right now!' she says.

Tommy pounces to his feet, races past Helen and through the two rows of snooker tables before reaching the top of the stairs.

22:25

Ciara

I SPIN THE BUS STOP TIMETABLE ROUND AND ROUND THE POLE AFTER I'VE caught my breath back.

'It says there's one due at half ten, but ye can never really go by these things, can you?' I say to Ingrid.

She's got her arms folded and is leaning her back against the glass of the bus shelter.

'Nah… they just get here when they get here… normally two or three at the same time,' she says.

I stare down the road, waiting to see the light of a bus number coming towards us. Nothing.

It's starting to get cold, so I turn around and hug my best friend; for a bit of warmth more than anything. Ingrid rests her chin on my shoulder while I stare at a fuzzy reflection of myself in the glass of the shelter, neither of us saying a word.

It's mad that we're getting close to the last hour of our lives. I know it's sad that we feel we have to do this. But I feel happy because I *know* we're going to do it. Being alive might be good for some people, but it's never been for me. I was born into sadness… can't remember either of my parents laughing in our home. Not in each other's company anyway. No wonder I'm bleedin' miserable.

The only person I ever remember laughing in our house was Debbie. And now I know why. She was probably out of her face on cocaine. I can't believe it. She was the only adult who I ever felt really liked me, really. I'd no idea she was so stupid that she would take drugs. Doesn't matter anyway. Whether I saw cocaine or not in her house tonight, we were still going to do this; still going to end it all. I just never thought I'd end it all while not loving Debbie anymore. I guess you never really know people — even the ones you love the most. Makes me wonder if Miss Moriarty has any dark secrets.

'You think Miss will be happy to see us?' I ask, still staring at my reflection.

'She'll be wondering what the hell we're doing knocking to her house on a Sunday night but... yeah... she'll be happy to see us. She loved us.'

I nod my head.

'Our very last goodbye, huh?' I say. And then I feel Ingrid nodding her head on my shoulder.

Her nose sniffles. I bet she's crying. Her mind better not be bleedin' changing again. Wouldn't surprise me. The two of us were giggling our little heads off as we ran to the bus stop. It wouldn't be unusual for me to be crying straight after I've been laughing. I think depression works that way. Does for me anyway.

I lean off her, place my hands either side of her face.

'You okay, Ingrid?'

She smiles her eyes.

'Fine,' she says.

'You sure?'

She looks downwards, at our feet, and then nods her head again.

I put my hand under her chin and lift her face towards me.

'Ingrid.'

'Yeah — I'm fine,' she says, shrugging her shoulders.

'Just over an hour left. Quick visit to Miss Moriarty's, then a bus ride back to Rathmines...' I arch an eyebrow.

She nods again.

I grab her in for another hug; this time to feel her love as much as the warmth.

It was almost twelve hours ago that we came up with this plan. Around eleven o'clock last night. I'd never seen Ingrid so upset; had never seen anyone so upset. I couldn't stop her sobbing, no matter how hard I held her close to me. Her chest, her shoulders, her head — everything was shaking quicker than I ever thought body parts could shake. It took ages for them to stop.

'Here we go,' she muffles into my ear.

I turn around and see a bus coming towards us.

'I'm gonna ask you one more time, Ingrid. You sure you are okay?'

Ingrid looks at me, then looks towards the bus.

'Ingrid!'

She releases her grip on me, strolls slowly towards the curb and places her hand in her pockets. When she steps on to the bus, she reaches a fistful of change towards the driver.

'Two fares to Crumlin,' she says.

The driver stares at both us of us, then taps away at his tiny little machine before scooping the coins out of Ingrid's hand.

'There y'are, girls,' he says, passing Ingrid two paper tickets, 'hope yis are havin' a good night.'

We both nod a thank you to him and head up the aisle, towards the back of the bus.

'Ingrid?' I say again as we sit down.

'Yes!' she says. She sounds a little bit annoyed. 'You don't have to keep asking me, Ciara. *Yes*. I'm fine.'

I hold her knee, squeeze it a little and then we both sit in silence as we stare out of opposite windows at nothing because the night is too dark.

'It's just,' I say turning back towards her, 'I don't want you doing this just for me.'

She turns her head to face me, then tilts it sideways. But she doesn't say anything. I hold my eyes closed and try to think everything through as the bus rattles its way down the canal road. I'm one hundred per cent certain I want to do this. And I'm one hundred per cent certain I want to do it this way; me and Ingrid doing it together. But I'm not one hundred per cent certain she wants to do it. I know she's really sad now. Last night broke her little heart. But she might be okay in a couple weeks time; just like Harriet said. Whereas I know I won't be. I'm depressed. And I'll be depressed forever… until I kill that depression by killing myself.

But I don't want to keep on asking her if she's okay and I certainly don't want to break the pact by asking her if she still wants to go ahead with it. So I bite my tongue. Literally. I hold it between my teeth and try to not say anything more about it.

The bus heaves over the speed bumps and our bums are lifted up and down on the seats but we keep our faces straight and our mouths closed. I try to look out the window again… see if I can make anything out in the dark. But all I can see is my own reflection staring at back at me. And I can almost hear my mind screaming at the reflection.

You have to ask her, Ciara. Go on. Ask her!

I bite my tongue, hard this time; until I can taste a bit of blood. Then my teeth unclench, my head spins around and my hands reach for Ingrid's pretty little pale face.

'Ingrid Murphy, I love you very much.'

She squints her eyes, then reaches her hands either side of my face, cupping my cheeks.

'I love you too,' she says, her eyes heavy.

'I need to ask you — I'm sorry to break the pact.' She holds her eyes closed and I swallow. 'Do you want to do this? Do you want us both to commit suicide as soon as we've finished saying goodbye to Miss Moriarty? I need to know you're ready.'

22:35

Ingrid

WE SIT IN SILENCE, EXCEPT FOR THE ROARING OF THE BUS ENGINE EVERY now and then when it struggles over the speed bumps.

Then Ciara turns to me and places a hand to each side of my face.

I know she's going to ask me if I still want to go ahead with this. I know she's going to break the first rule of our pact. And I get it; she knows me too well. She knows my mind was changing when we were in Harriet's bedroom.

'Ingrid Murphy,' she says, 'I love you very much.'

I give her one of those half smiles, then hold my hands either side of her face too; just to let her know that it's okay to ask the question she's desperate to ask.

'I need to ask you — I'm sorry to break the pact. Do you want to do this? Do you want us both to commit suicide as soon as we've finished saying goodbye to Miss Moriarty? I need to know you're ready.'

'Yes,' I say, without hesitating; without allowing any silence between her asking the question and me answering it.

Then I open my eyes to see her nodding at me, her lips smiling. She brings herself closer to me, so our foreheads touch and we just hold each other. Until the bus juddering over another speed bump makes my chin slap against Ciara's. Her teeth crack closed. She laughs at the strange sound it makes and so do I; the two of us bent over at the back of the bus, laughing on the outside, in pain on the inside. And all my mind is doing is wondering whether laughing at the noise of somebody's teeth closing actually makes life pretty shit... or whether or not finding the likes of that funny is what makes life pretty good. I've never quite understood what parts of life I'm supposed to enjoy.

I answered her question really quickly. Maybe because I knew the question was coming; I was prepared. Or maybe I answered her that quickly because I'm absolutely certain I want to do this. My mind keeps changing. I've just told her ten seconds ago that I'm ready to this. And now I'm not sure I am.

Suicide seems to make the most amount of sense to me, though. The only way I can get rid of the pain is to end that pain. One thing that's making me slightly nervy about doing it now is that I think the goodbyes we made to our favourite people have been pretty cold. It was my idea; the goodbyes. It was something I wanted to be part of the pact.

Ciara found me standing behind a bush at the entrance to that tiny park near Balfey's house. He was the one who had the free gaff last night. I kept playing what Stitch said to me over and over in my head as I stood behind that bush; tears pouring down my face. It wasn't really his words that were hurting me. It was the laughter from everybody else that followed his words. It made my stomach turn, my whole body shake. I wanted to throw up. But all I could do was cry. And cry.

'Oh, Ingrid,' she said when she found me. She hugged me tight and as she did I whispered into her ear.

'I want to commit suicide.'

She pulled away and stared into my face. She'd been threatening that she would kill herself for years. She said I was the only one keeping her alive. She brought the idea of us both doing it together up a few times before; when I used to agree with her that life was shit and that my parents were just as bad as hers. I'm not sure how much of that I really agree with. I think I was just trying to be supportive; felt I was being the best friend I could possibly be to her if I could relate. But that laughter last night — after Stitch said what he said — it just made me realise I can't go on. I can't go to school tomorrow. I can't do a whole six years in secondary school being known as Fishfingers.

We spoke for two hours about our pact, on that cold bench just inside the park. Ciara was all up for doing it last night. I said we should wait to do it tonight so that we could have a chance to say goodbye to our families and those closest to us. I wanted to say goodbye to Mum and Dad. And Sven. And I really wanted to say goodbye to Harriet. But I'm not sure I really did that well enough tonight. I'm not quite sure what I expected it to be like, though. How are you supposed to say goodbye to somebody for the last time when you don't want them to know it's the last time? I could barely look at Mum and Dad when I was leaving the house; in case they could see right through me. I rubbed Sven's hair. That's it. It's all I did to say goodbye to my little brother. And I hugged Harriet and told her I'd definitely read the book she gave me. I promised I'd catch up with her soon so we could talk. Then I just left in the back seat of Uncle Brendan's car as she waved at me from the doorway. At least she'll get the book with my note in it. That's nice, I guess.

'Maybe we should write suicide notes after all,' I say, as the bus jumps over another speed bump.

Ciara wrinkles her face up a bit.

'Really?'

I shrug my shoulder. I don't know. We both decided last night that writing suicide notes would be too difficult; not just difficult because of how emotional it would be, but difficult because we're both not great at writing. Our parents would have that note forever. And I just don't think we could have written something good enough. That's why we agreed to spend the day at home with our families to say our last goodbyes, and why we decided to visit the people we truly loved before we ended it all. We felt a last goodbye to all our loved ones would have more impact than a note. Now I'm not so sure.

'Oh... maybe not, I don't know,' I say. 'I think writing that small note in Harriet's book is making me think it would be nice to leave a little message for Mum and Dad and Sven.'

Ciara squelches her face even more. She was dead against suicide notes last night. More so than me. She doesn't seem to have changed her mind.

'Don't you think... don't you think our goodbyes were a little... cold?' I ask.

She makes a funny face again.

'They were natural weren't they?' she says. 'My goodbye to my mam was like any goodbye I've ever given her. Seems about right to me.'

'What about your goodbye to Debbie... I mean you slapped her in the face?'

Ciara sniffs a small laugh out of her nose.

'What... you want me to leave her a suicide note now?'

'No, no...' I say, sitting back in my seat and slapping my hands against my knees. 'I don't know.' I realise I must be sounding as confused as I feel. I'm probably doing Ciara's head in.

'Listen,' Ciara says, placing her hands either side of my face again. 'Do you want to go home and say another goodbye to your mum? If you do, we can delay this a little bit...'

I breathe in deep. To give myself time to think. Then I find myself shaking my head before I've thought anything through.

'Nah,' I say. 'Let's just say goodbye to Miss Moriarty. Then we can just get this over with.'

CHARLIE AND TOMMY ARE WELL OUT OF SIGHT BY THE TIME HELEN PUSHES at the door and steps outside. She had tried to run fast, tried to keep up, but she needed both hands to hold on to the bannisters either side of her as she trotted down the stairs, allowing them to race way ahead of her.

'Fuck me,' she says to no one when she gets outside. She looks right, then left. No sign of either of them. No sounds either. She reaches for her phone, scrolls through the screen and dials Tommy's number again; then cocks her ear out for any inkling of that annoying ringtone.

Nothing.

She assumes Tommy would have gone left when he got outside. It would have been stupid of him to have run towards the police car. So she walks — in her own unique way — past the row of closed shops and towards a housing estate that looks like a maze of terraced-lined streets.

'Little bollix could be anywhere.'

She contemplates calling out Charlie's name, but bites her tongue. He'll come back to the car soon enough; hopefully holding Tommy Smith by the scruff of the neck.

She's wondering why the little fucker ran; is starting to lose hope that her instinct was right all along about the two girls. She shakes her head in an effort to reduce the growing logic from her mind. But nothing she can think of to support her gut — that the calls Tommy made earlier were legitimate suicide concerns — seems to be adding up. They *must* have been distraction calls; he *must* be working for Alan Keating.

She turns back and stares at the flashing sign for Cue. Maybe all of them up there are working for Keating. That's why the CCTV is gazing down at them. It's planned that way. Bastards will have a proven alibi all night.

Helen stops walking, lets out a sigh and then washes the palm of her hand over her face.

'Your instinct was wrong, Helen,' she muffles into her fingers. 'There aren't two girls out there about to commit suicide. Scott's death hasn't led you to this moment. Scott died. Get fuckin' over it already. It's been twenty-two—'

'Fuckin' hell.'

An approaching voice halts Helen's whispered monologue. She squints into the darkness, sees Charlie approaching her, his hand to his face. He's on his own.

'Fuck ye, Charlie,' she mumbles to herself before walking towards him. They meet under a street lamp.

'Little bollix punched me in the nose,' Charlie says taking his hand away to show Helen the damage.

She stares at his face, notices a fine trickle of blood making its way to his top lip, then shakes her head.

'What the fuck happened?' she asks.

Charlie grunts the stinging pain away before answering.

'Fucker's quick, I'll give him that. I managed to catch up with him, grabbed a handful of his tracksuit top... but he just turned around, knocked me one. I went flying backwards. Stings like hell. By the time I got to my feet he was out of sight.'

Helen clenches her jaw.

'Christ sake, Charlie!' she grinds through her teeth.

'What? What did you want me to do? I was assaulted.'

'You're a bloody police officer; you are supposed to control these situations!'

Helen turns her back on Charlie, her hands on her hips.

He looks at the back of her, his arms outstretched in bewilderment at her lack of empathy.

'We'll get that little fucker for assaulting a police officer. We know where he lives!' Charlie says.

'I couldn't give a shit about arresting him for assaulting a police officer!' Helen barks as she spins back around. 'I'm only concerned about these two girls. Whoever they are. Wherever they are.'

Charlie holds his hand to his nose again, then winces in pain before squelching his entire face at Helen.

'If all this little fucker has is information on two girls planning to die by suicide, why did he run away from us? Helen... we've got to admit we're wrong. The rest of the force are out there looking to stop Alan Keating from carrying out something big tonight. This little prick running away from us proves they're right. He didn't call two Garda stations because he's worried about girls he goes to school with. He rang in a distraction call.' Helen holds her eyes closed, her hands still on her hips. 'C'mon, Helen, you've got to admit that—'

'Shut up, Charlie,' she snaps.

'What d'you mean *shut up*? You know—'

Helen takes a step towards Charlie, grabs him — with both hands — by the collar of his Garda jacket and pins him up against a shop shutter, causing a clang to echo the entire length of the street.

'You listen to me, and you listen to me very carefully,' she spits into his face.

Up this close, Helen can see more of the damage to Charlie's nose; a blue T-shaped bruise already starting to form, spreading itself under both eyes.

'We have to believe we are right. We need to chase down these two girls. If... *if* the rest of the force are right, and Alan Keating is planning something big tonight, so fuckin what? Another theft, another heist. Who gives a shit? It's nothing. Money, material things... it's all fuckin pointless. *But...* if the rest of the force are wrong, and we're right? Is anything pointless? Is saving two girls' lives pointless?'

Charlie narrows his eyes, slows his breathing down and then shakes his head.

'Exactly,' Helen says. 'We have been given an important job to do and we will do it whether we think they were distraction calls or not, ye hear me?' Charlie nods. And Helen releases her grip on him, before flattening down his collar. 'Our task is a hell of a lot more important than theirs. We have to be super thorough. Whether we are right or wrong!'

Charlie reaches his hand back up to his nose.

'I s'pose you're right,' he says as his jacket pocket begins to vibrate. He reaches inside for his phone, then looks up at Helen after he's noticed the screen.

'It's Newell — my SI.'

'Put him on speaker,' Helen demands.

Charlie swipes at his screen to answer the call, then presses at the speaker button holding the phone outwards.

'Guilfoyle, what the hell are you up to?' a voice barks down the line. 'Louis Kavanagh told me you were at Tommy Smith's house half an hour ago... what are you playing at, son?'

Helen shakes her head, pinching her forefinger and thumb together and running them across her closed lips.

'We eh... I eh... I got information from the local school Headteacher using the image of Smith from the CCTV footage. He was able to give me information on the boy; told me his name, gave me his address.'

A scoff is heard down the line.

'Listen, Guilfoyle, I appreciate you are doing your job as well as you can. But leave this to us, okay? You can get your ass back to the station and finish your shift out. Don't go chasing Smith. We're on top of it. You eh... haven't come across him yet, have you?'

Helen shakes her head, pinches her forefinger and thumb across her lips again, her eyes widening.

'Guilfoyle?' Newell barks, having been met with silence.

'No, Sir.'

Charlie holds his eyes closed in disappointment, his chin tucked into his neck with shame.

'Good. We don't want him getting away from us. Listen,' Newell says, 'Louis told me you were operating with some Detective from Rathmines. Who are ye with, son?'

Helen's eyes go wide again, her head beginning to shake rapidly. She has her finger pointed right in Charlie's face.

Charlie swallows.

'Eh... Detective Helen Brennan,' he says slowly, before mouthing a 'sorry' at Helen.

She grinds her teeth in his face, then spins around, her hands on top of her head as if she's just missed an open goal in the last minute of a cup final.

'Brennan? Never heard of her. Well... you tell her we have everything under control. Leave Tommy Smith to us — that is an order.'

'I hear you, Sir. All understood.'

As soon as the line goes dead, Helen spins back around.

'Ye little rat bastard,' she says, her finger pointing again.

'I had to... he bloody knew I was with somebody. What did you want me to say?'

Helen shakes her head while producing an overly loud grunt.

'I'm gonna get fuckin fired now,' she says.

'I think we both might,' Charlie replies, bringing his hand to his nose again. 'Fuck this, Helen... I have to ring him back. I have to tell him we confronted Tommy Smith. They need to know.'

'Then you *will* get fired,' Helen says. She kicks the shop shutter behind Charlie, causing the clattering sound to echo down the street again.

'Ah Jesus, I've fucked up my career haven't I?' Charlie says, almost sobbing.

Helen doesn't answer. She just stands under the streetlamp, her hands on her hips, her mind racing.

Then she notices them. Across the street. In the window next to the Cue sign. The gang of men staring down at them.

'Fuckers are laughing at us,' she says. 'Let's get back to the car and get our thinking caps on.'

Charlie paces after Helen, still holding his hand to his nose as if it's gonna make the stinging pain go away. When they're inside the car, they sit in silence; Helen staring out the passenger side window, the tip of her thumb in her mouth; Charlie gripping the steering wheel, trying to ease the pain away by sucking air in through his teeth.

'I have to ring Newell back, I *have* to,' he eventually says.

Helen looks at him, then sighs a deep grunt that is filled with disappointment.

'What's that going to achieve?' she asks.

'They are looking for Tommy Smith; the whole bloody force is. I know what direction he ran in... I need to tell them. Fuck it! I'm telling them.'

He reaches into his jacket pocket. By the time he's taken the phone out, Helen's fingers are wrapped around his wrist.

'Charlie; don't be a fuckin idiot,' she says.

'I've been a fuckin idiot all evening,' he replies, wrestling his arm away.

'I'm sorry to let you down, Helen. I'm sorry for... for everything you've been through, but...' he shrugs his shoulder. 'I have to do my duty. I have to ring it in.'

He pulls at the handle, pushes his car door open and holds his phone to his ear.

When he closes the door, Helen slaps both of her hands against the top of the dashboard.

'Mother fucker!' she screams. Then she holds both hands over her face, her breathing becoming long and slow. When she removes her hands, she fidgets at the rear-view mirror, sees Charlie walking slowly away from the car, one hand holding the phone to his ear, the other rubbing the back of his head. She winds down her window, her attempt to hear anything. But there's only silence — he's travelled too far from her.

She grunts again; still struggling to let logic overrule her thinking. She wants to believe there are two girls out there about to end their lives. She needs to believe it. Her life is worthless without Scott having some sort of inspiration on it.

'Help me out, Scott,' she says. 'Gimme a sign. Just something small.'

She widens her eyes, inches her face closer to the windscreen.

Nothing. Just a dark blue sky and — in her periphery — that flashing sign for Cue. Then she flicks her head.

'That's literally a sign,' she says. 'Cue. Cue. Cue. What are you trying to tell me, Scott?'

She stares at it, her eyes moistening. Then a tear escapes and runs down her left cheek. She's not crying because of grief. She's crying because of the realisation of her delusion. She hates herself when she talks to Scott. Hates herself even more when she asks him to send her a sign. It never makes her feel better. It only emphasises his loss more.

Helen's not stupid. She knows she'll never see her son again. They bloody cremated his body twenty-two years ago. Scott's gone. He's ash in a tiny urn that's buried six feet under the ground in a tiny plot at Mount Jerome cemetery. How the fuck could he send her a sign?

She slaps the top of the dashboard again with both hands, then wipes away the tear.

'You're a fuckin idiot, Helen,' she says.

She's sniffling up her nose, wiping all of the moistness from under it when the car door snatches open.

Charlie slouches into the driver's seat; his phone in his hand.

'Well...' Helen says. 'How did your SI take the news?'

'He eh... well, he's not happy. They're on their way here now to try and catch up with him. I've to get back to the station. Back to my desk. I'll be dealt with in the morning.'

'But sure, you were just doing your job. They gave you the job of looking into the calls as if they were legit—'

'Helen!' Charlie snaps, his voice filled with frustration.

Helen shuts up, folds her arms, the leather of her coat squeaking as she does so.

'I'm never gonna be a Detective, am I?' Charlie says.

'Course you will. They'll keep you on. Just tell them this was all my fault. My husband is the SI in Rathmines Station. I'll see to it that you're looked aft—'

'No, Helen,' he says, turning to her. 'I mean... I don't have the bloody skills to be a Detective, do I? I don't have the instincts, don't have the—'

'You do... you do,' Helen says, reaching a hand towards his shoulder.

Charlie laughs out of the side of his mouth.

'I don't though, do I? You walked right up to my desk about three hours ago, told me you were helping me out with this investigation, brought me to the tram station, to view CCTV footage at the Red Cow, to question two bloody Headteachers...'

'Yeah — you've done a good job with me.'

'Listen,' Charlie snaps. 'All that chasing around with you and y'know what? I never even asked you the first question I should have asked you when I first met you.'

Helen narrows her eyes, then shakes her head at Charlie.

'What question?' she asks.

'I should have asked you to show me your Detective badge, shouldn't I?'

Helen laughs.

'I'm serious, Helen — if that even is your name. Show me your badge.'

22:45

Ciara

BLEEDIN' HELL. INGRID WANTS TO GO BACK AND SAY GOODBYE TO HER MAM and dad all over again. Jaysus. Last night she was all talk about staying at home to say a final goodbye to our families. Now she wants to go back to do it all again. Maybe she doesn't want to go through with this. Maybe she's not ready.

I place my hands either side of her face again and stare into her eyes. I want to sound gentle.

'Listen,' I say. 'Do you want to go home and say another goodbye to your mum? If you do, we can delay this a little bit...'

She sucks in a breath, then shakes her head.

'Nah. Let's just say goodbye to Miss Moriarty, then we can just get this over with.'

I nod my head slowly and wrap my arms around her; squeezing her in for another hug.

'You're doing the right thing,' I whisper to her. 'If you keep changing your mind and going back and forth about all this, you'll just end up sad for years like me. The sadness never stops. It just keeps coming and going and coming and going. And every time it comes back, it feels worse. We're nearly there, okay? A quick goodbye to Miss, then we'll stop this pain forever.'

She squeezes me even tighter and when we finally release I can see the sadness has gone out of her eyes. That sort of half smile is back on her lips. Same sort of look she gave me last night when we wrote this pact.

I squint through the darkness of the side window, to try to make out where we are. Can't see anything. So I stand up, walk slowly up the aisle and look out the front windscreen.

'Almost at our stop, Ingrid,' I say, strolling back to her. 'I don't know the door number, but I'll know the house when I see it. It's only a couple minutes' walk from the stop.'

'Can't wait to see her face when she answers the door,' Ingrid says.

'Me neither.'

We've both been back to our primary school twice since we graduated last June. Miss Moriarty was delighted when we visited. I'm not sure how she'll feel about us knocking at her house late on a Sunday night though. But I'm pretty sure she won't mind. We agreed last night that we'd just tell her we were in the area and thought it'd be rude to walk by her home without calling in to say hello. She'll have no idea we're actually calling in to say goodbye.

She was our teacher for two years in primary school. We had her when we were in fourth class and then again in sixth — our last year in primary. She really cared about us; about our learning, about our lives. I remember her telling me once that me and Ingrid were really lucky to have each other. She's not wrong there. The teachers we have now in secondary school wouldn't even know me and Ingrid are best mates. That's the difference. They don't look up from their desks. They're only interested in doing their lessons; they're not interested in knowing the students. I'm not sure any of them will actually be upset one little bit when they hear the news in the morning. I'd bet any money that the most asked question in the staff room will be 'which two are they?' But Miss Moriarty, well... she will be sad. She loved us; cared about us. I wish, so much, that she was a teacher in our secondary school. That'd probably save our lives.

'C'mon,' Ingrid says, getting up from her seat. She stabs her finger at the small bell on the back of the seat and I follow her as she stumbles her way towards the driver.

'Thank you,' she says to him when he pulls over.

'You get home safe now, girls,' he says. Then he pushes at a button that closes his doors and leaves us standing on the pavement. It's starting to get really cold now.

'This way,' I say, wrapping my arm around Ingrid's shoulders.

I lead her around a corner just off the main Crumlin Road, and towards Miss Moriarty's little cul de sac.

Miss had told us she lived in Crumlin when she was our teacher. I managed to find the exact address when I was flicking through some paperwork in the Headteacher's office sometime last year. I visited the street and stood outside her house for ages one day. I didn't knock or anything. I just thought it was cool that I knew where my teacher lived. Her house isn't as big as ours. Which is a bit weird. Surely teachers should be paid a lot more than anyone else? My dad runs a company that sells boring insurance. And he's loaded. All Ingrid's dad does is talk on the radio for three hours every morning. How the hell are they rich and Miss Moriarty isn't?

'It's this one here,' I say, pointing towards Miss' front door.

We walk towards the garden gate and then stop outside it.

'Okay,' Ingrid says to me. 'We just say we were in the area visiting a friend and that we felt it was rude to walk by Miss Moriarty's house without knocking in to say hello, right?'

I nod my head.

'Yup. You first,' I say, pushing the gate open.

Ingrid takes two steps into her garden and then lifts and drops her crooked letterbox a few times. Within seconds the door is opened.

'Yes?' a man says.

'Oh,' Ingrid says turning to me. 'We eh… we thought our old teacher Miss Moriarty lived here.'

The man scratches at his head, then turns over his wrist so he can look at his watch.

'Brigid,' he calls out over his shoulder. 'There are two young girls here to see you.'

22:55

Ingrid

I CAN SEE MISS WALKING DOWN THE STAIRS. SHE'S WEARING A BATHROBE and her hair is all wet.

'Hey, you two,' she says, smiling, 'what are you doing here?'

I laugh a bit awkwardly, then stand aside, leaving Ciara to do the lying.

'We eh… we were visiting a friend around the corner and thought it would be rude to walk by our favourite teacher's house without knocking in to say hello… so eh… hello.' Ciara waves. And I laugh. Awkwardly again.

Miss Moriarty looks a little lost for words. She doesn't say anything; she just stands there, combing her fingers through her wet hair.

'I'm sorry, Miss. Have we come at a bad time?' I ask.

'Not at all. I'm just out of the shower… was going to dry myself off and get into bed. It's eh… it's late… what time is it?'

'Almost eleven,' a voice from inside the house calls out. It must be the man who answered the door to us. I wonder who he is. She's not married. Her name is *Miss* Moriarty. Not *Missus* Moriarty.

'Eh… well, come in,' she says standing aside and pulling the door a little wider for us.

We step into a square hallway that's no bigger than the welcome mat we have in ours. 'How did you girls know where I lived?'

'We eh… we've always known. Somebody pointed it out to us once,' Ciara says. She lies so quickly. I'd be still scratching my head if it was up to me to answer that question.

'We won't keep you long, Miss,' I say and then I lean into her and hug her. I miss Miss Moriarty so much.

'Oh, Ingrid,' she says, hugging me back. Then she reaches one hand towards Ciara and drags her in to our little huddle. This is what teachers should do; hug their students, care for them. The teachers we have now barely even know our names.

'Let me get the two of you a quick drink. Squash?'

Me and Ciara look at each other, then both nod at the same time.

'Thanks, Miss,' Ciara says.

'Hey, you don't have to call me Miss... it's Brigid, now that you're no longer students of mine.'

She waves her hand to make sure we follow her into the kitchen and then she begins to pour us both a raspberry Ribena.

'So, how you getting on in secondary school?' she asks.

Me and Ciara look at each other again.

'Not great,' I say.

Miss squints her eyes at me as she hands us our drinks.

'What do you mean "not great"?'

'Well... well...' I stumble, fidgeting with my fingers.

'The teachers barely know who we are,' Ciara says. 'It's not like primary school where you're with the same teacher all day. We change classrooms every forty minutes and... I don't know. It's just hard.'

'Oh... everybody says that about secondary school when they start,' Miss Moriarty says. 'You'll get used to it. It's only been... what's-it?'

'Eight months and two weeks,' Ciara says.

Miss Moriarty smiles.

'Exactly,' she says. 'It's nothing. By next year you'll be used to it. Don't worry. It'll get better.'

Ciara looks at me. I decide to just drink from my glass while staring up at the ceiling.

'Wouldn't you like to be a secondary school teacher?' Ciara asks, looking back at Miss Moriarty. 'You'd be great at it — and you could join our school. Be our teacher forever.'

Miss smiles again.

'Oh you're so sweet, you two.'

She runs her hand through her wet hair again. I don't think she likes us being here. We called at a bad time. Her conversations are very short. She's definitely not her usual self.

'Who... eh...' Ciara says, looking back over her shoulder. 'Who was the man who opened the door for us?'

'Ciara!' I say. She can be so rude sometimes.

'It's fine, Ingrid,' Miss says, 'that's Jamie. He's my partner. My boyfriend.'

'Didn't know you had a boyfriend, Miss,' I say.

She smiles again. I miss that smile so much.

'I don't tell my students *everything*,' she says, patting the top of my head. 'C'mon, come with me.'

She leads us out of her tiny kitchen, into another room.

'Jamie, these are two of my former students: Ingrid Murphy and Ciara Joyce.' Jamie stands up and reaches up his palm for us to high five. 'Ingrid is Terry Murphy's daughter.'

'Ah yes,' Jamie says, 'Brigid told me she had taught Terry Murphy's daughter before. How is your old man?'

I shrug my shoulder.

'Fine... I think,' I say and then everyone laughs a little. 'He eh... works a lot, I don't think I get to see as much of him as most people get to see their dads.'

Jamie and Miss look at each other and then Miss turns to us.

'Take a seat,' she says. All four of us sit in their small sitting room, the tele turned off, just a lamp in the far corner on. The chat goes silent; nobody quite sure what to say.

Then Ciara taps me on the hip. I look at her and see that her eyes have gone really wide. She's trying to mouth something to me. I've no idea what she wants to say. So I shake my head and squint my eyes at her.

'What?' I whisper.

She locks her fingers together, holds them out in front of her and tries to mumble something between her teeth.

What the hell is she trying to tell me?

CHARLIE'S HANDS ARE GRIPPED TO THE TOP OF THE STEERING WHEEL, HIS head hanging between his elbows.

'There's no need to be that upset with yourself,' Helen says. 'I *used* to be a Detective. I was a Detective for five years before… before…' she swallows. 'Before my life got turned upside down. After Scott's suicide I just… I couldn't continue working. I was in and out of therapy, in and out of hospital…' She looks over at Charlie. He still hasn't lifted his head. 'I do work at Rathmines Garda station. As I said, my husband runs the shop. He saw to it that I was taken back on in some capacity.'

She hears a puff, the first noise Charlie has made since Helen admitted she wasn't who or what he believed she was.

'In what capacity?' he asks, peeling his back up vertebrae by vertebrae until he's sitting upright.

Helen sucks air in through the gaps of her teeth.

'I do admin work.'

Charlie puffs a darting laugh out of his nostrils as Helen reels backwards in embarrassment.

'Listen, just… just drop me back at your station,' she says, her face reddening. 'My car's there. Please.'

Charlie looks at her, then back out through his front windscreen before he turns the key in the ignition.

'Admin work,' he whispers to himself, shaking his head.

He drives in silence, Helen now the one hanging her head; her fingers forming a diamond shape on her lap.

'I'll take the blame for everything. My husband will understand. I'll be able to talk him around,' she says.

Charlie makes a clicking sound with his mouth.

'I'm sorry you lost your son,' he says. 'And I get it... why you... why you were trying to track down these two girls. Suicide. It can't be... it can't be easy to deal with.'

Helen purses her lips at him.

'It never leaves you,' she says as she stares back out the window at nothing in particular. 'I didn't have one darn clue. Not one clue he was gonna do it. Him and his friends. I guess they were just depressed. But I didn't see one sign of depression in Scott. Not one bloody sign of it. I know he wasn't the best kid in the world. His teachers used to say he could get distracted at school. But at home he was just... just normal. A normal teenager. It's one hell of a body blow to lose your son. But to lose him to suicide... well... the worst thing is I still don't know *why* they did it. What I wouldn't give to know what happened that night. You know what my husband says to me all the time... he says "you *never* will know". Imagine having to deal with that your whole life?'

She holds her hand to her face, her shoulders shaking. Charlie reaches a hand over to her, gives her shoulder a light squeeze. She'd already informed him how her husband has dealt with the reality of Scott's suicide compared to her. It was just as gut wrenching for Charlie to hear the second time around.

'Don't cry, Helen,' he says.

She waves him away. But he keeps his hand on her shoulder, only taking it off every now and then to change gear as he navigates all the way back to the station; not a further word passed between them.

It's always eaten at Helen that she will never know what happened to her son and his two friends the night they decided to end it all. She's tried her best to get to the bottom of it. She discussed it with the other two sets of parents. None of them could come up with answers. One of them blamed Scott... argued that he must have orchestrated it all. The frustration of never knowing what happened has always prolonged Helen's grief. She believes — and has done for a long time — that only a new life in Canada will ever ease her depression.

When Charlie kills the engine outside Terenure Garda station, he waits on Helen to lift her head, but she doesn't move.

'Well I guess it was an adventure at least, huh?' Charlie says, allowing a little laugh to sniff its way out of his mouth. But his joke hasn't hit its audience.

'Helen,' he says. 'We're here.'

She wipes her hand over her face, then leans her head back on to the rest.

'I need to take a leak,' she says. 'Where are the toilets in there?'

Charlie cocks his head while taking the keys from the ignition.

'C'mon, I'll show you.'

They stroll solemnly across the tiny car park and then into the front desk of the station.

'Charlie,' the man at the desk nods, 'Detective.'

Charlie looks back at Helen then twists his face into an awkward smile.

'Through here,' he says to Helen, pushing at a door. 'The Ladies is in the corner.'

Helen smiles with her eyes at Charlie, then holds her arms out.

'You're right, Charlie. It *has* been an adventure. It was... it was good to investigate with you. You're gonna make a helluva Detective one day. I'm sure of it.'

Charlie raises his eyebrow as he leans in to accept Helen's hug.

'I'll see ye around, Helen.'

He releases and then turns away, swirling his key ring around his finger as he makes his way back to the desk Helen first met him at three hours ago. She stares at the items on his desk; it feels like a hell of a lot more than three hours since she picked each of them up and inspected them for no real reason at all.

She strolls to the corner Charlie had pointed her towards and pushes at a door that leads into a pokey toilet with two cubicles.

'Still better than my station,' she says to no one, before rushing towards the sink. She turns on the cold tap, holds her hands out to form a cup and then fills it, before splashing at her face.

'What are you fuckin playing at, Helen?' she says to herself in the mirror as water drops from her brow. Then she enters one of the cubicles, pulls at the toilet paper until she has a ball of it in her hands and begins to dab at her face. As she's leaving the cubicle, she throws the ball of paper over her shoulder, missing the bowl by quite a distance.

She pulls tentatively at the door that leads back into the station, inching it open slowly so she can stare at Charlie. He's scratching at his spikey hair; looks really disappointed in himself as if he's cringing inside.

'Breathe, Helen,' she whispers to herself. 'Calm down.'

'Sorry?' a woman calls out appearing at the toilet door.

'Oh... no, *I'm* sorry,' Helen says, offering a fake smile. 'Bloody talking to myself, aren't I? First sign of madness, huh?'

The woman smiles back, then pushes past Helen and into one of the cubicles. Helen steps out, into the station, and then tiptoes herself towards Charlie.

'Didn't wanna leave without another hug,' she says perching her ass onto his desk. Charlie laughs a little, then reaches his arm around her and takes her closer to him.

'Our little adventure, huh?' he says into her ear.

'Our little adventure,' she whispers back.

'If you ever need someone to talk to, to have coffee with, you know where I am,' Charlie says.

Helen pats him on the shoulder, then stands up.

She walks away, back out through the office floor towards the door and out past reception without paying the man at the front desk any further attention. As soon as she's outside, she swings the key ring around her finger, and heads straight to Charlie's car.

She clicks the button, releasing the locks, and pulls at the driver's door. As soon as she's inside she eyeballs herself in the rear-view mirror, then looks away quickly; her eyes focusing on the road ahead as the car inches forward.

She knows where she's going; made her mind up when she was holding her face as Charlie drove back to the station. She also realised then that she needed the police car. It was the only means in which she could justifiably pass as a Detective — it's a tough lie to carry out if you don't have a badge to flash. She knows. She's tried it before.

'You're doing the right thing,' she says to herself. 'You're doing the right thing.'

She picks up speed, then reaches for the button that sets off the siren before pausing.

'Nah... better not,' she says. She flicks her eyes to look at herself in the rear-view mirror again, then holds them closed.

'What the fuck am I doing?' she whispers. 'What the fuck am I doing?'

She opens her eyes, shifts into fifth gear and speeds down the canal road. She can hear herself breathing, her breaths growing sharper as the digits on the speedometer rise.

'What the fuck am I doing?' She shouts it this time, laughing.

Then her pocket vibrates, causing her to blink as she eases off the gas. She takes out her phone and presses the green button.

'What the fuck are you doing?' Eddie screams down the line.

23:00

Ciara

JAMIE HOLDS HIS HAND UP FOR ME AND INGRID TO HIGH FIVE — AND WE DO. He looks nice. But sure... of course he's nice. He's Miss Moriarty's boyfriend. She's way too lovely and clever to ever have a horrible boyfriend.

'Take a seat,' Miss says.

And we all do; me, Ciara and Miss sitting on the grey sofa, Jamie on the tiny green armchair across from us.

I watch as Miss struggles sitting down; pulling the belt of her bathrobe tighter across her belly. Her belly is big; never knew she was that fat... hold on.

I tap at Ingrid's hip, then try to mumble to her.

'Id ee egnan,' I say through my teeth.

Ingrid looks at me as if I'm mad, then shakes her head a little. She can't make out what I'm trying to say. I hold my hands out over my belly, make a bit of a round shape with them. She's still shaking her head.

'Yes, young girl,' Jamie says. 'We are pregnant.'

'What!' Ingrid says. She reaches her arms towards Miss and gives her a big hug. So I do the same, joining in.

'Congratulations, Miss. That's the best news, like, ever,' I say.

The three of us stay in a hug for ages.

'Twins,' Jamie says.

I hold my hand to my mouth as I sit back into the sofa.

'Yep,' Miss says. 'They're due the end of August.'

I'm so happy for Miss. This is the happiest I've been in… jee… I don't know how long.

'Ah… two little Moriartys running around the place. I can't wait to—' Ingrid stops herself talking, then sits back in the sofa. I know what she was about to say; that she can't wait to meet them. Until she realised she never will.

'Two Roses, you mean,' Jamie says.

'Huh?'

'Two Roses… my name.'

Ah… Jamie Rose. Makes sense that he'd have such a nice name. I bet he'll make a great dad. Better than mine and Ingrid's anyway. He won't be stuck at work all the time; he won't tut at them when they have their first period.

I had my first one late last year, just before Christmas. I didn't know what to do, had no idea what was going on. I just screamed.

'What the hell is wrong with you?' my dad said, poking his nose into the bathroom. He saw me standing there, staring into the bowl at all of the red that had just poured out of me.

'What *is* wrong with me?' I asked him.

'Ah, here…' he said, shaking head. 'It's eh… a subject your mam will have to talk to you about… or Debbie. Wait till Debbie gets here in the morning.'

'Debbie doesn't mind me anymore, Dad!' I said. Then I began to cry. He left the bathroom. I didn't see him again for a few days.

'You'll both make great parents,' I say to them.

Jamie smiles at me.

'It's two girls,' Miss says, rubbing her belly.

Me and Ingrid squeeze each other and let out little squeals.

23:10

Miss Moriarty

THE TWO OF THEM CLING TO EACH OTHER AND PRODUCE A CUTE LITTLE high-pitched squeal.

I love Ingrid and Ciara; always have. My heart has always gone out to them. They never really palled around with anyone in primary school, apart from with each other. And me. They'd try to include me in their plans for lunch and would spend break time trying to make sure I didn't get any work done. Even though I've a lot going on, I still kinda miss them. It's a shame they're not enjoying secondary school, but I can't get involved. At some stage you just have to let kids grow up. They have to take responsibility for themselves.

'You'll both make great parents. They're going to be lucky girls,' Ingrid says.

How adorable. Ingrid's going to an impressive woman when she grows up. She's intelligent, pretty, comes from good stock. Her mam used to be a model — made quite a big name for herself in Sweden back in the day. And her dad's a bit of a national treasure. He used to be a personality on tele; now has his own radio show. She's a little bit sensitive though; conjures mountains from molehills with way too much ease. But once she grows out of that, she'll be grand. I'm not so sure about Ciara, though. Ciara's parents aren't up to much. I'm sure her mam is too fond of the drink. She used to turn up for parent-teacher meetings a little squiffy. At least she turned up though; not like her husband. I tried to ring him a couple times over the years, just to let him know how Ciara was getting on at school. He always claimed he was too busy to talk. He runs Fullam's insurance and accountancy. I'm sure the business gets more of his attention than his family does. Ciara always seemed to focus on the negatives in life; her glass was always half-empty. I'm not surprised though; if parents show a lack of belief in their kids, then it's inevitable that the kids themselves won't have much belief. No matter how good a teacher is, there is only so much impact we can have. I've often worried about Ciara over the years. But having Ingrid as a best friend is good for her. She'll be fine.

I hold my hand to my mouth and yawn.

'Sorry, girls,' I say. 'I'm so tired.'

I'm not lying to them; not trying to rush them out of my house. It's just ever since I fell pregnant I've been feeling wrecked. And nauseous. Standing at the top of a classroom all day is torturous when you've got two little ones growing inside you. They seem to weigh me down that extra little bit every day. And I've three more months to go before maternity leave. I'm not sure how I'm going to get through it.

'Oh sorry, Miss,' Ingrid says. 'We know it's late. Maybe we should let you go to bed.'

'That'd be great, girls,' Jamie says, walking towards me and placing his hand on my belly. 'Brigid needs as much rest as she can get.'

'Tell you what,' I say, 'when the girls are born, why don't you two call by again? I'd love you to meet them.'

I smile at the girls; knowing how much they'll love that invite. But they don't smile back. Ingrid stumbles a reply and then shakes her head. That's odd.

'Eh... yes. Okay... okay,' Ciara says, holding a hand to Ingrid's knee.

I squint my eyes at them.

'You two okay?'

Ciara nods, and then Ingrid mirrors her.

They're probably jealous of the babies; because they've seen themselves as my babies for so long. That's cute. I've read an article about that before; students feeling envious when their favourite teacher becomes a parent.

'So how you two getting home then?' I ask.

'Bus,' Ingrid says.

'Bus? At this time of the night?'

'No... no... don't be silly, Ingrid,' Ciara says. 'She's...' Ciara winds her finger around her temple. 'We're getting a lift from Ingrid's dad. He's around the corner in our friend's house.'

I squint again. These two are up to something. I can sense it. Teacher's intuition.

'The friend's house that you say is around the corner... what's the family name?' I stare at Ingrid as I ask this, knowing I can read her better than Ciara. I think Ciara mastered the art of bullshitting from her father. It's probably the only trait she's ever picked up from him.

Ingrid looks at Ciara.

'Sally Sweeney,' Ciara says.

'The Sweeneys? I don't know any Sweeneys that live around here,' I say.

Ciara laughs.

'Ah they do... around two corners actually. They live just off the main Crumlin Road.'

I don't believe her.

'Eh... why don't I ring your parents, Ingrid?' I say.

'I've just got off a call from Superintendent Newell at Terenure Garda station.'

Helen holds her eyes closed.

'I'm sorry, Eddie,' she whispers.

'Off investigating the suicide angle? Bringing some rookie with you on a wild goose chase?'

'I'm sorry.'

'You told me you were tucked up on the sofa watching TV.'

'I'm sorry, Eddie,' she says, ensuring this time that each word is pronounced clearly and slowly.

'How bloody dare you? I don't know whether I'm more angry at you dipping your nose in further than you ever have before, or more angry because you lied to me.'

Helen stays silent. There's only so many times she can say the word 'sorry' — especially if it's making zero impact.

She's still cringing, outwardly anyway; her right shoulder slumped lower than her left, her head tilted, her teeth clenched tight. But inside she's feeling somewhat relieved. Eddie isn't aware she's stolen a police car. He only knows that Helen was out with Charlie, sticking her nose in where it doesn't belong.

'Christ, what were you thinking? You bloody chased away the most significant witness we have.'

'It wasn't me who chased him away, Eddie. It was the naivety of the young officer I was with—'

'You shouldn't be anywhere *near* a young officer. Nowhere near one!' Eddie's voice is getting sterner now; Helen wincing at the obvious fury in his tone. He's been so patient with Helen for so many years that she feels really guilty when she irritates him. Yet sometimes — especially when it comes to work — she just can't help herself. Though she's never gone this far; had never taken another officer on a wild goose chase, pretending to be a Detective. 'I'm mortified... imagine being told my administrative assistant is out leading an investigation, posing as a bloody Detective.'

Helen hangs her head when she stops at a red light, allowing another silence to settle between them.

'Where are you now?' Eddie says, trying to regain control of his tone.

Helen shifts her head slightly forward, so she can look upwards through the windscreen at the buildings surrounding her. She can make out the old Victorian houses of the Highfield Road to her right; the Rathmines Clock Tower standing tall in the distance.

'I'm on my way home,' she says.

Helen hears Eddie mumbling to himself. It's undecipherable, but the fact that he's even doing this is quite telling. Eddie doesn't normally talk to himself; not like Helen does.

'I hope to hell you are,' he grunts.

Helen says nothing; then shifts into first gear and takes off slowly across the junction.

'I'll speak with you first thing in the morning. Forget going out for breakfast; you and I need to have a serious conversation. We need to re-evaluate what you do in our station; whether or not you should be doing anything at all.'

Helen's nostrils stiffen.

'Eddie—'

'I'm serious, Helen. Deadly serious. I blame myself. I shouldn't have said a word to you about these calls. I shudda known as soon as you heard the word suicide that you would go off on one. I just... I can't keep taking the blame and dealing with the guilt every time you fuck up at work.'

'Eddie. Don't... I'll do anything. *Anything*. If I don't have my job... I have nothing.'

'We'll talk in the morning.' Eddie's tone is softening, his volume lowering. 'Just... just answer me this question, will you, Hel?'

Helen holds her eyes closed again.

'Go on.'

'Did you take your pill today?'

She opens her eyes wide and then rolls them backwards, just as she's rolling the car to a slow stop. She stares out the driver's side window and brings the phone a little closer to her lips.

'Yes!' she says.

'Good... good. I hate prying about that, but... y'know. Just felt like I should ask.'

'Good night, Eddie,' Helen says.

She presses at the red button; her eyes still haven't blinked since she started to stare out the window.

She shuffles in the car seat, so she can place her phone back into the pocket of her leather coat, then pushes the door open and steps outside, crunching the gravel beneath her feet as she strolls across the car park.

She takes one large breath when she reaches the small porch way and then pulls at the heavy door.

'Ah... hello again, Detective,' the barman calls out. He's stopped drying glasses; is resting his forearms on the bar, chatting with one of the punters.

Helen nods a hello back at him, then begins to peer around the square room at all of the faces in attendance. She spots him at the back of the room, holding a pint glass to his mouth, his eyes peering at her over the rim of it.

'You need to come with me again,' she says.

He places his glass back down on the table to a tsunami of mumbles floating around the bar, then rises slowly out of his seat, placing both sets of his fingers on the table for balance.

Helen watches as he brushes his feet against the carpet, shuffling his way towards the exit. She spins on her heels, takes in everybody's face, ending with the barman, and then paces out the door after him.

'Brother Fitzpatrick, you need to sober yourself up as quickly as you can,' she says. 'Two of your students' lives are in serious danger. And you and I have less than an hour to save them.'

Fitzpatrick bends over slightly, his hands resting on his knees.

'Course I'll help,' he says, a slight slur in his delivery. 'I'd do anything for my students.'

Helen stares at him, her hands on her hips.

'I bet you would,' she says, before storming towards the Garda car.

'Hey... what does that mean?' Fitzpatrick calls after her. He then burps into his chest while rising to a standing position and shuffles towards Helen. By the time he's climbed into the police car, Helen is staring him down. As if she's the Headteacher and he a student who's just got caught smoking behind the bike shed.

'Where you taking me?' he says, looking up at her.

'Your house.'

'My house? *My house?* For what? I don't want the neighbours seeing—'

'Brother! Two of your students are in grave danger. You need to understand the serious nature of what the hell I'm saying to you.'

Fitzpatrick holds both of his hands aloft.

'Okay… okay,' he says, blinking. 'You're eh… quicker walking to my house, down that lane-way back there.'

'The last time I ran down that lane,' Helen says as she reverses the car from its space, 'I ended up like you were a few seconds ago, Brother… my hands on my knees, struggling for breath. We'll take the car, thank you very much. Won't be long.'

Fitzpatrick lays the back of his head on to the rest and they both sit in silence, save for the odd clicking of indicator lights every so often, before Helen is pulling up the handbrake and removing the keys from the ignition. Fitzpatrick's head pivots to look out any window he can see out of in search of neighbours' curtains twitching.

'Right,' Helen says. 'We're gonna go inside. We're gonna sober you up. And then…' Fitzpatrick stops staring around himself to look at Helen, his eyes glazed over. 'And then I'm going to ask you about something you mentioned to me when I first met you earlier.'

'Huh?' Fitzpatrick says, tilting his head like a puppy dog.

Helen puffs out a small sigh.

'When I first brought you outside that pub an hour or so ago, the first words that came out of your mouth were "I'm sorry"…. As soon as you sober up, Brother, you better explain in detail to me just what the fuck it is you were saying sorry for.'

23:20

Ciara

'The friend's house that you say is around the corner... what's the family name?' Miss asks.

Ah bleedin' hell! I think she might be trying to catch us out. She knows we've been lying to her.

'Sally Sweeney,' I say as quickly as I can. Don't know where I pulled that name out of, but I knew I had to answer before Ingrid caved in.

'The Sweeneys? I don't know any Sweeneys that live around here,' Miss says.

I laugh a little, just to come across as if I'm calm. I always do this when I'm lying.

'Ah they do... around two corners actually, they live just off the main Crumlin Road.'

Miss Moriarty stares at Jamie, then back at me and Ingrid.

'Eh... why don't I ring your parents, Ingrid?' she asks.

Oh no. This isn't going to end well.

'No, there's no need,' I say, standing up. 'They're not in anyway. They're around in the Sweeneys' house waiting on us to get back to them. We said we'd pop around to see you for ten minutes and I guess... well, we really shouldn't be taking up too much of your time.'

Miss Moriarty's forehead wrinkles as if she's just become an old woman in the space of two seconds.

'Girls, are you sure?'

'Yeah, yeah, yeah,' I say, tugging at Ingrid's elbow. 'C'mon, Ingrid, it's getting on to midnight. Let's leave Miss and Jamie to it.'

Ingrid stands up but I can tell by her face that she's ready to crack. I need to get her out of here quickly. She throws her arms around Miss again.

'I'm gonna miss you,' she says.

'Miss me? Sure you can call by anytime you want. Don't be silly.'

'She's only getting sentimental because you're pregnant, Miss,' I say, laughing. Jamie laughs too. 'C'mon, Ingrid.' I yank at her elbow again.

When Ingrid finally releases her grip on Miss and turns to face me, I hold my hand up to high five Jamie once more. And then Ingrid does the same.

Miss follows us into the tiny square hallway and, after I've opened the front door, I turn to her and hug her myself.

'You're the best teacher in the world,' I say. Then I turn away from her for the last time ever and step into her small garden.

'Stay safe, you two,' she says, as we open her gate. And suddenly her door is closed and we both know we've finished our last goodbyes. I don't know how we managed it, but we did. I wasn't a big fan of the last goodbye thing; it was Ingrid's idea. But it's kinda cool that we got around to doing it. I'm glad I found out Debbie takes drugs. I can die knowing who she truly is. And I'm glad we found out Miss Moriarty is pregnant. She deserves all the happiness she gets. Maybe her having twin girls come into her life in a few months time will take away the sadness she will feel for us dying. They'll be like our two little replacements in life; our two substitutes.

'Hey, I wonder if Miss' twins will be us being reincarnated,' I say as we walk towards the bus stop.

Ingrid laughs out of her nose.

'Could you imagine Miss Moriarty being your mum? Wow. How perfect would that life be?' she says.

I know Ingrid doesn't believe in any of that nonsense about reincarnation or religion at all. I've always known, but we had a long conversation about it after we came up with the pact last night. We don't believe we're going to come back in other bodies, we don't believe we're going to end up in some Heaven. We just know that once we die, that's it — we're gone. And that's why we're doing it. Because we want to be gone. We want our minds to shut up; to stop going round and round and round in circles. I can't imagine going to Heaven and having to stay with these thoughts for eternity. That wouldn't be Heaven. That would be Hell.

Anyway; it's all bullshit. You'd have to be really stupid to believe life goes on and on and on forever.

'I wonder what she'll call the two girls; might call them Ingrid and Ciara, in memory of us,' I say.

Ingrid laughs through her nose again.

'Could do,' she says. 'It's a pity we'll never meet them though, isn't it?'

I stop walking and turn my face to her, just as we're stepping onto the main Crumlin Road.

'You're not changing your mind just so you can see Miss' twins are you?'

Ingrid laughs again.

'No... jeez, course not,' she says, and then she throws her arm around my shoulder and we continue to walk, like Siamese twins, to the bus stop.

'I really thought we were in trouble there,' I say. 'She asked a hell of a lot of questions, didn't she?'

'She just knows us so well,' Ingrid replies. 'I saw the way she was looking at us, she kind of knew something was up. She just couldn't put her finger on it.'

I nod my head.

'Yeah, I really thought she was going to catch us out when she was asking about our made up friend around the corner. And then... jeez, when she asked if she could ring your parents... I didn't know what to do. The last thing we need right now is your mam finding out what's been going on. She'd just want to ring the police straight away, wouldn't she?'

23:25

Harriet

UUUGH. I CAN'T SLEEP; CAN'T GET CONOR OUT OF MY HEAD. THE BASTARD. I bet he's curled up with her somewhere now, his arms wrapped around her waist, his cock hard against the crack of her ass. I wish he was doing that to me right now. I'm such a fucking idiot. Why do I always fall for the bad boys? I never learn. I hate being a girl. Boys have it so much easier.

I turn over in my bed again, facing my window and stare at all of the books sitting on the windowsill. I make a silent promise to myself that I'll read them… one day. But I've been making that same promise for months… maybe even years at this stage. I really need to grow up.

It's so difficult for me to try to face the reality that I'm an adult now. Eighteen. And supposed to have it all sussed. It's so shitty that people of my age are supposed to know what they want to do for the rest of their lives. I haven't a clue what I want to do next week, never mind thirty years from now.

I'm just going to take that job in the shop, bring in a few quid for the summer and then think about what I want to do with my life. I wouldn't mind travelling; going to Australia for a year or something. But I couldn't leave Dad alone. He'd be lost without me. Not that we do a lot together; he's normally downstairs slouched on the sofa watching TV while I'm up here listening to Take That CDs, thinking about boys.

I face the other way, away from the books and then try to breathe really slowly. I imagine a flock of sheep in a field, taking turns to jump over a bale of hay.

Uuugh. This is bullshit. Whoever said counting sheep will help you fall asleep? I can't get past nine without imagining Conor's perfect teeth when he smiles. I'd love to be kissing that smile right now, my tongue circling his mouth.

I circle my tongue in my own mouth and realise it's dry. I really should bring a glass of water to bed with me every night. I never do. I always seem to catch myself stewing whether or not it's worth it for me to get out from under my warm duvet, walk down the stairs and step onto the cold tiles of the kitchen to fill a glass of water.

Fuck it. I turn over again, stare at the window blind as if that's going to quench my thirst and help me fall asleep.

Then I let out a yelp and whip the duvet away from me. I step out of bed, stretch my arms over my head and decide to brave the coldness of the kitchen tiles.

I can hear the TV blare as I make my way down the stairs. He's watching some cop show; probably an old episode of *Hill Street Blues*. I wish he'd get up off that sofa; go down the pub or something and talk to some people. Perhaps he'd even meet another woman; a step mum that could help me answer the thousand questions I have about being a woman. But I know he never will. He's married to my mam until he dies too. It's kinda cute I guess... but also a little sad. He has lots of years left. And I just know he's going to spend all of them on that sofa.

I hiss as I tip-toe over the cold tiles to get to the sink, then I fill a glass and down it as quickly as I can before filling it back up and strolling towards the stairs again. I notice the time on the microwave clock as I pass it; 11:30.

'Holy fuck!' I say, my body jumping, some of the water leaping from my glass. 'Jesus, Dad, don't sneak up on me like that!'

'Sorry, love,' he says, 'I wasn't sneaking up on you. Was just gonna have meself another cup of tea.'

I let out a disappointed sigh; not because I got a fright, not because I have to soak up the spillage, but because I've snapped at Dad. Again. I hate snapping at him. He never deserves it. He just seems to get in the way of my shitty life every now and then.

'No, *I'm* sorry,' I say.

He grabs at a tea towel and begins to mop up my mess for me.

'Ye can't sleep, huh?' he asks looking up from his crouched position. I shake my head. 'You haven't been able to sleep right these past couple weeks... everything okay?'

'Course it is, Dad,' I say. 'I'm just stressing a little about the Leaving

Cert exams.' That's a lie. I genuinely couldn't give a shit about them; not now that I've decided I'm not going to go to college.

'You'll be fine, love,' he says, standing back up to nudge his knuckles against my cheek.

'Thanks, Dad,' I say, taking a sip. 'You eh... get the girls home okay?'

'No,' he says, folding the tea towel in half. 'The two of them legged it on me. They got me to stop off at the garage on the canal road and then just said "thanks" and ran off.'

I squint my eyes

'Really? I thought they were acting a little bit odd when they were here. Wonder what the hell they're up to?'

Dad shrugs his shoulders.

'It's the age they're at now, isn't it? They want to be independent. Oh...' he says, 'Ingrid gave you your book back. It's on the sofa. She said to say "thank you".'

I cock my head, try to remember what it was specifically that felt so odd about Ingrid and Ciara when they called by about an hour ago.

'Hmmm,' I say. Then I spin on my heels and stroll into the living room. Dad follows me and watches as I pick up my book and flick through it.

I love you Harriet,

Ingrid. x

My mouth opens wide.

'Look... why would she write that?' I ask Dad. 'They were acting really strange when they were here.'

'It's just their age, isn't it?'

I shake my head.

'Nah... something's up. I'm worried about them. We've gotta ring Auntie Greta.'

I slap the book closed then walk to the phone in the hallway, pick up the receiver and begin to dial.

HELEN PACES INTO THE KITCHEN, RUNS THE TAP AND THEN GRABS AT THE kettle. She fills it, places it back on its base and clicks the switch. Whilst it's bubbling towards a boil, she roots around in the cupboards until she finds where Fitzpatrick keeps his glasses. She fills two of them with tap water, then places one aside and gulps from the other.

She lets out a heavy gasp before filling the empty glass again and carrying both back into the living room.

Fitzpatrick is sitting upright on the sofa, fidgeting with his fingers. She flicks her wrist, flinging water into his aged face again.

He sucks in a long breath, then wipes at his eyes before staring up at Helen.

'How did ye not see that coming?' she says to him, handing him the second glass. 'Here... drink up, sober up. And let's get down to business.'

She watches as Fitzpatrick sips from his glass.

'Get it into ye,' she says. She takes a step towards him, holds the bottom of the glass up, helping the water pour.

He lets out a sigh, spitting and spluttering some of the drink back into the glass.

'Ye trying to kill me?' he says.

'Me? I'm the one giving you water... y'know, that liquid we all need to stay alive. You're the one poisoning yourself with alcohol.'

Fitzpatrick puffs his cheeks out, swirls the glass in front of his eyes and then tries to down it again; this time almost finishing the job. He holds the glass towards Helen who takes it from him, just as the kettle confirms it has boiled by producing a click sound.

'Where d'ye leave your tea bags?' she says as she makes her way back into the kitchen.

'Eh... in the press under the kettle,' Fitzpatrick slurs while wiping at his mouth.

Helen grabs a cup that had been left to dry on the drain, tosses a tea bag into it and pours the kettle. She whistles as she turns to the fridge, then pinches at her nose.

'Sweet fuck,' she says, balking backwards. 'The bleedin' stench of your fridge. You keep dead rats in here or something?'

After swiping the air away from her nose, she turns around, sees Fitzpatrick staring at her, leaning against the kitchen door.

'Rarely use it,' he says. 'I eat in the school, or down the pub at night.'

Helen spins back around.

'Have ye no milk?'

Fitzpatrick burps into his chest.

'Nope,' he says.

Helen rolls her eyes, then grabs at the cup and hands it to him.

'Here, drink this without milk. It's tea. The only hangover cure I ever found that worked when I used to drink.'

Fitzpatrick lifts the cup to his lips, then takes a step back, his eyes tearing up.

'Jesus, sweet Mary and Joseph,' he says, 'that's bloody boiling.'

'Well... looks like it's woken you up.'

Helen walks by him, back into the living room.

'Brother Fitzpatrick, time to start talking. These girls don't have the time to wait on you to fully get your shit together.'

She hears him shuffle his feet back into the room after her.

'Whatcha ye need to know?' he asks.

'You need to tell me what the hell you were apologising for earlier?'

Fitzpatrick brushes his feet off the cheap wooden floorboards of his modest terraced home and then sits back into the sofa.

'It's nothing,' he says, shaking his head.

'It's not *nothing* now, Brother, is it? You were worried about something when me and Officer Guilfoyle spoke to you earlier. It's vital you tell me what that was all about.'

Fitzpatrick has both sets of fingers wrapped around his cup, the heat offering him the only comfort he could possibly feel right now. He coughs, blinks his eyes and then shakes his head.

'It is nothing. Nothing to do with whatever you are here for. If you were here for that, you wouldn't need me to explain it now would ye?'

Helen squints her eyes.

'You've sobered up quite quickly, Brother. Used to it, are we? Sobering up after a heavy night on the sauce? It's what you have to do all the time, isn't it? Drink all night, run a school during the day.'

Fitzpatrick lifts one hand from the cup, only so he can pinch at his temple.

'You tell me why you're here,' he says, 'what's this about; two of my students being in danger?'

Helen stands tall, her hands stuffed into her coat pockets.

'Are they in danger because of you, Brother Fitzpatrick? Is that what you're apologising for? Do you abuse your students? Have you pushed two in particular too far?'

Fitzpatrick reels his head backwards.

'What are you talking about, Detective?'

Helen puffs out a tiny laugh; she's trying to act menacingly nonchalant, just as she used to when she first became a Detective all those years ago. She adopted her nonchalant persona from the best of the best; Colombo. The Peter Falk series was all the rage in the early eighties, just as Helen and Eddie were being promoted to Detective status — Helen being one of the first females in the entire country to ever hold such a rank. She was such a promising young Detective. It's a shame she never got to fill her potential.

Helen sits, keeping her hands in her pockets.

'Tell me what you were apologising for...'

Fitzpatrick shakes his head.

'I need to speak to a lawyer,' he says.

Helen shakes her head this time.

'Impossible. We don't have time for that. Two of your students have just over half an hour to live and you need to tell me who they are.'

Fitzpatrick holds his eyes closed.

'Hold on, Detective,' he says, 'why are you here? Are you genuinely here to find two of my students who you think are in danger — or are you here to find out about... about—'

'About what?' Helen says.

'I want a lawyer.'

Helen holds both of her hands in front of her face and grunts her annoyance into them.

'Are you telling me that whatever it is you wanted to apologise for earlier has nothing to do with two young female students at your school?'

'No... no, course not,' Fitzpatrick says, his eyes still closed.

Helen sucks on her lips, as she usually does when she has a quick decision to make.

'Okay... listen to me, Brother. Whatever it is that you need to apologise for, I'm gonna come back to that, you hear me? Whatever dark shit you've got going on... it won't be forgotten about. Unless.... unless you can help me. I believe two of your students are going to kill themselves at midnight. We need to find them before it's too late. Do you know of any girls from your school who are so depressed that they might want to take their own lives?'

Fitzpatrick blinks his eyes open, refocusing them on the strange face in front of him. Then he shakes his head; slowly at first, then more aggressively.

'Bollocks,' Helen says.

'Hold on... are you serious? Two of my girls are going to commit *suicide? Tonight?*'

Helen rolls her eyes.

'I've been bloody saying this to you since I first took you out of the pub you stupid f—' she stops herself.

'I thought this was all about something else,' Fitzpatrick says. He stands, holds both hands clasped behind his head. Then he blesses himself, mumbling a thank you to a God he doesn't even believe in.

'You need to talk to Abigail Jensen. She's the welfare officer at the school. She knows all there is to know about all of the students. If anyone can help you identify them, she can.'

Helen bows her head. She's no further along in her investigation than she had been four hours ago; hearing from a Headteacher that she should ring his welfare officer. Last time she did this she ended up with a list of one hundred and sixty-four names. She sighs as she stretches her hand towards Fitzpatrick, opening and closing her fingers.

'What?' Fitzpatrick asks.

'Your phone... with Abigail's number ringing.'

Fitzpatrick pats at his chino pockets.

'Oh, I don't carry my mobile phone. Hate the bloody thing,' he says. Helen's eyes roll. 'I eh... I eh....' Fitzpatrick stutters. 'I have a Filofax up in my bedroom. Her number is in that. I'll go get it.'

Helen stares around the Brother's living room as he stumbles up the steps, noticing the array of framed photos hanging on his wall; most of them of Fitzpatrick with his arm draped around celebrities. Fitzpatrick with Eamonn Holmes. Fitzpatrick with Brian O'Driscoll. Fitzpatrick with the Pope.

'Fuckin weirdo,' she whispers. 'Bet this guy's into some dark shit. Probably a kiddie fiddler. Aren't they all? Those bloody church fellas. Hiding behind the dog collar.'

She walks into the hallway as she hears him trudging back down the stairs, her right hand gripped to her phone.

'Here,' he says, stretching a piece of paper towards her. 'That's her mobile number.'

Helen takes the paper from him, then punches the number into her phone. Both her and Fitzpatrick stand in the cold hallway, the ring tone bouncing off the walls.

'Hello.'

'Hello, Abigail, this is Detective Brennan. I'm with Brother Fitzpatrick.'

'Oh no... is he in trouble?'

Helen lifts her gaze from the phone, to look at Fitzpatrick. He just holds his arms out wide.

'He's not, no,' Helen says. 'But two of the students who attend your school are.'

Helen hears a gasp on the other end of the line.

'Which two?' Abigail asks.

'Well... that's an answer I was hoping to get from you. We had an anonymous phone call made to our school from one your students a few hours ago. Tommy Smith. You know him well?'

'Yeah... Tommy. Of course. Is he okay?'

'Oh yeah — that little fella is more than okay... wherever he is. But he told us two of his friends — both girls — were planning on killing themselves tonight. He didn't give us names... I'm hoping you can.'

'*What?*' Abigail says, all high pitched. 'Suicide?'

'Abigail. I know this may be shocking news to you right now, but I really don't have the time for you to absorb it all. I just need you to get your thinking cap on. Are there two girls who know Tommy who you think could be depressed enough to want to end their lives?'

Helen holds the phone away from her ear as Abigail blows a puff of her cheeks down the line.

'Jee... well... the truth is, we have quite a number of girls who have come to me this year describing symptoms of depression. I don't know what it is about the modern age; online bullying I think more than anything, but girls and boys are developing depression now more than any time I've worked in education.'

'Sorry, Abigail, I don't need a lesson on the growing rates of depression. I just need to find these two girls before it's too late. *Think.* Think thoroughly. Two girls Tommy Smith knows who suffer from some form of depression or have shown you any signs of it recently...'

Helen stares at Fitzpatrick as the line falls silent, noticing he's leaning against the wall for support. He doesn't look drunk anymore, just tired. As if he could fall asleep standing up.

'Yes,' Abigail says. 'I'm pretty sure I know which two girls you're talking about.'

23:30

Greta

I STARE AT THE CLOCK ABOVE THE MANTELPIECE, THEN STRETCH MY ARMS above my head and yawn. I normally go to bed around eleven o'clock, but can't seem to shift myself tonight. I've been watching some awful movie called *French Kiss* that I thought might be alright because Meg Ryan was in it but... nah... too cheesy. Although, in fairness to the movie, it didn't have my full attention. I couldn't stop worrying about Ingrid. And Ciara.

Ingrid's going to be in a whole heap of trouble when she finally gets home. I'm going to ground her for two weeks; stop her pocket money for the rest of the month.

How dare she lie to me. I'm not sure I'm going to be able to cope with her being a teenager. I've too much on my plate looking after Sven.

I stretch and yawn again, then decide to click through the channels, even though I know I'm not going to watch anything. The phone ringing makes me cock my head and I hop off the couch to catch it as quickly as I can; not just because I'm hoping it's Ingrid and she's going to tell me she's okay, but more so because Terry will fume if it wakes him.

'Hello,' I say, snatching at the receiver.

'Auntie Greta... it's me... Harriet.'

'Oh hey, Harriet, please tell me Ingrid is with you.'

There's a pause. A pause that makes my stomach flip itself over.

'Eh... she's not with me right now. But she was here. She left about an hour ago and well... well... I don't know how to say this, but her and her friend Ciara, they seemed a bit… eh… they were acting a bit weird. As if they're up to something.'

I hold fingers to my forehead and close my eyes.

'Oh Jesus.'

'She eh… left a note in a book I had given her a loan of — she wrote that she loved me in it. She never does that. And Dad was giving them a lift home and half-way there they asked him to pull over at a garage and then they ran from him.'

'Oh Jesus,' I say again. 'She eh…' I hold my hand flat out in front of my eyes and watch it tremble, 'she eh… she seemed a bit distant when she left here earlier. They said they were going to spend the night at Ciara's house, but when I rang Ciara's mum a couple hours ago, she told me they'd said the opposite to her.'

I suck in a breath. 'Harriet, what did they say to you when they were at yours?'

Harriet clicks her tongue.

'Ingrid told me that she had been embarrassed by a boy in front of everybody at a party last night.'

'A boy. *I knew it!*' I say, covering my mouth after I've said it. 'Who is this boy, Harriet?'

'I don't know… he has a weird nickname. Stitch they call him, I think… something like that.'

'I had a feeling they were hanging around with boys. I said it to Terry. Terry wasn't having any of it.'

'Listen, Greta,' Brendan says joining in the call. 'They're just young girls. Whatever it is they're up to, I bet it's not as serious as you think. They'll be home soon.'

I hold my hand to my forehead again and try to slow my breathing. Maybe I shouldn't be overreacting. They both lied to their parents to say they were staying in each other's houses when they've probably called back over the see this boy. Is that such a big deal?

'If they call by again — or if you hear from them, Harriet — you make sure to ring me straight away, okay?'

'Course I will, Auntie Greta. I told Ingrid I'd bring her out soon and we can sit down and have a good chat.'

I put the phone down without saying goodbye, my mind racing. Then I stare up the stairs and before I even realise it I'm climbing them… slowly. When I reach our bedroom, I push the door open as gently as I can and watch his breaths heaving the duvet up… then down. He's almost on the verge of snoring. He'll go crazy if I wake him. I know he will. If he didn't have the big interview with the transport minister in the morning, I might be tempted. I close my eyes, to try to engage with the thoughts racing through my head, then decide to quietly pull the door closed and walk back down the stairs.

I shuffle my feet into my trainers, reach for my coat that's hung on the bottom bannister and then snatch at my keys. My hands are still shaking. I make sure I open the hall door quickly, so that it doesn't creak and, before I realise what I'm doing exactly, I'm out in the darkness, walking down our drive and turning right.

They only live four doors down. I say 'they'. I mean 'she'. He's never really there. I've sometimes wondered if they have an open marriage or something like that. It's certainly not conventional anyway.

I whisper an apology to nobody as I hold my finger against their doorbell. I must be going mad; talking to myself. Then I hear the latch turn in the door and suddenly I am not talking to myself anymore.

'I'm so sorry, Vivian, but I'm getting ever so worried about the girls. I don't suppose they came back here, did they?'

Vivian blinks her eyes. She looks jaded. Or drunk.

'No... no... they didn't come back here. What time is it now?' she asks.

'It must be gone half eleven, something like that,' I say. 'It's just... my niece rang; said the two girls called over to her about an hour ago and they were acting suspiciously. Do you mind if I come in?'

Vivian takes a step back, giving me room to enter. This is actually the first time I've ever been in their house. It's lovely. They've much more light in their hallway than we have and their walls have been more recently painted than ours. It's easier to maintain a home if you only have one child, I suppose. Certainly easier if you have cleaners like these guys do.

'My brother-in-law offered to give them a lift home, but he only got half-way with them before they got out of the car and ran off. There's definitely something going on. Do you know much about the party they were at last night?'

I rest both of my hands on my hips and stare at Vivian as she shakes her head, folding her bottom lip out.

'No, sorry,' she says. Then she walks by me, into her living room. 'C'min.'

I follow her; across their massive TV screen, over the expensive rug and past their Chesterfield sofa until we're in the kitchen.

'Cup of tea... anything like that?' she asks as she grabs at the stem of a wine glass and swigs from it. 'Or,' she gasps after she's swallowed, 'this is an expensive Merlot. My favourite. Fancy a glass?'

I blow out an unsteady breath and then find myself squinting at Vivian, trying to work out just how many glasses of that expensive Merlot she must have had tonight. There's a certain unsteadiness to how she's standing in front of me; her eyes almost narrowed.

'No,' I answer in what I know is an irritated tone. 'We need to find out where our daughters are. Vivian… we need to ring the police.'

23:35

Ciara

THE TWO OF US ARE FACING EACH OTHER, HOLDING EACH OTHER'S HANDS, staring into each other's faces while we wait on the bus to come and pick us up to take us to our last stop.

'Whatcha think our parents are doing now?' I ask.

Ingrid rolls her eyes up to the stars.

'Probably be in bed. Dad will be anyway. He goes to bed around eight o'clock.'

'Eight o'clock,' I giggle. 'Does he stay up later than Sven?'

Ingrid smiles back at me.

'He's got to get up at five a.m. to do his show, doesn't he?'

I nod my head.

'Of course. And your mum?'

'She'll probably be going to bed about now. I think she stays up until around eleven-ish, watches movies and stuff. What about your parents?'

'Well... I'm pretty sure my dad is out somewhere, probably still working. Or that's what he'll be telling my mam he's doing anyway. I never know where he is up to be honest. My mam... well... we both know where she'll be right?'

'Sitting at the kitchen island drinking a glass of wine.'

'A *bottle*, Ingrid!'

Ingrid closes her eyes and shows me her teeth.

'Sorry. Of course, a bottle. I always get that wrong.'

'I'm not sure what time either of them go to bed at,' I say. 'They don't have a routine. It's not like your house.'

Ingrid grips my hands even tighter and the two of us leave the talk of our parents there.

I'm not going to blame my parents for my death. I only blame them for my life. I never asked to be born. Nobody does.

I think having kids is the most selfish thing anybody could ever do. It's one of the main reasons I don't want to become an adult. Adults tend to do so many selfish things. They never think of others. I've often lay down on my bed and thought about it; there actually can't be anything more selfish in this world than deciding to have children. How can anybody be so bloody selfish to do that! Look at Ingrid's little brother. Poor Sven is going to be a vegetable his whole life. He can barely talk. He never asked for his life. But you don't even have to have a sickness to wish you were never born. I've never been ill, aside from the odd cold here and there, and I certainly wish I was never born. Unless you count depression as a sickness. Though nobody has ever offered me a pill for it. I did wonder once whether or not I should go see a doctor and ask him about my feelings. But I just wouldn't know what to say. I rang a Childline number once as well, but hung up as soon as the questions got a bit tough for me. Suicide is the only way out. It makes total sense.

'How long's the bus ride back to Rathmines from here?' Ingrid asks.

'Bout fifteen minutes this time of night. There'll be no traffic. You all set?' I squeeze her fingers tighter in mine as I ask my question.

She looks down, nodding her head.

'Ready as I'll ever be,' she says. 'Mad to think we only have about fifteen minutes left though, isn't it?'

I squeeze her fingers again.

'Suppose it is. But that's a good thing, right? Only fifteen minutes left of being depressed, fifteen minutes left with the bad thoughts going round and round our heads.'

She looks up and smiles at me with her eyes. Then nods her head slowly again.

'I can't wait for it to be over,' she sighs out of her mouth. And then, over her shoulder, I see our bus coming.

'Isn't it mad to think nobody has any darn clue what we're up to? Just me and you, buddy; that's all. Everybody will be totally shocked in the morning, won't they? I don't think one person we know will say they saw it coming. I read about that once y'know,' I say.

'Read about what?'

I stop talking as the bus pulls in and its doors flap open.

'Two fares to Rathmines,' Ingrid says to the driver. He doesn't say anything; he just fiddles with his little machine until our tickets come out and then he holds his hand out for Ingrid to pour her coins into.

There are four people sitting downstairs, so we decide to head to the top deck. We sit at the front, right against the window and when we sit down I finally answer Ingrid's question.

'I read about suicide. It was in one of my mam's old magazines. It said loved ones never see it coming. And that it's usually the people who act happiest that end up doing it.'

'Not sure people would call us the happiest, would you?' she says to me.

I puff out a small laugh.

'Suppose so. But they'll all be surprised won't they?'

'Definitely,' she says.

23:35

Vivian

I CURSE. BUT ONLY INSIDE MY HEAD. THIS IS THE LAST THING I NEED. They'll be fine for fuck sake. They're teenagers.

'C'min,' I say, leading her through the living room and out into the kitchen. I don't mind her seeing me drink; it's not as if it's eleven o'clock on a Tuesday morning; it's a weekend night. Nothing wrong with that.

'Cup of tea... anything like that?' I ask as I grab at my glass. 'Or... this is an expensive Merlot. My favourite. Fancy a glass?'

She looks me up and down.

'No,' she says abruptly; as if she's angry with me. I knew she'd be a bitch. You can't be as attractive as she is without being a bit of a cunt in some way. 'We need to find out where our daughters are, Vivian... we need to ring the police.'

I place my glass back down on the kitchen island and walk towards her.

'Aren't you overreacting a bit? They're just teenagers having some fun on a weekend night.'

'They've school in the morning, Vivian. Besides, they lied to us. They told me they'd be here, they told you they'd be at my house. This is...' she turns around, holding her hand to her forehead as if she's some God-awful Hollywood actress, 'serious. Something is definitely going on between them.'

I don't know how to handle this level of drama. This is why I like to drink alone.

I find myself turning around, pulling at my cabinet and reaching for another glass. I half fill it with Merlot and then hand it to her.

'Here, calm down and let's talk,' I say.

She eyeballs me and lets an awkward silence settle between us before she accepts the glass, nodding her head as she does so.

'Thanks.'

I take her by the elbow and lead her to the kitchen island.

'Greta, the police won't be able to do anything. The girls have been missing for what... a few hours? Don't they have to be missing for, like, twenty-four hours at least before the police will get involved?'

She sits, takes her first sip of my Merlot, her hand a little shaky, and then nods her head.

'Suppose you're right. I'm being a bit over-dramatic, aren't I? That's not like me.'

Yeah right that's not like you.

I just smile back at her.

'Nice house you have. You used your kitchen space really well. I keep saying to Terry that we should put a skylight in ours... you can't beat a bit of natural light.'

I look up through our skylight, into the black sky.

'I didn't even ask Michael for permission,' I say. 'I just got it done, gave the builder Michael's bank account details.'

Greta pushes out a small laugh. She seems to have relaxed. Wine works wonders.

'Where is Michael?' she asks, looking around herself.

I push out a huff.

'In work, probably.'

'On a Sunday night?'

I sip from my glass.

'He never stops. He's in that office more than he is here.'

She takes a fistful of that beautiful golden hair she has and tugs it over her shoulder, then rings her fingers through it.

'I think we might share ambitious husbands as well as troublesome thirteen-year-old daughters,' she says.

As I stare at her playing with her hair, I remember the amount of times Ciara came home to say that the Murphys would like to invite us to their house for dinner.

'Yeah... we've probably loads in common. We should — for the sake of our girls — get to know each other a bit more,' I say.

'That'd be nice.'

The kitchen falls silent. Seems as if we've run out of things to say already. I lick at my teeth, a habit I have when I drink red wine because I hate the thought of my teeth staining, and then refill my glass. I don't bother offering more to Greta; she's barely touched what I've given her already.

'Sorry,' she says, shaking her head. 'I hate to bring it back up, but I just can't understand why they'd run away from Brendan if he was giving them a lift home. It keeps coming into my head. I can't relax.'

She stands up. And so do I.

'There's not much we can do; let's just wait here until they come home.'

'We could go out and look for them,' she says.

I look down at my slippers.

'Let's think it through. Who else might know where they are? Do you know of any boys they hang around with at school?' I ask.

Greta puffs out her cheeks, then shakes her head again.

'No... jee. I thought they didn't have any other friends, never mind boyfriends. I thought Ciara and Ingrid were just two peas in a pod.' She looks up at me, her eyes widening. 'Do you know if they have any other friends?'

I scoff. Then tug at my ear. Jesus. I don't know anything about Ciara really. It's just... it's just so boring, parenting, isn't it? I haven't enjoyed any stage of it. I'm not quite sure what I would get out of questioning my daughter. It holds no interest to me. Not that I'd ever say that out loud.

'No, sorry. Same as you. I thought they were just two peas in a pod myself. Ingrid is the only friend Ciara's ever had. Well... apart from Debbie.'

Greta's head cocks up again.

'Debbie. The girl who minded Ciara for years right?'

'Uh-huh,' I say before taking another sip.

'Think they might have called out to her house tonight?'

I shake my head as I swallow.

'Course not, why would they do that?'

'Well,' Greta says, standing a little taller, 'I'm wondering why they called out to Ingrid's cousin. I know it's late... but maybe you should ring Debbie. See if she's heard anything from the girls.'

I sigh and hold my eyes closed for a couple seconds longer than I probably should.

'Really?' I say when I reopen them.

'Please.' Her hands are clasped, her eyes sad. I feel sorry for her.

So I place my wine back on to the island and shuffle my way to the phone.

FITZPATRICK HAS SLUMPED BACK INTO A SEATING POSITION ON THE STAIRS — his head in his hands — by the time Helen has hung up the call. She drops the piece of paper he had handed to her minutes ago with Abigail's number on it and then spins on her heels to head out the door. But she stops, turns again, takes two steps towards Fitzpatrick and leans over him.

'You better hope I catch up with these two girls before it's too late, Brother.' She breathes heavily at him, giving herself a moment to think of what to say next. 'Bloody drinking so much when you have such an important job to look after young people. How dare you. I bet... I wouldn't be surprised if you're somehow responsible for these girls suffering with depression. I know you've got dark secrets — and I'm going to find out what they are. I'll be back, Brother Fitzpatrick... and I'll find out just what exactly it is you wanted to apologise for.'

Fitzpatrick takes his hands from his face and sits into a more upright position just as Helen is pulling at his front door.

'It's not that bad!' he shouts after her as she storms down his narrow pathway, towards the Garda car she stole half-an-hour ago. 'It was only a few quid I stole from the school funds. I'll pay it back. I swear.'

Helen doesn't bother to look back at him. She's fully focused on saving these two girls. She got names, got addresses — all from Abigail — and is intent on being their hero; the hero she failed to be for Scott.

She speeds off from outside Brother Fitzpatrick's house, noticing curtains twitching in a couple neighbours' windows as she does so. By the time she's at the end of the road, she switches the sirens on, the sound blaring, the lights flashing.

'C'mon, c'mon, c'mon,' she instructs the car, tapping her palms against the steering wheel.

She dips her head slightly, to see the digital clock on the dashboard. 23:36. Then she smiles.

'You're gonna do this, Helen. You're gonna catch them. You're gonna save them. You're gonna save yourself. By the time the morning comes around, nobody will be bothered that you stuck your nose in, nobody will be bothered that you stole a police car. They'll be lauding you, offering you your old job back. Eddie might even ask you to help him run the station. Just as you and he planned when you first joined the force and fell in love.'

She eyeballs herself in the rear-view mirror, the grin widening across her face.

Two girls. Both thirteen. Both being bullied at school. Both have parents who don't give a shit. The information Abigail gave her over the phone wasn't surprising — not to Helen. She'd been researching teen suicides for over twenty years. Is obsessed with the subject. Boys are more likely to commit suicide, though not until they're in their twenties. That's when they realise they haven't met the expectations society has placed on them. They become disillusioned, begin to compare themselves to their peers — believing everyone else's bullshit — then they top themselves because they're confused and too proud to speak out about how they feel. Girls on the other hand are much more mature than boys from an early age. They realise as early as their teens that they might not be meeting expectations placed on them. They look to their peers, especially the popular ones, and feel mightily inadequate. Whereas males are most likely to end their own lives in their mid-twenties, females are more likely to want to do it in their mid teens. Though, fortunately, they're less brave than the opposite sex; less likely to carry out a suicide attempt to full fruition.

But it seems — to Helen — that these two girls are beyond that. They're not looking for attention. They *want* to do this. They're going to end their lives tonight. They've made a pact; just like Scott and his friends did twenty-two years ago. And they're not going to change their minds.

Helen knows all of this information from studying statistics released by the National Suicide Research Foundation every year; has noted the rapid increase in numbers across both genders with every report that gets published. Each year she tuts as she reads the latest figures, and on each occasion she thinks to herself 'if only I could have talked to one of them before they did it, it might make up for me losing Scott.' That's why her adrenaline is rising now; she is certain that tonight is the night — is adamant she's finally gonna save, not one, but two teenagers from doing exactly what Scott and his friends did.

She screeches the car on to the canal road, swerving around those who have pulled in to let her pass; her heart racing as quickly as the speedometer, her mind flashing forward to tomorrow when she will receive plaudits of heroism from all around her.

Then her eyes blink back to the present. But it's too late.

Her car comes to a sudden stop, crashing into the back of the Land Rover in front of her. She jerks forward, then back in her seat.

'Ah for fuck sake!' she yells, yanking at her door handle. She gets out, at the same time a middle-aged man gets out of the Land Rover.

'Jesus, did you not hear my siren?' she says.

The man holds both of his palms up towards her.

'I did, officer, I was trying to pull over, you just came too fast... way too fast.'

They meet where their cars met, and both bend down to survey the damage.

'It's not too bad, the man says... your car took the brunt of it. These things,' he says patting at the wheel arch of his Land Rover, 'can take a bashing.'

'You really need to be more careful when you hear emergency services on the roads,' Helen scoffs. The man stands back up straight, stares at her, his eyes squinting.

'You okay?' he says. 'You didn't hit your head, did you?'

Helen tuts.

'I'd feel better if you moved your bloody car so I can get on with my job.'

The man swivels his head, taking in the two pedestrians who have ran towards them.

'Don't we need to swap insurance details or whatev—'

'Contact Terenure Garda station tomorrow, we'll sort it out then,' Helen says as she strides away from him

'But eh... what's your name?'

Helen doesn't answer. She hops back into the police car, reverses it, the front bumper hanging off, and then waves her hand at the man as she speeds off again.

The noise of the bumper scraping against the road can be heard over the siren, but Helen doesn't care. She'll deal with the whole mess in the morning. Eddie will look after it. A new bumper will mean nothing in the grand scheme of things. Saving lives is the most important thing a copper can do; isn't that what the police force is for: serving and protecting the public? She's going to protect two members of the public in the most heroic way imaginable.

'I'm coming, girls,' she screams to herself. 'Hold on. Don't do anything yet. Helen's on her way.'

She turns the car, its wheels screeching, its bumper scraping and its siren blaring, onto the road Abigail said the two girls lived on and then slows down so she can make out the numbers on the doors of the large houses. She's not surprised the girls seem to come from good stock. That tends to be the way. It's rare that it's poor girls who attempt suicide. It's more likely those who feel they can't live up to the expectations set on them by their successful parents. She thinks that might have been why Scott did it. He showed no signs of depression. Perhaps he just felt inadequate because of their regarded status as Detectives. Though — having wracked her brain for twenty-two years — Helen really hasn't come to any conclusion. It eats at her that she will never know the answer. That's why she's eager for her and Eddie to move to Canada. The quiet, the calm. She's certain it will dilute the prominence of that question repeating itself over and over in her mind.

When she sees one of the numbers she's searching for, she abandons the car in the middle of the street, strides towards the front door and lifts the knocker before slamming it back down three times as loudly as she possibly can.

A light comes on in the hallway before the door inches open,

'Jesus, why you knocking so hard, everything alright?' a woman says. She notices the police car over Helen's shoulder and then holds a hand to her mouth. 'Oh Jesus.'

'Ma'am, I'm Detective Brennan from Rathmines Garda station… I need to speak with your daughter as a matter of urgency.'

'Oh my God, what's she done? What's she done?'

The woman takes a step backwards, her eyes widening, her fists forming into a ball.

'We believe your daughter's life is in danger. It's imperative I speak with her as soon as possible.'

The woman holds both balls of fists either side of her face, digging them into her cheeks.

'Mum, Mum. What's wrong?' a girl appearing at the top of the stairs, wearing polka dot pyjamas, calls out.

The woman looks up at her, then swallows.

'Louise, you need to get yourself down here right now! The police are here to talk to you.'

23:40

Terry

'THAT'S ALL VERY WELL AND GOOD THAT YOU THINK YOU ARE DOING THE RIGHT thing, Minister, but I put it to you that your opinion is wrong. Just give me a second here to read you out some statistics. In 2013, the number of road deaths in Ireland was one hundred and eighty-eight. The following year one hundred and ninety-three. In 2015, one hundred and sixty-two, then back up to one eighty-six in 2016. Yes, in 2017 there was small drop again, to one-five-seven, but in each of the past two years the number has slightly increased again. I put it to you, that labelling the methods you have introduced over the past six years as 'a fantastic success' is nothing more than a fairy-tale. Isn't that right Minist—'

'Terry, Terry... wake up.'

My eyes dart open. I can't see a thing, but I can hear her — and smell her.

'What the fuck, Greta?' I say, slapping the mattress.

'Terry, Ingrid is in trouble. Something's definitely up.'

I hold my eyes closed as tightly as I can, then open them wide, just so I can try to focus. I turn to the digital clock on my side table. 23:41.

'What are you talkin' about?'

'Terry — Ingrid and Ciara... they called over to Brendan and Harriet's house earlier, they were also at Ciara's former child minder. We've just been on calls to each of them; they all say the girls were acting really weird. I'm so worried, Terry, I ... I...'

I can feel her knees vibrate against the bed, so I hold my hand out to reach her; see if I can calm her down a bit. Then I pull back the duvet and manage to throw my legs out of the side of the bed, yelping out a yawn as I do so.

'Calm down, Greta,' I say, 'there's no need to get all dramatic. Start again. What did you wake me up for?'

She takes a deep breath, then sits down beside me.

'Ingrid and Ciara visited two houses tonight. Two that we know of. And they acted really strangely in both of them. I told you… I told you when they were going out that door tonight that Ingrid couldn't even look me in the eye. Something's up… something major.'

'Like what?' I ask, twisting the balls of my palms into my eye sockets.

I hear her shrug.

'I dunno,' she says.

'Well, then, how am I supposed to know? I've just been asleep, haven't I? How do you suppose I know what the hell our daughter's up to when I've been snoring my head off?'

I hear her gasp a little bit. Maybe that was a bit harsh. But she knows darn well I have a big interview in the morning.

'Terry, your daughter might be in trouble,' she says.

I stand up, click at the switch on the lamp by my bedside and then sit back down, holding the palm of my hand to my wife's lower back.

'How the hell do you get from her visiting her cousin to her being in trouble, Greta? Are you sure you're not being a bit dramatic here? Ingrid and Ciara — they're teenagers now. This is the sorta stuff teenagers get up to…. Listen,' I say, moving my hand up to grip her shoulder, 'I'll give her an earful tomorrow when she gets back from school. But…. I mean, there's nothing I can do right now, is there? I'm in my bloody boxer shorts, and I have to get up in five hours' time.'

'Terry… Brendan was giving them a lift home when they both got out of his car and ran. They left a book behind; a book Harriet had lent to Ingrid. Ingrid had signed it before she handed it back, writing 'I love you Harriet'. You know that's not like our daughter. I think she might be running away; her and Ciara.'

'Huh?' I say. 'What would they be running away for?'

Greta shrugs again. She's really good at posing questions; is shit at answering them. A bit like the politicians I interview.

'Well… have you checked her wardrobe, did she take any clothes or anything like that?'

Greta stands up, then sprints out of our room. I hear her as she rifles through Ingrid's wardrobe, sweeping hangers aside.

'No… no everything seems to be here', she shouts out to me.

'Shhh… Jesus, be quite will ye. You'll wake Sven.'

I hold both of my hands over my face and then sigh as deeply as I can into them.

'Terry, I'm really frightened. I don't know what's going on, I just know I don't like it,' Greta says, pacing back into our bedroom.

I *hate* that I'm awake right now. Hate that it'll play havoc with my performance tomorrow. But I know I can't really have a go at Greta, especially while she's shaking so much and almost in tears. It's just… I don't know what it is she wants me to do.

'Let me go get you a cup of tea and we can have a little chat, huh?' I say, standing up, tapping her on the shoulder as I walk by and then scratching my balls as I head down the stairs.

'What the fuck!?' I say, reeling back, cupping my hands over my boxers.

'Sorry,' the woman says. And then I recognise her. It's her from up the road, Ciara's mam. What's-er-name… 'I eh… didn't realise you were going to come down the stairs half naked.'

'Oh sorry, Terry,' Greta says, running across our landing. 'Yeah… Vivian's here. We're both a bit unsure what to do. That's why I decided to wake you.'

I stare up the stairs at my wife, then back down at Vivian.

'Well, first things first…' I say, 'How about I get some clothes on.'

HELEN STARES AT THE BACK OF LOUISE'S POLKA DOT PYJAMAS AS SHE follows her and her mother into their plush kitchen, all the while wondering what the hell Louise is doing dressed for bed when she is supposed to be killing herself in a half an hour.

The light is so bright in the kitchen that it makes the windowed patio doors look as if they've been painted jet-black.

Louise's mother pulls out a chair, motions for Helen to sit it in and then seats herself in the chair next to it, her hands shaking. Louise walks around the opposite side of the table but remains standing, her arms folded.

'There's no need to be shaking,' Helen says, gripping the mother's hands as she sits. 'I'm here now, everything is okay.'

'Wh-what is going on?' the mother stutters.

Helen purses her lips at her, then flicks her eyes towards Louise.

'Louise… whatever it is you are planning to do at midnight, I'm here to save you. I am the mother of somebody who—'

'*What?*' Louise screeches, her face contorting.

Helen grips the mother's hands even tighter.

'Tommy… Tommy Smith, he told us what you and Sinead are planning on doing tonight.'

Louise pulls at the back of a chair, scoots it towards herself, sits in it, then rests both of her elbows on the table and stares at Helen.

'What are you talking about, officer?'

Helen looks back at the mother, then at Louise again.

Silence.

'Officer... please, please tell us what's going on,' the mother says, her voice shaking as much as her hands.

Helen swallows.

'Louise, be honest with me now, be honest with your mother. As I was about to say to you, I am not just a Detective, I am the mother of a son who died by suicide... I have studied suicide for many years. Decades. You need to be honest. Are you and Sinead Longthorn planning on ending your lives at midnight tonight?'

Louise breathes out a laugh. Her mother's eyes go wide, her arms — releasing from Helen's grip — stretch across the table, so she can cling to her daughter's fingers.

'Mam,' Louise says, shaking her head. 'Relax. This is all... this is...' She rolls her shoulders, shakes her head with disbelief.

'It's okay, Louise,' Helen says slowly. 'Open up to us now; I'm here to tell you life is worth—'

'What the hell are you talking about, officer?' Louise says, standing back up. She walks around the table, to her mother, and places her hands atop both of her shoulders. 'I was asleep in bed until you came banging down the door.'

Helen swallows again, then her eyes dart from left to right.

'Officer?' The mother says, squinting.

'I eh... I... where is Sinead Longthorn?' Helen asks.

'The Longthorns, they're in Majorca aren't they, pet?' the mother says, turning to look up at her daughter.

Louise nods her head.

'Yeah, they've been away the past couple weeks during the mid-term, they're due home on Saturday.'

Helen holds her eyes closed, reality washing through her stomach.

'In Majorca,' she whispers. Then she opens her eyes. 'So you two aren't... you eh... you didn't make a pact?'

'What the hell is going on here, Louise? Tell me!' the mother says, standing up and turning to grip her daughter in a bear hug.

'Relax, Mam, I don't know where this officer is getting all of this from.'

Helen stands too, causing her chair to squeak across the kitchen tiles.

'The welfare officer at your school — Abigail — she said you and Sinead have shown signs of depression over the past few months, says you are dealing with a big bullying issue.'

'What!?' the mother says, leaning herself off her daughter so that she can stare into her eyes.

'Yeah... we reported some bullying that's been going on and Ms Jensen — Abigail — gave us some leaflets about depression and teen suicide statistics last week. But it was... it was nothing. Me and Sinead looked at the leaflets and wondered if Jensen was going crazy. It was way over the top. We're getting bullied at school... and a bit online... but it's... I mean, we're not going to kill ourselves. We never would. We were just reporting the bullying.'

'Oh sweet Jesus,' the mother says, grabbing Louise in for another hug. 'Why didn't you tell me... sweet Lord.'

'Relax, Mam... it's all okay. It's nothing.'

Helen stares at Louise and her mother holding each other in the middle of their kitchen, before her eyes flick to the microwave clock. 11:45. Fifteen minutes left to save... whoever it is she is supposed to save. And here she is, standing in the wrong fucking kitchen.

'Louise,' she says tentatively. 'Is there any reason Tommy Smith would ring in to two police stations to tell us two girls are planning on committing suicide?'

Louise releases the grip her mother has on her, then sticks her bottom lip out and shakes her head.

'I don't think anybody believes anything Tommy Smith says. I mean... somebody told me he's hanging around with a gang of older fellas now.'

Helen holds a hand to her face, covering her eyes so she can squeeze them shut in an attempt to defuse the migraine that is threatening to flare up.

'Are there any girls, that you know of from your school, who you think might be planning on ending their lives?' she asks, her hand still covering her face.

Louise puffs out her cheeks.

'No,' she says.

'No girls who might be depressed?' Helen asks.

Louise puffs again, this time almost laughing.

'Who isn't depressed these days?' she says. 'All of the girls talk to Ms Jensen about some problem or other. I think she just diagnoses anyone who has a small problem as being depressed. She's just ticking boxes, isn't she? Isn't that what working in a school is all about? That's what me and Sinead have noticed since we started going to secondary school. All the teachers are just following protocol. They're just protecting themselves in case anything happens. They aren't interested in the students, not really. They're only interested in themselves.'

'Louise, please. Think. I have good reason to believe two girls from your school are going to kill themselves tonight. If it's not you and Sinead... who is it?'

Helen removes the hand from her face, takes one large stride towards Louise and grips her shoulders. Louise is tiny, the top of her head just about reaching to Helen's chest.

'I'm sorry. I don't think there's anyone at my school who is suicidal. Of course I don't. If I believed that, I'd have reported it, wouldn't I?'

Helen's eyes glaze over as she stares down at Louise, then she lightly pats her on both shoulders and spins on her heels.

'I'm so sorry to bother you two,' she says as she walks out of the kitchen and down the long, narrow hallway before reaching the front door.

'Is that it?' the mother yells after her. 'Officer... officer, is that it? You're just gonna leave us with that bombshell?'

Helen doesn't answer. She pulls at the door and steps out into the garden, then sucks in some fresh air through the gaps in her teeth. It's more of a cringe than a breath.

She wobbles down the garden path, her head racing. Then she sees it. The police car with the bumper hanging off and the front light smashed.

'Oh for fuck sake, Helen,' she whispers to herself.

23:45

Ingrid

NEITHER OF US HAVE SAID A WORD TO EACH OTHER SINCE WE SAT UPSTAIRS on the bus. We were holding hands for a few minutes, then Ciara let go and leaned in to me. I have my arm wrapped around her; her head snuggled into my chest.

The bus seems to be moving in slow motion, swaying us a little as it makes its way out of Crumlin. We'll probably arrive in about ten minutes or so. Our last stop. Ever. At least I think it is. I'm pretty sure we're actually going to go through with this.

There's not much time to back out now anyway. There was a tiny part of me that had always felt Ciara was too frightened to commit suicide, no matter how many times she spoke to me about it. But last night, as we were coming up with our pact, I could see in her eyes how excited she was that she was finally going to do it. The fact that I was on board obviously made a huge difference to her. She told me I was the reason she had stopped herself doing it before. But if I wanted to die, then so the hell did she.

I stroke her hair and as I do, she places one of her hands on my knee. We're both just staring out the front window of the bus, at nothing because it's too dark to make anything out. The pictures in my mind are more clear than the picture in front of us. I've been thinking about Sven; about how he'll be affected if I commit suicide. I'm hoping it helps him more than anything, though. When he grows up and learns what happened to his older sister, he'll feel that his condition — whatever it is

704

— isn't so bad. He'll know life is only as good as his mind. And his mind will always be good because he doesn't know what bad is. I don't think he'll ever be clever enough to be depressed. I spent part of this morning lying on my bed wishing I had his condition.

Besides, Sven will get more attention from Mum and Dad if I'm dead. It'll all work out fine for him. There's no need for me to worry about my little brother. There's certainly no need for me to be going back over the thoughts I've had going through my mind all day anyway. I need to shut it off; can't wait to shut it off. I'm sure we're doing the right thing. It'll be better for everyone when I'm gone.

I look at my digital watch. 23:47. Almost there, the last minutes of our lives ticking away.

As the bus turns down the canal road, Ciara twists her head so she can look at me. She doesn't say anything, she just smiles, then turns her head back so that she's staring out the window again. So, I do the same; stare out the window. Only this time I try to take in what I'm looking at, rather than slipping back into my thoughts. It's tough to make much out in the dark, but the street lamps are lighting the way a bit, shining onto the calm water of the canal.

The bus pulls over, allowing a few more passengers to get on board. A couple of them climb the stairs and sit behind us. I wonder if that's why we've been so quiet on this bus journey; because there are others around us. But I bet it's more to do with the fact that we're just trying to soak in our last minutes alive. Maybe we've said all we have to say anyway.

I wonder what Ciara is thinking. She doesn't have a little brother; doesn't care for her mam or her dad. She's probably thinking about Debbie. Or maybe Miss Moriarty. I don't ask her though. I just continue to run my fingers through her hair and down her cheek. Until I feel wetness. I stop, then tilt her head towards me.

She's crying.

23:45

Greta

I SIT ACROSS FROM VIVIAN, BOTH OF US LEANING OUR ELBOWS ON OUR thighs in the quiet of my sitting room while we wait on Terry to get some clothes on. My fingers are fidgeting with each other as I try to get inside Ingrid's mind. I've probably been a terrible mum to her over the past few months. Sven's taken most of my attention.

It's beginning to dawn on me that we left her alone to face secondary school. I don't even know what subjects she's studying there; have no idea what any of her teachers' names are.

'Jeez, I just hope they're out flirting with boys,' I say to Vivian. She nods her head. The thought of Ingrid flirting with boys would have been my worst nightmare a few hours ago, but now it seems to be my biggest hope. That's how worried I am. I have no idea what Ingrid and Ciara intend on doing tonight.

'Right-ee-o,' Terry says as he plods down the stairs. He always says 'right-ee-o'; especially during his show. It's almost like a shitty catchphrase he clings to. He claps his hands once and then stands between Vivian and me.

'So, we know they visited Harriet and before that your former child minder, Vivian... remind me of her name again?'

'Debbie. Debbie Martyn.'

'Yes, Debbie. So what does this tell us? I wonder if they have been visiting older girls to get their perspective on boys. Maybe Ingrid — or

Ciara, it could be Ciara — has got her first boyfriend and perhaps they just went in search of advice.'

I nod my head slowly as I soak in the plausibility of Terry's theory. Then I look up at Vivian. She's still staring into her lap.

'Vivian, what do you think?' I ask.

She looks up, her eyes heavy.

'Sorry, but eh… could I have a drink? My throat's a bit parched,' she asks.

'Sure thing, a glass of water?' Terry says.

'Eh… do you have anything heavier… a red wine by any chance?'

My eyes meet Terry's.

'Sure thing,' he says, making his way to our kitchen.

'What do you think, Vivian? Has Ciara mentioned any boys in her life recently? Ever heard of this Stitch or whatever his name is?'

She shakes her head.

'I… I don't really… I mean… I don't even know when I last sat down and spoke with Ciara. It's been ages. Way too long.'

'Don't worry,' I say making my way towards her so I can rest my hand on her shoulder. 'I feel the exact same way about my relationship with Ingrid. I guess we're both guilty of feeling our girls have grown up enough to look after themselves.'

She looks up at me. I'm not sure if her eyes are glazed from emotion or from alcohol. I wonder how much wine she had before I called over to her.

'Here y'go, Vivian,' Terry says, swooping back into the room.

'Is this Merlot?' she says, sniffing into the glass he just handed to her.

'It's red. S'all I know,' Terry says.

I'd normally laugh at something like that. But I just stand back upright and fold my arms.

'Terry, I hope you're right. I hope the girls have just been trying to get a perspective from girls older than them about boys. And that they'll knock back on that door in the next few minutes. But the one thing that's niggling me is the note Ingrid wrote in Harriet's book. Why would she do that? It's sticking in my mind… it almost seems… I don't know… final.'

'Don't be silly. What do you mean final?' he asks me.

I dip my chin into my neck and begin to fidget with my fingers again.

'I don't know,' I say. I don't want to say out loud what is troubling me. Mainly because I can't make sense of it.

Terry sits on our sofa, then claps his hands again.

'She wants to ring the police, don't ye, hun?' Vivian says, swirling her glass.

'Sure the police will laugh at us,' Terry says. 'Don't children have to be missing for twenty-four hours or something before they'll look into it?'

'That's what I told her,' Vivian says.

I rub my face with my hand and then blow out my lips.

I keep seeing the note she wrote for Harriet in my mind; her cute little handwriting.

I love you Harriet

She never says those words, let alone write them. She has never told me she loves me; has never said it to her dad, to her little brother. It's just not how we talk to each other.

'Something's not adding up for me,' I say. 'I'm going to call the police.'

I pace out of the sitting room, into the hallway and pick up the phonebook to search for the local station's number. Terry joins me by the time I've found it and I begin punching it into the phone.

'Are you sure you're not overreacting, Greta?' he says.

I just stare at him as I hold the phone to my ear.

'Rathmines Garda Station, how may I help you?'

'Hi... my name is Greta Murphy. I have a thirteen-year-old daughter who has gone missing with her best friend. Her name is Ingrid Murphy, her friend is Ciara Joyce.'

'Okay, ma'am,' the voice says. 'And how long have these two girls been missing?'

I hold my eyes closed, then sigh a little out of my nostrils.

'They left here at about twenty-past seven this evening.'

'This evening?' the voice says back to me. 'Just over four hours ago?'

'Uh-hmm,' I say as I begin to nibble at my thumbnail.

'Ma'am, I understand your concern right now, but we suggest you only involve the Gardaí should your child be missing over twenty-four hours.'

'But I'm... I'm going out of my mind right now. I know something is wrong, I can feel it in my bones. Call it mother's intuition or whatever—'

'Ma'am... I am sorry you feel this way. But trust me; ninety-nine times out of a hundred, young people find their way home after we've received a call like this. What I propose you do is wait at home. Make sure somebody is there when your daughter arrives. There's no need for everybody to go out and search; somebody needs to be at home when your daughter gets there.'

I bite at my thumbnail again, then feel a rage burn up from my insides.

'That's it? That's all you're gonna do for me? Give me some obvious advice?'

Terry takes the phone from me and rests his other hand around my shoulder.

'Officer, this is the girl's father — Terry Murphy... y'know, off the radio? We'll eh... take your advice on board. Thank you very much.'

Then he just hangs up. As if everything is okay.

'Right-ee-o,' he says, squeezing my shoulder a bit tighter and leading me back into the sitting room. 'Ingrid and Ciara are clearly up to something. But I bet it's all very innocent. This is all we have to do: Vivian, I suggest you go home and wait up until Ciara arrives home. Somebody needs to be there. Greta, you need to do the same here. It's more than likely they'll arrive home soon. The Gardaí have said this is the only thing we can do right now.'

I watch as Vivian downs the rest of her glass, before handing it to Terry.

'What are you going to do?' I ask my husband.

'Well... I have an important interview in the morning. I'm going to go back to bed. Don't wake me up when Ingrid gets home; I'll deal with her tomorrow.'

I switch my stare from Terry to Vivian and then back again.

'That's it? That's all we're going to do? We're just going to wait for them to come home?'

'It's all we can do,' Vivian says, reaching her arm to my elbow. And then she winks at Terry before turning on her heels and strolling down our hallway and out our front door.

Terry leads me to the sofa and sits me into it.

'Just relax, Greta... throw on a movie or something.'

I stare up at him and then find myself nodding my head.

'Okay,' I say. 'I'll just wait here until she comes home.'

I take the blanket that hangs on the back of the sofa and drape it over me as Terry kisses me on the top of my head. Then I pick up the remote control and begin clicking through the channels.

HER HAND TREMBLES AS SHE TRIES TO PLACE THE KEY INTO THE IGNITION; failing six times before finally finding the slot.

'You're a fuckin idiot, Helen. A fuckin idiot!'

She stares over at the house she's just left as she shifts into first gear, sees Louise and her mother staring out at her. They watch as the bumper scrapes off the road, sparks darting in all directions as the car pulls off.

Helen eyeballs herself in the rear-view mirror, then shakes her head.

'A fuckin idiot!'

The speedometer's dial begins to shake as it pushes upwards; the car now doing seventy miles per hour in the narrow streets of a tight housing estate.

By the time she's reached a stretch of main road, the speedometer is inching towards one hundred. Then Helen forces her foot on the brake, the car coming to a noisy, sudden stop; parts of the bumper cracking and flying free.

And then she slaps herself in the face with both hands.

'A fuckin' idiot! C'mon, Scott, talk to me. Give me a sign. Are there or aren't there two girls out there about to kill themselves?'

She's startled when she hears a rattling on her window.

'Officer, officer… you okay?'

A man with square-framed glasses is staring in through her driver's side window, his nose practically pushed up against the glass.

She waves her hand up at him. 'I'm fine.'

'You sure?' he says. 'Did you have a crash? Would you like me to ring an ambulance for you?'

'I said I'm fine!' she shouts.

The man holds both of his hands up, then slowly backs away from her.

Helen pivots her head around, looks out the back window, the front windscreen, each of the windows either side of her. It's dark. Almost pitch black, save for a tiny street lamp about fifteen yards away that seems to only light the pavement directly beneath it. There are no other cars on the road, no sign of anybody but the silhouette of the man who had knocked on the window walking away from her.

She breathes in through her nose, then pops the breath out of her mouth. She repeats this over and over; each time the sound of the pop growing in volume and frustration.

'Nobody's gonna kill themselves are they? The calls weren't fucking suicide calls; they were distraction calls, Helen. You fuckin idiot!' She slaps both of her hands on top of the dashboard. 'As soon as I heard suicide I let my heart overrule my head.'

She grunts loudly, before a cringe runs down her spine. Then she slaps her hands on top of the dashboard again and screams, an eerie shriek that echoes all the way around the car and back into her ears.

'Fuck you, Alan Keating!' she says. 'Fuck you, Tommy Smith. Fuck you, Scott Brennan!' Then she gasps in some air. 'No... no... I'm sorry, Scott. I didn't mean that, honey. I didn't mean it.'

Her shoulders begin to shake. She wipes a tear that had rested on one of the bags under eyes, and then looks around herself again. The night is dead. Eerie. Creepy. Until car lights shine in the distance, coming towards her. The lights slow down, then a horn beeps.

Helen shifts into first gear, presses at the accelerator and drives off, waving her hand up in the air in apology to the driver behind.

She thinks back through the night as she drives in no particular direction at all; back to when she bluffed her way into Terenure Garda station to meet with Charlie; to when she took him to the Red Cow Luas HQ to view CCTV footage; to when she went to Patrick Tobin's house; to when she went to Brother Fitzpatrick's local pub and ordered him outside. Twice. To when she splashed his face with water. Twice. To when she confronted Tommy Smith in the snooker hall; to when she pinned poor Charlie up against the shop shutters and bullied him into lying to his SI; to when she sat on his desk and gripped onto his car keys; to ramming that car up the back of a Land Rover; to entering the house of an innocent school girl and telling her mother she was there to save her from killing herself.

She stops the car near the canal, its lights reflecting off the calm water. She's often thought about ending her own life. She wanted to do it straight after hearing of Scott's suicide. It was Cyril who woke her and Eddie up one Monday morning, just gone four a.m.

'I'm so sorry,' Cyril said. Helen knew by the look on his face that something awful had happened. 'It's Scott, isn't it? Isn't it? Scott! Scott!' she yelled up the stairs.

'He's not up there,' Cyril said approaching her slowly. He threw his arms around her, hugged her as firmly as he could. 'He's dead, Helen. Him and two friends. They took their own lives. I'm so sorry.'

She's replaying that moment now as she stares out of the windscreen and almost feels tempted to press down on the accelerator, drive straight into the canal. The car would probably take about twenty minutes to sink fully under the water. Two minutes after that she'd be gasping for breath.

'That'd be a fuckin stupid way to do it,' she mumbles to herself. 'Horrible. At least Scott and his mates did it quick. They were breathing in fresh air one second, the next they were gone. Forever.'

She sighs, then presses the balls of her palms into her eye sockets and wiggles her wrists.

'Wake the fuck up, Helen,' she says. 'Think. Think!'

She switches off the ignition, kills the lights that were shining onto the canal's ripples and then pulls at the lever beside her chair, so that it flicks backwards, allowing her to slouch into a lying position. Then she begins to suck on her lips; a tic she always produces when she's floating deep into her mind.

'It's so quiet,' she says, leaning up to peer out the windows. 'It wouldn't be this quiet if Alan Keating was up to something. If he's pulled something off, there'd be sirens all over this neck of the woods. Think, Helen. Come on. Think for fuck sake!'

She shakes her head with frustration, clenching her hands into a ball.

'Uuugh, what am I doing?' she says, pressing at the lever beside her seat again and pumping it back to an upright position. 'There can't be two girls out there... there just can't be. Why did Tommy Smith run away? It doesn't make sense. Does it? Come on, Scott. You're the only one who can tell me. Please. Give me a sign. Give me a sign, son.'

Her jaw drops open when she feels her phone vibrating in her pocket. She reaches for it, stares at the screen and notices a strange number. Her finger is trembling as she presses at the green button; almost as if she thinks Scott will be on the other end of the line.

'Hello,' she says tentatively.

'Helen,' a familiar voice says.

She sits upright.

'Charlie… is that you?'

'Yes, Helen. Listen… we've just had a phone call made to the station a couple minutes ago. I thought the right thing to do was to ring you as soon as I heard.'

23:50

Ciara

INGRID TILTS MY HEAD UP SO SHE CAN LOOK AT MY FACE. I THINK SHE FELT one of my tears when she was running her fingers through my hair. I smile up at her, then shift to sit more upright, resting my ear on to her shoulder. Neither of us says anything; we just stare out the front window.

I wonder what she's thinking about. Probably her parents and Sven. Why wouldn't she? She's going to miss them. And they're going to miss her. They're worth thinking about. Not like my family. I'm not going to miss one thing about my parents. I know they're the reason my head is so messed up. They shouldn't have had me. They clearly didn't want me. That's why I'm depressed. It's why my mam sits at the kitchen island every evening drinking wine and why my dad never comes home. None of us like being with each other. All of us are trying to escape in some way; him by working as much as he can, her by getting drunk. And me. By dying. At least I have the courage to end it all and get away from my crap life. Not like them. Chickens.

Won't be long till we get to our stop. Ten minutes or so. I knew it'd be around midnight when we finally did it. Me and Ingrid talked all of this through. It'll be over in the blink of an eye. No pain. No suffering. Then somebody will find our bodies. They'll ring the police. The police will ring our parents. There'll be lots of crying; lots of drama. It's the thoughts of that drama that drives me to suicide more than anything. They'll deserve all the pain they'll feel when they're told the news.

I let out a sigh, then lift my head off Ingrid's shoulder and wipe at both

714

of my eyes. I'm really tired. Though it doesn't matter. I'm almost asleep forever. The whole weight of tiredness that being depressed brings will no longer bother me; the whole stresses in school about being the short fat one will no longer bother me; the pressure of passing exams will no longer bother me; being lonely in my own home will no longer bother me.

I twist my head over my shoulder as the bus pulls over at another stop. And my heart flips.

It's not... is it? I widen my eyes a bit. Bleedin' hell... it is!

Stitch. In a grey hoodie sitting on the other side of the stairs. He's leaning his head against the window, looks like he's almost asleep.

My heart begins to thump really fast as I stare at him. Which is weird because I was enjoying how relaxing this bus journey had been. Me and Ingrid were just keeping really quiet and really calm as we headed towards our death. But seeing this bleedin' eejit sitting behind us has made me panic a bit.

I twist my head back around and stare out the front window, wondering whether or not I should tell Ingrid he's sitting six rows behind us. I don't want it to have any impact on her. If he starts talking to her; if he starts apologising for calling her Fishfingers, she might change her mind.

I let out a sigh. There's no escaping him. We'll be getting off in a couple stops. As soon as she stands up and turns around, she'll see him.

I breathe deeply and then rub my eyes.

'What's up with you?' Ingrid says. 'You okay?'

My head shakes slowly and then I turn to face her.

'Look behind you, Ingrid,' I whisper. 'Grey hoodie.'

23:50

Ingrid

CIARA'S TAKEN HER HEAD OFF MY SHOULDER. IT'S A PITY. I WAS ENJOYING how peaceful and quiet everything was. The bus was totally silent. Even though I know a few people got on behind us.

She turns around and begins to fidget. Then her breathing changes. Maybe she's getting a bit frightened seeing as we're nearly there. Only two more stops to go. I wonder if she wants to change her mind. Maybe she wants to change her mind. I think I'd be up for that. We could probably do this tomorrow instead.

'What's up with you?' I whisper to her. 'You okay?'

She shakes her head and then sighs a little bit. Something's up. I can always tell with Ciara.

She leans her face nearer to mine.

'Look behind you, Ingrid,' she whispers. 'Grey hoodie.'

I don't know why. But I already know who she's talking about before I turn around.

I twist my neck as slowly as I can and see his face almost hidden behind his hoodie, his eyes closed, the side of his head resting against the window.

I try to breathe as slowly as I can as I stare at him because I don't want him to have any effect on me. Not anymore. Then I turn back around.

'What are the bloody chances?' I say to Ciara. She just stares into my face as the bus pulls in at another stop.

'We're getting off at the next one,' Ciara says. 'Let's just stand up, walk down the stairs, and if he notices you or tries to say anything, I'll shut him up, okay?'

I can't believe he's on this bus. Just as we're about to do this. I nod my head and then Ciara stands up and reaches her hand to me. I grab it and stand up too before each of us tip-toe our way towards the steps.

I'm staring into his face when his eyes flick open. Then he gasps and sits up straight, whipping down his hood.

'Ingrid,' he says.

Ciara holds her hand to my mouth, then takes a step towards him.

'Stitch — you have no right to talk to her after the way you treated her last night. You shut the hell up and let us get off this bus.'

His eyes widen. He looks more shocked than I am. I wish he wasn't so handsome. Ciara doesn't think he is. But I've always thought he was one of the best looking boys in the school. I think it's his bushy eyebrows.

'I just… I just… I want to say sor—'

'I told you, Stitch,' Ciara says, raising her voice. 'Don't try to say anything to her.' She points her hand down the stairs and looks at me. So I do as she wants. I grip the handrail tight and begin to sway my way down the steps. 'Don't!' I hear Ciara shout. Then she follows me down and we wait quietly beside the driver as he makes his way towards our stop.

It seems to take ages for him to pull in. I'm a little scared Stitch will come down the steps to try to talk to me at any second.

But he doesn't.

The bus pulls over and me and Ciara wave a thank you at the driver before we find ourselves back out in the cold air. We stand and wait until the bus has pulled off and then we hug each other again.

'Wow. That was weird,' I say, resting my chin on Ciara's shoulder.

'I gave him the finger, did you see that?' she says. It makes me laugh.

The last time he'll ever have seen either of us will stay in his head forever; Ciara's finger telling him exactly how we feel about him. He'll have to live with that for the rest of his life if we commit suicide. He'll replay calling me Fishfingers over and over in his mind and feel guilty forever.

'You ready?' Ciara says.

We release our hug and then — at the exact same time — we both stare up to the very top of the Clock Tower.

It's one hundred and fifty feet high. They taught us that at school. I think everybody who lives around here knows that. You can see the top point of the Clock Tower from almost every street in Rathmines. It sticks out like a sore thumb. I don't know how many times in my life I've stared up at one of its four clock faces to make out the time. It used to make me dizzy when I was a kid. I'd stand under it and try to stare up to its highest point. Never in a million years did I think I'd ever stand on its ledge one day and jump off it. But here I am. About to do just that. I think we are anyway. Ciara certainly doesn't look like she's going to change her mind.

I squeeze her hand as we walk to the side of the tower and — as we planned last night — Ciara jumps to reach the ladder that leads us to the fire escape. When she pulls it all the way to the ground I suck air in through my teeth, shiver a bit, and then nod at my best friend.

We don't say anything to each other as we climb the shaky steps.

I've never been up here before. Ciara has. She figured out a couple years ago that this was the way she wanted to end it all. She says we'll be dead before we even hit the pavement. She's thought it all through. This is the best way to commit suicide; no pain, no suffering. Just one tiny leap and it'll be all over. She's stood on the ledge a couple times before. Just to test it out.

The wind seems to get stronger the higher we climb but suddenly the shaky stairs end and Ciara is stretching ahead of me, over a small ridge, and on to a concrete ledge. I can actually hear the ticking of the four clocks beneath us as if they're right next to my ears.

I take one step forward and edge my chin outwards, so I can stare down at the pavement.

Wow.

It really is high. I can feel my heart thump a little bit. I think we're really going to do this.

We both stand in silence, staring down onto the footpath where we're supposed to land as the wind gets a bit heavier around us. Then — out of nowhere — we hear a clanging sound.

Somebody's climbing the stairs.

HELEN'S EYES GROW WIDE.

'What'd the call say?' she asks really slowly.

Charlie puffs a disappointed sigh down the line.

'I'm sorry, Helen, but the Royal Hospital museum has just been stolen; they think there's about three million euro worth of paintings missing. Everybody here is kicking themselves; it's got to be Alan Keating. He played us. The calls were a hoax, a distraction. I eh... I just wanted you to know.'

Helen holds the phone in front of her face to stare at the screen. There's nothing to look at, except for the timing of the call flicking upwards in seconds. Eighteen seconds she's been on this call. Nineteen. Twenty.

She holds the phone back to her ear.

'Thanks for letting me know, Charlie,' she says.

'You okay?' he asks.

'Course I am... course I am,' Helen replies, her thumbnail in between her teeth as she stares out of her side window.'

Charlie sighs again.

'I mean... I know I'm going to be in trouble in the morning with Newell, but I just I... I thought you should know. We were wrong, I guess. But thank you so much for the adventure. It might be my last night as a cop, but I won't forget it. I'll never forget it. I hope you're eh... still up for that coffee some time?'

Helen nods her head as an answer… her thumb still between her teeth, her eyes still wide.

'Helen?' Charlie says.

'Yes. Yes. Coffee. Of course, Charlie. Any time,' she says.

'Cool. So where are you now?' he asks. 'Did you go straight home from here?'

Helen swivels her head slowly, staring around Charlie's car.

Then she inches her nose a little forward to try and make out any of the bumper damage.

'Yeah… I'm at home,' she says, before twisting the phone screen to her face again and pushing at the red button.

She doesn't scream, doesn't sigh, doesn't slap her palms against the dashboard. She just sits in silence, staring at the subtle ripples in the canal, the edge of her thumb back in her mouth.

Her past is playing in her mind in black and white like an old film reel. She's remembering walking into her bedroom one evening, her stomach flipping, a tiny white stick in her hand. She showed it to Eddie. His eyes narrowed immediately. It was a surprise. A huge surprise. But one they accepted. They'd both talked about not wanting kids — preferring to give their progressing careers all the time and effort they required. But they adored him as soon as he was born. They'd often switch shift patterns at work, just so one parent was always home with their precious boy.

'I'm so sorry, Scott,' she says to the glistening lights in the canal. Then she turns the key in the ignition and inches the car forward, before clicking into reverse and backing all the way to the main road.

She dabs at the tears in her eyes while she drives, unsure where she's driving to. She flitters between thinking about going back to Terenure Garda station and leaving the cop car where she found it — or driving straight home, going to bed and pleading with Eddie to deal with the mess in the morning. But she still can't get the two girls out of her head. No matter how much her common sense is screaming at her.

She drives up the main Rathmines Road, spots the Clock Tower in the distance. Then, as it gets nearer, she stares at the hands of it. Almost five to twelve. What an embarrassment this whole night has been for her. She cringes, then without even noticing, she finds herself back at the canal again; car stopped, headlights shining onto the ripples.

'You're literally driving around in circles, Helen. What the fuck are you doing? Make a decision. Make a fucking decision.'

She looks at herself in the rear-view mirror.

'What if they're still out there?' she says. 'Two girls about to kill themselves at midnight. Where would they be? Where would they go to do it? Come on, Scott... give me a sign. Give me a sign.'

She looks around herself, out both side windows, out the back windscreen. Then, as she tugs at the rear-view mirror, her eyes widen.

'Of course!'

She taps the steering wheel, adrenaline rising in her stomach. 'It's been staring at me all bloody night.'

She shifts into gear and speed reverses into the street.

A loud horn blares from a passing car that has to swerve out of her way. Then she wheel spins on to the main Rathmines Road and then pushes her foot, as hard as she can, to the accelerator.

She's almost grinning to herself when her phone vibrates in her jacket pocket.

'Hello,' she says, holding it to her ear.

'Hel, where are you?'

'I'm at home, Eddie.'

'You are not at home. I can hear you... driving.'

'Well, I'm going home.'

'You told me you were going home hours ago!'

Helen sniffs her nose as a response.

'I have something to tell you,' Eddie says.

Helen sniffs again.

'Keating carried out a hell of a heist tonight. The Irish Museum of Modern Art at the Royal Hospital.'

'Yep... over three million worth of art, right?'

'How did you know that?' Eddie asks.

Helen sighs. Says nothing.

'Hel... what are you doing? Where are you going?'

'I know where the girls are, Eddie.'

'What the hell do you mean *girls*?'

'It's obvious where they're going to commit suicide. It's been staring at me all night. I shudda bloody known.'

'Hel... Hel!'

Helen shifts into fifth gear, the car now speeding towards the moonlit shadow of her destination.

'Hel!' Eddie shouts again. 'Don't do anything stupid, you hear me?'

Helen sniffs wet snot back up her nose, then lifts the knuckles of her fingers to dab at the tears flooding her face.

'Goodbye, Eddie,' Helen says.

'Wait! Where are you? Where are you going?'

Helen blows out her lips, tears spraying on to the steering wheel.

'Hel! Hel!' Eddie sounds frantic... frightened. Then he gasps. 'I know where you're going... Helen! You stop. You stop right now. That is an order!'

Helen swallows back some tears, then sniffs her nose again.

'Bye, Eddie,' she says, before she tosses the phone on to the passenger seat.

It doesn't take long. She's there within seconds, grabs at her door and shoves it open. Then she runs — in her own unique way — as quickly as she can; not even bothering to look up at the top of the Clock Tower. She's certain the two girls are on that ledge. It makes total sense to her. It all adds up.

She stretches until she can reach the bottom rung of the ladder and yanks at it.

Then, without hesitation, she begins to climb.

23:55

Ciara

I PINCH AT INGRID'S TRACKSUIT TOP AS IT BLOWS IN THE BREEZE; THE TWO of us standing at the edge, staring all the way down to the footpath.

The Clock Tower looks huge from down there when you're looking up at it. But it always seems higher when you are looking down from up here. I'd know.

This is not my first time on this ledge.

But for some reason, I'm more frightened now than I was when I was last up here, even though my best friend is right beside me.

I guess the last time I was standing here I was doing research or something — testing out whether or not this is the best way for me to kill myself. But this isn't research no more. This is the real deal. Me and Ingrid are going to hug each other for the last ever time in just a few seconds, then we're gonna leap.

I decided this was the quickest way to do it. It'll take us two seconds to hit that pavement. Then our lives will be over; no pain, no suffering, no struggle. I could never imagine cutting my wrists, could never imagine drowning myself. This is the only way I was ever going to do it.

I wrap both my arms around Ingrid and squeeze her as tightly as I can.

She puffs out a sad laugh, then grips me and we hold each other as a quiet breeze whistles around us. Then I hear a clanging sound. It's the stairs.

Somebody's coming.

We both spin around.

'Ingrid! Ciara!'

Stitch is lifting his leg over the ridge between the stairs and the roof's ledge.

'What are *you* doing here?' Ingrid calls out, gripping me even tighter. We take a step backwards.

'No, no, no, no, no,' Stitch calls out, shaking both of his hands towards us. 'Please don't tell me you are both gonna do what I think you're gonna do.'

Shit. I can't believe this. The bleedin' ass hole followed us. Now it's ruined. Our pact is ruined.

'Stitch... you just climb back down those stairs and pretend you didn't see us up here,' I say, taking another step backwards with Ingrid.

'Oh my Jesus, no,' Stitch says. 'Seriously, You are really gonna do that? Jump? Kill yerselves?'

I've never seen anyone look so confused. His whole face has fallen, there are wrinkles on his forehead that I've never seen before and his eyes look heavy, his bottom lip is sticking out like a baby about to cry.

'Because of me? Don't be bloody stupid. I didn't mean to... I'm so sor—'

'It's not because of you. Don't flatter yourself.' I say, interrupting him before he gets inside Ingrid's head. I release my grip on my best friend and take two steps forward, my finger pointing. 'This has got nothing to do with you. Climb back down those stairs and don't get yourself involved.'

'Ingrid... Ingrid, I'm so sor—'

'Shut the hell up, Stitch!' I scream at him. He's not even bothering to look at me. He's staring over my shoulder. Trying to plead with Ingrid. But I won't let him. I take another step towards him.

'Get lost, Stitch. If you wanna stand there and watch us do this, you can live with that the rest of your life. But if I was you, I'd just get lost back down those steps and forget you ever saw us up here.'

He falls to his knees.

'Ingrid. Ciara... don't be stupid.'

'Get lost, Stitch!' I scream, taking another step towards him. I stretch out my leg, push the soul of my trainer against his chest.

He stumbles back, holding his hand to the ledge for balance.

'Jesus no, Ciara,' Ingrid says, grabbing me from behind. She drags me back a little. 'She's right, Stitch. Just go back down... forget you saw us here.'

Stitch gets to his feet, his face still all wrinkled, his mouth still open.

'I'm not gonna let yous kill yerselves. Are ye mad?' he says. Then he takes a step towards us and reaches out a hand.

MIDNIGHT

Ingrid

'Jesus no, Ciara,' I say, grabbing around her arms and holding her back.

My breathing's gone all funny. I thought she was going to kick him off the roof for a split second.

'She's right, Stitch,' I say over Ciara's shoulder. 'Just go back down... forget you saw us here.'

He crawls back to his feet, slowly, and stares at me. His eyes are really wide. So's his mouth. He looks different. It must be the shock.

'I'm not gonna let yous kill yerselves. Are ye mad?' he says. Then he takes a step towards us and stretches out his hand.

'Get lost, Stitch,' Ciara roars. I can hear the pain in her voice. She's angry. Really angry.

Stitch doesn't listen. He takes another step closer.

'Stitch... I said get lost!' she screams.

My breaths are getting sharp. I think I just want to jump.

Now.

Get it over with.

Stitch takes one more step closer.

'C'mon, Ingrid, take my hand,' he says. 'Let's all go back down the steps and we can talk—'

'Stitch, I swear to you, we're gonna jump. Now if you want to stand up here and watch us...' Ciara says, releasing from my grip and taking a step towards him. I cover my eyes with my hands, but through the cracks of my fingers I watch them square up to each other, their noses almost touching.

Ciara takes another step forward, forcing Stitch to take a step back. This is a mess. What an absolute bloody mess. I can't believe he followed us up here.

'Ingrid... don't mind this mad bitch, come with me,' Stitch shouts out. Ciara grabs him and then suddenly they're wrestling, their hands grabbing on to each other's shoulders.

'Leave her, leave her,' I scream as I run towards them. I grip on to Ciara's waist and try to grab her backwards. But Stitch has her held too tightly. So I thump at his hands... until he lets go. But then he reaches for me. I turn, force both of my hands into his chest and push him away as hard as I can.

All I can do is watch.

As he falls.

Not a sound coming out of him.

He just swirls through the breeze until he stops swirling altogether.

'Sweet Jesus. Holy fucking Jesus,' Ciara says grabbing me. I can hear her words in my ears, repeating over and over in slow motion. She drags me to the ground and lies on top of me. 'Sweet fuckin Jesus,' she says again, straight into my face. I blink at her. Really slowly. As if I'm a robot.

Then I shake my head. To try to turn back time. To see if Stitch will appear back on the ledge with us.

I crawl to the edge to the ledge and stare down. He's just lying there. Facing up to the moon.

'What'll we do? What'll we do?' Ciara screams as she gets to her feet behind me.

I swallow and then press my hands into the ledge so that I can get back to a standing position. I turn slowly, so that I'm face to face with my best friend again, and a tear drops from my eye.

'Our turn next,' I say. I sound really strange. As if I'm not me. 'C'mon.'

I stretch my hand out to Ciara. She just stares at me, her breathing is still really heavy and panicky.

'We killed Stitch... we have to report—' she says, her arms flailing in all directions.

'We don't have to report anything. We just need to jump,' I say.

Ciara shakes her head. She's in a different state of shock to me. Everything is going really slowly for me... but for her it seems to be going really quickly; her breaths, her head shakes, her hands, her thoughts.

'His parents... his parents are—'

'I know, Ciara… I know. Which is why we need to do this. Now. It's time.' My voice sounds really different. My whole body feels really different. As if I'm no longer alive. Maybe I've just accepted it. It's time to die.

Then suddenly Ciara's eyes return to normal and her head stops shaking. Her heavy breaths become normal, her arms rest down by her side and her whole body seems to slow down. She holds her fingers out to me and I grip them. Then, for some reason, I smile at her. And she smiles back.

'You're right,' she says. 'We really need to do this, don't we?'

I nod my head and then we both turn towards the ledge. But rather than stare down at Stitch, I stare across the tops of the buildings on the other side of Rathmines — as far into the distance as I possibly can.

'On three?' Ciara whispers.

I grip my fingers tighter around hers. And then nod my head.

HELEN'S ALMOST HALF WAY UP THE FIRE ESCAPE WHEN SHE HAS TO GRIP HER hands to her knees and bend over. But she doesn't want to stop for long.

She takes in one large breath, blows it out and then continues; the tick-tocking of the four clocks that sit each side of the tower rising in volume the higher she climbs; the wind starting to swirl, blowing her leather coat behind her like a cape.

She heaves herself over the ridge, then — after scrambling to her feet — she stares across the ledge.

At nothing.

'You're an idiot. A fucking idiot, Helen,' she says, grabbing a fistful of her orange hair. 'Course they're not up here. They don't even exist. They never existed. You've been chasing ghosts all night.'

She inches forward to the edge of the ledge and stares down at the pavement; down to where Scott landed. And Ingrid. And Ciara.

Then she wipes her face, smudging snot and tears across her cheek.

'I can't believe it's been twenty-two years,' she says, sucking back up her nose.

She stares off into the distance, over the rooftops of Rathmines, zipping her leather coat up fully so that the collar is fastened tight under her chin. It's not the first time she's been up here. It took a year after Scott and his friends died for her to stoke up the courage to visit the scene. Even though hundreds of people had laid flowers at the foot of the Clock

Tower in the aftermath of the suicides, Helen couldn't bring herself to visit. She kept her head low every time she left the house because had she looked up, the tower could be seen hovering above the rooftops of the terraced houses of her estate. The sight of it repulsed her. It still does. But one night, just before Scott's one-year anniversary, she found a strength within her to sneak out of the house and make her way to the exact spot they landed on. She circled her foot around it, then stared up to the highest point of the tower.

Seconds later she was heading to that point; grabbing on to the ladder that led to the fire escape stairway. She stood on the ledge, staring down at where she had just been circling her foot. She thought about leaping herself. But froze. Eddie kept coming into her mind. She adored him. Even more than she did when Scott was alive. He went out of his way to ensure she got counselling, went out of his way to make sure she had the best mental health support she possibly could have. He saw to it that she got a job back in the station when she was ready. Even though he knew she'd never be the same person again. She wasn't only heartbroken from Scott's suicide. She was mind broken. And neither her heart nor her mind would ever mend.

Even though the doctors insisted she shouldn't return to police work, Eddie conjured up some position at the front of the station for her — doing admin work. It meant he could keep an eye on her all day long. He knew she was capable of going off the rails at any point — especially if she didn't take her medication — and it was annoying to him that she would poke her nose into investigations every now and then. But at least she was still there, still near him, still existing.

She places her hands into her coat pocket and inches closer to the edge; the toes of her Converse trainers hovering over it, only the weight of her heels keeping her alive. Then she closes her eyes and sucks in a deep breath.

'Hell!'

She twists her head, sees Eddie clambering over the ridge. He has both hands held up and his palms out as he inches slowly towards her.

She wipes at her face, then darts at him.

'Oh, Eddie,' she says wrapping her arms around his head and neck. They squeeze each other as tightly as they possibly can. 'I'm so sorry. So sorry.'

Eddie brings one of his hands to the back of Helen's head, taking a fistful of her orange hair. Then he yanks it back a little, so that her head tilts and he can stare into her eyes.

'It's not you who needs to apologise. It's me. *I'm* sorry. I'm sorry for telling you to go home and watch your soaps. I'm sorry you found out about this case. I'm sorry I haven't been checking up on you as much as I should.... It's just been such a manic night, a manic investigation and... and...' He holds a hand to his face, to cover his tears. He hates crying, does Eddie. Only ever cried in his own company after Scott's suicide.

The two of them shake their heads, then they just grab each other closer again.

'I just want to know...' Helen sobs on his shoulder, 'what happened to them. What the hell went on that night.'

'Sweetie,' Eddie says pushing his wife away again so he can stare into her face. 'How many times do I need to tell you?'

'I know. I know,' Helen says, shaking her head. 'I will *never* know what happened.'

Eddie purses his lips.

'You can't keep punishing yourself. We have to accept that we will never know what happened. We'll never be able to get inside their heads.'

Helen takes a deep breath, then blows it out through her lips; tears spraying either side of her.

'I should have known as soon as suicide was mentioned in the station earlier that you would've been affected by it. I was too bloody concerned with Alan Keating that I... I...'

'Don't blame yourself, Eddie,' Helen says. 'You'd think twenty-two years later that I'd be able to hear the word suicide and not have it trigger me. I just... I'm not sure I'll ever get over it. Not in this life.'

Eddie wraps his arm around the back of Helen's head and pulls it towards him, so that her chin rests on his shoulder.

'Well... we're going to get away from this life,' he whispers. 'On the way over here I made a phone call.' Helen opens her eyes. 'I spoke with Dickinson, told him I would be handing in my resignation first thing in the morning. I'm done. I'm retiring. And you and I...'

Helen takes her head off her husband's shoulder, bringing her nose to touch his.

'We're moving to Canada?' she says, unable to hide a joy that bubbles up within her. She laughs as she says it, spraying tears onto Eddie's face.

Then Eddie kisses her forehead.

'We're moving to Canada,' he says.

Helen wraps her arms as tightly around her husband's waist as she can and uses all her might to lift his feet a few inches off the ground.

When she releases, allowing his heels to rest back down to the ledge, he laughs.

'It's the right time,' he says. 'To hell with this job. To hell with chasing around after ass holes like Keating and looking like a mug. I'm done. We spent the last twenty-two years chasing my dream of becoming a superintendent. Now — for the *next* twenty-two years — it's all about you. All about us. A new life.'

He brushes a strand of hair away from Helen's face and the two of them grin at each other as wide as they possibly can.

'C'mon,' he says, gripping Helen's hand. 'Let's get back down to earth.'

They make their way to the steps and clunk down them with their arms wrapped around each other.

'I'll book the flights in the morning,' Helen says. 'When do you think we can leave?'

Eddie puffs out a laugh.

'I'm supposed to give two months notice, but Dickinson said he'll do his best to shorten that for me and ensure I get the full pension too.'

Helen squeezes her husband into her hip. It seems strangely eerie that Eddie would inform her of her new life at the exact same spot her old life ended. But she's super excited. This is the giddiest she's been in twenty-two years.

'Okay then... well, I'll book the flights for two months from now anyway. It'll give us a chance to say goodbye to everyone, to get the house on the market.'

Eddie releases his grip on his wife, then jumps down to the pavement before holding his two hands aloft. He catches Helen as she leaps towards him and they wrap themselves in a tight embrace again.

'Did I get you into a whole load of trouble?' Helen asks.

Eddie sniffs out a laugh.

'Not much more than usual. Nothing I can't handle.'

They smile at each other again, then Helen leans her head onto her husband's shoulder, offering one more apology with body language rather than words as they stroll onto Rathmines' main road.

'I'm parked over here. Where's your car?' Eddie asks, pressing at his key ring, making his headlights flash.

Helen squints her eyes a little, then holds her hand over her mouth.

'What?' Eddie asks as Helen takes a few steps onto the road.

Eddie follows her, tracking her line of vision down a line of parked cars until he sees what she's staring at; a cop car, its headlight smashed, its bumper hanging off.

'Oh sweet Jesus,' he says.

The End.

DID YOU...

...miss all of the clues to that twist ending?

Well, watch this short interview with author David B. Lyons in which he talks you through each and every one.

Get ready to kick yourself!

www.subscribepage.com/thesuicidepact

It is estimated that 1.3 million people will commit suicide this year.

That means one person will die from suicide in the time it takes you to read the words on this single page.

If you suffer with depression, please reach out and talk to somebody.

Here is a list of helplines from certain regions of the world.

Ireland: *Pieta House* 1800 247 247
United Kingdom: *Mind* 0300 123 3393
United States of America: *ASFP* 1-800-273-8255
Canada: *The Lifeline* 1-833-456-4566
Australia: *Lifeline* 131114
New Zealand: *Lifeline* 0800 543354
India: *AASRA* +91 22 2754 6669

Or — from anywhere in the world — visit:

www.befrienders.org

FOR MORE INFORMATION ON DAVID B. LYONS'S NOVELS...

Please visit his website:
www.TheOpenAuthor.com

If you could spare the time to leave a review on Amazon for this box-set the author would be very grateful.

ACKNOWLEDGEMENTS

Each of these books have been dedicated to a specific individual. My late father — Ben. My mother — Joan. And my daughter — Lola.

However, the entirety of this boxset is dedicated to my wife Kerry without whom none of these novels ever would have been written. Every word I write, I write for you. For us.

I owe debts of gratitude to a huge team of brilliantly patient people such as Barry O'Hanlon, Margaret Lyons and Hannah Healy who are always the first three sets of eyes to read my works (bad drafts 'n' all).

I am also grateful for the support of Rubina Gomes, Livia Sbrabaro, Susan Hampson and Maureen Vincent-Northam.

.

Printed in Great Britain
by Amazon

43237445R00442